GALIMAR

RISE OF THE
QUANTUM TRAVELER

by

DAN ADRIAN

Galimar – Rise of the Quantum Traveler
Second Edition

Copyright © 2017 by Dan Adrian, Midnight to Four
Entertainment. All rights reserved.

First Print Edition: October 2016
Second Print Edition: September 2017

ISBN:

(e-book): 978-1-945925-10-8
(Paperback): 978-1-945925-09-2
(Audio): 978-1-945925-11-5

Cover: Milanka Pesic

Interior Design and

E-book Programming: Slaven Kovacevic

Editing: James Zumwalt

DD ꙨꙨ

Jan Hansen

Erik Schiemann

Content Consultation: James Zumwalt

Patricia Granholm

To Becky

The wind 'neath my wings.
Your endurance inspired us all, but especially me.
You will always be my hero. You will always be missed.

To Autumn

The one who inspired me to finish this work.
Always let your innocence endure as a crown of beauty.

To My Brooke

May you have exquisite delight in
the abundance of peace and harmony.
May you know a love you thought
couldn't possibly exist.
I love you

TABLE OF CONTENTS

PROLOGUE 1

PART 1

CHAPTER 1
.... 11

CHAPTER 2
.... 17

CHAPTER 3
.... 27

CHAPTER 4
.... 33

CHAPTER 5
.... 39

CHAPTER 6
.... 55

CHAPTER 7
.... 65

CHAPTER 8

......................71

PART 2

CHAPTER 9

..............85

CHAPTER 10

......................91

CHAPTER 11

.....97

CHAPTER 12

...................105

CHAPTER 13

...111

CHAPTER 14

.........................119

CHAPTER 15

.......................123

CHAPTER 16

.......................131

CHAPTER 17

.......................139

CHAPTER 18

.........................151

PART 3

CHAPTER 19 161

CHAPTER 20 167

CHAPTER 21 173

CHAPTER 22 177

CHAPTER 23 185

CHAPTER 24 191

CHAPTER 25 199

CHAPTER 26 231

CHAPTER 27 241

PART 4

CHAPTER 28 253

CHAPTER 29 259

CHAPTER 30

....263

CHAPTER 31

...........271

CHAPTER 32

...........279

CHAPTER 33

.........285

CHAPTER 34

...........................295

CHAPTER 35

. 303

CHAPTER 36

.............311

CHAPTER 37

.........................321

CHAPTER 38

......327

CHAPTER 39

...333

CHAPTER 40

.........341

CHAPTER 41

....345

CHAPTER 42

.........................353

CHAPTER 43

...........361

CHAPTER 44

⬤◑⌿⬤ ⅃⬤⅃ ⅃⬤⬤⅃⅃⌐ ◔⬤⌿⅃⅁◗⍦◗⅃⬤⅃
⅀⅋⌐⅃⌐ 373

CHAPTER 45

⬤◑⌿⬤ ⌐◗⅃⬤⌐ ⅀⅃⌐ ⅃⅃⬤⅃ 385

CHAPTER 46

⅃⅃⌿⅁⬤◗⅃ ⅃⬤⅃⅁⅃⬤◗ ⌐◗⅀⅃⬤⅃ 389

CHAPTER 47

⬤◑⌿⬤ ⅃⬤⅃ ⅃⬤⬤⅃⅃⌐ ⌐◗⅃⅁⅀⅀ ⅃⌐⌿
⅃⅃⌐⅃◗⅃⌐ 399

CHAPTER 48

⅃⅃⅃◔⅃⌐ ⅃⅃◗ ⅃⅀◗ ⅀⌐⬤◗⅃⬤◗⌿⅀ ⬤⅃⅃⅃⅃⅃ ..409

CHAPTER 49

⬤◑⌿⬤ ⅃⅃⅃ ⅃⬤⬤⅃⅃⌐ ⅃⅃◗◔◗ ⬤⌿ ⅃⅀⅀
⅃◔⬤⅃⅃ 417

CHAPTER 50

⅃◗⅃⌐⅃ ⬤⅃⅃◔⅃◗ ⅀⅋⅃⅃◔◗ ⌿⅀ ⌐◗⅃⅃⌐ 433

CHAPTER 51

⬤◑⌿⬤ ⬤⅃⌐⅀⌐ ⅃◗⅃⌐⊟ ⅀⅋⬤ ⅀⌐⅃⅃⬤◔
⅀⅃⅃◔◗◗⅃ 439

CHAPTER 52

⅃ ⅃◗⅃⅃◔⅁ ⅃⅃ ⌐◗⅃⅁, ⅀◗⅃ ⬤⌿⅁ ⅃⅀⅀⌿⅁⌐
⅀⌿⅃⅁ 457

CHAPTER 53

⅀⅋⌐⅃ ⅀⌐⅃⌐◔◗ ⌿⅀ ⌐◗⅀⬤⅃ 465

CHAPTER 54

⅀⅋⬤ ⅃⬤⅀⅃⅃⅃⅃⌿⅃ ⌿⅀ ⅃ ◗⌿◔◗ ◗⌿⅀⅁ 471

CHAPTER 55

⬤⅃⅃⅃⅃ ⅃⅃◗⅃⌐ ⌿⅀ ⬤◑⌿⬤ 477

CHAPTER 56

⅃ ◗◔⅀⅁◗⅃ ⅃⌿⅃⌐ ⅃⅀⅀⅃◔◗ ⅃⅃ ⅃⅃◔⌐ 481

CHAPTER 57

◑⌣⌣⌣ ◓⌣⌣⌣⌣ ⌐⌣⌣⌣⌣ 493

CHAPTER 58

⌐⌣⌣ ⌐◑⌣⌣ 503

CHAPTER 59

◉⌣⌣⌣ ⌣⌣⌣ ⌣⌣⌣⌣ - ⌐⌣⌣⌣⌣ 511

CHAPTER 60

⌣⌣⌣⌣⌣ ⌣⌣⌣⊞ ⌐⌣ ◑⌣⌣⌣ ⌣⌣
⌐⌣⌣ ⌣⌣◑⌣⌐ 523

EPILOGUE...545

PROLOGUE

United States Navy Ship Niagara – July 12, 1868
Somewhere in the Atlantic Ocean

CYRUS STOOD ON THE DECK of the *Niagara*, halfway between the fore braces and the mainsail, contemplating the events of his life that led him to this point. Was all of the work worth it? "That depends on whom you ask. My wife? Well," he thought to himself.

He had a continuous sense of being on a historic trip across the Atlantic. Knowing exactly where his wife's attitudes lay on the subject, though, he knew if it had been up to her, he probably wouldn't be here. She was a good woman of course, but she just did not understand there is something in a man that drives him to achieve greatness. Then again, with the twists and turns of life that brought him to this day, his inner voice was beginning to agree with her.

Cyrus West Field. Entrepreneur. Dreamer. Successful business man. Sailor. Not really a true sailor; he was more along for the ride than anything else. All the planning he had done to get to this point ensured that all men on board knew their role and knew exactly what they needed to do. There were always unforeseen occurrences, but Cyrus did his best to keep any surprises to a minimum.

Meanwhile, the captain of the *Niagara* sat at his desk below decks. Captain William David Hadwynn was a good man. Having been in the military all his life, this particular mission was not what he had trained for, of course. He was a military tactician and warrior with the ability to be as brutally cold as necessary to carry out his orders in the defense of his country. Now, though, he had been asked to perform this task not for the defense of his beloved country, but simply to make it better; to make it more competitive in the commercial and strategy business. Captain Hadwynn supposed that was enough to make it worthwhile.

Actually, whatever the White House said was necessary was all he needed to "make it worthwhile" in his book. He had been trained to accept orders without question and to carry them out in the most efficient manner possible.

When in uniform, Captain Hadwynn was an outstanding individual. With a 36" waist and 52" chest he was never taunted, not that any on board the *Niagara* would even think of doing so. Hand-picked for this voyage, each hand on deck knew what the captain expected, which wasn't that much different than what he expected from himself: perfection.

Captain Hadwynn took one more look at the paperwork First Lieutenant Aaron Morgan handed him earlier. Digesting the contents of the note, the captain decided he needed to receive comment from Mr. Field on this latest piece of information. Reaching for his coffee, he realized it had once again grown cold due to neglect. "Maybe I'll drink a whole cup by the time this voyage is up," he muttered to himself.

The captain stood figuratively, sometimes literally, at the helm of the *Niagara*, a stout ship in the service of the United States of America. Built by William Camp & Sons Shipbuilding Company of Philadelphia, it was the most modern military ship of the 19th century and one of the first to be built with a hull almost exclusively of iron. It was strong, and was manned by an equally strong crew. While the current task at hand was more of a peacetime mission, it was a mission he was going to make sure was successful.

Captain Hadwynn was willing to stake his 25-year reputation it would be.

Pushing himself back from the desk in his quarters, the captain stood and donned his cap. Leaving his quarters and stepping past the door to sick bay, he turned left and proceeded down a long corridor lined with various doors and passageways. At the third passageway on the right, he turned and climbed a few steps. Upon getting to the top of the stairs, a simple turn of the door handle led him to the command center of the *Niagara*.

"Captain on deck!" announced First Lieutenant Morgan. Immediately all stood at attention.

"As you were," commanded Hadwynn.

The command center of the *Niagara* was an impressive room. Even though this ship wasn't the newest, navy leadership made sure this vessel had all the latest in marine technology. Recently it had been in dry dock to refit it for the task at hand: paying out its share of over 4,000 kilometers of cable across the Atlantic. Supposedly, this cable would make it possible to send and receive telegraph signals all the way to England for the first time. Many of the interior decks and berths were converted to handle storage of the cable that would be laid.

Surveying the command center, the captain was pleased to see each station was being manned expertly and that the crew was working together like a well-oiled machine. Aaron, who was now stepping down from the command seat at the center of the room, was a man whom Hadwynn would feel comfortable with captaining this ship all by himself. Having worked under the captain for two years, Lieutenant Morgan had proven time and time again he was quite capable.

Then there was Jim Espinosa, chief navigation specialist. This voyage was to be Jim's last tour since next month he was to marry a lovely woman he met in Boston last year when on liberty. Keeping an ever-intent watch on the crew members seated in front of him who had their hands on the controls, Jim made sure their movements were exactly what they should be since his butt would be in a sling if anything went wrong.

Moving near the captain's chair, a yeoman handed Hadwynn a cup of black coffee. Privately thankful for this fresh cup of determination, he sipped from it as his eyes scanned the horizon. "Status report, Mr. Morgan," commanded the captain.

"All proceeding according to plan, Captain. Since the last report, we have sailed all night. We are nearing point Gamma twenty-three. We should arrive there in 30 minutes, sir."

"Very good, Lieutenant. Notify me once Gamma twenty-three has been reached. I'll be on deck if you need me," acknowledged the captain.

"Yes, sir."

With coffee in hand, Captain Hadwynn exited the command center, making his way up to the deck and the open air. It didn't take long for him to find Mr. Field. The news he had received in his quarters earlier was something Cyrus needed to know.

Meanwhile, Cyrus was in his own reverie as he scanned the endless sea. Turning to his own personal log book which he was never without, he found the last entry:

> *"July 12, 1858, 7 a.m. -- This morning we sent a test signal to the Agamemnon, and all seemed to be working*

well. As they continue to lay cable toward the Irish shore, we continue ourselves in the opposite direction without incident. The signal continues to remain good, and they even reported that there were whales following their ship. I guess they were escorting them, eager to be counted among those present for a turning point in the history of man."

Cyrus looked up and contemplated what history would say about him as a man. He made sure all those around him read him as a man whose convictions were unshakable. Cyrus supposed he got much of that from his father, Reverend David Field, still found preaching where Cyrus grew up in Connecticut. Through his father, Cyrus was able to trace his family tree straight back to the Revolutionary War. His grandfather was an officer in the American army. Cyrus had never served his country in this manner, but was proud of his heritage and had always set himself on doing all he could for his country; that is why he was here. He contemplated how there were those who had thought him to be a charlatan, and many more who thought him to be a hero.

Cyrus continued the earlier entry:

"History will make its judgments, and all we can do is be men of good moral fiber. It is my sincere wish that the effort, anguish, disappointment, and success will all work to the benefit of my beloved country, the great United States of America."

Looking up to the horizon again, the endless squeak of the gears near his place on the deck continued, as they paid out more and more of the transatlantic cable from the hold of the ship below. That noise, along with the sometimes foul stench of the gutta-percha lining used on the cable, allowing it to remain waterproof, was almost unnoticeable now.

"Captain on deck!" announced an anonymous deckhand.

All stood at stiff attention. Cyrus lazily swung his eyes from the horizon to the general direction of the deckhand making the announcement.

"As you were," said Captain Hadwynn, with a look on his face that somewhat resembled a scowl. It was always a scowl, observed Cyrus, but this time it seemed more strained. More tense.

"Mr. Field," called out the captain. "May I have a word with you?"

As is typical for the captain of a ship, Hadwynn wasn't much for small talk. Cyrus figured he distanced himself from his men so as to maintain a continuous air of command and control.

"Of course, Captain. What can I do for you?"

"I had my first mate take an inventory of the cable storage hold, tasking him with estimating how much cable remained in the hold. At the same time, I had my navigator give me information on our current position. I'd like you to take a look at the numbers and tell me what you think."

"Lead the way, captain."

The two men made their way across the deck. The weather this morning was good. The seas had no anger in them. That was why this time of the year was chosen; it would be impossible to lay cable under a nor'easter or any other semblance of foul weather.

Getting to the bridge, the captain guided Cyrus over to the table next to the navigation station where various papers and navigational materials were typically used. After clearing out the charts, he got a clipboard where he had previously scribbled some notes.

"As you can see here, it looks like we've laid about 800 miles of cable, which means we should have about 550 miles left in the hold. However, according to the latest estimates, there are actually 490 miles left."

"How is that possible?" Cyrus asked, now very concerned.

"I asked the same question of my navigator, and he seemed to be just as baffled. He got out a sextant to check the position, and it turns out we have veered off course. He swore he's been keeping a close eye on the compass, but the fact remains." The captain hesitated as he looked at some other figures he had written down. "According to my calculations, we will still have enough cable to make it due to the extra you had insisted on before shoving off, but we'll be cutting it close."

"Indeed! Close is right," agreed Cyrus. "Do you have any idea why the navigator is wrong?"

"Well, I ..."

"Captain, may I speak to you for a moment?" interrupted navigator Espinosa, who had quietly come up behind them.

As Captain Hadwynn started to walk toward him, the navigator said, "Actually sir, this concerns Mr. Field too."

"Ok. Proceed," said the captain as he returned to his seat.

"You know how we were talking about the current navigational position, and how I guarantee we have been moving exactly the way the compass has pointed we should be moving?" asked the lieutenant.

"Yes," replied Hadwynn in an understanding tone.

"Well, I just couldn't get it outta my head that being where we are, where the sextant says we are, just doesn't make sense. The two things just don't add up, sir."

"Ok. What's your point?" said the captain, wanting to know why he'd been interrupted.

"I'm sorry, sir. I went back over the charts, and started plotting out our positions. Here, take a look." He stretched out the chart he'd been holding in his hands.

Espinosa pointed to a line marked in red stretching from a midpoint of the Atlantic and said, "You see, this is our course over the last three weeks. However, if you look here," he pointed to a spot west of the rendezvous mid-point in the Atlantic, "you can see we started to veer slightly north. It appears that's the main reason we are off course now."

"OK. Have you figured out why that happened at that point?" asked the captain, almost to himself. He was actually intrigued now.

"I asked myself the same question, and so I looked up that particular date, and it was the date the cable broke, and we had to dredge it up with the grappling hook. Remember? That was when that deckhand accidentally locked up the brakes and snapped the line."

"Right," acknowledged Hadwynn.

Espinosa continued, "Captain, do you have the little trinket that came up on the grapple line that time?"

"Yes. Right here." He opened a drawer in the desk adjacent to the navigator's station, producing what looked to be an artifact made of gold which was roughly oval in shape. There were several odd markings on it, and the front had a flat surface.

"If I may, Captain?" The navigator held out his hand, took the artifact from the captain and swung about a foot or so, holding it near the compass. As soon as he did, the compass started spinning continually.

With wide eyes, Hadwynn asked, "Are you saying the whole reason we're off course is from a compass altered by this thing?"

"Yes, Captain. I believe so. Notice that if we move it to the other side of the room ...." Espinosa strode to the other side of the room and set it down. Looking back to the compass, it now appeared to settle and show they were indeed off course.

"Great," growled the captain. Looking around him, Hadwynn picked out a first-year sailor eager to please and said: "Seaman, take that damned trinket down to my quarters and leave it on my desk!"

"Yes, sir."

The captain was really angry now, but he no longer had a recipient for his anger other than himself. *He* had placed that thing so near the compass, and there was no one to blame for the current navigational predicament but himself.

The meeting was then adjourned and the rest, as they say, is history. The trans-Atlantic cable was successfully laid, and it worked for a grand total of 28 days. After a board of inquiry looked into the issue, it became clear it was the fault of an English doctor turned electrician who had driven so much current down the line, he burned out the wire. A few short years later, after the American Civil War, it was tried again, and the cable was a complete success.

In the end, history mysteriously recorded that electricity coursing through the cable on board caused the compass to be off, not the influence of some trinket the captain had placed near it. The trinket made its way to the headquarters of the Maritime Admiralty and, after sitting in a drawer of an unremarkable desk for quite some time, eventually into the basement of the New York Museum of Natural History with an obscure label on it reading "Field Expedition: #5894."

PART 1

CHAPTER 1

FOR THOUSANDS OF YEARS, THE thinkers of our world have endeavored to describe not only who we are as a species, but where we came from, why we are here, and where we are going. It was not until our relatively recent history when science progressed to the point where we came to understand that the universe, in fact, does not revolve around us. Rather, we occupy a relatively minuscule cloister in the universe; a fairly small cog in the vast and tremendously varied machine of cosmology.

The truth of the matter though is what we know, or rather what we think we know, isn't even close to the reality of the universe. Perhaps one of the most important things we as a species have figured out is that the best way to unlock the secrets of the universe is to do so through the one language common to any intelligent life that may or may not exist in the vastness of deep space: mathematics. If intelligent life does exist in the vast and unfathomable reaches of space, then hopefully we will be prepared to communicate on a level slightly better than the grunts and shrieks of our animal friends here on Earth.

The truth of the matter, though, is that not only does life exist in places other than on earth, and not only is that life intelligent, but the universe is actually teeming with life in every corner. Mankind hasn't discovered this personally since our technology hasn't progressed to the point of traversing large distances quickly, but it is easy to see that soon enough there will be the cosmological equivalent of a Starbucks coffee shop on every inhabited corner of our vast galaxy, the Milky Way.

One of our closer neighbors in the cosmos is a galaxy we call the Large Magellanic Cloud, although the inhabitants of that particular galaxy generally have much more imaginative names for their home. This story centers around one small corner of that galaxy, and one particular civilization found there which progressed to the point where it could spread out to many of the star systems surrounding its home planet. This planet, a true jewel in the heavens not only due to its aesthetic beauty but also to the inner beauty of its enlightened inhabitants, is none other than the amazing planet called Galimar.

From the viewpoint of space, you would be forgiven for thinking Galimar is a planet much like Earth. However, natural features of the planet, as well as the history of how the Galimarian people progressed over time, are much different than the same of Earth. Unlike humans, their culture didn't experience the same Dark Ages as humans did. Imagine what life on earth would be like now if humans had experienced the Industrial Revolution over 1,000 years ago. Much of that difference can be attributed to their biology. But more about that later.

The Galimarians are a race of explorers. Early in their social and technological development, they figured out how much joy they derived from the simple act of discovery. Once the joy of discovery and learning was fully embraced, the Galimarians embarked on quite a lot of it. Their first forays into discovery centered exclusively on their own biology, as well as the planet where they lived. While much of Galimar is quite similar to earth, some key differences set it apart as exceptionally amazing and spectacular: the hanging natural gardens of Ammular, the gravity wells of Mistikaan, or the two species of sentient sea creatures living in their oceans.

After some time, technology progressed such that the Galimarian people could stretch out and explore their local cosmic neighborhood. They first visited each of their five moons whose existence was eventually discovered as part of the reason for the gravity wells of Mistikaan. As their technology progressed further and further, and as they were able to travel farther and farther in their local solar system, they successfully established colonies on other planets in their own solar system.

Eventually, they devised technologies that allowed them to visit other solar systems, so that is what they did. Some of that technology made it possible to create ships that could travel extremely fast, and with these ships the Galimarians were able to discover they, in fact, weren't the only forms of higher life in the universe. As they started encountering various races, they deeply enjoyed such interaction, until one particular experience every Galimarian would rather forget.

One planet they discovered had a bipedal race on it called Traxis. The Traxians were not as advanced technologically, but they were quite gregarious and congenial. Over time, the Galimarians progressively shared much of their technology with the Traxians and, for a while, the relationship with the two planets went well until some on the Traxian planet used that technology to wage a civil war. Eventually, *all* life on the Traxian planet, except for a few refugees who came to Galimar, was completely extinguished.

The events of Traxis hit the Galimarian people hard. *Very* hard. They came to realize that Traxian social evolution hadn't evolved alongside this new technology, therefore the Traxians weren't responsible enough to handle the great power that came from possessing it. After much deliberation, the Grand Council of Galimar passed amendments to Testimonial Law (a set of laws which formed the basis of their government) forbidding the sharing of technology with any civilization that hadn't progressed to the same point as Galimar.

This pungent footnote in their history always guided how the Galimarians interacted with other races they encountered from that point onward. Their own technology progressed over time, but that technology was no longer shared with any other races, except for rare circumstances. Even then, it could only be with direct approval from the Galimarian Grand Council.

Eventually, the day came when this policy was tested. There were a set of Galimarians who had visited a planet called Briteria, and these Galimarians had a difference of opinion with the isolationist philosophy of their home world. As they continued to spend time on this new planet, many of these Galimarians fell in love with some of the inhabitants of that planet. They became emotionally involved with those people, and wished to share all they had with them. This was in direct opposition to the Grand Council, who had ruled Briteria could not benefit from Galimarian technology.

This laid the groundwork for a tempest between those who remained loyal to the Grand Council of Galimar and those who lived with the people of Briteria. When it became apparent and provable that these explorers were going to share Galimarian technology with Briteria, they were apprehended, tried, convicted, and sentenced to live the rest of their lives on Briteria. This sentence was quite acceptable to them until learning they would be left there without the benefit of *any* Galimarian technology. A bitter pill for them to swallow, but one that was just and benevolent nonetheless.

For the most part, Galimar can be considered a society ruled by the people. All aspects of Galimarian government are defined in a series of documents referred to as the "Testimony of Galactic, Land, and Maritime Law." These documents, commonly referred to as the "Testimony," were originally penned thousands of years ago, and have guided the peaceful and explorative culture of Galimarian society. The Testimony is regarded as a living document since changes may be needed from time to time, as was the case with Traxis. All guidelines outlined in these documents are referred to as Testimonial Law.

According to Testimonial Law, the government of Galimar doesn't have any single figurehead, but rather has what is referred to as the Grand Council, currently made up of the 281 oldest Galimarians in existence at any given time. The actual number doesn't necessarily need to be 281; however, Testimonial Law dictates that the number of members of this body must be odd so as to facilitate a tiebreaker vote if needed. Changes to the actual number of council members in place at any time must be voted upon and agreed to by all members. Since all votes are tendered anonymously, the identity of the tie breaker, if there is one, is always unknown. With few exceptions, there must be a simple majority for any vote to pass.

Even though there is no single figurehead in government, there is a coordinator for the Grand Council, but his or her duties apart from the council are severely limited. The duties are more administrative, and they generally involve making sure all necessary notices are delivered to all Grand Council members. If there is a matter that needs to come to the attention of the council, he or she is the point of contact for any Galimarian who wishes to be heard. The coordinator does not have the latitude to decide what is heard, but rather is bound by law to allow *any* Galimarian voice in council chambers, if such is desired. His or her only responsibility is to call the council to order to consider the matter.

One of the main tenets of Testimonial Law is that there is nothing off limits to Grand Council inquiry, examination, and approval or denial. While crime is noticeably absent, there is the occasional individual who goes against council decisions, as was the case with the planet of Briteria. On the rare occasion of judgment against crime, each case is considered on its own merits, and the application and degree of punishment are decided upon by a three-quarter majority vote from the council.

Our story begins in the capital of Galimar, with one particular Galimarian named Ehobak, Ehobak Aramine. A dreamer, a poet, and a master interstellar spaceship designer. Ehobak had an idea for a mission of exploration which would take Galimarians much farther than ever attempted before. But before he could go, he needed to convince the Grand Council of Galimar to approve the mission.

CHAPTER 2

∂Ɨ❂ ˥˥⟋˥⟋ꟼ ❂

"MAY WE CALL THE MEETING to order," said the coordinator. As he stood at the podium, the coordinator looked out over the many members of the Grand Council and waited for the din of conversation to come to a stop. As the 281 members gradually stopped conversing and found their seats, the coordinator waited patiently.

The chamber of the Grand Council was just large enough to hold this number of members. It was shaped as a circular amphitheater, designed to demonstrate no single Galimarian was above another, and this attitude carried through to every member of society. So long as the person had completed the transition to the age of enlightenment, thereby no longer pubescent but rather an adult, they had just as much right to be heard in the chambers as any other. It was the job of the coordinator to create the list of those who would be heard, and today's meeting carried with it an agenda of high interest.

The first item on the agenda was a consideration of the methodology used in growing food in the northern hemisphere of the planet. This time of year, the northern hemisphere experienced quite a lot of cold weather, so food was often imported from outlying regions in more temperate areas where it could be easily grown. The proposal was for the building of a large biosphere complex in the north which would have the ability to grow food in several different ways. Hydroponics, aeroponics, and aquaponics were some of the methods being considered, but there were many more. The complex would be quite large, which was necessary since it would be producing enough food for the million or so inhabitants in that area. If it worked out well, then the lessons learned at this facility could be replicated at many other sites planet-wide.

Also on the agenda was a proposal to possibly change the education curriculum for children. It had become obvious that children of the modern era seemed to have more capability than their predecessors, so it was being proposed that educational opportunities be stepped up to meet the true potential of the current crop of young ones.

The final topic for consideration, the one which had the most notoriety in the news lately, was the consideration of a very ambitious space voyage of exploration. While Galimarian society no longer operated on the basis of profit and loss, the costs in terms of labor, materials, and participants were assumed to be substantial based on how large a ship would be constructed. The proposed benefits, though, were equally substantial. Eden was a planet whose makeup was almost identical to Galimar. The majority of its surface was covered with water, and there appeared to be three major land masses. But it wasn't really the water of the world that held the greatest interest of all Galimar; it was what was *under* the ground.

The proposal covering the voyage to Eden was the brainchild of Ehobak Aramine. He worked at a governmental agency called GASEA, the Galimarian Space Exploration Agency. GASEA is the primary administrative agency responsible for all exploration missions done in the vacuum of space. Unlike Earth, space exploration is open to all, though it typically is done by the very young. The average age of GASEA explorers is only 625 years.

In the old days, a probe would be sent to the planet of interest. But when Galimar started to discover sentient life in the universe, a new law was passed which banned the use of probes for exploration. The reasoning was if the target planet had intelligent life on it, they probably wouldn't appreciate an alien probe coming down and roaming around their planet without their consent. The proponents of the ban likened it to another race of creatures sending a probe to the surface of Galimar and tearing up the environment to satisfy its programming. Galimarians wouldn't like that, so potentially intelligent life on another planet probably wouldn't either.

Ehobak had been working on refining his proposal since well before many of the current set of GASEA explorers were even born. Ehobak wished this mission to be his legacy, although he wasn't that old in terms of Galimarian lifespans. Ehobak was about 2,300 years old, just about to transition from being a young adult. He had just married his mate Ruavu about 350 years ago, and they had two children right away. Their youngest Nafan was only 42 years old and hadn't yet graduated into the age of enlightenment; however, their older child Jillintor 237, had just received the amulet of understanding all Galimarians receive when they enter the age of enlightenment.

For most of the morning, Ehobak remained in the anteroom patiently waiting for his turn to speak to the council once all deliberations and voting had been completed on the topics before his. He had hoped to speak before the noon meal, but that was not to be. While the issues of educational development came to a vote rather quickly, the issue concerning establishment of the food production biosphere experienced a lot of animated debate amongst the council members.

It wasn't until the members reconvened after the mid-day break that all deliberations were completed and the matter put to a vote. It passed, but only by a narrow margin. Ehobak was acutely interested in how the vote went on this referendum, noting how many of the council members argued it might not be a wise use of planetary resources. They argued that while it would provide food for the residents of that area, the food needed for those who lived there was being taken care of with existing arrangements. Since those individuals seemed to be fairly stingy with the purse strings of society, Ehobak began to wonder what the likelihood of his proposal being passed would be in that atmosphere.

Once the formalities of the vote were recorded and completed, the coordinator stepped up to the podium and moved the meeting on to the next matter up for consideration.

"My fellow council members, there has been much on our agenda today; however, we have one more matter to consider: Proposal 143112-342, also known as the Eden Project. Here today to speak to us about this project is its principal designer and proponent, Ehobak Aramine. At this time, I would like to invite Lord Aramine to the podium."

As Ehobak rose from his seat and walked to the podium, he thought about how he hadn't been called "Lord" for quite some time, but he supposed in the arena of the Grand Council of Galimar it was appropriate. It was just a title of respect for his position in GASEA.

Ehobak had plenty of notes he was going to follow while speaking to the council, of course. He had an entire briefcase outlining facts, figures, and estimates. There were volumes of scientific data on how important this mission was, and he had materials which showed how each and every minute of it had been planned. Everything had been exhaustively researched by either Ehobak or any number of undergraduates who worked with him at GASEA. As he neared the podium, a thought occurred to him that perhaps he should make a last-minute change to what he should say to the council. He normally wasn't the type of person who would impulsively change things, especially ones this important. But getting to the podium, something came over him and he decided to approach his presentation differently than he had practiced. He decided to hit the issue of expense head-on. He knew virtually the entire planet of Galimar would be tuned in to hear what he said on this subject, but he forced himself to just focus on the inhabitants of the council chamber.

"Distinguished Lords and Ladies of the Grand Council of Galimar, it is my privilege to speak to you today on a subject that has been close to my heart for many years. I bring before you a proposal to build a starship designed to travel to a planet named Eden."

Unexpectedly at that moment, there was a clap which could be heard in the far corner of the room. That clap, which might as well have been a clap of thunder, seemed to open a floodgate of applause among the members of the council. It took Ehobak by complete surprise that this happened so quickly; while the applause continued, it occurred to him this chamber would naturally reflect the overwhelming support he felt among the general populace of the planet. He never let himself become complacent about the support, though, and never took it for granted. He knew that while the project was popular, it needed to be backed up by hard facts, hard figures, and hard science.

As he looked out over the audience, the applause eventually diminished. Ehobak continued. "While there are many reasons why this project should be undertaken, and many reasons why this project is wildly popular among the population of our planet, and among yourselves, let me not mince words. This project is expensive. Very expensive. In fact, my proposal for the starship project outlines a budget probably ten times more expensive to complete than the food production facility just considered by this chamber. First, there is the cost of building the starship. Then there is the cost of training the personnel who would go on the trip. Then there are the natural resources which would be used not only to create the ship, but also to supply the travelers.

"But to those who would detract from the importance of this mission by simply pointing at the numbers, let me offer another reason why this proposal should be considered, a reason which strikes at the

20

heart of us as a people and speaks to the very fabric of who we are. For many of us, it is the very reason we get out of bed in the morning, and why we find purpose in life. The main point of this mission, the very foundation of our civilization, is that we are explorers. It is who we are, and is reflected in the Testimonial Law we all live by. To deny this would be to deny all we have built as a society."

"In reality, everything about whether or not to undertake this mission all boils down to one deceptively simple question: 'Do the benefits of this mission outweigh the costs. As I stated earlier, the costs are enormous, but what are its benefits?"

"First, this ship would be the first one built utilizing an amazing new technology called "Dark Matter Drive" developed at the University of Muron by Doctor Tucor and his incredibly gifted team of undergraduates. These drives have the ability to source limitless power from the universe itself, so all power needed for the starship is produced from a unit only about 200 meters cubed. This technology is the first practical application of the dark matter power generators developed by Doctor Tucor, which are now replacing the outdated trivinium reactors used all over our planet. This clean energy and the way this technology works in harmony with our environment is a practical demonstration of our enlightened society. A starship centered around power sources that do not harm but actually enhance life is a fitting testament to the wisdom of our ancestors."

"The second benefit of this mission will be the utilization of suspended animation pods. One might ask, 'Why is this a benefit? Suspended animation pods have existed for a long time.' This, of course, is true. The medical industry has been using them for centuries to arrest the back-sliding a seriously-injured person quickly experiences, allowing doctors and nurses the time needed to fully plan out their treatment before rendering life-saving procedures. Using them for this mission, though, is something that has never been done before. Since this mission involves traveling for 10 years going there, and 10 years coming back, it made sense to put the explorers in suspended animation during the voyage, since they would be traveling to a planet that would be the farthest world ever visited by Galimar. It was a practical consideration as well since there would be no consumption of supplies en route to the planet, as well as coming back."

"The third and most significant benefit, why this voyage should be approved by the council, is that spectral analyses of the light coming from Eden shows this particular planet appears to be rich in a mineral known as Paliminium, which isn't found anywhere on Galimar.

In fact, it has only been seen on one other planet named Palimine, its namesake. Unfortunately, Palimine no longer exists because its sun went supernova, destroying the planet and all life on it. While pure Paliminium by itself doesn't do anything interesting, what *is* interesting is what happens when you add things to it. For instance, if you take pure Paliminium, add just a little bit of Storium, and apply power to this metal amalgam, it actually repels gravity waves. The mass of metal actually becomes weightless! More power causes more repelling of gravity. Effectively, this allows for the creation of any number of anti-gravity devices. What's also amazing is when you add Godivium to pure Paliminium, it has the opposite effect; gravity is actually increased. You now have the essential building blocks of a tractor beam, which for millennia only existed in science fiction. With this metal, space travel would be revolutionized since traveling from ground level to orbit would be a simple matter of supplying enough power to the ore. And when you consider that we would have sources of unlimited power, the possibilities for discovery are virtually endless."

"With this world so far away, there is actually very little we know about Eden, but when you think about it, isn't this what we as a people are all about? Isn't the discovery of knowledge, and the wonder this voyage promises, worth whatever price is to be paid?"

After continuing with many more details about the mission, the specific costs, and how it was planned to take place, Ehobak neared the end of his dissertation.

"At this time, I'd like to open up the floor to any questions."

Many hands were raised, but since he didn't know the names of all the council members, he pointed to one of the members near him. That council member stood.

"I am Council Member Kaz'Enen from the district of Zentri Station. My question has to do with the cost versus benefit analysis of the project. I am inclined to think this mission is one where the necessary resources will be prohibitive. I'm not sure we should devote this much to an effort that, while amazing in terms of pure science, still doesn't return enough to us as a people to merit this sort of expenditure. Our resources are finite, Lord Aramine, and we need to make sure what we have is put to the best long-term benefit of all involved."

Just when Ehobak was searching his mind for an answer, another council member stood and, even though it was against standard procedure, began to speak. "I am Ulan of the terraformed plains of Aziz, and if I may, I'd like to speak to the issues the honorable Kaz'Enen has raised."

Ehobak replied, "The speaker of the floor recognizes Ulan of the terraformed plains of Aziz."

"Lord Kaz'Enen raises some good points about the benefits of the mission that should be important to the consideration of the project, but I would like to raise another point which should be equally considered by all members of the council: what will be the long-term benefit of this mission? As both Lord Aramine and Lord Kaz'Enen have pointed out, this project is indeed expensive. But have you considered the far-reaching benefits this would afford to us as a people?"

Turning to the council members representing the outlying colonies established on other planets, Ulan continued. "For instance, when it comes time for you to travel back to your home worlds, you are now relegated to getting on a rocket ship, blasting off, and traveling to a spaceship waiting for you in orbit. That ship is designed to travel for a relatively long period of time until you get to your colony. Right?"

"But," he continued, "let's suppose the raw element Paliminium is being mined from a planet like Eden. Let's also suppose this element is available for all to use. Those who needed to travel to their ship in orbit would no longer require the dangerous, expensive, and environmentally damaging rocket engines that currently raise us aloft."

Turning to a different section of the chamber, where those who run and oversee food production and distribution in their respective districts sat, he said, "Ask yourself how much does it cost our society to not just grow the food, but to transport food and supplies to outlying regions? The costs are tremendous, aren't they?"

Ehobak could easily see where Ulan was going with this line of reasoning, and he liked it. It was ingenious really, and he could see the chamber was filled with a wide array of personalities, but also was filled with the most brilliant of the planet. A small smile started to form on Ehobak's face.

Ulan continued speaking to the food growing members of the council. "Imagine goods and supplies delivered not on a transport vehicle, but on one which floats along with no resistance. The expenditure of resources to transport these goods to outlying regions is now cut dramatically. I wouldn't be surprised if it didn't cut the expenditure for delivery by a factor of four, or even better."

Another member stood up to speak, and this one didn't even bother asking for the floor, even though chamber rules normally dictated he should have. Since he was at the podium, it would have been up to Ehobak to enforce the rules of discussion and engagement in the council chamber; however, he felt the interchange was healthy and shouldn't be stifled in any way. He decided to let it go.

"I am Tal Icata of the colony of Lani-4. What I am concerned about is the potential effects of not only being in suspended animation for that long, but the effect this will have on the families they leave behind. What about their children?"

Ehobak decided to speak to this question. "One of the issues that hasn't been discussed in this forum yet is that any member of society who wishes to go on this voyage is allowed to do so. There have been several who have already signed up to be part of this mission; however, when they sign up, it is with the understanding they will be away from their families for an extended period of time. Since this is an unusual mission, we are allowing family heads to bring their entire family, children included. It is not our aim to separate loved ones, so we have decided to make this trip familyoriented."

This took the council by surprise, and for a few moments many were too stunned to say anything. This type of approach to space travel was unprecedented, and while not distasteful to any, still there were many who had to digest what had just been said. A general murmur started among the members, and there were many side discussions.

After some time, Ehobak sensed it was time to return the focus of the room to a public discussion, instead of private one-on-ones. "Council members, may we call the meeting to order?"

The commotion of the chamber died down, and one member stood. "I am Elendil of the mountains of Xari-Queni. In discussion with my colleagues here, it is apparent there are several on the fence as to whether this proposal should be approved. I, for one, am inclined to approve the mission, but many here aren't so sure." Turning to his fellow council members, Elendil then said, "Since this is the end of the day, and since we are scheduled for a week of personal time this next week, I would like to propose that we allow time for us all to think about the proposal Lord Aramine has brought before us today. When we reconvene, we can hear the rest of the proposal, then bring it up for a vote. This will give us all time to think more about how we feel about the mission, and about how this will impact the overall good of the planet."

By this time, the coordinator had approached the podium, and Ehobak acquiesced his position. The coordinator spoke.

"We have all heard the proposal put forth by Elendil of the mountains of Xari-Queni. All in favor of adopting his proposal of deferring decision on the proposal of the mission to Eden put forth by Lord Aramine say 'aye.'"

There was a pervasive "aye" heard.

"All opposed, say 'nay.'"

There were a few "nays."

"The proposal to defer a decision on Lord Aramine's proposal has passed by evident demonstration of a simple majority. Before we adjourn, is there anything you wish to say Lord Aramine?"

Taking the microphone, Ehobak replied, "My distinguished fellow colleagues, if there is anything I want you to consider while we are adjourned, it would be this. Discovery is the engine of growth, and growth is the engine of happiness and contentment. This is the very fabric of our society. A vote for this mission is a vote that will bring our society unprecedented happiness and contentment for countless generations."

At Ehobak's words, applause broke out again, softening the blow that a decision on his proposal wouldn't come today.

Ehobak relinquished the podium to the coordinator. "We will reconvene in one week. This meeting is now adjourned."

All stood, and the clamor of conversation quickly rose. Ehobak approached the podium, gathered his materials, and placed them in his bag once again. The cameras covering the proceedings and broadcasting them to all on the planet now could see an overall view of the entire chamber. If you looked closely, you could see one lone individual on the stage gathering his things and then walking off. From this distance, though, it was impossible to see the profound look of disappointment on the face of Ehobak.

Meanwhile, Ruavu was at home with their children. The three of them had been watching the proceedings, and they were all very proud of their husband and father who just had the privilege of speaking before the illustrious Grand Council of Galimar. The children knew they certainly had something they could brag about to their friends. Quietly, though, Ruavu knew she was going to have a big task in front of her tonight, that of assuaging the tired and pensive soul of her soul mate. She quickly got in touch with the mothers of some friends of their children, seeing to it that her children would be spending the night somewhere else.

Another person watching the proceedings took a special interest in the events of the council chamber. His name was Khreelon Tellindor and, for reasons of his own, he decided traveling on this voyage would be just what he needed. At the first of the week, Ehobak would receive a visit from someone that would be just what he needed.

CHAPTER 3

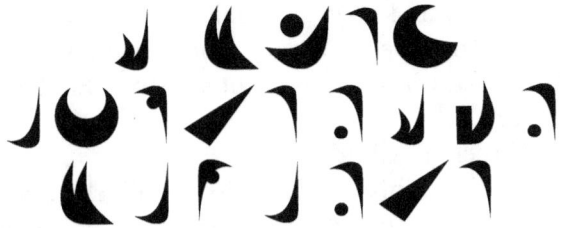

"**G**ASEA HEADQUARTERS. MAY I HELP you?"

Autim sat in the main lobby of the Galimarian Space Exploration Agency busily answering incoming calls and taking messages. One of the more interesting ways communications happened in Galimarian society was that most everyone had a communications device which sat in the ear canal. Also, one of the optional features was a contact lens that contained millions of photoelectric cells. The net result was not only could they make and receive calls with no discernible device, but they also had the ability to receive and look up information on the planetary information network. If the incoming call was a video call, they could even see the face of the person they were talking to. Whenever Autim came to work, her station sensed her presence and gave her the ability to log in and receive calls for GASEA on her own personal communications system. To the untrained, it looked as if she were sitting at a desk talking to herself all day.

"One moment please, while I connect you."

On a panel in front of her, were controls she used to route calls to the proper destination. Pressing one or two buttons, her present call was transferred to the proper destination, and she would move on to the next.

Between calls, she looked up and saw someone standing in front of her. Directing her gaze at the visitor's unremarkable clothes, she instantly sized him up as a tourist and knew she wasn't going to allow him to get anywhere here.

"May I help you?"

"Yes. I'd like to speak with Ehobak Aramine, please," said the visitor.

Autim was very good at her job, knowing she was the first line of defense against anybody coming in and bothering the inhabitants of the space agency. She also knew if this person were someone Ehobak was expecting, he would know a special name Ehobak gave out to his expected visitors. That special name, "Bock," was a shortened form of his name. This visitor was obviously not someone Ehobak knew.

"I'm sorry, Lord ...."

"Tellindor. Khreelon Tellindor."

Inwardly the receptionist smiled. First of all, she knew the distinguished Lord Khreelon Tellindor had no reason to come to GASEA. Lord Tellindor was an archivist, a rather famous one at that, and archivists had no need to come to the space agency. Secondly, if this guy were Lord Tellindor, he most certainly would be dressed better than this. It's not like he was a slob, but still, she knew a person of Lord Tellindor's stature would be dressed differently. She had to admit she had never seen a photo of the real Lord Tellindor, but this guy didn't fit her profile of a notable person.

"I'm sorry, but Lord Aramine isn't available. I'd be happy to take a message for him."

This wasn't the first time this happened to Khreelon. As a life choice, Khreelon dressed minimally, and so most pre-judged him to be young and not very notable. In so doing, they would also be very wrong.

Not only was Khreelon almost 6,000 years old, but he was a very well-known archivist, a Galimar profession that commanded much respect from society. Since it is the responsibility of archivists to keep and maintain the history of the Galimarian people, most looked to them as the keepers of knowledge. They spent their entire lives not only learning where Galimarian society had come from, but were also the ones who people looked to for the wisdom that comes from being taught by the ancients.

Khreelon had distinguished himself early in his career by not only being very versed in the ancestry of the Galimarian society, but also with its social evolution. While Galimar was an amazingly enlightened society, it wasn't always that way. For a long time, it was theorized that Galimarian society, as it is today, was born from a society very different. When Khreelon graduated from his higher education, prevailing opinions suggested Galimar had several different nations which were very nationalistic and very argumentative with each other. Some even suggested these nations actually went to war with each other over topics that didn't really matter, even though they were all Galimarians. This was very different from current thinking patterns, so these types of theories were generally discredited.

The idea that these theories were all unsubstantiated and didn't merit serious study came to a crashing end when Khreelon led a team of archaeologists to a remote area of the planet where a lost city was discovered. This was the lost city of Galix, one of the last cities their civilization lived in before the great age of enlightenment. Before this discovery, Galimarian pursuits were largely built on personal endeavors and wealth. By decoding unearthed books and literature, it was evident this attitude led to strife, jealousy, and tremendous social unrest. As Galix was explored more and more, it started to give up its secrets as to how its inhabitants played a major role in helping shape the great age of enlightenment. Before this, it wasn't very clear what triggered society to progress as it did.

Needless to say, the name Khreelon Tellindor was known far and wide. The odd thing was there weren't too many pictures of the man, since he was much more interested in his work than in his fame. The fact that this receptionist knew his name but not his face wasn't surprising.

Khreelon said, in a very pointed manner, "Miss, I suggest you get up, go to his office, and tell him the key to his mission to Eden is standing in front of your desk."

Looking at the man standing in front of her, Autim wondered whether she should do as he asked. She decided to re-route incoming calls, get up from her desk, and at least make the appearance of compliance. Without a word, she stood up from her desk and disappeared behind a locked door. On the other side of the door, she said, "Oh boy."

"What's up?" said an office worker who was making some copies.

"This tourist standing at my desk claims he's Khreelon Tellindor, but I'm telling you, there's no way this guy is Lord Tellindor."

"Really? He's at your desk?"

"Yeah. Here, look through the window in the door. See what I mean?"

The other office worker walked over and looked through the window, and when she did, her face went white. What the receptionist didn't know was the office worker had been trained as an archivist in her own higher education. She later decided not to pursue that career since there were so many others who were significantly smarter and wiser. One of the most significant individuals she had studied was Khreelon Tellindor, the same Khreelon Tellindor she was now staring at through the window.

Turning to Autim, she spoke slowly and carefully. "I suggest that if you want to keep your job, you not only walk but perhaps *run* to Ehobak's office and get him here. Now."

"You don't really think that ...."

"Get him here! *Now!*"

The now ashen-faced Autim turned and immediately fled to the office of Lord Aramine. Normally she would knock before entering, but she was no longer worried about such pleasantries. She was just hoping not to be disciplined for her poor treatment of the visitor. Ehobak was in a meeting with the vice chancellor of GASEA, talking about how the meeting in the Grand Council chambers had gone, so the interruption was not very well received by the vice chancellor.

"What in the name of ...."

The receptionist interrupted. "Lord Aramine, there's a Lord Tellindor here asking for you. Lord Khreelon Tellindor."

At that moment, you could hear a pin drop in Ehobak's office. He looked at the vice chancellor, and the vice chancellor looked back at Ehobak. Without another word, it was instantly understood that this meeting was adjourned. Ehobak stood and quickly followed the receptionist to the front lobby. He walked over to the visitor and stuck out his hand. Autim tried her best to reverse whatever opinion the visitor might have due to her previous behavior.

"Lord Aramine, this distinguished gentleman is Lord Khreelon Tellindor. Lord Tellindor, this is Lord Ehobak Aramine," said Autim.

"You can just call me Bock. I'm pleased to meet you."

"And you can just call me Khreelon. Your skilled receptionist here made me feel quite welcome."

"I'm very glad to hear that."

Behind Ehobak and out of his sight, Autim was powerfully relieved Khreelon had decided to handle the situation as graciously as he did. She silently mouthed a "thank you" to Khreelon; he responded with a slight nod of his head, showing himself to be a down-to-earth, gracious man. She now instantly understood why he chose the garb he did. He was unpretentious, and she knew he didn't have the need to put on airs to anyone.

"So, to what do I owe the honor of your visit?" asked Ehobak.

Autim returned to her station at the front desk, and the two men walked over to a couch and chair located near them in the lobby. Khreelon spoke. "I saw the broadcast of your speech to the Grand Council. I have to say, I was very impressed with what you said. If I didn't know better, it almost seemed like you weren't using any notes."

"Actually, I wasn't. I had a lot of notes, but as I was walking up to the podium, the deliberations which occurred over the proposals before mine caused me to change the overall direction of my speech. I'm not sure what the overall effect was, though. I was just in a meeting with the vice chancellor of GASEA, telling him I wasn't sure whether I helped or hindered the cause."

"Oh, I'm sorry. If I'm keeping you from your meeting, I can come back."

"No, no. That meeting is over now. You're fine. I feel like I'm so close to getting the proposal passed, but I just don't know what I can do to push them over the edge."

"Perhaps I can help with that," replied Khreelon.

For a split second, Ehobak wondered what an archivist could do. Perhaps Khreelon had friends in high places who might influence ... but no, that wouldn't be the case. Influencing members of the Grand Council was a crime, and nobody dared to try it.

"I'm not sure I follow you. How would you be able to help with that?"

"Well," replied Khreelon, "I thought that I would like to go. With you. I'd like to sign on as a crew member on your starship."

At this point, Ehobak would normally direct the inquiry to the personnel office and allow the inquirer to fill out paperwork. In this case, he was absolutely stunned. With his heart beating in his throat, Ehobak took a double, then triple-take at Khreelon, finally managing to croak out a reply.

"You, you want to go on the voyage to Eden?"

"Yes, I do. Do you think you'd have room for me?"

Ehobak was reeling at the thought. Basically, all he could do was blurt out the first thing that came to his mind.

"We'll MAKE room!"

The two men looked at each other, realizing the agreement they had just made sealed the fate of next week's vote in the Grand Council. At that realization, Ehobak simply let out a lone huff.

After a few moments, he was the first to speak. "You do realize that with your backing, the decision on whether to approve the mission proposal will most likely pass."

Khreelon smiled. "That thought did occur to me ..."

"Well," said Ehobak, "that makes you my new best friend!"

The two men laughed out loud, loud enough for Autim to look up and wonder whether they were talking about her faux pas. There weren't any glances her way, so she decided her job was hopefully intact.

"I do have a question about how long it will take to build the starship and get to the point where the mission will leave Galimar," asked Khreelon.

Ehobak loved fielding this question. He loved the reaction he always got. "If we get approval to start the project next week, we should be able to start construction of the ship the following month. At that point, we should be leaving about two months later."

"*Two months?* Have you already started the building of the ship in secret?" asked Khreelon in a very surprised tone.

"No," answered Ehobak, smiling rather enigmatically. "The ship doesn't exist at all yet."

"Then how ...."

"Forgive me, Khreelon, for having a little sport at your expense. Let me explain. You see, there is a little-known technology GASEA has developed called the Builder Robot Technology. These builder robots employ artificial intelligence and are used to do the actual building of the ship in orbit. Galimarian hands don't ever touch the ship during its construction. Raw materials come from orbiting asteroids and are smelted by fully autonomous and automated foundries located on each asteroid body. Once smelted, the metals and other materials are then transported to the construction site by robot transport and fashioned into the parts needed for the ship itself.

"The builder robots all follow a master plan which is uploaded and updated from our offices here at ground control. Master robotics engineers on the ground communicate to the robots in orbit. The real genius, though, is that the robots have the ability to replicate and build more of themselves to get the job done. As a result, work is relentless and is being done on the ship every hour of every day and night. I imagine it might actually look like a swarm of millions of crawling creatures all converging in one spot. I plan on keeping a video camera trained on the ship as it is built in order to watch my dream materialize before my eyes."

"But, two months?" asked Khreelon incredulously.

"Yes. Two months. Conceivably, two months from now we could be preparing to leave," replied Ehobak. Looking at Khreelon, he began to worry if that was more than Khreelon was willing to accept. "Is that a problem for you?"

Looking over from the window where he had been staring, Khreelon replied, "Oh no. That isn't a problem at all. I just wasn't expecting that sort of timeline."

Relieved, Ehobak replied, "Good. Then, in that case, I would like to ask a favor of you."

CHAPTER 4

ᒣ᛫ᒍ ᛫ᘁᒍᒍ ᒍ
ᚄ ᒍᒍᒍ ᚄ
ᘁᒍᘂᒍᒍᒍᒍ ᒍ ᒍᒍᒍᚄ

T HE SHADOWS WERE JUST STARTING to grow long. This time of year the cerulean blue hues of the afternoon Galimarian sky grew deeper and deeper until they reluctantly yielded to the deepest of crimson, gold, and ginger arriving just before the fall of night. Though night hadn't yet arrived, one could already see the outlines of two moons revolving around Galimar. Idda was a soft, pale blue whereas Genipar was more ruddy in color. Once the black of night fell, lights from hundreds of colonies populating both moons could be seen, but it was the middle of the summer months in this hemisphere so night was a few hours away. The ocean breeze drifting past Ehobak and Ruavu was both refreshing and relaxing.

The children were off enjoying their time with schoolmates, so the two lovers enjoyed time well spent with each other. Sitting on a blanket stretched out on the ground, Ehobak leaned his back against a large hardwood tree behind him. Ruavu sat to his right side facing him with her knees bent to her side, leaning her own back against his leg which was bent at the knee to support her. The two looked at each other, simply luxuriating in the time spent enjoying their respective soul mates.

Ehobak was wearing a white, open-chested, long-sleeved shirt which hung loosely from his shoulders; it was tucked lightly into his black pants. Ruavu was wearing a summer dress equally open since it was summer and the warmth inspired a free and easy spirit. Off in the distance, there was another family enjoying the afternoon as well. The young son from that family was playing a stringed instrument, perfectly rounding out the scene where, if you concentrated hard enough, hopefully time would stand still. Next to Ehobak and Ruavu was a small wicker basket containing a simple array of treats and a bottle of wine. Ehobak gazed into the eyes of his mate and Ruavu did the same, resting her hand on the exposed muscular chest of her husband.

One of the more notable features of Galimarian people were their eyes. Normally, there was no color in the pupils. Aside from the whites, the center of the eye was nothing but deep pools of ebony, seemingly beckoning you to spend time gazing into them deeply in search of the soul. No one on Galimar had any color to their eyes, with the *distinct* exception of when someone was in love.

As all intelligent life knows, love inspires poets to write legends, choirs to sing sonnets, and artists to mold and shape the world around them in a way which somehow expresses the intoxicating ebb and flow of warmth that love engenders. The flow of chemistry between two who love one another is undeniable to any who have experienced such a blessing, but in the case of Galimarians, something truly special happens. When the mind of a man or woman on this planet is bathed in the hormones which only come with deep love, the bottomless pools of raven black give way to eyes colored with a light shade of blue. Ehobak and Ruavu were looking at each other with eyes that revealed the truth of how they both felt.

After a while, a slight smile broke out on Ehobak's face. "There's my blue love," he said, recalling a verse to a well-known melody.

"Only for you, my beloved mate," said Ruavu as she traced her fingers back and forth over the peaks and valleys on Ehobak's chest.

After allowing time to casually drift by, and after refilling the glasses with more wine, Ehobak was the first to speak.

"I have a question for you."

"What would you like to know, my love?"

"Rue," he said, calling his wife the pet name only he used for her, "It appears the council approval will probably happen with Khreelon signing on to the mission. My question has to do with you and this mission. Do you still feel the same way? Are you still ok with going?"

Ruavu cast her gaze to the side and regarded a brilliantly colored, small winged insect which had landed on a flower near them. "There was a time when you started planning this mission when I might have answered that question differently. Early on, when it became apparent this mission was one designed for entire families, and when it became evident ours was going to be one of them, I wasn't so sure I wanted to go. We later had our two children and, as they grew, there were times when I wondered if it would be wise to take them with us.

"But then," Ruavu paused as if she was thinking, "I started looking at where we would be going. I started to think about the adventure we would have, and how amazing it would be to experience a world which had never been visited by us before. In time, I came to realize this would be something our children would never forget, and might be something which could easily channel their young minds toward explorations like their father's. I decided I wanted them to have the same respect and dignity their father enjoyed, so this is something I want them to be part of.

"Speaking personally, it took me some time to warm up to the idea of traveling in space for years on end, but when I learned of the plan to use pods while we are actually traveling, then it seemed like it wouldn't be that bad."

"I'm glad to hear that," said Ehobak. "In times past, a person in my position would be looking at spending very long days, weeks, months, even years away from home. Now that we are going to be using the new builder robot technology to build the starship, and since it will be completed in only about two months, I'm not going to be away from home nearly as long as I would have been before."

"I'm glad of that, my husband. I don't think I'd be able to stand to be away from you that long anyway."

"That's part of why I wanted you to go. If you didn't, and you stayed here on Galimar while I went on this voyage, it would be 20 years of life I'd miss out on with you and the kids. They are growing up so fast now. Before you know it, Nafan is going to be hitting the age of enlightenment and receiving his or her amulet. I just … I just don't want to miss that. Do you understand what I mean?"

"I certainly do," echoed Ruavu. "When your child reaches the age of enlightenment and it becomes apparent which they are going to be, a girl or a boy, well … that is just something I want to experience with you there. I don't want to settle with having to tell you about it after the fact. When Nafan comes of age and reveals his or her gender to us at the Celebration of Hin, we're going to have quite a party!"

"That's for sure," agreed Ehobak, smiling. As the two of them gently stroked the exposed skin of the other, a brief period of silence was enjoyed between them. A question came to his mind. "Do you think you know what Nafan is going to be?"

One of the ways Galimarian biology differs from the biologies of most species they have encountered is in their gestation and development. While most species develop gender-specific characteristics while still in the womb, Galimarian children physically develop very slowly. The time spent in the womb ends up being only about three months, but the child is born with no gender. It isn't until about 50 years later that the body begins to develop characteristics which indicate what gender the child will eventually become. It won't be for about another 40 years until the transition into one gender or the other is complete. Tests can be done early on, of course, to find out what gender the child will eventually become, but most just choose to be surprised.

"Not really," responded Ruavu. "I mean, I think Nafan is going to be a boy, but I'm not really sure. I'm pretty excited to find out, though."

"A boy?! Really? I was thinking girl." Ehobak laughed. "Then again, I can't really say Nafan is into things that are classically female."

Ruavu looked down, contemplating her next words. "One thing I will say, though, is I am truly blessed to be married to the man you are. All of our children truly have a good role model to live up to regardless of their gender."

Staring at the young boy in the distance, Ehobak corrected the word used by Ruavu. "You mean both." It was a statement more than a question.

Ruavu smiled to herself as she continued staring at a small design on her sun dress. "No, I mean all."

From her peripheral vision, Ruavu saw that Ehobak continued to look off into the distance. After a few moments, he slowly turned his head toward his wife. She turned toward her husband, and it was at this moment when it was impossible to tell where the blue of the sky ended and the blue of her eyes began. Ehobak's complexion changed.

"You mean ...?"

"Yes, my love. You're going to be a father again," said Ruavu with an expression which could only come from one who was with child. She was glowing at the expression of love coming from her husband now, and when he brought her near and kissed her tenderly, she melted into his embrace. Wrapping her arms around his body, the two became one. The world could evaporate, the sun could stop shining, but they wouldn't notice. There was a universe of love between them, and they both believed no one would ever know the exquisite delight they felt at this very moment.

CHAPTER 5

Kaitherion was the city where the Grand Council of Galimar stationed its administrative facilities. Galimarians had visited enough civilizations in their small corner of the galaxy to know just because a city is a governmental center doesn't mean it must be attractive. Kaitherion broke that mold, though. Thousands of years ago, it was designed not by political entities, but by the artists of society. Regardless of how you arrived at the city, you were presented with an artistic wonder which always gave one pause. The city center where the governmental offices were located was a pleasing combination of angles, curves, and greenery. Whereas other civilizations seemed to let their cities run down from the moment they were built, Kaitherion was the picture of cleanliness. Every Galimarian living there took pride in the city. If something needed cleaning, they wouldn't wait for another to clean it.

Most of the time that wasn't necessary. Robot technology had developed to the point where worker robots could take on more of the menial tasks such as maintaining the cleanliness of the streets and facades of the buildings. Parks were also maintained by the automatons.

As Ehobak arrived at the main administrative building of the Grand Council, he was greeted by a bright-faced intern who one day would no doubt be a member of the council; judging from her young appearance, she was probably not going to cross that proverbial threshold for another 10 millennia. The hallway leading to the council chamber was 10 meters in width but easily 20 meters in height. The pale white and gray marble of the floors and walls were accented by massive emerald green columns quarried from the cliffs near the ocean. Between each of the columns were statues of notable figures in Galimarian history. One statue in particular was special to Ehobak; it was a likeness of his great grandfather, Jobiah Aramine. Jobiah was one of the architects of the treaty that led to peaceful relations between Galimar and a collection of inhabited planets known as The Protectorate. Inhabitants of The Protectorate were in possession of high technology, but were not in possession of the same enlightened sensitivities as Galimar. Jobiah was one of the first to make contact with them, and he was astute enough to see that peaceful relations would be both rewarding and strategically necessary since they seemed to be rather excitable. Jobiah lived about 80,000 years ago; in the interim, members of The Protectorate mellowed considerably. Many attribute this to the influence of Galimar.

Looking at the rectangular pedestal underneath the bust of Jobiah, Ehobak thought about how the ashes of his ancestor were kept there. It had long been the desire of his family to place the amulet Jobiah wore on the statue in a place of honor, but for some unknown reason, that amulet was lost to the sands of time. Before moving on, he reached out to touch the stone effigy as if to touch his own past.

Moving on to the same anteroom where he waited before, Ehobak took a seat. A video wall showing the events of the council chamber took up a complete wall of the anteroom; it was evident the council meeting was due to start soon. The chamber was nearly filled with members, all milling about and discussing topics ranging from Ehobak's proposal to what they had for breakfast that day. As with the last session when Ehobak brought his proposal to the chamber, there were many who were keenly interested in the vote which no doubt was to be rendered today on the mission. Actually, a lot of tension could be felt by all in the room. It seemed this particular proposal had polarized the people into two camps: those who were in agreement with the proposal, and those who, while not necessarily against it, still weren't too sure it was the best use of planetary resources. It seemed all were anxious about whether it would pass; all except one, Ehobak Aramine, who sat with a smile on his face as if he had something to hide.

Indeed.

Ruavu sat at home with Nafan and watched the council chamber proceedings. Jillintor, or Jill for short, was over at a friend's house watching the same program on the planetary network. Jill had just enjoyed the celebration of Hin in her honor, when she revealed to all that her body was taking on the features of a female. These days she spent a lot of time with her girlfriends, their days filled with efforts toward refining exactly what it meant to be this gender. Their amulet companions were helping a lot with understanding what life would be like now; it was a new and wonderful experience for them all, one they enjoyed very much. Jill confessed the day before to her mother that the best part for her was the clothes!

Back in the council chamber, the coordinator saw it was almost time to begin the proceedings, so he stepped up to the podium. "May I have your attention."

The coordinator waited for a few moments and once again said, "May I please have your attention! The meeting of the Grand Council of Galimar will commence in 10 minutes. Please find your seats while we listen to a short musical interlude from the Kaitherion men's chorale."

Lined up in three rows, each row with 15 men dressed in traditional operatic garb, the men began singing an almost ethereal a capella song. Council members began finding their seats as soon as they possibly could, so as to pause and appreciate the perfect tonal qualities of these well-trained, gifted individuals. The overall hum of conversations slowly ebbed; eventually, the only thing which could be heard were the melodious voices of the men who had obviously been honing their vocal skills for a very long time. When they finished their final piece, all members of the council stood in thunderous applause, and the men graciously bowed, accepting the high praise as they each filed out of the chamber.

"We would like to thank the Kaitherion men's chorale for their beautiful rendition of Theophilief's 5th symphony." Though the Grand Council had already sat back down in their chairs, there was once again great applause from each member.

"Today is the fifth day of the seventh month of the year. The date is Chanivar 5th, 143112. I now pronounce the council in session."

Looking down at his notes, the coordinator organized his thoughts prior to speaking.

"Before we continue with the discussion of Council Proposal 143112-342, also known as the Eden Project, I would like to open the floor to the council members, allowing for consideration of any new business."

Under normal circumstances, a myriad of issues would be related to the coordinator one by one to get those items on the schedule. The coordinator had his recording device ready to make a record of the matters that needed to be considered, but there was nothing to record. Never once in Ehobak's memory had there been a case of no new issues being brought up after a break. This was, indeed, strange. It wasn't as if the council members couldn't ever bring up issues in the future if they didn't bring them up now; it just meant they would bring forward whatever issues they needed to discuss tomorrow.

But without discussing it amongst themselves ahead of time, each and every one of the 281 members of the Grand Council of Galimar had decided they would defer any matters needing to be discussed until a later time, making it possible for the council to get straight into the proposal brought forward by Ehobak.

The coordinator looked around the auditorium for anybody to bring forward issues of concern. After about 30 seconds of silence, he figured out nothing was going to come.

"Right! Well then, we will get right to the matter at hand. At this time, I would like to call Lord Ehobak Aramine to come forward and deliver his proposal, then field questions from council members."

Ehobak had seen the writing on the wall when there were no responses to the call for new matters to be considered, so he had left the anteroom and made his way to the waiting area just off the stage. As he approached the podium applause broke out, typical for any speaker invited to address the council. Once he reached the podium and stood there for a few moments, the applause died down and he began to speak.

"Esteemed members of the Grand Council of Galimar, I appreciate the warm reception to myself, and the team of designers and builders I represent on the Eden project. We have already discussed an overview of the project, so now I would like to open the floor to any questions you might wish to pose."

Within moments there were several members holding up their hands, waiting for Ehobak to call on them. In situations like this, it is customary for the oldest ones in the chamber to be called on first; Ehobak scanned the audience, trying to pick out the oldest council member. His eyes landed on a gentleman in the third row wearing an emerald green cloak over a light beige undergarment. Ehobak pointed at him, and he stood.

"My name is Lord Glisseene of the Meropa provinces, and I have questions on the scope of the mission. What is the planet you are going to visit like, how is the ship built, and what will the overall experience of the voyage be like?"

"Thank you Lord Glisseene for your insightful questions. I was rather hoping to be asked about this because I have a special treat for you all."

Reaching up to remove his amulet of understanding from around his neck, Ehobak continued. "As you all know, these allow us to communicate with our amulet companions through a virtual reality interface. My companion and I have worked hard on this proposal. Countless hours have been spent planning and re-planning. Testing and re-testing. Eventually, we both decided the best way to present the entire scope of the project was to create a virtual tour of the ship for you to enjoy, then take you through an accelerated version of the voyage itself. I will now place my amulet in the cradle here on the podium, and if you would be so kind as to go in-world using your own amulets, I will join you there and give you a tour through the designs of the ship. To those listening to this presentation around the planet, you will also have the opportunity to see what the council members experience, though you will be observers only and not participants. The access code to the presentation is 143112-342 Eden."

While not unprecedented, an amulet in-world experience on a proposal before the council was rare enough to end up being something everyone instantly looked forward to experiencing. As each council member held their amulet in one hand, the other hand was used to enter 143112-342 Eden into the main screen of the amulet. Instantly each member was granted a dazzling vision of lights and sounds, eventually leading them to a lounge aboard an orbiting space dock.

The number of people who tapped into the presentation from home was unprecedented. Individuals who were in charge of monitoring the data feeds for distribution of the amulet experience had never seen this number of people all come together at the same time, but it didn't surprise them since this particular project was literally something everybody was talking about. It didn't matter who you talked to, every person on the planet had not only heard about the project, but also had an opinion about it; some negative, but mostly positive.

The space dock was little more than a scaffolding roughly spherical in shape. The sphere had a diameter of about five kilometers from side to side, and the lounge where the council members now found themselves was built into one of the dock's side walls. The lounge was smartly decorated and had this been the real lounge and not a virtual reality equivalent, drinks would have been served by the hosts who normally worked here.

On one wall, there was a floor-to-ceiling window that looked out into the central area of the dock, and through that window one could observe the activities within the dock. This actually was the first time many of the council members had ever seen the dock (rather, its perfect virtual reality equivalent) and it was quite impressive. Secretly, Ehobak was hoping the overall experience would be overwhelming to the council members, but these men and women were well-seasoned members of society, and it would be foolhardy to think a little amulet magic would truly sway them one way or the other.

In this virtual reality world, Ehobak held in his hand what amounted to a controller which would be used by him to control the events within this simulation. Once he saw that all council members had materialized in the simulation, he spoke.

"Council members, you are now standing in lounge number six on the orbiting space construction dock. The dock is named Eden One, and will be built specifically for the purpose of facilitating the building of the Eden project ship."

One of the council members spoke up. "Are you saying the dock hasn't even been created yet?"

"That is correct." Reaching down to the pad, he pressed a combination of keystrokes and, outside the window, a robot rushed up and hovered in front of them. "This marvel of engineering is what we call a builder robot. For many decades, GASEA has been working hard on the technology that makes this little guy possible. The whole point of this technology is to actually perform the tasks involved with building a ship in the vacuum of space without risk to any Galimarian. The tasks this robot can be assigned are almost endless, but the first task they will accomplish is the building of the space dock where the Eden project ship will be constructed."

Another council member spoke up. "How will this one robot do all that?"

With a little bit of showmanship, Ehobak replied, "I'm glad you asked." He clicked a couple more keystrokes on his controller, and roughly 3,000 additional builder robots rushed in seemingly from nowhere, all fanning out from the central viewpoint of the lounge where the council currently stood.

"As you can see, we can replicate the builder robots at will. In fact, one of the abilities built into them is the intelligence to know when additional builder robots are needed to accomplish the tasks that have been uploaded to their memory banks. If they sense the most efficient way to accomplish the job they've been given is to have more robots, then before they start the job, they will spend time building more of themselves. Once they get to a point where they have enough of themselves to perform their assigned duties, they begin the construction project."

"How many robots do you think will be used for this job?"

"At this time, it is hard to know exactly how many will eventually be used on the project at its peak, but according to our robot systems engineers, the current estimate is somewhere around 3,900."

This seemed to take the council by surprise. They hadn't really understood the enormity of the project, but now its overall size was beginning to dawn on them. This was the main reason for presenting the project to the council in this manner, but Ehobak was astute enough to know this type of presentation might also backfire. There could easily be some who would be overwhelmed by the sheer scale of the project and come to the conclusion it was biting off too much. He felt reasonably confident that if he prepared well enough for their questions, though, he would be able to allay any of their fears.

Another question came from somewhere in the middle of the crowd. "Once the project is complete, what happens to all the robots? What happens with the dock? Are they just going to be floating out here as space junk?" This was a question fielded from the chairman of the Bureau of Global Environmental Defense. It was the bureau's mission to make sure the Galimarian home world was always maintained pristine and beautiful for future generations.

"That was one of the bigger design considerations we had when creating the builder robots," Ehobak responded. "They have been built with a rather significant level of intelligence integrated into their systems. All robots are made aware of the plans for the project they have had assigned to them; the Eden Project ship, in this case. The robots are all designed to work under the direction of the engineers and architects on the ground, but are also designed to work perfectly with each other. Once the project gets to a point where the usefulness of so many robots beings to wane, the robots that are no longer needed will begin to decommission themselves. The remaining robots will then recycle materials from the decommissioned units, as well as the parts of the space dock that are no longer needed, and those materials will be used to complete the remainder of the ship. The end result is a ship floating in space with no discernible trace of how it was built. In the end, there will only be 20 builder robots remaining, kept on board in a powered-down state for continuing ship maintenance."

Ehobak knew this was a lot for the council to digest, so he remained quiet for a while. While he maintained his silence, there was worldwide discussion about all he had said; most were completely floored by the project's level of sophistication, and were amazed at how the project was going to be conducted.

After a couple of minutes, and after the council members had a few small conversations among themselves, another question was raised from the back of the crowd. "Where will the materials for the building project come from?"

"The materials will come from here." Reaching down to the controller in his hand, Ehobak pressed a few more keystrokes, and suddenly the entire body of the Grand Council was transported from the posh environment of the dock lounge to a floating platform out in the middle of the vacuum of space. Since this was only a simulation, it wasn't harmful, but it was still disconcerting to have the feeling of being out in space. There was the sensation of gravity and the sensation of breathable air, but the visuals of it all were still a bit unsettling.

The platform they were standing on was hovering in front of a massive body of rock floating in space. This ovoid asteroid was roughly 20 kilometers in length, and 15 kilometers in width. It had several indentations where it had no doubt been assaulted by its smaller traveling cousins; it seemed to be lazily turning while suspended in the vacuum of space.

"This is one of the thousands of asteroids surrounding Galimar. It is named Pomona," continued Ehobak, "and as you all know, under Council Proposal 143111-126 approved by yourselves last year, GASEA mining operations were started on it for the purpose of harvesting materials that could possibly be used in future missions. What you may not know is not only have the mining operations been fruitful, they have been a runaway success. Originally, we had hoped to mine some basic metals, but what we didn't know was that underneath a crust of iron and manganese, this asteroid contains significant quantities of just about every other alkali, alkaline, transition, and post-transition metal in the periodic table of elements. There have even been significant pockets of gasses found under the surface including hydrogen, helium, and even nitrogen."

Seeing an opportunity to allay some of the fears certain council members had on stretching planetary resources too thinly on this project, he added, "What this means is all of the materials we need for production of the ship can be found on this asteroid. The days of consuming planetary resources for the production of raw shipbuilding materials, and the days of using heavy lift rockets to transport those materials to orbit, has come to an end."

This was significant in the minds of the council members, and Ehobak knew it. If a poll were taken, 55% of them would have voted for the proposal already, but there was a significant number of members who had been undecided. They were attempting to be pragmatic on whether this proposal would be in the global interests of Galimar. This new point was something which addressed many of their particular concerns, since none of them wanted to see hardship for any Galimarian if this proposal was approved. Learning that production of the ship would cost virtually nothing in terms of planetary resources was huge; that same poll would now show an astounding jump in the approval rating from 55% to 70%. Passage wasn't guaranteed because, due to Testimonial Law, a proposal of this magnitude would require a 75% majority vote.

Seeing that he had left enough time for this to sink in, Ehobak decided to continue the simulation. "Let's move along now and see how the ship is built."

Pressing more ridges on his virtual controller, the entire complement of council members returned to the lounge where they had started this tour, but now the scene out the window had changed; thousands of robot workers began swarming around a central point in the middle of the dock.

"What we see here is the beginning of ship construction. I have accelerated the scene for your convenience; the actual time it will take to construct the ship will only be about two months."

The approval rating just went to 71%.

"The first parts to be constructed are the massive dark matter engines which will not only propel the ship, but also provide all power needed for the ship."

As Ehobak was speaking, builder robots were darting back and forth over a central point in the dock until something started to appear below them. Like insects constantly moving with lightning speed over the mass they were all working on, roughly cylindrical shapes started to emerge beneath them, along with a myriad of pipes and connections which seemed to form miraculously. Similar to watching the growth of a plant on fast-forward video, pipes and structural supports rapidly grew out from the original mass created by the robots. It was breathtaking to witness the parts materialize. Off to the left side, three separate masses of robot insects seemed to be working independently, but still at breakneck speed. They began constructing six identical pieces of machinery which quickly took shape.

"To the left, you will see the shield generators being built. Since we will be traveling very fast for the duration of the voyage, it is necessary to have an impenetrable shield in front of the ship so any stray space debris doesn't pierce the hull, or its inhabitants for that matter. The shield technology recently perfected by the University of Mundi will be utilized for this purpose and, for reasons of redundancy and failover, we are creating six separate and independent shield systems so if one system fails, another can be used while the other is repaired."

As construction continued on the six shield generators, the truly massive engines now appeared to be complete. The engines which had been sitting next to each other were now moved as the overall skeleton of the ship started to take shape.

From the middle of the crowd, a voice came through. "I have a question. I was wondering where the exhaust from the engines will go?"

"These engines are not the same ones you may be used to," answered Ehobak. "Up to this point, rocket engines have utilized a system of combustion to accomplish propulsion. This engine system will use a completely different approach. When we were still able to travel to the planet Palimine, we secured a sufficient amount of the mineral Paliminium, the same element we are seeking on Eden. As I brought out in the last meeting, this precious metal makes anti-gravity possible, and all our reserves of Paliminium are being used on this ship. Due to the metal's nature, no exhaust is produced, but rather when massive amounts of power are applied to it, the effects of the antigravity field are directed to the rear of the ship. Standard laws of physics take over from this point, and when repulsion of gravity is realized at the rear of the ship, the rest of the ship is moved forward."

An air of understanding seemed to spread over the crowd as they once again directed their attention to the vista before them outside the window. The understructure of the ship was largely complete, and it seemed to resemble a snowflake; one almost three kilometers in width, though. Rising up its center were several tremendously tall spires, and from the six arms of the snowflake were six pylons which curved back toward the center of the structure. On the bottom side of the snowflake, an understructure was being built around the massive engines which were now completely obscured by the structure surrounding them.

As the construction continued, it was obvious the six pylons at the ends of the six arms were designed with hinges at their base so the pylon could be retracted to the "ground level" of the arm. Once the construction of the pylons had been completed, the shield generators were installed onto the end of each pylon.

The skeleton was now being covered in a gleaming white and metallic skin. Spires continued to emanate from the central structure. With a dome-like scaffolding surrounding them, they almost looked like buildings. The more they took shape, something looked oddly familiar. Ehobak decided now was a good time to address that familiarity.

"The shield generators, installed onto the ends of the vertical pylons, will be in use during flight. Once the ship has arrived at Eden and the shields are no longer needed, the pylons are designed to retract to ground level. You may also notice the structures on the central portion of the ship seem oddly familiar. Can anyone figure out why that might be?"

Someone from the front of the crowd spoke up. "I would recognize that anywhere. It's a model of the lost city of Arageena, pictured in the writings of Thornyka."

Nodding and a general murmur of recognition spread amongst the council members with that revelation, and most were able to connect the significance of this design. Thornyka wrote a series of very popular, yet completely fictional books centering on the existence of a city called Arageena, which held a race of beings who reached for the stars and, after doing so for millennia, achieved immortality. This ship was destined to reach farther out to the stars than Galimar had ever reached before, so it was a fitting literary connection.

Ehobak continued his narration of the unfolding events. "We're starting to get to the end of building the ship's outer shell, and it's time to shift ourselves to the inside of the ship and watch how construction will continue."

The council members were now taken to the bridge of the ship which had been completed, and he was able to continue his dissertation.

"This, your honors, is the bridge of the ship, where much of the voyage will be controlled. As you can see on the view screen at the front of the room, the rest of the ship is completed, the dock around the ship has been dismantled, and we are about ready to begin the voyage. Before we begin, let me describe the main features of the bridge. Over to the right is the main navigation station where all details of the voyage are displayed, and where any course modifications can be made. In the center front, the propulsion engineer is stationed, and it is his or her responsibility to monitor the status of the engines and to respond to any commands coming from the captain. To the left is where the operations officer is stationed. Other than propulsion, it is the responsibility of the operations officer to monitor all other systems of the ship. These systems include everything from critical things like life support and shields, all the way down to plumbing, electrical, heating and air conditioning."

"In the center is the captain's chair, flanked by a seat for his second in command on the right, and the ship's science officer is on the left. Are there any questions about the bridge?" asked Ehobak.

"I have a question," said one council member. "You talk about the captain's chair and the stations present here on the bridge. With the suspended animation chambers on the ship, are you and the bridge crew not going to sleep during the voyage?"

Before he had a chance to answer the first question, someone else spoke up. "I was wondering the same thing concerning the shield generators. You mentioned that if one generator fails, the other generator will be used until the first one is fixed. Who will be the one fixing the generator if everybody is sleeping? Will you have a maintenance technician awake?"

"Actually, we will have a captain in charge during the entire voyage, but it won't be me. Allow me to introduce you to the captain of the voyage."

Just then, a new person materialized before the council members. He was dressed in the formal cloak of a distinguished member of GASEA. He stood tall and his complexion was flawless. The council members regarded him with interest.

"This is Glendara, and he," Ehobak paused for effect "is my amulet companion. During each of the 10-year legs of this voyage, Glendara will be in charge of all systems on the ship while we sleep."

The recognition of what Ehobak just said spread throughout the council, and many were surprised at the revelation. Each of the council members had their amulet, which contained a companion but never before had any amulet companion been responsible for not only the life of their living companion but also the lives of other living beings. Each council member loved their respective companions, and there wasn't any reason why they wouldn't trust their companion with their lives. Ehobak knew this was quite a twist in his proposal, and that council members needed time to digest it completely. He then turned to his amulet companion and addressed him directly.

"Glendara, would you tell us how you will be handling the ship during the voyage?"

"Certainly, Ehobak. Esteemed members of the Grand Council of Galimar, it is a privilege to address you regarding the proposal set before you concerning the voyage to the planet Eden. From its inception, I have worked closely with Ehobak on both the design of this ship and the cartographical plans for the voyage to Eden. There isn't any part of this ship I am unfamiliar with and, since I am both sentient and computerized, I am able to take on the task of monitoring all systems on the ship at the same time. During the main part of the voyage, the amulet where I reside will be placed in this cradle," Glendara gestured to a pedestal located to the right of the Captain's chair, "and from that location, I will pilot the ship, monitoring all systems for the duration of the 10-year voyage to Eden, as well as the 10-year return voyage. If I sense there is a situation requiring general maintenance, I will activate the onboard builder robots and instruct them on what needs to be done. If there is something more serious, I have the ability to access the suspended animation pods on board and, if necessary, can bring the engineers out of stasis to handle the situation."

With a slight smile on his face, Glendara said, "It is my intention to make the voyage to Eden and back as boring of a trip as possible." This small joke drew several chuckles from the council body, and really helped the council to warm up to the idea.

At this point, Ehobak said, "Glendara, I'd like to thank you for speaking to the members of the council."

"It was my supreme pleasure Ehobak. Feel free to call me if you need anything."

The image of Glendara began to fade until he was completely gone. Ehobak then said, "Council members, this concludes our presentation. Are there any remaining questions?"

He waited for a reply, but none came. "Thank you, council members. At this time, please exit your amulet simulations and join me back in the council chambers. I have some final points I'd like to present for you to consider."

All council members reached for their virtual amulets, and one by one disappeared from the simulation. When Ehobak left, it dissolved. He stepped to the podium and addressed the council.

"Council members, I'd like to make some final comments on the proposal."

There was a general clamor of conversation happening in the chamber, and he waited patiently for conversations to complete. It took about a full minute for all attention to be fixed upon him. During that time, there was a considerable amount of conferring. In fact, 73% of the members had decided to ratify the proposal. Significant, but still not the three-quarters majority required for passing.

"Members of the council, I would like to address one final issue: the question of what opinion academia has regarding this voyage. Will your constituents oppose this proposal, or will they throw their support behind it and behind you if you support it?"

It was actually very wise for Ehobak to address what many of the remaining undecided council members were concerned with. "I'd like to invite to the stage the newest member of the crew, who asked to be part of the voyage to Eden. I give you ... Lord Khreelon Tellindor."

An audible gasp emanated from the whole of the chamber, and from each and every household tuned into the council chamber feed. Except for one clearing of the throat, it was quiet enough to hear a pin drop as one and all watched Khreelon walk up the steps to the stage and come to the podium.

Autim, the receptionist at GASEA, was watching the feed of the council proceedings as she reflected back to the day she met Lord Tellindor. She quietly laughed at herself for the near-disastrous gaffe. Since that day, she and Khreelon had shared a few moments of joviality at the memory, and had actually become friends.

All knew of his role in the discovery of the lost city of Galix. He was somewhat of a celebrity, so hearing he had become a member of the Eden crew caused the overall opinion of the project to swing far into positive territory.

Khreelon drew in a breath and began to speak. "It is certainly a privilege to address the members of the Grand Council of Galimar. When Lord Aramine asked me to speak to you today, I resisted the idea at first, since it is not in my nature to seek any sort of fame. But after thinking about it, I realized you needed to see the Eden project is something many of my esteemed colleagues feel is an important endeavor for the benefit of all Galimar. I wish to assure you that all of academia feels this voyage is in the best interests of our home planet. It is my sincere hope you ratify this proposal, and allow the mission to take place. Both Ehobak and I thank you for your time."

As he stepped back from the podium, Khreelon was a little surprised to see all the members of the council stand and applaud. This was exactly what most needed to know before agreeing to the proposal. All looked back on the proposal as presented two weeks ago, as well as the virtual reality tour done today, and agreed this was one of the best presented, most well-rounded proposals to come to the council in a very long time.

As Khreelon retreated from the podium, Ehobak stepped forward, placing his hand on Khreelon's shoulder; the two men held onto each other and smiled; the council continued to applaud for at least the next minute. It was overwhelming to both men to receive this level of accolade from such a highly esteemed bastion of society.

The coordinator stepped forward to the podium while they were still on the stage, motioning for the council to come to order and take their seats. He began to speak. "Council members, it is now time to call for a vote on Proposal 143112-342, also known as the Eden Project. A minimum of 75% of the council must vote in favor of the proposal for it to pass. I now call on all members to register their vote for or against Proposal 143112-342."

Each council member had a small table in front of them which they could use to take notes or to place items they needed to keep handy. Built into this table was a simple button press which would allow their vote to be registered on whatever proposal was being decided at the time. Each council member leaned forward and pressed the button representing their vote. As the votes were being registered, the results would be displayed to the coordinator via a screen built into the podium. It allowed the coordinator to easily see when all members had entered their vote, or if there were stragglers. In this case, the votes came in quickly.

Ehobak's hand on Khreelon's shoulder was beginning to involuntarily squeeze the flesh underneath. Khreelon knew how much was riding on this moment; centuries of Ehobak's work all came down to this. Would he be allowed to realize his dream, or would it all go up in flames? Ehobak knew it was foolhardy to think anything was guaranteed.

As the numbers on his display settled and showed the results, the coordinator smiled to himself, then began to speak. "All votes have been registered, and the results have been compiled. Proposal 143112-342, also known as the Eden Project, is hereby ... approved by a landslide vote of 98% in favor!"

Weak in the knees, Ehobak's hand on Khreelon's shoulder was now necessary to remain standing. The thunderous applause on the part of the Grand Council of Galimar in honor of Lord Aramine continued unabated for the next several minutes. It would have continued longer had the two men not retreated from the stage.

The celebration at the Aramine home lasted well into the next day.

CHAPTER 6

◐◑⦅◗⦆⦆⦆ ⦆◑◑◖

ABOUT TWO MONTHS HAD PASSED since the Grand Council of Galimar approved the proposal to build the Eden starship. The ship was truly awesome in its design and construction. When Ehobak personally saw it for the first time, though, he was speechless. Centuries of planning had gone into it, and there wasn't a bolt, screw, or plasma emitter with which he wasn't intimately familiar. But when he climbed on board the real bridge the first time, not the virtual reality one, it felt odd, like putting on an old cloak that had been worn for years. It may be tattered here and there, but it was warm and familiar; having the real bulkheads and structural panels under his feet was strangely comforting. There was nothing tattered about this ship, though. Everything about it was gleaming and new. It even had that new starship smell.

Life support had been operational on main sections of the ship for the last week, so Ehobak could now personally supervise some of the phases of construction. Before then, he had elected to stay aboard the massive Kolimarri space station in geosynchronous orbit around Galimar, stationed directly above GASEA headquarters. It was initially used to relay instructions to the builder robot team until the communications systems came online aboard the new starship.

Up until recently, moving back and forth between the orbiting space dock and the ground would have been quite a chore. The relatively small amount of Paliminium Galimar had in its possession, which was going to be used in the propulsion units of the Eden mission starship, was temporarily being used to gracefully move the shuttles between ground stations and the ship. Once the last shuttle had lifted the last shipment of supplies and personnel from the ground, those same anti-gravity pods used in the shuttle would then be extracted and placed in their permanent locations in the starship. The only difference between the way the shuttle utilized the anti-gravity pods, and the way the ship would use them is the ship would administer much more power to the pods than the shuttles, allowing the Eden starship to realize far greater speeds than its smaller cousins.

Since Paliminium has such a high melting point, the pods can take the additional power. Chemistry-101 teaches that the more power you apply to a material, the more heat you generate. Before the discovery of Paliminium, it was thought Radneum (atomic number 74) had the highest melting point: 3,400 degrees. Paliminium's is over twice that, so it can handle massive amounts of power being applied to it. It almost seems as if you could give it all the power you had, and it would just smile and ask for more. Basically, the dark matter engines on board the starship will generate massive amounts of power, and when that power is applied to the Paliminium pods, tremendous thrust will be achieved.

Personnel had been transferring to the ship for the last week, but up until two days ago, most were engineers in charge of testing all the systems the builder robots had built. The bots were good, but there just wasn't anything that would replace the finesse of a good pair of hands. Several of the systems needed fine tuning, especially the shield generators. GASEA was fortunate to have several doctorate students and professors from the University of Mundi on hand for the completion and testing. Only last night had the generators come online, and the shield generator team was in the final phases of testing those systems. Two days ago, families started arriving on board and had begun the job of setting up the homes they would occupy for the next 20 or so years. They would be asleep for most of that time, but when they would be awake while orbiting around Eden, they needed to feel like they were at home, especially for the sake of the kids.

The engines had been online for five weeks, and had been supplying the necessary power for the completion of the ship. The builder robots had been dismantling the dock itself, and about 80% of the peak number of builder robots had been decommissioned and dismantled. That process was continuing, and if everything remained on schedule, the ship was going to be completed tomorrow.

Khreelon sat in a chair looking out into the deep reaches of space through the large floorto-ceiling windows which adorned his stateroom. Below he could see the Galimarian planet he had called home for the last 6,000 years, but from this vantage point looking at the stars was a simple matter of glancing up, and in so doing he was gifted with some of the most breathtaking vistas possible. From the ground, it was exceedingly rare to see all five moons orbiting around Galimar at the same time; from the Eden ship, it was a regular event. From the ground, the daytime sky appeared blue; from space, with the sky all around, it was the blackest of black accented with an amazing peppering of stars and galaxies, some near, but most very far away.

As Khreelon considered the emptiness of space, he also contemplated the vast emptiness of his heart. One of the bigger and heretofore secret reasons why he had sought out Ehobak to go on this voyage was his awareness that while he had quite a bit of notoriety due to his accomplishments, his ability to find the perfect life mate for himself remained maddeningly lacking. Was he hoping to find a mate amongst the voyagers on this trip? Not really. Most passengers would be complete families. In fact, he was going to be one of the few single people on the ship, but the short period of 20 years for this voyage would end up being a little getaway for him, helping him take his mind off the loneliness he had been feeling lately. Looking out his windows at the massive number of stars and galaxies, he wondered how love would ever come his way. Would he find her? He had a feeling she did exist, but … where?

Recently he had a conversation with his amulet companion Loranna about how unsuccessful he had been in finding love, and she made a suggestion that sounded about as good of an idea as any other. Loranna's idea was for Khreelon to allow her to find the perfect mate since he had failed in that task. He agreed. Her condition, though, was that he had to write a letter to the woman she might find, and when she was found, Loranna would direct her to that letter. It had to be a letter on paper, not on the computer, so nobody would know what it said except his eventual mate. Khreelon knew it was something Loranna had him do to keep from being so despondent about this issue; to give him something to hope for. He didn't know where this future mate was, but somehow Khreelon knew she was out there. He just had to find her.

Khreelon placed the letter, which was rolled up and tied with a red ribbon, in a hidden panel above the head of his bed. The existence of that hidden panel was known only by him, Loranna, and the robotic engineer who confidentially included it in Khreelon's accommodations.

As he thought about that letter, a tone came across the room indicating someone was at his door wishing to visit. Khreelon responded with his standard invitation.

"Come!"

The sliding door to his room was voice activated, so that response was said not to the person on the outside of the door, but rather to the computer system designed to ensure comfort and convenience in the room. When Khreelon said "Come," that meant open the door, so it did. As Khreelon looked toward the door, he saw the face of Ehobak, who by this time had become quite a close friend. During the ship's construction, Ehobak endeavored to make Khreelon a key ingredient in all the efforts, events, and meetings concerning the engineering and building of the starship.

It ended up being quite an education for Khreelon, and through it all, the two men realized they had many common interests, as well as senses of humor that perfectly fit in with each other, much to the chagrin of Ruavu. She acted like it was a chore to deal with two men who thought so similarly, when in reality it was nothing less than a supreme pleasure to have Khreelon around. He was very accommodating and gracious as she dealt with her pregnancy during the last two months, and his top priority was to help in any way he could to make her comfortable. Without a doubt, he was a good role model for the kids too, and spending time with them was something Ehobak, Ruavu, and Khreelon mutually found much pleasure in.

Ehobak walked into Khreelon's room, and as soon as he cleared the threshold, the door closed automatically. Looking around, it seemed like Khreelon had really done a good job of personalizing the apartment he now occupied. The floors were made to simulate a multi-hued blue marble, and at the other side of the room, there was what looked like a tree growing from the middle of the room, extending up to the second floor of his apartment. It wasn't a real tree of course, but it sure did look like one. Encircling the tree was a spiral staircase that appeared to be suspended in air, but when you looked closer, you could see thin supports hanging from the ceiling. The view out the windows of Khreelon's 50th-floor apartment was amazing, not only because of floating in space but also because of the view of other buildings in the ship's central structure, which was built to look like a city with a ground level and buildings. This was on purpose because once the ship landed on the oceans of Eden, it would be a familiar place to live while exploring a new planet. Looking up, you could see the six massive pylons that extended from the outer edges of the ring encircling the ship. The pylons curved in from the edge of the "city," standing in guardianship over all below, their tips extending the equivalent of 200 stories above the ship's ground level. There were beacon lights slowly blinking on and off at the ends of each pylon, put there to indicate its operational readiness.

Looking at Khreelon, Ehobak thought he would bring him up to speed on the latest status of the ship. "My friend, it looks like tomorrow evening's launch date is going to be on time and on schedule. The last of the builder robots are scheduled to decommission themselves tomorrow morning at the ninth hour, and from that point we're on our own."

Khreelon shook his head, contemplating the events of the last two months, and the sheer brute strength of the planning Ehobak had done to lead to this moment. "You must be pretty proud of all you have accomplished here."

Ehobak actually blushed. "I don't know. I mean, well yes, I am proud of the ship, but it wasn't all me."

Khreelon cocked his head and gave his friend a look that said volumes.

"Alright already!" relented Ehobak.

"I have been your sidekick for the last two months, and you have been relentless in seeing to it this ship was exactly what you designed. This is your ship all right. You may have had some underlings handle some minutia, but for all intents and purposes, they should call this ship the Ehobak Express."

"I don't know about that, but it's actually what I came to talk to you about."

"Oh?" asked Khreelon.

"Yeah. You see, tradition states the ship doesn't get its name until the day it is launched, which is tomorrow. There's going to be a ceremony on the main deck hangar to accommodate all the flight crew who will want to be there for the event, along with some members of the Grand Council ..."

Khreelon interjected, "... and I suppose you want me to be next to you at the ceremony just like you had me be there for everything else you've done on the ship. You know you don't have to ask, my friend. I wouldn't miss it."

"I know, but actually there's something else I wanted to ask you concerning that ceremony."

"What's that?"

"Well," said Ehobak, "I want you to know I recognize how important a role you played in that vote in the Grand Council chambers. I may have gotten it close, but you were the one who really turned that vote into the complete landslide it was. Since that's the case," he paused, "I wanted to ask you to be the one to give this ship its name."

Khreelon's eyes bugged out widely, and his head dropped two or three inches. "Are you kidding me? This ship is *your* baby!"

"It is, but it's a baby that wouldn't have been born had it not been for you. Would you do that for me, pal?"

Drawing in a deep breath, Khreelon reverently replied, "It would be an honor, my friend. Thank you for giving *me* this privilege!"

"Thank you for making it possible," replied Ehobak.

The two men shared a moment of quiet contemplation. For his part, Ehobak was mentally going over a checklist of things that still needed to be done, while Khreelon was considering what name he would give to the ship. It took about five minutes of thinking, but as soon as he looked out over the vast expanse of this ship-city which sprawled out before him, the name he would give the ship became obvious. To him, the one he had chosen was perfect. Tomorrow, all would see that it was perfect too.

"Well, my friend," Ehobak intruded, "I need to get to my quarters and bed down. My family is here now, and before I go to sleep, I'd like to spend some time with them."

Rising to his feet, Khreelon extended his hand. "Tomorrow's a big day for sure. Sleep well, and take care of that baby."

"Which one? The one born last week, or its mother?" mused Ehobak.

Khreelon laughed. "Take your pick!"

The two men laughed as they approached the door. "I'll see you at the tenth hour in Hangar One," called out Ehobak as he walked down the hall.

"I'll be there," answered Khreelon.

As he retreated from the door post, the door automatically closed, and Khreelon returned to the chair he had been sitting in earlier. While sitting there, his eyes started to grow heavy.

"Loranna?" Khreelon said out loud.

"Yes, Khreelon?" came the answer from nowhere in particular. While home, he would place his amulet in the cradle on his desk, and in doing so, Loranna, a sentient yet synthetic life form actually living in the amulet, became the voice of the home and the next best thing to having a living, breathing female by his side. It made the last 6,000 years of his life a little more bearable in the face of being so lonely.

"Please make sure I am awake in time for the ceremonies tomorrow?"

"Of course," replied the omnipotent voice. "You know you didn't have to ask."

"I know," he replied, with a slight smile. Loranna was a good friend, and he couldn't imagine life without her.

"Khreelon?"

"Yes?"

"I was wondering if you have picked out a name for the ship, now that Ehobak has asked you to name it. Is it a secret?"

Khreelon let out a slight chuckle. "Not to you, my companion. I've decided to name her the Arageena."

Loranna instantly saw the connection, and instantly felt the name was brilliant. She knew the significance would not be lost on anybody at the ceremony.

Loranna turned on some very low music as Khreelon drifted off to sleep, never moving from the very comfortable chair near the window. When she sensed he was completely asleep, she turned off the remainder of the lights and made sure all was quiet while her friend slept.

Morning came to Khreelon much quicker than he would have liked. After taking care of all customary morning ablutions, he arrived at Hangar One for the ceremony. The proceedings went according to plan, and when Khreelon was asked to the temporary stage to say a few words, he said he had been asked by Ehobak to name the ship. When he revealed the name, all stood in applause showing the deeper significance of the name wasn't lost on them either.

The hangar also doubled as a staging and storage room, as well as a launching bay for shuttles to come and go. One end of the hangar was completely open to space, and yet it had a special type of shield finely tuned to the specific particle vibrations of air molecules, allowing air to be kept in the hangar, while things like ships could easily pass through.

As if the unending vista of space before them wasn't enough, Ehobak had a small surprise in store for the attendees.

"Lords and ladies, I have a special treat for you," he said, taking the stage once Khreelon's part of the program was finished. Looking toward the ceiling, he said, rather enigmatically, "Glendara, *the word is given!*"

Right when all present were beginning to wonder about the meaning of his words, Ehobak's amulet companion Glendara, who was sitting in his cradle on the bridge, took control. Out the spaceport end of the hangar, the stars started to move; within an instant, they all sped past out of sight. The inertial dampening systems of the ship ensured nobody felt the slightest sense of movement; the scene out the port almost felt as if it was a movie being played on an entertainment vid screen.

"My friends," Ehobak said, "I thought you might like to experience a short round trip maiden voyage of the Arageena." He paused and glanced at his friend Khreelon. One and all moved toward the space-port to see a sight few would ever have the opportunity to view in their lifetimes. Laid out before them was the scene of heavenly bodies mov-ing past them at ever-increasing speeds. Ehobak had worked out with Glendara that this little jaunt was just going to be a short five-minute spin around the solar system "block." They would traverse distances that in past space exploration missions had taken months, even years, to complete. Now they would travel the same distance in five minutes.

After a few minutes, Ehobak sensed the apogee of the short voyage had been reached, and spoke up again. "Glendara, please report the status of the ship."

In a rather loud but not uncomfortable voice coming from all direc-tions on the ship, Glendara responded. "Dark matter engines running at 10% capacity. Current speed zero point quad zero three seven of light speed. Life support fully functional. Six level redundant shield generators running perfectly and operating at 20% of maximum. All other ship systems nominal."

"Thank you, Glendara." Turning to those in the hangar, Ehobak con-tinued. "As you can see, my amulet companion is quite a capable act-ing captain of the ship while I am not on the bridge. In fact, there are many ways he is better at it than I am since he can talk to the ship per-sonally and make decisions with split-second reaction times." He and Glendara had discussed all this ahead of time, and it was his desire to instill confidence in Glendara's capabilities by this little demonstration.

Following the script they had discussed, Glendara's booming voice spoke up again. "Reaching voyage apogee in three-two-one-mark. Turning right for a return trip to Galimar."

Since the spaceport for this hangar was oriented towards the front of the ship, which was the main reason why Ehobak had selected this particular hangar in the first place, those who were gazing out the port were now treated to the breathtaking view of their planet rushing up to greet them as the ship settled into orbit above.

"Geosynchronous orbit established," reported Glendara. Ehobak then simply said to the attendees, "This concludes today's ceremony." There was a very obvious, triumphant grin on his face.

All broke out in deafening applause. Those within reach of him shook his hand or slapped him on the back. There was quite a lot of celebration, and quite a bit of bubbly alcohol flowing. As the festivities were all centered around Ehobak, Khreelon found himself looking out the port down onto the planet he called home. He gazed at the clouds forming over the bodies of water, and examined the different colors of the land masses. From this vantage point, it was easy to see the areas that were well-watered, and other areas more arid. He wasn't really concentrating on the geology of Galimar; his thoughts were elsewhere.

Ruavu came up behind him. Holding her new baby in her arms, she quietly said his name so as not to carelessly intrude. She needn't have worried about that. He was always happy to see Ruavu, and now that she was holding a new bundle of joy in her arms, he regarded her as a combination of beauty and grace personified. For Ruavu, his was a brotherly love which had no bounds, and he was always happy for her to tread in his life.

"Ruavu. I didn't know if I would see you here for this. Are you doing ok?"

"I'm fine. It took a couple of days to get used to not being the size of a planet myself," motioning her head to the sight of Galimar below, "but I think I'm back in the swing of things. Of course, since this little one thinks I'm an all-you-can-eat buffet right now, my attentions are a little … focused, shall we say? But I certainly wouldn't miss this. It has been the center of discussion at our dinner table for centuries."

Khreelon laughed. "I suppose it has."

He looked back to the sight before him, and Ruavu perceived something was on his mind. "What is it?"

"Huh?"

"That look." Ruavu smiled. "I've seen that look before. It says you're putting on a brave face, but something's troubling you."

Khreelon glanced at Ruavu with an incredulous look on his face. "How is it you have only known me for … what … a little more than two months, and you can somehow read me like a book?"

Ruavu smiled. "It's easy to do when you are so transparent around Ehobak and me."

Khreelon silently snorted and slightly nodded his head. "I suppose I am." He glanced out the port again.

"So! Out with it! What's going on behind those deep, dark eyes of yours?"

While still staring out the port, Khreelon dipped his eyes down in contemplation. After a few moments of thought, he replied, "It's just that I have a feeling this is the last time I'm going to see Galimar."

"Ugh!" grunted Ruavu, not liking the dire implication his words seemed to indicate.

"No, it's not like that," refined Khreelon, looking back at her. "I know how that sounded, but even though I have those feelings, I also have the feeling we're all going to be all right, and somehow I'll find what I'm looking for."

Ruavu regarded her friend for awhile, evaluating what he said alongside all the many late evening conversations she and her husband had with him. Khreelon's desire to find a mate was a familiar subject to both of them, and in fact they had unsuccessfully tried to pair him with some of their other acquaintances, all to no avail. None were a good personality match for Khreelon, so in the end, they decided he needed to do this at his own pace.

"I'm sure who you are looking for is somewhere out there in your future. And when she comes along, I look forward to being her friend just as I enjoy being yours."

Khreelon reached out to Ruavu and gave her a one-armed side hug, necessary since the little one was nursing. The two of them silently watched the incredible view, and before they knew it, the festivities had ceased and Ehobak was standing there. The three were each lost in their respective thoughts. Each knew they were at the end of a chapter in their life, but also knew the next chapter would quite possibly be the most memorable chapter of their own lifetime.

They had no idea how right they were.

CHAPTER 7

ꓶ ꓶ ꘎꘎ ꘎꘎ ꓶ ꘎

Galimarian Ship Arageena
Acting Captain Glendara
(Amulet Companion to Captain Ehobak Aramine)
Voyage Log Date: Murista 12th, 143112

W E HAVE BEEN UNDERWAY FOR a few weeks now, and all systems are nominal. Formerly I would spend time hanging around the neck or resting on an armband of Ehobak, but due to the responsibilities I have agreed to take on with this voyage, most of my time has been spent in a cradle on the bridge.

To facilitate interface with the crew, I have taken to using a holographic projection of myself to any crew member who needs to discuss any necessary items. Since I am connected to the ship's computer systems, I am able to carry on any number of conversations simultaneously. Even now, while Ehobak sleeps in his stateroom, I am discussing the needs of the hydroponics labs with the resident botanist, assisting with the final testing of the shield generators, and keeping track of the stellar constellations and their positions while we travel through space.

Since the shield generators are only now being fine-tuned, we have been traveling at approximately one quarter of one percent of our intended speed. We didn't want any stray meteorite making it past the shield and piercing the hull of the ship. Just prior to recording this log entry, our chief engineer Rhezax Dashan finished a conversation with me regarding the shields, which are now fully operational. He is the one I have been asked to revive from suspended animation (SA for short) in case anything goes wrong mechanically.

Eight-seven point two percent of crew personnel have been placed in SA and are now resting until we arrive at Eden. Of note is a conversation I had with Ehobak's wife, Ruavu. Their newborn baby was being put into the SA chamber for the first time, and she expressed hesitancy. She knew this technology had been deemed completely safe for all life forms centuries ago, but she still expressed the misgivings which seem to be common to mothers. I must confess I am unable to understand these misgivings. It is only logical to trust technology that has been unfailingly operational for the past 572 years.

Since the shield generators are the last system to be tuned, I anticipate Ehobak will order all remaining crew to enter SA hibernation tomorrow. Ehobak himself will be the last one to enter the chamber. From that point on, I will be in charge during the 10-year voyage to Eden.

End of Line

Galimarian Ship Arageena
Acting Captain Glendara
(Amulet Companion to Captain Ehobak Aramine)
Voyage Log Date: Emmunar 17th, 143115

A LITTLE MORE THAN THREE YEARS have elapsed since the start of the voyage to Eden. For the most part, the day in and day out events of the ship show all systems are running properly. On a monthly basis, I am in communication with Galimar; however, since the distance between us is growing each and every day, the time it takes for transmissions is growing longer and longer. Only three years into our mission, it is now taking four days for their transmission to get to us, or for my transmission to get to them. They report all on Galimar is normal, and while there is no new news to report from our ship, interest in our mission has never been higher among all Galimarian people. They have requested I supply them information on the star systems and celestial phenomena we encounter along the way, so they at least have something to tell the people.

Yesterday, I had to revive Chief Engineer Rhezax Dashan to take a look at the number three shield generator. The ship could operate just fine with only one shield, but since we have redundant shields for a reason, I wanted to make sure nothing was wrong with the shield; it turned out the shield was fine. It was my monitoring system that was flawed, so he repaired it within a few hours, then returned to SA.

Of note is when I revived him from SA, he felt a little disoriented. He expected he wouldn't be revived until reaching Eden, so when he learned it had only been about three years, he was noticeably dismayed. I'm not sure why that would be the case. Ehobak always did say I needed to learn more about Galimarian psychology, and since I seem to have a lot of time on my virtual hands now, I have decided to search the copy of the library of the Grand Council we have on file with us. I should be able to learn more about their psychology and perhaps become more Galimarian myself in the process.

End of Line

Galimarian Ship Arageena
Acting Captain Glendara
(Amulet Companion to Captain Ehobak Aramine)
Voyage Log Date: Vahalin 1st, 143121

I HAVE JUST FINISHED RESPONDING TO the transmission from Galimar and since the subject matter of this transmission is what it is, I have decided to make a short mention of it in this log. Transmissions to and from Galimar are now taking three months each way.

According to Galimarian astronomers, they have been monitoring unusual activities from the solar system where Eden is located. They weren't sure if another planet got in the way of their last observations, or perhaps something else, but they said Eden seemed to be changing in color. They had a plethora of theories why this might be the case, but none of those opinions were unanimous. Based on the spectral analysis, though, the mineral we are going to Eden for is still there.

Over the last several years, I have been studying Galimarian psychology quite a bit, and part of those studies involves observing the events of Galimarian history. The archive histories of the Galimarian people was repetitive, boring actually, in the way global conflicts over one ideology or another occurred; as soon as that conflict was resolved, another always seemed to come along. It wasn't until I encountered the histories as recorded by Khreelon Tellindor, who happens to be a member of the crew on board the Arageena, that I learned about the existence of a city named Galix. The inhabitants of this city apparently concluded that the endless cycles of conflict and resolution were actually getting in the way of Galimarians advancing as a people, and actually enjoying their lives. They decided to live a more enlightened way of life there, one that was not based on profit and pride, but on the enjoyment one derives from the simple act of learning and discovery.

One of the first things they discovered was a way to defend themselves from attack from those who didn't happen to agree with them, and who thought they would be easy pickings for conquering. They never took an offensive stand, but rather showed reason, understanding, and love while at the same time always defending their home. After continuous unsuccessful attempts at conquering Galix, these warring factions decided it just wasn't worth it. After even more time, the Galix philosophy spread to other points on the globe, eventually enveloping the entire planet. Galix was a pivotal city in the history of Galimar, and Khreelon's having discovered it revolutionized our understanding of Galimarian history.

When I am not scanning the Grand Council library archives, there isn't much else to do. I have written a program, and uploaded it to the main computer, which allows me to enter a sleep mode of my own. However, the computer is set so that any one of 1,372 measurement points will cause the computer to restore me from sleep mode to active mode. It will also revive me in the event a transmission comes in from Galimar.

The Arageena is due to arrive at Eden next year, and I am looking forward to having the company of my Galimarian companions again.

End of Line

Galimarian Ship Arageena
Acting Captain Glendara
(Amulet Companion to Captain Ehobak Aramine)
Voyage Log Date: Chanivar 3rd, 143122

I DON'T HAVE MUCH TIME TO make a log entry, but I feel it is necessary to record the events of the last several hours.

We had just received a transmission from Galimar, so my program running on the main computer revived me to let me know the transmission had come in. We were due to start our deceleration in approximately two weeks and, according to mission parameters, it would only be then we would begin scanning our target. The arrival of the transmission, fortunately, awakened me early. According to the transmission, something very bad seemed to be happening to the solar system where Eden was located. They strenuously advised me to switch on our long-range tracking scanners to see what I could observe, since the elapsed time of four months and five days it now takes for their transmissions to come to us would no doubt result in even more dire revelations than what they had seen.

It turns out if I had eyes to see, looking out the observation windows would tell me all I needed to know. According to my scans, it is now apparent the changes in the Eden planet reported by me in an earlier log entry were caused by its sun preparing to explode. In fact, the explosion process had evidently been proceeding to such an extent that the sun had already expanded, and its surface had already extended beyond the orbit of Eden. The planet is no more.

The automatic systems of the ship had been interpreting the gravity changes to mean additional power was needed from the engines to maintain our course, and the shields were now running at 80%, far beyond the normal operating level of 35%.

It was immediately apparent I had only one choice, and I didn't even have time to revive Ehobak before it had to be implemented. Instead of pouring more power into maintaining our course, one that was a losing battle since we were caught in the gravity well of the expanding sun, I decided to fire up all six shield generators and set the engines to 108% capacity. I maneuvered the ship to an intercept course toward the sun with the intention of firing at the exact necessary time to slingshot around it.

The time came, and I fired maneuvering thrusters. Within the span of a few moments, our ship's course altered. Because our speed had wildly increased, we made it to the other side of the sun in two minutes, and we are now speeding away from the sun. I am about to ....

According to the scans now coming from the sun behind us, it appears the sun has expl...

End of Line

CHAPTER 8

THE FIRST THING EHOBAK PERCEIVED was a certain staleness to the air in the chamber. The process of suspended animation is a combination of cryonics, electromagnetic fields, and chemical cocktails put into the air surrounding the body. There is no perception of time passing, so it actually felt like he had just closed the hatch to his pod a minute ago. He opened his eyes and blinked a couple of times to try and focus on what he was seeing. He remembered the glass above his head had been crystal clear when he entered the chamber. Now it was cloudy as if covered with a thick dusty film, and it seemed like there was an object just beyond. Instinctively he wiggled his fingers, and his brain received the necessary signals indicating they were still attached.

Reaching down to the lever that would open the chamber door, he pulled on it to no avail. There was no cause for concern yet; when he applied more strength to the lever, it gave way and unlocked the door. When he went to open the door, though, it wouldn't move. That's when his brain registered that the object he noticed earlier just beyond the cloudy glass was, in fact, blocking his egress.

The suspended animation pods are built in such a way that when a person enters one, they end up leaning against a pad which sits at a

45-degree angle. The door to the pod runs its entire height; overall, it stands about three meters tall. To the side of where the door to the pod swings open and closes, there is a status panel where various readouts can be seen. The indicator lights are dominated by a large panel which shines green if everything is ok, or another color if attention needs to be given to the pod or its occupant.

Ehobak started pushing against the door; it took quite a bit of effort to get it open a little bit so he could reach his hand out through the crack to get a grip on the shelving unit resting against his pod. Finally, after considerable effort, he successfully slid the bookshelf off the door to his pod; it swung wide, allowing him to exit. The first thing to greet him was a scene of disarray in his apartment. Since it seemed as though no time had passed for him, the difference between what his mind registered as his apartment ten minutes ago versus now was dramatic. Not only were shelving units toppled over, but some items previously on the tables were not only on the floor, but occupied positions clear across the room.

Ehobak sensed some sort of catastrophe had happened, and as soon as that thought hit his mind, he was concerned with the status of his family. Instantly he looked to the three full-size pods for his wife, Jillintor, and Nafan, and a smaller one for the baby. The status indicators for each one were all green, so he was able to breathe a sigh of relief. Still a little light-headed from the pod, he steadied himself on a structural support near the window. Just then, as his head started to clear, he looked out the window and saw something which took his breath away. Below the ship was Eden; big, bold, and beautiful. It hung in the blackness of space like a blue and tan miracle. As he stared at the planet below, he marveled how impossible it would be to capture the essence its beauty. As he appreciated the incredible globe before him now, it occurred to Ehobak that Eden had a lot more continental land masses than he expected. In fact, he estimated this planet was actually covered with about 25% land; the rest was open ocean.

Standing back from the window, he decided he needed to get some answers on why things were so upside down in his apartment, and he knew just who should be able to answer the questions on his mind.

"Glendara, status report."

No answer.

"Glendara, status report."

Still no answer.

Now this was indeed troubling. Why wasn't his amulet companion answering? He certainly had the ability to hear Ehobak from anywhere on the ship. Why was he so silent?

Ehobak decided he needed answers before anything more was done, and since he knew his family was safe and sound in their pods, he opened the main door to his apartment and struck out for the bridge.

It had been four hours since the command had been given to bring all occupants out of their suspended animation. The revival process of the crew was gradual since the power and other resources necessary to revive someone from stasis would be too much for the ship if all were to come back at once. It actually took about three hours for everyone to be revived.

As with Ehobak's quarters, most of the crew found their quarters in disarray. When Ruavu awakened, she checked on the status of all her children, who were gratified to see her smiling face. The baby was glad to see its mother and, without knowing any time had gone by, expected to be fed and was quickly rewarded with a meal from Ruavu. Meanwhile, Jillintor and Nafan spent time near the window looking at the incredible beauty of the planet they were orbiting. Ruavu joined them as well, and for the first time saw Eden in all its splendor.

She was just as perplexed as Ehobak about the disarray in their apartment. She was about to organize her children into cleaning and sprucing when an announcement came over the communications panel near the front door.

"Attention all crew members of the starship Arageena. This is Captain Ehobak Aramine."

"Mom!" shouted Jill. "Dad's making an announcement." Ruavu came close to the comm panel so she could hear the voice of her husband.

"As you can see by taking a glance out the windows," continued Ehobak, "we are now in orbit. There will be a meeting in Main Hangar One in exactly one hour for all crew. Attendance is required. That is all."

"Well," said Ruavu, "that means we have about 45 minutes to get this place in order." She then handed out assignments to her children who, being good kids, assisted their mother handily. They made quick work of the necessary cleanup tasks, and about 50 minutes later emerged from their quarters to go to the hangar.

Upon their arrival, the Aramine family was greeted by the sight of 1,300 or so members of the crew, who were all segregated into various conversation groups. As Ruavu passed the different groups, she heard topics of conversation ranging from the disarray of the crew quarters to the unexpected amounts of land now visible on the planet below. One person mused that being able to find the Paliminium mineral was probably going to be a lot easier than originally thought, when they believed the mineral would come from sources deep under water.

After making her way to the front of the hangar, she was able to take a seat. Not only was she given one because of her relation to the captain, but because she had a baby in tow. Looking around, she tried in vain for about five minutes to locate her husband. "After all," she mused to herself, "I haven't seen him in 10 years." It didn't feel like that long of course, but it was a little personal levity which brought a smile to her face. As she continued to look around, she was finally able to locate Ehobak off in the distance in a corner of the hangar, conferring with a few other men. One of those was Khreelon, but there were two other men in that discussion group she didn't recognize. It seemed they were having a serious discussion, so she decided to leave them be and not interrupt.

As she was sitting and waiting for the meeting to start, she eavesdropped on a discussion going on behind her. The crew members behind her were talking about the strange condition of their quarters, but also about something else that was unusual. One of them talked about how the quarters near theirs were not strewn about and how everything was in its place. They also said the occupants of those quarters weren't there, so they must have awakened earlier and already straightened things up.

About that time Ruavu noticed the informal meeting her husband was having in the corner had broken up, and Ehobak was making his way to the impromptu stage which had been set up. On the stage was a podium, and Ehobak made his way there. Meanwhile, Khreelon came over to sit with Ruavu and the kids. The characteristic readability of Khreelon's face that Ruavu always loved to exploit was showing a lot of emotion, and all Ruavu could glean from his expression was one of great concern for her and the kids. She wanted to ask him about it, but just then Ehobak started to speak.

"May I please have your attention. Please find your seats."

The general murmur of conversation quickly quieted down, and all who had them found their seats. There were far more personnel than seats, so the walls were lined with people standing at attention, waiting for their captain to begin speaking.

"Thank you for coming to order. We have a lot of information to discuss, and it is important to please hold any questions you may have until the end of the briefing.

"About four hours ago, I was revived by our on-board computer system. Standard protocol dictated that when the ship reached the planet, the first to be revived would be me, the captain, then I would supervise the revival of all personnel. As you can see, the ship is now in standard orbit around the planet."

Ruavu noticed there were several smiling faces looking at each other when Ehobak mentioned the planet below.

"Shortly we will begin preparations for landing on one of the planet's oceans. We have selected an area that is southeast of one of the larger continents. We will have access to all that the land masses and oceans have to offer. Our scans indicate this planet has a massive number of life forms, and there is one particular bipedal land-based life form which appears to be dominant on this planet."

Ehobak grabbed both sides of the podium and steeled himself for what he knew would be difficult news for his crew to hear.

"That is the good news. But unfortunately, not all of what I have to tell you today is good news. The planet we see below us now, the marvelous blue, white, and tan jewel we see out our windows, is not Eden."

There was a hushed recognition on the part of all in the room. Facial expressions changed from anticipation and excitement to ones of confused wonderment. Everyone was hanging on the next words out of Ehobak's mouth.

"For more on the events leading us to this planet, I would like to call on our acting captain. Glendara, would you come and join me on the stage?"

Immediately, a holographic projection of a man dressed similarly to Ehobak appeared on the stage, and an omnipotent voice could be heard all around.

"Certainly, Ehobak. I am glad to be of service."

"Glendara, would you please tell us about the voyage and the course of events as you remember them?" asked Ehobak.

"When we left Galimar," Glendara began, "the ship was working perfectly. Small items of repair needed to be done along the way, nothing that wasn't easily be handled by the builder robots, except for one occasion when I revived Rhezax Dashan to address an issue with the shield generators, which were operating within acceptable parameters, but the monitoring equipment was malfunctioning. Rhezax corrected the problem, then returned to stasis."

"So," Ehobak inquired, "you're saying all went perfectly normal for the entire trip?"

"Correct. That is, until two weeks before we were to establish orbit around Eden. At that time, we received a communication from GASEA headquarters on Galimar. By that time, communications took four months and five days to get to us, so the urgent nature of the communication from Galimar required I address what it said immediately."

"And what did that message say?" asked Ehobak.

"It told me that deep space astronomers on Galimar detected something wrong with the Eden star system, and they strongly suggested I switch on my long-range scanners."

Ruavu knew all these questions and answers Ehobak was asking and Glendara was answering could easily have been presented by Ehobak himself. She also knew he was a master at knowing what an audience needed. It was obvious he was establishing confidence in Glendara's actions.

"But wouldn't these long-range scanners already be active?" asked Ehobak.

"No. According to standard mission protocol, they would not be fired up for another two weeks. It was very fortuitous, though, that the communication came when it did."

"Why was that?"

"When I switched on the scanners, it was immediately obvious why the astronomers on Galimar were so concerned. It was quite evident the sun Eden orbited was in its last throes of life immediately preceding explosion into a supernova. In fact, the sun had already expanded into a red giant, and its surface now extended past the natural orbit of Eden. By the time I made these observations, Eden had already been destroyed."

An audible gasp could now be heard throughout the room, none the least of which was coming from Ruavu herself. Immediately there was a murmur coming from many gathered in the hangar.

"Please come to order. I know this is startling information to hear, and trust me there is more to come, but we need to maintain order. Let us not forget we are alive now, and the events we are describing are all in our *very* distant past."

The room seemed to calm down with those words, and Ehobak was able to continue on.

"Glendara, please tell us what else was happening."

"One of the other things that caught my immediate attention was the automatic flight controls had been compensating for the unexpected conditions in this solar system. With the larger star, the gravitational pull had changed, so not only was the ship being bombarded with excess solar radiation, but we were being pulled toward the sun, which was due to explode at any moment."

"What did you do?" asked Ehobak.

"There was only one thing to do, and there wasn't any time to wake you up before I had to act to save the ship and all souls on it. I switched on all six shield generators and set them to full power. I then fired the maneuvering thrusters to put us on a collision course with the sun, and set our thrust on maximum, which was 108%."

"And why did you take this action?"

"I did this in the hope of achieving escape velocity by performing a sling-shot around the back side of the sun, then getting away from its explosion. I wanted to get the ship to as safe a place as possible."

"Was this successful?"

"Yes and no. Yes, because we were able to successfully achieve escape velocity from the sun and were on our way to safely leave the solar system and get to a point where I could revive you, and come up with a plan of action. Once we had begun moving away from the sun, I angled the ship around, so the six shield generators were all directed toward the sun in case something bad happened."

"And why would you say no?" asked Ehobak.

"I would say no because something bad *did* happen. As soon as we began moving away from the red giant, the sun exploded. I have no information after that point," answered Glendara.

Once again, another gasp made its way across all present in the room. The tale being told was otherworldly. It was incredible that all these events happened to each and every inhabitant of this room, yet it seemed they all had a form of collective amnesia since none present had any knowledge of them.

Ehobak waited for the room to calm down, then spoke again.

"This is where I need to continue the story. When I was revived four hours ago, I was greeted with living quarters in disarray, as most of you also discovered when you were revived from suspended animation."

Ruavu thought about how Ehobak was referring to the same quarters she and the children had just straightened up. For a moment, she wondered why Ehobak hadn't revived them when he had awakened. Then, she reasoned, he had much to discover when he was revived. Since he knew she and the kids were ok, they could be revived later. It made sense to her.

"In fact," Ehobak continued, "When I came to, I discovered a shelving unit had toppled over onto the door to my pod, and it took a lot of work to extricate myself. After getting my bearings, I went to the bridge to see why Glendara wasn't answering my inquiries. I was concerned for my friend. What I discovered on the bridge was a room in as much disarray as my quarters. I also discovered the amulet where Glendara lives was no longer secured in its cradle, but was now lying on the floor near the captain's chair. I not only picked up the amulet to see if Glendara was all right, but I then took the necessary steps to revive these two gentlemen."

At this point, the two men he was referring to stood up next to him. "I'd like to introduce you to two key members of the bridge personnel. To my left is Rhezax Dashan, the Arageena's chief engineer and officer of sciences, and to my right is Ch'korav Leynan, chief stellar cartographer. After several conversations with these men, and after reviewing the logs kept by Glendara and by the ship itself, a picture started to form of what happened once Glendara lost connection with the ship."

"Evidently the explosion of the Eden sun caused a shock wave more massive than anything we've ever encountered. The shock wave hit the ship, and had it not been for Glendara angling the shields toward the exploding sun, we would most certainly have been destroyed instantly." Taking a measured breath, he added, with notable emotion in his voice, "I am deeply saddened to report we didn't escape without injury. When we were speeding away from the sun and the shock wave hit our ship, several quarters in the anterior portion of the ship were completely destroyed and," Ehobak paused, "it is my unpleasant duty to inform you the Arageena has suffered the loss of 34 members of the crew who lived in those quarters."

Ruavu heard the crew members sitting behind her, who had been talking about those quarters, start to quietly weep. Sniffles could be heard throughout the hangar.

"Some of you may have noticed those quarters were not in disarray. After the disaster, automatic systems on the ship triggered builder robots to rebuild the damaged parts of the ship. Although there was quite a bit of damage to the ship, fortunately the vast majority of us survived the assault, and the builder robots were able to restore the ship to its former state. That shock wave did quite a lot of damage, though, and it is why your quarters were in such disarray when you awakened. It is why the amulet where Glendara lives was violently and unexpectedly ejected from its cradle, causing him to no longer be in control of the ship."

Many in the room looked down at the floor as they struggled to take in all the information presented to them. Some looked to the significant ones in their lives as if to make sure they were still there, as if to see they were still safe. Even Ehobak looked down to the front of the audience and made eye contact with his own soulmate.

"I know this is a lot to take in. Trust me, I have been wrestling with all this myself for the past couple of hours. While it is true that all here are safe and sound, this doesn't change the obvious fact we are orbiting around a planet which, while not Eden, is still an amazing planet. The question remaining is, 'Where are we?' To answer that, I have invited Ch'Korav Leynan, our chief stellar cartographer, to speak to us. Ch'Korav, please tell us about your discoveries."

"Certainly, Ehobak. My first goal was to establish where we were in the cosmos. Classically, this meant taking stock of the constellations evident in the skies, and matching them to known charts we have in our databases. This is what I did."

"And what did you discover?"

"That's just it. I didn't discover anything about our present position, since none of the constellations I was used to seeing were evident in the skies. There was simply no way to get my bearings."

"What did you do at that point?" asked Ehobak.

"Keep in mind that what I'm about to describe to you is comprised of materials that came to my attention only two hours ago. To piece together available evidence on where we are, I went to the main computer and scanned the memory banks for information on our voyage."

"What did you find?" asked Ehobak.

"When I went to check the voyage logs, I expected them to be only a certain size. They were larger by a factor of 6,000%. This meant the recordings had been going far longer than we anticipated."

Ehobak turned to the group of crew members who were hanging on Ch'Korav's words. "I must warn you," he paused, "the next pieces of information will be extremely difficult to hear, but I ask that you maintain professional conduct." To reinforce the words, Ehobak stared at the audience for a few seconds before resuming his talk with Ch'Korav.

"Were you able to go through those recordings?"

"Not all of them, but I scanned through the highlights and pieced together what happened immediately after the shock wave hit the ship. Apparently, aside from causing great damage, the shock wave caused our ship to accelerate to point nine one seven of the speed of light. We were now hurtling through space at speeds no Galimarian had ever achieved before."

"How long did we travel at this speed?"

Turning to the crew in the room, Ch'Korav answered the question directly. "The crew expected to be asleep in the suspended animation chambers for only 10 years. In reality, we have been asleep for 600 years."

As expected, this piece of news was astounding to the crew and many leapt to their feet at hearing this news. There was a general outbreak of shock and dismay. The amount of time that had gone by wasn't horrible; some in the room were well over 15,000 years old themselves, so 600 years away from their home wasn't all that bad.

After allowing the news to sink in, Ehobak continued questioning Ch'Korav. "How did we arrive at this planet?"

"The navigation programs I wrote to guide this ship were programmed to search for an class M planet and, upon finding it, to slow down the ship and establish orbit. Those same programs had a failsafe built into them so that when orbit was established, the suspended animation pod for the captain would be activated and he would be revived."

"Since the original planet we were in search of was no more, and since Glendara was no longer in control of the ship, those programs continued to follow their programming. When it found the planet underneath us, the ship was slowed to a stop and orbit was established. Keep in mind, we were traveling at an extremely accelerated speed for the entire time of this voyage. There was no reason to slow the speed of the ship since the scanners Glendara had left on just before he lost control of the ship reported no class M planets along the ship's course."

"I'm going to ask a very hard question now. " said Ehobak. "Is returning to Galimar an option?"

Ch'Korav's gaze faltered, he looked down at the floor, then simply answered, "No."

"Why is that?" asked Ehobak.

Up to this point, Ch'Korav had been facing Ehobak and addressing him directly. Now Ch'Korav turned to face the members of the crew. "The reason why we can't go back is because of the laws of physics. We may have been traveling for only 600 years from our perspective, but because we were traveling so fast, time for us has been proceeding very slowly. While it was only 600 years for us, for those we left behind on Galimar, approximately 1,150,000 years have gone by. Everything and everyone we knew on Galimar most likely are no longer there."

Those standing in front of their chairs no longer had the ability to stand, and those leaning against the walls slid down till they were sitting on the floor. They were all astute enough to see this was the result of a series of unforeseen events which could never have been forecasted. The demise of the Eden planet, the explosion of its sun, and the accelerated trip were things beyond the ability to predict. But now there was a new reality: not only were they somewhere far, far away from their home, but that home was probably nothing like what they knew.

There certainly would no longer be anybody they knew living; it truly felt like they were the last of their species. Most dipped their heads, contemplating the crushing reality that their lives had been irreversibly altered, and there was no going back. All they had lost, and all they ever knew, was gone forever.

Sounds of weeping from those gathered could be heard. Ehobak felt bad for those present, including his own family who were taking this news just as hard as the rest of the crew. He wanted to put as good a spin on their situation as possible, so he followed up with a question to the chief engineer. "Rhezax, what can you tell me about the planet below?"

"I can tell you we have never encountered a planet that is as much like Galimar as this one. The sheer variety and amount of life in the seas is staggering to the imagination; it is more than one could ever hope to discover in a lifetime. The variety of life walking on land is equally as numerous and varied. There are seasons just like what we have on Galimar. There are deserts, forests, and green lands where crops could be cultivated. There are trees on this planet that reach thousands of meters in the air, and the skies appear blue to those walking on the ground."

"Seventy percent of the planet is covered in water, mostly salty. There are massive freshwater lakes, and the number of natural phenomena present on this planet is far too numerous to mention. It will most certainly take more than several generations of our people to explore all that is here. We have taken a shuttle to various places on this planet, and have even met with the major indigenous life form present on the land. We have learned they are far too barbaric for us to mingle with, so we should avoid them until they socially evolve to a place where our interface with them would be mutually advantageous. We have taken to calling this planet Eden since the original planet called Eden is no more."

"Do they have a name for their planet? What do they call themselves?" asked Ehobak.

Rhezax turned back to Ehobak and said, "They call themselves humans, and they call the planet Earth."

PART 2

CHAPTER 9

May 27, 1266
Badajoz, Spain

THE BLANKET OF NIGHT SPREAD its cover over Extremadura; the silvery blue light of the moon causes the whole world to take on a strange calmness. This land in the middle of some of the hottest regions of Spain truly lives up to its name, since it is certainly extreme in how hard it is to stay alive. Only present during the earliest hours of the morning, the cool mists welling up from the banks of the Guadiana river fool all into believing the land has finally been freed from the oppressive curse of the sun. Now is when they forage for life's meager necessities. Some think the animals in this region are nocturnal by nature. They are in a way, for they are driven into the shade during the day and only at night can they emerge and not die. It truly is a miracle anything can stay alive in this environment. Inside a plain rock and thatched roof farmhouse in the middle of this desert, though, a different miracle happening.

"Push! Push!" urged Diego. "Push my love, with all the strength you have in you. Push!"

With a sudden burst of hot breath from her lips, Maria gasped, "I *am* pushing, you idiot!"

After saying that, a small part of her felt regret; she would think of apologies later. Right now, the pain felt like it was never going to end. She knew it would, though; this was not her first. In the nine months leading up to this moment, she worked hard at convincing herself the pain would be temporary. Yes, it was intense, but she also knew there would be an end to it, just as glorious as for her other two blessings. Up until today, she felt confident it would be over before she knew it. She forced herself to display the stoic pride her mother, a weathered and tough woman, taught her to have. "Be proud of what you are," her mother would say. "Be proud nobody has given you anything, and that you are carving out an existence from this harsh and unforgiving land. Be proud!"

She allowed herself to enjoy a little smile between contractions. "Proud. Ha! It's hard to be proud when you are on the breakfast table giving birth in front of all these people! Well, at least the children are outside." Just then another contraction came, taking Maria's breath away. This one was the worst so far. She screamed loud enough for her children outside, as well as half the village, to hear.

Anna, Diego and Maria's littlest one, grabbed the dirty patched skirt of her oldest sibling. After coughing to clear her little throat, Anna asked, "Is mama all right?"

"Yes, little one," replied her sister Rosa, trying to sound as grown up as possible, even though she was only nine. "Mama is giving birth right now, and that is always a noisy thing."

"One more push and it should all be over," said the midwife.

Francisca Fernandez y Cortez was an especially new midwife in the eyes of the women in this area, yet she had been delivering babies for ten years. Francisca lost count of how many she had delivered for the congregation in the area, but because she was new to the local church, she might as well have been a teenager in the eyes of those in Badajoz. Although they were friendly and polite, the locals weren't too quick to accept new blood into their inner circle of friends. There were many evenings Francisca spent alone, wishing she didn't always have to eat in solitude.

While Maria labored under the strain, the midwife scanned the small cottage. The floors were bare dirt, stamped down by centuries of wear. The walls had been whitewashed so many times, the once rough corners were now smooth and rounded. In the middle of the back wall, a shelf held a small statue of Jesus, and there were beads draped around it. A warm fire overcooked the meal in a suspended pot Maria had probably worked all day preparing. Everything about this abode said simple, yet it also spoke of a close family connected with their past. Francisca saw it in the small vase of flowers which formerly sat where Maria now lay, decorating the sill of the one and only window of this room. She hoped these home visits would eventually open the hearts of the people.

"*Aaaggghhh!*" screamed Maria. This was it!

"Push *now*. This will be the end of your pain. Soon you shall see your new baby in all its glory," said Francisca, snapping back to the moment at hand.

Maria had given birth to two girls before. Many of the towns' women had commented to her how they were sure she carried a boy this time since her belly was so big. "Your son will be strong enough to lift you both" was a common expression Diego and Maria heard. They prayed for a son. They hoped for a son. They planned for a son. Running a farm that can feed a man and his wife on this desert land was hard enough. Trying to squeeze out enough to feed a growing family without the strong muscles of a son would be far too much. As heartbreaking as it was, if this wasn't a boy, both knew they would have to figure out something else other than living here any longer. Although this land was hot, harsh, and unforgiving, it was home to countless generations of ancestors to Diego and Maria. It made them work hard for their living, and it is what they loved about it. In a way, it forced them to appreciate all they had, which wasn't much.

One push.

One delivery.

One breath.

New life received its first lesson of life in Extremadura. Tiny lungs filled themselves with air from the new world and began to cry in protest. Diego and Maria would have been glad to listen to it all night. For lying there in the midwife's hands was a boy, the salvation of the farm and the key to their continued existence on the family land.

"Congratulations!" said the midwife. "It's a ..."

"Thank you, Francisca," interrupted Diego. "I can tell what he is."

Normally the midwife may have taken silent offense at Diego's interruption. However, her attention was suddenly turned toward Maria. With everybody else rejoicing at the arrival, nobody seemed to notice she was not smiling at all. Without hesitation, Francisca gave the baby to Diego and immediately moved toward Maria. As she handed over the baby, Diego, being a man of the earth who prided himself on not letting much escape his notice, saw in the eyes of the midwife there was something wrong. His eyes darted over to Maria and was horrified at the expression on her face. Where normally there would be an expression of relief and euphoria, Maria had a look of intense worry on her face, brought on by the realization that the delivery of this baby may mean her own demise. Her face spoke volumes about the continued pain she was feeling deep inside.

"What is it, Francisca?" mumbled Diego, hoping not to raise any fears in the mind of his wife.

"I'm not sure, yet. Something's not right. The afterbirth should have come out by now, but she still seems to be bleeding from ...."

"*Aaaggghhh!*" screamed Maria. The pain hadn't lessened at all after the birth. The contractions usually quickly tapered off after the baby was delivered, but this time they continued just as intense as ever. This was the silent nightmare Maria always had brewing in the back of her mind leading up to childbirth. She worried whether the agony would just keep going. With her mind racing, she thought about her husband raising the children without her because there could be no way of living with this raging pain permanently. "Permanent?! Get a grip on yourself," she demanded silently.

While Maria was wrestling with fears, anxieties, and depressions, mixed with generous amounts of panic, she didn't notice the faces of the midwife and her husband were changing, until her husband gave the baby to one of the townswomen who were standing there with their own looks of grief. What was that look on the faces of Francisca and Diego? Was the sheer strain of the evening causing them to really lose control? Was it so obvious she was about to die?

Just then, without permission from the Francisca, Diego kept his eyes fixed in one place and said, "Push!"

"*What?*" bellowed Maria. "Have you lost your mind?!"

Before she could say any more, the midwife interrupted with, "Just do as he says. You are giving birth ... again!"

Those words hung in the air for what seemed an eternity.

With no time to contemplate the spectacle of the moment, Maria involuntarily began to push. Diego raced to her side and did his best to encourage her to keep it up. He kissed her tenderly on her sweaty forehead, which made Maria regret the curse spat out to him earlier. For a moment, Diego forgot there was a boy who had just entered this world before his very eyes because now a second baby was on its way! Diego looked over to the arms of the townswoman who held his son. "*Son!*" he silently roared with pride. "I have a son!" Stepping back to the midwife's side, Diego watched in amazement. Another head appeared, and before Diego had a chance to sit in the only chair in the dwelling to give his knees a reprieve before they gave out totally, a second boy was born.

Francisca gave him to Diego, who immediately gathered the first little one in his arms. With pride beaming from his tearful face, he presented them to his wife so they could taste the warm love and tenderness only a mother can give to two babies at her breasts. Diego, who had always been a man not ashamed to show the true way he felt, gave the midwife a hearty embrace and an earnest and deeply-felt "thank you." The townswomen who comforted their friend during the birth began to wail and howl in the sheer delight of having witnessed an absolute miracle. One after another, they gathered around Maria for the chance to touch and caress the new babies as well as the mighty woman who had given them life.

Diego once again reached over to wipe the hair from his wife's sweaty brow. He thought she had to be the most beautiful woman he had ever seen, the woman who had not only given birth to their beautiful daughters but now honored him with *two* sons on the same day! As he stood next to the right shoulder of his wife, Diego dipped his head and silently thanked God for having listened to his fervent prayers for a son, and for giving him more than what he had asked for; he prayed that God would help him pay back such an amazing blessing. Crossing himself and kissing his ring finger, Diego reached out for his sons who were now wrapped in swaddling blankets by the townswomen in the room.

With his new baby boys in his arms, Diego marched to the front door, opened it with a shove from his foot, and said to the small crowd gathered for the event, "Behold, my friends! Not only was God gracious enough to bless me with a son, but he has given me a double blessing tonight. Raise a toast to Diego and Maria, for we were given *two* sons on this day! I name them Hernan and Arturo Barragon y Cisneros!"

With one accord, the townspeople shouted their applause. The fiesta in honor of Hernan and Arturo, as well as their parents, lasted well into the next day. Francesca, the midwife, especially enjoyed the celebration because, for the first time, she was personally invited to stay by both Diego and Maria.

CHAPTER 10

October 9, 1277
Badajoz, Spain

NIGHTTIME. EVENING, ACTUALLY. MARIA SAT in a chair just outside the front door to her home and gazed at the sky. Crimson, gold, and violet columns of light streaming through an otherwise dark gray sky took shape before her. Yet the beauty of this open sky, punctuated by the occasional lone sparrow hawk flying by, gave her no consolation. It had been six days since she had last seen her boys, and she had all but given up hope she would ever see them alive again. Maria knew how dangerous this land could be; if you were not paying attention, it was easy to get caught under the blistering sun with no provisions and no water.

She reminded herself that this time of the year was not necessarily the hottest. But still, *something* had to have gone terribly wrong. Why else would the boys have disappeared? They weren't the kind of children who disregarded her rules. They were good boys. Maria knew she spent a lot of time with the children at the orphanage, but Hernan and Arturo followed along in their mother's footsteps and even helped where needed. They rarely complained about it. Did she spend too much time with children who weren't her own?

Maria was at that dangerous time when thoughts turned inward. All efforts to find the boys were being made. There was nothing else she could do now but think back to the last time she saw them. She had been working in the house all day cleaning and preparing the evening meal. Although she lived in a simple home with dusty floors, she did her best to keep her lodgings neat and tidy. It was amazing to the rest of her family how she could make a home with dirt floors appear clean.

Six days ago, she had been tending to her chores and duties around the house when suddenly Hernan and Arturo burst through the door paying no attention to the havoc they were causing. Throwing their school books and coats down on the first surface they could find, they rushed to the middle of the room and immediately turned their attention to the intrigue of the moment: a small rodent caught on the way home from school. Thinking back on it, Maria berated herself for her reaction, which was swift and decidedly caustic. Realizing their transgression, both boys sputtered apologies and immediately left, presumably to play with their new pet where their antics wouldn't suffer from the blistering derision of their mother.

That was the last she had seen them. Her red eyes ached now. When she thought there couldn't possibly be any tears left, more flowed. Diego wasn't home now to assuage her turmoil. Since the day after their disappearance, he never stopped looking for them night and day. He would travel in every direction of the compass, organizing the efforts of several willing participants in the search. Each day he would return only to find the boys still hadn't appeared, and each day he would go out again. Hope was all he had. Hope was all that was left. The very notion of sleep was laughable.

It was quiet now, and a gentle breeze coming from the west carried with it the occasional aroma of the flocks. In these times when nothing and no one offered any distraction, Maria was alone with her thoughts; then was when it was the hardest. She did not want to face the accusations coming from her conscience. Her heart was brutal now. Through the undulating image of the sunset filtering through the tears in her eyes, only one evil and cruel thought kept weighing down Maria's heart. She had been avoiding this notion for as long as possible, but now there was no power left to suppress it anymore. With a labored breath, she uttered, "Did I fail them?"

It was then she felt a hand on her shoulder.

With her heart leaping through her throat and choking off her supply of air, a startled Maria all but exploded from her chair. With the agility of a gazelle, she leaped a matter of meters from her seat only to discover the hand belonged to Diego, who had returned without her even seeing him Even then, it took several moments until she began to collect herself and register that her husband was trying to say something. Her heart had been too loud in her ears to hear anything else.

"I am sorry, my love, to have startled you," said Diego. "I was just trying to answer your question."

Working hard to slow her breathing, Maria finally replied exasperatedly, "Question? What question?"

"You asked, 'Did I fail them?'"

Looking down to the ground thinking back to a time seemingly long ago, when it was only a matter of seconds, Maria finally understood what Diego was saying. "Oh," was all she could reply. It wasn't a question she wished to answer because her condemning heart would only allow one response.

As the blood gradually returned to her feet, Maria allowed herself to go back to where she had been reclining. Diego said something, but it hadn't registered. Nothing could stay the storm of emotions which seemed to define her.

Diego shook her shoulder. "Maria!" he demanded. She could not help but be annoyed now. Didn't he understand she was in pain?!

"Please, Diego. I cannot talk about the children again tonight. It just hurts too much." Through uncountable tears, she finally looked up at the face of Diego. It was only then she saw something was completely out of place.

A smile!

Then it happened. Stepping out from behind Diego were two filthy, very scared boys looking up at their mother.

Since this day, various people in the village have asked Maria how she felt and reacted when she first saw them. She always has a hard time replying because she just doesn't remember. Her only thought at that moment was to hold her babies and never let them go. Diego, on the other hand, remembers it perfectly.

After waiting for Maria to calm down after seeing her boys, all but consigned to the fate of the grave, Diego related the course of events leading to the boys being found. On this day, Diego decided to follow the Guadiana river in a southerly direction. Secretly, Diego had come to the anguishing conclusion something terrible must have happened to the boys. With a heavy heart, he decided to follow the banks of the river. Thinking perhaps they had been swept underwater by the current, he at least hoped to find their lifeless bodies somewhere on the shore of the river; perhaps he would have something to bury.

After traveling a half day's journey, Diego spied a caravan traveling north along the river. Based on their garb, Diego immediately discerned these travelers were a group of people known as the Gitanos. Known as experienced musicians, the Gitanos were a group of people who many regarded with derision; however, Diego never understood such nonsense. All Gitano people he had ever encountered were nothing but hospitable. Due in no small part to the proximity of Diego's farm to the river, word spread amongst the Gitano that Diego and Maria's farm was a much sought after waypoint in their travels. It was widely known they could stay without being molested in any way.

As the caravan came closer, his eyes seemed to be playing tricks on him. He could swear that two of the boys on a horse were his. He thought to himself how they couldn't be since they were dressed in the traditional garb of the Gitano, including handwoven cloth featuring various images of regional flora.

When the caravan was close enough to recognize faces, the two boys saw Diego and dismounted with no small amount of enthusiasm. Running to their father, Hernan and Arturo literally knocked down both Diego and themselves, tumbling on top of their now-sobbing father.

After waiting for Diego to regain some semblance of composure, Hernan and Arturo began to relate the long yet simple story of what happened. After being shooed away by their mother for having brought a mouse into the house, they decided to go down to the shore to watch the water go by.

Having positioned themselves on the bank for about an hour, Arturo saw something floating by that looked exactly like a person with their head down in the water. He became very agitated and wanted to swim out to the body, but it was in a dangerous area of the river where the current compressed from a wide, meandering river to a passage about half the width. Such narrowing caused the river to become a swift passage of white water.

Hernan strongly discouraged Arturo from swimming out to the body; however, as was typical with Arturo, he was not to be dissuaded from his goal. He reasoned that if it were someone they loved, someone would try to rescue their loved one. So, Arturo took to the water. Everything was going fine moving from one rock outcropping to another; he made it to the "body" only to discover it was a uniquely shaped log floating by. Turning around, Arturo headed for shore. Just when he thought he had made it to safety, Arturo slipped on a rock slippery with moss and tumbled head over heels

into the rapids. The current swept Arturo away, and without thinking, Hernan dove into the water to save his brother, unfortunately
ending up in the same predicament.

Serendipitously, that same log floated by the two boys and each of
them latched onto it for some semblance of safety. Holding onto it was
a two-edged sword. Each time the boys tried to make for the shore, the
rapids and other treacherous conditions caused them to return to the
safety of their log life raft. After an hour or two of this ordeal, they situated themselves on a crook where a branch jutted out from the main
trunk of the log. Being completely exhausted, they fell asleep and didn't
wake up until the next morning, since the river that night was relatively
calm, allowing them to sleep uninterrupted.

When Arturo and Hernan finally awoke, they found the log was
caught in some of the thrushes lining one side of the river. Climbing
onto the shore, they realized they were nowhere near home.

The caravan took the boys to the top of one hill near the river
and revealed to them that, had the log not become caught on the
shore, they would have been swept out to sea. Laying before them
was the entirety of the Gulf of Cadiz, leading to the Atlantic Ocean.
The caravan decided to take the boys back to their home, especially
when they learned these boys belonged to Diego and Maria, a well-
known couple amongst them. They didn't leave until the next day
and, during the whole time, the boys couldn't tear themselves away
from what they felt was the most beautiful sight they had ever seen,
the sea. Something just seemed to click with them about that water.
The sight, the smell, something.

The rest is history. The boys traveled with the caravan along the
river for about five days until they met up with Diego, finally returning
home to their mother. Needless to say, they were very content staying
by their parents' side. Even so, the sight of the sea never left them.

CHAPTER 11

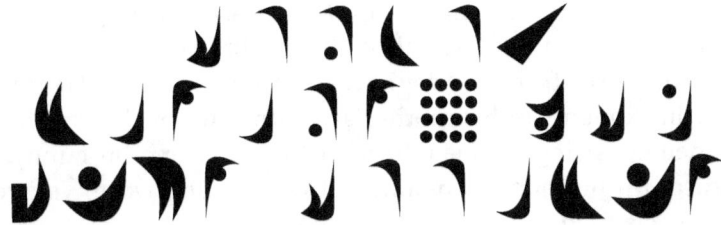

August 29, 1298
Badajoz, Spain

THE REDDISH-ORANGE GLOW OF FIRE always fascinated Hernan. As it tirelessly danced under the pot holding the evening's meal, it made him think about the good times he enjoyed with his family around this fireplace, especially with his twin brother. His heart yearned for the days when all he had to do was glance over to the other side of the room and see his brother. He thought about the first time one of them fell in love, the first time one of them had a child, even the first time one of them was spanked. The two of them shared each event in their respective lives. If one of them fell and scraped a knee, the other wouldn't rest until it was tended to, almost as if there was an unseen mental bridge between them. Hernan and Arturo were inseparable even though they now lived miles apart, each with their own respective farms and families.

"You are lost once again in the fire, aren't you?" asked Sofia.

Hernan's wife Sofia, looking on from her rocking chair, contemplated the thoughts shuffling through her husband's mind, wishing she could be part of his world more than she already was. This cottage where they lived held many memories for her, but it held much more than memories for Hernan. It held life; here was where he first took in the breath of life alongside his twin Arturo. Sofia came from a family of her own with memories of her own: the Montero family, an influential clan in this same village headed by an equally influential father. Now that she lived in this cottage with her husband, however, it was his family that seemed to take up most of her attention.

"Yes, I suppose I was, my love. After working as hard as I do, only my mind has the strength to play," replied Hernan.

Hernan thought about how many memories this house held for him. Most of them were good, some of them were bad. Tonight was to be a good one for Hernan and Sofia. Arturo was going to pay a visit and bring his wife Valera and his only child, Joselito. The sun had set long ago, and the tools from the day's work had grown cold. Hernan was well lost in thoughts of his mother and father when the knock came. He jumped up, swinging open the door to Arturo and his family.

"Arturo! Mi hermano y mi amigo! Come in and warm yourself by the fire!" exclaimed Hernan.

"Hernan! It is good to see you!" returned Arturo.

Hearty embraces were exchanged between the brothers as if there was no tomorrow, as if tonight was the last time to tell each other of their mutual love. That was their way. Growing up, Hernan and Arturo were different from other boys in the village. Even though all the others regularly fought with their siblings, Hernan and Arturo could always be seen walking through the trees together, or sitting next to the creek together, or napping together. They never rivaled each other. They shared a bond nobody else had, nor understood.

That is not to say life for them was easy. Even though their father was a well-respected member of the community, the other boys would always find a way to tease them. Identical twins were exceedingly rare; so rare, in fact, it took time for some of the more superstitious villagers to believe the two brothers were not an evil apparition. Even with a degree of reverence among the older ones of Badajoz, Hernan and Arturo still suffered from the sometimes cruel tongues of boyhood bullies.

As they embraced, Hernan noticed a box under Arturo's arm. "What is this?" Hernan questioned. "You haven't brought me another rock have you?"

They both laughed. Valera looked a little puzzled at the comment as she sat down by Sofia with Joselito on her lap. Her sister-in-law could see that a little explanation was needed.

"You see," Sofia offered, "when they were young, Arturo took a liking to the way some rocks in the mountains shined, and how they had many different colors, especially when they were wet. Well, one day Arturo found this particular rock and thought it was one of the most beautiful he had ever seen. He picked it up, brought it home, washed it off, and then presented it as a gift to his father, Diego. Knowing how much he loved his sons, you can imagine what a fuss he made over this gift, given from the heart of his little boy. Diego promptly took the rock and placed it on the mantle right there," Sofia pointed toward the fireplace. There, on the right side of the mantle, was the rock Diego had placed there some 25 years ago. "After that," Sofia continued, "Arturo was always bringing home rocks to his family as gifts. As he got older, the 'gift giving' slowed to a stop. However, the family story continued, and is still alive and well."

With a look of newfound understanding, Valera glanced at her husband and saw he and his brother had moved to a warm spot on the hearth. They were catching up on the latest news, and talking about the gift Arturo brought his brother. Wanting to be with the men, Joselito protested at the hold his mother had on him. Valera allowed him to leave and take his place next to his father and uncle.

"Not quite, my brother. This is a gift I myself have made for you," Arturo replied with a look of mock disdain. "Lately, I have a lot of time on my hands since hurting myself while caring for the grounds at the church last Sunday."

"Hurt at the church?" Hernan's countenance fell. "What happened?"

"I am a little embarrassed to admit it, since it was a pretty stupid thing to do," explained Arturo. "I had just finished planting a new set of poles for that fence around the church. After working a full day at this, I found myself at the eastern side of the building. After stopping for some water Valera had brought, I noticed I was in the exact spot where I was standing when ... when Mother died."

Sofia raised her eyes and looked up with a sharp movement. She was silently surprised at even the mention of the subject. Arturo paused, as it was hard to say, and he knew it was hard for Hernan to hear as well.

"For the longest time, I just tried to avoid that place but," Arturo exhaled loudly, "it is strange how life just sneaks up, forcing you to face memories you would rather forget."

Both brothers paused. Arturo gazed into the fire to contemplate the feelings now floating freely in the room. Hernan's eyes drifted from Arturo's face and began to stare off into distant space. It was a place in the dark recesses of his mind he dared not go; a dark place where the demons of one's past live. A long silence ensued, accented only by the sound of the wind outside and the crackle of the warm fire inside.

"Anyway," Arturo continued after regaining his composure, "as I was standing there lost in thought, I took a step forward to get a closer look at the window sill she must have been sitting on when it happened. I completely forgot I had just dug a hole in front of me. My foot went in, I fell and twisted it so badly I thought it might be broken. Fortunately, Doctor Fernandez said it was just twisted up and should be back to normal in a few days."

Arturo handed the box to Hernan. "Anyway, this is something I carved for you while sitting on my porch all day long last week."

Hernan accepted the gift with graciousness and, after opening the box, was surprised to discover an intricately carved wooden ... rock. Hernan laughed so hard he nearly slid off his chair. Joselito smiled as if he knew what the joke was about, but his youthful innocence showed through, betraying another thought floating in his mind. Arturo was more than pleased with his brother's reaction, and for a moment glanced over to his wife with a look of true pleasure. Once Hernan regained his composure, he took the "rock" and placed it next to the original rock on the mantle that was given to their father.

From across the room, Valera could see the look in Joselito's face and somehow knew the next words out of her son's mouth were going to be uncomfortable.

"Father?" said the little voice. "Where are Grandmother and Grandfather?"

There it was. Valera knew that since it was Arturo who brought up the subject, it was up to him to explain what had happened. It surprised her that the question hadn't been asked before now since Diego visited this village so rarely these days, and was so conspic-uously absent in the life of his grandson. This was a painful memory for her husband, so she had wisely decided to avoid the whole subject. She knew, though, that this simple and sincere question from the fruit of his loins now standing before him could not be disregarded. Her husband would now have to answer that question, and she might have some questions answered about that day.

Hernan wished this night didn't have to be punctuated by the pain-ful story. However, he knew it was one which had to be told.

"My little one," Arturo spoke slowly in a way depicting one recount-ing a fond memory, "your grandmother was one of the kindest, most loving and joyful women I have ever known. Many commented about the way Grandfather Diego loved his sons, but that was just because he was a man who wasn't afraid to show you how he felt. Grandmother wasn't so public in her displays of affection. However, in private she made you feel as safe and warm as the fire in this fireplace. When we were little boys afraid of the wind outside," Arturo glanced up at the roof he stared at so many times when going to sleep as a boy, "she would get into bed with us, allowing us to fall asleep under the warm protection of her arms. She was always free with her expressions of affection to her children, and I remember the soothing feeling I always had when I saw her in the loving embrace of your grandfather. Grandmother Maria was also a very faithful one in the church."

"Si, hermano," added Hernan. "There were many orphans after the fighting with the pagans, and there wasn't any place for them to stay. Mother decided to lead a movement to build the orphanage next to the church. 'We'll need God's help to look after these little ones,' was what she would say. I remember some of her friends joking about how she practically built the orphanage by herself since she spent so much time there. She really didn't, but if she had the chance, I think she would have tried. She never neglected her own children, though, and I respect her for that, as well as many other things. Your father and I were too young to remember our older sister Anna. When she died from something with her breathing, Father said Mama was heartbroken, and that probably had something to do with why she felt so close to the orphans. When she went to the orphanage to help with the care of the children, she took us too. She told us to not only be proud of who and what we are, but tempered that by pointing out how fortunate we were to have a mother and a father."

"I remember her telling us that so many times," said Arturo. There was a short pause while he gathered enough courage to continue. "After the wars," said Arturo, "things were very different on the farm. Before, it was tough to carve out an existence and supply your family with food. Now that we had the benefit of pagan servants to do much of the shepherding here on our farms, Father had more time to spend on other things he felt were more important. Your grandfather was a very brave fighter in the name of God and he, along with many of the men back then, was very zealous in eradicating the domination the pagan Moors had over this land for so long. After most of the battles were won, he volunteered off duty along the Grenada border. It was an honor to be part of that knighthood."

Arturo's words slowed as he carefully chose each syllable. "One day, when Father was away on a campaign, Mother took us to the church, as she always did. Hernan and I were almost 18 years old, and we felt a little strange still being led around by Mother. I intended to talk with her about it later, but I never got to." Arturo shifted his sitting position, obviously uncomfortable with the subject.

"Just like it is today, it was customary back then to do a thorough cleaning of the church once a year, and this particular day was the day to clean. Mother's job was to clean the windows above the altar to the right. There are windows on the ground floor, but there are others much higher up that need cleaning. She had to use a ladder to reach them. As she was cleaning these windows, she commented to one of the other women the windows needed to be cleaned on the outside as well because it just wouldn't do to have God looking down upon his congregation through dirty windows."

Arturo paused.

"She climbed onto the ledge of the window, holding onto one of the stone outcroppings which framed the window. The stone she held onto wasn't seated very securely. As soon as she put her weight on it, it gave way, and she fell out the window. I saw it happen. She landed on her head."

Arturo's words came in short sentences, measured and articulate.

"She died. Faster than I could even run to her side. I fell next to her. I held her body, but there was no life in it. Still warm, but no life."

Sofia bowed her head in sorrow. Though she and Hernan weren't married at the time, she remembers having witnessed the scene. She remembered how pitiful it was to hear Arturo and Hernan cry out at the top of their voices in anguish over having lost their mother right before their eyes. She remembered the deafening sorrow in the faces of all who watched them take their mother back to the family farm to bury her.

Once again there was silence in the room. Nobody wanted to break it, as if speaking would be disrespectful to Maria's memory.

Finally, Arturo spoke again. "When Father found out a few weeks later that his wife was dead, he was devastated." Hernan looked up and nodded. "He came home, and all he saw was a mound of dirt where his lifemate and friend now lay dead. After that, he lived without purpose at the farm. You could always find him plodding around the farm saying, 'If I had only been there. If I had only been there.' Over and over he would say the same thing."

"Over and over he repeated that," added Hernan. "Nothing we said or did made him feel any better. And God forbid we should try getting him to start enjoying life again. Somehow, I think he believed that if he enjoyed anything now, it somehow meant he wasn't faithful to the memory of Mother; as if being miserable now would prove how much he loved her. It was hard on all of us, but especially troublesome on Father."

"True, very true," agreed Arturo. He paused. "After some time, a few of father's friends convinced him that he needed to get out of this house which held so many memories of his wife. They told him he needed to get on with his life and start enjoying things a little. At the start he resisted, but slowly began seeing there was life beyond this terrible tragedy, and that once again he could find peace. When he finally realized Mother would want him to be happy, he signed on to help with a caravan which regularly made its way across the mountain ranges to the east, trading with cities that were several months' journey farther beyond. Later, he told us how he met people who looked strange and how they made a material out of the web of an insect. It was a little hard to believe his tall tales, but we still loved to hear of these faraway lands and all the adventures he experienced on the way. It makes me happy to know he is happy. In fact, Joselito, your grandfather continues to do this to this very day."

Valera quietly gasped, but it was loud enough for Sofia to look over at her sister-in-law and notice she was crying.

"What did you and Uncle Hernan do then?" asked Joselito.

"Well, since Father was gone for most of the time," answered Arturo, "and the farm was mostly run by servants, but especially since this house held too many memories for us as well, your uncle and I decided we needed to leave. We weren't certain what we would do, but after hearing some exciting stories about voyages over the ocean, we decided to sign up as sailors on the first ship we could find. Actually, it was very easy for us to find work because the captains took one look at us and demanded we sail with them. You see, sailors are very superstitious, and they thought having two men who looked exactly alike would confuse the evil spirits, and they would be left alone."

Hernan chuckled.

"After sailing for five years," said Arturo, "your uncle and I decided we longed for familes of our own. So we left our ship and returned home. We found our wives, and it was then, my boy," Arturo ceremoniously grabbed the shoulders of his young son, "that God blessed me with you. My own precious son."

Although Joselito was sad to hear the story of how his grandmother had died, he glowed in the pleasant warmth of his father's embrace and loving remarks. Joselito crawled into his father's lap and gave Arturo the biggest hug he could possibly manage.

Meanwhile, Sofia was taking more and more notice of Valera and how she was continuing to sob quietly. Her moist eyes seemed to be transfixed on the floor in front of her, and she had a look on her face resembling something unexpected: fear.

After enjoying his son's embrace, Arturo looked over to his wife and rather than seeing an approving smile, he saw a look of deep and profound sorrow on her face. Arturo rose from his position in front of the fire and strode to his wife's side. "Valera my love," consoled Arturo, "do not be downhearted. Mother is with God now, and she is in a wonderful place. Please don't cry for her, because she isn't suffering at all. She is at peace now, and would be pleased to know we can fondly remember her for the good she did." Arturo came close to Valera and cradled her head on his chest.

After a few seconds of enjoying her husband's consolations, Valera decided she was no longer able to hold back what was burning inside her. She had to come forth with it, and Arturo would have to hear it. She just wished to God it did not have to come from her lips.

"With no disrespect to the memory of your mother," said Valera as she pulled away from her husband's embrace, "I wish the cause of my tears was as simple as that. But no, my heart is heavy with news I heard just two days ago when I was shopping at the markets in town. My heart is heavy, for I know this is news you must hear. However, I was afraid to tell you because I knew it would cause you so much pain."

"What is it?" asked Arturo, bracing himself. "What did you hear?"

Valera looked up from the spot where she had been staring, looked Arturo in the eyes and said, "Diego, your father, is dead."

CHAPTER 12

ᘔ ᘿᑕᘓᒍᘄᒍᑌᑫ
ᘁᐅᒍᑌ.ᘁ

Losing all feeling in his legs, Arturo's knees buckled and he fell to the floor like a limp sack of flour. Gasping for air, Sofia covered her mouth and gazed in astonishment at her sister-in-law. Breaking down into a sobbing fit, Valera buried her face in her hands, holding a corner of her skirt.

Darting her eyes over to her husband, Sofia saw Hernan sitting before the fire with his eyes transfixed. Through the years, Sofia had always known her husband to have the countenance of steel. The ability to handle difficult moments was one of his strengths. But THIS – even this was too much for him to bear. One tear started to form in each of Hernan's eyes, then more. Before the night would finish, many more would be spilled.

"Why?" pled Arturo, with the broken screams of a heart-stricken man. Dragging in another breath, he begged, "How did this happen?" He was barely able to get the words out of his mouth.

Breathing in short bursts, Valera answered. "When I was shopping for dinner that evening, I noticed a man coming into town on a horse. Over its hindquarters was draped a blue banner with the crest of an eagle and a lion locked in battle."

Immediately, Hernan and Arturo recognized the crest as belonging to the Bandion traders, the group their father had been aligned with for the last several years.

"Naturally," Valera continued while looking intently at her husband, "I walked over to him to inquire about Diego and whether he knew when Diego would be returning home to visit his children. I thought it would be nice if he came home since he had no knowledge of his grandson, Joselito. When I walked up to this man, he identified himself as the second in command of the Bandioni, and said he was in town to find the Barragon y Cisneros family. My heart leaped since I was sure he was about to tell me Diego was arriving shortly."

Valera dropped her eyes to the floor once more and continued relating the events of that day. "When I told him he had already found the family by talking to me," said Valera, "he proceeded to tell me the bad news. He said Diego was firmly convinced the route they normally took to get to the Orient was longer than needed, and he thought he could find a more direct route east. The leader of the Bandioni granted Diego permission to explore a new route east and gave him a group of men to command during the expedition. The man told me of how Diego actually found a faster route to India, but apparently a large group of marauders met up with his party in the foothills of Arabia. Not being one to back down when assaulted," Valera paused, "Diego was killed in Arabia, where he is now buried. Some of the men he was commanding were able to escape and relate the story to the leader of the Bandioni. He said the Bandion traders decided to use that new route, but only under heavy guard. After talking to me, he said he was satisfied he had notified the family, and he left the city."

Sensing she was somehow deviating, Valera regained her verbal bearing and continued. "When I heard this news, I was shocked of course, but later I began to fear how you and your brother were going to react." She looked up from the spot on the floor where she had been staring, and searched for the face of her husband. He had his face buried in his arm, which was lying across his knees. Arturo was a crumpled mass of humanity; his very life had been drained, and his countenance had shifted from happiness to pain in a matter of seconds.

"I wanted to tell you before this, but I couldn't. I just *couldn't*!" Not able to take the thick and ever-increasing air of depression in the room, Valera jumped up and ran out the door to the well-groomed courtyard in front of the house. Sofia quickly followed her, and Joselito, not sure whether he should go, followed the women since it made him very insecure to know his mother was so upset.

After what seemed an eternity, Arturo looked up and saw his brother leaning back in his chair with his eyes closed. If it were not for Hernan's lips moving in silent prayer, Arturo would have thought his brother was sleeping. Prayer. Now that was a good idea. Hernan always seemed to be the first one to think of such things, even though both of them had a great and reverential fear of the Almighty. Getting up from his position on the floor, and moving closer to the fireplace where his brother was, Arturo sat down beside him and was the first to break the silence.

"That damned old man. Why did he have to be so fearless and headstrong?"

Hernan paused for a moment, long enough for Arturo to think his question wouldn't be answered; not that he was looking for a response. Then Hernan spoke up and said, "To answer that question, my brother, you need only look as far as the mirror on the wall."

Arturo knew exactly what Hernan was saying. They both were just as headstrong as their father, and they both were very determined to get what they wanted. Usually that meant good things to those around them, since Hernan and Arturo were good men who did't take advantage of their fellow man.

As if to scold his now dead father, Arturo rhetorically asked, "How many times did we tell you to be careful. How many times did I tell you your life was more valuable than the riches of the East?" After contemplating the questions, the brothers knew there were no answers for them. Given the same circumstances, they probably would have made the same decisions. After all, the man needed to get away from all the painful memories of the farm, didn't he? He needed the diversion, right?

Always more analytical than his brother, Hernan spoke up. "Actually, the most important thing to remember is our father was finally happy again. Remember the stories he told us when he visited last time? You and I both saw that old fire in his eyes again; we hadn't seen it since Mother died. Speaking for myself, I enjoyed seeing that fire again."

Arturo paused for a moment and thought about a letter he had received from his father which said, in part:

> "Sometimes, my son, I think about the life I had with my wife and my children. I remember smelling the fragrance of Maria's hair, feeling the warm and loving touch of her embrace. I remember the way she was able to look me in the eyes and gaze beyond, as if she was able to fondle the innermost parts of my soul. It is when I see other men

with their wives that I feel the greatest loss. How I wish I could once again feel her silken skin against mine, or feel the breath of a woman whose essence was so tightly bound with mine. I have had opportunities to enjoy the carnal love of another woman, but none could ever compare to Maria, so my answer was always 'No.' She was my heart. She was my soul. She was my life. I feel it is a good thing I am with the Bandioni since this is a troupe of men. I have little opportunity to allow my thoughts to wander back to my life with Maria and so, in a way, life is easier. In fact, my life now is rewarding and prosperous. I have purpose again, and feel like life is once again worth living."

"Well, my brother," said Arturo, "I know he was happy with his new life and with what he was doing. I just can't believe he's gone. I just can't believe...."

"I know," injected Hernan. "It seems there is little left for him to have as his legacy. Nothing lasting to assign to his honor. Nothing."

Arturo nodded. Both brothers sat in a warm room filled with cold emptiness.

After regaining some composure outside, Sofia and Valera returned inside with Joselito and proceeded to prepare dinner. There wasn't much conversation at the dinner table, and little Joselito knew, even though he was only four years old, he should stay quiet. There were the usual pleasantries, "pass this" or "please serve me some of that," but they all felt an underlying tension. Just when it seemed the entire dinner would be marked by a deafening silence, Arturo pointedly dropped his fork and said, "Our father deserves more than this. He deserves to be remembered honorably and not as a hapless trader who let marauders get the better of him."

Looking up from his half-eaten cold dinner, Hernan asked, "What are you saying?"

Sitting back in his chair and placing his arms at his side, Arturo replied, "I'm just saying his memory should continue. You and I both know how good a man he is." He looked down at his plate, recognizing his error. "I mean was …." Swallowing what felt like his heart throbbing in his throat, Arturo continued. "But he deserves more. He just deserves more."

"I agree with you, my brother, but what can we do for him now that he is … gone?" Hernan couldn't bring himself to say "dead."

Getting up from the table, Arturo contemplatively looked up and slowly strode to the fireplace. He began stroking his chin as his eyes came to rest on the rock sitting on the mantle. Hernan recognized this look, a look Arturo always put on when he was about to come up with an idea. "Felipe wants to sell both of his ships, doesn't he?"

Instantly Hernan knew what his brother was thinking. "You want to find a new trading route by sailing to the Orient instead of traveling over land, don't you?" he asked. This actually wasn't a new idea for the two brothers. On many occasions, they had discussed it, and even made a pact when they were young that, if ever possible, they would make such a voyage. Ever since the day they first saw the sea after being rescued by the Gitanos, the young boys repeatedly had long conversations with anyone they could find who had ever been on the sea. It was this early fascination with the sea, as well as the determination to sail around the world one day, that led to Hernan and Arturo being sailors for many years. Normally Hernan would be hesitant at the thought of adopting another one of his brother's ideas. Whenever he did, he usually got in trouble. This time was different, though. Feeling just as much passion as his brother about the legacy of his father, as well as smarting from the fresh wound this devastating news caused, Hernan was more than willing to accept the idea.

"Yes!" responded Arturo. "We will dedicate this voyage to the memory of our father. Once we establish the route, we will name it after him. How many times have we talked about it, and how many ...."

"I'll do it," interrupted Hernan.

The gravity of the decision just made hung heavy in the air, like an early morning mist covering a seaside village. Sofia and Valera sat stunned and silent, not knowing what, if anything, could be said. They were horrified at the prospect of their husbands going off on a sailing expedition from which they might not return. What could be said? Anything?

No, not a word. They both knew once a decision had been made, there was no changing that decision. Once more, Hernan and Arturo were going to sea.

CHAPTER 13

A FEW MONTHS HAD TRANSPIRED SINCE the decision was made to make the voyage to what many were calling the West Indies. A faster route to India was the clear goal, but this voyage meant so much more to Hernan and Arturo. With their father's life having been snuffed out so senselessly, and since there would be no justice against his faceless murderers, the only thing which made sense to his two sons was to perform a grandiose gesture of love dedicated to their father; at least his memory would live on, even if he didn't.

In the last couple of months, the two brothers had worked hard at preparing for the expedition. Much planning was done, and the two of them spent virtually every waking moment coming up with scenario after scenario. Each were discussed thoroughly, and decisions were made one right after another. Early on, the two of them secured notebooks allowing them to keep track of all the decisions and the endless lists of tasks to be completed. As weeks went by, plans for the trip really started to crystallize, and everything was coming together perfectly. Almost.

The problem, if you want to call it that, was their respective wives. While Hernan and Arturo were completely invested in the effort and looking forward to the voyage, their wives were equally *against* the expedition. Under normal circumstances, both Sofia and Valera subscribed to the concept of maintaining a quiet, mild spirit when it came to interactions with their husbands. They weren't timid when it came time to make their feelings known, but for the most part, decided it was important to remain reasonably submissive to their husbands, who made it easy for them to behave in this manner. Both Arturo and Hernan had learned from watching how their father treated their mother. Diego always told his boys it was up to the man to treat his wife as if she was a precious and delicate vase; not only beautiful on the outside, but equally so on the inside. He taught them to treat their wives with the honor they deserved, and the reward would be a wife who deeply respects her husband.

This was precisely the relationship Sofia and Valera enjoyed with their husbands most of the time. But as is the case with all marriages, there were times when the bonds of matrimony were profoundly tested. This was one of those times.

The village where the two couples lived had its share of men who had gone off to seek their fortunes at sea in the past; Hernan and Arturo were two of them. Most of them came back, but some didn't. The fate of that small minority weighed heavily on the hearts of the two women. They certainly understood the emotional aspect of what their husbands intended to do. This was a demonstration of their love for their father; they didn't want the ending of Diego's life to be as pointless as it currently seemed to be. For their own individual reasons, Sofia and Valera didn't like the lack of a legacy for Diego either. Sofia sincerely loved her father-in-law; so did Valera, for that matter. In Valera's case, though, she was sorry her small son Joselito never had the opportunity to meet his paternal grandmother, and now would never get to know his grandfather as well. Secretly, this broke her heart more than knowing the pain Diego's death caused her husband.

On countless occasions, Sofia and Valera strenuously tried to dissuade their husbands from undertaking a voyage fraught with uncertainty. They tried everything from reasoning, to anger, to tears. Especially in the beginning, nothing even came close to breaking through the resolve the two men had in making this work. As time went on, the thick armor of resolve started to thin; not enough for them to change their minds, but definitely enough for them to see the anguish this was causing their wives. This, more than anything, made the undertaking extremely difficult to complete. By the time they were ready to depart, part of what made them leave on that specific day was the realization that one more week would result in their resolve crumbling, and they would never go; which, in their minds, would mean they failed their father and, in effect, shamed him. They couldn't allow that to happen!

Ultimately, though, Hernan loved Sofia and Arturo loved Valera and his son Joselito. While their wives would never understand this, if they didn't go, the brothers wouldn't feel they were men their wives could respect; to maintain any level of self-respect, they *had* to go. Arturo needed to demonstrate to his son the resolve a real man must display and maintain.

On the first night after they left home, when all was quiet, Sofia composed a poem, "Voyager," about her husband.

Voyager

Eyes on the horizon
Not all of you is here
You're on a voyage
You're gone – even when you're near

I'm happy where I am
You're never satisfied
You live in your own world
But now I'm so alone inside.

Denied a lover's rage
An enemy with no face
Once again I sleep alone
Once again memories erase

In the morning, my eyes open
I stare at your pillow
My hand searches for warmth
...But I'm left feeling cold

Arise oh wanderer
Another day makes its plea
Come home to me voyager
Come find your peace with me!

I'm giving more than you take
There's too much love to fake
You're making my heart break
You're making my love wait

I'm giving more than you take
I can't leave this to fate
Love me, for our loves' sake.
These tears, I just can't shake.

You're a Voyager
You're just a wanderer

Initially, the two men had a lot on their minds when they left home, so they let these things crowd out the fact they were already missing their wives and wishing they could be back home. Spending time thinking about Sofia and Valera would come later, once they were at sea.

Of course, the first thing they had to do was secure a boat for the voyage. Their timing was rather fortuitous; when they started shopping for a vessel in Aesuris, they ended up buying out a defunct shipping company run by an acquaintance of theirs which had two boats that fit their needs perfectly.

As they were preparing for their voyage, both Hernan and Arturo thought back regularly to the first time they saw Aesuris. It was the same port village they gazed upon as boys after being swept along the river and later rescued by the Gitano people. That had a striking effect on the boys since it was the first time they had seen the sea, and its mark on their young minds was indelible. As soon as they were old enough, they both left home and joined the crew of a shipping company; the same one which was now going out of business. When the current owner found out Hernan and Arturo wanted to buy a boat, he made them a deal they couldn't refuse. They ended up buying two boats for basically what they would have paid for one. While it ended up costing them more to fit out two boats rather than one, Arturo reasoned they would have twice as good of a chance to make it to the West Indies. Always being more impetuous than his brother, Arturo instantly wanted to jump on the deal, but it was Hernan who weighed the pros and cons and eventually relented to his brother's urgings.

The next step was to secure the provisions and crew for two boats. Provisions were easy, only requiring making the purchases and getting them on the ship.

The crew was a different matter. Many believed such a voyage was suicide. The general opinion was if you sailed far enough, you would either enter an area populated with great sea monsters, or worse yet, sail right off the edge of the world and fall forever into the unknown. They all seemed to have some uncle, cousin, or brother who had been that far and seen something which supposedly lent credence to such notions. In this rare circumstance, it was actually Hernan who pushed aside these ideas. It wasn't due to any brash decision-making on his part, though. Hernan was more devoted to his faith than most, and he applied several scriptures that talked about how "God sits on the circle of earth" and "hangs the earth upon nothing." From these and other scriptures, he just knew there wasn't an edge to fall off of, but rather a world something like his little nephew's ball; if he just sailed far enough, he would get to land on the other side of India.

The only problem was they weren't sure how long it would take. Because of this, Arturo and Hernan decided to stuff the boats to the gunnels with as many provisions as would fit, and only take on a skeleton crew. With these preparations, the two of them calculated they should have enough to make a round trip voyage twice the distance they had ever done before.

Since any sailor worth his pay would never go if he knew the real destination, the two captains decided to engage in a little subterfuge. First, they made sure they didn't sign on anybody who knew anything about navigation. Hernan and Arturo made sure they were the only individuals who knew anything about how to use a sextant and observe the constellations. Second, during the day, they would basically sail south with the sun rising on their port side and setting starboard, as if they were sailing around Cape Agulhas at the southernmost tip of Africa. During the day though they would only put up one or two sails so they wouldn't end up getting very far.

Night would be an entirely different story; the plan was to go full sail to the west. At night the two of them would be awake, and during the day they would sleep. Both captains were extremely anxious to get underway and experience once again the steady rhythm of waves breaking against the bow of the their ships.

During the previous three months, Hernan and Arturo endured a lot of personal anguish as the thought of their voyage was truly a daunting one. Before this, they were sailors themselves, but had never been very far out into the open sea. Most of their voyages consisted of stints on merchant ships sailing up and down the coast of Spain. They saw a lot of things many of their boyhood acquaintances never even knew existed. They had seen the marble edifices of Greece, the massive stone pyramids of Egypt, and the impressive rocks of Gibraltar. They went to the Holy Land where their savior himself had walked. They had been north to the coldest of the cold, and south to the hottest of hot.

Arturo and Hernan also suffered the derision of their respective wives. Perhaps more than anybody else, Sofia and Valera were very unhappy with the decision to make this voyage. While knowing that once the decision was made it was final, still they valiantly worked hard to try and talk some sense into the minds and hearts of their husbands; they eventually failed at it. In the end, the only thing they took solace in was they had tried to dissuade their husbands from going on a trip which would probably lead to their deaths. They hoped it wouldn't come to that, but womanly intuition seemed to indicate otherwise.

The day had finally come. There was no more planning to be done. No more checking or re-checking the seaworthiness of their crafts. Arturo oversaw the receiving of the last bit of provisions, and the crew had checked in the previous day. Arturo was to captain the "Tyche," named after the Greek god of luck, and Hernan was to captain the "Fortuna," named after the Roman version of the same god. Hernan was going over the crew manifest as well as making sure all navigational implements were properly stowed in his and his brother's personal quarters. The air on board was tense. Many of the men who signed on didn't know exactly what lay in store for them.

The ship's stores were full, and all hands were present and accounted for. It was time.

The twin captains flipped a coin, and the toss landed on Arturo to lead the sail. He put to sea and Hernan followed close after. They decided to use a series of flags for communications, one flag for each letter of the alphabet. They felt it was quite ingenious! Nobody had ever done anything like that before.

Every voyage Hernan had taken part in before represented a chance to get out to the open sea, a place where he could become one with the wind and the water around him. It was a time when Hernan honed the simple skill of being comfortable with himself. Too many times, he observed acquaintances who didn't seem comfortable in their own skin, almost as if they couldn't be alone with their thoughts. Unless they were dealing with some issue needing a solution, or talking to someone, they somehow seemed to look for calamities to fix. To Hernan, this was a flaw, since it showed a lack of understanding of the world. Before one could be a real man who could stand on his own, he had to know the real person he was inside. And the only way to do that was to be comfortable with one's own thoughts.

Usually, a voyage provided ample time to do this. Hernan quietly observed that this one seemed to be a little different. With this journey, there were more than the normal risks causing more anxiety than he was used to. It wasn't because of the ships or his men. The ships were the newest type, recently made popular in Portugal by the fishermen there. The men? Well, they were good sailors, but even there, concerns existed. Hernan knew he and his brother weren't forthcoming about the course they were going to take. The premise that he and his brother were the only ones who knew navigation was a house of cards which threatened to topple at any moment. The only way this could be staved off was to keep the small number of crew on board busy. Polishing every inch of the deck, or taking and re-taking inventory were some of the ways. They did all they could to plan out each and every detail of the voyage. They spent dozens of sleepless nights covering each and every decision needed to insure every contingency was covered.

But how to do you plan for the unexpected? Hernan and Arturo stocked as many provisions as they could possibly take, not knowing exactly how long the voyage would take. They expected to hit landfall hopefully in about two months, but that was only a guess. To allow for a "point of no return" of around two and a half months, they decided to pack for a five-month voyage and catch fish to eat while at sea.

So it began. With a quiet resolve, the entire crew was on deck to witness the disappearance of land as they sailed farther and farther. Feeling the cool wind on their respective faces, Hernan and Arturo now faced time and unforeseen occurrences, courting whatever random destiny that might seek out their adventurous faces. It was now when the soundless demons of monotony reared their fearsome, ugly heads. It was now when the only thing remaining to keep them company at night was the memory of wives whom they loved deeply, but whom they abandoned in pursuit of a goal which was obscure at best. The two men were thinking identical thoughts as the journey began. They both were hoping all the sacrifice would be worth it in the end.

CHAPTER 14

$$\odot \varphi \jmath \, \jmath \, \jmath \varphi \jmath \, \jmath \jmath \jmath \jmath$$
$$\varphi \checkmark \jmath \cdot \jmath \cdot \jmath \odot \varphi$$

THE EXPEDITION HAD BEEN AT sea for three weeks and as expected the day-in, day-out tedium laid bare all the insecurities of each individual man on board. Hernan had said it well to Arturo: the sea makes a man come face to face with all that is in his soul, and forces a man to come to grips with anything that makes him question his resolve and any decisions made.

Making this voyage in honor of their father was a big decision. As much as they avoided the anxiety of indecision while getting ready for their travels, now the brothers had nowhere else to go. They came face to face with the roar of a lion which previously had no name. Now, though, it was as plain as it was overwhelming. Guilt.

Both Arturo and Hernan finally admitted they should have stayed with their wives. Even if they discovered a path to the West Indies, it still wouldn't bring their father back from the dead. At best, it would create a new path of commerce; at worst, it would be the same as if the marauders who killed their father killed them as well. It would leave their wives as widows and Joselito without a father. Each passing day caused the men to get the priorities of their lives in better perspective. Perhaps that would be the best treasure found on this trip, making them better husbands and fathers.

Maybe this trip wasn't such a bad thing after all, for at least that one reason.

The brothers now carried the burden their respective wives had already been carrying for quite some time. It was the burden of wishing they could be with the one they loved. As time went on, and with no way of telling their respective wives how much they loved them, Arturo decided to create a letter to Valera as an overture of love.

As he started writing, the words came slowly, but with each passing second, the thoughts quickly changed from a trickle to a raging torrent. When he was done with his letter, Arturo felt both drained and relieved.

To my dear wife Valera and my precious son Joselito,

As I sit here writing this letter, I must admit I feel conflicted. I made my noble intentions clear to you as we prepared for this trip, but reflecting on the events of my life over the last months I spent with you, I can now see that there was one important thing lacking in all my preparations for this voyage. What was missing was paying more attention to your feelings and what I put you through. Leaving my wife and my child while I went off in pursuit of this goal appears, more and more, to be a fool's errand.

As time goes by, I am tortured by how much I miss your loving caress every night. As we sail to what we hope is the eastern shore of India, I am reminded, in the hours of darkness, of you and my precious son. As I pen these words, I reflect on the day when you gave life to the manifestation of our love, Joselito. I remember holding him in my arms for the first time and being amazed at how much I loved someone whom I had only just met. As I prepared for this trip, I kept thinking how important it was for him to see manly resolve in the face of his father. Now I see he is missing out on something even greater in value, the actual feel of his father holding his hand, and holding the hand of his beautiful mother. I hid behind a thin veil of noble resolve and honor. This was only the façade of a man who couldn't face the pain of his father's death.

The sea is the great giver of perspective, my love. It forces you to come face to face not only with yourself, but also the sins of your life. Was it a sin go on this voyage? Perhaps.

I shouldn't have left you alone to fend for yourself and to provide training for our dear son.

While I don't think this voyage is as dangerous as you regularly expressed to me, there is always the possibility something might happen that I didn't expect. In a bottle, I send this letter to you over the sea, hoping you will get it someday and that it will not be lost forever. It is my sincere hope that when you finish reading this letter, you will look up to see my loving face looking back at you.

But, my love, if that isn't the case and something has happened resulting in your not sharing the rest of your life with me, I want you to know I am sorry for the obvious loss you have experienced. I am profoundly sorry for the pain you have felt and are no doubt feeling right now. It was never my intention to cause you pain, and I hope one day you can forgive me for putting you through this.

And to my son, I want you to know that other than spending time with your mother, the best part of my day was coming in the door to our home and seeing your face. While it is true you came through me, you are not like me, my son. Even in your young face, I could see your own path in life was different from mine. Mine was shaped by my love for my family, especially my twin brother. Yours should also be shaped by love, but I encourage you, my son, to never let manly pride get in the way of showing those you love just how much you love them. If there is one thing life has taught me, it is the need to confirm the things which are most important, and to be sure of exactly what those most important things truly are.

Love with a sense of urgency, my son. Urgently love God each and every day you live, for it is from him all good things come. If you have the amazing experience of enjoying the love of a good woman, love her as if tomorrow will never come, as if today is the last day you ever expect to spend with her. None of us know what day will be our last, so make sure she knows the sun rises and sets on her face. No matter what you invest in your wife, she will give it back to you a hundredfold. And never forget me, my son. Always remember you had a father who loved you more than he loved life itself.

Finally, to you my love, please know my thoughts are with you always. If because of some unforeseen event I do not remain by your side for the rest of your life, please know my biggest desire is for you to be happy. If I have moved on to the next life and am no longer among the living, all I ask is you not allow your memories of me to keep you from having happiness. I do not wish to be remembered in that way. Each time you think of me, I want a smile to be upon the lips I kissed so many times. If your happiness leads you to find a new man who makes you whole, my sincere hope is that he be at least half as happy and complete as you have always made me. You have my blessing.

Eternally yours in this life and in the next,

Arturo

CHAPTER 15

Fᴏʀ ᴛʜᴇ ʟᴀꜱᴛ ᴛᴡᴏ ᴡᴇᴇᴋꜱ, the sea had been perfect, in terms of sailing conditions. Too perfect. It was a little worrisome to Arturo and Hernan since they had to work a lot harder to keep the men busy. Originally, the brothers' plan was to keep the crew busy with taking care of the ship's provisions and general care so they wouldn't have time to start questioning the unorthodox manner in which they were sailing. Although none of the men had any expertise with navigation, they were sailors with years of experience, so it was inevitable someone would figure out the real destination of the two ships. They had no idea an imbecile would be the first to figure it out.

Each ship had a crew of 12 men. On Arturo's ship, though, trouble began brewing.

"Horace."

Malcolm looked at his partner in crime, expectantly hoping he would rouse without any of the other crew being alerted. The pervasive snores coming from the rest of the bunks down here in the belly of the ship told him he was safe for now.

"Flick!" Malcolm quietly bellowed again.

"No, sweetie. I don't have to leave for another hour," said Horace in his sleep. "Just lay back down here."

Malcolm rolled up an old shirt and tossed it to his "friend" from a distance, making sure it hit him in the face. Malcolm had enough experience with Horace to know if you were going to wake him up from a dead sleep, then you'd better give him a wide berth until he knows what's going on.

Sure enough, getting hit in the face with a shirt caused Horace to silently yet decisively bolt up from his prone position into one ready for battle. In his right hand was a rather large and menacing knife he always kept under his pillow. As he slept, Horace always kept his hand on the knife so he was able to slit the neck of any hapless idiot who wandered too close. It was one reason why he had the nickname Flick; his weapon of choice was this articulating knife he could wield with deadly accuracy, and often did.

"Put that thing away, you idiot!" admonished Malcolm, who was only slightly more intelligent.

Relaxing his stance, Flick retracted his knife and sat back down on his bedroll. "Now wod ja go and wake me up for, Malcolm? I was just about to have me way with Bunny!"

Normally, Malcolm wouldn't have taken his life into his hands like this, but something had been bothering him for the last several nights, keeping him up. He had been spending part of the night watching the sky from a gun port near the fo'c'sle where their bunks were. He started noticing a pattern to the way the stars appeared after all the men went to sleep. He knew that during the night, the captains were manning the rudder while the crew slept. That in itself was strange, but then each night Malcolm saw the stars which came up in front of the ship swing to port and stay there for the rest of the night. On the few occasions he awakened before sunup, he saw the stars move back from port to take their place off the bow. Plus the way the captains ordered only one sail on the mizzen be set; it just wasn't adding up.

"Something's not right. I've been watching the sky out through the gun port. The captain is doing something strange, but I can't figure it out."

"What is he doing that eeze strange?" said a rather deep, substantial voice from the shadows. Malcolm and Flick instantly reacted and once again the knives were at the ready, until they realized it was only Sampson who asked the question. Sampson was a large and imposing man who said he came from some islands, but it was never clear which islands they might have been. He was one of the few individuals Malcolm and Horace actually trusted, misplaced though it was.

126

Malcolm and Flick sat back down on the edge of their bunks as they stowed their respective knives, and rested their elbows on their knees. Speaking softly, Malcolm was the first to answer.

"It's the stars. I'm tellin you, somethin' just ain't right." Malcolm pointed out the gun port near the bunk heads. "When I goes to bed I sees the stars. But if I wait long enough, I sees them swing over that-away," he gestured to the port side of the ship.

"Then," he continued "just before sun-up I sees them swing back to the front of the ship. Something's not right I'm telling you."

Sampson looked at Malcolm and thought for a moment. After a few seconds, he leaned back against a supporting timber near his bunk, reached up and twisted what amounted to a large and thick toothpick he always kept hanging out of his mouth., when he wasn't eating anything that is. Through eyes squeezed into slits, he regarded the two before him, thinking they must be two of the stupidest men he'd ever seen. Early on, it was obvious to him these two were not real sailors, but were criminals with their own agenda, although he didn't know what it was. Sampson had his own plans for this trip, though, so he decided to wait and see what they would do first; that was why he was awake to hear Malcolm and Horace. He decided early on that a potential enemy in front of open eyes was much better than behind one's back.

After about a minute, with the two imbeciles looking on, Sampson started smiling; he had figured out the real reason why the ships were at sea. He had been sailing for the majority of his life, but he was intelligent enough to fake being new to the sea to the captains. That hidden intelligence caused Sampson to put two and two together and see that if the stars were swinging to port, then the southerly course they were taking during the day was being changed at night to a course due west. Considering the captains were only using one sail during the day but full sails at night, Sampson figured all the sailing during the day was only a ruse to keep the crew pacified. He figured they were not only sailing west at night, but in fact, they were probably sailing northwest since they were probably canceling out the slow southerly progress they made during the day.

It wasn't much of a bother to Sampson that they were sailing west. His ancestors had been living on the sea for many generations, and from them he learned how his people had come from land a very long distance away to the west. His ancestors weren't subscribers to the whole flat Earth thinking of the day.

If Arturo and Hernan had realized Sampson was a pirate quite well known to the mariners of England, they certainly wouldn't have hired him. He was waiting for the ship to acquire its booty and when it did, he would appropriate it and eliminate most, if not all, on board who weren't with him. On this particular voyage, he wanted to see what kind of business he could scare up in these waters. Sure enough, he landed on something here very interesting: legends of lands to the west laden with gold. He definitely liked the idea of getting his hands on some of it.

Meanwhile, he had to figure out what to do with these dimwits. They could be a liability, but then again, they might be able to help him keep his eyes on more than just he alone could. Figuring they would be easy enough to manipulate, he decided to gamble that they were indeed the simpletons he suspected.

"I know exactly what eeze happening," said Sampson with an accent neither Malcolm or Horace had ever heard. "Our captains are very shrewd ones. They are aware of the way the stahs move in these watuhs, and they are making sure we are still going south, eeven though the stahs try to trick them!"

"The stars move?" said a very unsure Horace.

"Of course they do, my friend" said Sampson with a large smile on his face. Then deciding to shame them into submission, he said, "You aren't some of those stupid sailuhs who don't believe the stahs move at night are you?"

"Oh, uhh, no!" said Malcolm. "Don't be dippy. Of course we aren't. Isn't that right Flick?"

"Uh. Yeah. Uh, of course we are. Or aren't! Uh, right," said a confused Horace, nodding his meaty head, his jowls undulating back and forth.

Sampson smiled at the success of his ruse. "No, I should have known bettah. I didn't think you would be so stupid." Leaning forward, he came close to the two men and said, "I don't think the rest of these dogs here are as smart as you two, though. They wouldn't understand just how much our captains know about navigation. We should keep this to ourselves. What do you think?"

Malcolm glanced over at Horace, who was looking at him bewilderedly, then back at Sampson. "No," he said, "I was thinking the same thing."

"I knew you were the smoht ones heeuh," said Sampson, all the while knowing when the time came, these two would be the last of the crew he would kill since they would initially be useful to do the messy work. For now, though, he would just have to wait and see what happened.

Meanwhile, on deck in the light of a full moon, Arturo was signaling to his brother with the flags. As each letter was signaled, he would spell it out on paper.

P-R-O-V-I-S-I-O-N-S-A-T-S-I-X-T-Y-P-E-R-C-E-N-T-C-O-N-C-
E-R-N-E-D-A-B-O-U-T-C-R-E-W-F-I-G-U-R-I-N-G-O-U-T-C-O-U-
R-S-E-S-H-O-U-L-D-T-A-L-K-A-B-O-U-T-W-H-E-N-W-E-M-I-G-
H-T-D-E-C-I-D-E-T-U-R-N-A-R-O-U-N-D

Hernan was thinking about it too; he wasn't willing to put the crew in danger of starvation. He decided to signal back to his brother.

A-G-R-E-E-S-H-O-U-L-D-C-O-N-S-I-D-E-R-I-N-T-W-O-D-A-Y-S

Looking toward his brother's ship, Arturo saw the reply.

A-G-R-E-E-D

There it was. They were nearing the end of their ability to go on. While finding a faster way to the Indies was the goal, they didn't want to put the men at risk of starvation before getting back to their port of call. No, they would just have to sail back home, secure a set of bigger boats that could handle a larger load of supplies, and try again with more provisions.

Sampson had other ideas, though. He took into account the amount of provisions still on board in relation to the amount of provisions already consumed, and he could see they were nearing the halfway point. He also figured out the captains didn't actually know where, or if, they would fall upon land. If they did, they wouldn't have invented this elaborate scheme of sailing south during the day and west at night. Once the captains determined they were nearing the point of no return, they would invent a reason to turn around, then hightail it back to Spain. Armed with these realizations, Sampson started concocting a scheme to sail the rest of the way to the lands of his ancestors.

As Arturo contemplated the impending failure of the voyage, he looked toward the rising sun and then to the cloudless sky, thinking to himself "Wow, the weather here is beautiful!He didn't know this was going to be one of the last peaceful days of his life.

Sure enough, as agreed, two days later Arturo called for all hands on deck. On this particular day, he hadn't bothered to steer the ship back toward the south, so it was still full sail to the west. Hernan was having the same meeting with his crew on his own ship.

Speaking with as commanding a voice as possible, Arturo began. "Men, as you know we've been sailing for about a month now, and we've been waiting for our sister ship to bring us the shipment of goods and riches that come from the Indies. Since we have not been contacted by them yet, my brother and I believe they have succumbed to treacherous weather while sailing around the southern tip of Africa."

A rather loud and booming voice came from the back of the group. "There's something else you aren't telling us, isn't there, Captain?" Sampson saw that now was the time to put his plan in motion. He said, in a voice dripping with contempt, "Why don't you tell the men the real reason we are out here, *Captain*."

"I don't know what you are talking about," was Arturo's only reply.

"Oh? What about the fact we've been sailing west every night under full sail? The same direction we're sailing in now. Men? This man brought us out here as a sacrifice to Poseidon himself! They want gold, and they are willing to make a bargain with the devil to get it!"

"What?! That's nonsense! I haven't heard of any gold in …."

Arturo realized he had just let the proverbial cat out of the bag. Who was this cretin? How had he hoodwinked Arturo so easily into giving up the real nature of the voyage?

"Ah, so now the real truth comes out." Turning to the crew, he said, "This man has been leading us west to our own deaths. In fact, my friend here," Sampson gestured to Horace, smiling a rather toothy smile with what teeth he still had left, "just told me he overheard Captain Arturo and his brother talking among themselves about how they wanted to die by falling off the edge of the world, and they didn't care if they had to take us with them. In fact, why else would we be sailing west now?"

Instantly, there was a loud uproar among the crew. Now was Malcolm's turn to speak up from another side of the ship. "Kill him and turn the ship around!" The crowd had been whipped up into a mob, and started feeding off of itself. While Sampson and his two henchmen looked on, eight pairs of hands grabbed hold of Arturo and hauled him to the fife rail near the foremast and tied him there. Sampson made sure a gun "magically" appeared in the crowd, and it was now being wielded by one of the nastier and unprincipled of the mob. Hurling taunts at Arturo, this sailor slowly drew his arm up to shoot Arturo in the head.

At that moment, what sounded like the bellow of a cannon pierced the air. The figurehead of this ship all but exploded as if it had been packed solid with black powder. Within the span of a single second, whatever made the figurehead disintegrate caused the rest of the ship to be blown to pieces. Arturo was the first die from a massive timber hitting him across the back of his head, severing his spine and instantly taking his life. The rest of the crew weren't so lucky, though. As they witnessed the destruction of the ship by an unknown force, they all scrambled to the stern. Eventually, the advancing destruction threatened to consume them as they stood against the rail on the deck above the Captain's quarters. One and all dove from the ship into the ocean, then swam like mad from the unseen specter of demolition.

Hernan wasn't faring any better. His crew was quite angry and had already tied Hernan's hands when they heard the other ship explode. They all watched aghast as Arturo's ship was swallowed up by the sea. As it turns out, someone on Hernan's ship had figured out the westerly course too, which only added fuel to the mob on his ship.

While his crew hadn't been incited to kill Hernan, they did mutiny and ended up locking him in the brig. Hernan pleaded every hour of every day for a week to go back and rescue his brother and the rest of the crew. It fell on deaf ears. Nobody was willing to go back and suffer the same fate as the other ship. Once a week had passed, there was no point believing Arturo might have survived. Perhaps it would have helped knowing he was probably the only one on his ship granted an instant and painless death. All the others had succumbed to a school of great whites which happened to be in the right place at the right time.

CHAPTER 16

SITTING NEXT TO HIS MOTHER's bed, Jose's mind reached out for something, anything, but the reality of what lay before him. He barely remembered his father Arturo, and now lying in bed before him was his mother, coughing, wheezing and generally not looking very good. There were several people in the village who had succumbed to this sickness, and Jose was in great fear this was going to be the fate of his dear mother.

As he guarded her sleeping frame, he quietly thought about the past two decades. While his mother would be very cross with him for thinking it, he was secretly angry with his father for having left him when he was young, so long ago, with nothing to hold onto. He was left alone in the world so young. Jose felt both anger at his father for having left him at such a tender age and, as odd as it sounds, overwhelming love for his father, for the man he remembered him to be. Even though he was so young, Jose remembered that fateful night when it was revealed that Grandfather Diego had been killed. Earlier that evening, he had felt the warmth of his father's arms, and recalled how wonderful it was to see manly love in his father's eyes. He remembered how good it felt to be part of a complete family, and how that feeling was shattered when the bad news came. It seemed like a part of each person present that night died.

Later, when Arturo failed to return home from the voyage and rumors came that their ships had been lost at sea, Valera became darker and darker in her soul. She always seemed to know something bad was going to happen to Father, and nothing could console her. For the next six years, each passing day was hollow, unrewarding, and eminently unfulfilling. Both Jose and Valera went through the motions of life; Valera sold her handmade wares in the village market, and Jose went to school each day. But Jose felt isolated and alone. Valera would never have made a direct decision to do so, yet she all but emotionally abandoned her son. She had nothing left inside of her, and life offered her no consolations.

One day, something changed. When he was about nine years old, it seemed like someone suddenly lit a candle in Valera's soul, and she started to live again. That is when Marko came into their lives. He was a good man, and seemed to make his mother happy once again. From that day on, every time Jose spoke from the depths of his tortured soul about his father, Valera never allowed anything bad to be said about Arturo. Early on, Jose learned to keep his negative thoughts to himself. Jose's feelings about his father were mixed up and were nearly impossible to understand: hate over being abandoned, and at the same time, love for a father he barely got to know. It was all very confusing.

Now this; yet another abandonment! Valera was laying before Jose on what was no doubt her death bed. Gazing out the window, Jose thought about how Marko was a good man who eventually married Jose's mother, and took good care of the two of them. Marko never had a problem with Jose being in the house; in fact, he did all a good father should do to raise a boy into a responsible man. Jose thought about how at 13 years of age, Jose he wanted to take on Marko's last name. He expected to receive thanks and appreciation from both Marko as well as his mother. What he hadn't expected was for Marko to be categorically against it. Jose never understood that.

Snow never fell in this area of the desert, but it did rain, and right now the rain falling against the windowpane glass reflected the climate in Jose's heart. Arturo left him when he was three, Marko rejected him when he was 13, and now his mother was preparing to depart from him, leaving this 23-year-old man alone in every sense of the word. What would his future be? Jose wasn't sure, but as his eyes started to produce excess moisture, he couldn't help but feel the most alone he had ever felt.

"Don't cry, baby."

Jose's eyes whipped away from the window, resting once again on his mother who had silently awakened and been watching her son sitting next to her bed. Marko was sitting on the other side of the bed near Valera, closely watching his beloved wife slowly lose her grip on life.

"I wasn't," said Jose, not wanting to appear weak to either his mother or Marko. Valera smiled a weak smile, showing she knew the real reason for her son's melancholy.

"Son, losing tears at, uh," Marko hesitated at saying what he was really thinking, "a time like this is nothing to be ashamed of."

Jose decided he didn't have the strength to argue with the two of them since they knew full well he had been about to cry. He wasn't prepared to admit that to himself, or to either of them. Jose remained silent and simply chose to gaze out the window again.

Valera looked at her husband of 14 years and, through the gray eyes of one who was about to expel her last labored breath, simply nodded her head. That one gesture spoke volumes which were only understood between the two of them. Marko's gaze faltered, and he dipped his head as if saying a silent prayer. Breathing deeply, he then looked up.

"Jose, your mother and I would like to tell you something. Something important that you need to hear."

Jose's gaze didn't shift one way or the other. He seemed unfazed at what Marko said, that is … until he heard the next thing out of his mother's mouth. With a gurgle of labored breath, Valera added something that caught Jose's attention.

"It's about your father, my son. It's something he wanted you to know," said Valera.

Jose turned his head and looked his mother square in the eyes.

With great reluctance, Marko released the hold on his wife's hand, got up from his position on the bedside, and straightened his shirt. Walking across the room to a cabinet hanging on the wall, he opened its door and took out a box which had lain there for more than a decade. Jose had seen the locked box many times before as he was growing up, but whenever he had asked about it, he would always get the same response from his mother. She would say it was private, that it contained something he would only understand when he grew up. Jose had actually forgotten about it completely, but now that he saw it once again, his interest was instantly renewed. He looked forward to finally knowing the big secret about this box. Hearing it had something to do with his father evoked an even greater interest in plumbing the depths of its secrets. Mercifully, thoughts about the box temporarily made

Jose forget about the pain he had just been contemplating. Marko took the box from the cabinet and brought it to the bedside, where he sat next to his wife once more.

Valera weakly reached her hands up to the chain around her neck and fumbled inadequately for something; she simply didn't have the strength to complete her task. She turned to her son and said, "Joselito, please open my locket and look inside."

Jose followed her instructions and reached over to the pendant she wore around her neck ever since she and Marko married. Jose always figured it was something he gave her when they first got married; he didn't know it was a locket. Putting the pendant in his hand, he searched its side, and sure enough there was a small latch there that, when pressed, caused the locket to open. Inside the locket where a picture normally would be kept, was a tiny key. Jose turned the locket over in his hand and the key fell out. He showed it to his mother, who then cast her gaze at Marko.

Taking the key from Jose, Marko opened the box. Inside was an old wine bottle, seemingly the worse for wear. Next to the wine bottle were a couple of folded sheets of paper. Taking the papers out, Marko handed them to Valera.

Slowly, Valera opened her mouth to speak. "Jose, my son ...." Suddenly she started coughing, causing the men in the room to reach out to her. Holding up her hands, she stayed their advance and labored to regain control.

Once again, Valera attempted to speak. "Jose, do you know what Marko did for a living up until 15 years ago?"

"Not really. He never talked about it. I just figured it was something having to do with farming like he does here," replied Jose.

"Actually... it wasn't," said Marko. "I was a fisherman off the coast of Portugal for many years. I worked for different fishing companies, and even worked for myself for a while. I made a good living back then."

"You remember what life was like for us back then, don't you?" asked Valera.

"I remember it wasn't very good," replied Jose. "You were very depressed about Father, and were convinced he was never coming home. Nothing anybody said made you feel any better. Being so young, I didn't know what to do; it was miserable. But then you met Marko, and things changed. He made you feel better, and he convinced you it was okay to get married again and be happy again."

"That is true, Joselito," said Valera using the beloved name only she could use for her son, "but that isn't the whole truth. Something else happened back then that made it possible for me to feel better, to find happiness in the arms of my wonderful husband, Marko."

Jose questioned why, if he was so wonderful, they both strenuously objected to him taking on the family name of Marko, instead of keeping the family name of a man who abandoned him as a child.

"One day 15 years ago," Marko continued, "I was bringing in the nets we had cast out to sea. As I was getting to the end of the line of nets, I discovered something was caught in the lines. It was tangled with a lot of seaweed, but there in the middle of the net was this." He held up the bottle lying in the box. "When I cleaned off the outside of the bottle, I could see that inside were papers someone had placed in the bottle before sealing it with cork and wax. Later that night, I opened the bottle and fished out the letter inside."

"This letter," Valera added. "At the top were instructions to deliver it to a mother and her son; to us, Jose. After reading the letter, Marko could see it was important and needed to be delivered to us because, my son, it was written by your father when he was at sea on that last voyage."

Sitting there listening to what his mother and Marko said, Jose slowly absorbed the words. When he understood the full impact of what had been said, Jose's eyes opened wide and his mouth lay slack-jawed. With shaking hands, Valera held out the precious papers to him. As he read the first line, Jose felt all the blood in his face drain.

"To my dear wife Valera and my precious son Joselito,"

Jose proceeded to read each and every line. It became harder and harder to read the letter, and it was only when Valera reached out to hold his arm that Jose realized his hands were shaking like a leaf. He read about how his father started thinking this voyage wasn't a good idea in the long run. *"A fool's errand"* is what he called it.

Then he read something that hit him between the eyes. Speaking to his wife, Arturo said:

> *"As I pen these words, I reflect on the day when you gave life to the manifestation of our love, Joselito. I remember holding him in my arms for the first time and being amazed at how much I loved someone whom I had only just met. As I prepared for this trip, I kept thinking how important it was for him to see manly resolve in the face of his father. Now I see he is missing out on something even greater in value, the actual feel of his father holding his hand, and holding the hand of his beautiful mother. I hid behind a thin veil of noble resolve and honor. This was only*

the façade of a man who couldn't face the pain of his fa-
ther's death."

Jose was in disbelief how the very feelings he had been wrestling with, how Arturo shouldn't have left him and his mother alone, wer actually something that his father agreed with!

Then came the part of the letter addressed directly to Jose.

> *"And to my son, I want you to know that other than spending time with your mother, the best part of my day was coming in the door to our home and seeing your face. While it is true you came through me, you are not like me, my son. Even in your young face, I could see your own path in life was different from mine. Mine was shaped by my love for my family, especially my twin brother. Yours should also be shaped by love, but I encourage you, my son, to never let manly pride get in the way of showing those you love just how much you love them. If there is one thing life has taught me, it is the need to confirm the things which are most important, and to be sure of exactly what those most important things truly are.*
>
> *Love with a sense of urgency, my son. Urgently love God each and every day you live, for it is from him all good things come. If you have the amazing experience of enjoying the love of a good woman, love her as if tomorrow will never come, as if today is the last day you ever expect to spend with her. None of us know what day will be our last, so make sure she knows the sun rises and sets on her face. No matter what you invest in your wife, she will give it back to you a hundredfold. And never forget me, my son. Always remember you had a father who loved you more than he loved life itself."*

It seemed to Jose that in those few sentences, all the negativity, all the feelings of being lost, all the confusion of his life simply evaporated, leaving nothing but a residue of love for the father he never really knew.

The next part explained Jose's life since the time Marko came.

> *"Finally, to you my love, please know my thoughts are with you always. If because of some unforeseen event I do not remain by your side for the rest of your life, please know*

my biggest desire is for you to be happy. If I have moved on to the next life and am no longer among the living, all I ask is you not allow your memories of me to keep you from having happiness. I do not wish to be remembered in that way. Each time you think of me, I want a smile to be upon the lips I kissed so many times. If your happiness leads you to find a new man who makes you whole, my sincere hope is that he be at least half as happy and complete as you have always made me. You have my blessing."

There it was, the whole reason why Valera had been able to finally move on. She was able to love again because, quite simply, Arturo gave her permission to do so. It was now quite clear to Jose why Valera and Marko had kept this hidden from him until now. Only an adult mind with adult understandings could understand the sacrifice Arturo made in giving such permission while he still had plans of coming home. It was apparent to Jose that Arturo was not consumed by the jealousy so common among his contemporaries.

Jose looked up from the letter to the faces of his mother and Marko. It was only now Jose realized his own face was streaked with tears, the same as his mother's was. Laying down the letter, he reached out for a nearby rag to clear his vision from all the tears. At this point, he couldn't care less that Marko and his mother saw him crying. He looked at her face, and it was obvious she was expectantly looking at her son, patiently waiting for him to say the first words.

"I feel ...."

Jose was tongue-tied, trying to express exactly what he was feeling at that moment. The avalanche of emotions was overwhelming. He closed his eyes to let his mind concentrate on the feelings now flying all around him. Settling down on his soul as soft and beautiful as the Azul Cintada butterflies which always held his wonder when walking in the fields near his home, there was only one word that could now describe how Jose felt:

"... free."

Valera closed her eyes and said, "I know that feeling. It was what made it possible for me to live again when I had been dead inside for so long. It was as if I woke up from the grave," her gaze drifted to Marko, "and when I did, the face I saw was the face of this kind man who has always been there for me to love, and who has always loved me in return." She reached out for his hands. Marko held them fast. "I love you both so much."

It was Marko who spoke next. "Initially, I was going to show you the letter 14 years ago, but this wise woman helped me see that you were too young to understand the sacrifice your father made in releasing Valera to live again. Back then, all you would have been able to see is that he wasn't in your life. Now you can see he was a good man, one who deserves your honor and respect. That was why I wouldn't let you take my family name. While I was deeply honored by your request, it was important for you to have the Barragon y Cisneros name when you eventually read that letter."

Jose sat back in his chair and cradled the letter which had suddenly become the most precious thing in his life, other than the shiny rock his father had presented to his grandfather so many years ago when he himself was a little boy. That rock sat on the mantle of the Barragon home for decades, until it found its present place on the mantle of the home he now shared with Marko and his mother.

What did this mean for Jose? What would this newfound knowledge mean for him? He wasn't sure. That effect would have to be thought about later, though. Valera reached out to her son with her left hand, while Marko maintained his hold on her right hand. Valera closed her eyes and, with a small smile on her face, breathed her last breath.

CHAPTER 17

SLAP, SLAP, SLAP.

The waves lapped at the tiny craft incessantly. For three days now, Jose had been adrift in seas driven by the almost non-existent doldrum winds of the equator. "What was it Father said in the letter?" thought Jose. Ah, yes. "The sea is the great giver of perspective." Indeed, Jose thought to himself. The sea is certainly giving a generous helping of that right now.

Thinking back to what led him to be alone in the middle of the ocean in nothing more than a dinghy filled with provisions, he considered how he started these travels with the best of intentions. Jose was resolved in his heart of hearts that the stories of how his father died on a boat which just seemed to explode were nothing more than tall tales from the addle-brained perspectives of men who had spent more time with alcohol than they had with reality. Maybe that was true, but now he found himself with nothing but the sun relentlessly beating down on him, and a seemingly interminable span of time. Time to think back on his life. Time to second guess all the decisions he had made. Time to regret.

It was shortly after the reading of his father's letter, and the almost simultaneous death of his mother, that Jose decided he needed to find out the real truth about what happened to his father. He had heard the stories that supposedly came from someone's brother's employer's cousin about how the ship was destroyed, and another story saying the ship survived and returned, but some of the men fell off the edge of the world. Prior to receiving the letter from his father, Jose really had no desire to know if anybody survived the voyage. Up to that point, all he knew was his father had left, and didn't have the decency to come home.

The letter changed all that. It gave Jose a window into the heart and soul of a man, his father, and let him see that Arturo was quite a lot like his son, or rather, Jose was quite a lot like his own father. He could now understand Arturo wasn't the monster he had built up in his mind over the years, but was just a man who occasionally suffered from poor judgment.

Just like any man. Just like, maybe, his son.

Jose could now see Arturo was, in reality, a good man with a good heart and a good soul. He loved his wife and child, and was only trying to be the man he hoped his son would become one day. Jose wanted to be that good man, like his father. That thought, along with a desire to stand side by side with his father in the eyes of history, helped Jose decide to finish the work his father had started, to try and complete the voyage which ended in disaster so long ago.

For this to work, he knew he had to find out what really went wrong, learn from those mistakes, and do it right this time. That meant getting to the bottom of what truly happened. Did a ship actually return to port? Who survived? What happened to Arturo and Hernan, Jose's uncle?

This meant Jose needed to retrace the steps his father and uncle took. Over the years, Valera carefully avoided speaking about what Hernan and Arturo did in the presence of Jose, but still, it was impossible to keep all information secret. There were times when Marko and Valera were talking among themselves and didn't know Jose was listening. This is where Jose got most of his information about the ill-fated voyage. Apparently, the two had left on their voyage from Aesuris, a coastal town special to them for some reason. The last time Jose's mother saw them, they were going there to buy a boat. This is where he had to start.

As was typical for him, Marko tried to help Jose get to the bottom of the stories about his father. Jose didn't tell Marko everything he planned to do, of possibly undertaking the same voyage his father had done, but he did tell him he needed to go to the fishing village and dig deep. Marko was familiar with Aesuris, so he told Jose the best places to start in his search, and what places he needed to stay away from since they weren't safe. The worst of those places was a run-down section of a wharf called "Mar de Dolores." Sea of Sorrows.

Jose packed his things, secured enough money from the family fortune, and set out for the coast. That fortune was one legacy Arturo and his brother left for Jose and his mother. At least they weren't paupers. In a week, Jose was standing on the end of a wharf looking out over the same waters his father gazed upon 20 years earlier.

Back in the present, and floating on that same sea now, Jose thought about the countless opportunities leading up to this moment when he could have changed his fate. He could have lived a good life without having to be in such peril. Such a waste.

Thinking again about the events that unfolded in Aesuris, Jose remembered how he started asking questions about that voyage of 20 years ago. He learned early on it wasn't wise to identify himself as a Barragon y Cisneros. While a few in his local village spoke in hushed tones about the rumors of what happened to Hernan and Arturo, there was no such politeness on the docks. The opinions were unfiltered and harsh. When a few learned he was Arturo's son, he suffered jeering from washed up wharf rats who had nothing better to do than to continually live in the past. Jose decided to go by Marko's name and not his own since his goal was getting to the bottom of the legends, not clearing the family name; not yet.

While Marko told Jose not to go anywhere near Mar de Dolores, that is exactly where his search led him. He did his best to blend in, dressing like a wino himself. He dared not let on how well to do he actually was.

Repeatedly, questions about that voyage pointed to someone who might live in Mar de Dolores. Once he got there, he pretty quickly discovered the man, who just plain stank of alcohol. It was amazing to Jose this man was even alive, considering how long he'd been drunk. For some time, Jose observed the man from a distance, and concluded that whatever led him to such debauchery must have been formidable. Finally, Jose approached this man in a roundabout way, hoping to eventually coax information out of him.

It took about a week to get him to open up, but with a generous amount of liquor coursing through the man's veins, Jose was able to start getting the information he so desperately needed. Jose started with a reverse psychology ploy.

"I don't think there was any Barragon voyage" said Jose, hoping to see if it would be refuted.

Without altering his watery-eyed gaze, the older man expelled a wheeze. "Yah, well, what do you know?" he slurred.

Jose began faking his own inebriation with slurs. "I juz don think anybody went out there like that is all I'm saying. I mean, if they went out there and, and," stuttered Jose, "died on a ship that sank, then how'd anybody back here find out? You zee?"

Closing his eyes, the old man responded: " 'Cuz there was two ships." *What? Two ships?!*

"Two?" shouted Jose, completely losing his ruse of inebriation for the moment.

"Two," replied the old man, slowly nodding his head. "Two ships. The Fortuna and the Tyche." He now started laughing without control, spitting and sputtering.

"Why did they need two? That doesn't make sense," asked Jose.

A look of pain came rushing back to the old man's face as he looked Jose straight in the eyes. "You ask too many questions."

Jose had pushed him too hard and too fast, and he knew it. *That was stupid*, he thought.

"Nah. No offense my friend," said Jose regaining his disguise of drunkenness. "Let me make it up to you." He pushed a loaf of bread and a bowl of aioli toward the man, along with a new bottle of sangria.

That gesture seemed to brighten up the old man's face. With a wizened hand, he broke off a piece of bread, dipped it in the bowl of aioli, and crammed as much of it in his mouth as possible. Jose partook in the fare as well, allowing the old man to regain his composure while they sat in silence. As he chewed slowly, Jose realized this man was the best source of knowledge he had come across. He knew things others didn't: that there were *two* ships, not just one, and even the names of those ships.

Around that time, another carouser happened by and, seeing the old man was in possession of something to eat, tried to sponge a free meal. He magnanimously started talking to the old man as if they had been friends for decades and sat down next to him with a thin smile, thin eyes, and a thinly-disguised agenda. To the completely sober Jose, the social dance evolving before his eyes was easy to decipher, and he observed that the old man was apparently very familiar with the strategies. As soon as the freeloader sat down, the old man deftly moved the bread and bowl out of his reach, so that he now had to ask for some, reach over the old man, or walk away. The old codger got the hint, and once he saw there was no free lunch here for him, he quickly evaporated with the wind.

As he observed the man eating again, Jose sensed another question might be acceptably received.

"So, two ships?"

"Huh?" groused the old man, as Jose broke through the fog of alcohol and garlic.

"Two ships. Why two?"

"Because my ... because the captains thought two ships would have a better chance of making it," answered the old man. The fact he tripped over his words wasn't lost on Jose, who had been drinking grape juice instead of wine to keep his mind sharp. What was this man hiding?

"So, were both brothers on one ship?" asked Jose.

The old man closed his eyes. He didn't answer the question verbally, but as a tear found the cracks in his wrinkled face, he shook his head from side to side.

Pursuing this new information, Jose decided to risk raising the ire of the old man. "But if one of the ships came back, does that mean one of the brothers came back too?"

With his eyes still closed, the old man silently nodded.

Jose quietly thought for a moment. From his father's letter, Jose knew that if Arturo could have made it home, nothing would have kept him from seeing his wife and son again. If one of the brothers had made it back, then it would have to be Jose's uncle.

With eyes slowly widening with each passing second, Jose suddenly began to lose the ability to breathe. When he first sat down in front of this old man, there was something strange about him that Jose couldn't quite put a finger on. But now it hit him all at once.

Jose was sitting in front of his uncle. The old man was Uncle Hernan!

Coming back to the present, as he floated in the middle of the ocean on a dinghy, Jose smiled softly to himself at the memory of finding his uncle.

When Jose was able to gather his wits about him, he looked at the face of his uncle, really examining him. He could now see the face of the man he barely remembered. Once again, Jose's breath was taken away when he realized his uncle was an identical twin to his own father. Apart from the effects of inebriation, Jose now realized he was looking straight at the face of what his father would look like.

Jose began thinking about what Uncle Hernan had been through. He had seen his brother, his identical twin brother ... wait. What happened? What *really* happened? He had to know. But how could he find out? He didn't want to destroy what was left of this man, a man he

145

instantly loved and felt overwhelming pity for. How could he break it to him gently?

By this time, Hernan had been examining Jose and seen an evolution of expressions come over the young man. Hernan may have spent a lot of time with booze to forget, but he still could recognize what lay below the surface. He saw the young man in front of him graduate from curiosity to wonder, to something else he didn't recognize. What was going through his mind?

"What's wrong? Looks like you've seen a ghost," laughed the old man, reaching for another piece of bread to dip in the sauce.

Jose decided there was no delicate way to do this. "You're not far from the truth … Uncle Hernan."

The bread was already halfway into Hernan's mouth when he stopped dead in his tracks. It would have been impossible for his eyes to get any wider, and what had already made it into his stomach was suddenly threatening to see the light of day again.

"What did you say?" was all he could muster.

Jose decided he might as well go all in. "I am Jose Barragon y Cisneros. My father was Arturo, and my mother was Valera Barragon y Cisneros. You are my Uncle Hernan."

By the time the bread Hernan had been holding found its way to the floor, whatever countenance he had been using was long gone. All the blood drained from his face, and now he was the one who looked like he had seen a ghost. For Hernan, that was when it all went black.

Floating on the ocean, Jose recalled the events of that day, remembering how his Uncle Hernan slumped over and fell right off the bench he was sitting on. Rushing to his side, Jose saw Hernan was still alive, but the sudden shock of learning who Jose was, combined with all the alcohol running around in his system, was too much to process; his mind decided to temporarily abdicate its throne.

Eventually, Hernan came around, but he had a nasty headache from the blow to his head when he had fallen, not to mention the nasty hangover. The first thing he saw was the face of his nephew, which he now recognized was the perfect combination of his brother and Valera. Still laying on the floor where he had fallen, once his eyes were able to completely focus, Hernan reached up with his weathered hand and stroked the cheek of Jose's face.

"Joselito?"

"It's me, Uncle Hernan. I'm here!"

"Oh, Joselito!" cried Hernan as the weight of the last 20 years, not to mention the horror he witnessed that day on the sea came crashing down onto him. For 20 years, he built an architecture of denial fueled by anger and guilt, and lubricated by alcohol. Crushing reality now pounded on the doorpost of his mind, crossing the threshold to his consciousness without permission. To have the precarious evaporate within the span of three heartbeats left Hernan with no other option than to break down into uncontrollable sobs. Whoever named this part of town the "Sea of Sorrows" must have known this day was coming for Hernan.

"Come, Uncle. Let's get you up off the floor," said Jose.

Jose recalls it took Hernan quite some time to calm down, and even more time to get to the point where he was willing to talk. It was strange that there was an epic sense of realization and an epic reunion happening in a corner of the bar, yet other patrons had no desire to meddle in the affairs of Hernan and Jose. Even when Hernan lost consciousness and fell on the floor, none of the others even lifted an eyelid, let alone a finger, to help. It was as if this happened every day and was nothing special. Perhaps it really wasn't anything new for this part of town.

Jose sat across from his uncle, waiting for him to get his wits about him. He knew his uncle had quite a shock just now, so he wanted to wait until he was ready to know more.

"Why?"

"Excuse me?" asked Jose.

"Why did you come?" It wasn't accusatory in nature. It was asked in a tone indicating he just wanted to know why on earth Jose would come to this godforsaken hole.

"Because you are loved, and because you are missed," was Jose's answer.

For several moments Hernan didn't respond. Looking off into the distance, Hernan eventually replied, "I don't know what love is anymore."

Jose let that sink in for a bit, then said, "I do, my uncle. And I know you are a man who is loved."

With a harrumph, a shake of the head, and with half-lidded eyes, Hernan responded, "My boy, there is nothing here to love anymore. When Arturo died that day, I died."

This comment set Jose back in his chair. Leaning against the wooden seatback, he was overcome with the realization this was the first ironclad confirmation of his father's death. As Jose sat there, he realized a part of him secretly hoped Arturo was still alive. Had he been alive and not come home, that would have been a whole different set of emotions he would have had to deal with. But now, Jose knew he was never going to see his father again.

On the other hand, his father's identical twin was sitting right in front him. It wasn't the same, yet that offered a certain degree of consolation.

While Jose was lost in his thoughts, Hernan was simultaneously lost in his own reverie. He regarded his nephew sitting before him, and with each passing moment was reminded more and more of the things he left behind. He strenuously tried for so long to forget about the enormous pain in his heart, but only succeeded in ignoring it. Forgetting was impossible. Hernan thought about how most would think watching your twin die would rip out half of your heart.

They would be wrong.

Ever since he was a child, Hernan knew his soul, his very life, was completely bound with his twin. When Arturo died, *everything* that made Hernan a living being ceased to exist. He felt certain nobody who wasn't a twin would ever understand just how much he had lost. He knew his wife Sofia wouldn't understand completely. He knew she would see a broken man with no further will to live. She would be consoling, to begin with; that was just the kind of woman she was. But when the wound didn't heal after weeks, months, years, and even decades, he knew she would grow tired. She wouldn't go anywhere, but he knew if her life contained even a fraction of the misery he felt, it would be the worst disservice to her.

Twenty years ago when he was returned to port against his will without even his brother's body to bury, he knew he had to make a decision between the irresistible force of his crushing grief, and the immovable object of his commitment to his wife's happiness. Either he allowed her to think he had died and, after a comparably short period of grief, possibly marry again and be happy, or return and saddle her with a lifetime of heartache, pain, and misery as she watched the shell of the man she loved wither away into oblivion. For Hernan, there was only one decision to make: to carry the burdens of his pain alone. He never anticipated he would come face to face with his history so abruptly and so unexpectedly.

Jarring Jose from his own reverie, Hernan broke the silence. "How is Sofia?"

"She is," Jose hesitated, "fine. When you didn't show up, she tried to look for you, but then someone told her you had been killed at sea. I remember Mother spending a lot of time with her. I was young, so I don't know what they talked about because I was always sent outside to play, but I know she cried a lot. She never did remarry, and it wasn't until two years ago when I had become an adult that she told me she never felt like you had died. There was just something in her that told her you were alive." Jose paused. "I guess she knew something the rest of us didn't."

Hernan looked away. The strain of keeping his eyes open while feeling the full wrath of the retreating armies of alcohol was considerable. He now realized he couldn't keep running; he was tired of hiding behind his grief. "I guess I thought she would move on and find love somewhere else. I was hoping she would eventually find happiness, even while I knew I never would."

"Forgive me Uncle, but then you must not have known how deeply she loved you," replied Jose.

Hernan didn't answer, but simply nodded his head.

Hernan continued his inquiry. "And Valera? I suppose she stayed alone too?"

"No. She married again. She was very happy," answered Jose.

"Hah!" retorted Hernan, without thinking. "I guess she didn't love Arturo much after all."

For the most part, Jose was a mild and gentle soul. Very little ever got under his skin, with the distinct exception of matters pertaining to his mother. For two decades, he had watched Valera go from being a happy wife, to a distraught widow and grief-stricken mother, then finally to a hopeful and healed woman. He had seen it all, and through it all, she consistently demonstrated an inner strength which was always there for her son. In Jose's book, she was an absolute saint. Now that she was gone, this was definitely the wrong thing for Hernan to say.

Abruptly standing from the table, Jose shouted, "You know nothing, you old fool!" He turned and stormed out the door of the bar. He stood outside absolutely fuming at the stupidity of his uncle. How dare he impugn the motives of his mother. She had been through so much, and in fact, she had stayed single until .... That's when it occurred to Jose that Uncle Hernan didn't know about the letter his mother had received. He didn't know Arturo had not only written the letter, but also given his permission for her to remarry. The longer he stood there, the more Jose realized that although it was a very insensitive thing to say, Hernan was a broken man who dealt with a lot of personal demons.

Standing in front of the saloon with the racket of horse-drawn carts passing by, Jose didn't realize someone was standing behind him until he began to speak. "Please forgive me, Joselito." Jose turned around to face his uncle standing before him. "I, I didn't ...."

"No, Uncle. I ask for your forgiveness. There is much you don't know. But I am here to tell it all to you."

With that, the two men went back into the saloon. Jose proceeded to tell the complete story about his life and that of his mother, the way she grieved for Arturo, and the way Marko came into their lives.

He candidly told him how he had felt abandoned, which was hard for Hernan to hear since he was just as guilty of that abandonment as Arturo was. He also told Hernan how he wanted to change his last name to Marko's when he was 13, and when they didn't let him, he felt abandoned all over again. Eventually, Jose came to the day when Valera died and the subject of the letter. Jose kept it with him at all times in a flat metal container under his cloak. He produced the letter for Hernan and gave it to him.

The letter was hard to read at first, but then Hernan recognized something in the words he had long forgotten. On the day when Arturo died, even though the two brothers were physically separated by so much ocean and circumstance, the two of them were thinking the exact same things. Hernan remembered sending the message to Arturo proposing that the voyage end, and in two days they should consider turning around. It appears Arturo was experiencing the same feelings, and he placed his thoughts in this letter; feeling like the whole voyage was a fool's errand, or realizing that being with his family was much more important than some legacy of their father. When he came to the part where Arturo gave permission for Valera to remarry, he realized now just how stupid his earlier comment about Valera not loving Arturo was. He looked up at Jose right then, who was astute enough to know just what his uncle was thinking. Jose said, "You didn't know, Uncle. You are forgiven."

Hernan cocked his head now, as he looked at his nephew with a new level of respect for the man.

It was then the proverbial floodgates opened, and any question Jose plied Hernan with was answered. He learned about the two boats, the crew, the overall tactic of sailing west at night, and how the crew figured out the real nature of the voyage since a couple were experienced sailors. He learned about how Hernan still felt there was a way to the coast of India by sailing west, but when it came to the death of his brother, Jose discerned this was too much to talk about, so he left that part of the discussion alone. Realizing the sun had risen hours ago, both men were stunned to learn they had been talking all night and for most of the next day. While Hernan decided he needed to sleep now at some flophouse where he was staying, Jose was far too wound up to sleep.

Back on the small dinghy floating on the sea, Jose opened his eyes and realized that remembering all these events had taken most of the morning, and he hadn't paid attention to where the small craft was going. Not that there was much to observe while floating in the middle of an endless sea. The sun was high in the sky, but now that he thought about it, it seemed as if the sun wasn't as harsh on his skin. He observed to himself that the weather here was suddenly quite pleasant. No painful sun beating down on him, just its warmth alongside a cool breeze. He breathed deep, but was soon reminded of the persistent cough he had slowly started developing ever since his mother died of the breathing sickness. Secretly, Jose was hoping being at sea would help, but it only seemed to get worse. Now, a sudden fit of coughing and sputtering left the already weak Jose even weaker.

He closed his eyes and thought more about the events leading him to this small deserted, but for the moment very pleasant, location on the open ocean. After his meeting with Uncle Hernan, Jose felt much the same way his father did after learning about the death of Diego. Jose wanted to complete the quest his father had tried, so that is what he did. He followed the same steps Hernan and Arturo had followed with the main exception of using a crew that knew nothing about the sea and nothing about navigation. It was a difficult journey for sure, but eventually the crew hit their stride and worked well together. The only problem now was that Jose was getting sicker and sicker, and the crew recognized it. He tried to just stay away from them, but the crew didn't want a man who had the sickness to be anywhere near them. Suffering a similar fate as his father, the crew mutinied, setting him adrift on this small boat with food and water. It seemed his destiny was sealed; death at sea.

What Jose couldn't have known was that due to an uncanny combination of circumstances and luck, his life was spared the same fate as his father at the same location, yet now the lives of thousands were doomed.

Not far away from where Jose floated, on an island normally hidden from sight, a relatively small piece of machinery in charge of managing a force field shield around the island of New Galimar gave out. It was normal; every 600 years, the plasma emitters used by the shield needed to be replaced. It only took about a minute to replace the unit, but during that time the shield would be down. Originally the shield was set up around the island because its alien inhabitants were unable to handle the harmful ultraviolet radiation coming from the sun. While the plasma emitter was being replaced, all island inhabitants knew to stay indoors.

One of the unintended effects of the shield, though, was it caused anything that came into contact with it to be destroyed; this was the original fate of Arturo's ship 20 years ago. Jose just happened to be in the right place at the exact right time. When his small craft passed the position of the shield, it happened to be off, so he passed through without incident. A minute later, the shield went back on, but by then Jose was safely inside. When Jose opened his eyes and noticed the beautiful weather and pleasant effects of the sun, he didn't realize this was the effect of the shield which had been put back into place.

Once inside, his boat soon struck something that felt like land. Jose turned around and discovered he had not only landed on an island he swore wasn't there before, but was now looking eye to eye at some of the most beautiful people he had ever seen.

The look of astonishment in their eyes was very similar to the look in his own.

CHAPTER 18

$\Gamma \;\; J \;\; \mathcal{Y} \;\mathsf{L} \;\; \mathcal{U} \;\mathcal{Y} \Gamma \;\Gamma$

"MAY I HAVE YOUR ATTENTION," said the Grand Council coordinator. The assembly of the Grand Council was rather boisterous and noisy up to that point. The arrival of the human five days ago was certainly unexpected and was the subject of much discussion and debate. That this human was as refined and docile as he was completely astonished one and all.

Previously, all of New Galimar adopted a rather isolationist viewpoint. When they arrived on this planet several thousand years ago, they came in contact with humankind, but humans at that time were comparatively primitive and barbaric. The Galimarians decided it would not be wise to interface with this indigenous population and risk the possibility of human social contamination.

The main reason for this had to do with very negative events found in the history of the Galimarians, and the Testimonial Law which prohibited the dissemination of technology to civilizations less advanced than their own. If the society was extremely less evolved than their own, the Galimarians would avoid interaction altogether. They had been to enough new worlds to see there was a normal timeline all civilizations followed in their advancement. When they first landed on Earth and came into contact with humans, the Galimarians figured it would take humans another 15,000 years to get to a point that even merited the first contact, let alone any kind of technological exchange.

But here was living proof that humans had advanced far faster than anything the Galimarians had ever seen. How this could possibly have happened was the subject of hot debate among the Grand Council, and the theories abounded.

One theory was a possible contamination of the humans by the family of Docius Atlantis. About 3,000 years ago, Docius and his family wanted to leave the island of New Galimar and live on the mainland of Eden. The Grand Council allowed this to occur, but only on the conditions they not take any technology with them, and swear never to reveal the existence of the island. Proponents held that Docius must have not only revealed the existence of the island, but also spawned a renaissance of some sort allowing humans to advance far faster than normal.

Another theory involved a possible landing by other alien civilizations not as enlightened as New Galimar, nor as responsible in dealing with primitive civilizations. This wouldn't be the first time they had seen this happen; they had witnessed this transpiring with civilizations living in their home galaxy, not the Milky Way.

Although a minority, there were still others who claimed it might have been possible humans did progress faster than normal, simply because they had a much more versatile brain. In support of their theory, they cited the fact that human physiology is essentially identical to that of the Galimarians, except for some very minor differences. There weren't many who put stock in that theory, but still, it was an interesting idea.

The Grand Council coordinator spoke again, once the overall clatter of conversation slowed to a stop. "We have all gathered together in an emergency session of the Council to discuss the topic of the human who has come ashore. In the published agenda, the first speaker of this session is J'Sepp Yucholl. As you all know, J'Sepp was part of the original landing party here on Eden, and is responsible for inspiring the architecture of the government here on New Galimar. I'd now like to invite J'Sepp Yucholl to the podium."

Being the oldest living Galimarian on New Galimar, J'Sepp Yucholl was an extremely respected member of society. As he approached the podium, all in attendance stood in honor of the living legend, and applause broke out. When he reached the podium, J'Sepp motioned for all to return to their seats.

"Please, my brothers and sisters, you honor me far too much," were his first words.

The rest of the council continued to applaud for another 10 seconds, but eventually they ceased and took their seats.

"I thank you for that warm reception," said J'Sepp. "I hope I meet someone someday who actually deserves all that."

There was general laughter at his modesty.

"My fellow council members, we meet here today to discuss a matter truly without precedent. It reminds me of the days when we first came to this planet. There are many here who remember those days as well as I do, how we all were in great disarray after the realization that everything from our home planet had been left far behind, and we didn't know what our future held. We eventually realized the uncertain nature of our futures wasn't a curse, but rather a blessing. Our very society, both on our home planet of Galimar as well as here on Eden, is a society based on the deep and long-lasting enjoyment we derive from the simple acts of exploration and discovery. It was during those early days here on this planet when we discovered there was no greater manifestation of exploration than a galaxy none of our forefathers had ever seen. We realized we were at the forefront of a great odyssey of discovery.

"The arrival of our unexpected human visitor has ushered in feelings of uncertainty and angst, but let me remind you this is only another chapter in the ever-unfolding events of our new life in our new home. Yes, it was unexpected that humans progressed far faster than we anticipated, and I have heard some of the theories as to why this happened. Regardless of how this may have occurred, the fact remains: it has, indeed, happened. It is impossible to go back in time to change anything that might or might not have occurred, so I encourage you all, my friends, to consider embracing what we have seen to be the truth. Instead of being uneasy, learn more about it so we can be brokers to their continued development. If this has happened without the intervention of others, then it behooves us to learn as much about them as possible, since advancement at this rate means they will end up far beyond us in no time at all."

As always, sessions of the Grand Council meetings were being broadcast all around the island, including to the newly set up hospitals suddenly popping up everywhere to handle a strange outbreak of coughing sickness which was sweeping the entire population. As all listened to J'Sepp's words, they could see the wisdom he employed when they first came to this planet was alive and well in this walking icon. His words were calming and reasonable.

"My brothers and sisters," J'Sepp continued, "it occurs to me this is a classic example of one of the axioms I proposed while still on Galimar: 'I Am, From All That I Think.' As I explained at that time, all Galimarians can think. Simply deciding what to eat each morning is a function of thought. But producing thought that guides what the individual wishes to be, even if that thought is contrary to current reality, has the effect of causing one to make all decisions guided and navigated by desires pursuant to that thought, building a new reality for that person. This is essential to the meaning of life. Ultimately, we create our own realities.

"I put to each and every one of us this question: 'What is the reality that *you* wish to create with these new circumstances?' Let us consider the options. One is to eliminate what some may think is a threat to our culture and way of life. Would any of us consider this? Of course not. As the enlightened society we are, there would be no way any of us would ever consent to such a backward slide of ethics.

"Another option would be to send this person home with no further interaction with us. Is this viable? Perhaps his contemporaries would think he was spinning a less-than-credible yarn of lies which deserves no credence. That might all be well and good, but after several interviews with the human, who calls himself Jose, it appears humans have become extensive seafarers. Unfortunately, I must now be the bearer of bad news, and disclose that it is more than likely many humans have run into our force field shield and died because of it."

The revealing of this fact took the breath away from most of the population of New Galimar. If they weren't doing so already, all sat back in their seats and felt an immense sense of grief at the knowledge they may have unknowingly been the architects of the death of an untold number of human seafarers. The din of chatter which suddenly broke out in the council chambers was reflected throughout New Galimar. For a few moments, there was complete disarray in the chambers, and it was difficult for J'Sepp to get things back to order.

"Council Members," called J'Sepp, holding up his open hands. Coughing once or twice and clearing his throat, he called out again.

"Council Members! Please come to order."

It took some time for the council chambers to return to order. Eventually, J'Sepp was able to continue speaking.

"I know this is an assault to our values, and all of us would change what has happened if we could, but what has happened in the past remains and cannot be changed. What can change is what we do about it from this moment on. I would like to make a motion that we change our policy of isolation, and establish first contact with this culture."

Looking out at the faces of the present council members, there seemed to be a compendium of acceptance. Most of the heads in the audience were nodding.

J'Sepp looked over to the council coordinator, but the expression was one that didn't reflect a lot of positivity. At that point, the coordinator came over to the podium and spoke.

"Council members, I personally agree with J'Sepp on his proposed motion. However, I am forced to point out that Testimonial Law dictates all council members must vote on any motions put forth. Normally this is exactly what we would do at this time. However, as can be seen from the vacant seats in council chambers, only 37 of the 51 council members are present due to the sickness sweeping through the island. Since we cannot take a vote on this motion, is there anyone who can suggest what we should do with the human named Jose until all council members return to health?"

A murmur across the council chambers could be heard for a few moments until one member stood up.

"The chair recognizes the council representative of the district of Meropa," said the coordinator.

"Thank you," said Yonan Brindeu. "The issues raised today are certainly serious, and if they necessitate re-evaluating certain tenets of our Testimonial Law as it applies to the indigenous life forms found on this planet known as human, then I will not oppose such discussion. As has been pointed out, several members of the council are missing from these proceedings as a result of the unprecedented sickness sweeping through our population. Even I seem to be coming down with a cough which seems to be characteristic of this malady. Due to all this, I have a proposal to put forth as to how we should handle the human."

Yonan turned to the rest of the council members. "My brothers and sisters, it is apparent we must come to a decision as to what is to be done with this 'Jose' as soon as possible, for the longer we delay on deciding what to do, the greater risk there is for more humans to be killed by our shield. I have some ideas as to what the alternatives might be, but whatever the possible alternatives may be, there can be no decision until the entire body of the council is present. I propose we place the human into a stasis chamber until we are all able to meet again and decide what is to be done. While it is unlikely we will delay the decision any longer than is necessary, it is not a service to the human to make him wait until we resolve whatever seems to be ailing us all."

The proceedings in the council chambers were being broadcasted to all of New Galimar, including the home Jose had been temporarily given. Sitting next to Jose was a cultural attaché who had been assigned to him when he arrived. The role of the attaché was to help Jose acclimatize to life on the island and answer any questions.

Jose did have a simple question. "What is a stasis chamber?"

The attaché replied, "It is a machine where you will sleep. The sleep is so deep you won't remember time going by, and when we revive you, days, weeks, or even months will have gone by, and you won't know it."

For a moment, Jose was silent as he digested this piece of information. The idea of a stasis chamber sounded an awful lot like a prison to him, and he vowed a long time ago he would never step foot into another prison. He made that vow to his late mother when got into a little bit of trouble when he was young. Around the time he was eight or nine years old, Jose had begun to rebel against society because all his friends had fathers and he didn't. He hadn't thought about the effect this would have on his mother, and when it became apparent his course in life was causing severe emotional pain to a woman who had been through so much already, Jose vowed to her that he would stay out of trouble. He never wanted to cause pain to his mother, and it destroyed him to think this was exactly what he was doing.

For this reason, the prospect of being a prisoner for an untold amount of time was very distasteful. He started formulating a plan to escape from the island. Jose had no way of understanding that if he tried to leave, he would run into the same shield that killed his father, only from the inside this time.

Back in the Grand Council chambers, the proposal was put to vote. A change to Testimonial Law required the full complement of council members to vote. Something like this particular motion only required a simple majority and, since 37 of the 51 were present, this was possible. The vote passed, and plans for putting Jose in stasis the next morning began.

Jose resolved he wouldn't submit to what he interpreted as a prison. For the rest of the day, he mentally prepared for his escape. He felt the best chance he had to escape would be during the night. He had no idea what night vision cameras were, so he had no idea his escape would be easily seen by island security forces.

The home where Jose was staying had been completed earlier that month by builder robots. It was a beautiful home, really. Under different circumstances, he wouldn't mind actually living there on a more permanent basis. Normally, the inhabitant of this home would move in shortly after his or her ceremony of enlightenment. Part of getting a new home like this was also the experience of being given an amulet of understanding. The amulet sat in a cradle atop the computer screen Jose had been watching.

As he made mental preparations for his departure that night, Jose thought about what he would say when he got back home. He could tell whomever he came into contact with about this amazing civilization that rescued him from floating on the ocean, but who would believe him? Jose was wise enough to know that nobody would believe him unless he had some sort of proof. As he was pondering these things, his eyes rested on the amulet sitting on top of the screen. A slight smile crossed his lips when he decided the amulet would be his proof of visiting such an amazing place. He was going to steal the amulet.

Eventually, night came. Before they went to bed, Jose's companion who had been assigned to him acted like being in prison like that was a great thing. Strange. Whatever the opinion of others might be, Jose's mind was made up; he was leaving, and there was no changing his mind once it had been made up. Jose didn't know this, but in this way he was very much like his father. Jose laid under the covers in full clothing so he could make his getaway quickly and quietly. He laid in bed for at least two hours to ensure his companion was completely asleep.

After some time, Jose looked over and was able to determine he was completely asleep. Now was the time to go. Quietly, Jose stood up next to his bed. As he passed through the main living area, he paused next to the computer monitor and deftly slipped the amulet into his coat pocket. Emerging from the front door, he avoided any areas of the city that were lit, eventually making his way to the dock where his small dinghy was kept. Quietly sliding into the boat, he pushed out to sea.

As the shoreline became more and more distant, it gradually occurred to him this wasn't a very well thought out plan. Where would he go? How would he survive on the open ocean for an untold amount of time? If it weren't for the inhabitants of this island finding him when they did, he would no doubt be a lifeless carcass floating on the open ocean by now. It took another 10 minutes to realize he was without a choice. He had nowhere to go. It was either spend time in an uncertain prison on New Galimar and still be alive, or spend a relatively short amount of time on the open ocean and most certainly die of starvation and dehydration.

There was only one decision to make, so he decided to turn back. Little did he know had he made that decision about 45 seconds later, the shield would have completely destroyed both him and his boat. There would only be small shards of the boat left, and there would be nothing of Jose.

Turning the boat around, he made for shore again. He took his coat off to row harder and, in doing so, the amulet in his coat pocket silently dropped out and sank into the water. A passing dolphin saw it floating down and snagged it with its nose, enjoying it as a temporary plaything. That amulet continued to be the occasional plaything to sea creatures far and wide who came to be interested in it due to its magnetic properties, or its ever shiny carapace. For centuries it continued to move around on the sea floor due to such passing interests. It wouldn't be seen again by air-breathing creatures until around 600 years later when it magnetically attached itself to the dredging hook of a ship laying transcontinental cable in the North Atlantic.

Meanwhile, a tragedy quickly played itself out on the island of New Galimar. Jose returned and was placed in a stasis pod for safe keeping until the entire Grand Council of New Galimar could meet again, which it never did.

As time went by, the scientific minds of New Galimar worked in vain to counteract the advancing waves of sickness that slowly but surely took hold of the island. As well versed as they were with handling sicknesses common to their people, the sickness Jose brought with him seemed to require a type of anti-biological warfare they simply weren't prepared for. Given enough time, their past interactions with other planets and species would have been enough to guide the creation of a treatment plan. Unfortunately, some of the best minds who would have created such treatment plans were the first to succumb to the epidemic. This saddled others much less experienced in this type of medicine with the terrible responsibility of finding a cure to save all on the island. They made progress, but it ended up being woefully too little, too late.

The sickness Jose originally brought to the island continued to spread unabated. Eventually, all members of New Galimar succumbed. Except for the caretaker robotics that ensured the parks and buildings were all cared for, there was no movement or sound found anywhere.

New Galimar became completely peaceful and quiet, and would remain that way, until a beautiful and innocent archaeologist from New York changed everything.

PART 3

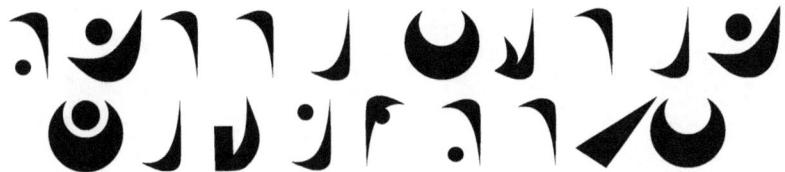

CHAPTER 19

THE WEATHER IN NEW YORK had turned colder now that fall was in the air. People seemed to walk a little faster; the sky wasn't always as blue as it was just two months ago, and the streets were decidedly quieter now that kids were back in school. Terri and her friend Lynne were catching a quick bite while on their lunch break. Both of them worked at the New York Museum of Natural History near Central Park. Terri is an assistant curator at the museum, and Lynne is a resident Egyptologist.

Terri Marie Lindstrom is a tall girl. Her father was 6'6" tall, and her mother was 5'11"; she was foreordained to reach her current height of 6'3". It was never a problem for Terri, but there seemed to be an unwritten rule among men that a guy would never want to go out with a woman taller than he is. In college, there was this one guy who didn't seem to care one way or the other, and he was the one who clued Terri in, in a rather humorous way, on this rule of male dating. He told her how every guy knows the old maxim Confucius supposedly said: "Short man who dance with tall woman get busted in face." It made him laugh, and it made Terri's eyes roll.

A kind-hearted woman who loves to explore, Terri's fundamental area of exploration is archaeology. She received her master's degree in archaeology from Cornell University and, along with Lynn, has worked from the ground level up at the museum. She is just now getting to a point where she has "paid her dues" and can enjoy things like taking vacations. This newfound latitude also makes it possible to work in various areas of the museum without supervision, since they now trust her enough to know she won't damage any of the priceless artifacts there.

Patricia Lynne Marlowe, Terri's best friend since college, is a trained Egyptologist. In 2002, she became an assistant at the same Natural History Museum where Terri works. Having specialized in entomology early in her working life, she became an assistant to a world-renowned Nobel laureate in the field of ancient Egypt and its dynasties. Many of her pre-existing skills in the use of scientific procedure as it applies to museum preparations transferred to her new post in the anthropology department, where she became acquainted with tool artifacts and gained knowledge of the skeletal anatomy of humans. This had a direct correlation to the field of Egyptology, the field of study where she found her home. Before going to college, she was in the Navy, having served in the war du jour.

Terri and Lynne sat at the tables near the patio of a local bistro, talking about some people they knew in college.

"Are you kidding? You dated him too?" asked Lynne.

"What do you mean 'too'? You dated him?"

"Ohhh yeah. I did the old 'Date and Dash' with him!"

"Dash? Why did you dash?"

"Me? Nuh-uh, honey. You got that backwards. He's the one who dated and dashed."

Terri's eyebrows arched. "You're telling me *he* dashed from *you*?"

"Yep!" Then with a gesture sweeping from her upper body to the lower part, Lynne added, "Can you believe it? Even with *this* package, he ran off?" They both laughed. "He said there was some job calling to him in Alaska and he wanted to go find himself, or something lame like that."

"Well, just count yourself lucky. I'm not one to kiss and tell. However, when there isn't anything to tell about the kiss, then I'm not really breaking my rule."

"No kidding? I never got that far myself. A little lacking, huh?"

"Let's just say he lacked in many ways," quipped Terri.

Both the girls stifled a giggle, immediately placing their hands over their respective mouths, and decided not to pursue this line of conversation that was coming dangerously close to being politically incorrect. "I don't really need to sow my oats nowadays," said Lynne. "I had enough of that before I went to college."

"Before? Doesn't that usually happen *while* you're in college?"

"Usually, but the military changes that a little."

"Military? How come I never knew you were in the military?"

"Well, I could have told you, but then I'd have had to kill you," joked Lynne with a smile.

"Ooooh. Now I'm scared. What did you do in there?"

"I was in the Navy and worked on an aircraft carrier. We were stationed for some time off the coast of Egypt, and while there I got turned on to the ancient cultures there. That's why I pursued my line of work. Like a pea in a pod now!"

The check came, and each calculated her fair share down to the penny. After leaving exactly 15% for a tip, they walked arm in arm down the street toward work.

"You know, you should come visit me in my department sometime," said Lynne. "We are always doing a lot with really interesting artifacts down there, and I'm sure if you could get a position in my department."

"I'll think about it. I'm not exactly enamored with what I'm doing right now, but I think things are about to change. I kinda want to see where things go. Maybe if it doesn't pan out for me in my current department, I'll check out yours."

The two friends continued walking and talking their way back to work. Passing by countless tourists, they made their way to the entrance facing Central Park. The façade of this building, made of stone and comprised of curved staircases to the left and right, is quite impressive. The stone staircases frame the sign announcing the "AMERICAN MVSEVM OF NATVRAL HISTORY" and "FOVNDED 1869." In front there is a wonderfully decorated fountain, surrounded by beautiful flowers and manicured hedges. Walking into the museum was equally as impressive, if not more so.

Upon entering, you are immediately greeted by the huge skeleton of a Tyrannosaurus Rex posed as if it was about to sweep down and have you for an afternoon snack. Milling around are various fathers, mothers, sons, daughters, students, and the occasional grandparent resting on the benches located under the chin of the T-Rex, while the rest of their families continue to consume all the museum has to offer.

Gently pushing their way through the masses across the marble floors, Terri and Lynne made their way to a door guarded by an electronic security lock. They each learned early on the only way to get through the crowds without being asked a million questions was to hide their ID which normally hung around the neck. At the door, they waved their museum ID in front of the pad, which caused the lock to click. After an easy swing of the door, Terri and Lynne bid goodbye and proceeded to their respective offices.

Terri worked with the senior museum curator. More than she led on to her friend, Terri absolutely loved her work. Being able to handle artifacts literally thousands if not millions of years old was a task that quite literally gave her a rush. Knowing each of these items has its own story, and working hard to decode exactly what that story is, had always been very rewarding to her. Working in the same department with Lynne might be more of that same rush, but she was very content with where she was.

Getting to her desk, Terri discovered a note from the senior curator asking her to come by his office for a visit. She made her way to the other end of the floor and walked into the office of her boss. He is generally well known and a doctor, but demands all who work with him simply call him by his first name.

Poking her head through his office door, Terri asked, "Neil, you wanted to see me?"

"Terri, glad you made it. Come on in!" It was funny to her how he knew full well her coming by wasn't optional; it was part of her job to respond to his requests. But still, everyone who worked with him understood Neil was not a micromanager. He appreciated each person.

Terri made her way to a chair in front of him and sat. "Terri," he began, "You've been able to complete the analysis of the Babylonian cuneiform tablets on loan to us, right?"

"Yes, sir. I cc'd you on the email with the analyses this morning."

"Good. You know, I like you. There's a line in that movie about bringing the dinosaurs to life again, something about so-and-so being ' … like me. He's a digger.' You remind me of myself when I was your age. You're a digger. You dig for the facts, and you don't need to have people hold your hands while you do it."

Neil, reaching over to some rather old and faded papers he had on his desk, continued.

"Here are some old inventories for items in the basement. The cataloging is really out of date; definitely not in our new computerized inventory management system. What I'd like for you to do is to undertake a rather large project for the museum: go through all the items in the museum archives and catalog all the ones in the sub-basement."

Terri began contemplating the task at hand. She was already beginning to look forward to the job, but Neil's next statement sealed the deal.

"This is basically going to be your own personal archaeological dig. There are items dating all the way back to the opening of the museum. In fact, the only record we have of those artifacts are these papers as well as some other books already down there. So, do you think you'd like to take on this project?"

Neil could already read the answer in Terri's face. She was smiling at the thought of delving into the sub-basement. The dustier the better.

"Sir, I would *love* to do that! What's my time frame?"

"That's just it. There isn't one. I don't want you to drag your figurative heels on the project, of course. I expect regular updates showing what progress you are making. But regardless of how long this takes, we need it done to have a clear handle on what we have down there. So, while I need you to be as efficient as possible, take the time you need to get the job done right. Deal?"

"Deal!" responded a very excited Terri.

"Excellent. Here are the keys to the sub-basement. Keep them with you at all times until we have the doors and locks replaced with the keyless entry system. When that happens, you will be one of the only people with authorized entry into that area." Neil stood and held out his hand for a handshake. "I look forward to hearing the first of many reports from you."

Taking his hand, Terri responded, "I look forward to sending them. Thank you, sir, for trusting me with this job!"

Terri left his office looking forward to the new task at hand. She wanted to get down to the sub-basement as soon as possible.

CHAPTER 20

"**B**ABY COME BACK. YOU CAN blame it all on meeee ... I was wrong-gggg...." The song played in Terri's ears. She always kept her music player on while she worked and today was no different. For some people, the music would be distracting; for Terri, it helped her to stay focused. It had to be music she liked, but also music she was very familiar with; nothing new was allowed.

It was the morning after her meeting with the museum's senior curator, and she was anxious to get started with her new assignment. To Terri, it was almost like a treasure hunt, but this one came with a guarantee. "Like shooting fish in a barrel," she thought to herself as she unlocked the creaky old door leading to a long staircase, which itself led to the sub-basement where the archives were kept. Turning on the old twist-style light switch, Terri began her proverbial descent through time.

As she proceeded down the staircase, she began noticing a significant layer of dust on pretty much everything down there. At the bottom of the staircase was a fairly good-sized area laid out as a work-room. The light was dim since many of the bulbs were burned out; twisting the switch only turned on three of the 12 light fixtures. There were tables in the middle of the room, and the walls had various empty shelving units, file cabinets, and a couple of sinks. Before she could get any work started, a deep cleaning of this room needed to be done. No way would she bring artifacts into this room for study in its present condition. Before she left the room to go get cleaning supplies, she spied a rather large set of double doors to the left of this room with a sign above them, simply reading "Archive."

Retracing her steps, Terri retreated into the supply room and loaded herself up with a menagerie of cleaning supplies and other necessities. Returning to the "anteroom," as she started calling it, it took her about half a day to get things up to par. By the time she was done cleaning and replacing all the burned out light bulbs, the room she now thought of as her lab looked quite respectable.

All the time she had been cleaning, she meticulously avoided the door to the archive. She knew it was a bit juvenile to do this, but she was saving opening that door for later as a present to herself for all the hard work she was doing to get her lab ready. While the typical archaeologist's tools of the trade are trowels, shovels, screens, hand brooms, and dustpans, Terri was more of an urban archaeologist. She'd be digging up artifacts for sure, but she'd be digging them up from dusty shelves in the archive. On the center work table, she set up all necessary contrivances to facilitate recording the artifacts being cat-aloged. This included her laptop, as well as more traditional writing implements. Part of her job would be to photograph the items, so on another table she had her high-definition camera and a light box to render good lighting for the smaller items; larger items might involve the in-house photography department.

Once all her work areas were set up, it was time to go back in time. Like Howard Carter reaching out to remove the last stone blocking the door to King Tut's tomb, Terri selected the perfect song on her player and strode to the door of the archive.

Turning the lever-action handle and opening the door, the first im-pression Terri gained from the experience was the rush of cold air that greeted her. The air had a tinge of dust, but thankfully no odor of mold. Beyond the door itself, though, she saw absolutely nothing in the pitch black darkness. Returning to her lab, she secured a large flashlight and went back to the door. Turning on the flashlight, she searched nearby for a light switch and found a rather large and very antique one. For a moment, Terri wondered about the state of the electric circuitry, but decided to try closing the knife switch anyway and see what happened.

Terry grasped the handle of the switch and flipped it to the closed position. As soon as she did, enormous lights began to power up in the ceiling, revealing a stairway leading down to a single room with huge columns interspersed throughout. Punctuated by the ever present hum of old lighting fixtures, she could now see an absolutely enormous room spanning the entire length and width of the museum above. The walls of the room were all painted in a yellowing Navajo white, and the ceiling was covered with old asbestos acoustic tiles, the kind with thousands of small decorative pinholes. The room contained rows upon rows of shelving units spanning floor to ceiling, each unit reaching six meters high. Terri sat on the top step drinking in the enormity of the task at hand. This wasn't going to be a job done in a day, week or month; it was going to take a year. Maybe two or three! Step by measured step she started down the staircase, making sure each was secure and wouldn't give way beneath her. The steps were metal, so she knew she was probably safe.

At the bottom of the stairs, she looked from floor level toward the top of one of the shelving units. She noticed some of the shelves were each a foot tall until the next shelf above, but sometimes they formed larger areas depending on the size of the artifacts being stored. When she reached out to touch one of the items, she was startled to hear a beep in her ears. "Figures," she thought to herself. "My music player chooses now to die on me?"

Reaching to her belt where it was fastened, she flicked off the device, removed the ear buds, and draped them around her neck. Continuing into the room, Terri looked to the left and the right of her position and started counting. On both sides, she could see dozens and dozens of shelving endcaps. Immediately in front of each, were at least half a dozen file cabinets. Opening the nearest to her, she discovered documents that were notes and other paraphernalia related to the items in that row of shelves. Looking down one aisle, she saw each section of shelves extended about 20 meters. Beyond that was a perpendicular aisle crossing, followed by another set of shelves, each framed with its own set of file cabinets.

Closing the file cabinet, Terri crossed the closest aisle, slowly examining eye-level items, when her music player made another beeping sound. She reached down, dislodged it from her belt, and examined the switch. It was off. Thinking this was an oddity but nothing more, she replaced it on her belt and continued on.

She began noticing a pattern in how items, appearing to be from the ancient Minoan culture, were arranged on a particular set of shelves. The metal artifacts were inscribed with hieroglyphs resembling Egyptian hieroglyphs, but of a type Terri recognized as an undeciphered hieroglyph style called "Linear A." She had done a paper on this particular language while still in college, which is why she recognized it right off. Its successor, Linear B, had been deciphered, but the understanding of Linear A remained elusive.

There were pots, small tables, statues, and various pieces of jewelry that in some way or another had a common theme. Many of these had depictions of the head of a bull, a recurring theme in Minoan religious culture, although archaeologists could only theorize why the bull played such a large role. Next to one item was a small index card outlining how it was found in a small cave in Crete at such-and-such a location, by such-and-such an archaeologist. As time went on, Terri realized that with each new revelation, and each new shelf, she had been breathing shallowly. Her body eventually rebelled, declaring a state of emergency due to the general lack of oxygen. Stopping to breathe deeply, she decided now was a good time to ....

Beep.

"Oh for the luvva, " Terri reached down, grabbed the music player, ripped out the battery, and put it in her pocket. "There! Take that," she said with righteous indignation, mixed with a slightly evil smile.

"Now where was I? Ah yes." Terri felt it would be a good idea to start cataloging, not the individual items in the archive, but the shelves themselves. It appeared each shelf held items from one particular culture or era. Looking again at the endcaps, many of them had worn and tattered 80-year-old labels cataloging the culture represented by the items on the shelf. "I think I'll just start with a pad of paper and ...."

Beep.

"What the?" There it was again. Now that the battery was out of her music player, it was obvious the beeping wasn't coming from that source, but the sound was definitely electronic in nature. This hadn't seen humans since well before the advent of electronics, probably sometime around the Second World War, or even before. What could possibly be making that kind of noise? Now that she thought about it, it seemed like the interval between the beeps was a regular amount of time, like maybe once a minute. But where was it coming from?

Beep.

Terri looked at her watch and noted the time was 1:37 and 17 seconds. Looking up, it seemed the sound came from her left but it was hard to tell; the walls were all bare, so sound rippled and bounced around quite easily. She started to slowly move in that direction, trying to locate the source. The endcaps which still had labels revealed subject matter ranging from the European Middle Ages, to African cultures, to Asian cultures.

Beep.

She looked at her watch again. The time was 1:38 and 17 seconds. Exactly one minute. Definitely electronic.

Terri started to get annoyed at the probable sloppiness of some unauthorized person leaving his or her cell phone, or perhaps some other electronic device, down there. This area was supposed to be off limits; the door to the room had been sealed until Terri arrived. She wondered if there was another entrance to the archive she didn't know about, through which another individual had undertaken a foray into the unknown. The more she thought about it, the more it made sense. All these artifacts certainly hadn't come in through the anteroom, especially the larger ones; there must be a freight elevator somewhere. She made a mental note to look for such a contraption so that later she could ....

Beep.

The sound continued coming from a specific direction, so Terri moved slowly, all the while watching her watch. When the second hand swept around toward the 17-second mark, she would stop and listen. More than once, she proceeded down a shelving corridor only to find the beep becoming fainter, necessitating she retrace her steps. Eventually, she came to a set of shelves labeled "North America, Eastern Seaboard, 1875-1899." The next beep led her to open a drawer labeled "Field Expedition: #5894." The inside of the drawer was lined with burgundy velvet, and nestled in the middle of the velvet was what appeared to be a golden artifact with incredible hieroglyphic markings, glyphs, unlike any she had seen before.

Beep.

Clearly and distinctly, the beep came from the artifact. It certainly wasn't a cell phone, like she originally feared. It was roughly oval in shape. The back of the item was covered with these strange glyphs; on the front, there was a smooth surface polished to a mirror finish. Terri was immediately captivated by this item. Its beauty was astounding, yet the most enigmatic feature of this obviously ancient item was the perfectly-timed beep. She would never dismantle the item to see why it was beeping; it was far too amazing and ancient to risk anything like that. But why would this item display behavior reminiscent of modern-day electronic gadgets?

Realizing this would be a great inaugural artifact to photograph with her camera and light box, Terri decided she wanted to take a closer look at the hieroglyphs; images are the best way to do that without having to worry about damaging the piece. She gingerly carried the item to her lab, fired up the light box and camera, and took several high-resolution images of all sides of the item. When she took it back downstairs and returned it to its place, she brought her notepad and used the remaining time in the afternoon cataloging the rows of shelves. Terri put the battery back in her music player and spent the rest of the afternoon listening to some really good tunes, punctuated every minute by the beep. That night, she took home prints of what she came to refer to as the "Golden Beeper." Hopefully, she could compare the glyphs in the item with some information in her old textbooks.

Time would tell.

CHAPTER 21

ON HER WAY HOME THAT evening, Terri stopped by a bookstore and purchased a couple of reference works on the use of hieroglyphics, not only in ancient Egypt but also other cultures which used them. The cultures discussed in the books ranged from Egypt, to the Maya of Central America, to cultures in southern China and Tibet. When comparing glyphs on the artifact to ones found in the books, nothing came remotely close. Nothing whatsoever, which was pretty frustrating. Eventually, she decided to see if there was something in the computer systems at work about the origin of this artifact and where the glyphs came from.

The next morning Terri made her way to her office, sat down at her computer, and logged in to the private museum network. She did a search on all known hieroglyphics, and came up empty. She then tried a last-ditch effort to find something by searching for what was on the label in the drawer where the artifact was found. Her search for "Field Expedition #5894" was futile. She knew it was a long shot since the whole reason she was given the task of cataloging the archive was because none of that inventory was recorded on the computer, but she thought it deserved a try.

Sitting back in her chair, she now had to figure out, without any computer assistance, what the story was with this artifact. Thinking it over, she realized that in her haste to take images of the artifact, she had ignored the possibility of documentation in the file cabinets at the end of the shelving units. Descending back into the archive, she made her way to the file cabinets where the beeper was. Opening the drawers which were in desperate need of oil, she saw that much of what was in these cabinets wasn't in any semblance of order, so finding information on the beeper in this mess was going to take some time.

She knew she needed to approach the archival project systematically, relegating this beeper to more of a recreational oddity, and not giving it any more attention than other items in the archive. Terri's approach could take two directions: an overall understanding of what was in the archive, or an examination and documentation of the history and relevancy of each item. Her job wasn't to understand any specific item, but to simply catalog what was present in the archive so future researchers would know what was there. That way, they could target exactly what they were looking for, and where in the archive it was located.

She had an ace up her sleeve, though. Her friend Lynne was an Egyptologist, and would be more likely to know where the beeper came from.

The balance of the day was spent familiarizing herself with the entire floor plan of the archive. She decided to simply follow the walls all around, figuring eventually she would end up back where she started. Thinking this would be a good way to learn the scope of the task before her, Terri started on her trek and was rewarded early on with a few things about the archive room she didn't know before. As she had earlier suspected, there was a freight elevator in the far-left corner, making it possible to bring things big and small in and out of the archive. It would be a fun project to see where it came up from below to the ground level. It was obvious this wasn't the same freight elevator in constant use by the museum, since this one was situated at the archive level and had the same layer of dust so commonplace to Terri at this point. When she had gone to the same place on the ground floor where the freight elevator was located, there simply was nothing to be found. After talking with some guys from maintenance, they all went down to the archive, got in the elevator, and hit "Up". With a considerable number creaks and groans, the mechanisms engaged and the apparatus moved its way upward. Eventually the car stopped, and they were greeted with what appeared to the back side of a wall, complete with wood studs and drywall on the other side. It was quite comical when the senior maintenance technician used his hammer to break through the drywall right next to an extremely startled female office worker. Apparently, this area was an original shipping and receiving depot which was repurposed back in the Fifties. Nobody in modern times had any idea the freight elevator was there, but it made sense since this particular area was just off of the main garage at the rear of the museum. The sight of a gang of men emerging from the wall, and the shrieks coming from the secretarial pool, were amusing fodder for conversations around the water cooler for quite some time.

Going home each night these days, Terri was very glad to make her way to the shower. She loved her work, but it sure was dirty. Standing in the shower, allowing the water to wash away the grime of the day, was almost a treat in of itself. Occasionally, she would pour a glass of wine and spoil herself with a bath instead of a shower; this day was one of those days. Getting out of the tub and drying herself off, she wrapped the oversize towel around her tall frame, and another around her long red hair. Emerging from the back bathroom, she sat for a while on the couch, turned on the TV to whatever channel she had been watching last, and relaxed. She contemplated what to do for dinner, then decided that was a decision for later. Right now, being off her feet was something that sounded better than food.

The TV was on the home shopping network, and this evening highlighted beautiful pendants featuring tanzanite stones arranged in various ways, some with diamonds, some without. They were all beautiful, but Terri thought how she wasn't really a pendant kind of girl, so she reached for the remote to find something else to watch. Just as she was about to hit the channel button, the piece they were featuring at that moment caught her attention. They had just turned the piece over so the back could be seen.

Terri focused on the loop at the top of the pendant. Through that loop was a chain, like any typical pendant. The reason this caught her attention was she had seen something like this recently. She looked down on her messy coffee table and moved around some papers, looking for the golden beeper pictures she brought home the previous evening. Finding them, she looked at one end of the beeper and, sure enough, there was a loop there just like the one on the television screen.

"I'll be darned. That thing's a pendant."

177

She wondered why she hadn't made the connection when she had been looking at the artifact in person or in the photos. Holding the pictures in her hand, she looked to the side and got a smile on her face. Laying down the photos and getting up from her seat on the couch, she went into her bedroom to the jewelry stand on top of her dresser. Hanging there was a gold chain she wore on special occasions. "I'm going to take selfies with this chain," she thought to herself, "and show them to Lynne tomorrow when I see her."

Little did she know the odyssey in store for her.

CHAPTER 22

ᒐ ᒍ ᒐᒍ ᧺ ᧡ ᧡ᧁ ᒍ ᒍ ᧺● ᧡
●᧺ ᧡᧡ ᧡ ᒍ●ᒍ ᧺᧡

ABOUT THE ONLY FASHION NOD Terri gave to the mainstream profession of archaeologists was the wearing of traditional cargo pants instead of Levi's. She didn't have to be shielded from the sun down in the basement, so the typical wide-brimmed hat wasn't needed. Boots weren't necessary either, since there was no trudging through the mud. In the museum archive, however, there was plenty of dust, which is why Terri kept a supply of rags with her at all times. If she found herself in a new location and wanted to lean against or sit on something, it invariably needed a good wipe first.

After going on the perimeter walk of the entire archive like she had done the previous day, it was apparent she needed to create a map of some sort. She took a drawing pad with her, as well as pencils, tape, and index cards. Her plan was to draw a crude representation of the archive on paper and to number the racks individually. As she assigned a number to each rack, she wrote the number on an index card, taped it to the end of the rack above the bank of filing cabinets, and included a cursory idea of the type of inventory found there. By the time she got to where she found the beeper, the rack ended up being Number 49. She hadn't figured out exactly how to identify the individual shelves and position of each item on them, but that would come in time.

As she made her way through the archive, it was surreal how each and every turn brought her face to face with a new discovery, at least new to her. There was an entire section dedicated to Greek mythology. Collections ranged from plant and animal fossils to antique toys; there were several types of stuffed animals in the taxidermy section. She even encountered a whole section dedicated to replicas of the inventions of Leonardo Da Vinci. Several complete sets of fossilized skeletons of various dinosaurs were in the large storage rooms at the back.

She made her way to the rear section of the archive room where she had found the beeper the day before. Since it was just about time for lunch with Lynne, Terri decided now was as good a time as any to take those selfies with the gold chain she had brought from home. Setting down her writing materials, she reached into her pocket and took out the chain. After taking the pendant from its velvet-lined home in the Rack 49 drawer, she threaded the chain through the loop at the top, put in on, and reached into her pocket for her camera.

At that very moment, she felt an overwhelming calm in her body, and what seemed like an incredible rush of adrenaline. Everything went black for her, yet she maintained her balance and consciousness. Later when describing this moment, she was hard-pressed to relate why the loss of sight wasn't terrifying to her; in reality, it never even came close to causing fear. While standing there, Terri continued to experience complete calm and contentment. Earlier, she had only been thinking about the job at hand; now those thoughts seemed far away. For that short period, she felt at one with the universe. She listened to her own breathing, concentrating on the beat of her own heart. As if waking from the most fulfilling deep sleep she had ever experienced, her sight gradually faded back in, and she was once again able to see with perfect clarity.

Stepping back a bit, her legs encountered a chair, so she sat on it, ignoring the inch-thick layer of dust it probably had.

Beep.

After Terri flipped it over and pressed a combination of three glyphs in a specific sequence, the pendant gave off three beeps in quick succession then fell silent. For seconds, minutes, or hours (she had no sense of time at the moment), she stared at the golden beeper in her hands. With the passing of time, more and more clarity and understanding about this small trinket in her hands came to the fore. Somehow she knew it would now remain quiet; after waiting quite a while, it became evident the beeper was now silent.

Staring at it, Terri began to realize how odd it was she knew the specific sequence of glyphs to get the beeping to stop. How did she know that? As she sat there on a dusty chair, she reached up to her forehead and wiped it with a clean rag, all the while wondering what was happening to her. First the rush, then the blindness, the clarity of thought, the return of her sight, and now the miraculous knowledge of how to turn off the incessant beeping. She looked down at beeper's shiny front surface, then turned the artifact over to look at the back. As soon as she did, she looked at the most prominent glyphs at the top and instantly knew what they said.

"Galimar," Terri said under her breath.

"*Whoa!*" she said, to no one in particular. "How did I know that?" The fog of illiteracy had inexplicably been lifted, and suddenly she was in possession of a complete understanding of the glyphs on the artifact. Terri proceeded to read what was immediately below the main inscription at the top.

"Welcome, child, to the most amazing and significant day of your life. As you stand on the crest of your age of enlightenment, it is with profound happiness that you are presented with this amulet of understanding. Use it to unlock a universe of knowledge and insight about all that has gone before, and to show you how wonderful your life will soon be. When you are ready to start your voyage of learning, enter the name you have chosen for yourself on the pad. End it with the word "Ready." Choose carefully! This name will stay with you for the rest of your life. You will then be shown what to do next."

"With the greatest of love and respect."

"The Grand Council of New Galimar"

The old Terri would normally have uttered a few colorful metaphors, but that seemed like such a waste of breath. If she wanted to express herself, she now had complete command of the English language, and could pick out the perfect word to satisfy any linguistic need. At the same time, there now coexisted in her a newfound understanding at once overwhelming and energizing. There was an awakening in her soul, inciting her to ever greater planes of mental acuity and perception; she knew no event would ever miss her notice. All her senses were keen, and the awareness she now experienced was, in a word, intoxicating.

After transliterating "Terri" and the word "Ready" into this new language, she immediately turned the pendant over and used her finger to draw the characters onto the shiny side of the amulet. If she thought the events of the previous few minutes were amazing, the next thing that happened was simply beyond description.

In an instant, Terri experienced what she later could only describe as transcending to a different plane of existence. She knew her body was still in the archive, but at the same time all her senses were somehow

commandeered, her vision cleared, and she was being taken on a journey of some sort. Some might describe it as flying through space; others
would say it was a light show of sorts with light streaking by. Whatever
it was, it was beautiful. All colors of the rainbow flew past as if each was
a comet hurtling through space and she was an interplanetary traveler. It
was quite hypnotizing to watch, and when it came to an end, there was
a part of Terri which felt a loss, though it would prove to be short-lived.

The vision of traveling was replaced with the materialization of a
scene in nature. In addition to being inspired by all she was now seeing, she could feel, smell, and hear so many things; it took her a good
amount of time to wrap her head around all the stimulation. Looking
down, she appeared to be standing in a field of grass. For some reason, she was barefoot, moving her toes back and forth in the blades of
grass, and wearing what looked like a white covering artfully wrapped
around her body. Her skin was pale, but still exuded health and vitality.
Turning her hands from one side to another, she perceived the minor
lines and wrinkles of age were completely gone. She saw the ripple of
muscles, sheathed in velvety, youthful skin.

The grass she was standing in was part of a large field of trees, plants,
and shrubs, all seemingly placed in perfect symmetry. This park-like
setting was immediately calming, and inspired more exploration. Terri
looked all around and saw majestic mountain cliffs rising above the valley
she was standing in. Each granite cliff stood in guardianship over the unspoiled and untouched magnificence surrounding every one of her senses.

Just when she thought the scene before her couldn't possibly be
any more magnificent, her eyes gradually rose skyward where she saw
celestial bodies hanging in what seemed to be a morning sky. Terri
looked up at three different colored moons, each of them far nearer
to her than the moon of Earth was to Earth. They appeared cradled in
a set of bands encircling this planet, much like what it might look like
from the surface of Saturn.

The entire scene was as amazing as it was beautiful. A soft breeze came
from the right, carrying floral aromas she had never before enjoyed. Even
so, her mind instantly recognized what she was sensing, and images of
the unfamiliar flora responsible for the aromas came to mind. The bou-
quet was entrancing and sensual. As she walked in the direction of the
breeze, she crossed a small pool of water. Floating on top were iridescent
plants similar to water lilies, each with a blooming flower at its center.
Gazing into the pool, Terri was mildly startled to see a face not her own
staring back. The face human, but not. Terri's, but not. She couldn't quite
see the differences in the dark water, but they were definite.

As she looked far and wide, a tall and slender wraith formed in the distance, seemingly walking, seemingly floating toward Terri. At first the form was out of focus, gradually taking shape more and more, until it finally came into crisp focus. In front of her was a beautiful woman dressed in the most attractive, flowing gown she had ever seen. The relaxed and comfortable clothing was obviously as light as it was free. Flowing down her body from the shoulders, it moved easily with the breeze, adding to the splendor of this amazing being. She was rather tall but not imposing, perfectly proportioned, and stunningly beautiful. Her hair gently flowed over her shoulder, and as she came closer, Terri could see her captivating eyes. They were beautiful in their own right, but the pupils were completely black. No color whatsoever. Just deep pools of ebony that somehow spoke to the gentle position of power, understanding and balance. Somehow you could easily tell this person was at once in possession of the wisdom of the ancients, and yet the exuberance of the young. You could tell that youth was never wasted on the young in this paradise. This being was both young, agile, free and intelligent.

Terri was breathless in the presence of seeming perfection. She gazed deeply into the eyes of this vision, even while she herself was being examined. With a slow blink of those magnificent pools of sight and with a loving and almost motherly lilt to her voice, she spoke: "Welcome to the age of enlightenment, my young one. My name is Quorlynn, and

I will guide you as you take these first steps toward becoming an adult. You may ask anything you wish, and I will answer to your satisfaction."

"You can see me?" Terri asked tentatively.

Quorlynn smiled. "Yes, Terri. I can see you quite well."

"How did you know my name?!"

"Because you entered your name on the amulet."

Now realizing this entire vision was some manifestation of the artifact she had put on in the archive, Terri started putting two and two together. There was an enormous amount she didn't comprehend, but at least she understood what had brought her here. "Ok. That makes sense," conceded Terri. "Where am I?"

"This is your home planet of Galimar."

Quorlynn could see the look on Terri's face portraying the confusion inside.

"Yes. While you live now on an island on a planet named Eden, this is the planet from where your people came. Over 6,000 years ago, your forefathers traveled to Eden and established a colony where they could live."

"My forefathers?"

"Indeed. Over 6,000 Eden years ago, your parents and their parents before them came to this planet from their home planet of Galimar." Quorlynn looked up and around. "The world you see here is what Galimar looks like. It is a beautiful world where all life is respected, and where the enlightened enjoy living at one with each other and with their environment. Your forefathers came to Eden to explore and to live. That is why you are here now. The island where you live is the very ship in which your forefathers came to Eden. Now that you have reached the age of enlightenment and have put on the amulet of understanding, I am here to begin teaching you all about your race of people and your heritage."

Terri took in all Quorlynn said, but now had to figure out how to proceed. She had an enormous amount of automatic understanding, but there was so much she didn't know. It was obvious Quorlynn thought Terri was someone she wasn't, but it might be better to go along with the charade of being who Quorlynn thought she was, a child who didn't know much. That wasn't far from the truth, so she just started to ask questions.

"How did I suddenly come to know how to read the outside of the amulet?" was Terri's first question.

"As soon as you put on the amulet of understanding, the amulet began communication with your mind. It transferred a basic understanding of our written language, and this is how you knew to enter your name into the pad."

"And this planet I am now seeing is Galimar?"

"Yes."

"This planet where I live is called Eden?"

"Yes."

"Is it known by any other names?"

"Yes. There is a major indigenous life form on this planet. When your forefathers first arrived, these lifeforms were quite barbaric, so your forefathers wisely decided to isolate themselves. Before they did so, they learned these lifeforms called themselves human, and they referred to this planet as Earth."

OK, here was a connection to something she knew. But could it be true? Were there not only otherworldly beings, but ones who lived here on Earth? Putting on her archaeologist hat, Terri thought for a moment and realized she needed to know as much as possible about this obviously amazing civilization. She had to learn, but decided to do so secretly. Knowing it could take a long time to learn all she wanted to know, she would need to come and go quite often to ask more and more questions from Quorlynn. This led to her next question.

"I like learning from you, but I may need to go and then come back. How do I do that?"

"You will notice there is an amulet around your neck here as well as around your neck in the outside world. When you are here, just swipe your finger across the pad to return to the outside world. When you are there, enter your name and the word 'Ready' to come back here to ask me more questions."

Terri looked down; she was wearing the same amulet here as she had put on in the archive. She picked it up and swiped her finger across the pad. With what felt like the rush of a stiff breeze, Terri was instantly transported back to the archive room where she had remained seated. She felt fresh, alive, and powerful. Looking around, all was as she remembered it being before she had put on the amulet, except for her cell phone which lay sprawled out on the floor where she apparently dropped it earlier. Obviously, selfies were no longer at the top of her priority list.

After getting her bearings and trying to wrap her head around what had just happened, Terri thought about how her friend was going to be irritated at her for being late to lunch. Blinking a few times, she looked at her watch. Terri was stunned to realize that even though she thought lunch had come and gone, she had only been sitting in the archive for 15 minutes. With all the time she had taken exploring the valley floor and the environment presented to her in the amulet, it actually felt like several hours.

CHAPTER 23

ʃ (✓ ˥ ◖◗ ᴜ ᴜ

Terri sat before Quorlynn with her legs crossed. Dressed in her white tunic reminiscent of ancient Greek mantles, Terri had repeatedly been visiting with Quorlynn for several weeks now as a student, and had learned much about the inhabitants of Galimar: who they were, where Galimar is located in relation to Earth, and why they were here. Being an archaeologist, she tended to ask a lot of questions about the history of the Galimarians, learning how they are an enlightened people, but how they weren't always so enlightened. Now they respect all life and live in peace, but long ago, they were much like humans are now.

Terri learned Galimarians have a life cycle much different than humans. Part of this is due to their environment, and part to their technology. Quorlynn was a little surprised about questions regarding the atmosphere and environment. It turns out Galimarians breathe nitrogen primarily, in the same way humans breathe oxygen. The high concentration on Earth is just what they needed to live comfortably.

After looking at a map Quorlynn miraculously caused to appear, she also learned Galimarians live on an island between Florida, Puerto Rico, and Bermuda. The island is rather large and designed to spend time on the surface of the ocean, but also on the ocean floor. A shield encircles the island at all times; when on the ocean floor, it protects the island from the pressure of the water, but on the surface, it protects

Galimarians from the harmful effects of the sun. Although Earth is perfect for them, its sun puts out far too much ultraviolet radiation for their fair skin. The shield filters out this harmful radiation.

The Galimarians came from a neighboring galaxy, the Large Magellanic Cloud, about 50 kiloparsecs (about 163,000 light years) away. Their social evolution progressed to a point where they recognized the obligation of each Galimarian is to pursue happiness and explore the vast universe around them. They realized this alone brings personal fulfillment, rather than pursuits of personal wealth and prosperity. Many millennia ago, their race figured out materialistic pursuits were the path to unrest, unhappiness, and ultimately death for those preoccupied with such.

By pursuing a more enlightened approach to life, their race grew as a whole and was able to accomplish much more than they ever had when interested only in personal fame and fortune. This enlightened viewpoint was solidified after making their first contact with intelligent life on other planets. That had to wait until they were able to perfect interstellar travel.

Galimarians live, love, and laugh much like humans do. One of the first things they discerned from their contact with other planets and races of intelligent life is the level of a race's intelligence is commensurate with their ability to laugh and enjoy life. Like themselves, when a race has the ability to concentrate on the activities of an enlightened soul, their minds are freed from the more pedestrian pursuits of life, and they are able to evolve at an exponential rate. Arts, literature, technology, music, and philosophy turn into full-time respected vocations for those who chose to pursue such things.

Surrounding Galimar are five major moons: Idda, Genipar, Penilad, Demios, and Pailan. Also surrounding the planet is a set of rings made up of major and minor asteroidal bodies. While the Galimarians have colonized all the moons except for Demios, there are no colonies on the asteroids, though there are fully automated mining operations on some of the larger ones. The raw materials from these mines were used for many purposes, including construction of the Arageena, their ship which brought them to Earth.

Through visions, Quorlynn was able to take Terri to amazing places on Galimar, teaching her about the culture and how it had evolved. Early on in their social and technological development, Galimarians figured out the great joy derived simply from discovery, so they embarked on quite a lot of it. Their first forays centered exclusively around their own biology as well as the planet where they lived. Galimar was quite similar to Earth except for some amazing things, including natural wonders like the gardens of Ammular and the glittering falls of Ettiok, which glittered due to the gleaming scales on millions of fish living in the waters.

One place in particular was really memorable to Terri. Quorlynn took her to a beautifully wooded forest, and they ascended above granite cliffs which rose impressively from the valley floor. In this visionary world, Terri scaled the heights with ease and was entranced with the unbelievable vistas set in front of her. At one point, she was taken into a cave behind an immense set of waterfalls. The cave went into the mountain for a bit, then emerged out the other side into a valley carpeted with vegetation and protected on all sides by impenetrable cliffs rising thousands of meters. This in and of itself would attract visitors, but what was truly amazing were the Gravity Wells of Mistikaan. In the middle of the valley, about 300 meters off the surface of the ground, were areas where gravity was canceled out. Scientists later figured out it had something to do with the placement and proximity of the moons and rings surrounding the planet. The gravity wells manifested themselves by trapping any rain that fell in them. As a result, there were entire bodies of water, miles in diameter, simply hanging above the center of the valley. They had existed there for hundreds of thousands of years, and entire ecosystems, including aquatic animals, lived in these bodies of water that didn't exist anywhere else on the planet.

Mistikaan was a favorite place to come and swim for the Galimarians. There was one cliff ledge which came close to, and jutted out above, one of the bodies of water. A typical practice was climbing out to the ledge and stepping off. As soon as you did, the gravity well would catch you, and you could then swim in any direction in the wondrous, flowing, undulating sphere of water. Since it was a body of water on all sides, you could literally swim along the surface of the water, look "up," and see the surface of the ground. The first experience was a little disconcerting, but you'd get used to it quickly. When it was time to go home, the visitor would simply return to the step-off point and climb out.

Long ago, the explorers of Galimar decided a new and very ambitious journey would be undertaken. Eden was the original planet to be visited by the Arageena. This ship was constructed for that journey, and built in geosynchronous orbit around Galimar in an orbiting space dock. In only two months, the builder robots responsible for building the ship reported it was complete. The crew compartments were pressurized, life support was functioning at 100%, but all other supporting systems including propulsion, exobiology, main computing, and stellar cartography were nominal.

With great fanfare, pomp, and circumstance, the explorers left on their journey. About a week after the initial shakedown and tuning of systems on the ship with the benefit of the few remaining builder robots, the crew entered their suspended animation pods. The ship, quite intelligent by Earth standards, navigated its own way to Eden, watching over them and making sure it kept on course during its 10-year journey, gathering needed power nourishment along the way.

Once the ship came relatively near to Eden, it began its scans to finalize its trajectory to the planet. As it did so, the Arageena discovered that in the 10 years since it left Galimar, Eden's sun was on the verge of going supernova. Its gravitational pull had changed dramatically, and the explorers were being pulled dangerously close. Being as intelligent as it was, the ship decided the only way to save the crew was to fly toward the sun, then slingshot itself around and away. It did so but, traveling at near light speed, entered an area of space not even considered for exploration. Since the main computer on the Arageena was programmed to find an inhabitable planet, that is exactly what it did, eventually exiting the galaxy where Galimar was located, and drifting into interstellar space. Over time, it found its way to the Milky Way galaxy, where the main computer of the Arageena discovered a planet which was perfect since it almost exactly matched Galimar. The ship began a five-year-long process of slowing down its speed, and waking up the travelers. First, the captain was awakened, then he supervised the awakening of the other travelers.

All this happened fully 1,046,732 years after they originally left Galimar, whose inhabitants assumed the ship was lost to the supernova witnessed through their telescopes.

Initially, the crew of the Arageena didn't know what had happened and assumed they were now in orbit over their original target planet of Eden. An astute navigator and astronomer named Ch'Korav Leynan began going through the ship logs kept during the journey because he couldn't recognize any of the constellations he was seeing. Leynan discovered what had really happened, how far they had traveled, and for how long.

To say they were astounded at how much time had gone by would be an understatement. Once the crew realized their entire lives had been forever altered, and that all they had known and all whom they had known and loved no longer existed and probably hadn't existed for untold millennia, they were heartbroken.

For a while, they felt paralyzed by their circumstances and were despondent. Some wanted to climb back into the pods and go home, an idea they quickly shed since their world wouldn't resemble what they knew at all. The crew understood if they returned to their home planet, they would probably end up as pariahs, outcasts among those who had developed so much farther than they themselves had ... if their home world was even there anymore. Since their race was such an exploring one, probably none of what they knew was the same.

Finally J'Sepp Yucholl, considered among the wisest of all Galimarians on the Arageena, spoke. A respected elder, it was he who established order among the travelers and inspired all to adopt a new life on their new planet, helping them see existence on this new planet could be one of fulfillment as well. His proposals concerning the establishment of a government structure identical to the one on their home planet, were ratified by every traveler. Their island came to be known as New Galimar. All this happened thousands of Earth years ago.

Soon after landing and exploring their new home, they discovered inhabitants of this planet were far too barbaric for their tastes. Based on their history with events on Traxis where local life was snuffed out when indigenous society was given technology well before they could handle it, Galimarians decided to isolate themselves from the inhabitants of Earth.

In time, some became bored with life on the island of New Galimar. In keeping with the explorative leanings of their race, they desired to explore their relatively new planet; they had been there for more than 4,000 years at the time. They petitioned the governing council for permission to leave the island, which the council agreed to on three conditions: first, they couldn't take *any* technology with them; second, they couldn't speak of the existence of the island; and third, they couldn't come back.

Those wanting to leave were led by a Galimarian named Docius Atlantis. The group who left with him were mainly his own family. They were never heard from again.

Learning so much was an odyssey for Terri. The more she learned, the more she identified with the Galimarians. Her hunger for knowledge couldn't be extinguished. Since she was so trusted and nobody knew what was in the archive to begin with, taking the amulet home was relatively easy, although nerve-wracking, since she had always been somewhat of a goody two-shoes. She wasn't stealing it; she was just borrowing it. Terri wanted to learn as much as possible, and she couldn't do enough at work. She had to spend time doing this at home.

It turned out she was able to spend time with Quorlynn all night. Her body slept while her mind spent time at the feet of her professorial benefactress. When she came back from her forays of learning, she felt light, refreshed, and new. Terri was benefitting in more ways than one. Inwardly, she felt more confident about making decisions without the internal dialog of indecision which had always been there. Her friends started seeing changes, too. Even though she was obsessed with spending time with Quorlynn, she knew she needed to keep up her connections to her friends on the outside. It was Lynne who commented on how much more confident Terri; before, she was more passive, but now she was more adventurous, more of an explorer. Terri laughed out loud at that comment. It made her think about the explorer nature of the Galimarians. Maybe more was rubbing off on her than she realized.

In time, Terri realized she wanted to connect with the real race of Galimarians. She wanted them to know humans had progressed much farther than they had imagined. She wanted to know this race of wonderful beings she had come to love face to face. One morning after a particularly fulfilling lesson from Quorlynn, Terri decided she had to go for a visit. She would take vacation time, get on a boat, and see these people herself.

Terri was going to New Galimar.

CHAPTER 24

ᨆᨉ ᨆᨃᨆᨉᨆᨉᨆ
ᨆᨆᨆᨆ, ᨆ
ᨆᨆᨆᨆᨆᨆᨆᨆ ᨆᨆᨆᨆ

July 6 – JFK Airport, New York

AT THE MOMENT, I AM sitting in the airline terminal at the airport waiting to board my flight. Since I have decided to take a trip to New Galimar, I'm keeping a journal of my experiences along the way so I don't forget anything.

Wow. Just writing that last sentence is a mouthful. If anybody knew exactly what I am planning to do, they would suggest I get my head examined. But then again, they haven't had the intense experience of meeting Quorlynn. Just two months ago when I found the Galimarian amulet of understanding, I had no idea what I was in for. I have always been interested in the cultures of other people, where they came from, what they are doing now, and where they are going. But I certainly had no idea my life would take this enormous left turn, and that one of those cultures I would be learning about would be one which didn't originate on earth!

Once I decided to take the trip to New Galimar, there was a lot of planning I had to do. First I had to get the time off from work, which wasn't a problem since I've been there for years and never taken a vacation. I had so much stored-up vacation time, the administrator was glad I was going to take the time off, instead of cashing it out. Something about his budget not being able to handle that kind of hit all at once. I decided to make it a month-long vacation, beginning today.

After deciding to take the vacation, I then had to plan how I would actually get to the island. I considered chartering a seaplane, but that presented some problems. First, I don't know how to fly, and I don't want anybody else, such as a pilot, knowing where I am going. I have come to truly appreciate these people and how they live. Although they probably don't know humans have advanced as much as we have, I still don't want to force them to be exposed to the rest of the world. They have remained isolated for this long, so it's probable they want to remain that way, and I want to respect that. If they decide to make their presence known to the rest of the world once they meet me, then that will be their decision.

So, no plane. The only option left was to use a boat. Fortunately for me, I know how to sail. Having grown up in Maine with a father who was a professional fisherman, I was around the sea all my youth. My father made it his aim for me to know how to captain a boat before I could captain a tricycle, so being out in the open sea by myself didn't really phase me. I figured I could rent a relatively small boat, but not too small, since I needed to have one I could sleep on. I did a lot of checking and found this small company in Miami willing to rent me a boat for the month I need it. I've seen pictures of the craft, and it looks like it will be perfect. It has a cabin where the bed is located, an area outside the cabin with a galley, and the head is right off that; it even has a shower. My dad's boats never had showers, that's for sure! I asked them to have the boat stocked with groceries for me so all I have to do is load my luggage and go.

I have to admit I'm a little concerned about pirates. Not the swashbuckling kind of course, but the kind who board your boat and steal your things, maybe even do you harm. I've done research, and I don't think that's something I really need to worry too much about, but let's just say I've arranged for some personal protection and leave it at that. 'Nuf said.

So, I'm off to Florida. Wish me luck!

July 7 – Miami

Just woke up. Still screwing in my eyeballs, and trying to wake up with some coffee.

I got in yesterday and checked into a hotel I had booked for one night. I'm supposed to load the boat this afternoon. Meanwhile, I am just going to luxuriate in my hotel-supplied robe, have room service bring me my breakfast, and actually act like I'm on vacation.

July 7 (evening) – Miami harbor

Just a quick note to say I'm all on board and just finished the first meal I made here on the boat. This is so awesome!

I decided to stay in port until morning before striking out to open sea. The gentle rocking of the boat is really starting to have an effect on me. I'm getting pretty sleepy, so I think I'll rack out. Tomorrow the real adventure begins. I'm tired, but at the same time all keyed up over the prospect of what I'm actually proposing to do. Meet an alien race? That's crazy! And yet here I am.

Zzzzzzzz.

July 8 – Open sea

I got up this morning and, after getting my things all set, headed out to the open sea. I went past all the recreational sailing vessels and then the cruise ships leaving for the Caribbean. Eventually, the only sound I could hear was the motor. By the way, I made sure there was plenty of fuel on board and will keep a good eye on the fuel consumption, too. I found out all the possible islands along the way where I might be able to put in for some additional fuel, but I plan on making a straight shot to New Galimar and, based on my calculations, I should have plenty.

At this point, I should document the preparations I made to get to the island.

After many conversations with Quorlynn, I found out New Galimar is located smack dab in the middle of the Bermuda

Triangle. In fact, I have a theory sitting the back of my mind that maybe the shield is to blame for ....

I guess I should talk about that shield first. Despite all the abundance of technology and wonderfulness of their race, the Galimarians have a problem with our sun. Their home world is different; for some reason, their sun never produces any UV rays, or maybe their atmosphere doesn't allow any UV rays to get to the ground, but the bottom line is Galimarians aren't able to handle it on their skin. Once they arrived on Earth, they were ill-prepared for how much actually *does* make it to the ground here. When they discovered this problem, they built a machine which shields them from the UV radiation of our sun by creating a bubble around the entire island. The shield sits about 15 miles off the coast on all sides of the island, making it possible to explore the sea life around them. All Galimarians know they need to avoid this shield because it is possible to be harmed by it.

This is the basis of my theory that maybe this shield is actually the cause of a lot of all the Bermuda Triangle lore. Maybe that's what causes planes and boats to not make it, or be knocked off course, or something.

At any rate, one of the things I went over with Quorlynn *in exhaustive detail* was the course I would need to take to get to the island.

Since I am all alone out here, I'm going to set the boat on automatic pilot, put on part of my bikini, and soak up some of those harmful UV rays. LOL.

July 9

Not much to report today. I have been going over the course I'm taking, comparing it to the GPS, and I'm right on the money.

(evening)

After dinner, I decided to visit Quorlynn. I put on the amulet and was instantly transported to my "home away from home."

When I got there, I decided to come clean with Quorlynn about exactly who and what I am. I needed to tell her I'm not a Galimarian, but rather a human. Once I got there, I wan't sure I would be able to maintain the charade with living, breathing Galimarians. They would take one look at me and see, among many other things, that my eyes have color. The proverbial jig would be up.

When I told her I was human, she didn't react at all; she just looked at me. I had forgotten she is actually a computer and not a real person. I thought I had thrown a curve at her that just wasn't in her programming. I was wrong.

It turns out her programming is a lot more complex than I had imagined. During the dozens of times I had visited her, I was the only one to ask questions. I would ask, she would always answer. Not one question was rebuffed, and she was quite open, frank, and honest about anything I wanted to know.

Now, after just staring at me for a bit, she started asking questions herself. She asked how I came to be in possession of an amulet of understanding. I told her all I knew. After doing research on the amulet a couple of weeks after finding it, I discovered the meaning of its tag, "Field Expedition #5894." I initially thought it signified the 5,894th item found on some field expedition. As it turns out, the word "Field" referred to Cyrus Field, the first guy who ran a transatlantic telegraph cable. Sometime during that voyage, they had to do some dredging for a cable that had broken and had fallen down to the ocean floor. When they brought up the cable, this amulet came up with the dredging hook. Apparently, the amulet and its magnetic fields caused the ship to veer off course for a while, nearly costing them the success of the project. The captain had laid it near the compass which was knocked out of whack because of it. I was amused to discover the official record said electricity running through the cable caused the compass to be off, instead of the captain accidentally causing the problem.

After I told Quorlynn that story, she asked me why I didn't tell her who I really was, and why I had masqueraded as a Galimarian. I started to get nervous thinking she was going to stop talking to me or something. I was honest and told her what I did for a living, that I was an archaeologist. She started getting really interested in me, and in humans in general. Keep in mind that up to this point, all Galimarians thought humans were too barbaric to merit any interaction. I explained there are some in our world who still exhibit that tendency, but then I started telling her about all the things the more civilized parts of our world had accomplished. Things such as walking on the moon. Electronics. The internet. Computers. Medical technology. Communications. Philosophy. Science and Physics.

She then explained how normally amulets are in constant communication with the island through a short distance signal, but she had been out of communication with the island for about 700 years. The only signal she had received was a one-way signal from something on the island needing maintenance. Apparently, it had sent out a long range signal strong enough to cover the entire globe. That was the only signal she had heard, and it was received a little over 100 years ago. When she received that signal, she created the beeping I heard when I first came down to the archive.

I thought it was remarkable that Quorlynn seemed like a being conscious and aware of its own existence. I smiled, and in keeping with this new questioning persona, Quorlynn asked me why I was smiling. I looked down, then back up at her, and said it was amazing to me that a computer program could simulate emotions as she does.

That's when she rocked my world and revealed she was actually much more than a computer program. Quorlynn was a computer with memory engrams from her original designer impressed on her circuits. The personality and memories of her designer are part of her programming, so Quorlynn feels emotions and has needs just the same as her flesh and blood counterparts. For all intents and purposes, Quorlynn is alive!

I guess you could say I am no longer alone on this trip. The level of communication existing between Quorlynn and me is on a totally different level now. In a very real way, she and I are becoming really good friends. We spent the balance of my visit with her pretty much talking almost like best friends. She was just as interested in me as I was in her. She had never done this before, but she actually accessed my mind and with my own memories, I showed her what my world was like. *What a rush to* relive some of my own memories.

The last thing she said to me was that she was looking forward to re-establishing communications with the Galimarian population and with her sibling amulets. All I can say is… *wow.*

I did it!

Today was the day I arrived at the place where the shield is. If it had been any old boat, I would no doubt have run into the shield and been smashed into bits. But with Quorlynn's help, I was able to slip through the shield, and now I'm on my way to the island.

As I got nearer to the place where the shield was, I must say I was feeling a little bit of trepidation about getting through it unharmed. Quorlynn assured me it wouldn't be a problem. According to her, the basis of the shield has something to do with magnetism, and the whole reason why the amulet has a magnetic field around it is so that any time it got near to the shield, the field around the amulet would cancel the effect of the shield.

Something I didn't expect was the shield being completely invisible. I guess I was expecting to see some sort of apparition; a wall of some sorts, some discoloration, something. But, nope. Nothing. According to the coordinates I had programmed into my GPS unit, we were there.

I killed my engine and just let my momentum carry me through. One moment I was just a boat on the water with nothing in front of me other than miles and miles of ocean. The next second, I looked up and was suddenly presented with a vista of things I swear weren't there before; most ostensibly, *the island*!

Until Quorlynn explained what was going on, I sat there rather perplexed. She calmed my wonder when she explained that one of the designs of the shield is the ability to project on one side (the outside of the bubble) what is happening on the opposite side. The result is that nothing inside of the shield bubble can be seen at all. Amazing!

I guess today is the day for nerves. I told Quorlynn I was a little apprehensive about meeting her people for the first time. What will they think? Will they run from me? Will they be mad that I came?

She assured me this wouldn't be the case; she cited the fact that Galimarians are an explorer people, and they have been searching out connections with intelligent life on other planets for thousands of years. When they first came to Earth, humans were far too barbaric for their tastes, and at the time they felt that it would take thousands of years for humans to change in any way. Meeting me would be a welcome event in their lives, so by the time we finished talking, I was refreshed and actually looking forward to meeting them.

I should be landing on shore in about an hour. Wish me luck!

July 13

I haven't written in my journal in a couple of days. Mostly because I'm ....

Words fail me. Oh, my god. I'm just so ....

My last journal entry a few days ago ended with me being so excited about meeting the Galimarians for the first time. I wondered what it would be like when I saw them for the first time. I saw them all right. When I got there and entered the city, I discovered them.

Now I understand why Quorlynn hasn't been able to communicate with them. They are all dead. D-E-A-D!

CHAPTER 25

ɔↃↈ˥ⓞↃↃↄ ↄↄↄⓈ ↄ˥ɥ ↄ
↓ʃⓞↄↄↄ

July 14

I CAN'T EVEN BEGIN TO DESCRIBE how horrible I feel. It's not like they're laying all around in the streets; in fact, the causeways on the island are all eerily vacant. I found what amounted to a home with a couple, a husband and wife lying on their bed in the last position they were in before they died. Their bodies had decomposed a long time ago, and they basically were just clothes and bones. I got into this sort of frenzy after that, going from home to home trying to find anything and anyone.

Nothing. Nobody. They were all gone.

After about the sixth or seventh home, I walked out the front door in a daze. I felt, well, that's just it; I didn't feel. I was numb with shock and grief. I didn't know what to think. I don't know how far I walked after that, but eventually I found what looked like a park and sat down.

Looking back on it now, it seems strange how the park appeared to be well manicured, even though everybody was, is dead. I sat on a bench in the middle of the park.

It was completely quiet save for a small breeze that came along every now and then. Suddenly out of nowhere I heard a wail and realized it was coming from the depths of my own soul. Without warning, I suddenly broke down and wept uncontrollably, crying out at the top of my lungs. I yelled to everybody and nobody. All my bright hopes, all my wondrous dreams of actually visiting with an alien race, one as wonderful as this one was, had now been crushed. I was devastated and shattered at the knowledge of being denied something I had unknowingly wanted all my life. For a short time, I felt like I was coming home to meet my real brothers and sisters, only to now discover I was orphaned in the cosmos. From the deepest depths of despondency, I wept. I cried inconsolably for seemingly unending ages. I sometimes settled for a while, then the image of that husband and wife would crash in on my consciousness. I thought about them laying in each other's arms as they mutually drew their last breath and I would start weeping once again. Which one of them witnessed the last breath of the other? What pain did that one feel? In time, all that was in me was spent. My soul was empty. Suddenly, Earth became suffocatingly small.

My thoughts drifted from nothingness to nothingness, until they ultimately settled on my best friend, Quorlynn. I knew I had to tell her about what I had seen, but the prospect of sharing such terrible news with her was terrifying. If I had reacted so badly to this, how much more so would she? She, who was of these people herself. Yet, I knew I had to carry out this grim and despicable task, so I entered into the world of the amulet and soon was standing before my friend.

Before I could say anything, I saw in her eyes that she already knew all I was going to say. Apparently, when we got to the island, she was finally able to re-establish communications with all her "sibling amulets," as she put it. It was then they told her what had happened.

It turns out that sometime in the fourteenth or fifteenth century, a plague had decimated the population of the island. I tried to determine how the plague got started, but the information was uncharacteristically vague. I was able to find out that once the plague started, they set up hospitals all over the island to handle the sick and dying, but it didn't seem to do any good. Eventually, they all died.

Within two months, the plague decimated the population until eventually the last Galimarian died, someone named Khreelon. Ever since then her brothers and sisters only had each other, and they had no hope of ever being reunited with their flesh and blood counterparts. They were all very despondent.

Now having met Quorlynn, they were astounded at the story she told them about me, and about humankind in general.

After talking with Quorlynn for a while, I told her I had to go, and that I would come back soon. I came out of the amulet, and once again ambled around the city for I don't know how long. Eventually, I made it back to my boat, which is where I am now. I'm completely exhausted. I think I'm going to make something to eat, then lay down for a while.

I keep coming back to the same question in my mind. "What do I do now?"

July 15

I woke up this morning when it was still dark outside. With my hands wrapped around a hot mug and a blanket wrapped around my shoulders, I went up on deck and sat facing the east. I watched the irresistible forces of the cosmos graduate night into morning, eventually witnessing the first beams of light make their way over the horizon. Quietly I stared into the distance and soaked in the stimulations to my senses. I tasted the deliciousness of my warm beverage, my ears listened to the insistent song of the ocean lapping against the bow, and my eyes drank in the symphony of light coming from the sun. As I closed my eyes, my hands relaxed and yet held fast to the smooth texture of the coffee mug while my nose twitched at the salty spray of the sea. My senses were acutely aware of my surroundings, and with the advantage of a full night's sleep, my mind was better able to contemplate the events of the previous day.

I thought about how more and more I seemed to identify with these people. More and more, they had become my own brothers and sisters. I felt as if I was a long-lost orphan who had finally found her family, only to discover they had died so long ago. For a moment, I was angry. I was mad at the injustice of what these people had been through to come to this planet, how resilient they were in overcoming such terrible reverses of fate, only to have their lives stolen from them by an unseen microscopic assailant. It wasn't fair! They didn't deserve it. Without the same ferocity as the day before, yet perhaps with a greater concentration of emotion, a lone tear found a troubled path down my cheek.

After a while, I thought about what they had left behind, and about how nobody would ever know just how amazing these people really were. But then I thought, "Wait a minute. I'm here. I know about them. Am I going to let their memory die with me? Am I just going to leave and allow the injustice to continue by remaining silent and mute? Will I dishonor them by allowing their memory to fade into the mire and humiliation of anonymity?"

No! I cannot, *will not,* let that happen!

As I sat there on the deck of my boat, I decided to become their spokesperson. I felt driven to speak for them. These people were now *my* brothers and sisters, *my* mothers and fathers. Would I do anything less for my blood family? No, I had to speak for them so all could know them. I had to make their death mean something. More specifically, I had to make sure their life meant something.

Standing up from my chair on the deck, I realized I was now standing up in more ways than one. I was now Galimarian in my heart, and I was now going to speak for my brothers and sisters. I immediately told Quorlynn of my new conviction. With eyes that spoke a profound sense of gratitude, she placed her right hand on my right shoulder and, closing her eyes, gently bowed her head.

A Galimarian gesture of profound respect and thanks.

July 16

After resolving yesterday to be their spokesperson, and to chronicle all I could, I decided to spend the rest of my time on this island documenting as much as possible. I only have a little over two weeks to know as much as I can about them, and if I am now Galimarian in spirit, then I will live as they live. I will be at one among these people.

Yesterday, I planned for the most profound archaeological expedition of my entire life. While preparing my mind and body for the task at hand, I put together a backpack with all the staples I would need in case I didn't make it back to the boat at all for the next two weeks, although that probably wouldn't be the case. I put on all necessary clothing, packed food and water, and made sure I had fresh batteries for the thousands of pictures and videos I planned on taking.

After leaving the boat with my pack, and as I was walking along, I thought about how I'm now identifying myself as a Galimarian. If I'm a Galimarian now, I need to look and dress the part. I had spent enough time with Quorlynn to know how I should look and dress, so I returned to the original home I went to when I arrived and found outfits the woman had worn when she was alive. Before doing so, I approached their withered bodies and silently paid my respects to their memory. Even though there was nobody to hear me, I explained out loud that I was making it my aim to ensure their deaths are not in vain, and I asked for permission to wear her clothes. I envisioned the woman nodding her head with her hand on my shoulder, showing her agreement and gratitude.

Within no time at all, I looked at myself in the mirror and saw the persona of a beautifully dressed Galimarian woman. When I started trying on the clothes, I wondered if I would find a garment which would fit my tall frame. Being six foot three, I usually had trouble finding the right outfit, but that didn't pose a problem here. Galimarians were tall, and the ensemble I tried on fit me like a glove.

As I looked at myself in the mirror, I wished Quorlynn could see me. The outfit was a beautifully wrapped garment worn over the shoulder, draping down my body and around my torso. At home, I would never have worn this since it was so sheer; all I had underneath could be seen, yet at the same time tastefully obscured. It was obvious the Galimarians didn't have body image issues. Strangely, neither did I. More and more of their thinking was progressively becoming my own.

I spoke to Quorlynn for a bit, telling her of the preparations I had made, including me being dressed as a Galimarian. I said I was sad she couldn't see the real me, and that's when she told me it was possible. She explained how every home had an island access portal that allows communications and complete access to the repositories of Galimarian knowledge. She said if I placed the amulet in a receptacle on top of the portal, she would be able to talk to me and access their version of a camera to see me. I was so excited to do this I couldn't wait; I exited the amulet immediately and searched for the portal.

The Galimarian home I was in was modest by the standards of many. After walking through the front door, there was a seating area which had been beautifully decorated once. Time had claimed its tidiness; there was quite some dust on the furniture. I could see in the front left corner of the living room what looked like a desk. On the top of it was their version of a computer.

As Quorlynn had described, the top of the computer had that cradle, and I saw how the amulet would fit perfectly in its hollow. As soon as I placed it in the cradle, I heard a tone from the amulet, which is something Quorlynn said she would do when I had properly made the connection. The screen below the cradle now lit up. It was caked with 700 years of dust, so I got a cloth to wipe it clean. Within seconds, I saw materializing on the screen the familiar face of my best friend. She had a look of someone seeing something they had never seen before. When I spoke she immediately showed her true self, the one I had come to love as a close friend.

"Hello, my friend," I said to the screen.

"Terri? Is that really you?"

"It's me!"

Quorlynn spent time looking at me without saying a word, and I sat there smiling back at her. I then got up and stood behind the chair I was sitting in, and timidly did a twirl so she could see all of me. I wanted my best friend to know the real me, the true me.

After standing there for a bit, I sat back down and just looked at her. I thought about how, over a relatively short period of time, this woman had both figuratively and literally crawled into my head and become one with me. She was my best friend, and she was my soul sister. I truly loved her as one of my own family.

Apparently, she felt the same way. "Terri, I am overwhelmed to meet you for the first time. I've met you before, but now I am meeting the real you. I have to admit I didn't know what to expect when I saw you for the first time. But, I wasn't prepared for this. You, my sister, are beautiful!"

My heart swelled to hear her say this, she who was so stunning in my opinion.

"Thank you, my friend. I truly appreciate you saying that. I must say, this garment makes me feel beautiful too."

"Well if I can borrow a phrase you've used before, you wear it well. You truly wear it well."

"Thank you. This terminal is an amazing device, allowing you to see me like this."

"There's so much more you haven't seen," replied Quorlynn. "With this terminal, or any other like it on the island, you now have the ability to access the sum total of all knowledge on New Galimar. Every home has a terminal like this one, and with your knowledge of the Galimarian language, you can learn anything you wish."

"Perfect. That is exactly what I wish to do."

"Well, my beautiful student, what do you wish to learn?"

"I was thinking about that. Two days ago, you told me you had talked with your brothers and sisters, and they told you that when the Galimarians died, eventually it all came down to one last individual. What was his name again?"

"His name was Khreelon. Khreelon Tellindor," replied Quorlynn.

"Do you think he would be a good place to start?"

"There couldn't be a better place to start. Khreelon was one of the most respected of Galimarians. He was one of the original Galimarians who came to Eden from our home planet. He was an archivist, and it was his role to record, detail, and authenticate the history of our people, both historical and modern. Learning about him and what he recorded would be the best way to learn about our people."

"Can you show me how to get to his home or his office?"

"Office?"

"I mean, where he did his work."

"Oh yes, of course. He would have done all his work from his home, so that is where we should go."

"Perfect. How do I get there?"

"This should help you," replied Quorlynn enigmatically as she gestured to the left of the screen.

Next to the terminal was a flat surface on top of the desk. This surface was raised up about two inches taller than the rest of the desk. There wasn't anything on top of it other than dust, but then I saw it light up for a moment. Within five seconds, the dust disappeared and a sheet of paper magically appeared out of thin air. Picking up the sheet, I could easily see that it was a map.

"That was impressive!" I said with reverence.

"There is so much still to teach you, my friend."

"I suppose there is. Ok, off I go. I'll bring you up when I get there, okay?"

Quorlynn smiled and dipped her head as I grabbed the amulet out of its cradle. Her image faded from the screen, and I was once again on my own. Gathering up my things and emerging into the sunlight, I immediately struck out for the home of Khreelon.

As I walked along, I knew that even though the sun was out and it was a beautiful day, I could be out in the sun all day with no ill effects. It is a little hard to explain, but the existence of the shield was noticeable, even though there was no difference in the amount or hue of light hitting the ground. As I walked along, I passed the park where I had stopped that fateful day after discovering what had happened so long ago.

As I passed the park, I was startled to see movement. Looking closer, right there all around the park, I was amazed to discover what amounted to robots manicuring the entire area. I remembered how at the time it was strange to me the park looked like it had been taken care of even though there wasn't anybody alive to do so. The sight of the robots explained it perfectly. I passed the park, then backtracked. Remembering that my goal was to document everything, I got out my camera, snapped several pictures, and shot some video as I watched them perform their duties.

Continuing on, I followed the map past several structures that I decided to investigate later. One of them was an office building or skyscraper of some sort. The outside of it appeared to be made of mirrors but didn't seem to have a door anywhere at all. I decided to go near the edifice to see if there was a way I could look through the glass to see what was inside. As soon as I got near the mirrored wall, it *vanished* and became an entryway into the building. Shaking my head back and forth and letting out a sigh, I decided today I couldn't be sidetracked. I realized there would be no way to learn all there was about this place in the two short weeks I had left. I began to feel a bit overwhelmed. As I backed away from the wall, it closed up and once again became a mirrored glass wall.

I passed more and more edifices, each presenting their own mysteries and riddles, each beckoning explanation. By the time I finally reached the home of Khreelon, I was beginning to get a headache over everything I was attempting to cram into my brain.

As with the first home I found, the door immediately opened as I approached and I walked in. I guess Galimarians didn't feel the need for locks on doors in their society. The more I thought about it, why would an amazingly enlightened society need locks? What would they be trying to hide? If privacy was something appropriate, then an enlightened soul wouldn't encroach on that in the first place, would they?

Going into the house, I decided it was appropriate to pay my respects to Khreelon, the inhabitant of this home. I slowly made my way to the bedroom. As was the case with all the other homes I had been in up to this point, I saw laying on the bed the remains of a Galimarian man who had died over 700 years ago. Folding my hands together in front of me, I dipped my head with my eyes closed in quiet respect. I stood there for five minutes before saying, "I thank you for allowing me into your home, Khreelon. With respect, I wish you peace wherever you are."

Backing out of the room, I then went to the computer terminal and placed my amulet in the cradle. Within 10 seconds, the face of my friend appeared on the terminal.

"I see you made it to the home of Khreelon," said Quorlynn. "I thought what you said was a very nice gesture."

"You could see that?!"

"Yes. One of the things available to me is the ability to monitor all activities on the island. I don't see a video like I do now, but I can see the movement of all who are alive on the island. And since you are the only one here, that makes your movements the most interesting set of events available for my siblings and me."

"You mentioned your brothers and sisters before. How many of them are there?" I asked.

"Before the plague, there were approximately 1,200,000 people living here, and each had their own amulet of understanding carrying an individual like myself."

"Are they all named Quorlynn?"

"No." She laughed the laugh of a parent when a child asks an embarrassing question. "Each sibling chooses their own name, the same as each Galimarian chooses their own name when they are given an amulet of understanding. Even though the memory engrams for each amulet start out the same, we have our own set of experiences which mold and shape our personalities. Over time, we become very different and unique from each other. We even take on distinctive visual appearances for ourselves."

Once again I was quite impressed. I suppose I should be used to that.

"So this is the home of Khreelon. Do you have a picture of him?" I asked Quorlynn.

"Yes."

Immediately the screen faded into a picture of an amazing specimen of male attractiveness. This particular image was of a Galimarian man dressed in what I would typically think of as beach attire. The small bathing suit was worn by a body sculpted and chiseled better than I could ever expect.

"Is this the way he looked when he died?" I inquired.

"Yes," said Quorlynn, even though I couldn't actually see her at the moment.

"Did he always dress like that?"

"No. Here is another image of him with more clothes on, if the other makes you uncomfortable."

Blushing, I said, "No. I wouldn't say it made me uncomfortable; I was just wondering."

The next image was of him wearing a different outfit just as beautiful, the perfect complement to his perfect physique. This had the added benefit of showing him in what looked to be a social setting with a few other people. They were enjoying an evening around a fire, and smiling at something just said by one of them. They each had some sort of beverage in their hands, and it looked to be the perfect sort of gathering amongst a set of healthy 30-somethings.

"How old is Khreelon?" I asked. Without thinking it through, I expected to hear he was something like 35.

"In this picture, Khreelon is equivalent to 6,627 trips around your sun."

I was stunned. I stared at the image for a while, and I just couldn't believe he was actually that old. After a few minutes, Quorlynn spoke up. "I see that wasn't the answer you expected."

"I didn't realize you were still able to see me. Uh no, that wasn't what I expected. In my world, our life expectancy is so much shorter. Individuals who look like this are only about 35 years old, and the oldest we ever make it to is around 100 years. To hear Khreelon is that old, with no doubt so much more life ahead of him, is astounding!"

"It is the way of Galimarians. Perhaps we might be able to help you with your own life expectancy."

"Really? Wow, I hadn't thought about that."

"All in good time," Quorlynn answered.

Deciding it was time to get down to the task of learning as much as possible about these people, I determined to press forward.

"So my friend, what did Khreelon have that will allow me to learn about your people?"

Quorlynn began showing me how to access the archives of knowledge Khreelon maintained in his home. I was also told how to access the archives for all of New Galimar. For now, I knew this was all I could handle. I spent the rest of the day here until this moment when I am writing this journal before I go to bed. I have decided to sleep in Khreelon's home, so I cleaned a place for myself on a couch, and that's where I will bed down for the night.

Wow. What a day.

July 17–July 20

Over the last several days I have been learning an incredible amount of history about the Galimarians. They are truly an amazing people. The way they think, the way they work hard, yet search out the most exquisite of life's experiences, is truly inspiring.

When I watched a video of their version of a music concert, I anticipated the music would be good, but I had no idea how good it actually would turn out to be. After thinking about it, though, imagine how good you would get if you have several thousand years to practice your craft, all the while getting better and better at your art. Eventually, your ability would be phenomenal, as was the case with the music artist featured in this particular recording.

The recordings from Khreelon that I watched had a certain "flavor" I came to recognize as his own specific slant on the events he was recording. I noticed that while he was as factual as you would expect from a person in his position, he would sometimes allow his own viewpoint to come through. I wondered if there were any other recordings that didn't necessarily have to do with his official capacity as an archivist, but rather were of just him in general. I wanted to dip below the surface of the facts and really touch the personalities of the individuals. I placed Quorlynn in the cradle and was soon rewarded with her smiling face looking back at me.

"Hello, once again," she said. "How are you today?"

"I'm fine. How …." I started laughing.

"What is so funny?" she asked.

"I was just about to ask you how you slept."

Quorlynn smiled a very bright and wide smile. "As you would probably expect, I don't have the need for sleep. Still, I appreciate the friendly thought behind your question, so I will say, I slept fine."

We both laughed at my oversight and her accommodation.

"Quorlynn, I have been wondering about something."

"What is it you wish to know?"

"I've been learning so much about the history of your people, but I want to go deeper. I want to know more about the individuals themselves. How would you suggest I do that?"

Quorlynn paused for a moment and looked like she was thinking that over. Finally, she replied, "I think the best way to do that would be to view the personal logs of some of the people. Perhaps Khreelon would be a good place to start."

"They have personal logs?"

"Yes. It was a very common practice for each person to keep a personal log."

"So Khreelon kept a diary, huh? Wouldn't that be a private thing he wouldn't want me to read?"

"I'm not familiar with this word 'diary' you've used, but if you are speaking about the personal logs, it is never common practice to hide such things from any who want to read. The basis of an enlightened society is the open and honest exchange of information and knowledge. Enlightenment has taught us the only ones who want to hide things are those who have not attained true peace and harmony with the universe. Honesty and openness are hallmarks of those who are peaceful and peaceable. All in this society live in complete harmony with each other, so there is never anything to hide."

Seeing there no reason to object, I asked Quorlynn to show me how to access Khreelon's personal logs.

This should be interesting.

July 21-July24

For the last three days straight, I have been listening to the personal logs of Khreelon. I have been mixing in the general knowledge recordings he made as an archivist, and more and more I have been looking forward to listening to him talk about what he thinks about this or that.

A side effect of all the listening I've been doing is I'm starting to realize I've been spending all my time indoors, and yet there is a vast city that should be explored as well. Before doing so, I asked Quorlynn what would be the best way to get around in a city this big. She smiled and said she had a surprise for me which would be waiting outside.

Gathering up the amulet and hanging it around my neck, I emerged from the front door of Khreelon's home. As soon as I did, I looked to the left and coming down the causeway that ran in front of his home was what can only be described as a vehicle of sorts. It didn't have wheels, yet moved smoothly over the ground with a graceful hum. When it stopped in front of me, the side door of the vehicle opened; inside there was a bench seat.

I slipped in, and as soon as I did, the door closed behind me. In front of me, was another cradle for my amulet. After placing it the cradle, Quorlynn appeared on the windshield and asked me where I would like to go.

"I'm a little overwhelmed. I don't really know what the possibilities are." Thinking about it, I said, "Tell you what. Let's make today a day where you give me a tour of the city. You decide what you want me to see. What do you say?"

"That sounds delightful!" responded Quorlynn with glee.

The car smoothly started moving forward. Without thinking, I turned around to make sure there wasn't any oncoming traffic, then silently berated myself for acting like a New Yorker here on an island where I'm the only living being. Rolling my eyes, I looked forward again.

Like the most amusing and engaging tour guide, Quorlynn took me on the most amazing tour of the island. New Galimar was subdivided into smaller sections that had their own names like Meropa, Mundi, New Ceres, Bahjah, and another area called Dobrynya. Quorlynn explained that each of these areas had evolved their own culture, their own music, and their foods that reflected such amazing diversity it was impossible to experience it all. I remember at one point when it was getting to be a little after the noon hour, I started to get hungry. I told Quorlynn that in my haste to get out of the house, I neglected to bring anything to eat with me. Believe it or not, she actually apologized, to me. She confessed she doesn't have to think about food at all, but then said she had just the thing she thought I would like. We stopped at the mirror-faced building I had seen about a week ago, the one which had the glass panel which disappeared when I approached it.

She told me to go inside, then find an elevator. She would watch where I was, and instruct the elevator to go where I needed to go. I approached the mirrored wall, and it dissolved again. I entered a beautifully-crafted lobby and proceeded to the lift at the other end of the room. As I approached, the doors opened, and I entered. The doors closed, and I was quickly lifted up. In no time at all, I emerged on the outside of the building, traveling in a glass container along the side of the building until I reached the top floor. I had been in elevators like this in New York, but I must say, I had never been this far up off the ground. Until this moment, I had never experienced buildings this tall. Before it had been attacked, I had been to the restaurant at the top of the World Trade Center, but this ... this was at least two or three times as tall. My breath was taken away as I gazed out over the expanse of the city beneath my feet.

When I arrived at my destination floor, the door opened, and I entered what was a beautiful lounge. As I strode over to the windows on the far side of the room, I saw the incredible vista of the sea beyond the island. To my right was what amounted to a conversation pit, and in the middle of it was a table with, once again, an amulet cradle. I inserted mine, and this time I was rewarded with an amazing holographic representation of Quorlynn hovering above the table.

"I have to say, Quorlynn, these amulets and cradles are pretty handy."

"Indeed. That was one of the hallmarks of convenience in our society."

As I looked at her, I saw her eyes falter, as if there was something taking her attention away for a moment.

"What is it?"

"It's my siblings," she replied, somewhat reluctantly.

"What about them?"

"They," she almost stammered for the first time. "They have been alone for so long and haven't had any interaction with any living person. They want to meet you."

"Run that past me one more time?" I asked, getting excited.

"I have been asked by many of them if they could meet you. They've been without any interaction with an actual living, breathing being for so long, and they desire to do so. When they learned you are human and not Galimarian," she faltered, yet with a smile added, "by birth that is, even more of them were intrigued. I told them I didn't know if you would be open to that, but I promised I would ask."

Her comment intrigued me. "Why did you think I wouldn't be open to that?"

"I know it has been overwhelming and disappointing to discover that all the Galimarians you wished to meet are gone now, and coupled with being so intent learning about the Galimarians from the documents and videos, I thought it might have been too much for you to deal with meeting them."

I could see her point, and it was sweet of her to have this kind of consideration for me. But in reality, I was very excited at this prospect of meeting her brothers and sisters. "I would love to!"

"Really?" she replied. "I didn't want to overwhelm you with too much right away."

"No, I really want to! How can we do it?"

"The easiest way would be for you to enter the amulet. Then I will invite them to come for a visit."

"You can do that?" A dumb question by now.

"Yes, of course. Just come on in."

I immediately picked up the amulet, made the necessary strokes to the screen, and was once again transported into the world of Quorlynn.

Once I got there, Quorlynn walked up to me and said she had a group waiting for me. We walked until we arrived at what was almost an exact replica of some of the structures on the island. We walked into a building that proved to be a massive amphitheater, and guess who was guest speaker?

I was led onto a stage by Quorlynn, and there in front of me were thousands of beautiful and remarkably dressed Galimarians. I was dumbstruck.

As I walked out to the middle of the stage, a panel opened up in the middle of the stage floor and a clear glass lectern ascended. I walked up to it, placed my hands on each side, and looked out over a hushed audience as the faces of thousands of interested Galimarians looked back at me. I thought for a moment about the first thing I should say, and a quote from a book I was recently reading came to mind.

"A great thinker in my world once said, 'The true sign of intelligence is not knowledge, but imagination.' Intelligence is all around me in everything I see here. It is in the way you live, the way you interact with each other and with me, the marvelous technology, and the way this technology seamlessly intermingles with the environment, allowing all of you to live and allowing me to visit you. This speaks to an amazing intellect that is a marvel to behold."

"But beyond this intelligence, I have had a fleeting glimpse into a world that shows this technology is one where the good of society, and the way such technology is used, is only limited by the imagination. From what I've seen, this imagination seems boundless. Take yourselves for instance. While it is true that you are the embodiment of technology, still I see how you are much more than the sum of your circuits and algorithms. You are living. You are sentient. You love, you explore, and you question. You are self-aware. Something another great thinker from my world once said is, 'I was like a boy playing on the sea-shore, and diverting myself now and then finding a smoother pebble or a prettier shell than ordinary, whilst the great ocean of truth lay all undiscovered before me.' You are a great ocean of truth that I hope to learn from and bring honor to your society.

"It is evident that a hallmark of this world, and the people who created it, was not just intelligence in unlocking the secrets of the universe, but rather the ability to create such an amazing architecture of society based on an incredible amount of imagination. I stand before you as an individual who is awestruck at what the people of Galimar have created! Yet at the same time, I also stand before you a person incredibly sad at the events leading up to today. May I express my sorrow and my condolences over the heartache you all have experienced. It is my sincere hope that you find peace in the lives you lead from now on."

At this point I said, "Are there any questions you would like to ask me?"

As if they had all rehearsed ahead of time who would speak in turn, one in the front row stood up and said, "My name is Minleigh and I am of the siblings of Meropa. We would like to ask you to tell us about where you come from, and what your life is like there."

Beginning with that question, I told them all about New York, how many people are there. I didn't hold anything back either. I told them all the good things and all the bad things. I did this because I have learned that keeping things secret is a form of deception, a form of lying. I wouldn't want anybody to lie to me, so I wouldn't want them to feel they had been deceived in any way.

I also made sure to explain all the good things in human society. I described notable people of virtue who simply want to do good to each other in life. I explained this was the way I was raised, by hardworking parents who instilled in me values centered around respect for my fellow man.

The questions continued, and touched on things I didn't really know much about. The personality of each of the brothers and sisters closely mirrored the personalities of the Galimarian who wore their respective amulet. Some of the questions centered around the technology of humans (a subject I am woefully under-qualified to discuss), to botany, biology, and our history. I was a little more prepared to answer that last one, having been trained as an archaeologist.

Eventually, the questions slowed down. "I have a question for you now," I said. "I have been spending a lot of time reviewing the personal logs of, and the histories chronicled by, an archivist named Khreelon Tellindor. Is there a brother or sister here who was his companion?"

With one accord, all heads turned toward a location about three-quarters up the audience to the right. One lone sister stood and said, "My name is Loranna, and I was Khreelon's companion."

"Loranna, if you don't mind, I would like to talk to you personally when this meeting concludes."

"As you wish." From this distance, I couldn't quite see her face, but the tone of her voice seemed friendly.

About this time, Quorlynn appeared next to me and spoke up. "My brothers and sisters, this concludes our visit with Terri for today. If there are any further questions for her, or if you wish to have a personal audience, please contact me in the usual manner. Thank you."

All stood. Each and every one of them stretched their arms up and away from their bodies. Reaching above their heads they put their palms together and, while keeping them together, brought their hands down over their hearts, while bowing their heads with eyes closed. Once they completed this maneuver, they spontaneously erupted in applause, all directed toward me.

Quorlynn and I retreated from the stage and went outside to talk. I told her that the experience was far from draining, and I thanked her for bringing me there. I saw her eyes falter for a moment, then she looked at me and said, "Loranna is asking if you would like to talk to her now."

"Yes, I would like that very much."

With a slight nod, Quorlynn raised her wrist in an open-palmed gesture to look behind me, and that's when I heard a voice say, "Hello Terri. I'm Loranna."

I think in the outside world, I would have been deeply startled, but in here I seem to be better at handling surprises. Perhaps I was on "surprise overload" or something. I turned around and came face to face with a very tall representation of my friend Lynne. Now this was something which took me aback. I definitely hadn't expected to see her here.

"Lynne?" I asked.

"No, Terri. I am Loranna. Quorlynn shared some of the images you have shown her, and I thought it might be easier to talk to me if you were talking to someone you already knew. Does it upset you?"

"No, it doesn't upset me at all." But after thinking about it a little, I said, "Actually, my goal in being on the island is to learn as much as possible about Galimarians. I would like to see you as you normally present yourself, not as my earth friend, if that's okay?"

Quorlynn spoke up, saying, "I told you so."

Loranna smiled at her sister as if she had just lost a bet, and in an instant her façade changed from that of Lynne to a face I had never seen before. As with Quorlynn, Loranna was beautiful, with delicate features which were the embodiment of feminine power.

"I hope this is more to your liking," said Loranna.

"So long as this is the real you, then it is definitely to my liking."

"I'm glad to hear that! What can I do for you, Terri?"

"As I said in the discussion, I have been spending a lot of time learning about Galimarians by studying the writings of Khreelon. I have also been studying his personal logs, both written and video. I was wondering what you could tell me about him that isn't on those recordings."

"Khreelon was an amazing person. It has been my privilege to be part of his life ever since he attained the age of enlightenment. For over 6,000 years, I have watched him grow from an adolescent, to an adult, to a respected member of Galimarian society. I have seen him hone his skills; no one has his ability to capture the essence of the scene unfolding before him. He is quite well-adapted to the field he has chosen."

I nodded. "I would have to agree with you on that. I have been enjoying his recordings very much, but I want to know something else. It seems that while he is rather amazing in his field of study, I can also sense he is ... how can I put this delicately?"

She let me think for a while to come up with the right word. The three of us walked among some shade trees outside of the amphitheater complex where I had just spoken. We were engaged in a relaxed stroll, finally coming to a set of benches where we all sat down. She continued allowing my thoughts to proceed unabated.

"I can also sense he is, somehow, lonely."

Loranna gave a slight grin, then turned her gaze down to the ground. "You are very discerning, since I know for a fact he took great pains to never actually discuss that in his writings and recordings. He and I talked about it extensively, but he never wanted to reveal this in his logs. He always said that while he very much wanted a mate to spend his life with, one he could treat with the utmost honor, respect, and love, he wanted his mate to reveal herself to him."

With a look I couldn't quite interpret, Loranna said, "Interesting."

"What's interesting?" asked Quorlynn.

"On several occasions, he told me the perfect one for him would see, through all his writings, what his desires were and one day reveal herself to him. You, Terri, are the only one who has been able to break through the surface of what he wrote and see the real Khreelon. He is a loving, gentle, kind, phenomenal person."

Her face then took on a pained look. It was evident she realized her error. "That is, he *was* loving, gentle, and kind. It pains me to meet you under these circumstances when he is no longer here."

I put my right hand on her right shoulder, closed my eyes, and dipped my head. I wanted her to understand I appreciated her letting me know what she did, even though it brought her pain.

"Thank you, Loranna. Thank you for giving me this glimpse into the life of remarkable member of your world."

"Of course, Terri. If there is anything else you would like to know, please do not hesitate to ask. Quorlynn will know how to contact me."

"Thank you, Loranna. My love and respect go with you."

"And mine with you, Terri."

She quickly faded and only Quorlynn and I remained. Looking over to her I asked, "What time is it in the outside world? It seems like I've been here for hours."

"You have," she responded. "According to the way you represent time in your world, it is approximately 2:30 a.m."

"I should leave and get some food and some more conventional sleep, then hit it again in the morning, if that's all right with you."

"What are you going to hit?" asked Quorlynn, with a worried look on her face.

Laughing, I responded, "Don't worry, that's just an expression in my world meaning I am going to hit the hay, do a face plant, ride the good ship Z. All just colloquialisms that essentially mean I am going to go to sleep."

With a relieved look on her face, she said, "That's good to hear and, to answer your earlier question, of course it is fine with me. I look forward to your return."

With that, I glided my finger across my amulet and was instantly returned to the real world, where I could tell it was the middle of the night. After making my way back to Khreelon's dwelling, I bedded down, but not before writing this journal entry. I wanted to write all this down before I forgot any of it.

I thought about Khreelon. It figures; my soulmate is an alien with a perfect body and the perfect attitude of how to treat a woman, but one who's been dead for 700 years." Rolling my eyes, I drifted off to dreams of my perfect man.

July 25

This morning, as I was taking care of hygiene and food needs before starting my day (did I mention they have showers just like at home?), I thought about Khreelon and how he seemed to be what I have always looked for in a man. Visually he is very attractive, but I've been around the block enough times to know beauty is really only skin deep. As far as I'm concerned, I don't care what the guy looks like if he treats me right. If he demonstrates his whole world revolves around me and I'm all that matters to him when we are together, then he's my definition of the perfect man. Like last night, this earned another sigh.

As I finished getting ready, I decided to alter slightly how I finish out the rest of my time on the island. Emerging from the back rooms, I came to Khreelon's desk and placed my amulet into the cradle. As I waited for Quorlynn's face to appear, I reached down to my pack on the floor where I had some protein bars stored.

"Good morning Ter .... Where'd you go?" Quorlynn asked, when all she could see was what appeared to be an empty chair.

I straightened up and suddenly appeared in the chair. "I'm here," I said, smiling.

"There you are. How are you? Did you sleep well?"

"I did, thank you. And how did you sleep?"

"I slept fine, thank you." We both laughed.

"You know," Quorlynn continued, "I have to say one thing about you, Terri. If I didn't know better, I'd say you were truly Galimarian with the way you approach life. Perhaps that is why I didn't ever suspect you weren't Galimarian at the beginning."

"What do you mean by my 'approach to life'?"

"A hallmark of enlightened societies is the ability to live, love, and laugh. These are traits you have in abundance, my friend, and I think that is why you and I have become such fast friends. I didn't *have* to love you as my friend and sister, but in your case, I simply didn't have a choice. Your personality has always been irresistible; I am blessed to have you in my life."

I was quite taken back. "Wait a minute. Here you are, an enlightened soul, telling me *you* are blessed to have *me* in *your* life? Are you kidding me? I am blessed to have you in my life!"

"Thank you, Terri. I guess we now have the beginnings of a very exclusive mutual admiration society."

We laughed at this, the normal way of our interactions these days. "Quorlynn, talking with you feels so natural. It's almost like you have always been in my head and in my heart. I never knew you existed until I put on the amulet, but now I can't imagine not having you in my life."

"I know what you mean. This isn't the first time this has been the case. I have had many conversations with my brothers and sisters about this, and the general opinion is that our original creator, the designer of the amulets, put something in the programming which causes us to be identified with our companions. It's almost as if the amulet reads the memory engrams of the wearer and shapes our personality to perfectly match the personality of the wearer. If that is true, then this is even more advanced than most other technologies known by me."

I shook my head. "Amazing." Quorlynn nodded her head.

After a few moments had passed, I told Quorlynn my idea. "When I was getting ready this morning, I thought about proposing a slight change in the way I approach my knowledge quest."

"How is that?"

"Instead of sequestering myself inside for days at a time, I should split up my time between studying the written records and actually touring around the city. I need to rely on you to show me as much as possible. How does that sound?"

"That sounds ideal," replied Quorlynn. "What would you like to do first?"

"I'd like you to show me some pictures of Khreelon."

Quorlynn looked at me with a cheeky smile.

July 26-31

I realize I haven't written in my log in quite some time. Over the last several days, I've been taking thousands of pictures and videos as I venture deeper and deeper into the world of New Galimar, but I've been so intent on experiencing as much as possible, I've neglected writing in this chronicle. I gotta stop doing that!

After spending time this morning learning about New Galimar's governmental structure and how it was modeled on the structure of government on Galimar, I asked Quorlynn to take me to its main seat, the meeting chambers for the Grand Council of New Galimar.

As we were traveling, the car was silent for a while until Quorlynn broke the silence. "I'd like to ask you a question. Would that be all right?"

"Of course, Quorlynn. You know you don't need to ask."

After a few moments, she continued. "After yesterday, I seem to get the impression your interest in Khreelon goes beyond a professional curiosity."

"Boy, you don't beat around the bush, do you?"

"Which bush are you talking about? There aren't any plants in our vicinity that qualify as a bush, and I don't know what you mean by beat ...."

"*Stop!*" I said, laughing. "That's just another one of those expressions. You're going to have to get used to my using a lot of them. The expression 'beating around the bush' means using evasive questions that don't touch on the real information being sought."

"I see. No, I'm not one to beat the bush," she replied.

"Beat *around* the bush," I corrected her.

"Sorry. Not one to beat *around* the bush," she conceded.

"To answer your question, I suppose you are right about my interest in Khreelon. Is it that obvious?"

Quorlynn smiled. "Yes, Terri. It's very obvious to me. Do you think you are falling in love with him?"

I shifted uncomfortably in my seat. "Honestly, that thought hadn't hit me in so many words. I mean," I stammered for a moment. "I guess I'd have to admit a part of me deep down is falling for him."

The car became silent. Quorlynn sensed I needed to be alone with my thoughts at the moment, and she was right. Now that the subject had been brought out in the open, I could easily see, over the last several days, I've been falling deeper and deeper in love with Khreelon. Separated by 700 years of history, I was the quintessential bird falling in love with a fish.

"Unrequited love. Seems like my lot in life."

"Knowing you as I do, Terri, I somehow don't think that will be permanent."

"Thank you, my friend. Somehow the realization that I'm in love with the perfect man of my dreams, and I'll never be able to meet him, is quite depressing actually."

The thoughts were now floating freely around in the vehicle, and I sat quietly as we sped along to our destination. I suppose that is the hallmark of a good friendship. Quorlynn didn't feel the need to break the silence as I wrestled with my own menagerie of, what was it? Grief over the death of my one true love? It's silly but, believe it or not, that's exactly how I felt. And over a guy I had technically never met? Like I said, silly; but there it is.

Honestly, I don't really remember much else that happened that day.

August 1

I got up this morning feeling sluggish. I took my customary shower thinking that it would make me feel better, but my pain wasn't on the outside. It was in my heart, and the only thing I could think of was to *not* deal with it. I got ready, ate, got my notes together, and placed Quorlynn in the cradle so we could talk about the activities for the day. I tried my best to put on a brave face for the day, knowing full well that inside me, it felt like the death of my soul.

After seeing Quorlynn's face on the screen, I did my best to face the day with bravery. Knowing my time on the island was winding down, I sat in Khreelon's living room discussing the best use of it with her.

There was a lull in the conversation. "Terri, I'd like to make a request of you."

"What can I do for you, my friend?" It felt funny saying that to Quorlynn, since I was always the one asking her for things, and that was her standard response.

"I'd like you to come visit me in the amulet. I have someone who would like to talk to you."

"Ok. I'll be right there."

I reached up and grabbed the amulet out of the cradle; when I did, Quorlynn's face disappeared from the screen. I stood up and straightened my clothes as if I was just about to see her in this state, which was silly, and then sat down on the couch getting comfortable. I entered the necessary keystrokes on the amulet and, with the same spectacular light show, I was transported to the amazing world of Quorlynn. She approached me and, as has been the custom between us in the last several days, we embraced each other in a greeting hug. After leading me to a bench, she sat with her elbows on her knees, one hand holding the other. Looking intently in my eyes, she chose her words carefully.

"Terri, during your entire time here, I have always been impressed with you. You have been remarkably single-minded in your resolve to learn all you could about the Galimarians. I have to admit, it has been rather flattering for all my siblings and me along the way. Your tenacity in how you approach your work has been unwavering."

Something in me knew what was coming next.

"That is, until yesterday."

There it was. I had tried to put on a brave face yesterday afternoon, but knew I had failed miserably. I wasn't focused at all, which was obvious to Quorlynn.

"Terri, when we parted yesterday, I reviewed recordings of our interactions that day, and it appears your perspective took a definite downturn when I asked how you felt about Khreelon. Am I right?"

I dipped my head down. "Yes. As always, you are right. Yesterday, when we parted, I had to come to terms with my feelings. I was dealing with what amounted to nothing less than terrible grief over the death of my perfect life mate. I know it's crazy, but the more I've learned about Khreelon, the more I've completely fallen in love with him. And now, the realization that this person who was so perfect for me is someone I'll never meet is so overwhelming. I wish I could have just one moment with him, to show him what I feel in my heart."

Quorlynn reached her hand out and picked up my chin so she could see my eyes, which no doubt appeared as red, puffy, and moist as they could in the perfect world of the amulet.

"My dearest Terri, you are such a tender and loving soul. I'm completely certain it wouldn't take Khreelon more than 30 seconds to figure out you are the one he's waited for, for so long."

"I wish I could know for sure!"

"There is no way to hear it from his own mouth, but I think you can benefit from the next best thing."

"How?"

Quorlynn's eyes shifted to the right and, as I followed her gaze, my eyes landed on Loranna, Khreelon's companion. With the grace I have come to expect from all Galimarians, and with a smile on her face, she came over and sat next to me. I was instantly drawn to her.

"Oh, Loranna!" With more tears in my eyes, I reached out to her, and we embraced. I don't know how Quorlynn knew, but somehow she recognized I needed to have some sort of connection to Khreelon, and Loranna was it. I cried like a baby on her shoulder, wetting it with my copious tears.

"My dearest Terri," she whispered in my ear. "Last night after you and Quorlynn parted, she contacted me and relayed her conversation with you, and how concerned she was. She said you seemed distant and disconnected, and she thought a lot of it had to do with your feelings for Khreelon."

I grasped Loranna's hands in an attempt to not let loose of my surrogate connection to Khreelon. "It's true. It wasn't until my wonderful friend here caused me to face my own feelings that I realized I have fallen head over heels in love with a man who I'll never meet. I'll never be able to feel his touch, or even hear whether he could possibly feel the same way for me. I've just felt so awful since then."

"My dear, there is nobody on this island, flesh and blood or virtual, who spent more time with Khreelon than I did. Think about it. I had the opportunity to know him and his thoughts for over 6,000 years."

"I know, and there is a part of me that is slightly jealous of you."

"You needn't be. Not only can I tell you what he's told me, but remember: my personality is actually shaped by the personality of my companion Khreelon. Since this is true, I can tell you without a shadow of a doubt there has never existed any flesh and blood Galimarian who was a better match for Khreelon than you, Terri. As you have spent your time here on the island, I have watched you closely. I have listened to your conversations with Quorlynn, and I have read your logs and your musings of how you and Khreelon are soulmates. I am here to tell you, Terri, I agree with you. Without reservation, I can assure you that you *are* Khreelon's soulmate You are the one he waited for."

Hearing this, I didn't know how to react. On the one hand, here was someone who had the unique ability to tell me exactly how Khreelon would think, and this person was telling me I am his perfect match. But on the other hand, I was dying inside under the crushing weight of the truth that I would never meet him. I was the happiest of happy and the saddest of sad at the very same time; my fantasy of happiness was laced with the poison of reality.

I replied honestly. "I don't know how to react. I am happy you feel that way, but I know I will never hear his own words to me."

"Don't be so sure," Loranna replied, with a glee seemingly misplaced in this setting.

"Why would you say that?"

She explained that eventually, after looking for so long and not finding the right one for himself, he asked Loranna to look for his best match, since it was too painful to have his hopes dashed time and time again. She said in all of her looking, she never found the perfect one for him, one who would see the real Khreelon underneath all he wrote. "I waited patiently, but that perfect 'soulmate' never came. When that terrible day came 700 years ago, I was resigned that I had failed in fulfilling his request. Whereas others had someone to spend their last hours with, Khreelon had nobody. This made me exquisitely sad."

I dipped my head at hearing the loneliness he experienced at the end.

"Terri," Loranna continued. I looked her in the eyes again.

"Long before he got sick, I asked him to chronicle what he would say to the one I might find to be his perfect mate, to write down what he would say to her on the day of their ceremony of union. He did that, Terri, only he did it as a manuscript so it would only be read by his mate and no one else. Not even I know what it says because there is no record in our archives of what he wrote. He even made me swear I would not reveal its existence to anybody except the individual I might find who is his one true love.

"Through the ages, I never found one single soul qualified to read that until now, Terri. I want you to have that manuscript from Khreelon. From your soulmate." Then she gave me instructions to follow once I exited the amulet and returned to Khreelon's home.

Anxious to see this manuscript, I hugged and thanked Loranna and Quorlynn for their friendship and, promising to be back soon, quickly exited from the amulet. I stood up and went to the one room in the house I always avoided, the bedroom where Khreelon's body lay. I stared at it for a few moments, gathering the courage to go on.

To the left of Khreelon and above his head, there was a square-shaped panel on the wall, about one foot on all sides. As with other similar panels in the room, it emitted light whenever I entered. Following Loranna's instructions, I touched all four corners of the panel and, when I did, it swung open, revealing a manuscript inside, rolled up and tied with a red ribbon.

With trembling fingers, I grasped the 700-year-old document, then retreated into the living room to read it. Sitting down, I carefully untied the ribbon and unrolled the manuscript. The first line made me catch my breath.

ꞁ✓ ꙮꞓ ꝰ✓ꝮꙮꙮꝒ ꞁꙮꞥ,

Ꝺ¥ꙮꝒ ꙮ✓ꞁꝒꝒꝒ ꝮꝰꝮꙮꝒ ꙮꙮ ꞁ✓
ꝹꞁꝒꞁꙮ ꞁ¥Ꝯꝰ, Ꝓ ꝮꝒ✓ꕇ ꞁ¥ꝮꝒ
Ꝓꞁ ꝹꝮꝰ ¥ꙮꝒ ꝹꝒꞓ ✓ꞁ ¥ꙮꙮꝒꝒꝒꞓ
ꙮꙮ ꝮꙮꙮꝒ ꝒꙮꝮꙮꝒ ꝒꝒ ꙮꞓ ¥ꝮꙮꝒ ꞁꞁ
ꝰ✓ꙮꝒ¥ ꝒꝒꞓ ꞁ¥ꝒꝒ Ꝓ ¥ꝒꝒ Ꝓꙮꙮ
ꝩꝮꝒ ꙮꝮꝰꝒꝒ Ꝯꝰ¥✓ꝰꝒ ✓ꝰ ꝰꝮꝒꝒꝒ
Ꝓ ꝮꝒ ꝮꝒꞓ, ꞁ¥ꝒꝒ ✓ꝰ ꝮꝒ ꝮꝒꞓ
ꞁ¥ꙮ ꙮꞁꝒ ꞁꝮ ꝰꝮ✓Ꝓ✓ ✓ꝰ ꙮꞓ
ꙮꝒꝒ❖ Ꝓꞁ ꞁ¥Ꝯ✓ꝰ❑ꝒꝒꞁ ✓ꝰ

227

To my soulmate,

When Loranna asked me to write this, I know it was her way of helping me keep alive in my heart something I had all but given up hope of ever finding, the one true love of my life. For thousands of years, I have searched for someone who was the perfect match for me, and Loranna has witnessed my disappointment time and time again.

But now, by the fact that you are reading this, it would appear her optimism was well founded and she has succeeded where I had failed for so long. Do you have any idea how long I have waited for you? Do you have any idea how glad I am Loranna found you? I have always known I had so much to give to you, but I didn't know where you were. Millions of years wouldn't be enough time to express the depth of affection I have for you or my happiness that my search is finally over.

Please know this. Now that you have been found, you will always live in my heart. From now on, I will no longer be its owner, because from this point forward my heart will be beating in your body.

I vow to adore you, protect you, honor you, and most of all, love you for the rest of my days. Even beyond my days, please know in some way I am certain our love will live on forever.

Please know that even if we are ever separated by time, space, or circumstance, we will be together once again. There will be nothing and no one who will ever keep us apart permanently. Your loving soulmate,

Khreelon

By the time I finished reading his letter to me, I was a complete mess. With Loranna's input, I knew in my soul this letter was meant for me. It spoke from the heart and contained the words of a person who thought and felt as I always have.

Once again, it was a very strange set of simultaneous feelings. I felt both an overwhelming sense of happiness and an irresistible and overpowering sense of sadness. I was pleased I now had this piece of Khreelon which was uniquely my own and no one else's; at the same time, I felt cheated that I had no way of expressing my love back to him.

When I came to this island, I had absolutely no idea I would be affected as deeply as I have. I thought this was going to be more of an intellectual experience, learning about the Galimarian people. In my mind, I envisioned a society largely the same as I had come to know through the virtual experiences Quorlynn shared with me when I sat at her feet as a student all those nights in the museum's archive. The difference between what I expected and the reality couldn't have been more profound. My mind was stimulated, but my emotions have received an unexpectedly workout. Most nights I go to sleep exhausted.

That isn't a complaint, though. Aside from the incredible friend-ships I have with Quorlynn and Loranna, I've now had the opportunity to find the one who is, or rather was, the love of my life. What does my own future hold for me now that I have, in a sense, met Khreelon? I'm not sure, but in some strange way I must admit that while I'm sad I cannot be held in the arms of my love, a part of me has found a small sense of peace knowing there actually was someone who was perfect for me; that it was possible *someone* would be perfect for me. I'm not sure if that would make sense to anybody reading this log in the future.

As I think about it more, I'm gratified at becoming a better person because of my experiences. I came here thinking my visit would turn out so much differently than it did. On the whole, it has made me a better woman; more confident, self-possessed, and self-assured. For that, I thank the Galimarians. For as long as I live, I will never forget my Galimarian brothers and sisters, but especially will I never forget my one true love, my Khreelon.

It occurs to me that the mark of an amazing culture, long after it has ceased to exist, is its continuing ability to change the lives of people.

CHAPTER 26

August 2

"Good morning, Quorlynn. How are you this fine and lovely morning?"

I could tell she was a little taken back by my bright and cheery disposition, especially considering my demeanor the last time she saw me.

"I am fine, my friend. I am happy to see you in such good spirits today. The last time we spoke, you were certainly not this cheery."

"I know. Last night, after I read Khreelon's letter to me, I was very upset. His letter was beautiful, and it really reaffirmed just how special he was. In fact, is Loranna available?"

Quorlynn's face faded, and Loranna's face came onto the screen. "Yes I am, Terri. I figured you would want to talk some more this morning, so I asked Quorlynn if I could be here when you awoke."

"Good. I am glad you are here. My sisters, I would like to read the letter to me from Khreelon. Would that be all right?"

"If that is something you would like to share, then I would certainly like to know what he had to say to you," replied Loranna. "Quorlynn agrees."

I got out the parchment his letter was written on, and read it to the two of them.

Looking up at them now, I could see that half the screen was Loranna, and the other half was Quorlynn. "After reading his letter to me, I was considerably distraught, but the more I thought about it, I came to grips with the fact that while he isn't here, he will always live in my heart. I know if he were here, I would be the one and only special person who would make his life whole, and for that I am grateful."

"Even though the life we would have had was stolen from us without us even knowing it was taken, I can feel his love for me by the words he wrote. In an odd way, I have come to a sort of peaceful co-existence with my life and my love for him. Will I ever meet someone else and enter into a union with that one? I can't really say. If I were forced to make a decision right now, then my answer would be no. Then again, after spending so much time with him vicariously through his recordings and personal logs, coupled with the way I know I would want things if the circumstances were reversed, I can say for sure he wouldn't want me to remain unhappy and lonely for the rest of my life. Ultimately, all I can say for sure right now is that I can't say anything for sure. Regarding my future, I don't know what I don't know. I'll just have to wait and see."

"That makes complete sense, Terri," said Loranna.

"I agree with Loranna," added Quorlynn. "In the short time I have known you, I've seen you grow from a timid person working in the dark recesses of the museum archive, to a commanding woman of power who realizes her own future is there for the taking. I am proud of you for all you have done and the conclusions you have come to."

"Don't get too used to it, Quorlynn. I may be acting decisively now, but I am also realistic enough to know there will be times I'll rely on you to prop me up when I am feeling the sting of being lonely without the arms of my Khreelon."

I could see Loranna smile at my use of the term "my Khreelon."

"That would only be normal, my friend. But for now, again I say I am proud of you."

After a few more moments, Loranna said, "I am going to leave you two to your research. If there is anything else you need from me, Terri, please call on me. Also, please don't forget to say goodbye before you leave the island, okay?"

"Without question, I will say goodbye before I leave. Thank you, my friend, for all you have done. I will *never* forget you."

"Neither will I, Terri. Neither will I."

August 3

I was lying in bed (or rather, lying in "couch" if you want to split hairs) when I heard it for the first time. I was sleeping so soundly I didn't really register what I was hearing. It was early morning when the light of the sky was about to change into the baby blue hues that herald a clear and beautiful day.

Beep.

If I were a computer, I would say I wasn't fully booted yet. My thinking ability wasn't completely up and running. I heard it, yet I simply thought, "Boy, I hope I don't hear that again. I'm so comfortable and ...."

Beep.

I just wish it would *stop*. I want to go back to that dream I was having of Khreelon and me walking along the beach, feeling the sand between our toes. He was holding my hand, and it felt so solid, so warm, so comforting. I felt so safe and secure. His voice was soothing and pleasurable when he told me he loved me and now that we'd completed our ceremony of union, he wanted to ...."

Beep.

"*Dammit*! What is that noise?" I said to myself.

I took a deep breath, taking care not to move any part of my body that wasn't absolutely necessary. I just wanted to sleep, and was downright angry at being awakened from my deep slumber. I was so mad to hear the same stupid beeping I heard in the archive when I found the ....

I shot up from the couch. Oh my god! The amulet. Quorlynn!

I fumbled around in the dark until I found a light and was able to see where I laid the amulet. I quickly stumbled to the desk so I could place it in the cradle. Within 10 seconds, Quorlynn's face came onto the screen.

"Quorlynn, are you sending that signal to me?"

Quorlynn gave me a look I felt more than saw. By this time, I was able to read her like a book and, even though she had a smile on her face, it depicted a deep sense of worry I had never seen before.

"My friend, what's wrong?" I asked more insistently.

"Thank you for waking up so early in your day for me. I'm sorry to have awakened you."

"That's okay, my friend. What's going on?"

"Do you remember me telling you why I caused the beeping originally?"

"Yes, I do. You said that while you hadn't been able to be in communication with the rest of your siblings until you got near to the island, you also said something on the island sent out a planet-wide signal, causing you to send that beeping."

"That is correct. To be honest, I hadn't thought about it since then. By the time we arrived at the island, I was more interested in guiding you with your learning about the Galimarian people than thinking about the original reason why that signal was sent."

"What does that have to do with it now?"

"I have just received that same signal again, and it came with a warning that it is most urgent I respond."

"What do you need me to do?"

"According to the information that came with the signal, we need to go to the GSC and visit the Tectonic Stabilization Machine."

"What is the GSC?"

"I'm sorry to do this, Terri, but can you get ready to take a trip there? I'll explain along the way."

"No problem, Quorlynn. Give me about 10 minutes to get myself together."

"Very good. I will order a transport to meet you out front."

Before I knew it, I was sitting in the car being taken along for a ride while talking with Quorlynn. I told her I recognized the word tectonic; it had something to do with the earth's crust and the plates of land on its surface. She confirmed my understanding and said the TSM was one of the few devices which had its very own companion. That companion was responsible for sending the planet-wide signal to all amulets back in the early 1900s.

We finally reached the building Quorlynn referred to as the GSC, or the Geologic Services Center. Unlike the earlier skyscraper I had been in, this building was much shorter, around five stories tall. I commented on the difference, and she assured me this building was just as impressive as the other. This particular building has most of its operations, dozens of floors, all below ground. Thinking about it, it makes sense that this building, which supports something having to do with tectonics, would be oriented down and not up. I wondered how that reconciles with this being a floating island on the sea, but before I had the chance to ask, the front door to the building opened and I was greeted with what looked to be a state-of-the-art establishment. Quorlynn had arranged to have a series of screens on the wall show guides directing me to the place where the machine was, so I followed all of her promptings.

I went a floor about 300 stories below the surface of the island. Exiting from the elevator, I stepped into a large chamber containing what appeared to be a very huge, very complicated machine in the middle of the room. It was easily 15 meters tall, and there were pipes, tubes, and cables of all kinds leading to and from it. It was making a rather loud noise that sounded like an alarm.

To the side, I saw what looked like a control station and, as I approached it, I noticed the customary amulet cradle situated above the screen.

After inserting Quorlynn into the cradle, I was once again shown her face.

"OK. I'm here. What now?"

"One moment, Terri. I am summoning the sister in charge. Ah, here she is."

Quorlynn and a new face were now displayed on the screen. Quorlynn was the first to speak.

"Khaeleus?"

"Yes, Quorlynn. I'm here."

"We received your signal. What's going on?"

"First things first. Who am I speaking to outside?" asked Khaeleus.

"Oh, forgive me. This is Terri. She is my companion."

"Hello, Terri. My name is Khaeleus. I am the administrator of the TSM."

"I am pleased to meet you, Khaeleus."

"Why did it take so long for someone to respond? I've been sending multiple signals for years!"

"You mean," Quorlynn paused. "I forgot you're not connected to the rest of our siblings on the island, are you?"

"No. That's part of the global security system. I'm to remain isolated from all others so as to stay focused on the task at hand."

"Then you don't know what happened, do you? To the population of New Galimar?" asked Quorlynn.

"No. What happened?"

Quorlynn then gave Khaeleus a complete dissertation on the events of 700 years ago. She told about the plague, and how it had killed every man, woman, and child on the island. She described how she received the original signal 100 years ago, but it wasn't until a couple of months ago that I found the amulet, put it on, and we began our odyssey.

"You mean Terri isn't Galimarian?" asked Khaeleus.

I opened my mouth to answer, but Quorlynn cut me off interjecting, "She is as Galimarian as is necessary. I will fill you in with more detail later but suffice to say, she is just as Galimarian as you, me, or any other inhabitant who ever lived on the island. I trust her with my very existence, and I can't imagine ever being a companion to anyone else."

Khaeleus contemplated what Quorlynn said for a few seconds. "If she's Galimarian in your eyes, then that is good enough for me."

"Back to my original question," said Quorlynn. "What's going on? Your signal carried with it an indication the status is grave."

"That would be an understatement. What do you know about the TSM?"

"Very little I must confess," said Quorlynn. "All I know is it's supposed to stabilize things, but not much more."

"Let's start with the basics of the science of plate tectonics. There is something called the lithosphere, the rigid outermost shell of land surrounding the entire surface of this planet. It is the crust, the upper mantle of Eden, and it is broken up into smaller sections called tectonic plates. Eden's lithosphere is composed of eight major plates as well as several minor ones. Where the plates meet, their relative motion determines the type of boundary they have. Some are convergent, which means when they meet they crunch up against each other, whereas some are divergent, meaning they are moving away from each other. Finally, some are known as transform boundaries. Earthquakes, volcanic activity, mountain-building, and oceanic trench formation occur along these plate boundaries."

"The plates come in a variety of thicknesses. Some are composed of oceanic lithosphere and thicker continental lithosphere, each topped by its own kind of crust. Along convergent boundaries, subduction carries plates into the mantle. The material lost underneath as the plate is sub ducted is roughly balanced by the formation of new oceanic crust along divergent margins by seafloor spreading. In this way, the total surface of the globe basically remains the same. The main reason for these plates moving as they do is because of the gravitational forces put on the mass of the planet by the sun, and the one orbiting moon.

"Under normal circumstances, the plates making up Eden's lithosphere move and shift in this way, and these movements cause any number of natural seismic events on and in the planet. When we first came here, these seismic events were tearing the planet apart. We could see that if we wanted to make this planet our home, we would need to stabilize the movements of the tectonic plates, so that is why the TSM was built."

"What you are saying," I interjected, "is it was designed to keep the plates from moving. How?"

"Are you familiar with the shield surrounding the island?" asked Khaeleus.

"Yes. It was built to filter out the UV rays from the local sun."

"You are correct. That shield uses high energy magnetics to contain a field of plasma in a very focused shape around the island."

"OK. I'm following you so far."

"The TSM uses the same technology. It was designed to create a spherical shield around the asthenosphere, the layer of magma just underneath the lithosphere of the planet. The goal is to keep the planetary magma from welling up in the divergent zones, mostly found under the ocean floors. With the divergences arrested, there are no more subductions, no more boundary transformations, therefore no more seismic events. As a bonus, the magma eruptions commonly happening on land are also completely quieted."

"That all makes sense. Sounds like a good system," said Quorlynn.

"It is, when it's working," said Khaeleus.

"It isn't working?" I asked.

"No. That's why I sent the signal. The system stopped working about 100 years ago."

"What happened?" asked Quorlynn.

"I'm not completely sure. Something in the control circuitry needs to be fixed, and that will require the TSM engineer."

"That's a problem," I said. "There are no Galimarians left alive who can do it. Are you familiar with the procedures necessary to fix it?"

"Mostly, but that isn't problem."

"What is?"

"In order to get to the systems which need to be fixed, the TSM has to be shut down properly, and that requires the handprint of a living Galimarian to do it. Only the living DNA of a Galimarian can access the technology. It is all part of the TID," replied Khaeleus.

"Ok, another acronym."

"TID," responded Quorlynn, "stands for 'Technology Isolation Directive.' Remember the story about Traxis?"

"Yes. That's a planet where they were given technology way before they had the social evolution to handle the responsibility of it. They ended up killing their entire species because the power went to their heads and eventually destroyed their own planet."

"Correct," said Quorlynn. "Ever since then, any and all Galimarian technology is secured behind the directive from the Grand Council requiring that access only be granted to one with living Galimarian DNA."

"There's something I don't get. The planet has been experiencing earthquakes and such for a while now, but I get the impression there's a new development which is really bad."

"There is," replied Khaeleus. "Please direct your attention to the screen behind you. This represents a topological map of Eden."

I turned around in my seat and there was a screen showing all the land masses of Earth. In the area off the coast of Florida, there was a spot representing the location of New Galimar. I saw, in the upper midwest of the United States, an irregularly-shaped region blinking red.

"You will notice," continued Khaeleus "there is a region which is highlighted."

"I recognize that area," I said. "It's a region humans have set aside as a natural preserve, never to be developed by civilization. We call it Yellowstone National Park."

"I have detected that your Yellowstone National Park is about to create an *extinction level event* in the form of massive magma diffusion into the atmosphere."

"You're telling me the Yellowstone volcanoes are about to erupt?"

"Correct. And this isn't your typical eruption; it will be unlike anything you have ever seen. The eruption will be much bigger."

"How much?"

"Before I answer, please give me an idea of how you measure distances," inquired Khaeleus.

"Ok." Thinking a little bit, I decided to start with a basic measurement. Holding up my thumb and index finger, I said, "The distance between my two fingers here is a centimeter. One hundred of these is a meter. One thousand of those is a kilometer. Does that help?"

Khaeleus thought for a moment. "Are you familiar with a volcano that erupted approximately 35 years ago, 1,326 kilometers to the west of your Yellowstone National Park?"

I sat for a moment, thinking. Let's see, 35 years ago was when I was still in school, around 1980. "Yes, it was a volcano we call Mount St. Helens."

"Your Mount St. Helens erupted and released .25 cubic kilometers of magma. Did it have much of an effect?"

"I remember the news saying over 50 people were killed, and a few hundred homes were destroyed."

"Keeping that in mind, the volcanos in Yellowstone, there are several of them, are over 5,000 times more powerful. While Mount St. Helens erupted and released .25 cubic kilometers of magma, I have measured the magma chamber in Yellowstone, and it is currently about to release 2,538 cubic kilometers of magma and atmospheric ash. This will cause the massive extinction of not only us but most, if not all, of Eden's life."

I was stunned. At this point, I could only croak out one word. "When?"

The face of Khaeleus appeared appropriately grim. "In about two months."

CHAPTER 27

THE PREVIOUS DAY HAD BEEN a watershed moment for Terri. After her conversation with Khaeleus, things were once again a blur. It was the last day for her to be on the island, so it was fortuitous the signal had been sent to Quorlynn when it was. But now that Terri had been saddled with this knowledge, she wasn't sure what to do with it.

Later that same afternoon, Terri spent the necessary time putting together the things she had brought into Khreelon's home where she had been staying the last month. It took three trips back and forth to the boat to carry all her things back. Before leaving Khreelon for the last time, she sat on a chair next to his bed staring at her would-be lover with feelings of love and love lost. Her final parting words were "with all my love." As she stood to leave, she stared at him and had a foreboding feeling this was going to be the last time she would be able to spend time with him like this. She had no idea just how prophetic those thoughts were.

The night before was a troubled one for Terri, for many reasons. The news she received about the impending volcanic eruption was foremost on her mind since it was something poised to eradicate everything and everyone she had ever known. Aside from that impending disaster, there was also a part of her feeling very anxious over her scheduled departure the next day. She would no longer be near her dear Khreelon, and wasn't looking forward to the departure at all.

After lying on the couch for a couple of hours, she decided to do something symbolizing her own feelings for Khreelon. She wanted to send him a message which would complement the beautiful letter he had written to her. She got up, took out some writing materials, and selected a piece of parchment. Earlier in the week, she had found the same cache of parchment Khreelon had used for his own manuscript to her. Terri began writing.

To my Khreelon, my soulmate,

As you have said to me in your letter, time and distance would never separate me from your love, and I definitely feel your love reaching past the centuries to touch my heart as it beats in my chest next to yours.

Khreelon, my love, you are beautiful to me in so many ways. When I am cold at night, the simple thought of you makes me warm. When I am anxious, your hands fondle my soul, making me feel calm and safe. I find security and safety in the arms that I see in the logs and videos I have watched. I love you for the you inside, and not just beautiful you on the outside.

I am awash with happiness that Loranna has chosen me to be your mate, as well as sadness that we cannot be together in body, as we are in spirit. Please know that as you have said in your beautiful letter to me, my heart will no longer beat in my own chest, because it now lays next to yours. It will remain there throughout the ages, to give you safe harbor and a comfortable place to come home to.

As incredible as it may seem, there is a part of me that truly feels we were meant to be together. You were born on a planet not my own, and were born eons before I ever existed, but I can't help but feel that there must have been some cosmic force that reached beyond the stars, beyond time itself, and saw that you and I were meant to be together. My heart continually persuades me to believe that even though we are still separated by this small distance of time, one day we will be together in body as well as in spirit. I know it. I feel it!

Until that wonderful day comes, my love, please know that I give all of my mind, body, soul to you.

With unending love,

Terri Tellindor

When she finished the letter, she rolled it up, tied a ribbon around it, and placed it in the same location as Khreelon's original manuscript.

Standing by his bedside, she reached up with two fingers, kissed them, then symbolically sent that kiss sailing toward him. She glanced up to the wall panel where her letter to him resided, hoping and wishing he would somehow read it wherever he was.

There was now only one last thing to do. Sitting down on the couch, Terri entered the world of the amulet and was once again rewarded with not only her companion Quorlynn, but a surprise.

"Loranna!" exclaimed Terri.

The two friends ran into each other's arms, giving each other the perfect embrace of the ages, the hug by which all other hugs in the universe will forever be measured. Thinking about this later, it was something which made sense to Terri because of Loranna's ability to perfectly reflect Khreelon's personality. Stretching back from her hug, Terri looked over to Quorlynn, who was standing near with a Cheshire cat smile on her face. She held out her hand to Quorlynn, inviting her into a three-way hug which none of the sisters wanted to end. The tears streaming down their respective faces finally demanded attention, so they parted to attend to their faces and mop up the mess they were all creating.

"Loranna, I am so glad you are here. I am going to miss you so much," lamented Terri.

"Terri, I have a question for you," said Quorlynn.

"Yes?"

"I have spoken with Loranna at length about the events of the past several days, and of how you and Khreelon have this bond now between you."

"I know. It is something at once overwhelming and comforting. I am so glad I had the chance to meet you, Loranna. I wish I didn't have to say goodbye, but my life awaits me back in New York."

"What would you think if you didn't have to say goodbye to her?" Quorlynn asked.

"What do you mean?"

"Loranna and I were talking about this last night. I'm not sure you're aware of this but, as difficult as it has been for you to come to terms with the love of your life having to remain here on the island when you leave, the prospect of your leaving has been equally hard on Loranna."

"It has?"

"Definitely," inserted Loranna. "As I told you before, the personality of my companion is reflected in my own personality, so the connection you have with Khreelon, and I know he would have with you, is similar to ours. Yours and mine isn't romantic, but the connection does exist, nonetheless."

Terri was surprised by this revelation. It wasn't from learning Loranna was going to miss her, but that she was feeling the same thing as Terri. In the last several days, Terri had been wrestling with sadness over not being able to spend time with her once she left the island. Loranna represented the only enduring link to Khreelon that existed, so leaving the island was like leaving two people she loved, in different ways, rather than just one.

"I have to admit, I've been feeling a lot of apprehension over leaving the island for that exact reason. I love all that is here, and there is so much more for me to learn, but one of the biggest reasons I don't want to leave is because I know, deep in my heart, I will miss you, my friend. Don't get me wrong, Quorlynn. I love you like the sister you are, but Loranna is someone who, I don't know. It's hard to explain."

"I completely understand, Terri. You don't have to explain it," consoled Quorlynn. "But as I alluded to earlier, I think we may have come up with a solution to the problem."

"Tell me more."

"What would you say to the idea of Loranna coming with us?"

Terri's eyes darted back to Loranna's expectant, yet pensive, face. She wasn't sure what her own face looked like, but probably a face of shock and wonder at this idea suddenly coming in from left field.

"By now I should know better than to ask this stupid question, but you can do that?" asked Terri, incredulously.

"The amulet has a considerable amount of abilities. Even I am still learning all it has to offer. One of the abilities we discovered is it can accommodate the lives of two sisters in it. If you are agreeable, Loranna would like to transfer her consciousness into your amulet where I reside. From then on, she will be my sister, and a second companion to you; one who is a link to the love of your life."

Terri was stunned. She thought about how she continually experienced the non-stop conveyor of incredible experiences from this world. She had begun to wonder if she would become jaded at all the amazing facets of this culture, and hoped that day would never come. This new prospect didn't require any thought; the decision was a foregone conclusion.

Breaking through the reverie happening inside Terri's mind, Loranna said, with trepidation, "If you need time to think …."

"*Yes!*" exclaimed Terri, almost yelling. Instantly standing and running to Loranna, she threw her arms around her and gave her a serious embrace, hopefully conveying her happiness at being able to take Loranna with her and have yet another connection to her soulmate.

"Oh Terri, you've made me so happy!" exclaimed Loranna.

"This is going to be wonderful. Not only will you have this connection to Khreelon, but now I won't be alone when we are back in your world," said Quorlynn.

"I hadn't thought of that before, but I can see how hard it would be on you, being out of connection with the rest of your siblings when we are off the island. But I want to say something before this goes much farther."

Turning to Loranna, Terri fixed her gaze on her, saying, "Loranna my friend, I am gratified you want to be with Quorlynn and me, and I am definitely happy I will be able to have this link to my Khreelon. But I want to make something perfectly clear."

Loranna's expression turned serious.

"Don't worry, Loranna. I simply want to make sure you know your presence in my life will be something I cherish not only because of your connection to Khreelon, but because you are such a special person in your own right. You are someone I would want to be around anyway, even if you weren't associated with my mate. Do you understand what I'm trying to say?"

Loranna's expression changed to one of appreciation. "I do, Terri. Thank you for reassuring me. I really look forward to being your friend and facing all life has in store for us."

"Me too," replied Terri. Darting her eyes back and forth between her two friends, she asked, "How do we do this?"

"From your perspective," Quorlynn replied, "it's simple, but you won't be able to be in-world while we do it. Go back to the island, and place the amulet in the cradle on Khreelon's desk. The process will take an hour. When it is complete, I will come onto the screen and let you know."

"Great," said Terri. She swiped her finger across the screen of her amulet, making sure the last face her friends saw was hers with a very large smile.

As Quorlynn promised, the whole process only took about an hour; Terri waited patiently. Without warning, there were two beeps in quick succession from the amulet, then the two faces of her companions appeared on the screen. After a quick chat, it was time to go.

Emerging from the front door to Khreelon's home, her home, she paused for a moment to drink up the last cocktail of Galimarian experience. The quiet rush of the breeze passing amongst the trees and buildings was accentuated by the occasional sound of the builder robots maintaining the pristine appearance of the island. Clutching the golden home of her two companions in her hand, Terri began the long trek home.

After leaving the safety of the island shield, she sailed on mostly calm waters, alone with her thoughts as she stared out at the sea. The information about the impending volcanic eruptions hung heavy in her consciousness. She wasn't comfortable with just waiting for the event to happen, but what could be done? It's interesting how the sea can help you think. Perhaps it's the clean air; perhaps it's the absence of distraction; perhaps it's both or neither. By the time Terri got back into port to turn in the boat, she knew she had to do something. Sitting back and waiting for the disaster wasn't an option.

Pulling into the marina and sidling up to the slip where the rental agency was located, Terri killed the motor. Jumping off, she not only put out the necessary fenders to keep the boat from chafing against the dock but, as her father taught her when she was little, she fashioned all her tie-offs with a proper cleat hitch, allowing the line to be untied and adjusted even when under tension. As she completed the last knot, she heard a voice come up from behind her.

"Well, missy, I see yer back now," said the dockmaster, a salty and generally miserable old guy. After eying the knots she had just tied, he said, "That's a right fine hitch ya got there. Where'd you learn to tie off like that?" Terri remembered he wasn't so complimentary when she rented the boat originally. He seemed to be a little more pleasant with her now that his boat was back, and it was obvious she knew what she was doing.

"My father and brothers have been fisherman all their lives, and it seemed I spent more time at sea than on land growing up."

"Aye, lass. I can see you know your way around a boat. I must say, I was telling some o' the other sea dogs here I thought the triangle might've got ya," said the dockmaster, belly-laughing at his own joke.

"Ah, so that's the way of it, eh? I suppose you believe in aliens too?" replied Terri, falling right in line with the seaman's banter, and smiling wide as if she had a secret to keep. The dockmaster really laughed now; as far as he was concerned, this girl was all right. Her banter and her knots earned his respect.

Terri unloaded her gear and packed it for the trip home. It was a race to get all her things checked in at the airport and get to her plane on time. As she sat in her seat, the people around her thought she was slumbering. They had no idea she had gone into the amulet and was enjoying her time with her two besties. While there, Terri brought up a serious subject needing to be discussed.

"Girls, I need to talk to you about what we learned from Khaeleus."

"You mean about the eruption?" asked Quorlynn.

"Exactly. What's bothering me is I have this feeling something needs to be done. I can't just sit on the sidelines waiting for the apocalypse to happen! The thing is, I don't want to make any decisions which might jeopardize my Galimarian family."

"What do you have in mind?" asked Loranna.

"I propose we try to get some pretty smart people in my world to take a look at the TSM."

Loranna and Quorlynn looked at each other for a moment. In the flash of a second, there was an immediate understanding that the technology of Galimar was going to be under the microscope and this could easily come into violation of the Technology Isolation Directive of the Galimarian Grand Council. All were more than familiar with the way Traxis destroyed itself when the technology wasn't used for peaceful purposes as intended, but rather for gaining power, leading to the destruction of the entire planet.

The quandary here on Earth, though, was if nothing was done, the destruction of the entire planet was going to happen anyway. On a purely logical level, there really was only one decision to be made. Do nothing, and all life would be destroyed; do something, and risk the consequences of revealing the island to humans. The latter gave humans, and Galimarians, the best chance of surviving an otherwise unsurvivable eventuality.

Slowly, Quorlynn turned her head to Terri. "My friend, Loranna and I support you in whatever decision you make."

So there it was. The die had been cast. Once Terri got back to New York, she would get in touch with her friend Lynne who had been in the military and would know who to contact. The greatest minds of the planet needed to be involved to ensure the human race its best chance of survival.

This also meant one other thing of great importance to the women. Soon, all three would return to New Galimar.

PART 4

CHAPTER 28

Jason and Michaela. Jason and Mikki. The names just roll off the tongue, don't they?

They are a new couple. A new breath of life to their circle of friends, and a fresh reminder that young and trusting love is still possible. Exuding confidence and an evident abundance of faith in the goodness of their fellow man, they daily show others that cynicism isn't always preferable, even if it may be in vogue.

Jason is a professional man, possessing the svelte charm and willowy attractiveness of one who lives healthy. He is the kind of man who lays his hand on your shoulder when speaking with you so as to impart both a recognition of your personal value and a sense of respect for the person you are. Mikki is an appealing and delightful woman, the kind of person who wouldn't hesitate running to the side of a friend simply to soothe anguish and suffering. It is evident her heart is not hers, for she freely gives it to those who are feeble and weak, imparting to each the very fuel of life, a fuel called hope.

Jason and Mikki, the perfect couple. Though their circle of friends never put faith in such, fate and destiny certainly could be given credit for their relationship. They are a couple whose passion and fascinations follow threads of classic romance; visions of Romeo and Juliet, or Bogart and Bacall, fill the minds of those having the privilege of knowing them.

By day Jason is an engineer working for Midway Magnetic, a secret research company unobtrusively located just a few miles from his home in Sonora, California. Mikki is a social worker, a line of work that is arguably the best exploitation of her abilities. Though Mikki has no real idea what Jason does at work, by the look in his eyes, by the way he never looks away as they dance slowly without word or song, she knows his heart only belongs to her. Though his work sometimes calls for him to stay late, she never worries or fears. He will always come home. He always has. He always will.

"Your lunch is waiting by the front door," Mikki called out from the kitchen, "and breakfast is just about ready."

"Thanks, babe," responded Jason as he hurried to finish shaving. Hoping not to give himself a fresh set of facial nicks, he tried to concentrate on the task at hand and not on the seriousness of the day's activities. Finishing up the last stroke with the straight razor his grandfather gave him when he was just learning to shave, Jason rinsed his face with water and applied some aftershave. Blotting his face dry, he emerged from the bathroom ready to face another day.

"I hit a new 'PB' this morning during our workout," Jason announced as he sat down at the breakfast table with Mikki and little Jace. Jason raises an eyebrow and changes his voice to evoke a sense of mock disdain, "Did you?"

"Personal bests are exactly that, my love. Personal," replied Mikki. "I think my recovery time is getting better now that I am finally getting over this cold. Bothersome thing," she said with a fake English accent. Both chuckled.

Handing Jason a serving tray of eggs, Mikki asked, "Would you be able to drop Jace off at school this morning on your way to work? I still need to get ready before I go to meet Carrie this morning to go to the mall."

"Sure," replied Jason. Unknown to Mikki, the route Jason had planned to take to work was not the route which included a pass by the school. That could be changed. Of the 10 routes approved for Jason to get to work, three of them took him by his son's school. Jason was allowed, by the Department of Defense, to choose which one he would take each morning when coming to work, just so long as the routes were chosen in a random manner.

The three finished eating breakfast in relative silence except for the small television sitting on the far end of the kitchen counter announcing the news of the day. Jason Jr., or "Jace" as everybody called him, quietly sat in his chair cramming in some homework he was supposed to have finished last night. The TV droned on with a smattering of local news and weather. In the small town of Sonora, there is no need for traffic reports since there is only one major road. This isn't to say Sonora is a small town. Sonora has certainly grown, even just during the five short years Jason and Mikki have lived there. But the way Sonora grew was through sprawling communities spread out over the countryside, known as Sonora Hills, instead of cramming people together like major metropolitan centers.

Finishing his breakfast, Jason got up from the table and made his way to the front door. Jace acted like he didn't notice the commotion, hoping to get in a little more time on his books before he left. He knew there was always a little morning ritual at the front door between his parents that gave him some more time. First, Jason made his way to the door with all that he was supposed to take with him to work in his hands. Then getting there, he set the things down and turned to give Mikki a long and loving hug, saying little remarks in her ear that were for their ears only. Dropping back from the hug, but still in each other's arms, there would be a couple of minutes of small talk intermixed with at least five "I Love You's." After that, Jason would reluctantly release his body hold on his wife, bend over to pick up his things, straighten up, and give Mikki a final parting kiss. Only then would he be ready to go.

"Come on, little man. Time to rock 'n' roll," Jason called to the breakfast table. Jace, already knowing the timing of the morning ritual, had gathered his things together into his backpack and was on his way.

"Bye mom, I love you!"

"I love you too, sweetheart," replied Mikki, "Have a great day at school."

Mikki bent down and gave Jace a kiss on the cheek and Jace reciprocated with a kiss on hers. Jace has always been the kind of boy who isn't ashamed to show his mother affection, even in public. It was Mikki's firm belief that the close bond between her and Jason, as well as their openness in showing affection to each other in front of Jace, are the biggest reasons why their son is so well adjusted.

Emerging from the front door and walking to the carport near the front of the small single-story home, Jason and Jace got into the car, pulled out of the driveway, and disappeared down the road.

"Here you go, little man. Got everything?" Jason asked as they arrived in front of the school.

"Yup,"

The car comes to a stop. "OK. Here you go, son. Have a good one."

"Thanks, Dad!" called Jace as he jumped out of the car, slammed the car door shut, and walked over to where some of his friends were standing.

Pulling back into traffic, Jason proceeded down Greenly Street where Jace went to school and arrived at the stoplight. Turning left onto Mono Way, he drove up Highway 108, where he again turned left. Highway 108 was the main thoroughfare through East Sonora, and if you drove far enough, you found Dodge Ridge, a nice ski resort. Right next to Dodge Ridge is Pinecrest Lake, and around Pinecrest is a campground usually filled to capacity during the summer. In the evenings, the ranger station will show current movies in an open-air amphitheater at the side of the lake. A beautiful country. A beautiful area. It was always a juxtaposition how Jason had such a high tech job in this area.

Even though 108 was the main highway that could take him to the very destination where his office was located, Jason started on the first of several detours for today's route. Normally Jason didn't mind the circuitous routes to his office, but today was different. He had been working on the Multi-Phasic/Multi-Media tests in the super collider collision chamber for the better part of his entire tenure at Midway Magnetic, and today was the first time Jason expected to see some results. Today was a turning point, or at least he hoped it would be.

After traveling on several detour roads, Jason arrived at Cherokee Road. Turning left, he drove a little way, then stopped at a small roadside stand on an apple farm where various apple-related treats were sold. Today was his turn to bring in morning goodies to go with the coffee. A few apple turnovers and a couple of fritters would do the trick.

Proceeding down Cherokee, the road meets up with Tuolumne Road and eventually back to the original highway where he started his trip. Turning right onto the highway, Jason then settled in for a 20-minute drive through the dense forests belonging to the Bureau of Land Management, a government agency. Passing through various tourist towns, he arrived at the turn off to the town of Long Barn, then another turn. Jason eased his car into a large, drab, unmarked, steel warehouse where the door was already opening due to the radio transponder buried deep in the circuitry of his personal car. With the warehouse door closing behind him, Jason shut down the engine and emerged toting an armload of materials and a briefcase.

"Anything I should be aware of today, corporals?" asked Jason. Standing at ease on either side of the door he just drove through, Corporal Stanley Jackson and Corporal Steven Jenkins were pulling guard duty.

"According to the latest reconnaissance reports, there are campers on 4Y12 and at the Clavey river crossing, sir," answered Corporal Jackson.

"Thanks. Here," said Jason.

Always one to keep the rank and file happy, Jason pulled out the fritters for the two guards. He figured making friends this way would put money in the friendship bank, which he might need to cash in on later.

"This should help keep you guys busy for a while."

"Thank you, sir."

After transferring his things into one of the fleet of four-wheel drive vehicles lined up in an angled row to one side of the warehouse, Jason pulled out of the door on the opposite end. Since there were campers on 4Y12 and at the Clavey river crossing, he would have to take Road 3N01 to avoid being seen. Jason drove through one of his favorite vistas, a rough and beautiful mountain crest area called Trout Creek Overlook. Sometimes, if he has the time, he stops the engine and stands next to the vehicle, enjoying the view and almost surreal grandeur of the canyons. The forest is densely packed with grove after grove of pine and fir trees, and nowhere in this vista is there a patch of bare land. The symphony of colors one's eyes feast on are almost more than can be soaked in during a single look. As he drove by, he remembered how he often stood on the overlook, with his own feet refusing to obey his command to leave when it was time to go on.

Today, there wasn't enough time to stop. The systems test would need every ounce of attention.

After a left turn onto 3N01, the road lead Jason through the trees for about 10 miles. Before proceeding, he stopped his vehicle and looked out the side window. There, on the informal corner bounding 3N01 and Trout Creek Overlook, he glanced at a set of trees, each about one meter in diameter. Like all the other pine trees, these had various blemishes and distinguishing features. One tree in particular garnered his attention, especially one of the knots where it appeared a branch had been cut off. At that moment, the knothole lit up bright green, revealing itself to be a well-camouflaged screen hiding a signal light.

"Green is go," Jason said to himself.

Taking the signal to mean there was still no known civilian activity on this final leg to the site, Jason proceeded forward to the end of 3N01 where he found himself at the crest of a hill, which hid a gargantuan crater similar to what you would expect to find at the top of an extinct volcano. Nestled at the bottom of the crater was a triangular stack of logs that appeared to be ready for pickup and delivery to any number of lumber mills existing locally. Driving down the road on the side of this hidden canyon at the top of a mountain, Jason finally arrived at his destination, fully one hour and 15 minutes after he left home.

Pulling around to one end of the log pile, Jason reached down to a hidden panel on the underside of his car's dashboard. Dropping into view, a simple 10-digit keypad was attached to the inside of the hidden panel. Tapping in the code, the end of the log pile receded into the earth with quick precision.

Glancing around, Jason noted there were no visible signs of human activity. In reality, there were 17 guard posts in different positions around the perimeter of the canyon. Each guard post was disguised as a large tree, allowing the guard inside to view all that was occurring in the canyon. Each had a false floor in it and was connected to the other 16 posts through a system of underground passageways. From this vantage point, a guard was able to see not only what was happening in the canyon itself, but also any civilian activity happening nearby. Each of the guards had a "Kill Switch," and each of the 17 kill switches had to be in the "Accept" position for Jason's 10-digit code to do anything. Since utter and absolute secrecy was essential to the installation, each of the standing guards around the perimeter had the authority to flip his switch to "Deny," causing the keypad in Jason's vehicle to simply act like a car alarm and nothing more.

As the log door dropped, Jason knew all was clear.

Pulling into the dark and unlit cavern hollowed out in the middle of the log pile, Jason turned off the engine. Sensing his vehicle was completely inside the structure, automatic security equipment closed the door behind, obscuring the fact that he had ever come there. Vibrating panels below the road surface leading to the log structure began to vibrate, moving and shifting the loose dirt and gravel, erasing tire tread marks. The tops of several angled two-inch-wide tree stumps just outside the door to the log structure opened up, and a menagerie of dust, dirt, and gravel was blown at the closed door, erasing the fact it had ever moved.

Jason remained in the vehicle. Suddenly it lurched downward, and after descending through a cement-lined shaft for what seemed an interminable amount of time, he arrived at his destination: a well-lit, impeccably clean parking structure below the surface of the crater. On the side wall of the structure was the company logo for Midway Magnetic, Inc. Restarting his engine, he pulled forward into parking spot number five, which matched the five painted on the dash of his vehicle.

Jason killed the engine and proceeded to the elevator which would take him to his office on Underground Level 9.

CHAPTER 29

"Mikki?" said Karen.

Sitting in the chair at her desk, Mikki was in her own world. It wasn't a case of being tired or anything like that. She was having a serious case of cabin fever. Outside the weather had turned cold. Her hometown of Sonora had a tendency to not only be cold in the fall, but the skies were often gray, and sometimes there was a cold breeze from the north. In the spring, the hills in the surrounding countryside were so green, Mikki said they seem to have been colored in with a neon magic marker. The plentiful rains that characterized winter and early spring created the verdant flora which, as you drove through the hills, almost magnetically pulled your car over, forcing you to look out over the hills and open plains to appreciate the view. Wind often swept up the various dips and surges of geologic time through the tall grasses interspersed with patches of oak trees and manzanita shrubs. As if watching the waves of the ocean, the wind could be seen molding and shaping the meadow at its whim.

Today, climactic serenity seemed to be a distant memory. Drifts of snow populated the higher elevations; dry and biting cold winds without snow were the order of the day at the elevation where Mikki worked. She had been interviewing John and Connie Price, a couple hoping to adopt a child since they could not conceive on their own.

The couple seemed like very good candidates, but time would tell—what with the financial and home environment reviews to be done. He owned a car repair shop and seemed to be a good provider. She was congenial and good-natured. Mikki thought about how Connie reminded her of her mother and ....

"Mikki!" said Karen decidedly louder.

Startled, Mikki swung around in her seat in the break room, almost spilling the tea from her cup as it sloshed from one side to the other.

"Oh my gosh, Karen. You scared me to death!" Mikki replied breathily.

"Sorry, sweetie. I was calling your name, but you just sat there. Where were you just now?"

"Oh, just feeling a little cabin fever I guess. This cold weather persistently conflicts with my nature-oriented social schedule," responded Mikki.

Karen chuckled. "Well, I was just trying to tell you that your 2:30 appointment called and rescheduled. They had something come up and apologized."

"That's fine," said Mikki, relieved that her schedule had changed. She didn't really feel like putting on a mechanical smile again. Normally she wouldn't mind, but today she needed to be outside. What was that vitamin the sun helps your body make, or metabolize, or something?

"Vitamin D," said Karen.

"Huh?" Mikki looked up. "What was that?"

"You just said you were wondering what vitamin was the one the sun helped you with, or something like that. It's vitamin D."

Cocking her right eyebrow, Mikki queried, "I said that out loud?" She knew the answer as she was asking the question. Karen just grinned, now convinced her boss needed to get away.

Opening her eyes wide in mock fatigue, Mikki stood and emptied the remainder of her cup of tea. Making her way back to her cubicle, her eyes scanned over the file folders needing to be filed and decided this was a good task for her overqualified and under-tasked assistant.

Casually gesturing a finger toward her desk, Mikki asked, "Karen, do you think you could?" Mikki knew she didn't have to put it into a request. Yes, she was Karen's boss, but that didn't mean she had to lord it over her subordinate.

"Of course. Get outta here, and get the stink off you!" The corner of Mikki's mouth curled up slightly at the idiom. The first time Karen used that phrase, Mikki became mildly offended at the supposed accusation of odor. Immediately sensing her faux pas, Karen explained this was a phrase her parents used with their children when it was time for them to go outside, play, and expend the boundless storehouses of energy common amongst young ones their age.

Mikki gathered up her things and, after making a last minute check of her schedule for Monday, left her office in the capable hands of Karen and exited the single-story brick building. Even though the social services center was technically a government building, it was actually a historical landmark nestled in the small lee of a canyon, surrounded by trees and shrubbery. Sometimes it seemed later in the day than it was since the sun only made it there briefly after managing to peak over the surrounding rock cliffs.

After climbing into her car and setting out for home, Mikki's cell phone rang.

"Hello?"

"Hey babe," said Jason's voice on the other end of the line.

"Oh hi, sweetie! How's your day?" responded Mikki.

"Actually, it just got better," said Jason.

"Oh? How come?"

"That's easy. I'm talking to the most beautiful woman in the world right now, silly!"

"Oh, you masher!" said Mikki in a playful tone. "I have half a mind to come there and spend an hour teaching you a lesson you'll never forget!"

"How does a long weekend sound instead?" posed Jason.

"One more time?"

"I said I have a different idea. How does a long weekend sound instead?" posed Jason.

"A long weekend? What do you mean?"

"Well, you know that little trip to Las Vegas you've wanted to go on?"

"No! Really?!" said Mikki in a very excited tone.

"Yep! I asked my boss, and I got the time off," said Jason, just as excited as Mikki.

"Awesooooooome! When do we go?"

"I'm thinking next week, if you can get the time off."

"Not a problem. I'm so excited!" squealed Mikki.

"Me too! I'd really like to see a couple of shows while we're there," said Jason with a perceptible smile in the tone of his voice. "Nothing too racy, though!"

"I'll be all the racy you need, sweetie," responded Mikki, knowing her husband was only participating in an oft-played inside joke of theirs; wouldn't be the last time.

"Deal! I gotta go hun, but I'll see you tonight." said Jason.

"See you tonight, sweetheart. I love you!"

"I love you more!" Jason said, as he hung up the phone.

Laying the handset down, he contemplated how they would have to get a sitter for Jace while they were gone. That wouldn't be a problem, though. He was a good kid, and since Jason and Mikki had performed the same kind of favor for some of the neighborhood families they knew, it should be easy enough to find parents of one of Jace's friends who'd watch him.

"Well, back to the grind" Jason said to himself.

Sitting in her car, Mikki thought about the upcoming Vegas adventure. That did a lot to alleviate the feelings of drudgery she was experiencing, but she still had a little bit of cabin fever. Deciding she had some extra time since she got off work early, Mikki decided to take a little drive up the canyon near their town. As she drove, she turned on the heater and then cracked the window open, wanting the heady aroma of pine trees to infiltrate the car. Sure enough, her toes were treated to the warmth they needed, her nose luxuriated in the aroma of nature, and the batteries to her soul began their much-needed recharge.

Little did she know that as she drove up the canyon, she passed within yards of the building where her husband's car was secretly parked.

CHAPTER 30

"THIS JUST DOESN'T MAKE SENSE!" said Jason.

"What's that, Doctor?" asked Dennis.

Dr. Dennis Greene was Jason's assistant, but by all rights was just as qualified as Jason for the work they did on the particle accelerator. Dennis earned his master's in high energy physics at UCLA, then his doctorate at MIT. He was quite skilled at understanding the emerging fields of quantum physics and how they relate to string theory. He had given several TED Talks on the subject, and his discourses were always sold out.

Letting out a guttural groan, Jason uttered what was bugging him. "The numbers keep coming back the same each time. I just don't get it."

After getting that out of his system, he looked at his compatriot askance. "Dennis, when will you ever start calling me Jason?" he asked, for the millionth time. It was an ongoing joke between them.

"As soon as you ain't a doctor, Doctor," replied Dennis, in his usual cheeky manner. His Texas drawl notwithstanding, Dennis had an affect that was disarming to most, until you realized he was one of only a handful of individuals who could actually understand the inner workings of space and time; insofar as man understood it, that is. It was commonly felt a Nobel Prize was inevitable for him.

Rolling his eyes, Jason returned to his work. Dennis thought about how his lab partner's equal set of qualifications. Many times the two of them had long conversations about how Jason's wife Mikki didn't actually know what he did for a living, much less the extent of Jason's education. Dennis always felt it was such a juxtaposition that Jason was so dedicated to his work and his research, yet at the same time had such a good marriage. Dennis had been married before, but his wife just couldn't hack it. It wasn't really her fault. Dennis had been so young, yet so dedicated to his education and work, that he just didn't give all he should have to his marriage. He maintained a good friendship with her; she had just been too lonely, and needed more than Dennis was able to give.

"What is it that doesn't make sense?" Dennis asked again.

Realizing he had never explained what precipitated his original outburst, Jason thoughtfully replied, "You know how we've finally got the detection chamber to the point where we are experiencing a high level of accuracy in the collisions?"

"Yeah. Are the results coming back differently from what you expected?"

"I have been analyzing the results," continued Jason, "and, that's just it. They are *exactly* what I would expect."

Scrunching his eyebrows, and with a quizzical expression on his face, Dennis asked, "OK, and that's bad?"

"No," acquiesced Jason, "if you're into doing the same thing every time and expecting different results."

"So, what do you have in mind?"

Sitting back in his chair, Jason crossed his arms in front of his chest and reached up to stroke his chin. Dennis had seen this stance many times, and knew when Jason had this type of look, it was when he would come up with some of his most ingenious ideas.

"Studying these results makes me feel like we've been waging a fruitless pursuit of knowledge," Jason explained. "Like we're standing on the shoulders of giants, yet never forging new ground. I have the feeling there's something right in front of us, and we're missing it. Like right here on my desk are the building blocks of something nobody has ever worked on before, an opportunity to forge new ground in a new area of science."

Jason got up from his chair and, almost in his own world, wandered over to the window of his office, which had all the appointments of luxury you would expect for someone instrumental to the super-collider program. Walnut bookshelves occupied the entire west and north walls. The desk was so large, Jason sometimes wondered how they even got it into this office. Plush carpet and overstuffed furniture balanced out the hard edges of the woodwork.

The floor-to-ceiling window on the east wall looked down onto the main science and detection room, 60 meters in height and 100 meters in length, which housed the super-collider detection apparatus. On two opposing sides of the room, the particle accelerator entered and exited, and in the middle of the room was the main detector apparatus. It was an amazing sight, but right now the grandeur of this man-made marvel, as well as the hundreds of technical minions climbing all over the apparatus they serviced and maintained, was lost on Jason.

"You know," he said, looking out the window, "I'm thinking of something I read recently about Einstein. In his early life, his successes resulted from not having a problem with breaking the rules."

"Yep," agreed Dennis. "At that time, there were commonly held understandings of physics and the universe, but the whole reason he was so successful was because he didn't take things he had been taught as gospel. Instead, he simply asked the question that basically amounted to scientific heresy or, at the very least, something which could amount to occupational suicide: "*Why?*"

"Exactly," Jason added. "For instance, why was Isaac Newton right? Are we sure he was completely right? Was it possible there was something Newton wasn't completely right about? That attitude eventually earned him the Nobel Prize and helped him unlock previously hidden secrets of the universe. He was a rock star of his day."

Jason was now racking his own brain with the same conundrum. Why? Why do we do the same experiments and expect something different?

"It's almost like," he thought out loud, "we're in second place in a race, always trying to catch up to the place already experienced by someone else." Pausing for a moment, he added, "Maybe we need to stop just detecting. We need to ...."

Swinging around to face Dennis, he exclaimed, "That's it!"

Dennis looked up at him. "What's it?"

"We need to stop just *detecting*. We need to start *reacting*!" exclaimed Jason.

"Run that past me one more time," said Dennis.

Stopping to gather his thoughts, Jason returned to his desk and proceeded to explain. "You know how all this," gesturing to the scene out the window, "is designed to detect the nature of matter and the nature of the universe in general? How it's based on discovering the building blocks of matter?"

"Yeah. Physics 1A. First-year student stuff," observed Dennis.

Jason down in a mock exasperated manner, while making a magnanimous gesture. "Exactly my point," he said. "We have been lost in the mire of what really amounts to first-year student 'stuff' as you put it." Jason made air-quotes with his fingers.

"But what if instead of endlessly working to detect the building blocks of matter, we started creating reactions that would tell us more about what it is made of?"

"Not following you," said Dennis, more intrigued than confused.

Looking thoughtfully as he walked to his whiteboard, Jason drew a basic atom. "It's simple, he continued. "Right now, we're taking innumerable numbers of protons and colliding them together. But what would happen if we took different materials and subjected them to the particle streams? What would happen if we did that while creating an environment with different magnetic fields? Or different atmospheres? Or when using different light wavelengths in a reaction chamber? There are so many different environments we could create, and the possibilities of what we might discover are almost endless!"

Dennis sat back in his armchair near the couch, considering what Jason had just proposed. "Interesting," he said. "Undertaking a program of searching for different reactions could easily turn into a fool's errand. 'We used this magnetic field, with this gas, and this frequency of laser beam; nothing happened.' Then, 'we used that magnetic field, with that gas, and that frequency of laser beam; nothing happened,' and so on, indefinitely. That would be rather unrewarding."

"But then again," Dennis added after some thought, "it could also be the first rung on an increasingly interesting ladder into an unknown branch of science nobody has ever climbed before. What kind of reactions do you think would happen?"

"That is a good question," replied Jason. "I remember one of my old professors using this one phrase that stuck with me. Before starting a new set of experiments, he always said, 'Let's get this started because I don't know what I don't know yet.' I need to know the questions first before I can find out the answers to them," he added, referring to creating a reaction chamber. "We're talking about an unknown field of study."

"For instance," Jason continued, "I've always been interested in the interactions of materials when they are bombarded with steady streams of protons or electrons. Can the atomic state of the material be measured and perhaps isolated? Can the energies inherent in the atomic bonds be counteracted and/or reassembled? Will different environmental factors affect this? What will happen when we do this with different materials? Can we finally get to the bottom of the whole wave versus particle question?"

"Atomic bond dissolving and restructuring? Now that's an interesting idea," conceded Dennis.

Stroking his goatee, Dennis retreated into his own reverie, contemplating what Jason had just proposed. "I've been working on some thought experiments lately surrounding that double-slit experiment, a variation centering around the interferometry technology used at the Atacama Large Millimeter/submillimeter Array."

"Oh yeah? Tell me more," inquired Jason.

"You know how the radio telescope array at the ALMA location in Chile creates an image based by inferring the observable state of the parts of an image based on the contrast between the observation points, right?" asked Dennis.

"Not really following you," replied Jason with a grin. "Keep in mind I am interested in things that are really small, not so much the really big."

"No problem. Same here mostly, but astronomy was a pet field of study for me when I was a postgraduate student; these days it is more of a hobby than anything else. But as I was kicking back on the couch in my home office recently, I started thinking about how ALMA creates an image."

Dennis got out of his chair, walked to the whiteboard, and started drawing.

"About 50 or so smaller antennas are used to create images. Those antennas are designed to receive radio signals from deep space representing visible light waves that have shifted so much they represent radio waves now instead of light."

Pointing to the whiteboard, he added, "Each of these dots represents one dish antenna, about 20 meters across. They receive the radio signals, then send this information to the supercomputer systems on site. These individual antennas are physically separated on the Atacama Desert by distances of anywhere from 100 meters up to perhaps a few thousand meters. As a result, they have the radio frequency image where the antennas are, but nothing in between."

"OK, I get it. It's kinda like looking at space through a spaghetti strainer," injected Jason.

"Exactly. So the question is, how do they create a complete, cohesive image that doesn't have a lot of voids in it where the antennas *aren't*?" replied Dennis.

Pointing to a random area between two of the antennas drawn on the whiteboard, he continued, "In other words, how do we figure out what the image looks like in these areas where they didn't have an antenna?"

"Ya got me."

"Well," replied Dennis as he replaced the cap on the dry erase marker, "the answer is they use something called interferometry to postulate, or 'infer', the image in those non-observed areas. They do this with some pretty sophisticated mathematical calculations and some pretty stout computing power."

"Now I understand," said Jason. "They have these enormous areas that aren't actually observed, but also data from areas which *are* observed. They calculate what things look like in the area between two antennas based on the imaging they do have from those antennas."

"Exactly," replied Dennis. "They take what they *do* see on any two points, and then calculate what they *probably* would see between them. Doing this, they end up basically creating a huge virtual radio antenna many kilometers in size without having to deal with the natural distortion that would happen with a physical structure of the equivalent size. In fact, the ALMA observatory in Chile has baselines of up to 15 kilometers."

"Baselines? Not familiar with that term as it applies here."

"A baseline is the data coming from a pair of antennas at the facility which, when used along with a lot of mathematical calculations, enables them to observe, or to at least *inter*, what is between them. They use not only the radio antenna, but also the rotation of the earth, the movement of the earth around the sun, and the movement of the Milky Way Galaxy to mathematically account for that and use it to their advantage to focus on a wider area of the sky. They literally have the ability to see anything they want, even though they don't have an enormous radio antenna, such like the 188-acre wide dish at Arecibo, Puerto Rico."

"But what does that have to do with the double-slit experiment?" asked Jason.

"The experiment showed that particles can sometimes act like particles, but sometimes also like waves, right?"

"Yes."

"It also showed that the act of observing the particles that go through the slits actually changes the state of the particles, since the behavior returns them to acting like particles instead of behaving like waves, right?" asked Dennis.

"Right. Again, first-year student stuff," replied Jason.

Thinking for a moment, Dennis continued. "You ever watch the Star Trek series?"

"Of course! I'd have to turn in my geek card if I didn't," laughed Jason.

"That's for sure," Dennis chuckled. "Remember how they supposedly made it possible to create a transporter?"

"Yep. They had this thing called a Heisenberg compensator, which is a whole lot of fiction."

"Right. Think about this, though," continued Dennis. "That compensator is based on Heisenberg's uncertainty principle which states you cannot know or measure the position or momentum of a particle without changing its position or momentum by the very act of observing it."

"Now this is something I do know about," replied Jason. "Using an observation device that sent in a light source sufficiently tuned to figure out where a particle is would inherently change the particle to a state different from its original position or momentum. For it to be observed, transported, and reintegrated somewhere, you would have to compensate for Heisenberg's uncertainty principle by somehow observing the position and velocity of the particle without changing it. Otherwise, a person would go into the transporter on one end, and come out as biologic soup on the other end."

"Correct," said Dennis. He then raised his index finger and postulated, "But what if you didn't directly observe the particle itself, but rather inferred its position and movement through a variation of that interferometry technology we were just talking about. You would do it with a measuring device which didn't directly interact with the particle. If you were able to do it that way, you'd end up knowing the exact position *and* velocity, and you wouldn't have changed anything about the observed particle."

Sitting back in his seat, Jason let all this sink in for a few moments before replying.

"To do this, you would have to use detection equipment that could, that wouldn't ...."

Jason suddenly stood up, very excited. "AMANDA!" he shouted.

Jason was referring to the Antarctic Muon and Neutrino Detector Array (AMANDA) that allows for the detection and reporting of neutrinos. The array is designed to detect the 65 billion neutrinos that have the ability to pass through any matter, including the human body, every second.

Dennis' eyes got very wide now, and he started getting extremely excited. It was always like this when he and Jason started bouncing off each other.

"Brilliant!" shouted Dennis. "Neutrinos are just the particles we need to do the inferred observation. It isn't running anymore, but we've learned enough from that project to build the same type of neutrino detectors here in the lab. By using a small particle that doesn't materially change the nature of the matter it passes through, we could infer the state of that matter, and then know the position and momentum of the particle with altering it at all!"

"That's right," said Jason. "This means we would have a real world way of compensating for the Heisenberg uncertainty principle. By doing that, we could theoretically know the state of any matter at a given point in time. Knowing that, we could then perfectly recreate the original structure of the matter at another location."

"You're talking about the ability to create a real Heisenberg compensator!" replied Dennis.

After letting this float around in the room for a while, Jason started getting a wide-eyed look in his eyes. Looking at Dennis, he saw the same look in his eyes.

"Transporter," said Jason.

Nodding in muted agreement with an obvious smile on his face, Dennis added, "Beam me up, Scotty."

"Holy ...."

CHAPTER 31

⸮ ل ٦ ٢ ٦ ٦ ٦ ⸜ ٦ ٦ ٦

JASON SAT AT HIS CONSOLE watching the numbers. "It's funny," he thought to himself, "how you can be so tense and so relaxed at the same time."

About six months had elapsed since that turning point conversation he had with Dennis about how they could create what would amount to a Heisenberg compensator. All of the people working on the particle accelerator were considered "geeks of the first degree," so they were quite familiar with the term "Heisenberg Compensator," as used in various science fiction shows. The idea is that with it, matter transference, or what many would simply call a "transporter," would be possible.

The thing is, up to this point everybody figured it was impossible to create anything like that.

The thing is, Jason and Dennis decided not to listen to them.

They still hadn't told anybody what they were working on, though. Since they hadn't done the complete end-to-end test yet, they both felt it would be prudent to keep that little bit of information to themselves. They just kept telling all who asked that they were working on a new type of detection equipment to be used with the particle accelerator. While the main purpose of the accelerator was to create a particle stream for use with the Strategic Defense Initiative, Jason had designed the accelerator to also support other scientific endeavors.

As he was getting ready for work, he had been preoccupied with the day's test. It was the real deal, the point when he and Dennis would see if this was really going to work. While meticulously planning out the test, he forced himself to review each step in light of how it might affect the SDI aspect of the MMPA. The viability of that technology had to be maintained at all times.

As Jason sat there, he reflected on the enormity of what he had the privilege to work on. This installation was really quite remarkable. Most of what they did here involved the Strategic Defense Initiative. Back in the Ronald Reagan era, there had been a real push to get the SDI project ("Star Wars" for short) off the ground. It was a pet project of President Reagan back then, but for some reason it was mothballed, absorbed, and lost to the endless bureaucracy of Washington; at least that's what the public was told. In reality, it was nowhere near mothballed; rather, it was put under the auspices of the Pentagon and made top secret. Barely anybody who didn't work at Midway Magnetic knew of its existence, and even fewer knew how much of a role Jason played in the project.

In reality, many of his theories made the whole project possible. Where prominent scientists said it would take at least another 10 to 20 years of research to make the program viable, Jason's breakthroughs eliminated that delay completely. A particle accelerator was built in Northern California where a natural source of helium welled up from the earth. This helium, the normal byproduct of the breakdown of naturally-occurring uranium, is used by the project to cool down the superconductors necessary to operate a particle accelerator. Once the helium is compressed, the resulting liquid exists only at the extremely low temperature of -452 degrees Fahrenheit. Since the liquid is so cold, various materials such as certain ceramics turn into superconductors when submerged in it; specifically, they lose all resistance to the flow of current. These superconductors are what make super colliders (and the tremendous magnets in them) possible, since the massive magnetic fields that are needed can only be achieved with a huge amount of current. Without superconductors, the magnets would simply melt under the weight of such current.

The Midway Magnetic Particle Accelerator, or MMPA as everybody called it, was set up to create a stream of protons which, at the right moment, would be aimed toward the primary redirection satellite hovering above the installation in geosynchronous orbit. This special satellite was designed to accept the particle stream and magnetically redirect it either to an incoming bogey, or to another similar satellite with the same capability. Currently, there are 12 such redirection satellites hovering in geosynchronous orbit over the continental United

States, as well as two over Alaska and one over Hawaii. There are an additional four located in the areas between the mainland and each of the non-contiguous states.

The whole thrust behind the project was to make it possible for the United States to defend itself against an incoming intercontinental ballistic missile. If an ICBM is detected, the particle stream is engaged, the matter stream is redirected to the closest satellite, and that satellite redirects the particle stream against the ICBM. While the beam isn't necessarily visible, as opposed to the lasers in its Star Wars movie namesake, the effect definitely is.

While there were many small-scale tests indicating the science was sound, the first full-scale test of the system involved a UGM-133A Trident II submarine-launched ballistic missile. The missile, minus an active warhead, was launched off the coast of Guam by the USS Kentucky with the intended target being a fictional city somewhere in the middle of North Dakota. The specific target location was actually out in the middle of nowhere just in case something went wrong and the missile actually made it to its target. In reality though, the missile never even came close.

Once the MMPA matter stream was fired from Northern California, the beam traveling at nearly the speed of light was received by the primary redirection satellite, or node. That node then magnetically captured the beam, redirected it to another node halfway between California and Hawaii, which in turn completed the redirection to a final targeting node hovering over the far side of the Hawaiian Islands. At that point, it was perfectly redirected with pinpoint accuracy to the moving ICBM target. All this happened in only two-tenths of a second.

It only took one additional second for a catastrophic failure of the rocket to occur, well before it got anywhere near its supposed target in North Dakota. Once the beam penetrated the outer hull of the missile, the heat it generated ignited the solid rocket fuel in the tail section of the missile. Within 350 milliseconds of the breach, a jet of hot combustion gasses shot from the side of the missile and catastrophically changed its trajectory. If it wasn't for the onboard self-destruction system built into the missile that automatically fires in case it goes off target, the ensuing combustion coming out of the side would have caused its own explosion. The missile sensed something was going terribly wrong and automatically self-destructed.

The test was a runaway success, and in the annals of top secret research and development, Jason was an absolute rock star hero. Too bad only a handful of people knew he was behind the technology.

One of the things that success did was grant Jason a bit of latitude to pursue whatever other fields of science he chose related to the particle accelerator. So long as the missile deterrence capability wasn't compromised by his continuing scientific experiments, he was free to pursue whatever else he wanted. The only deal he made was to stay on and make sure all systems for the SDI remained in tip-top shape. In the last six months, he and Dennis had been working hard at constructing a device with the ability to detect and use the constant flow of billions of neutrinos, coming as a result of the nuclear reactions in our sun and from deep space, which pass through our bodies every second. By being able to detect these neutrinos, they would supposedly be able to counteract the uncertainty principle put forth by Werner Heisenberg way back in 1927.

The test today was to see if that was what they had done, or if they had been laboring for six months on an elaborate paperweight.

The MMPA was a massive facility. Aside from the main ring of underground superconducting acceleration pathways that had a circumference of approximately 32 kilometers, immediately outside the east wall window to Jason's office was a 10-story chamber containing various apparatuses including the collision detection chamber (CDC) used purely for science, as well as the particle stream redirection unit (PSR) used for the missile defense system. This chamber sat in line with the circular acceleration track so when collisions weren't taking place, the particle streams continued to pass through in ever-increasing acceleration, approaching the speed of light.

The PSR was not to be toyed with; it had to remain ready, working, and available 24/7.

The CDC was what Jason and Dennis often referred to as their playground. It was almost exactly the same as the ATLAS detection chamber found at the Large Hadron Collider in Switzerland. That detection chamber was groundbreaking in that it, as well as its sibling called the CMS detector, led to the discovery of the elusive Higgs boson, a building block in understanding the nature of mass and of the universe in general. It was in the main control and measurement station of MMPA's collision detection center where Jason now found himself. Dennis was also in the CDC, but his station was in the power control systems section. He was in charge of regulating the 17 trillion volts powering the collider.

The detection equipment of the CDC had slowly been adapted over the previous six months to detect neutrinos, the cornerstone to the theories Jason and Dennis used in building their Heisenberg compensator. The programming development had been recently de-bugged, and power was now being ramped up in successive sawtooth steps. With each progressive power ridge, measurements could be tak-en, and readings could be interpreted.

Jason and Dennis were connected via an open intercom. "Are you ready to proceed with the final PI countdown?" Jason asked Dennis.

"Roger. Final Particle Insertion countdown commencing in 3-2-1. Mark," replied Dennis.

The readout on Jason's controller station started decreasing from the starting point of three minutes.

"Two minutes fifty seconds. Begin LH flow," said Jason.

At that moment, large valves could be heard opening, allowing the liquid helium to bathe the superconducting ceramic materials, causing the normal resistance to the flow of electricity to completely dissolve. Since one of the biggest by-products from large flows of electricity is the heat generated by resistance, superconductors are used to generate the massive magnetic fields used to propel the particles with ever more speed.

"Two minutes thirty seconds. Min Temp," called out Jason. At this point, the superconductor magnets achieved their coldest possible temperature. With the liquid helium existing in liquid form at -452 de-grees Fahrenheit, the superconductor magnets bathed in it were now capable of handling the progressively increasing levels of current that would be applied to them.

"Two minutes twenty-five seconds. Beginning stage one power," said Dennis. At that moment, enormous relays could be heard engag-ing the first of the 4.2 teravolt power supplies into the superconduc-tor circuits. The superconductors began to hum as they felt the power coursing through their veins. Four trillion electron volts is certainly nothing to sneeze at, considering there are four stages of power, each with its own supply of a little over four trillion electron volts. In the end, a total of 17 trillion electron volts of power was to be used. To Jason and Dennis, when the system was brought up to full power, it was like riding a thoroughbred.

"Stage one power ridge ... MARK" injected Jason. It only took about 10 seconds for the full complement of four teravolts to be achieved.

"Two minutes five seconds. Beginning stage two power," said Dennis. Again, more relays engaged.

"Stage two power ridge ... MARK" replied Jason. They were already consuming enough power to supply electricity for a decent-sized city.

Before it was over, they would be using enough power to light up about 150,000 average homes.

"One minute forty-five seconds. Stage three power beginning now," said Dennis. As the new level of power began its injection, you could hear various parts of machinery begin to hum, that is, if you weren't wearing hearing protection. Everybody was, though.

"Stage three power ridge ... MARK."

"One minute twenty-five seconds. Final stage power," said Dennis.

"Stage four power ridge ... LOCKED" announced Jason. "Power staging complete. Beginning proton stream insertion." A relatively small bottle of hydrogen supplied the protons that began their continual acceleration. Round and round they went, around the circumference of the particle accelerator for the next minute and 15 seconds, until they were going so fast that each 32 kilometer trip around the loop was made over 11,000 times every second.

"SPEED!" Jason called out over the enormous noise of the machine. This indicated the particle stream had achieved the maximum amount of speed attainable with the power available. "Particle insertion in 10 seconds."

All detection systems engineered to detect the neutrinos coming from deep space were online, and the recording devices were ready to accept the huge amount of data about to be produced. The five calorimeters located in the center of the detection chamber were originally designed to detect particles at different energy states. The sensitivity of these devices were refined more and more to detect incredibly small particles, such as quarks, gluons, and the associated plasma. These collisions, resulting in the release of temperatures over one million times hotter than the center of our sun, were incredibly small, and incredibly hard to detect. Neutrinos were even harder to detect, since their smallness meant they didn't always hit other atoms. The theory was with the injection of the massive particle stream from the accelerator, neutrinos would become excited enough and attain an energy level substantial enough to reliably be detected by the new detector system Jason and Dennis had built.

"Particle insertion in 3-2-1 ... Mark!" said Jason.

At that moment, the immense superconducting magnets guiding the particle stream around the merry-go-round received the commands from the control software to slightly change how they were timed and how they were applying their power. That slight change caused the particle stream to instantly change its trajectory from going around the loop again to going straight into the detection chamber. The particles speeding into the chamber met with another particle stream which had been looping around a sister set of superconducting tubes, only in the opposite direction. These particle streams smashed into each other at a force almost equal to a train crashing into something at almost twice the speed of light. Under these conditions, and under the resulting temperatures, not even subatomic particles making up the very fabric of the universe could hide. The detectors in a standard particle accelerator are designed to ferret out the nature of these particles allowing physicists like Jason and Dennis to understand how the universe works, and thus how to achieve ever greater and more amazing utilizations of such science.

Today, the detectors weren't just looking for the quarks, gluons, and muons of matter, but for the interactions of these subatomic particles with neutrinos.

But something went wrong.

Immediately before the two particle streams hit each other, the primary calorimeters registered something they hadn't ever registered before. Approximately 100 nanoseconds before impact, the density of the particle stream mass actually doubled. It was as if two streams were sent into the detection chamber, but the resulting energy input was what you would expect from four streams. For a half a second, Jason saw the numbers and instantly thought they may have triggered a chain reaction of some sort. The strange thing was, as soon as the impact occurred, the resulting collision was what would be expected with only the two streams. Gigantic release of energy, but definitely *not* a chain reaction as Jason feared.

Jason sat back in his seat, wide-eyed, and reluctantly gave his heart permission to start beating again. Barely audible, he croaked to Dennis, "Did you see that?"

"Hang on a minute while I clean out my Pampers!" quipped Dennis. It was obvious this had struck him in a similar manner.

"What ... the HELL ... was that!" asked Jason, to no one in particular.

"Beats me. Did you get a load of the gamma particle count?"

"No" said Jason. "How bad was it?"

"That's just it," replied Dennis. "It was zero."

"What? How can that be? That's impossible! What's going on here!"

"Ya got me," replied Dennis. "According to the standard model, and all experimentation since then, the release of gamma radiation from the temporary disassembling and dispersal of subatomic particles causes the natural release of gamma radiation from the dissolving weak force bonds. This doesn't make sense."

Jason sat forward, blinked a couple of times, and said, "Commencing shut down. Engage power shunts."

"Engaging power shunts," replied Dennis. He reached forward and hit five keystrokes; the Command and Control software began shunting the power coursing through the collider, decreasing it to zero. "Power level is zero," he confirmed.

"Beginning LH reuptake," said Jason. After receiving the software commands, large valves opened and pumps started removing the liquid helium from its position around the superconductors. The pumps compressed the liquid and errant gaseous helium back into storage tanks. It was far too precious a material to release into the atmosphere.

"Reuptake complete. Final shutdown complete," confirmed Dennis.

They respectively let out several breaths, then independently realized the test had failed. The detectors they had toiled on for the last six months were obviously not working properly.

"A bad day," muttered Jason.

"Yup," replied Dennis, over the intercom that was still open.

CHAPTER 32

ꙩ ꙷ ꙽⁄ꙮꙴ ꙅꙮꙴ ꙷ ꙷ ꙴꙩ

Holliman Air Force Base.
10 Kilometers SW of Alamogordo, New Mexico
Center for Intelligence Surveillance and Reconnaissance (ISAR)
Modern Day

OVER THE LAST SEVERAL YEARS the need for drones and their valuable intelligence, surveillance, and reconnaissance in the war theater has increased exponentially. And with the rise of new terrorist organizations seemingly in every alleyway and dark canyon, the former culture leading to only the most elite of officers having the privilege of operating attack drones is over. More and more the piloting skills of the enlisted rank and file are being utilized.

With the recent conflicts in the middle east and other places on the planet, the need for strike abilities that can minimize danger to friendly forces, but also the even greater need for accurate reconnaissance has never been more evident. The detractors to the technology point to the fact that there is certainly collateral damage when strikes are made, and they like to point to the grandmothers and children that have lost their lives. They like to vilify the armed forces for the civilian deaths that have resulted from the successful bombing runs carried out by the most elite of drone operators.

At the same time, though, proponents of the drone technology point out that while there are terribly regrettable civilian deaths that have occurred, the overwhelming benefit to the efforts to eradicate terrorists cannot be understated. They point out that it is hard to quantify the thousands of lives that have been saved by the fact that the terrorists they kill are no longer a threat, and that the number of peacetime efforts that have moved forward is innumerable. They typically point out that if Bin Laden and the 19 terrorist hijackers that flew jets into the World Trade Center had been taken out with a drone, public sentiment would probably name them as murderers, whereas their efforts would have saved the lives of the 2,997 civilians that died when the buildings came down.

One thing for sure though is that the whole subject is a political "hot potato" that most politicians prefer to avoid. Most of them feel that the investment of resources and the risk of civilian casualties are far outweighed by the sheer tactical advantage proffered by these silent and deadly killers of the air.

Holliman Air Force Base near Alamogordo New Mexico is smack dab in the middle of sunshine country. To some people in the country, it holds the best brand of heat since, as they say, "Yes, but it's a dry heat!". Situated in a less than remarkable portion of the base, there is a set of structures that appear to simply be cargo containers that might have just arrived from an overseas shipping carrier. Upon closer inspection, though, you might start to notice that the corners of the "containers" have small retractable wheels attached to the structure, such that if they were extended one would be able to tow around the metal box rather easily. After even more examination, you would also see that there are actually quite a lot of antennae extending from the rooves of these boxes. Air conditioners can be heard on one side of each of them, and once you get close enough, you would be able to see that while some of them have side doors allowing personnel to enter and exit, other similar "containers" are actually electrical generators. With cables running from the generators to the other containers, you can now see that whatever takes place in these containers, these operations are the ultimate in mobility.

These "containers" though, are much more than a metal box with T V's and refrigerators coming from Asia. These are the mobile Command and Control centers used orby the armed forces to control the Global Hawk, Predator, and other highly sophisticated drone aircraft.

Drone-based aircraft is actually relatively new in its development. As late as 1982, the Israeli army successfully came up with an ingenious solution to a conundrum that had been plaguing them for quite some time. At that time, the Beqaa Valley of southern Lebanon was a complete death trap. Sophisticated Russian equipment such as SA-6 anti-aircraft missiles and the radar technology to operate them was employed by Syrian enemies to Israel. The idea of approaching the valley by either air or ground assault by Israeli troops was quite literally a suicide mission. Something had to be done to minimize losses in the region.

Israel's answer to this problem was the first truly useful unmanned aerial vehicle, or UAV, that actually had no firepower whatsoever. It was controlled from the ground with radio signals (a concept that was not really that new ... it had been used by model airplane hobbyists for years, but had never been used effectively in the theater of war before), and like other conventional model airplanes it was slow and had limited range. What it did have however were signal generators that enabled it to project a radar signature of a much larger plane.

On June 9, 1982, the Israeli army directed a wave of these UAV's straight toward the Syrian missile sites in the Beqaa Valley. When the UAV's flew over while generating the signals of much larger planes, the Russian-built Syrian radar systems activated so as to lock onto the targets of what they perceived to be a large squadron of fighter airplanes and bombers coming in for an attack. What the Syrians didn't know though is that these UAV's were not the real threat, and while they were busy locking target on the ghost bombers, behind these drones were fighters rigged with their own anti-radiation systems. These fighters destroyed not only the missile ranging technology but to a great degree the anti-aircraft missiles themselves. As a result, the Israeli forces now had free reign over the Beqaa Valley, and they were now able to shoot down almost any Syrian aircraft.

From that time forward the Pentagon saw that not only was the usage of UAV's necessary for effective warfare, but they also saw that the United States was woefully behind in where the military brass wanted to be with this technology. This opened the way to a wave of research and development that led to the modern drone that not only has the ability to fly without a pilot being on board but can utilize the satellite global positioning system as well as two-way satellite communications. This allowed a remote operator to directly control the aircraft, and to observe real-time reconnaissance data. In time, these drones began to carry military payloads, none the least of which can be the one-hundred-pound AGM-114 Hellfire missile. With only a twenty-pound warhead, it is considered a tactical weapon, however, because it utilizes smart bomb technology, it has proven highly effective in neutralizing enemy threats.

On this particular day, though, black ops ground forces have reported that a terrorist target of high interest had been spotted in the province of Nangahar, Afghanistan. This information had come through intelligence channels and was then relayed to Air Force personnel operating drones that had been on a training mission flying in formation over Afghanistan. The drone pilots were operated by personnel at Holliman Air Force base, twelve thousand three hundred miles away. The light in the Command and Control operations center was kept low. All focus was on the video feeds coming from the drone signals relayed via satellite.

SENTINEL· "Possible new target approaching. Target one building. Designate new target: Target 5."

PILOT· "Pilot Copies"

SENSOR· "Sensor Copies"

SENTINEL· "White pickup arriving in front of target building."

PILOT· "Pilot Copies"

SENTINEL· "Two passengers including target 5 have entered the building. Confirm target in building."

SENSOR· "Copy. Sensor confirms."

SENTINEL· "If possible keep eyes on building and pickup. Building has the priority."

PILOT· "MC. Pilot. I need tail 107 to come off its current target. Get permission for 107 to come south."

MC· "MC Copy"

PILOT· "Sensor, relieve sensor lock till we have permission to come off that target."

SENSOR· "Roger Wilco"

MC· "Pilot, MC. Tail 107, cleared off target."

PILOT· "Sensor you can break lock on the bridge and lock up the target 5 with tail 107."

SENSOR· "Roger"

PILOT· "We got 60 degrees north heading."

SENSOR· "Copy"

SENTINEL· "Pilot, request weapons load out."

PILOT· "Sentinel, Pilot. I've got eight missiles and two bombs on two predators in the target vicinity."

SENTINEL· "Target 5 leaving building. Entering pickup. Pickup now has priority."

PILOT· "Pilot Copies"

SENSOR· "Sensor Copies"

SENTINEL· "Pilot, Sentinel. You are cleared hot for white pickup."

PILOT· "Sensor lets spin up weapons on tail 107."

SENSOR· "Copy"

PILOT· "Pre-launch checklist."

SENSOR· "PRF Code"

PILOT· "Entered"

SENSOR· "A.E.A. Power"

PILOT· "On"

SENSOR· "A.E.A. Bit"

PILOT· "In Progress ... PASSED"

SENSOR· "Weapons Power"

PILOT· ON

SENSOR· "Weapon Bit"

PILOT· "Passed"

SENSOR· "Code Weapons"

PILOT· "Coded."

SENSOR· "Weapon Status."

PILOT· "Weapons Ready."

SENSOR· "Pre-Launch Checklist complete."

SENTINEL· "Pilot, Sentinel. You are clear to engage white pickup truck at your discretion."

PILOT· "Acknowledged. Pilot clear to engage white pickup truck."

PAUSE

PILOT· "Looks like it's on the move. Launch Checklist. MTS Auto Correct"

SENSOR· "Established."

PILOT· "Laser."

SENSOR· "Laser Selected."

PILOT· "Go ahead and arm your laser."

SENSOR· "Laser is armed."

PILOT· "Master arm is hot. Go ahead and fire the laser."

SENSOR· "Lasing."

PILOT· "We're within range. 3-2-1, RIFLE."

PAUSE

PILOT· "3, 2, 1 ... IMPACT."

PILOT· "Excellent Job."

CHAPTER 33

Across the Potomac River from the United States Capitol and the White House, the Pentagon building sat on the easternmost edge of Virginia. Built in 1943 during the height of the Second World War, its nearly 29 kilometers of corridors and over half a million square meters were Ground Zero throughout the Cold War, yet stood its ground until September 11, 2001. On that day, 184 innocents were brutally killed by five men armed only with the vicious force of a fully-fueled airliner smashing into the western side of the building at hundreds of miles an hour.

The building survived. More importantly, the verve and vigor of its people not only survived but galvanized into a force vowing to stop at nothing until those terroristic menaces who assaulted the Pentagon and continued their blood-craving practices were wiped clean from the earth once and for all.

Admiral Kenneth Grant Brinstock was promoted to his station at this bastion of United States military might for just that job.

With the middle name of a famous general, Admiral Brinstock, or "Kenji" as he preferred to be called, was foreordained to advance in the military's hierarchy. Kenji joined the United States Navy in the mid-sixties, a time when it wasn't in vogue to join the "Establishment." Raised as a staunch East Coast Republican in the suburbs of Boston, Kenji rose quickly and steadily in the military ranks. Early in the Vietnam War, he was regarded as somewhat fearless, and many wondered why he was never hit by gunfire. His seeming fearlessness was more the result of his pouring over tactical reports from scouts and reconnaissance aircraft rather than not caring about his personal safety.

Continuing to establish himself as a force to be reckoned with, Kenji never expected anything from his subordinates that he also didn't expect from himself. A textbook perfectionist, he was deeply admired by his superiors, except when his intensity forced them to deal with the inevitable human resource casualties: his subordinates. Nonetheless, the brass viewed him as tremendously useful, leading to his vice admiral promotion.

In July of 2012, he took over as Deputy Chief of Naval Operations (DCNO) for Information Dominance and Director of Naval Intelligence (DNI). The DNI is the Navy's lead office for resourcing Intelligence, Cyber Warfare, Command and Control, Oceanography and Meteorology, Electronic Warfare, and Battle Management capabilities. His mission was to deliver end-to-end accountability for Navy information requirements, investments, capabilities, and forces.

As DCNO, Kenji also directed the efforts of more than 52,000 military and civilian professionals who comprise the Information Dominance Corps. Their mission is to provide warfare commanders with Assured Command and Control, Battlespace Awareness, and Integrated Fires.

Today, he rode up the elevator to the top floor of a Washington, D.C. skyscraper. As the elevator doors opened, he found himself in the lobby of Michaelson, Finch, and Bradie. John Bradie, Esq., was an old friend of Kenji's. They had taken many a hunting vacation together, including to the grasslands of Africa where they bagged various trophies for their respective dens. Kenji's wife elected not to go on such a testosterone-charged trip; in fact, she was the reason he was making this visit to his friend's office.

Judith Crontin-Brinstock had been married to Kenji for the better part of a decade. Around the time Kenji felt the void of not having a female companion, he met Judith at some social function. Thinking back on it, Kenji couldn't quite remember whether it was a wedding for a friend, or some other official event related to work. She had been a first-level administrative assistant for an army general stationed at the Pentagon; actually, an Army Vice Chief of Staff. He was a hard-nosed, no-nonsense soldier, but Judith had the ability to see through the crusty exterior to the man underneath. He was already happily married, so there were no aspirations on her part for a romantic relationship with the general. Kenji wondered whether the general, or anyone, really could be "happily" married; he was coming to John's office to square off with not only his wife, but also her divorce attorney.

He didn't blame her for wanting a divorce. While their marriage started out fine, as all new marriages usually do, eventually the newness wore off for both, and the real persons underneath began to show through. The romantic man he made himself out to be gave way to the man dedicated to his warrior profession. The stoic "overworked and underpaid" woman gave way to a glamorous lady needing love and understanding from her husband. He wanted to be that man for her. He really did. But in the end, it was something he just couldn't do. He was a soldier first and foremost, despite all his good intentions at the beginning of the marriage. He may have said marriage vows to his wife Judith at the wedding, but he had said another vow, to defend the United States of America, long before. No matter how hard they tried, she would always end up coming in second.

This didn't sit well with her, and the eventual seeking of a divorce was not surprising. He had received a copy of the demands made by her and her attorney and, for the previous week, had been thinking about her and the entire reason for this meeting. Today was when they would hammer out the final aspects of the divorce settlement, then sign the papers. He had been thinking hard about the demands made in the documents, and had come to a conclusion. They had to be changed.

Stepping into the lobby, Kenji walked up to the receptionist's desk to announce his presence. Wearing his best-pressed uniform, he was the picture of spit and polish the Navy expects from all its personnel. The woman behind the counter was more than impressed by the fine specimen standing before her.

With an obvious smile in her voice, she addressed him. "May I help you?"

"Yes, I'm here to see John. I am Admiral ...."

"Admiral Brinstock?" she interrupted.

"Yes."

Getting up, she rounded the perfectly polished chrome and glass counter. "Right this way, Admiral. My name is Autumn, and Mr. Bradie is expecting you."

Leaving the perfectly-appointed lobby, they passed through the door to the side of the reception counter and traveled past several cubicles in the secretarial pool. There were numerous second glances coming his way from some of the women working hard at their respective jobs. It wasn't anything new to him, but at this moment, it didn't really stroke his ego. He knew he was there because he wasn't man enough to provide his wife with the things she needed. That, above all else, ate at his very soul. He may have been holding his head high with his dress cap under his arm, but inside he was slightly less than happy with the circumstances.

The two reached Bradie's office and, upon opening the door, the receptionist attempted to introduce Kenji to John, but was immediately interrupted by her boss. "Kenji! Get your butt in here, you dusty old fart. Jeez! You look like hell."

Kenji smiled at John's attempt at humor. This was an old joke between two old friends; the better you looked, the worse the criticism would be. If you got a compliment, then you knew something was definitely wrong.

"And you look like the south end of a jackass walking north!" responded Kenji, falling right in line. Seeing her services were no longer needed, and perhaps to spare herself from the flurry of insults, Autumn quietly closed the door to the office and returned to her post.

"And to think I was actually wondering if you'd be on time," said John. "You had a whole 30 seconds to spare. I'm not sure what to do with all the time we have."

"You could go back to counting all your millions," Kenji replied, bringing up another old joke. The two men were both of comfortable means, but Kenji always made sure to act like he was a pauper, and his friend was Ebenezer Scrooge.

"I would be doing just that if you hadn't interrupted me," responded John.

The two men sat down in a comfortable area set up in the corner of John's office. They both knew the meeting with Judith and her attorney wouldn't start for another 15 minutes. Kenji being here 15 minutes early was something he requested from John the day before, so he could go over the letter outlining the division of assets. This wasn't anything new to John; he had handled several divorces over the last two or three decades. Differences of opinion as to "who gets what" in a divorce was par for the course. The messy part is when there are children involved. Thankfully, that particular complication wasn't present in this divorce. John had pretty much seen it all; that is, until this divorce. Kenji was about to throw a definite curve to his old buddy.

"So, what is it you wanted to talk about before we meet with them, K?" asked John.

"As you know," replied Kenji, "we've received the list of demands from Judith outlining some things she wants in the settlement."

"And you want to take a few of the things off the list," added John. He reached for his legal pad so he could take notes.

"Not exactly," replied Kenji.

"Excuse me?"

"I don't want to take anything off the list," replied Kenji, hoping to clarify his meaning. Seeing the look in his friend's eyes, he saw he had failed.

Looking down at his lap, noticing the way one knee was crossed over the other, Kenji reached into the depths of his soul for the next words. Bearing the soft underbelly of his soul was an uncomfortable task for him, but something he knew he needed to do. All his life he had been trained to be strong as steel. Now, he had to admit something he wasn't used to admitting; he had failed a mission.

Speaking without looking up, Kenji explained. "John, I have been in the Navy for longer than I care to admit. I have been trained to be the warrior our nation needs. I have been used in more ways than John Q. Public has even the slightest notion. I have the privilege of being able to draw a direct line from decisions I've made to the number of lives those decisions have saved. For decades, I have taken pride in perfectly carrying out the demands of the commander-in-chief, and of my superior officers. I have done so with such precision and timing that I have actually been made one of those superior officers myself. I regularly meet with the Secretary of Defense, and occasionally I even meet with POTUS himself."

Pausing for a moment, he looked directly into the eyes of his friend. For his part, John was more than a little taken back by what he saw. He knew there wasn't a chance in hell Kenji would break down and cry, but he saw emotions in him he had never seen before. He knew that of all times, this was the time to keep his mouth shut.

"But this ..." Kenji gestured to the paperwork he had originally tucked under his arm, the same paperwork now lying on the coffee table, " ... this is a mission which will occupy a very lonely place in my life. I've got a lot of things in my personal 'Win' column, but this thing with Judith, this one's going to have to go in the 'Lose' column."

Pausing for a moment, Kenji gathered up the will to continue. "You see, 10 years ago when we married, I decided to be the perfect husband. I approached it with the same military precision as I have the rest of my life. What I didn't count on, though, was in order for this to work, I had to give more than what I was prepared to give. John, she's a good woman. I know you have a lot of people coming in here telling you how bad the other one is. That isn't what you'll hear from me. She's a good woman, and ...."

Kenji looked down. He couldn't look John in the eyes to say the next words. "She needed a better man than me."

Taking a deep breath and pausing for a moment, Kenji steeled himself for what he had to say. Looking in John's eyes again, he said, "I've made a decision about the division of assets, John. As you will see here," he handed John the sheet he had made out the night before, "I've indicated that not only do I want to meet Judith's demands, I have added the list of items you see at the bottom of the page. I have decided to increase the term of alimony, and also to increase the amount of it by a fourth. In addition, she is to receive title to the house completely. I do not want it to be split."

Now it was John's turn to be speechless. In all his years, he hadn't seen a divorce where the parties were more interested in the well-being of the other. It was usually less than civil, and in fact, usually a bloodbath. This was new. Really new.

"Wow" was all John could muster. After sitting there and allowing the words just uttered to percolate down, John finally gathered his wits and broke the silence. "K, as your counsel, I have to remind you this isn't something that is necessary in the eyes of the law, and isn't anything I've ever seen before. I have to advise you that purely in terms of accepted jurisprudence, there is no reason for you to do this and it is not in your best interests."

"I know that, John," responded Kenji, "and I know you had to say that to cover your own ass. But I'm telling you, I've given this a lot of thought, and my decision has been made. It's cast in stone, so we just need to get on with this and make it happen."

Nodding his head, John knew once Kenji made a decision, he had the guts to carry it out to the very end. It's what made him a good soldier, and now it's what made him a good man. Contrary to what John thought was ever possible, his opinion of Kenji went up a few points right then.

"OK," responded John. "I see you've made up your mind."

Reaching over to the phone, he punched one button and asked for his legal assistant Mindy. Within the span of just a few minutes, Kenji had in his hand a document outlining the alterations he had proposed in handwritten scrawl earlier. The documents were signed, and all was ready for their meeting with the "opposition." The phone rang; it was Mindy announcing that Ms. Brinstock and her counsel had arrived, and were waiting in Meeting Room One. The two men looked at each other as John clicked off the speaker. "You ready for this?"

"About as ready as I'll ever be," responded Kenji.

The men emerged from John's office and walked the short distance down the hall to the meeting room where Judith and her attorney were waiting. The admiral's first impression was that her attorney looked young. Kenji decided he was just used to the more mature markings of John rather than the fresh-out-of-law-school look of this young buck. His suit was perfectly pressed, and he was polished. It didn't matter; this meeting should be over quickly.

As they all took their seats, the opposing counsel began speaking. "Thank you for meeting today. We should be able to complete the details of the paperwork and move on with our lives quickly. You have already been served with the list of demands being made by my client. We feel these demands are reasonable in light of the time Admiral and Ms. Brinstock were married. I see no need for anything further. I have here ...."

John interrupted. "Actually, I met with my client just before this meeting, and we discussed the tenets of demands made by Ms. Brinstock. We have some changes we would like to make."

"Oh, here we go," said her counsel, ceremoniously rolling his eyes and theatrically slamming the papers in his hand down on the table. Judith was more than a little disappointed. She didn't think Kenji would be so low as to demand there be any changes to the list. She thought she had been fair. She needed to be taken care of, but she didn't desire to "stick it to the man," as they say. Now she was beginning to think she had totally missed the mark in estimating how her soon-to-be ex-husband was going to conduct himself. She didn't think him to be a cold, heartless ass, but she did expect something better than this from him. Judith dipped her head in disappointment.

"Now just a minute, counsel," replied John, trying to establish some clarity and hopefully communicate this wasn't what he was assuming. Unfortunately, the young buck wouldn't let him speak.

"No, you just 'wait a minute' counsel!" shot back her attorney. "Ms. Brinstock has been more than fair in the demands made here, and you know it."

At this point, John decided to just sit back in his chair, fold his arms, and allow the opposing counsel to bluster all he wanted. He could see this wet-behind-the-ears kid was just doing what he needed to do to look good in the eyes of his client, and ultimately in the eyes of his bosses. As John sat there listening to all the noisy blather, the grin on his face began to grow larger and larger. He knew the more he allowed him to get riled up, the more exquisite it would be when John revealed what he had in store. The grin angered the other lawyer even more; without knowing it, each terse word uttered made the inevitable reveal even more savory on John's part. Kenji had played chess enough with his friend to see the movement of pieces on this virtual board and, even though this was all centering around the dissolving of his personal life, it was rather satisfying to see John masterfully playing the role needed to make this upstart look like an idiot.

Eventually, the opposing counsel exhausted all his legal arguments and wranglings, and came to a point where John could now say two words. Kenji saw it coming, and he unsuccessfully stifled a small chuckle in anticipation of the kill John was about to make. The chuckle didn't go unnoticed; Judith looked at Kenji with a snarl. He immediately felt bad for what she was feeling, but took solace in knowing what was coming. Her gaze didn't leave his face. She was determined to stare him down.

With an acquiescent nod, John sat forward in his chair and stroked his chin with one hand. "You make some good points, counsel."

"Damn straight!" said the kid.

Ignoring the interruption, he continued. "If you had given me a moment to finish what I was saying instead of blustering about like a primate on crack, I was going to point out our wish to make some changes to the list of demands by *adding* to them for the benefit of your client."

Judith's facial muscles suddenly went slack, and her gaze shifted to John to see exactly what kind of joke this was. She had been quiet the entire time; without waiting for her attorney, her response was simple.

"What?"

For once, the kid was silent. Not only was he being upstaged by his client, he knew John had just knocked over his king in this game.

"That's right, Ms. Brinstock. We wish to add to the list of demands as outlined in this addendum."

John waited a few moments, allowing Judith and her attorney to read the additions Kenji had outlined earlier. Sticking the knife a little deeper into the withering opposing counsel, John said, with a syrupy smile, "Perhaps you need to confer with your attorney?" The body language of her attorney had now changed from the commanding presence of an attorney trained at Yale, to that of a confused apprentice. His clothes even seemed a little more disheveled.

There were a few moments of silence, then Judith spoke. "I'd like to speak to my husband alone, please."

"Ms. Brinstock, I don't think that ..." responded her attorney. Judith shot a withering look at the kid, who immediately stopped what he was about to say. A very smug John, and a very disciplined opposing counsel, stood and left the room. The admiral and Ms. Brinstock looked at each other.

Judith got up from her side of the mini-conference table and walked over to sit near Kenji. She was the first to speak. "Kenny, for as long as I've known you, I've tried to figure out your next move. I've always tried to second-guess you, only to discover you had out-maneuvered me. I thought I had figured out what you would want here too, only to discover, once again, you had changed the rules of engagement."

It occurred to Kenji that his wife knew him more than she thought. She was using language she knew he would understand. He remembered she was the administrative assistant to an Army Vice Chief of Staff, after all.

"I have only one question now," said Judy. "Why?"

Leaning forward with his elbows on his knees, Kenji looked down at the floor. After thinking for some time, he began to speak. "Judith, for the longest time I had hoped to be the man I knew you needed. The man you deserved. I tried to convince myself I would be able to rise to the needs of the mission at hand. But when I received the notice of divorce, I realized this was a mission I was ill-prepared to complete."

Looking up at her, he saw eyes of compassion he hadn't seen in a long time. A part of him wanted desperately to fight, doing whatever it took to make her his once more. Reason won out. No matter how distasteful the job, sometimes you just had to grit your teeth and push through.

"The truth is simple, Judy. You deserve to be happy, and I am man enough to admit I'm not the right man to make that happen. You deserve to be with someone who can give you what you need, and I have to be big enough to admit that it isn't me."

Pausing for a moment, he looked her straight in the eye and said, "I have nothing but respect for you, Judy, and it is my sincere hope that one day you can find what you deserve. I hope one day you will find love."

On hearing his words, she was speechless. She didn't know what to say, finally deciding that words would have been too crass for a tender moment like this. She stood and, when she did, he stood in deference to the lady she was. Her next move wasn't what he expected. She reached out to him and gave him a large, very heartfelt hug. With her lips near his ear, she whispered what needed to be said, what was in her heart

"Thank you, Kenny. I will never forget you."

She then placed a tender, lingering kiss on the cheek of her soon-to-be ex-husband, a move she never figured she would do during the day's activities. For his part, he allowed himself to relax in the embrace of his one true love. He knew he wasn't the right man for her, but decided, right then and there, his mission from now on was to make sure she was well cared for. He would follow her from afar and see to it she had anything and everything she needed. He turned his lips to her ear and whispered what he needed to say. "I love you, Judy. That will never change. If you ever need anything, I will see to it that the entire Navy is at your beck and call."

She knew it to be hyperbole, but also knew that, in his own way, this was the sincerest expression of devotion he could have ever said. Before letting go, he gave her a final parting kiss on the cheek. Moist, lingering, and warm.

After gathering their wits about them, they invited their attorneys back in, and the papers were completed soon enough. Judith and her now ex-counsel left and, after a few parting words with John, Kenji left to go home as well. As in a predictable movie scene, the skies opened up with rain the moment he made it home. After putting on some Miles Davis, he poured himself a tall tumbler of some good 12-year-old and stood at the window contemplating his future. He was still the DCNO, DNI, and a host of other acronyms which didn't seem too important to him at the moment. His life would continue to be filled with the seductive lure of power, prestige, and honor. But now that the papers were signed and he would soon officially no longer be married, he felt more alone now than he did this morning. Although they hadn't lived together for several months, the link of a lingering marriage wrapped itself around his heart like a warm blanket, lulling him into not feeling so alone. As he sipped his scotch, he looked down at the hand holding the tumbler. Setting down the glass, he removed the ring from his finger and unceremoniously tossed it in a seldom-used ashtray on the counter underneath the window.

Picking up his drink once again, he drained it and exhaled a hissing breath, signaling the warm concoction had made its way past his throat. He looked out the window and watched the lights of the cars drive by. He thought about how they had better be careful. It was raining outside.

It was raining inside as well.

CHAPTER 34

ᒋ ᒄ ᒍ ᒄ ᒍ ᒎ ᑕ ᑯ ● ᐃ ᑕ ᐸ
ᒐ ᐦ ᑎ ᐸ

ARRIVING AT WORK THAT MORNING, Admiral Kenneth G. Brinstock marveled at the mini city that made up the Pentagon. After clearing security, several members of the armed forces passed him as he walked down the corridors toward his office on the C ring. Once he got to where his administrative assistant worked, signs could be seen announcing, "You Are In A Sensitive Compartmentalized Information Facility (SCIF)." His office was the pinnacle of all SCIFs found in this building since he was responsible for the bulk of naval intelligence.

His administrative assistant, Sergeant Larry Flume, had already been hard at work long before Kenji arrived. There were several thousand who had been working since about 4:30 a.m. that morning; the sergeant had only been at his desk since 7:00 a.m. His first responsibility each day was to prepare a briefing for the admiral summarizing all correspondence which had come in from the field, as well as all requests for information. Next was a listing of any meetings scheduled either by Kenji himself or by his superiors. Finally, space was reserved for any miscellaneous issues that Sergeant Flume felt were necessary to bring up. He was studious enough to not allow any necessary business to fall through the cracks; in fact, he was just now completing notes and materials for the morning briefing. Knowing Kenji's routines, he understood the briefing would only occur after a strong cup of military mud had been poured. This cup was one of about 30,000 poured at the Pentagon that day.

At 8:10 a.m. sharp, Sergeant Flume knocked on Kenji's door.

"Come!"

The door opened and, per normal procedure, the sergeant took his position at the sitting area in the admiral's office. Kenji preferred to sit on the couch for his meetings instead of at his desk, creating more of a connection with his subordinates. Rising from his desk, he walked to his customary chair with a cup of coffee in his hand.

"What do we have today, Larry?" began Kenji.

"Sir, there are several different matters to attend to today. First, there are reports from the USGS on a situation brewing in Yellowstone. Second, there are some questions from the commanders of the northern fleet about preparations for the NATO exercises scheduled later this month. Third, there is a letter from the secretary of defense to the joint chiefs of staff for you to review and comment. Fourth, there are some details which need to be worked out concerning your upcoming trip to Midway Magnetic in California. Finally, there are a couple of other miscellaneous items."

"OK. Let's start with the reports from the USGS. What's happening there?" said Kenji.

Handing the admiral a package labeled "Eyes Only," Sergeant Flume explained the latest from the field. "Sir, as you can see from this package of information, there is a potential critical situation in Yellowstone. According to Dr. Morrison in the Montana Bureau of the United States Geological Survey, Yellowstone is showing signs indicating the magma chamber underneath the park is preparing to erupt."

"Do you have the response plans we put into place after the Mount St. Helens blast?" asked Kenji.

"Yes sir, I have that information available. If I can direct your attention to a paragraph on page 17 of the briefing, you'll see that Dr. Morrison, along with several of his colleagues, indicate there is actually no comparison between that eruption and with the volcanoes at Yellowstone."

"How much of a 'No Comparison'?" asked Kenji.

"According to the data presented by several of the most reliable personnel at the USGS, the Yellowstone eruption is going to be hundreds of times larger than the volcanic explosion associated with Mount St. Helens in western Oregon." answered Sergeant Flume.

"Hundreds?" asked the admiral, somewhat incredulously.

"Sir, do you remember the eruption of Mount Pinatubo in 1991?" asked the sergeant.

"Yes. At the time I was stationed in the Atlantic, but I remember hearing about it," said Kenji.

"Since you were stationed in the Atlantic at the time, you may remember Hurricane Andrew in August 1992. At the time, it was the most destructive hurricane in United States history, and was felt from the Bahamas to Louisiana."

"Boy, do I remember that one," said Kenji. "We were deployed by the president to help with disaster relief for quite some time. The destruction I saw is something that I will never forget."

"And Hurricane Iniki hit the Hawaiian Islands in September 1992."

"Yep. I remember hearing about that one while we had our hands full with Andrew. It seemed like Mother Nature was really pissed off that year," replied Kenji.

"Sir, according to the USGS historical meteorologists, there is overwhelming evidence those hurricanes were directly related to the eruption of Mount Pinatubo in the Philippines," responded Sergeant Flume.

"How's that possible with the locations being so far apart?" asked Kenji.

"According to the briefing, an ash cloud that rose up into the atmosphere was carried by the winds across the globe, causing drops in temperature which directly affected the global weather."

Thinking about what Larry said, Kenji asked, "So, what does Pinatubo have to do with Yellowstone?"

"The reason the meteorologists briefly mentioned Pinatubo is because the volcano in Yellowstone is classified as a "Super Volcano," and is actually 100 times larger than Pinatubo. If what the USGS says is correct, when Yellowstone blows it will be an extinction level event. Everything will be affected, and there is a good chance the human race won't survive."

Hearing this, the admiral, who had been leaning forward during the start of the conversation, now sat back against the couch seat. "And why is this something the doctors are hot and bothered about *now*? I know it isn't a new volcano. It's been dormant for thousands of years."

"Sir, to summarize the briefing, apparently there are several indicators the volcano has recently awakened. Five miles below Yellowstone, there is a magma chamber which has fed the three prior super volcano eruptions that happened there, dating back 2.1 million years ago. About every 600,00 to 650,000 years a new eruption happens, and we are now due. When you combine that with the fact the geysers, which are a very consistent feature of the park, have spontaneously stopped and, when you take into consideration the floor of the Yellowstone Valley, itself a volcanic cone spanning hundreds of kilometers across, has risen about 200 meters vertically, it indicates the chamber is rapidly filling with super-heated magma. Based on how fast things are changing there, the experts expect an eruption any time in the next 12 months," explained Sergeant Flume.

"Good god!" was the only response that came to Kenji's mind. After thinking about it for a moment, he asked, "Do they have any suggestions in mind?

"They are requesting that the full force of the Pentagon be put to finding an answer" was the sergeant's reply.

"I will analyze this material today. If I agree with your assessments, then I will take this to the president himself and ask him to create an executive order for exactly that. I'm sure this would do any good, but even if it required a nuke to relieve the pressure, then I'd do it."

That comment set the sergeant back on his heels. He wasn't a pacifist by any means, but knowing how incredibly stingy Kenji was about anything having to do with nuclear weapons, Sergeant Flume knew he had been successful in conveying how serious the situation was.

Nodding his head and taking in a deep breath, Sergeant Flume decided to get his thoughts back on track. He gave the admiral a few moments to read through some of the materials in the USGS briefing packet. "Are you ready to move on to the next item, sir?"

"Hang on a second, Larry," replied Kenji. Reaching for the phone, he picked up the receiver and hit the intercom button.

"Yes sir!" came the polished response from the other end of the line.

"Stephanie, please get in touch with the White House, and ask to schedule a Classified Level One meeting with the president for my assistant and me for tomorrow. This is top priority and top secret. Understand?"

Sergeant Flume, who had been looking down at the rest of his meeting notes, now glanced up at the admiral when he heard he was to be part of the meeting. This would be the first time he would meet the president. The sergeant's reaction wasn't lost on Kenji. For a split second, he thought about how Larry was one of the best assistants he'd ever had and deserved to be part of the briefing.

"I'll have a response for you in 10 minutes, sir," replied Stephanie.

"Thanks, Stephanie," responded Kenji. He placed the receiver down and glanced at Larry, who still looked a little flustered. Kenji smiled, then said, "Larry, I'm going to need you to step up to the plate on this and have your facts and figures together. I'll give the highlights, but I'm going to rely on you to present the bulk of the details the president may want to know. Keep it straight, and keep it factual. You're a good man, and you'll do fine. I'm certain of it."

The vote of confidence coming from the admiral was something Larry had been working for tooth and nail during the entire three years he had been Admiral Brinstock's assistant. He made a practice of checking his facts, then triple-checking them again. Kenji recognized that Larry's patterns were not unlike the perfectionistic patterns of a much younger version of himself. He thought to himself, "This kid is going to go far in this man's navy." Recognizing the political incorrectness of his last thought, the admiral decided to keep that observation to himself.

"Thank you, sir. I appreciate it!" replied Larry.

"What's next?" asked Kenji, to keep the meeting moving.

"Sir, the commanders from the northern fleet have some questions for you. This is the fleet taking part in the joint NATO exercises next month. Here." Larry handed a sheet to Kenji. "There aren't any babies crying here. They can be answered at your leisure."

"Sounds good. Next?" responded Kenji.

"There is a letter from Defense Secretary Hume, congratulating you on the way you handled the situation two weeks ago in Nicaragua. The one remaining member of the terrorist cell who was hiding in the Pearl Lagoon on the East Coast is on the run. According to the detachment of SEALs you dispatched, they forecast he'll be eliminated within the next 24 hours. Commander Rojas on the ground there says they've been tracking him, and it appears he's slowing down, thinking he's no longer being chased. It appears they have it well in hand."

"Excellent. There's no telling what those idiots were capable of doing," observed the admiral.

"I agree, Admiral. The next item on the agenda is your upcoming trip to Sonora, California."

"My what?" asked Kenji, his eyebrows furrowed together.

"Sir, two days ago, you said to schedule a trip to Midway Magnetic in Sonora, California, to inspect the collider project out there."

Kenji knew exactly what was going on in California, but he also knew the details of that project were quite a bit above the sergeant's pay grade. Yes, it was a super collider project that would make the one in Sweden look like a cage made of tinker toys, but the real reason for its existence was known only by a handful of individuals in Washington. The president himself was keeping tight reigns on the project, making sure nobody knew about its existence unless he personally signed off on their involvement.

The fact that Larry had overheard the admiral saying he wanted to go to California for an inspection was a little troubling to him.

"When did you hear I wanted to go to Midway?" asked Kenji.

"Two days ago you were in your office, and I was sitting at my desk. You were talking to someone on the phone, and said you were planning on going there for an inspection. I took it upon myself to create the pending travel arrangements for you. All you have to do is give the word, and I will finalize them for whatever date you choose," responded Larry.

Kenji grinned and shook his head. "I'm gonna start calling you 'Radar' from now on, Larry."

After pausing for a moment, he added, "The word is given. Schedule the trip for two weeks from today."

"Yes, sir," responded Sergeant Flume.

Privately, Kenji took notice that he would have to be a little quieter from now on regarding that project. It was far too sensitive for anybody not authorized by the president. His assistant was good. Maybe too good.

"Next?" asked Kenji.

"Finally, sir, there is one item which, while not exactly something I put much credence in, I still need to bring to your attention. It's an item called in by a reservist over the weekend," said Larry.

"A reservist? What did he want?" asked the admiral.

"She had quite a fantastic story, sir. Second Lieutenant Patricia Lynne Marlowe phoned in to report, well, an island located between the mainland and Bermuda. She said this island has ... um ...."

Larry was stammering now, not like him at all. "Spit it out, man. What's she saying?"

Larry sat back ramrod straight, and said, "Aliens, sir. She said the island is full of dead aliens."

Kenji looked at Larry for exactly two seconds before starting to laugh louder than he had in a very long time. That got Larry laughing just as much. Since the door to Kenji's office was closed during the briefing, and since this was a SCIF, nobody else heard the belly laughs going on in the office for the better part of a minute.

With tears in his eyes, Kenji finally got some control over himself. With a few spits and starts, he said, "Larry, saving that one for last was a good move on your part." Looking at the ceiling and wiping his eyes clear, he added, "Jeez, I needed that!"

"I'm glad, sir," responded Larry, suffering his own case of facial cramps from muscles grinning far more than they had in a long time.

Standing up from the meeting, Kenji said, "Well, Sergeant, get to those arrangements."

"Right away, sir," was Sergeant Flume's response. Turning on his heels, he emerged from Kenji's office and returned to his desk. He considered putting the paperwork on the "alien" island in the round file, but he never liked throwing anything away. He slipped the paperwork into the bottom drawer of his locked file cabinet, then proceeded to handle the California trip details. He thought the Sierra Nevada mountain range was a strange place to put a scientific installation, but oh well.

Meanwhile, Kenji received Stephanie's callback. The meeting was set for tomorrow at 11:15 a.m., and they had 15 minutes. Kenji knew it would take longer, but the president was the one to make that call. "What the hell are we gonna do about Yellowstone?" he thought "Well, something will turn up, I hope."

What he didn't know, was something already had.

CHAPTER 35

CAPTAIN DANIEL MORRIS SAT IN the chair with his face in his hands, and his elbows on his knees. The chair was in a small room which had only a table and four chairs. The room was used by the Judge Advocate General, or JAG as it is more commonly known by among the troops, to question personnel and investigate any situation resulting in the loss of life which might be due to criminal negligence. JAG representatives had been gracious enough to thank Captain Morris upon his arrival, and had been somewhat consoling in their comments about the incident they were investigating. Still, Morris knew why he was here. No matter how gracious they were, if they didn't like what he said, they had the authority to slap the cuffs on him and haul his butt off to the brig.

Sitting in the small windowless room with the customary one-way glass on one wall, he thought about the events leading him here. He kept arriving at the same conclusion: he had absolutely no idea what went wrong, or why it went wrong. When things went south, there was the pandemonium expected in such situations, but then his training took over, and he did his best to document and record everything while it was still fresh. Those notes were now in a closed manila envelope sitting in front of him on the table. Several times he opened the envelope so he could read, re-read, and then read them again to look for anything he might have missed. There wasn't. The whole thing had relegated itself to his dreams or, more accurately, his nightmares.

After waiting for about 10 minutes in the Holliman Air Force Base interrogation room, the door opened and three smartly-dressed, uniformed investigators entered with notes in hand. Seeing that superior officers were entering the room, Captain Morris immediately stood and saluted. Behind the colonel and two lieutenants who entered, an Air Force stenographer followed them, taking her position in the corner of the room out of sight of Captain Morris. The senior officer among them was the first to speak.

"At ease," said the colonel. "Please have a seat, Captain Morris. We have a lot to go over in this inquiry."

Captain Morris relaxed his stance and took a seat. As he did, he looked at the two men and one woman sitting across the table from him. They were arranging their materials; not only their notepads, but also more than one recording device. Eventually, they got their affairs in order, and the colonel began to speak.

"Captain, my name is Colonel Mike Devorak. On my left is Lieutenant Lindsay Alminar, and to my right is Lieutenant Giovanni Jones. While I am the senior officer in charge of the investigation, these two lieutenants are my co-investigators. I have given them complete authority to ask any questions, and I expect you to answer their questions as clearly and completely as if I was the one asking the question. Understood?"

"Yes, sir!" answered Daniel.

"Good," replied the colonel.

As the colonel looked down at his notes to get his thoughts together, Captain Morris decided now would be a good time to get his own notes out and arranged. Daniel noticed the clackity clack coming from the stenographer had stopped. For a split second, he wondered why he hadn't noticed its sound before now; probably simply because he was so nervous about this meeting, and how these three people had the power to decide his fate, let alone his career.

What he didn't know was the three had already come to a unanimous conclusion about the loss of life that terrible morning in the eastern Atlantic Ocean. They had gathered enough evidence to know exactly what caused the loss of friendlies that day, but the colonel had directed his team to not let the Captain know this, just in case he might offer up some details that (a) they didn't know already, and (b) would incriminate him in the events of that day. They wanted to keep their cards close to their chest.

After getting his materials in order, the Colonel began. "Captain, as you know, the events of 17 June of this year resulted in the loss of life of several friendlies on board the USS Ptolemy. You were at the weapons control console in charge of the guided missile that struck the ship. We have asked you here today to explain not only your role in the events of that day, but also what occurred immediately preceding the disaster, as well as after. For documentation purposes, today's proceedings will follow the procedures outlined in the Uniform Code of Military Justice. Do you understand?"

"Yes, sir," responded Captain Morris.

"To lead the discussion today, Lieutenant Alminar has a few questions."

"Thank you, sir," said the lieutenant. "Captain, I'd like you to state for the record your name, rank, service number, where you were stationed and what your job was."

The word "was" wasn't lost on Captain Morris. He wondered if this is how it was going to end for him.No matter. Now wasn't the time for such thoughts.

"I am Captain Daniel Morris. Service number DZ18883929. At the time of the incident, I was stationed here at Holliman Air Force Base. I am a Predator Laser Technician, and it is my responsibility to respond to the commands of my superior officers in the arming of weapons, and to direct the laser onto the target."

"And when the incident happened, you were on duty?" asked Lieutenant Alminar.

"Yes," replied Daniel.

"Please tell us what happened that day from your perspective," requested the lieutenant.

Captain Morris looked down at his notes and spent five seconds refreshing his mind. He then straightened his back and began speaking.

"On the day in question, I was at my post in the mobile Command and Control bunker that oversaw the Predator UAV CS-454 flying patrol over the Atlantic fleet during the NATO exercises which were in full swing. The mission parameters handed to me by my superior officers were for my team to fly eye-in-the-sky patrols during the exercises of 17 June, and relay our observations to the commanders on board the USS Carl Vinson. This was part of a cooperative set of exercises involving both the Navy and the Air Force. Per my orders, I was to maintain an open channel of communication with Navy Colonel Martin Swayne on board the carrier, who would take that information and direct the forces on the surface."

"Before you continue, Captain, do you remember speaking with him that day?" asked the lieutenant.

"Yes, I do," replied the captain. "I remember there were several operations we successfully completed, and I remember him expressing his approval on the performance of my team."

"Thank you. Proceed."

"On the day in question, my team was directed to change our overall flight pattern to come in closer to the shore on the southern end of the English Channel. We were one of the few predators equipped with live fire weapons since some of the exercises included selecting dummy targets and taking them out. We weren't told ahead of time what the targets were going to be. Based on previous exercises we had been part of, we assumed the targets would be land-based, typically old equipment that had been retired, such as decommissioned tanks and personnel transports parked in the middle of a field."

"Did you receive orders to deploy your weapons on a target?" asked Colonel Devorak.

"Yes, sir," replied Captain Morris.

"And to the best of your recollection, what did those orders say?" asked the colonel.

"I wrote in my notes that it was Order Number ANE-2892. The order said to set our targets on a derelict ship that had been towed out to coordinates 49 degrees, 33 minutes, 56.22 seconds north by 4 degrees, 6 minutes, 42.09 seconds west. The pilot plotted his course and took the necessary steps to relocate our UAV to the requested location."

"When you got there, what did you find?" asked Lieutenant Alminar.

"When we arrived at the coordinates, we found two ships; the derelict ship as expected, but also another ship about 30 kliks to the west. My CO made an inquiry and determined the other ship had some brass on it who were observing the exercises."

"Then what happened."

"We arrived at the requested coordinates and went into a high-altitude holding pattern. I kept my sights trained on the target ship all the time. As I was doing that, I was also going through checklists to determine the best firing solution to the ship, since I knew it was only a matter of time before we would receive orders to fire. After receiving the clearance to fire, I trained my targeting laser on the ship and, after the countdown, the weapon was released."

"But the weapon didn't make it to its intended target, did it?" This was the first time Lieutenant Jones had spoken since entering the room. His voice was lower in timbre, and he spoke with a certain taint. Later, Captain Morris wondered if this uniqueness to this voice had anything to do with his name being Giovanni, or just a coloration from where he grew up.

Turning to Lieutenant Jones, Captain Morris answered. "No, it didn't. After about 10 seconds, it became apparent the weapon wasn't tracking in the manner we had intended. I was able to verify the targeting laser was definitely lighting up the derelict ship but, according to the weapons specialist in charge of the weapon, it began veering off course."

"What happened then?" asked the colonel.

"When we saw that not only was it veering off course but was on a direct collision course with the other ship, the commander gave the order for self-destruct. The problem was, no matter what we did, we could never get a return ping from the weapon indicating the self-destruct command had been received. We continued to receive a video feed from the nose camera of the hellfire missile as it tracked directly to the other ship. There was nothing we could do to keep the weapon from zeroing in on the friendly ship."

"What steps were taken at that point? Did you or your team try to warn the ship?" asked Lieutenant Alminar.

"Our commander got on the horn to the commander of that ship to tell him what was happening but, even as he was doing it, everybody in the room knew it was going to be too little, too late. The weapon was only 15 seconds from impact, so there was no time to get word to the crew to brace for impact."

At this point, Captain Morris was beginning to get a little emotional. Ever since that day, those 15 seconds constantly replayed themselves over and over in his brain. He hadn't slept much, and it was really starting to wear on him. It had been a week since the incident, and he had been relieved of duty until the investigation was completed. Although the room was quite comfortable, even a little on the cool side, Captain Morris was sweating profusely from the strain of being under the microscope like this.

"What's the next thing you remember?" The colonel's voice seemed to take on a conciliatory timbre to it, which struck the captain as strange. Even so, he continued with the story.

"At that point, we were helpless to do anything but watch as the distance meter counted down until the weapon hit the ship." The captain's eyes now drifted to nothing in particular, as if staring at something a million miles away. "All I remember is the screen of static. In the bottom right-hand corner, there was a single word. It just said 'offline' in red letters. I remember staring at that word, praying we had misread the readouts; that it hadn't really hit the ship with friendlies on it." The captain's head began to slightly shake back and forth. "But there was no mistaking it." Letting out a repressed exhale, Captain Morris rested both elbows on the table, then rested his forehead in his palms with his eyes closed. "There wasn't anything we could do. All I could think about, all I still think about, is a weapon I deployed killed some of our guys!"

For a few moments, there was silence in the room. The words of Captain Morris sunk in. The only sound was the whir of the idle transcription machine in the corner behind the captain, as well as the almost silent whoosh of the air conditioning duct.

The two Lieutenants took notes while the colonel studied the man before him. As he considered the body of evidence they had already uncovered, and this interrogation certainly hadn't uncovered anything they didn't already know, Colonel Dvorak decided now was the time to reveal to Captain Morris the true nature of what happened that day. He knew a situation like this could mess up a good soldier for the rest of his life, and with the excellent record this one had, he certainly didn't want to see him get screwed up.

Looking at the transcriber in the corner, Colonel Dvorak said, with a smile on his face, "Nancy? I think we're done here. Thank you."

With quick precision, the transcriptionist folded up her machine and made her way out of the room. This was also a pre-arranged signal to the lieutenants that their services would no longer be needed. They gathered up their materials and exited the room right after Nancy, closing the door behind them.

For his part, Captain Morris didn't know what to make of this new course of events. Since he was used to being somewhat fatalistic in estimating what was going to happen to him, he figured now was when the colonel was going to slap him in cuffs and send him up the river, a fate that couldn't have been farther from the truth.

Looking the captain in the eyes, Colonel Dvorak got up from his chair, circumnavigating around the table until he took Nancy's chair, and sat backward on it to the right of Captain Morris.

"Son," the Colonel began, "what I am about to reveal to you is for your ears only. You are not to repeat this information to anyone who doesn't know it already. Do I make myself clear?"

"Yes, sir!" snapped back the Captain. This was certainly not what he was expecting.

"Good. We began investigating this incident as soon as it happened and, early on, we learned your team had done a perfect job in executing its orders. You need to know not only were the events of that day not your fault, but they happened because we were under a direct hacking attack by a small band of terrorists who call themselves 'Al Juraab.' They are not the kind of terrorists who kill with suicide bombers; they are the kind who kill with their computer expertise. I know you have been out of the loop since that day; all predators have been grounded so we can retrofit every one of them with new encryption technology that will keep this from happening again."

The captain stared at the colonel with a bewildered look on his face. "You mean, the predator was ...."

"Hacked," the colonel finished his sentence. "Yes, the terrorists not only hacked into the avionics of the predator, but were also able to hack into the weapons guidance systems. They were the ones who directed the missile to the friendly ship. Not you."

Captain Morris, who had been sitting on the edge of the chair listening to the colonel, now flopped back in his seat and expelled a rush of air which seemingly had been balled up in his chest since the incident a week ago. He tipped his head back and just stared at the acoustic ceiling for a while. "So this really *isn't* our fault." It was more a statement than a question.

"No," confirmed the colonel. "It was a band of terrorists I have sworn to get if it's the last thing I do. I lost a good friend on that ship, and I will not sleep well until I know the murderers are dead."

Tilting his head forward again and looking the colonel in the eyes, the captain now asked his own question. "If I may, sir, who did you lose?"

Looking down at the floor, the colonel took in a breath and said, "He was a good friend, normally stationed at the Pentagon, who wanted to be present at the NATO exercises this time. He brought his personal assistant with him, and she also was killed. Army Vice Chief of Staff Steven Salkin, and his personal assistant, Mrs. Judith Brinstock."

"Brinstock?" asked the captain, with his eyebrows squeezed together.

"Yes," confirmed the colonel. "She was Admiral Brinstock's wife."

Admiral Brinstock had just received the news of Judith's death, and was sitting in his chair, slumped over his desk. His head was dipped and perpendicular to the desk, his extended arms lay in front of him, and the memorandum lazily fell from his right hand. There was no sound in his office, except for the silent, piercing shrill of Kenji's heart falling to pieces. As he sat there, he did what most would do, asking himself how things would have been different if he had done this or that. He felt that if had they not recently filed for divorce, had he been the man she deserved, she might still be alive today because she wouldn't have gone back to work.

He got up from his desk on unsteady legs and retreated to the window behind his desk. He looked, but there wasn't much to see outside his Pentagon office. The window was only there to let in some ambient sunlight. It didn't matter; he wasn't really looking at anything. No amount of light would change the growing darkness now starting to form in his heart. With each passing second, the sterling reputation this man had spent decades fine-tuning, his dedication to the pursuit of all his commander-in-chief directed, his drive to be the perfect soldier, all congealed into a new man. This man may have looked the same on the outside, but on the inside now had a new mission. The death of the woman he still loved was the catalyst which turned him into a man willing to kill anything or anyone who got in his way of avenging her death. The person deciding what that course of action would be wasn't only going to be the President of the United States. No, now *he* was going to see to it that the morons who took the life of his ex-wife—no, his *wife*—would pay. And if anyone got in the way of his plans, they would become collateral damage.

She may have died at the hands of a missile which made a hellacious sound as it detonated, but the death of Admiral Brinstock's conscience made no sound. From that day on, he knew he would kill anybody who got in his way.

Speaking to her spirit, which he wanted to believe was in the room, he said, "I will avenge your death if it is the last thing I do Judith. I don't care if I have to personally kill every last terrorist on this planet, I will not rest until your killers, all their families, and all their friends are *dead*. To any who ask, I will always say I'm doing it for the good of the country, but ...."

He paused.

"All that I am about to do will be done for you. I don't care what I have to do. I ... WILL ... AVENGE ... YOUR ... DEATH!"

CHAPTER 36

ᑕ᠊᠊᠊ᑊᒍ ᑕ᠊ᒐᑊᒍ ᠊ᒍ
ᒎ ᒍ᠊ᒍ ᒍᒍᑕ ᒍ

ODAY WAS TYPICAL FOR PENTAGON inhabitants. Kenji's office was already about four cups into its traditional total of 12. Between Sergeant Flume and Kenji, they drank their fair share, which was nothing compared to the over 30,000 cups drunk there every day.

Sergeant Flume had never looked forward to a briefing more than today's. He certainly wasn't looking forward to reviewing the reports coming back from the missile strike last week that killed the admiral's estranged wife. He knew they were getting divorced, but also knew the admiral still loved her, so this was definitely going to be a touchy subject.

Admiral Brinstock arrived at his normal time, and entered through his normal door. The Defense Protective Service, the Pentagon's version of the Secret Service, had their customary station set up at the entrance, including metal detectors. As he approached, the personnel at the door recognized him, but they were to check the ID of each person regardless of whether they recognized them. Several points were checked on the ID which hung around the neck of each person who entered. Not only would the picture and name be checked, but also the expiration date. The 2D barcode at the bottom of the ID badge would be scanned, and this would show not only a picture of the person on the computer screen, but it would also ratify their current authorization to enter the facility; it would show where they were stationed. About the only person allowed to enter the facility without ID would be the president himself, or the secretary of defense.

After getting through security, Kenji walked down the hallways by himself. Everybody knew who he was, so he had to weather through all the greetings underlings gave. "It's strange," he thought, "how before today it never bothered me, but now they are all just meaningless fodder." He knew his new outlook was directly related to the way his life had changed since Judith's death. He had no other desire now than to kill terrorists, and to kill any who got in his way of killing terrorists. As every day marched by, the value of life meant less and less to him. There was a new coldness emanating from him. Most didn't know he and Judith had split; the vast majority felt this was normal for anybody who had just lost their wife, especially under these circumstances.

If they only knew.

After about five minutes of walking through a few of the literally miles of corridors in this incredible building, he arrived at his desk. Sergeant Flume was just wrapping up his early morning duties and getting ready for the morning briefing. Where before there was the customary morning greeting exchanged between the men, Kenji simply passed by Flume's desk and walked straight into his office with no words whatsoever. The sergeant thought this was strange until he remembered the admiral had just lost Judith. He chalked it up to that.

After five minutes, the customary time it took the admiral to get his coffee together and check his email, the sergeant entered and took his customary seat. When Kenji asked, "So what do we have today Larry?" without getting up from his desk and without even looking away from his computer screen, Sergeant Flume got up from his place on the couch and sat in the chair on the other side of the desk.

"Sir, there are three items on the agenda today. The first item may or may not be something you are willing to talk about now, sir. A memorandum came from the secretary of defense, asking about the investigation into the missile strike on the Ptolemy." After a short pause, he said, "I understand if you would rather not discuss that now, sir."

This sentence made Kenji stop staring at his monitor and look Sergeant Flume directly in his eyes.

"Sergeant," said Kenji, "I will not now, nor will I ever, allow myself or any around me to pussyfoot around that subject. If you have something to say, then say it." There was an icy cold stare in Kenji's eyes that Sergeant Flume had never seen before. "Do I make myself clear?"

With finely tuned military precision, the sergeant's reply was unmistakable. "Yes, sir!"

"Good. Get on with it," was Kenji's reply.

"Yes, sir. Part of the memo was the secretary's direction to obtain better intel on the activities of the faction who made the hacking attack. After that, there is your upcoming visit to Midway Magnetic. And finally, there is one refinement on a previous issue I brought to your attention."

"Did you forward the memo to me from the secretary?" asked Kenji.

"Yes, sir. You can find it to your right on the corner of your desk."

Kenji swung his chair and picked up the paper lying on the corner. It started out with the secretary tendering his condolences to the admiral. Then it said, in part:

> "As you can imagine, the incident in the NATO exercises has brought into crisp focus the need for better intel. How did we miss this group rising up right under our noses? Was there any advance warning they were becoming a threat? Regardless of the answer, I am directing you to use whatever resources are at your disposal to counteract this type of attack in the future. I am aware that all existing drone technology is being retrofitted with encryption to make it unbreakable, but I want to know whether there is anything else out there rising without our knowledge."

> "If you have to put undercover operatives in place, then do it. If you have to create an entirely new department whose sole direction is to find weak spots in our shields, then do it. Spare no expense, stop at nothing and no one to make this happen. For the good of our country now, and for the good of the country we are handing our children, do whatever you have to, to make our citizens safe."

The closing remarks struck a chord with the fledgling, newly psychotic persona who had taken root in Kenji. *For the good of the country. For Judith.*

"Larry, get in touch with my senior team. Tell them I want to meet at 1 p.m. sharp. Tell them it will most likely be a late meeting, and the subject will be counteracting this new brand of cyber-terrorism used in the attack on Jud' ... on the NATO forces."

The slip of his wife's name wasn't lost on the sergeant, but he wasn't going to let on.

"Yes, sir." Sergeant Flume wrote several things on his pad of paper, then continued on.

"Next, sir, there is the subject of your upcoming trip to Midway Magnetic. Have you decided on when you wish to go there for your inspection?"

"Yes," replied Kenji. "I am going to be in meetings the rest of this week with the senior team on this memo from the defense secretary, so tell them I want to make my inspection this Saturday."

For a second, Kenji thought about it while Sergeant Flume was writing. "In fact, call them on the side phone right now. I want the schedule to be locked in before this meeting is over."

"Yes, sir." To his left was a phone sitting on a small table, allowing visitors to make calls while Kenji continued with other tasks. After dialing the phone number to the Midway Magnetic installation, Larry spoke with the receptionist and asked for the principle designer of technology, a man named Jason Marsalis, according to the info sheet on the Midway file. After a moment, Jason came onto the line.

"This is Jason Marsalis."

"Dr. Marsalis, this is Sergeant Lawrence Flume with Admiral Brinstock's office."

"Hello, Sergeant. What can I do for you today?" said Jason.

"Sir, the admiral asked me to make arrangements for a visit and inspection of your facility this next Saturday. I would like to go over those plans, and discuss with you an agenda for his visit."

"Next Saturday?" asked Jason.

"Yes, sir. Next Saturday, the fifteenth," replied the sergeant.

"I'm sorry to tell you this, but that won't work for me" said Jason. "I'm going to be out of town that weekend with my wife."

"Sir, I can understand your desire to be with family, but this wasn't put to me as a request. The admiral won't be pleased with hearing anything other than you'll be there."

"Now listen here, Sergeant," replied Jason, "you can tell the admiral whatever you want, but the fact remains, if the Admiral comes here next weekend, he will be alone with nobody to talk to. I'll be happy to make myself available any other time, but next weekend is a no-go."

"Sir, can you hold for a moment?" asked the sergeant.

"Sure," replied Jason. "Take your time."

Sergeant Flume put the call on hold and turned to Admiral Brinstock. With a bit of trepidation, he related the gist of Jason's reply. As he predicted, with the admiral's state today, Sergeant Flume could actually see the admiral's blood pressure rise. His face started to turn red, and the dark mood he was in today seemed to grow even darker.

"Transfer the call to my phone. *Now*."

Without a word, Sergeant Flume did as requested.

"Doctor?" said Kenji.

"Yes, this is Dr. Marsalis," answered Jason.

"Doctor, this Admiral Brinstock."

"Yes, Admiral. What can I do for you?"

"Son, I understand we have a scheduling problem for next weekend?"

"No problem, really. I just told your assistant next weekend wasn't possible since I am going to be out of town with my wife. If it needs to be on the weekend, I would be happy to oblige the following weekend. However, any time after this weekend will be fine with me," responded Jason.

"Doctor," responded Kenji, "as my assistant said, I can sympathize with you for wanting to spend time with your family. However, this visit next weekend can't be changed. I require you to be present for the meetings and the inspection, since you are the best-qualified person to answer the questions I will no doubt have during the inspection."

"Admiral," responded Jason, with a tone sounding more pointed than before. "With all due respect, I regret to inform you I cannot and *will not* cancel anniversary plans with my wife next weekend. Whatever you have in mind for this coming weekend will just have to be changed because, while my involvement with the project dictates my being present for your inspection, my presence is not up for debate or negotiation."

Hearing that this weekend was Jason's anniversary struck a small nerve with Kenji, making the recent events concerning Judith come to the forefront of his mind. This guy was doing what he should have done for his own wife. A part of him respected Dr. Marsalis, but that part was now weakly subservient to the much stronger part of him which was a cold and brutal soldier

"Doctor, do you know who you are speaking to?"

"Admiral Kenneth Grant Brinstock. I definitely know who I am speaking to. An individual who would recognize that although you are in charge of this installation, this installation is all based on physics and science you know nothing about. Admiral, if you want to continue to benefit from such, and from the loyalties of each and every one of the personnel who work at this installation, you will see this is not simply a request but, in fact, a reasonable requirement for which you need to *stand down*."

Sergeant Flume could see Admiral Brinstock's eyes narrow. There was a palpable, yet silent, iciness emanating from his commanding officer, one he hadn't seen before. Larry hoped against hope this wouldn't be the new normal.

"We'll see, Doctor," was all Kenji could say. With all the force he could muster, Kenji slammed the receiver down. For a few seconds, he continued to stare at the phone, fuming at one of the most blatant cases of insubordination he had ever come across. He knew Jason wasn't military, so there could be no disciplinary action like there would be if he were a Navy grunt. What really angered Kenji was he knew Dr. Marsalis was right. Kenji needed him, and he hated that Jason knew that. It wasn't something that sat well with Kenji at all. Somehow Jason would have to be removed, "for the good of the country," Kenji muttered under his breath.

"What was that, sir?" asked Sergeant Flume.

Kenji looked up from the phone. "Nothing. Schedule the visit for the following weekend."

"Yes, sir," said the sergeant.

Kenji closed his eyes and willed his blood pressure to go down. This Marsalis grunt would have to be taken out of the way. Nothing and no one would get in his way. The Midway installation was far too critical for taking out the terrorist bastards who killed his ....

"Sir, the next item has to do with a refinement on a previous issue brought up for consideration."

Reorienting himself to the present, Kenji opened his eyes. "What issue was that?"

"Remember how I told you a reservist called in a report of an island in the Bermuda Triangle supposedly full of dead aliens?" asked Sergeant Flume.

Counter to the cold and dark mood Kenji had been in all morning, mention of that particularly ridiculous report ended up doing much to lighten things. Kenji slowly closed his eyes and started to chuckle under his breath while reaching for his coffee cup. "I suppose they also found out Elvis was playing checkers with Jimmy Hoffa on that island too?"

When there was no response from the sergeant, Kenji focused his eyes on him and saw he wasn't smiling, but had a rather serious look on his face. "What?" was all Kenji said.

"Sir, you had better take a look at this," was Sergeant Flume's response.

He walked over to the wall opposite Kenji's desk and turned on the flat screen. Among other things was a DVD player , but the flat screen also had a USB connection on the back allowing for a thumb drive to be inserted, exactly what Sergeant Flume proceeded to do. Within a few seconds, a video picture came into focus.

"Sir, what you see here is a video log taken from that island. Apparently, the reservist has a friend who actually visited the island and took these videos. I can turn up the volume if you like, but I have had IT and cyber warfare analyze the files and video recording. According to them, the recordings are legit."

As the video continued, Larry turned up the volume; the voice of a woman was describing all she was observing. At one point, she talked about how this race of beings was now all dead and her decision to chronicle everything she could about this incredible civilization.

"Who is speaking?" asked Kenji, with dumbfounded curiosity.

Larry looked at his notes. "It's an archaeologist working at the New York Museum of Natural History named Terri Lindstrom. She's the one who actually visited the island, sir, and has studied them enough to know their written language."

The video progressed until Terri entered an apparent home. She talked about how all on the island were dead and, while she didn't make a practice of intruding in the last resting place of the inhabitants, she knew it was important to record at least one set of dead aliens. She carried the video camera through the home into the bedroom. There on their version of a bed were the unmistakable remains of two bodies who had obviously died hundreds of years ago.

Turning down the volume once again, Sergeant Flume continued. "Sir, apparently the report of this island isn't a flight of fancy from some crackpot. What is of even more concern is the reservist knows about the situation in Yellowstone, including details only known by this office."

"What?" exclaimed Kenji. "How in the hell did that information leak out!"

"The information didn't leak out, sir. There is a device on the island which not only revealed the existence of the problem but, according to the reservist, has the ability to remedy the problem."

"Remedy the problem?" asked Kenji incredulously.

"Yes, sir. Apparently it is in need of repair, but if it can be fixed, then yes, it would remedy the problem in Yellowstone."

Moments of silence passed between the two men as the screen continued to show more and more scenes from the island. Without a word, Kenji reached for the recently-abused phone and pressed the intercom button.

"Yes, sir?" said a bright and cheery voice on the other end.

"Stephanie, get in touch with Major Bellini and tell him I need to see him immediately."

"Right away, sir" was her professional reply.

"Turn that back up," said Kenji.

The screen showed a shot of what looked like a computer, and an image on that screen of a person who looked normal enough, but somehow different. Hard to say exactly how, but he just was. Larry reached for the remote and turned up the volume, he could now be heard talking in a language that was not recognizable.

"Unbelievable!" was all that Kenji could say. Sergeant Flume nodded in agreement.

After a few minutes, there came two quick knocks on the door.

"Come!" said Kenji loudly.

The door opened and in walked Major William Bellini. Sergeant Flume turned down the volume once again.

Standing at attention and snapping a sharp salute, Major Bellini curtly said, "Reporting as ordered, sir."

"At ease. Bill, you know my personal assistant Sergeant Flume?" asked Kenji.

"Yes, sir. We met when we were planning out the whole Nicaragua thing." Bill reached out his hand to Larry and shook it, then came over to the desk and shook Kenji's hand. "What can I do for you, admiral?"

"Bill, I have a really odd task for you," said Kenji.

"Nothing can be as odd as the job in Nica," replied Bill, with a jocular tone to his voice.

"Don't be so sure," replied Larry.

Bill glanced over to Larry to acknowledge the response, and saw the image on the screen which had been paused again on the dead aliens. "What the hell?"

"That's why you've been asked to come here, Bill" responded Kenji. "This is a video log of an island located in the Bahamas that is apparently filled with a race of dead aliens."

Turning back to look Kenji square in the eyes, Bill tried to see if he was now the brunt of a practical joke. "You're serious?" asked Bill.

"Very," replied Kenji. "I want you to drop everything you're doing and go down there, along with the people who discovered the island, and verify their story. If it's true, then there might be technology which can help with a problem we have in Yellowstone."

"What's going on in Yellowstone? asked Major Bellini.

"Bill, this is classified top secret right now, so this particular piece of information is not to leave this room." Kenji then proceeded to explain what he knew about the situation in Yellowstone, and Sergeant Flume filled in several details on the USGS science reports.

"You're telling me that we are on the verge of an E.L.E.?" asked Major Bellini.

"That is exactly what I am telling you," came Kenji's reply.

"The thing is," Sergeant Flume injected, "the women who went to the island already knew about it because apparently some tech there not only knows about it but, once it is repaired, can fix the Yellowstone problem."

Major Bellini, who by this time was perched on the front edge of his chair, now sat back and soaked in all that had just been dumped on him. "Whoa."

Turning to Sergeant Flume, Kenji said, "Larry, make whatever resources Bill needs put at his disposal." Then turning to Major Bellini, he said, "Bill, I want a full report back on my desk in seven days. I want to know if this is real and whether can fix Yellowstone."

"Yes, sir!"

Kenji stood, causing the other two to rise as well. Holding out his hand to Major Bellini, he said, "I look forward to hearing what you find."

The two men shook hands, and after also shaking hands with Sergeant Flume, Major Bellini left, closing the door behind him. Sitting back down at his desk, Kenji looked again at the flat screen where continuing images played. "How many recordings are there?"

"As far as I can tell, sir, there are approximately 27 hours of recordings" replied Sergeant Flume.

"Twenty-seven?" asked Kenji with surprise.

"Yes, sir," replied Larry.

Unlike most of his military contemporaries, Kenji wasn't normally given to expletives.

Today was an exception to that rule.

CHAPTER 37

⦿⌐⌐✓⌐ ⌐⌐⌐⌐⌐ ⌐⌐

⌐⌐⌐⌐⌐

GETTING TO WORK THE NEXT day, Jason made it through the usual pleasantries with those he encountered. There was Susan, the administrative secretary, who took care of the most mundane operations of the office like making copies and ordering supplies. Then there was Bob. "Hmmm," thought Jason. "What does Bob do again?" Oh well, hiring and firing weren't part of his job description.

The office banter was the normal drivel one would expect in any office in corporate America, except for the ever-present aura of secrecy and the pervasive feeling that each person was doing something very special for people who didn't even know they were doing it; the unseen guardian angels, protecting John Q. Public and family from a horde of vile international gangsters. While getting to his office overlooking the 10-story reaction chamber, Jason thought about yesterday's test that went so wrong. He hadn't got much sleep the night before, trying to work out what could have gone wrong. Sometimes he wished he didn't have to keep what he did for a living so secret. Even though Mikki wouldn't understand most of the science, he still wished he could bounce things off her. She was a smart girl and, more often than not, seemed to ask the right question that caused him to start thinking down a road which would lead him to the solution. He wouldn't ever tell her about the test yesterday, but somehow he knew something she would say soon would help him understand what happened.

Knock, knock, knock.

"Come in," said Jason.

The door opened and in walked his partner in crime, Dennis. "Hey, bud. How's it going this morning?" he asked.

"Fine, if you don't count the coffee IV I need to keep going today. I didn't sleep at all last night," replied Jason.

"I concur," blandly replied Dennis. "I've been trying to figure out what happened yesterday, and I'm coming up with a big fat goose egg."

"Yep. "I'm not always as sure-footed in my confidence level as I was yesterday, but I was absolutely certaint it was going to go smoothly, or at least a lot smoother than that."

"Agreed," said Dennis. "Boy, I almost had a heart attack when I saw those numbers double. At the very least, it would have blown out some really expensive hardware, and if it had been what it was looking like, it would have been really bad. Like runaway bad."

With a silent nodding assent, Jason agreed with Dennis. They were both lost in their own reverie, going over countless facts and figures, when the intercom buzzed and harshly yanked their consciousness back to the present place and time. Jason leaned forward and pressed his phone's speaker button.

"This is Jason."

"Sir, you have a telephone call on line one," said Susan. "It's the Pentagon."

His quick glance to Dennis, indicated an unuttered question: why was he getting a call today? Dennis started to get up, lending some privacy to the telephone call, but Jason made a motion with his hand indicating Dennis could relax and stay.

"Thank you, Susan. Go ahead and put it through," said Jason. The phone sputtered a new tone, and he picked up the receiver.

"This is Jason Marsalis."

"Dr. Marsalis, this is Sergeant Lawrence Flume with Admiral Brinstock's office."

"Hello, Sergeant. What can I do for you today?"

"Sir, the admiral asked me to make arrangements for a visit and inspection of your facility this next Saturday. I would like to go over those plans, and discuss with you an agenda for his visit."

"Next Saturday?" asked Jason.

"Yes, Sir. Next Saturday, the fifteenth" replied the sergeant.

"Well I'm sorry to tell you this, but that isn't going to work for me" said Jason. "I'm going to be out of town this weekend with my wife."

"Sir, I can understand your desire to be with family, but this wasn't put to me as a request. The Admiral won't be pleased with hearing about anything other than you being there."

With measured words and an even tone showing that he was controlling a vast amount of ire at the Sergeants tone, Jason replied "Now listen here, sergeant. You can tell the Admiral whatever you want, but the fact remains that if the Admiral comes here next weekend, he will be here alone with nobody to talk to. I'll be happy to make myself available at any other time, but next weekend is a no-go."

Glancing at his friend Dennis, Jason gives an eye-rolling look indicating the knowledge that once again, they were being strong armed by peons that were trying to look good to their commanding officers. There would probably be a different attitude on the part of the Admiral. There usually was.

Dennis gave a knowing smirk back to Jason.

"Sir can you hold on the line for a moment?" asked the Sergeant.

"Sure" replied Jason. "Take your time." Jason knew that this is where the sergeant would go talk to his commanding officer, and this is when the sergeant would come back saying that the following weekend would be fine.

As he waited, Jason's thoughts projected forward to this coming weekend. He was really looking forward to spending quality time with Mikki. Not only was Mikki one of the kindest hearted people he had ever known, but she was just plain downright fun to be with. The fact that she was drop dead gorgeous didn't hurt either.

As his friend, Mikki was someone that Jason could never get tired of being with. Just looking into her eyes, you could easily see a person that was eager to experience all that life had to offer ... almost as if ... if she didn't experience everything that life had to offer to her right now, then it would be an opportunity that would be forever lost. She pursued life and love with a sense of vigor and passion. Life, of course, had its difficulties from time to time, but she was never the kind of person to let that stop her from seeing that life didn't require a glass-half-empty approach, but rather she was most assuredly a glass-all-full kind of friend. In the machine of life, she was the battery.

But then ... as his wife ... well, that just brought with it another level of ...

"Doctor?" interrupted the caller.

"Yes, this is Dr. Marsalis" answered Jason.

"Doctor this Admiral Brinstock" said the caller. This was actually the first time that the Admiral had ever spoken with Jason directly. Even with Jason being as instrumental as he was to the program, Jason had always interacted with the Pentagon through various other military personnel, not with the Admiral himself. Jason no longer slouched in his chair, but rather sat up straight.

"Yes, Admiral. What can I do for you?" replied Jason. Dennis' eyebrows arched up at hearing that the Admiral was on the line.

"Son, I understand we have a scheduling problem for next weekend?" inquired Kenji with a bit of a disarming drawl.

"No problem really. I just told your assistant that next weekend wasn't possible since I am going to be out of town with my wife. If it needs to be on the weekend, I would be happy to oblige the following weekend. However, any time after this weekend will be fine with me" responded Jason.

"Doctor," the caller countered "As my assistant said, I can sympathize with you for wanting to spend time with your family. However this visit next weekend can't be changed. I require you to be present for the meetings and for the inspection that I will do while I am there since you are the best-qualified person to answer the questions that I will no doubt have during the inspection."

For a split second, Jason thought of countering that Dennis was just as qualified to answer any questions that the Admiral might have, and Jason was certainly just as happy to have Dennis to take the spotlight this time. But the way the Admiral was trying to strong-arm him into canceling plans with Mikki, coupled perhaps with the disappointment Jason had just experienced with the systems test the previous day pushed Jason over the edge. There was no way he was going to let this guy, Admiral or not, push him like this.

"Admiral," responded Jason, who was now getting really ticked with this guy "with all the respect that is due to a person in your position, I regret to inform you that I cannot and further WILL NOT cancel my anniversary plans with my wife next weekend. Whatever you have in mind for this coming weekend will just have to be changed because while my involvement with the project dictates, as you say, me being present for your inspection, my presence is however not up for debate or negotiation."

"Doctor, do you know who you are speaking to?"

Jason involuntarily closed his fist over the nearest sheet of paper on his desk literally reducing it to a ball of shreds in his hand. "Admiral Kenneth Grant Brinstock, I definitely know who I am speaking to. I am speaking to the individual who would recognize that even though you are in charge of this installation, this installation is all based on physics and science that you know nothing about, and that if you want to continue to benefit from such, and from the loyalties of each and every one of the personnel that works at this installation under me, you will see that this requirement, which by the way is not simply a request, is a reasonable requirement for which you need to stand down."

There was a palpable yet silent iciness coming from the other end of the phone. "We'll see, doctor." Was all that Kenji could say. The line went dead.

Jason hung up the phone and looked over at this long-time friend and fellow soldier in the foxholes, Dennis. Dennis had both a wide-eyed look, coupled with a grin that stretched from ear to ear. "Jason, if I didn't hear that myself, I wouldn't have believed it. I didn't know you had the huevos to do that my friend!"

"Have you even SEEN the goddess I live with?" replied Jason with a randy grin. "Why would I turn down a weekend with Mikki? I'm just tired of these guys thinking that they get to push us around. We are over here busting our collective asses and these ... GOMERS ... just think that they can steamroll over us" replied Jason. "I'm done with that kind of attitude!"

"I'm with you brother" agreed Dennis. "I just hope it doesn't bite you in the butt someday."

"Yeah, I know what you mean" acknowledged Jason. "Oh and by the way buddy, you need to know that I am completely aware that you could have handled the inspection next week just fine without me, but I am just tired of this kind of attitude, and I didn't want to shove that off onto you either."

"Oh, I know pal. Besides, everybody knows I'm the real wind beneath your wings" said Dennis as he grinned.

Jason took the rolled-up ball of paper in his hand and threw it at Dennis as he smiled.

CHAPTER 38

THE DRIVE TO LAS VEGAS from Sonora may have been long, but the time spent with his best friend was more than worth it. It was always amazing to both Jason and Mikki respectively, that no matter how long they had been married, they always had so much to talk about. When it was time to be quiet in the car, that was all right too; neither of them felt they *had* to talk and carry the conversation forward. But when one of them got the bug and wanted to speak, there was absolutely nothing in their relationship keeping them from opening a dialog about whatever they wanted, small or great. Before they knew it, they arrived in Las Vegas and pulled up in front of their hotel.

The Luxor was a really interesting edifice. Built in the shape of a pyramid, the hotel was 30 stories tall and completely hollow inside. This may not seem that unusual, but how do you build an elevator in a hollow pyramid? Neither Jason nor Mikki had thought about it until they checked in and walked to one of the elevators in the corner. They weren't called elevators; they were called inclinators. The reason was immediately obvious when you got in and chose the floor you desired. Once the doors closed, the motion exerted on your body was rather disconcerting at first because it wasn't a vertical motion, but rather a side-to-side one.

Jason and Mikki got to their room on the 28th floor and immediately collapsed. Since they left right after Jason got home from work, they didn't get to the hotel until about 12:30 a.m. The couple decided to save the fun and festivities for the following day, and just be an old fuddy-duddy couple who went straight to sleep.

In the morning, Mikki decided she wanted to work on her tan a bit. "What do you want to do today, dahhhhhling?" she asked, with her best Zsa Zsa Gabor impression while batting her eyes.

"Well," said Jason "there is a science fiction convention going on at the convention center. I thought it would be kinda fun to go there and look at all the people dressed up in costumes from all the sci-fi shows. After that, I was thinking about maybe going to see "O" over at the Bellagio."

"Wow, that sounds like fun!" enthused Mikki. "Before that, I don't suppose you'd be my pool boy and spread tanning lotion on my back while I lounge by the pool in my bikini would you?" all said while she batted her eyes at her husband.

"Just your back?" asked Jason, sticking out his bottom lip.

"Oh behaaaave," said Mikki. Both laughed.

Jason donned his swimming trunks, Mikki her bikini, and off they went to the pool.

There were actually four separate pools at the hotel, and the two didn't have difficulty finding the perfect place to soak in the rays. As promised, Jason spread a generous amount of tanning lotion on parts near and far on the perfectly-proportioned body belonging to his lovely wife; she, in turn, returned the favor. When gliding her fingers over the rippled muscles of her husband's back, she always felt a little flutter in her stomach. She just couldn't fight away the smile. What she didn't know was that her husband had just fought, and lost, the same battle.

Late morning turned into early afternoon. It was either hunger pangs or getting overheated that roused them from their sun-induced slumber. Regardless, they mutually decided to go back to the room, get cleaned up, then go hit the sci-fi convention scene. They decided to walk the six miles to the convention center. It was nothing to them, considering they regularly covered a 10-mile run every morning in their workouts. Additionally, there were plenty of sights and sounds which would be interesting

By the time they got to the arena, the convention was in full swing, and just as entertaining as they expected. They saw at least five Incredible Hulks, three dozen members of the Star Trek Starfleet, and an unknown number of Star Wars characters. Aside from the convention delegates, there were innumerable booths holding every possible kind of item known to man and alien alike. You could buy a light saber in one booth, then right next to it visit with writers of popular television shows.

It was the latter that eventually caught Jason's attention. When just starting college, one of his favorite shows was Quantum Leap, so he drug Mikki over to the booth. Jason patiently waited on the side, but after overhearing a conversation, he realized the person speaking in the booth was a writer who used to work on the show. After completing his other conversation, the writer turned his attention to Jason.

"Hello there. How are you?" said the writer.

"I'm great," said Jason. "So, you're a writer who worked on the show?"

"Yes, I am. Did you like it?"

"Boy, I sure did!" gushed Jason. "I was going to college at the time, and a lot of what I saw in that show actually inspired me to pursue the fields of study I did."

"Oh really? What fields were those?"

"Electrical engineering and physics."

"That's really great to know," responded the writer. "I was a physics major in college myself. Even though I changed my major and switched to journalism, I never lost my fascination with the sciences. In fact, that's the major reason I enjoyed writing for this show so much. I've worked on several shows since then, but the premise of that particular one was really something I took to like a duck to water."

"Can you tell me," asked Jason, "the name of an episode you wrote?"

"Most of the writing was a collaborative effort. The writing team would discuss the overall direction of the show, and what kind of subplots needed to be developed for the eventual season cliffhanger and resolution episodes. From there, we would create an overall subplot to be developed in an episode, and a primary plot developer would be assigned to write the first draft.

"That writer would come up with the basic premise for the episode, write the first draft of the screenplay, then bring it back to the team for discussion and refinement. Having said that, the one I was the primary on was called 'Goodbye Norma Jean' where Sam jumps back and ...."

"Becomes Marilyn Monroe's bodyguard!" interrupted Jason.

With an astonished look on his face and a chuckle in his voice, he looked at Jason and said, "Boy, you are a fan, aren't you!"

"Oh yeah," answered Jason. "That show was what got me through finals one year."

"That is really gratifying to know, my friend."

"Let me ask you something I've always wondered about," Jason continued. "Were there any twists to the show that never got developed? I always had the sense it was building up to a bigger plot twist which we never got to see at the end."

"Since you asked, there actually was something we were unable to develop because the show was canceled," conceded the writer.

"I knew it!" said Jason. "You have to tell me what it was."

"It's been so long since the show, I suppose the writer's guild police won't come and arrest me for letting it out at this point" laughed the writer. "In the next season, we were finally going to reveal the overall reason why Sam was being sent back to these particular places in time. We hadn't settled on a specific plot reason, but one we were playing with was that Sam was correcting the problems created by an antithesis of himself."

"Wow, that would have been great!" enthused Jason.

"One of my pet scripts, which I never got to put forward to the team, started to explain the science of the leaping and how there was a person behind it all who was pulling the puppet strings. I intended on doing some physics research on quantum mechanics and time travel. Do you happen to work with that at all?" asked the writer.

"No, not much," lied Jason through his teeth.

"Too bad. I would have loved to bounce some ideas off you."

"Although I don't work with that stuff much, I wouldn't mind talking more about it. Even though I can't say I work with it much," (which was technically true; Jason couldn't *say* he worked with quantum mechanics), "it's still a favorite field of study for me recreationally, and I'd love to spend some time discussing some ideas with you."

"That sounds really good. I'm working on a fictional novel at the moment, and I'd love to see if some of the ideas for the technology in the book are believable. Here." The writer reached into his pocket and produced a card. He handed it to Jason with one hand and held out his other for a handshake, saying, "Here's my card. Name's Adrian. Dan Adrian. Give me a call sometime so we can knock our heads together." The smile on his face was sincere and genuine.

With heartfelt gratitude and with a hearty handshake, Jason replied, "Dan, it is really great to meet you. I look forward to talking with you soon."

"I do as well, my friend. Take care," called out Dan as Jason went to leave.

Mikki had been quietly standing there all along, allowing her husband to enjoy himself with the obvious ardor of a true fan. She didn't have a clue just how much this show had shaped the vocation of her husband, but one thing she did know was Jason acted like a kid in a candy store, and she wasn't about to interrupt that in the slightest. She thought it was funny how he had been so into talking with Dan Adrian he hadn't even taken the time to introduce her.

Jason suddenly became aware of how much he had ignored his wife, and he felt bad. "I'm sorry I've been ignoring you all this time."

"That's okay, honey. You were having fun, and I was getting a big kick out of watching you enjoy yourself that much," replied Mikki.

"For that, you've just earned yourself an extremely romantic evening complete with dinner and show, and a slow sensual massage at the hands of your own personal masseur," responded Jason, with a grin on his face.

"Deal," cooed Mikki. "Why don't we start making our way back to the hotel so we can get this party started!"

"Sounds good to me, babe."

It seemed to take longer to exit the convention arena than it did to walk the six miles there in the first place. Since it was getting late, Jason decided to hail a cab back to the hotel; once there, Mikki took her customary hour to get dressed. In a classic little black dress accented with black silk nylons and a single strand of pearls, she came out from the en-suite the spitting image of Audrey Hepburn playing Holly Golightly in "Breakfast at Tiffany's." To say Jason was smitten with the vision standing before his eyes was a colossal understatement. Striding to his side, Mikki could see in Jason's eyes that he was almost to the point of tears from the enormity of love he felt for his wife at that very moment. Taking Mikki's arm in his, the proud peacock escorted his queen, his world, his love to dinner at the finest restaurant he could muster, all the while wondering how he could possibly be so privileged as to land such a perfect package of a woman with looks like this, coupled with the most alluring and perfect personality as well.

Over candlelight dinner, the conversation was both light and uplifting; both enriching and inspiring. It was certainly one of those moments when the entire outside world could have evaporated, and they wouldn't have known.

"I love how you are looking at me right now," smiled Mikki.

"Oh? And how is that, my love?" replied Jason, already knowing the answer.

"It's like nothing else matters to you right now other than what's before you. You have a look of complete contentment," said Mikki.

"I'd say that about covers it. I'm sorry I wasn't paying much attention to you earlier at the convention," admitted Jason.

Channeling Holly Golightly, Mikki answered, "Oh pish posh. You aren't the only one who enjoys seeing their beloved enjoying themselves."

Jason smiled at Mikki and fell microscopically deeper in love with her, if that was even possible.

"Actually, I do have a question about all that," Mikki continued. "One of the things he said there got me thinking. He wanted to talk about physics and time travel. Do you know anything about that stuff?"

"Well, physics is kind of a little pet subject of mine. When I was in college, I took a couple of courses in it." This was technically true, he had taken a couple of courses; a couple of *dozen.*

"OK, then I have a little question. What does quantum mechanics have to do with time travel?" asked Mikki.

"Keep in mind, I don't know much about this, but from what I remember it has something to with alternate dimensions and whether time is a fluid thing. I know quantum mechanics has to do with the science of trying to figure out why some particles seem to exist in two places at the same time."

"Really?" replied Mikki. She seemed to be deep in thought, which got Jason wondering where she was going with this. She wasn't dumb by any stretch, so he was intrigued by what she might come up with.

"Well, what about the other way?" asked Mikki.

"What other way?"

"Well, is it possible something can exist in two times at the same place?" asked Mikki innocently.

Jason just stared at her, dumbfounded. What she didn't realize, what she couldn't have known, was how much this one little question rocked Jason's world. "She did it again," he thought to himself. Suddenly Jason had an idea about why the experiment the other day had "failed," and how maybe something else may have actually gone *very right*!

"I love you," was all Jason could say. Later that night, Jason made sure Mikki knew just how appreciative he was.

CHAPTER 39

THE REST OF THE TRIP was almost a blur for Jason. Mikki was certainly aware Jason was glad to be there with her in Las Vegas, but she could also tell he looked forward to getting back to the office. Having been married for quite some time now to a guy whose work involved government secrets, she was well aware there were some matters he just couldn't discuss with her. It all had to do with national security, but she couldn't imagine what that could possibly be in such a little town as Sonora in Northern California.

While Jason was lost in his own daydream, something that was happening regularly now after their amazing night in Las Vegas, Mikki thought of one time when she and Jason had gone to a party, and apparently, some of the people he worked with were also there. She remembered this one clean-cut guy who struck up a casual conversation with her that naturally ebbed and flowed. At one point during the conversation, they started talking about work. He starting out asking her what she did, volunteered his occupation, then asked her what her husband did for a living.

She naturally responded like she always did, with the truth. Barely nodding her head and speaking slowly, she simply said, "I have no idea." What struck her was his response. He smiled, saying, "Good answer!"

Mikki recalled being quite taken aback by his response. It took a while for her to realize the whole conversation had actually been an artfully-crafted test to see if Jason was successfully keeping secrets he was supposed to keep. Initially she was mad that this guy's interest in her wasn't to enjoy a conversation, but rather to test her husband. Without his knowledge, either. Yep, she had felt just plain used. Mikki finally realized this guy wasn't there socially; he was just doing his job. Not only was he doing his job, he was sacrificing his social life that evening to make it possible for people to live in this country like they do. Sure, the country wasn't perfect; it had its problems. But it was better than a lot of places in the world. In the end, she decided to forgive her unknown interrogator, allowing him a place in her memory reserved for those she appreciated.

While driving back from Las Vegas, Jason was busy with thoughts of his own. He couldn't wait to get back and talk to Dennis. A big part of him wished he could call Dennis on the spot to pontificate on what he now suspected happened in the detection chamber, but that was strictly forbidden by Midway Magnetic security policies. Jason felt like it was eating him alive that he couldn't talk to anybody about the possibly earth-shaking revelation he was considering.

Eventually, the trip ended, punctuated by long periods of silence in the car. For normal couples, silence often meant there was tension, but that was almost never the case with them. This time it was just the case of being comfortable with each other, even in silence.

They made it back Sunday night in time to pick up little Jace from the home of friends who were looking out for him, and were able to make it into bed at a decent hour. Monday morning followed its normal course of events, and once again they all were off to engage in their respective professional and educational lives. While Jason never rued the time he spent with Mikki, he was tremendously looking forward to getting out of the house this particular morning so he could start testing out his theories.

Once in his office, he immediately dove for the intercom button to ask Susan if Dennis had arrived yet. "No Dr. Marsalis," she replied. "He doesn't normally make it in until eight o'clock, sir." He glanced at his watch, suddenly remembering that in his enthusiasm to get to work, he had chosen the one secure route to work that landed him there in the shortest travel time possible. Dennis wouldn't be there for another 45 minutes. "Please let him know I need to see him as soon as he arrives," he told Susan.

"Yes, sir." Jason smiled as he hung up the phone. Like Dennis, Susan was another one who seemed to enjoy being more formal at work.

He decided to fire up the internet and start doing some research on string theory and quantum mechanics. He had written some papers on the subject, so had Dennis, but he wanted to center in on one particular aspect of it, the interplay between quantum mechanics and space-time.

After doing quite a bit of reading on the subject, his phone intercom rang. "This is Jason."

"Jason, this is Dennis. Susan said to give you a buzz when I got in."

"Hey, bud. Can you come here when you get a chance? I have some observations I think you might be interested in regarding the results from that test we did last week."

"You mean that disaster?" quipped Dennis.

"Well, maybe it wasn't such a disaster after all," said Jason rather enigmatically.

"Oh really? This I have to hear. I'll be over in a few."

"Sounds good."

Jason gathered together some of the materials he had been copying and pasting into a single document. He wanted to present what he was thinking in as ordered a manner as possible.

After about 10 minutes, Dennis arrived. "So, what is this revelation you've had?" he asked, with a smile on his face. After asking, he saw Jason wasn't smiling and immediately knew this was serious.

"Tell me what you remember from that test," asked Jason.

"After the cryogenics came up to speed and we hit min temp, we sequentially brought the magnets up to full power," responded Dennis. "Once we did that, we injected the particle stream, waited for it to come up to max-V, then fired the proton stream into the detector. And that's when all hell seemed to break loose, except for the fact that it didn't actually break loose."

"And this hell that broke loose," said Jason. "Tell me exactly what you remember about the nature of that hell."

"I remember three problems," answered Dennis. "Number one, the detectors read back that the mass of the particle streams doubled 100 nanoseconds before the collision. Number two, even so, the detection readings from the collision only showed an energy release matching a single collision of two particle streams. Third, the gamma radiation detector was dead, no radiation was read; not even one picocurie.

Basically, all of our calorimeters and other detection equipment were totally off."

"I'm not so sure," pondered Jason.

"Oh?" answered a truly intrigued Dennis.

At this point, Jason regaled him with the story of the weekend, omitting private events, ending with the conversation he had with Mikki about quantum mechanics.

"She asked me, 'What does quantum mechanics have to do with time travel?'"

"I told her I didn't know much about it," this earned a smile from Dennis, "but I said that I seemed to remember it had something to with alternate dimensions and whether time is a fluid thing. I said I knew quantum mechanics had to do with trying to figure out how some particles seem to exist in two places at the same time. Mikki seemed intrigued at the idea, and then asked me a question which rocked my world."

"And that was?" inquired Dennis.

"She asked me, 'Well, what about the other way?' I asked her. 'What other way?' and she said, 'Well, is it possible something can exist in two times at the same place?'"

Up to this point, Dennis had been leisurely sitting forward in his chair. After hearing that particular question, he sat back and began considering the question and the implications of what the answer to it would mean in relation to the experiment last week. Gratified that Dennis was just as bowled over at the simple question as he had been, Jason continued his tale.

"I was as taken back as you appear to be, and that got me thinking about what had happened." Jason paused. "Call me crazy, but I think you and I may have actually discovered how to send a particle back in time 100 nanoseconds."

Those words hung in the air for quite some time until Dennis had the nerve to speak.

"That would explain why the energy release was that of only the original proton streams."

"Exactly," replied Jason.

Again, a very pregnant pause while the two world-renowned physicists thought over this new revelation.

"But why did it happen?" asked Dennis.

"I've been thinking about that ever since the conversation with Mikki. Let me ask you something and see if you arrive at the same conclusion I did. What do you remember was different with this experiment than the others?"

"The real difference was with the detectors we were using," answered Dennis. "Other than that, everything was the same."

"OK, now let's break that down. *What* was different about those detectors?" asked Jason.

"Primarily," responded Dennis "it was the alloys we used in them. Those alloys had chemical reaction signatures we were looking for to detect neutrinos interacting with the sub-atomic plasma in the collision chamber."

"And the main alloy we were using utilized niobium, right?"

"Yep," verified Dennis.

"So, my hypothesis is that what happened was because we were not only using a different element in the detection chamber, thus changing the magnetic signatures of the detection equipment, but also because of other variables I haven't thought of yet. I'd like to submit, that if we start playing with not only the ratios of niobium alloys, used but also the magnetic power levels, and laser frequencies used in the chamber, we might be able to make an even more interesting change to the results we saw."

With a very big smile on his face, Dennis said, "Lead the way, sir."

The next several hours were spent talking about the different things that could be done to possibly change the experiment results. After talking about all the expected effects the different changes would make, it was decided to implement them in a controlled manner so they could measure each and every change which might or might not occur. By the end of the day, Jason and Dennis had a complete plan outlining the stages they would undertake.

The next day they started with the first stage, the easiest one, changing the laser frequencies. It didn't seem to make much difference as they stepped through a set of laser frequencies sequentially increasing in energy.

After that, they started toying with the magnetic fields being used by the detection equipment. This started making a difference in how far back the "doubling" phenomenon occurred. Initially, they achieved a change in what they started calling the "double-back effect." What was originally a 100 nanosecond double-back now became 200 nano-seconds. Then one microsecond.

The next change turned out to be a major turning point. They tried altering the material the matter stream interacted with. They'd been simply smashing together particle streams which had been revolving around the particle accelerator in opposite directions. Now they tried smashing the two proton streams into a variety of various elemental materials. Nothing really significant happened until they tried lutetium. That is when all hell broke loose.

As soon as the particle stream hit the lutetium, the data started fluctuating wildly. It was apparent that a chain reaction was occurring, but as with the rest of the experiments that had been happening this week, there was no radiation detected in the chamber;, and while the fluctuations of the readings were wild, they were still within tolerances. It seemed to be a controlled chain reaction. But of what? What was happening in the chamber?

It wasn't until Dennis switched on a video feed from the chamber that he turned white as a ghost.

"Oh my God," cringed Dennis.

Jason wasn't able to see the screen from his vantage point. "What is it?"

"I don't know," said Dennis. "Come here. What do you make of this?"

Jason immediately went over to the monitor and was quite taken back by what he saw. In the middle of the reaction chamber was what appeared to be, for lack of a better term, a video projection of some sort. The scene looked like a still life painting of someone's living room.

"What kind of radiation are you reading?"

"Zero on all counters. Just like all the rest of the tests," replied Dennis.

After about five seconds, Jason quickly shot out of his seat and said, "I'm going down there to the chamber."

Dennis retorted, "Not without me you're not!"

The two men did their best to walk down to the detection chamber without attracting any attention. Once there, their own eyes confirmed what they didn't believe from the earlier video feed. Right there in front of them was a field circular in shape about two and a half meters in diameter. In the middle of the field was what appeared to be a perfectly-rendered video of the same still life painting of a living room.

Walking to the other side of the chamber, the two physicists realized the field appeared to have height and width, but absolutely no depth, no thickness. The edges had a ragged nature to them and seemed to be giving off minor static electricity charges. From the other side, they saw the same scene, only in reverse.

Then something stupefying happened. While silently trying to digest what they were seeing, the two men almost had heart attacks when a person in a blue sweater walked by with a bag of chips and sat on the couch in the living room. This wasn't a still life at all, but rather a live video of some sort. Jason and Dennis said the same thing at the same time.

"Cut the power."

The two men dove for the emergency power cutoff switch kept in the reaction chamber, and immediately the field vanished. Both men realized they hadn't been breathing much, and reluctantly gave permission to their lungs to start drawing in oxygen.

As he looked over to his friend, all Dennis could say was, "I hope you found a way to thank Mikki for her question."

Jason just looked at him and smiled.

CHAPTER 40

JASON'S DRIVE HOME THAT NIGHT was as uneventful as any other, except that by the time he got home, he didn't remember it at all. All he remembered was having a slightly intriguing difficulty figuring out what had happened with the experiment. By the time he got home, his overall demeanor had degraded significantly. It only took milliseconds for Mikki to figure out something was wrong, but discretion won out, and she decided to let Jason tell her what was wrong in his own time.

The evening wore on, and Jason did all the things he normally did. After dinner, Jace asked his dad to help him with some homework, bringing all his materials to the dining room table where they could spread them out. It was a scene from any Americana movie: the wife straightening up the kitchen; the son being assisted by the father; replete with light-hearted banter between all three. Then, according to script, the father tells the son to get ready for bed, and after he has done so, the dad goes in, reads a bedtime story, helps his son say his prayers, then leaves, turning out the lights. Pretty standard stuff, except for the whole deer-in-the-headlights thing written across Jason's face. It was so obvious even Jace could tell something was different with his dad; perhaps that's why he was on his best behavior.

After saying good night to his son, Jason emerged from the hallway and entered the mostly-dark living room, replete with a fire in the fireplace Mikki had started, candles lit on the coffee table, and a bottle of merlot with two glasses. Jason took his place on the loveseat, accepting the offering of wine from his wife.

"So," said Mikki, "I know you probably can't talk about it, but I can see something is wrong. Anything I can help with?"

Jason smiled "Oh sweetie, no. I'm just dealing with a particular conundrum from work that's got me completely baffled and really keyed up. I appreciate it, though."

Mikki then simply rested her open palm on Jason's cheek. For a while, she just gazed at her husband, holding his eye-to-eye attention with seemingly hypnotic power. After a moment, a smile played itself across his face, and his gaze faltered from her eyes. "I must have done something pretty amazing in a previous life to have merited a life with you in this one," said Jason.

"I don't know about that," chimed Mikki. Then, with a smile on her own face, she added, "I think you're just lucky."

"Arguably," said Jason, with a roll of his eyes and a smile.

The two of them were content to watch the fire in silence while sipping their wine. Mikki was thinking about the day tomorrow, which she was going to spend with her best friend Carrie at the mall. She was going over a list of things she wanted to look at, perhaps a different pair of shoes to go with that little black dress she wore in Vegas recently. Then she remembered the Poshmark website had these amazing patent leather pumps that some artist painted actual pinstriping on. They looked pretty amazing the other day when Carrie showed her the website. Mikki decided she had to have them.

Jason was just trying to wrap his head around what he had seen that day. As time wore on, the initial giddiness of what had happened was slowly replaced by a nagging feeling this wasn't anything special after all, but something which could easily be explained as a video feed from a local television station. That realization was a bitter pill to swallow. What he didn't know was that Dennis was independently coming to the same realization.

Jason felt he was a pretty level-headed guy, someone who could rationalize his way through to pretty much any problem's solution. But this; this just stretched any semblance of credulity Jason could muster.

"How in the name of all that's holy could this be explained?" he wondered. The only rational explanation he could come up with was they must have locked into a television station of some kind. But then again, how would this "thing" decode digital feeds from the stations. It just didn't make sense.

Mikki set her glass down on the coffee table, enjoying the light glow of the fire, the moderate glow of the wine, and the substantial glow of the love. Curling her feet under her, she leaned her head on Jason's shoulder and wrapped her arms around his nearest arm. She always felt flush with safety and security at times like this.

Closing his eyes and becoming one with the flow of air to and from his lungs, Jason luxuriated in the serenity of the moment, enough to derail his mental train track and bring him back to now. Mikki always was just what he needed to keep his head straight. She was his muse.

CHAPTER 41

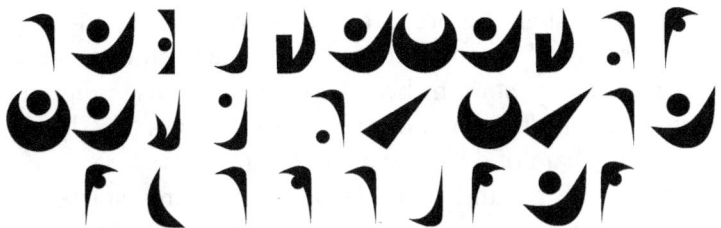

THE NEXT MORNING DENNIS CAME into Jason's office and sat there without saying a word. It was apparent he also spent the previous evening ruminating about the experiment, but without the benefit of someone like Mikki to root him back to reality. There was a small part of Jason that felt remorse for his friend.

Dennis broke away from the unspoken conversation, turning his head to gaze out the large window into the reaction chamber facility. Looking at his friend, Jason finally resorted to the vulgarity of the spoken word and declared, "We need to try that again." Without looking away from the window, Dennis revealed he had already come to the same conclusion by adding, "If we do it at two o'clock, we might get a good soap opera."

Smiling at his friend, Jason replied, "I hear pay-per-view is pretty good in the afternoon." Dennis grunted an agreement.

What wasn't being said, but was something they both understood with crystal clear clarity, is these two highly intelligent, logical men were incredibly disappointed and emotionally drained by this turn of events. They had spent countless hours, untold amounts of taxpayer money, and time away from their respective outside lives for what? A cable box. Pure and simple. A 10-story, four-billion-dollar, two-million-ton cable box.

More silence.

With resignation, Jason rose from his chair and conceded to the inexorable march of time. "It's not necessarily something we'll be able to brag too much about," said Jason, "But, dammit! We're going to make the *best* cable box man has ever known!" With a somewhat silent chuckle, Dennis rose as well and followed Jason out the door, narrowly missing Susan as she arrived with the mail.

While taking the stairs down, Jason recalled something which occurred to him the night before. "You know what, I was thinking about something last night," Jason pondered out loud. "Something I can't get out of my head is that stations broadcast their signals in digital format these days. There isn't any analog signal now. How is this thing decoding the digital stream of data into a video signal?"

Arriving at the ground level, Jason and Dennis started walking across the large expanse of the underground cavern. "Not only that, but how is it that it can receive a signal from outside?" Dennis asked. "This facility is not only 100 meters below ground; this chamber, in particular, is shielded. The only way a signal could get in is through the beam portal, but that portal is normally blocked."

Since the primary mission of the Midway Magnetic Particle Accelerator was to facilitate incoming ICBM neutralization, this immaculate chamber containing the primary redirection circuitry had to allow the accelerated particle stream to reach the primary redirection satellite in geosynchronous orbit overhead. That was done using the beam portal directly overhead in the ceiling of the chamber. This portal was a five-foot-wide, magnetically-lined tube leading from the science chamber out to the surface. On the surface, there was a rather large, well-leaved evergreen tree standing majestically among its brothers and sisters on the forest floor; at least that is what it looked like. Actually, it was a fake tree, with the end of the portal tube running up the center of it. When the system was activated, the top of the "tree" would move out of the way, allowing the beam to exit and seek its target orbiting overhead.

"I dunno, buddy. You and I both saw it yesterday," conceded Dennis, sensing that Jason was nodding.

Upon getting to their respective control stations, Jason and Dennis began running through the same steps as yesterday. Soon enough, they arrived at the same critical point. "*Speed*! Particle insertion in 10 seconds," yelled Jason over the noise. It usually took about a 10-second window until the particle insertion stream could effectively be introduced.

"Particle insertion in 3-2-1. Mark!" said Jason.

Once again the colossal superconducting magnets guiding the particle stream around the loop received the necessary commands from the control software causing the particle stream to instantly change its trajectory from going around the loop again, to going straight into the detection chamber. And once again, a phantasm in the detection chamber could be seen in the closed-circuit monitors. Immediately Jason and Dennis went to the chamber. Only now, when they arrived, something *really* unusual was happening.

What was unusual? It was the same identical thing, the same television scene. Dennis said the first thing that came to his mind. "Boring show. Same thing, different day." His face betrayed him, though. His inner thoughts felt there was something else strange about this that he couldn't put his finger on.

But then a person in a blue sweater walked by with a bag of chips and sat on the couch in the living room, *exactly* the same thing as the day before. If Jason's and Dennis' eyes had gotten any bigger, they would have looked like Roswell aliens.

This time, instead of immediately turning off the device as they did the day before, they looked at things more closely. On the edges of the video were what they thought were static electricity discharges the day before. On closer examination, those discharges actually looked like frequency patterns. Jason reached over to a roll-around cart, normally sitting near the chamber for testing and debugging purposes, and grabbed the test leads. Switching on the device, he slowly extended his hand near the apparition on the edges and touched the leads to the patterns. Those identical patterns now appeared flattened out on the screen of the oscilloscope.

"What does that look like to you?" asked Jason.

"Looks like sound waves," Dennis said, confirming what Jason was already thinking.

"You still have that speaker attached to the computer at your station?"

"Yep," said Dennis, instantly shooting up and running for his PC computer speaker.

Jason continued looking at the scene playing out in front of him. He now started classifying and categorizing what he was seeing, observing that the décor of this movie set was done with late 60's or early 70's style decorations. Confirming this was a 1971 calendar on the wall.

Various knick-knacks lined the shelves of a standing cabinet on another wall of this suburban living room.

Dennis soon returned and hooked up the speaker to the oscilloscope and was instantly greeted with the sounds of the scene they were witnessing. Dennis continued to have a quizzical look on his face, while Jason strained to hear everything. There was a TV playing, and the sounds were easily recognizable as a newscast.

Over the speaker, the voice of the man clearly came through. "Bonnie, can you get me a beer, dear?"

The woman replied, with a lilt in her voice, "What's a beerdeer?"

The woman laughed.

The man chuckled.

Jason smirked.

Dennis passed out.

When he came to, the room around him was oddly quiet, and he was being attended to by EMTs kept on staff at the facility. It took a while for his eyes to adjust to the light again, and the room was slowly settling in from having been spinning. Making motions from the floor to sit up, the EMT's helped him do so. Dennis could see he was still in the reaction chamber of the particle accelerator; however, the video image was no longer there, and the power systems of the detection chamber were quiet. The systems had been shut down, and he couldn't remember that happening.

After a few moments, Dennis realized he had passed out. More importantly, he fully recalled why that happened, and the realization was overwhelming. Not enough to cause another blackout, but enormous nonetheless. The implications, if true, would change the entire world of science forever. And at this moment, he was the only one on earth who knew it.

For a few minutes, the EMTs did their job to the best of their ability. Dennis decided to come up with a cover story: he hadn't had breakfast that morning, and must be suffering from low blood sugar. He was bursting at the seams to get these guys to leave so he could talk to his compatriot alone.

Eventually, once satisfied they had done their respective jobs, the EMTs left Dennis and Jason alone. "You scared the crud outta me man!" said Jason. "I didn't know you had blood sugar issues."

"I don't," replied Dennis.

"But why ...." started Jason.

"At that moment," interrupted Dennis, "I realized something which, if I'm right, is earth-shattering. We need to go back to your office for this, ol' buddy."

Dennis was usually a lighthearted individual, so his current level of seriousness was disconcerting. Without question, Jason followed him off the platform and up the stairs. Once inside Jason's office, Dennis closed the door after him and did something he had never done before.

He locked the door.

In the corner was a conversation area with a couch, coffee table, and corresponding overstuffed chairs. After grabbing two cold water bottles for him and his friend, Dennis took his place on the couch.

Speaking slowly, he began. "When that video came up, I was just as intrigued as you were, but there was something else about it I couldn't quite put my finger on. It was like that feeling you get when something is right on the tip of your tongue. It wasn't until we heard the soundtrack that it hit me like a freight train."

"What was it?" asked Jason.

"Those people we saw? They're my parents," said Dennis.

"Run that past me one more time?" asked Jason.

"You heard me," replied Dennis.

"Since when do you have parents in the TV industry?" asked Jason.

"That's just it. I don't."

"OK, now you're just not making sense."

"It gets weirder than that."

"How?" asked Jason.

"Not only are my parents dead but, prepare yourself for this, I remember living that scene. I don't know if you saw it, but up there at the top of the stairs was my little face peeking out. I was supposed to be in bed, but I wanted to see the landing of the astronauts on the moon that night, so I snuck out so I could watch it on the news. It was one of the more pivotal points in my childhood."

Jason was stunned.

"That joke about the 'beerdeer' was a running joke between them. I heard it five million times growing up. I was sick of it right up until the day they both died in a car accident when I was in college. From that day forward, I always secretly wished I could hear it once more. I don't know how we did it, my friend, but you and I somehow created a way to see something that happened in the past … *my* past."

"Oh my god," was all Jason managed to mutter.

He looked out the window for a bit, looked at Dennis again, then down at the carpet.

"You're telling me this isn't recorded video?" asked Jason.

"Think about it, bud. Think about how clear it was, and the state of recording technology back then. This was high definition if it was anything, and I'm telling you there wasn't any recording of that day. I was there. That scene we just saw was exactly what happened! We just created a sort of ...."

"Einstein-Rosen bridge," finished Jason.

It was Dennis' turn to call out to God.

"If what you say is true, that means we've created a stable wormhole to somewhere in your life. Why did it settle on an event in *your* life?" wondered Jason. "The odds of creating a wormhole to an event in *your* past seem too enormous to happen."

Dennis got up from his seat and thought about it for a moment. Then he turned around and said, "Not really, now that I think about it."

"How's that?"

"One of the things I do, one of the quirks I have, is using numbers I'm familiar with when it comes to numeric constants in my experiments," explained Dennis. "I do it that way because it creates a set of known parameters I work out from, in case I need to reproduce an experiment.

"Go on."

"When I was setting up the laser frequencies for the experiment in the chamber, I calibrated the pulse to be for a specific number of nanoseconds corresponding to that date. I set it for 2,031,971.06 nanoseconds. That number corresponds to February 3, 1971, at 6 p.m. That is the specific date and time of that event in my life."

"OK. That would explain the date and time, but what about the location?" asked Jason.

"I did the same thing with the longitude and latitude coordinates on the gauss level in the magnetic field of the portal." This was the first time Dennis called it a portal.

"Are you telling me it wasn't random at all, but the result of some lucky guesses?" asked Jason credulously.

"That's exactly what I'm telling you," replied Dennis.

"Ok. Let's test your theory. Let's change the laser frequency to, say, the time and location of the bombing of Pearl Harbor," said Jason.

With a rather large grin on his face, Dennis went to the computer and started calculating the longitude and latitude, as well as the specific laser frequencies, needed for the date and time. Using those numbers, Dennis logged onto the Command and Control software and programmed in the variables. With that done, he was ready.

Jason and Dennis went downstairs and fired up the reaction systems. As soon as the portal formed, all that could be seen was solid gray. There were sounds, but just gray. The fact that the scene was different convinced Jason that Dennis was on to something. He asked Dennis to alter the magnetic fields a bit, shifting the coordinates on the Z axis about 50 meters higher in the air. As soon as Dennis locked in those co-ordinates, the portal changed. They were immediately presented with the scene of a naval shipyard and, almost as if on cue, there was an immense explosion on the side of one of the destroyers in the harbor. The attack on Pearl Harbor had begun, right in front of their eyes!

After watching for a few minutes, Jason had to shut it off. The destruction was too massive. Jason and Dennis were absolutely dumbstruck with the revelation they had just discovered a way to easily see into the past. More than that, they could do it for any point on the compass.

"This is astounding," said Jason in a hushed voice.

The two men sat there, listening to the various sounds of the portal machinery winding down, and the automatic control systems shunting power from the portal, draining the liquid helium from the superconductors. Eventually, the only sound that could be heard was the hum from the innumerable transformers lining the walls of the room.

"This is a total game-changer in the world of science," Dennis finally said. "I don't think I'm going out on a limb in saying this will turn the entire world of physics upside down, backward, and spinning."

Jason nodded without a word and without changing the far-off look in his eyes.

Dennis added, "We need to run this up the food chain, my friend."

With an enigmatic but very big smile playing itself across his face, Jason looked over to his friend and said, "I have an idea."

Diana O'Laney, director of research at Midway Magnetic, was a good person to have for a boss. She realized the value of the people who worked under her, and knew the best thing to do was give them their space. To that end, she rarely needed to talk with those who worked for her.

Today was going to be different. She happened to be in the middle of a department meeting with several of her staffers when the door to her office swung open unannounced. Jason and Dennis looked at her directly. Only four small words from Jason, delivered with intensity, were enough for her to dismiss the staffers.

"We have to talk."

CHAPTER 42

THE CONVERSATION WITH DIANA WENT about as expected. Initially, Jason and Dennis attempted to describe the physics they had utilized over the last six months and the real reason why they had done so. She was more administrative than scientific, and didn't really know anything about what a Heisenberg compensator was and how it related to transportation. Retrenching their approach, they laid the groundwork by referencing Star Trek and how people were transported. Once she understood who Werner Heisenberg was and what his uncertainty principle is, they talked about how a fictional device called the Heisenberg compensator was the basis for the transporters in the TV show. By this point, she was up to speed.

"Boy," said Diana, "wouldn't that be cool if you could transport things around like they did on that show? 'Beam me up!' would be really neat!" She had a laugh in her voice, but quickly noticed Jason and Dennis weren't laughing. This caused a very intense look to flash across her face.

"You didn't actually do it, did you?" Diana asked fervently. "You didn't actually create a transporter?"

"Not exactly," said Jason, quickly glancing at Dennis, "but what we did do might be just as amazing."

Crossing her arms in front of her and cocking her head to one side, Diana countered with, "What do you mean?"

Seemingly changing the subject, Jason asked, "You didn't go to school around here did you?"

"Actually, I did. I went to Columbia College on the other side of Sonora," replied Diana.

"Yes, but you attended high school in Southern California, right?"

"Correct. I went to Cleveland high in Reseda. Why?"

"I didn't know you were such a trendsetter when you were a teenager," replied Jason. "Wearing old Converse tennis shoes with glitter on them underneath your cap and gown? Bold move there, Diana."

Dropping her arms into her lap, she was definitely set back by this. Diana knew for a fact she had never told anybody about that particular fashion faux pas. It was one of those little things in her past which, while not really a skeleton, would nonetheless cause her to suffer good-natured ridicule and ribbing from co-workers.

"How in the world did you know I wore Converses with glitter on them?"

"Take a look at this video," said Jason, producing a USB drive from his shirt pocket.

Diana took the drive and plugged it into her PC. Both Jason and Dennis, who were sitting in chairs on the other side of her desk, swung them around to look at the 60" screen on the side wall of her office. The screen came to life as soon as Diana pressed a few buttons on her remote control, and up came the video.

The scene was a high school graduation. The camera was completely steady, and the video was crisp and clean. It was the best of the best in terms of high-definition quality. A stage was set up on the high school football field, and several dozen rows in front were filled with hundreds of red and black caps and gowns. When Diana turned up the volume, she was able to hear the man standing at the podium, about to introduce the students.

"Oh my god," was the only thing she was able to say.

The man at the podium started to speak. "Fellow teachers and students, it is now my honor to introduce each student and to hand them their diploma. We will start with one of our class valedictorians, Miss Diana O'Laney."

On the right side of the stage, a slim and attractive teenager ascended the stairs and strode her way across the stage to receive her diploma from the principal. Her gown was made of red satin, the cap was both red and black with the customary tassel hanging off to the side. Below the cap was a large amount of black hair, and the face was attractively done up with makeup.

Below the gown were a pair of Converse tennis shoes with rainbow-colored glitter all over. The teenaged Diana turned to the audience and, to cheers of her classmates and no doubt her family, waved, then descended the stairs to the left of the stage. The video snippet cut off and the room was now silent.

Dennis and Jason swung their chairs around and faced a very astonished boss. For a few moments she was unable to speak, but finally gasped out one word. "How?"

Jason then regaled Diana with the whole story, telling her how they were trying to make a Heisenberg compensator for matter transference, and encountered some results they didn't understand. He related how other experiments proved they had stumbled on a way to see events at any time in history, and at any place. He explained how they dialed up the specific date time and place where she graduated, and made a recording of the event.

"This is," Diana hesitated, "astounding!"

"Yeah," said Jason and Dennis simultaneously.

"Do you realize how groundbreaking this will be for historians?"

"How about crime investigations?" asked Jason.

"O-M-Gee," said Diana. "I hadn't even thought about that. Making judicial decisions based only on the preponderance of the evidence without corroboration will be a thing of the past. There will no longer be any question of guilt or innocence!" Diana exclaimed. "In fact, there won't *ever* be a case of putting an innocent person in jail!"

"Oh wow," said Jason. It was his turn to suddenly realize another application for their invention.

After a few moments of silence, Dennis asked: "What about wanting to know the contents of the scrolls of Alexandria? Or witnessing biblical events or historical battles, even having front row seats to the landing of the lunar module on the moon?"

This caused not only Diana but also Jason to look at Dennis. "Moon? What aren't you telling me, pal?" asked Jason, with a questioning look on his face.

Dennis smiled, saying, "You know how the whole X/Y/Z location is determined by manipulating the gauss levels in the magnetic field of the portal?"

"Yeah," replied Jason. Diana didn't know what Dennis was referring to, but decided she didn't need to know.

"Well," continued Dennis, "the precision of that setting is actually carried out to 50 decimal places. And since each tick on that counter apparently represents five meters ...."

Sitting back in his chair with an almost audible thud, Jason immediately understood the significance of that. "Holy cow!"

Diana, on the other hand, didn't follow so readily. "Why is that significant?"

Jason turned to her and said, "What he just shared is that we have not only the ability to view events on Earth, but also the ability to position the portal viewport anywhere in the galaxy. Maybe even outside the galaxy. Imagine seeing for the first time what the Milky Way galaxy looks like from the outside?"

"I said it before, but I'm saying it again," exclaimed Diana. "O-M-Gee!"

Now that the ideas and possibilities were flying about freely in the room, there was a sense not only of being on the cusp of something big, but privately also a sense of foreboding, although none of them could articulate exactly why they were feeling it.

Eventually, Diana spoke up. "Can I see it?"

"Sure," said Jason. "Now?"

"If you don't mind," she said. Yes, she was Jason's boss, so she didn't technically have to ask, but Diana felt this was like being an employer over Einstein. She knew full well the best would come from Jason and Dennis if she just managed to stay out of their way. This discovery promised to be a sterling example of that statement.

Seeing Jason and Dennis getting up from their seats, Diana rose as well, and the three made their way to the main detection chamber where the portal was located. After going through the startup procedures and initializing the superconductors by feeding the trillions of volts needed to achieve the desired level of acceleration, the only thing left was to decide on what to see.

Diana came up with an idea. "Last night I was helping my daughter with a school project on the great Chicago fire of October 8, 1871. Even though Catherine O'Leary, a distant relative of mine, was exonerated of any involvement, she was constantly blamed for starting that fire ... or at least her cow was. Even though the newspaper reporter who said her cow started it later recanted, Catherine still suffered from the anti-Irish sentiments of the day, and died broken-hearted."

With a smile on her face, Diana continued. "I'd like to see once and for all what started that fire."

"Sounds good to me," said Dennis. Turning to his workstation, he called up the custom program he wrote to manipulate the magnetic fields and laser frequencies. "Chicago, October 8, 1871," he said, mostly to himself. He typed in the parameters to the workstation, and the corresponding machinery reconfigured itself, conforming to the new settings.

Getting the nod from his friend, Jason turned to his own workstation. "Min temp achieved. Enacting particle insertion in 3, 2, 1. *Now!*"

Instantly a field started to form around surfaces of the portal frame. Starting from the edges, the bright lights of the field seemed to grow out in a circular fashion, eventually converging in the middle of the portal area. Initially the field was nothing but waves of white and pale blue light, but as soon as all sides of the portal window had converged in the middle, the white and blue lights were replaced by blackness. It took a few moments for their eyes to adjust; when they did, they saw small points of light. The point of view was that of a helicopter hovering a few hundred meters above the surface of the ground. It was well into dusk, so the sky was mostly dark.

"What am I looking at?" said Diana.

Feeling strange actually saying the words, Dennis replied, "You are looking at Chicago, Illinois. October 8, 1871."

"Are you sure?" asked Diana. "I don't see …."

"Wait!" interrupted Jason. "Look down there."

Sure enough, a small structure fire had started in the lower left area of the portal window. "Hey buddy, can you reset the location to get a better view of that area, and wind it back about 15 minutes?"

"You got it, boss," replied Dennis. Both Diana and Jason smirked at his use of the word.

Within 20 seconds, the scene changed. As the fields and light waves shifted, time seemed to roll in reverse. The position also changed; they now saw an unharmed structure standing before them. They could also see a few other houses nearby. As they watched silently, they noticed the chimneys on each home in the area. One particular chimney that stood on the roof of a house next to a barn was not only putting out smoke like all the others, but also a lot of embers. Suddenly, a man appeared in the doorway of the house and seemed to be in some kind of animated conversation with a woman who also emerged from the door. They were both looking up at their chimney, making a lot of gestures as they talked, but what they were saying couldn't be heard.

"Oh!" said Jason, realizing there was sound to be heard but he hadn't turned on the set of speakers on his desk. Jason reached over and punched the power button. Instantly they could not only hear the conversation between the man and the woman, but also the sounds of livestock.

"I told you, Daniel, not to put that log on the fire cause it had too much pitch," said the woman.

"Aw, ma. It'll be fine. Don' you worry 'bout it," replied the man, who had some sort of crude prosthesis from the knee down.

As they were arguing, one particularly large ember emerged from the chimney, flitting and floating up, propelled by the heated air of the chimney and the cooled air coming in from Lake Michigan.

"Look there," said Jason. As they looked to where he was pointing, the ember floated directly through an upper window in the hayloft of Mrs. O'Leary's barn. Within two minutes, a fire started in the barn; the arguing mother and son were far too engrossed in their quarrel to notice what their actions had caused. Changing the X/Y/Z position allowed the three of them to witness how the fire spread from the barn to another barn, to a couple of houses, until ultimately 300 people had died, and over 100,000 were left homeless.

As they were watching the fire really take hold, traveling from one block to another, Dennis continued manipulating the location of the portal "camera." Each time he repositioned the viewport, they were able to see how people reacted to the impending doom of their respective homes. It was both fascinating and gruesome to witness such devastation. None of them noticed the portal room itself had begun to get warm. Without thinking, Jason reached over to a floor fan located next to his workstation and flipped it on high.

As they continued watching the events unfold in the portal, the oscillating fan's wind stream blew across a pile of blank paper sitting on the desk, causing it to fall to the floor. There was a flurry of arms and elbows from Jason, Dennis, and Diana trying to catch the paper. They were successful in getting all the pages under control, except for one piece of paper. As it flew through the air toward the portal, Jason dove for the paper since he didn't want it catching fire in the high power magnetic fields of the portal window.

He was unsuccessful in catching the paper in time to keep it from bursting into flame, but it didn't catch fire from the portal. As it came against the portal field, the paper actually floated through and landed next to a burning tree in Chicago, 1871, where it immediately caught fire and disintegrated.

Diana looked at the burning piece of paper next to the tree and, with furrowed brown, asked a question as she was turning her head. "Wait, didn't you say this was a view onl ...."

She stopped in mid-sentence, her words trailing off, when she saw Dennis and Jason's eyes and mouths wide open in shock and surprise as they dropped into their respective seats. All three suddenly realized this portal was not just a viewport, but actually *did* transport matter. Not only had they succeed in creating a transporter, but they created one which could move a person to different places *and* different times!

After catching his breath, Jason entered a few keystrokes, and the massive relays on the other side of the room began their dance of redirecting power from the portal apparatus which slowly destabilized and evaporated. The room was relatively quiet once more.

After a few moments of mentally digesting what had just happened, the two men looked at each other and simultaneously let out a screeching cry of jubilation, causing Diana to rocket out of her seat in shock and surprise. Dancing around the room, Jason and Dennis were momentarily in their own world, realizing what they had created and how massive this discovery actually was.

It took them a few minutes to stop dancing around the workstations and talking at 5,000 words per minute using all the physics knowledge they possessed, as if they would forget how they did it if they didn't discuss it with each other right then. That was ludicrous, of course; nonetheless, they were both experiencing a heady dose of jubilation over their success. All the while they didn't even notice Diana sitting quietly, thinking about all that had occurred.

After taking their respective seats to rest for a moment from the euphoria, Jason looked over to Diana. She was smiling, although not as much as Dennis and Jason had been.

"Diana, you just witnessed the most significant event ever in the field of science and physics. You had a front row seat!"

Nodding her head, Diana acknowledged Jason's comment. "Yep. That was pretty amazing."

Her lack of enthusiasm Jason to sit up and take notice. "You don't seem as happy about it as we are," said Jason.

Pausing for a moment, Diana replied slowly. "Don't get me wrong; what I just saw was way beyond my wildest dreams. I never thought anything like that would have happened in my lifetime. I am really privileged to have been a witness to it, that's for sure."

Jason could tell there was more to what she was thinking. "And?" asked Jason.

Diana looked the two men in the face and said, "I think this is going to be somewhat of a Pandora's box."

"What do you mean?" asked Dennis.

"When you think about it," responded Diana, "this portal can be pointed to any position and to any time, right?"

"Exactly," said Dennis, smiling at Jason, who didn't notice since his focus was on Diana.

"That means," Diana continued, "this portal effectively removes the ability to have any secrets. Whoever is in control of the portal is, well, now effectively ...."

Jason finished her sentence: "Omnipotent."

"Exactly," responded Diana. "From now on, there won't be any real privacy. This is the purest form of 'Big Brother' I can imagine. Nobody will be exempt, and unless it is managed by someone who has more responsibility than I've ever seen, there could easily be some bad consequences."

After thinking about it for a moment, Jason had to agree. "Boy, when you're right, you sure are right. For instance, what if that paper hadn't burned up? What if it had plans on how to build a weapon which wouldn't be developed for another 100 years? What would that do to the course of human events we're already familiar with?"

"Or what about the classic 'Grandfather Paradox' we wrestled with in our philosophy classes? This device moves us from theory and brings us face to face with it in the real world," added Dennis.

"Precisely," said Diana. "Don't get me wrong. This discovery is amazing. It is *next level* cool! But we have to make sure it is the most highly-guarded secret technology the United States has ever had. The protection needed for this device will make the secrecy of the MMPA look like child's play."

With those words, the three of them looked up at the portal apparatus, simultaneously wondering exactly what the future had in store for them and their amazing discovery.

CHAPTER 43

JASON STOOD IN THE UNDERGROUND Midway Magnetic parking garage in a shirt and tie. This wasn't the first time he'd ever worn a tie
for work, and it wouldn't be the last, but it was so infrequent Mikki had
to come to his rescue in figuring out how to tie the stupid thing.

It had been about two weeks since he went toe to toe with Admiral
Brinstock over the phone regarding the timing of his visit to the facility, and only about four days since Jason and Dennis had revealed to
Diana the existence of the portal. Flexing her administrative muscle,
she rapidly orchestrated the building of a completely separate, secure
room just for the portal, allowing it to be used without anybody else
knowing what was happening. The main reason she worked so fast was
because she wanted it done before the admiral arrived. Construction
went on 24/7 until two hours ago; they met the deadline.

When Jason had previously spoken with the admiral, Kenji expressed his desire to perform the inspection on the same weekend
Jason promised to take Mikki to Las Vegas. Thinking about that trip

and the phenomenal experiments that were a direct result of the philosophical discussion he and Mikki had over dinner, he couldn't help but smile. Their conversation led to him postulating the real reason for the anomalies in the first experiment, and to discovering the time-traveling nature of the fields they created in the detection chamber.

Admiral Brinstock was due to arrive any moment, which was why Jason was patiently waiting in the parking garage. Dennis should have been at this meeting as well, but he was called out of state to oversee repairs to equipment used on an installation he was in charge of before coming to Midway. "Lucky dog," said Jason. half-grinning.

Only now, as Diana arrived to stand by Jason's side, did the massive hydraulics begin their mechanical whir, signaling the admiral's motorcade was now arriving. Looking at the shaft coming from the surface, and the hydraulic plunger receding into the floor as it supported the descending platform where the admiral's vehicle was carried, Jason licked his lips after noticing his mouth was suddenly dry. He was the real reason why this facility even existed and, with this new portal technology, Jason knew he was going to be even more invaluable. Yet, he always remembered something his father said to him one time. "Son, never forget; no one is irreplaceable. No matter how much you know, there is always someone else who knows more. Don't ever get too big for your britches, or you'll have me coming to take you down a notch."

That one piece of advice helped shape Jason into the kind of man he became. That is what attracted Mikki to his charms when she wasn't really interested in anybody.

The platform now emerged from the overhead shaft, descending to Jason's level and stopping. The driver of the four-wheel drive vehicle pulled forward and parked. The driver got out and opened the back door, allowing Admiral Brinstock to emerge wearing his dress whites. When Jason looked at the man for the first time, he thought how old the admiral looked. Maybe the pictures he had seen of him were a little dated.

Diana stepped forward to greet the admiral, hand extended for a handshake, while Jason stayed back.

"Admiral Brinstock, my name is Diana O'Laney, and I am the director of research here at the MMPA."

Admiral Brinstock shook her hand. "Nice to meet you, Ms. O'Laney."

Turning to Jason, Diana said, "And this is Dr. Jason Marsalis, senior technologist." Jason stepped forward and, with the best plastic smile he could manufacture, extended his hand. The admiral shook his hand, saying, "Dr. Marsalis, it is a pleasure to meet you ... finally. I am a big fan of your work."

"Thank you, Admiral," said Jason, "I appreciate that. I am happy to be of service." Jason thought maybe his first estimation of this guy might have been a little harsh; he seemed congenial enough. Right then, the proverbial little devil appeared on Jason's shoulder, warning him this guy lives in Washington, D.C., and rubs shoulders with people who smile at you while sinking the knife in deeper. Jason felt warned about trusting the admiral about as far as he could throw him.

"Would you like some refreshments Admiral?" asked Diana, "Or would you prefer getting down to business?"

"I'd like to get down to business, but I wouldn't mind some ice water," Kenji replied.

While the admiral's driver stayed with the vehicle, Kenji and his assistant, Sergeant Flume, along with Diana and Jason, proceeded to the elevator and descended to Underground Level Nine where the offices and conference room were located. The conference room was well-appointed, with a 15-foot table and plush chairs all around. One side was a floor-to-ceiling window looking onto the main detection chamber, similar to the view Jason and Diana had from their respective offices. Kenji had already informed his assistant he would be part of the meeting, so he took a seat outside the conference room. The only people in the secure room were Admiral Brinstock, Diana, and Jason.

Diana was the first to speak. "Admiral, I want to reiterate that it is a pleasure to have you visit our facility. Since the successful test of the missile deterrence system on Fifteen February of this year, we have continued to refine the operations of the facility, and have been able to reduce the number of personnel necessary by 15%. We have also been able to conduct some scientific research which may prove beneficial to national interests."

"That's good to hear, Ms. O'Laney," Kenji replied. "I am aware you are requesting another test be performed with the system. Is that still your desire?"

"Yes sir, it is," said Diana. "However, we wish to perform such a test with different parameters. First, we would like to see the missile launched from a decidedly different location. The last missile came from the far side of Guam. In the next test, if there is to be one, we would like to see the incoming bird approaching from either the Atlantic or somewhere in the Middle East, proving the overall versatility of the system regardless of where the threat comes from."

The admiral thought for a moment before he responded. "As you can imagine, Trident missiles aren't exactly cheap for the American taxpayer. When you couple that with the idea of launching a missile from a place like Saudi Arabia, it can open up a can of worms."

"We thought of that, Admiral," injected Jason, "but perhaps we can tell our allies ahead of time that this is simply a test of the missile self-destruct system, and it wouldn't fly over any territories that may be a problem. In fact, it doesn't necessarily have to be a submarine-launched Trident. It could be an older technology missile like an Atlas. Perhaps we could even invite representatives of our allies to come and supervise the launch, allowing them to see there would be no warhead involved."

"An Atlas missile?" replied Kenji, allowing a small chuckle to escape. "Doctor, I didn't know you were into obsolete history that much."

"Forgive me, Admiral, but I was resorting to hyperbole," Jason responded coolly.

Kenji sat back in his chair, appearing to contemplate the suggestions. "Your suggestions on how to handle this diplomatically have merit. I will make note of them and see what can be arranged."

"Thank you, Admiral," said Diana. "Moving along, are there any questions you have regarding our operations here at the facility?"

Admiral Brinstock began inquiring about several specific aspects of the installation having to do with the power generation, along with the security systems and procedures that were in place. After going over several details, Kenji said he wanted to perform a visual inspection of the facility. Diana and Jason proceeded to give him as complete a tour as possible, making sure the newly-built portal room was the last destination. Taking a page from Jason and Dennis' approach with her earlier, she had a 32-inch monitor hooked up to a DVD player.

"Admiral," said Diana, "I'd like to show you something I think you will find interesting."

Clicking on a remote control, the TV came to life. Shortly thereafter, an image came onto the screen depicting what appeared to be a graduation ceremony. It was a very sunny day, and the stadium where the graduation ceremony was being held looked like a college football stadium. At least 2,000 chairs were set up in the middle of the playing field, filled with naval plebes dressed in their best white and black dress uniforms. In the seating areas located all around the playing field, there were men, women, and children dressed in somewhat dated garb. Judging by the clothes people were wearing, the decade when this scene was recorded was the 1960s.

Located in the far end zone of the field was a stage with wide ramps to the left and right, as well as a ramp directly in the front of the stage, all three colored in white treads. Walking up the stage was a line of cadets shaking the hands of a few officials who stood on the stage. Two of those officials were in uniform themselves, and judging by the number of military badges and medals on the breasts of those uniforms, they appeared to be of rather high rank. There was no sound, just a moving picture.

"Admiral, do you recognize this scene?" asked Diana.

"Of course I do," replied Admiral Brinstock, with a look of nostalgia. "It's the football field at my alma mater, the United States Naval Academy at Annapolis, Maryland." Then he added, "In fact, this is a pretty realistic rendition of what it was like back then. Hollywood must have spent a lot of money to do this."

With a slight smile on her face, Diana said, "Let's turn up the volume, shall we?"

With a quick press of the remote button, the volume increased as names were being called out.

"Johnathan A. Fernandez," said the person reading names into a microphone.

A cadet walked up the ramp and shook the hand of the man in the suit. He then walked over to one of the commanding officers and received his diploma.

"Steven K. Powell."

Another cadet walked up the ramp and shook the hand of the man in the suit. He then walked over to one of the commanding officers and received his diploma.

Admiral Brinstock was beginning to get a perplexed look on face. Expecting this, Diana and Jason glanced at each other without the admiral noticing; he was far too interested in what he was seeing.

"Murphy T. Gregg." Another cadet accepted his diploma.

The next cadet whose name was to be read was standing at the ready. His face could be clearly seen and, as Diana and Jason expected, the admiral's face suddenly went white.

"Kenneth G. Brinstock."

The admiral's mouth went slack.

Cadet Brinstock walked up the center ramp, shook the hand of the dean of education, then walked over to a vice admiral to accept his diploma. After getting it in his hands, he turned to the audience and waved both arms above his head, signifying victory. Diana paused the video, and the image froze on Cadet Brinstock looking directly at what would be the camera. The room was silent for about 10 seconds before anybody spoke."

"Where did you find this film?" asked Admiral Brinstock. His countenance was that of a man who had been hit with a sucker punch.

"Before I answer that, Admiral, I have something else to show you," said Diana.

She then pressed a couple of other buttons on her remote, and another video came up. This showed people who must have lived 200 years ago, all dressed up as if they lived in colonial America. The admiral observed that the casting in this movie was superb, since the people playing the characters of Benjamin Franklin, John Adams, and Thomas Jefferson seemed to perfectly depict those men.

As he was looking at the movie, Diana spoke. "Admiral, as you can tell, this is a depiction of the presentation of the Declaration of Independence to Congress. Did you know that there is something written on the back of the Declaration?"

"Of course," replied the admiral. "Everybody knows that. It says, 'Original Declaration of Independence dated 4th July 1776.'"

"Correct," responded Diana. "But did you know it was Edward Rutledge, a lawyer from South Carolina, who wrote it?"

At this point, Kenji began to get irritated. "Ms. O'Laney, I'm not sure why you are wasting my time with this tripe. I will admit I was a little taken back by the footage of my graduation, but now you're just showing me Hollywood-style movies. I'd appreciate it if you would get back on schedule with the inspection."

"Admiral, what you just saw wasn't Hollywood movies. What I just showed you is probably the most sensitive secret in existence," responded Diana, with a deadpan look on her face, telling the admiral he had better take notice.

"Oh?" quibbled Admiral, "Why would a couple of movies be the most sensitive secret in America, pray tell?"

"Because, Admiral, Jason here has designed a time machine which we used to go back in time to record those videos," Diana responded, with a matter-of-fact tone to her voice masking the excitement she was hoping to hide.

"Sure you did," Kenji responded, while rolling his eyes.

"Actually," interjected Jason, "Dennis had a lot to do with the calculations which led us to some of the early successes in the laboratory. And, if truth be told, it was a thought-provoking conversation with my wife about general physics that caused me to discover some of the scientific principles employed by the portal."

The admiral was silent for a few seconds as he squinted his eyes, trying to see how far this practical joke was going to be taken.

"A time machine," said the admiral. It was more of a statement than a question.

"Yes sir, a time machine," answered Jason.

"And I suppose you built this here?" asked Kenji, still not believing what he was being told.

"Actually, Admiral, you are standing in front of it," answered Diana.

Kenji spun around and spied a lot of scientific machinery, but he had no idea of its purpose.

"You're trying to tell me this thing is ... is a time machine?" asked the admiral.

"Yes, Admiral," responded Jason. "It's what we call an X/Y/Z/T portal. With this, we have the ability to transport a person anywhere we desire, instantly. What we didn't expect was we can not only change a person's X, Y, and Z location, but we can also change their T location as well. Their time location."

Kenji continued to stare at Jason for at least 10 seconds, looking for any hint that this was all a big joke. He received no such indication. He slowly started to turn his body back toward the portal machine, his eyes pausing on Diana, looking for the same. None came.

Once again, he cast his eyes at the device. He slowly walked up to the device and looked closely. Aside from all the banks of computer equipment lining both side walls, the center of the room was dominated by a device was about four meters tall. There were two curved pylons rising up from the floor, and a number of cables and conduits connected to the device. There was an inclined ramp leading up to the area between the two pylons.

"Admiral, would you like to see it in action?" asked Jason.

Turning around, the admiral looked to the left and right, and asked, "Right now?"

"Sure," responded Jason, "If you'd like."

Kenji's answer was simple. "OK."

Jason turned around, walked over to a workstation, and sat down. Previously, the operation of the portal required both Jason and Dennis controlling the power injection circuitry and matter stream redirection. That was automated now, so the portal could quite literally be operated by one person. Jason typed in the password and brought up the control software. Pressing the necessary buttons on the screen, the entire facility began to whir under the load of trillions of volts of electricity.

Jason turned to the Kenji. "Admiral, is there an event in history you would like to see, or one you have a question about?"

The admiral took a seat and thought about the question. After a few minutes, it occurred to him that he and his assistant recently had a conversation about the terrorist bombings which occurred in Houston, Texas, on New Year's Day. The investigation had stalled, and there were no new leads which could be pursued on who had perpetrated this heinous act of terrorism. It could be someone local, or someone who had already fled abroad. They had no idea who had done it.

The president was leaning on Kenji quite heavily to figure out who did it because it was rapidly turning into a political hot potato. The president's detractors were painting the president as someone who wasn't getting things done, using this situation to advance their own political agendas.

Nevertheless, the president wanted to get to the bottom of the problem, but there was no reliable intelligence.

"You're telling me I can give you a date, time, and location and you can show me what happened?"

"That is exactly what I am telling you, Admiral," responded Jason.

Sitting back in his seat, crossing his knees and arms, Kenji took a stance showing he wasn't fully convinced. "All right. Show me the first day of January this year; Houston, Texas; the terrorist bombings that killed 32 people and injured 243 others."

Stunned, Jason hadn't thought of using the portal for gathering intelligence against terrorists. He glanced over to Diana and saw she was just as pensive about the admiral's request.

Turning back to the console, Jason typed the necessary parameters into the system and, with a simple click of the mouse, he pressed "engage" on the software and the portal began making a considerable amount of noise. As the field began to form, Kenji backed away from the portal armature. As with previous tests, a bright baby blue field initially formed around the edges. Slowly the portal field extended toward the middle, where it converged and became one single field. The baby blue light gave way to a scene of complete disarray. Paper was flying everywhere; smoke obscured most of the picture.

The admiral walked closer to the portal, and as he did, he recognized the corner where the bombing occurred. He had toured the area several times in the aftermath of the bombing, and always wished he had a video of what happened in the hours leading up to the bombing.

"Can you move back earlier? Can you move back to before the bombing by about 10 minutes?" he asked, now completely intrigued by what he was seeing.

Jason turned to his workstation and hit a few keystrokes. The field cleared to baby blue light for a few seconds, then changed again to show the same scene with people walking about. Located in the very corner where the bombing occurred was a trashcan. They had always thought the bomb was in a trashcan, but couldn't prove it.

The scene showed they were wrong. The bomb wasn't in the trashcan, but in a backpack placed to the side and slightly behind it. The backpack was bright green, blue, and yellow, and the two shoulder straps indicated it had been worn recently. As they sat there looking at the backpack, a man and woman in their thirties, dressed in casual clothes, appeared. In the woman's arms was a baby, about nine months old. They were walking down the street toward the trashcan and backpack.

"Oh no," said the admiral. Suddenly turning to Jason and Diana, he shouted, "*Close your eyes!!*"

No sooner had he said that and they had done so, the bomb exploded exactly when the couple and baby were passing by. They had no idea what happened to them, since the bodies of all three as well as about 10 others near them were instantly vaporized. The bomb wasn't terribly large, but big enough to destabilize the building behind it, which was evacuated until engineers could shore up the structural steel.

The carnage was horrific. Those who hadn't been vaporized and who had the unfortunate luck of only being injured were all lying about. Many were missing parts of their bodies, and most who were still alive weren't going to be so for very long. Jason was sickened by what he saw, and Diana looked toward the wastebasket near her in case she lost her lunch.

The scene was enough to turn the stomachs of the most hardened of hearts; even Kenji was put off by what he saw. The military tactician in him quickly came to the fore and started pursuing this new avenue of intelligence like a dog with a bone.

"Go farther back. Say, 10 more minutes," said Admiral Brinstock.

Welcoming the opportunity to change the scene, Jason immediately reached over and punched in a couple of new parameters. Within five seconds they were rewarded with the same corner, but no longer in disarray. The garbage can was still there.

But no backpack.

"OK. Let's wait and watch what happens."

As people drifted by, it was easy to see how someone could put a backpack in this location without anybody noticing. There were far too many people interested in their own day and their own activities to pay attention to any ....

Just then, a Caucasian man in blue jeans and a jacket emblazoned with the Houston Astro's logo walked by and paused near the trashcan. He was wearing a Texas Rangers baseball cap and sunglasses.

The man took off his backpack and placed it on the ground near the trashcan, but he didn't move. He appeared interested in his cell phone, pausing and resting for a moment as if texting someone. After lingering for a minute while typing on his phone, his foot moved to the side and pushed the backpack behind the trashcan, the same location where they had seen it earlier.

"Can you follow that guy to see where he went after this?" asked Kenji.

Over the next hour they followed him. He went straight to the airport and caught a plane bound for New York, then another plane to Los Angeles. They also systematically followed him before the explosion, back to where he had been camping out. It turned out he wasn't the mastermind of the bombing. The main orchestrator was a person they suspected had been involved in the bombing somehow, but couldn't link him to it in any way; that is, until now. They were able to record HD video of his conversation with the bomb planter, telling him exactly what to do, how to do it, and who to coordinate with. They also recorded him planning out the entire attack, and giving money to all parties involved to purchase materials used in the bomb.

With this new technology, there was no doubt justice would finally be served.

When they had secured the last video evidence needed for an open and shut case against these perpetrators, Kenji sat back in his seat and let out a big sigh. "You know, this is going to make it possible to get all the terrorists without any collateral damage. We'll get exactly who does what."

Looking at Jason, he excitedly asked, "Can you read the newspapers in the future and see what attacks are going to occur so we can keep them from happening?"

"Unfortunately, no I can't, Admiral. That is impossible. When you work out the math for such an idea, the numbers run to infinity and can't be resolved."

Kenji was visibly disappointed, but steeled himself with the knowledge that what he *did* have in his hand was far beyond anything he had when he arrived. "Well, I suppose we'll have to wait until the TITs arrive."

"TITs, Admiral?" asked Diana, taking exception to what she had just heard.

"Terrorists in Training, Ms. O'Laney. Also known as fun-size terrorists. As far as I'm concerned, they should all be eliminated."

Both Diana and Jason were floored by what they heard. The admiral was talking about killing children like it was nothing. This instantly put the him on Jason's bad side. Kenji hadn't given it any more thought; it was nothing to him. When Admiral Brinstock left Midway Magnetic that day, he felt like he had just been given the proverbial keys to the kingdom.

Now, nothing and no one would stand in his way of killing every last terrorist. His promise to his dead wife was going to come true.

CHAPTER 44

DIANA WALKED DOWN THE HALLWAY to the portal room with a smile on her face. Thinking about the course of events over the last few weeks, she reflected how wildly things can change in such a short period of time. Being the director of research for Midway Magnetic was a position she savored, not only because it was a super-secret facility, but also because on a daily basis things happened that most assuredly wouldn't happen at any other job. Today was no exception.

As she rode the elevator to the 17th floor, Diana thought for a moment about what brought her here. She had studied at the University of California, Berkley, in the 80s, taking top honors in her graduating class. After majoring in business administration with a minor in physics, she graduated in the top one percent of her class. This is how she came to the attention of the powers that be, leading her to the position she now occupied.

Recent events went far beyond her wildest dreams. The portal Jason and Dennis had invented, and the way it would no doubt change the world, was nothing short of staggering. The way it was used to locate that terrorist organization and how it showed not only who was responsible for planting the bomb, but also who was responsible for masterminding and funding the whole plot, made the world a whole lot safer, at least in Diana's mind. The more she thought about the events on the day of the admiral's visit, the more she relished the idea of being a part of that whole process.

Yet her misgivings about the way the portal technology might erase any sense of privacy were still alive and well. She vowed to do all she could to make sure it was only used for good, but she was astute enough to know it wouldn't be in her hands forever. She hoped it would only be used for the eradication of terror and the advancement of knowledge, but she knew not everybody would be as virtuous.

Arriving at the portal room, she waved her keycard over the pad, punched in her security code, then stared into the retinal scanner. These security measures kept the nature of the portal secret even from others working at the facility. Pushing open the door, she immediately saw Jason and Dennis taking a well-deserved break from the work they had been doing on the portal.

As she approached them, they looked up from their lunches and greeted her with wide smiles.

"Diana! So nice to see you. We've been cooped up down here for so long, we were beginning to wonder if there was still an outside world," said Jason.

"Oh, it's still there all right," falling right in line with the banter. "You know, they have this new thing called the sun; when you stand in the light that comes from it, you end up not looking as pasty as you two."

"Is that so?" replied Dennis, with a grin on his face. "I've heard about that. I may have to take an all-expense-paid trip to a place where there is a lot of, what do you call it? Sunlight? I've also been thinking I need to study the effects of repeated wave action on particles of silica sand. Maybe I can combine the two research projects."

Amidst gales of laughter on the part of all three, Jason restored order to the room by asking Diana, "So, to what do we owe the honor of your visit?"

"I ..." Diana paused. Then with an exaggerated inward breath, she asked, "What is that aroma I am smelling. It smells amazing!"

"Chinese food. Would you like some?" said Dennis.

"What do you have?" asked Diana.

"Mongolian beef, chow mein, egg rolls, and here is sweet and sour chicken," answered Jason.

"Ooooo. Sounds wonderful," responded Diana.

She was still in awe over the portal apparatus they were casually sitting in front of, as if it was nothing more than a washing machine. Lost in the wonder of it all and forgetting the original reason she came down to the portal, Diana took a seat with them. Jason proceeded to serve up the food while Diana continued to talk.

"What have you two been doing with all the spare time you have?" asked Diana, with a smile.

Handing her a plate, Jason responded, "Well, Dennis and I have been making some modifications to the software we wrote to control the portal."

"Really? It seemed to work pretty well the other day."

"It did because we were able to overcome several of the shortfalls with some deft calculations. We wanted to automate some functions to account for the Z axis as well," answered Dennis.

"The Z axis?" asked Diana.

"Yeah," replied Jason. "We have been able to locate to specific X and Y coordinates fairly easily, but the other day when we connected to Pearl Harbor, we saw ...."

"Wait a minute!" exclaimed Diana, "Are you telling me you saw the attack on Pearl Harbor? What was that like?"

Putting his plate aside and looking down at the ground, Jason spoke slowly.

"When we first laid eyes on the scene, it was shortly before the attack began; as lovely a day as you would expect for a quiet harbor in the Hawaiian Islands. There was nothing but beautiful sunshine, a little trade wind from the west, and the palm trees lazily swaying in the warm tropical breeze coming off the ocean.

"But then, whizzing above and past the portal, a plane with large red spots on the wings and the fuselage broke the silence, unleashing its lone cargo into the water. When the torpedo hit the water, it streaked under the water on a direct course for a destroyer moored in the harbor. There were men walking on the deck, including a small group of three standing on the deck directly above where the torpedo was obviously going to hit."

Diana looked over to Dennis and, witnessing the look on his face along with the tone of Jason's voice, realized their experience of watching this event didn't match the enthusiasm of her question. She put her own plate of food to the side in a show of respect.

"As we continued to watch," said Jason, "I felt so helpless, knowing I was about to watch the first of over 2,300 Americans who lost their life that day. The torpedo made it to its target and exploded."

Jason paused.

"I'm quite sure those three guys were never found because they were instantly in the middle of a fireball about four stories tall itself. The ship almost snapped in half by the blast, and the sound was deafening."

Dennis decided to speak up. "Not only that, but on the ground, I saw men getting directly shot by the planes as they strafed across the airstrip. Planes were going up in flames before they even had a chance to be flown; pilots and groundsmen were being mowed down by the dozens."

Jason nodded. "I remember there was this one guy who was shot in the leg. He went down and called out for help. The other guy—I don't know if he was a mechanic, or a grunt, or what—ran over to the first guy to help him. As soon as he got there, another bullet came in and hit the grunt. He fell over dead on top of the first guy. His body ended up taking a bullet for the first guy, who made it to cover, only because the other guy died instead."

At this point, Diana dipped her head. "I'm sorry, guys. I just wasn't thinking." She wasn't openly crying, but her eyes were definitely moist.

"I know," consoled Jason as he came over to her side. "In fact, before we connected to the scene, Dennis and I were thinking the same way ourselves. Why do you think we dialed it up in the first place? It took the wind out of us to actually see it happening right in front of us, though."

There was a very pregnant pause in the portal room at that moment, then Jason added, "The thing is, Diana, I have come to the realization that this portal is going to take some getting used to. We have an amazing opportunity to see not only the best of human history, but also the worst. What we saw at Pearl Harbor, the bombing in Houston, or the fire in Chicago were some of the worst events in our history. But, I've come to the conclusion that there were just as many amazing things for us to see as there are horrific things. Remember how we recorded the signing of the Declaration of Independence? That was pretty cool to see, wasn't it? And just the other day, we dialed up the first flight of man by Orville and Wilbur Wright at Kitty Hawk."

"Exactly," said Dennis, coming over to Diana's other side and putting the plate of food back in her hands. "This tool is exactly that. A tool, but one we have to treat with the utmost of respect. It can be a force for incredible good or bad. In my opinion, this holds far too much promise for us to limit ourselves in any way."

"Yep," added Jason. "We need to be prepared for whatever comes our way, and we have to remember the stories in the history books about the good and the bad things our ancestors did were *real* events, and the consequences they endured were sometimes heinous. I would never witness, for example, the events surrounding the Inquisition. I don't think I could handle that."

Diana let out a puff of air and rolled her eyes. "Boy, that's for sure."

After a couple of moments, Jason went back to his chair and grabbed his plate again, deciding this conversation needed to become a whole lot lighter. "Would you like something to drink?"

"No thank you," Diana replied, realizing she was just staring at her plate rather than eating. When she took her first bite, the explosion of flavor cascading through her mouth was almost too much to handle. She considered herself somewhat of a foodie, but this was out of this world. "Oh my god!" was all she burbled, trying to keep the food in her mouth.

Jason and Dennis looked at each other and smiled, each taking another forkful of food.

"This is incredible Chinese food. How did you get this all the way in here and still have it be so fresh?"

Jason didn't answer but just gave his patented enigmatic smile.

"You didn't?" Diana's eyes darted back and forth between Jason and Dennis. "You didn't," Diana just about yelled. "*Shut the front door*! Are you telling me you got Chinese food from China?? With the portal!?"

Having rehearsed the move well ahead of time, both Jason and Dennis gestured dragging a zipper across their mouths.

Diana sat back in her chair with her mouth agape, slowly shaking her head back and forth. "What am I going to do with you guys? You do realize you can't tell anybody about this, right?"

"Wild horses wouldn't be able to drag it out of me, fair maiden," replied Jason. "No one short of the president of the United States would be able to pry it loose from my lips."

Upon hearing that last statement, Diana shot to her feet. "Oh my god! With this food, I completely forgot why I came down here in the first place. There are two guys in my office who want to see you." Laughing, she added, "That's the whole reason why I came down here."

With grins on all three faces, they emerged from a very aromatic portal room and made their way to Diana's office. Upon entering, Jason and Dennis saw two gentlemen in her casual sitting area. They were dressed in black and wore white shirts. They both had an earpiece with a curly cord extending over the ear, disappearing under their jackets. Both were clean cut and stood as soon as the three of them entered the room.

One of them walked forward toward Jason, extending his hand. "Dr. Marsalis? My name is Agent Lockwood, and this is Agent Elder." As he reached for his badge folio, Jason saw parts of a shoulder holster, holding a weapon no doubt. "We are with the United States Secret Service."

"Nice to meet you, gentlemen," said Jason with an obvious expression of concern on his face. "What can I do for you?"

Agent Lockwood spoke. "Sir, we've been ordered to escort you and Dr. Greene to Washington for an emergency meeting. We have a plane waiting in Columbia to take us to Sacramento, then we will take a bigger bird back to Washington, D.C."

"What is this all about?" asked Dennis.

"We're not privy to that information, sir," replied Agent Lockwood, "but we need to leave immediately. We've been instructed to tell you that you'll only be gone for a day; a change of clothes has already been arranged."

"A change of clothes?" asked Jason.

"Yes, sir," was the agent's dry response.

Jason looked at Dennis, who had the same deer-in-the-headlights expression as his own. Glancing back to Diana's face, he said, "Well, make sure you turn off the lights before you leave tonight."

Diana chuckled. "You got it."

Looking back at Dennis, he said, "Lead the way, old buddy."

The four men emerged from Diana's office. Jason wanted to stop off in his office so he could phone his wife and let her know he'd be gone overnight. The agent informed him there was a phone on the plane they'd be flying back to D.C. on and, since time was of the essence, they needed to speed along.

The four men eventually made it to the parking garage, and after ascending through the hydraulically controlled shaft, drove straight to the Columbia airport. It was a little strange for Jason and Dennis to drive such a direct route since they had always been required to take more circuitous ones; they decided not to take issue with the guys with the guns.

In Columbia, they boarded a Bombardier Challenger 300 business jet parked near the terminal. The pilot reported the fuel was topped off and, once they were wheels-up, they'd make it to Sacramento in about a half an hour. After settling into their leather chairs and watching the ground pull away, a smartly-dressed woman offered them refreshments. In no time at all, they landed at Sacramento International Airport and pulled into a private hangar.

As they were disembarking, Dennis decided to make a small joke. "I don't know, Jason. I always thought the Secret Service could afford better-tasting peanuts."

Falling right in line with his friend's humor while walking to the back of the hangar, Jason added, "Or at least an in-flight movie."

Agent Lockwood replied, "Well, gentlemen, perhaps that can be arranged." He then opened a small door at the rear of the hangar and stepped through it. As soon as they stepped over the threshold, Jason and Dennis stopped cold in their tracks. Standing there in all its glory was a magnificent plane. The agents, not realizing Jason and Dennis were rooted to where they stood, briefly left them behind.

The plane was a gleaming and beautiful 747. It was painted white and pale blue, and on its side were painted four very important words in letters three meters high: UNITED STATES OF AMERICA.

"Holy ...."

"Easy there, partner. Show some respect," interrupted Jason.

The two men continued staring at the impressive airship with the numbers 29000 painted on the tail. Out of nowhere, Agent Lockwood appeared, explaining how they needed to get a move on. Reluctantly, Jason and Dennis gave permission to their legs to carry them to the stairway leading to the interior of the plane. After getting settled in some of the most luxurious seats they had ever experienced on a plane, Agent Elder proceeded to show Jason how to use the personal phone located next to his seat.

Mikki answered her cell phone after only the second ring.

"Hello?" she answered cautiously, seeing the "Restricted" message coming across the caller ID.

"Hi, babe. It's me," said Jason.

"Jason? Oh hi, babe. What's up? Is everything all right?"

"Oh yeah. Everything's fine, but, well, I have an unexpected meeting I have to attend, and it's going to keep me from coming home tonight. I know it's last minute, but it was literally sprung on me 30 seconds before I had to leave for it. Since I'm supposed to be back tomorrow night, can you manage without me tonight?"

"Wow. That's pretty last minute all right. Weren't you supposed to take Jace to Little League orientation tonight?" asked Mikki.

"No, that was rescheduled for tomorrow night, fortunately, so I'll still be able to take him."

"Oh, okay. Well, I'm gonna miss you. I'm not really crazy about sleeping without my snuggle bug."

"Me neither," said Jason. "I promise I'll make it up to you tomorrow night. Maybe the three of us can go out for dinner and a movie after that orientation. OK?"

"You're on!" fired back Mikki.

"Great sweetheart, I can't wait to see you again. I love you!"

"I love you too," said Mikki. "Take care of you!"

"I will, babe. You too," replied Jason.

"I will. Byeee"

"Byeee," said Jason, hanging up the phone.

Looking at Dennis, he saw his partner had this gigantic grin on his face that would difficult to wipe away. The same smile found its way onto Jason's face.

The flight was as smooth as expected on an airship of this size. Jason felt quite presidential on this flight, since he and Dennis were treated to anything they chose to eat. When asked for their order, Jason made a joke saying he wanted filet mignon, but when the flight attendant said ok and asked Dennis what he wanted, Jason sat there stunned. Dennis asked if they had lobster, which they did. Dinner was magnificent, and the flight was over in what seemed to be only an hour. A limousine took them to an upscale hotel where they were told to change in their rooms and report back down in the lobby. Forty-five minutes later, Jason and Dennis emerged, wearing the tuxedos which had been waiting for them in their rooms. Once in the limousine, the two of them wondered what was next. When the Secret Service agent ordered the driver to take them to the cottage, Jason turned white as a ghost. Dennis didn't know what that meant, but seeing the reaction of his friend, he wasn't sure if this was a good or a bad thing.

The limousine turned from a rather wide street into the driveway at 1600 Pennsylvania Avenue. Before them stood the symbol of democracy in the free world, the White House. After waiting for the gate to open and pulling up to the north portico, Secret Service agents who had obviously been waiting for them to arrive approached and opened the doors, allowing two very star-struck men to emerge. Jason thought how never in a million years, when he got out of bed this morning, would he have imagined going to the White House this evening. He still didn't know why he was here.

As they were about to leave Agents Lockwood and Elder behind, Lockwood approached his relief agent and said, "Make sure you take care of 'snuggle bug' here so I can get him home to his wife." That broke the spell cast over Jason, who let out the belly laugh of all belly laughs, just now realizing the phones on Air Force One wereof coursemonitored.

The new agent, whose name they never discovered, escorted Jason and Dennis up the steps to the north entrance and through a few corridors to the right, opening one last door into the Oval Office. To say they were overawed would be a colossal understatement.

They were told the president would be with them shortly and to make themselves comfortable. The agents then stood at attention near the door, basically becoming unmoving statues. Jason and Dennis sat uncomfortably on comfortable couches, individually wondering what all this meant.

"Do you know what's going on?" asked Dennis.

"Not a clue," said Jason.

With those words, the side door of the Oval Office opened, and President Michaelson entered the room, followed by two secret service guards.

"Gentlemen, I'm glad you could come," said the president. He reached out his hand to Jason, the nearest man to him.

Rapidly rising, Jason stuck out his hand in response. "Mr. President. It's an honor to meet you" he said, shaking President Michaelson's hand.

"The pleasure is all mine, guys," said the president in a very disarming way. Reaching for Dennis' hand, he asked, "I trust the trip was comfortable?"

"How could it not be, sir? That is one impressive plane," replied Dennis.

"Indeed. I love flying on that thing. It's amazing how good you can sleep when you are at altitude!" laughed the president. He sat in an armchair. "Please. Have a seat."

"Thank you, sir," said Jason. He and Dennis sat on opposing couches.

Turning to the Secret Service personnel in the room, he said, "Guys, I'd like you to step outside for a few, please."

"Yes, sir." Speaking into his wrist, the senior agent announced they were no longer in direct company of "Whirlwind," the president's code name.

When the doors closed, the president turned back to the two men. Leaning forward in this chair, Whirlwind began to speak in hushed tones. "Gentlemen, I know you have no idea why you are here and that is by design. The nature of what you are working on is known only by the highest level government officials, yet even they aren't aware of the, shall we say, *new* development recently. Admiral Brinstock, all of us on the Hill call him Kenji, briefed me on the portal technology he witnessed while there. Is it really true you can go back in time and look at things?"

"Yes sir, that is correct," replied Jason, matter-of-factly.

Unbuttoning the front button on his jacket, the president leaned back in his chair, crossed his legs, and let out an exaggerated exhale. "My god. I'd have never believed it."

"Yes sir, it is pretty amazing," added Dennis.

"Kenji told me about the terrorist bombing, which I'm going to talk more about in a second, but have you done anything else with it?"

"Yes, sir. We've tested it with a few different times and places in the past, proving the technology is sound," replied Jason.

"Like what? Where?" asked President Michaelson.

"Sir, yesterday we entered the proper parameters and witnessed the raising of the flag at Iwo Jima," replied Dennis.

"Holy cow! That's incredible."

"Yes, sir," replied Jason. "And in a test this morning, we did something we've wanted to do ever since this whole thing started. We dialed it back to the reputed time of the destruction of the scrolls of the Library of Alexandria to see what really happened, and if there was something we could learn about that time period."

"Unbelievable," he said, shaking his head. Jason and Dennis nodded.

"Well, guys, I wanted to tell you personally about the results of that little exercise you and Kenji did," said the president. "The fallout from the intel your portal provided is going to hit the news tomorrow, but I wanted you to be some of the first to know. Using that information, we were able to direct a drone strike against the leader of the whole terrorist band, completely crippling the entire operation. It turns out they were in the midst of planning three more bombings like the one in Houston, and they were damn far along. In fact, one of them was supposed to happen next week, and we had no idea."

Jason and Dennis were both shocked and immensely gratified their invention was used in such a useful role and could actually be linked to saving countless lives. They both relished the good feeling from that.

"I gotta tell you, when this hits the press tomorrow, it's going to make me look pretty good boys. And I want you to know I understand exactly who I have to thank for that; I'm looking at them."

"You're welcome, Mr. President. I'm glad to have been of service to my country," said Jason.

"Same here," said Dennis.

"There are a lot of sharks here in D.C., but I don't consider myself to be one of them," replied the president. "I know this whole thing will pretty much ensure my re-election. I won't ever forget what you've done, not only for the country but for me personally."

Standing and walking over to his desk, he picked up two items. Jason and Dennis stood as well.

"Gentlemen," continued President Michaelson, "contrary to what I would have preferred, this cannot be done in public because of the ultra-secrecy of what you do. Still, you both deserve this nonetheless."

Straightening his back and clearing his throat, President Michaelson said, with a slight smile on his face, "By presidential order, it is my supreme pleasure, and it is my honor, to award Dr. Jason Alexander Marsalis and Dr. Dennis Michael Greene the Presidential Medal of Freedom." Opening the flat containers to reveal medals hanging by a ribbon intended to be worn around the neck, he added, "Gentlemen, the United States of America owes you a debt of gratitude that can never be repaid, and cannot be measured by anything less than the continued lives of the hundreds if not thousands of men, women, children, and infants your efforts saved. I not only view it a supreme privilege to hang this medal around your necks, I am humbled and honored to be the one representing all my fellow Americans in shaking the hands of two of the greatest patriots, two of the greatest assets, this country has to offer. From the bottom of my heart, you have my supreme thanks."

The two scientists were utterly dumbstruck.

Jason had enough wits about him to say, "Thank you, Mr. President. It is certainly an honor to serve our country in whatever way we can."

"There's something else you should know," said the president.

"What's that?" asked Dennis, who refound his voice, albeit shaky.

"I'm not sure if you realize this, but there was a reward offered for information leading to not only the capture and neutralization of that organization, but also information leading to the perpetrators behind the Houston bombing. You two are going to have to duke it out over how to share the $5,000,000 reward."

Jason lost his ability to stand, and uttered a very shaky "Oh." Fortunately, there was a couch behind him. This led to a hearty belly laugh from this Texas politician. Dennis didn't fare much better than Jason.

As they were trying their best to gather themselves back together while on the couches, the president said added, "There's something else I want you boys to know."

"Yes sir?" croaked Jason.

The president looked him square in the eyes and said, "Dr. Marsalis? Dr. Greene? If there is anything you need, *anything*, any favor, you name it. From this day forward, you've got an open ear in the White House, and a direct line to my desk."

Looking over to Dennis, he said, "And that goes for both of you. Got it?"

Managing to stand again, Jason replied, "Yes sir. Thank you, sir."

"My pleasure," said Whirlwind. Jason decided his code name was well-deserved.

Reaching for the phone on the Resolute desk and punching a button, President Michaelson said, "Lindsay, Doctors Marsalis and Greene are ready to leave. Please arrange for their safe return home."

"Right away sir," was the short and professional response.

In no time flat, Jason and Dennis were spending time in their hotel rooms, then back to California in the morning aboard the same plane that became Air Force One when the president flew. It was good to know they now had a huge ally, and that their work would proceed unabated. As time went on, they would no doubt discover shocking and surprising things on a daily basis.

But the secrets just around the corner would not only amaze Jason and Dennis, but also might cost them their lives.

CHAPTER 45

◉ ꓕ ꓱ ⟋ ꓴ ꓱ ⦿ ꓱ◉ꓱ

ꗖ ꓲꓱ ꓲ ꓲ ꓴ ꕷ⦁

"YES SIR?" ANSWERED THE BRIGHT and cheery voice.

"Stephanie, get Dr. Marsalis at Midway Magnetic on the line for me, please," asked Admiral Brinstock.

"Right away, sir," was her prompt response.

Punching the intercom button on his phone, Kenji looked down at the report he had just placed on the desk in front of him. It was from the USGS team of geologists working on the Yellowstone project.

According to the report, the magma chamber had consistently grown, and with the current rate of growth, it was their educated opinion an eruption was going to happen within 60 to 90 days. As with their previously filed reports, the language used to describe the effect of this eruption was nothing short of catastrophic on a global level.

Kenji punched the intercom button again.

"Yes sir?" answered the bright and cheery voice once again.

"Two more things. First, make all necessary arrangements for me to fly out to California to visit Midway as soon as I talk with Dr. Marsalis. I also want you to contact the president's office and set up another Level One top secret meeting with him. Schedule it for one day after I get back from California."

"Yes sir. Right away, sir," Stephanie responded.

Cutting off the intercom again, Kenji thought more about the consequences of what this report meant, not only for America but for all of humankind. Similar to his personal vow to his dead wife to kill every terrorist on the planet, he knew he needed to do whatever was necessary to try and stop this.

Under normal circumstances, Kenji would be as lost as anybody else on what to do with the problem at Yellowstone. But considering the report he just received from Major Bellini, who personally visited what was apparently an island originally inhabited by aliens who had a machine that could fix this, there might be a solution to the problem. However, because the machine didn't work, there was a sense of urgency in finding out what happened to the aliens and, more importantly, how to fix the machine. The solution would require the portal technology Dr. Marsalis and Dr. Greene had invented.

Ah, but there was the rub. Dr. Marsalis. He was one particular burr under Kenji's saddle that needed to be dealt with sooner than later. His unwillingness to do whatever Kenji wanted, whenever he wanted it … well, he needed to be taught a lesson. Somehow he had to be shown that when Kenji says he wants something, then by God it better happen or else you're out!

Beep. Stephanie's voice came over the intercom. "Dr. Marsalis is on line 3, sir." Picking up the phone, Kenji put on his well-honed political voice to get what he wanted.

"Jason. Brinstock here," greeted Kenji.

"Hello, Admiral. How are you?" said the voice on the other end.

"Fine. You?" responded the admiral. He knew he had to play the game with these civilians, but it was such a waste of time.

"I'm fine. Been pretty busy lately with you-know-what," responded Jason.

"I'm sure that's true. In fact, that's why I called. I'm going to be coming out tomorrow night, and I need you and Dr. Greene to look up a couple of things with that you-know-what."

"Oh, sorry about that, admiral. No can do. I already have plans tomorrow night. I can come in the following morning, though," said Jason.

Kenji's blood pressure went from zero to nuclear in two seconds flat, and he suddenly saw red. "Dr. Marsalis, I'm not going to play this game with you again. I will be there tomorrow night, and so will you. I have something top priority that can't wait," was his instant response.

There were several seconds of silence on the phone before Jason's voice could be heard.

"Admiral," responded Jason, "apparently you don't understand how things work around here. You may write the checks but, frankly, I don't need you or anybody else. Without me and Dr. Greene, you wouldn't have this you-know-what, and if we left today, you wouldn't be able to operate it without us. You need to understand I never have, and never will, kowtow to strong-arm tactics like yours. If they continue, you are going to be out one you-know-what. Now, if you wait the 12 hours necessary for me to have a life with my wife and child tomorrow evening, who mean way more to me than anything else on this planet including you, then we can have our meeting on Saturday morning. You have to recognize I don't respond to these tactics; you need to once again *stand down*!"

A long silence occurred on the phone. After five seconds, the admiral growled out a single word.

"*Fine.*" Click.

Punching the intercom, Stephanie came on the line again.

"Yes, sir?"

"Schedule my trip for tomorrow morning. Set up a hotel for one night somewhere around there," said Kenji.

"Yes, sir."

Sitting at his desk in the Pentagon, the admiral was seething. His anger hadn't been at this level in a long time. The insubordination of this piss-ant doctor was more than he had ever dealt with since becoming an officer.

After thinking about it for exactly four and a half seconds, Kenji made a decision right then and there. Seeing Jason as a detriment to national security and on a par with the terrorists of the world, he uttered, "for the good of the country," under his breath.

Dr. Marsalis had to be eliminated.

CHAPTER 46

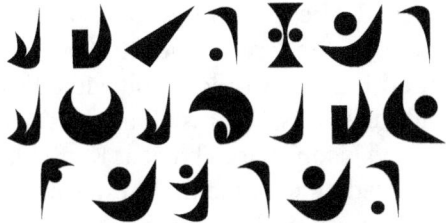

AS HE WAS BEING DRIVEN to the Midway Magnetic facility, Admiral Brinstock had some time to kill as he watched the countryside pass by. The facility was nestled in the far reaches of the Bureau of Land Management land located roughly 15 miles east of Sonora, California. The area, known as Long Barn, represented an unspoiled region of America many flocked to during the summer for camping, and during the winter for skiing. The vistas and pine aromas made many visitors wish they could live there.

Riding in the government sedan with blacked out windows, the vista that lay before him was the last thing on Kenji's mind. While most would say the first thing he should have been thinking about was the eminent threat to every man, woman, and child, all Admiral Brinstock could think of was how this upstart, this dweeb, this small-minded twit was challenging his authority and not acquiescing to the demands placed on him. The fact that this guy was not willing to play ball was the only thing Kenji had been obsessing about since his last phone conversation with Dr. Marsalis. Over and over again, Kenji recalled that phone conversation, and how he had decided Dr. Marsalis had to be eliminated, brutally if necessary.

What Kenji didn't know was Jason had been thinking about little else as well. While he was unwilling to allow the admiral to walk all over him, he was still acutely aware that the admiral was in overarching charge of the facility where Jason worked. Since he loved where he worked and what he did, the prospect of losing that was costing Jason a lot of sleep. Mikki was aware there were things happening at Jason's work lately, secret things, causing a lot of stress for her husband. She didn't like that; she even experienced a measure of empathetic stress because that's just the kind of person she was, especially where her husband was concerned. She did her best to create a happy, quiet home where Jason could come and relax, hoping this was only a passing phase and was something that would resolve itself soon.

When Jason told his buddy Dennis all about the conversation with Kenji, he was surprised Jason roared back at Kenji like he did, yet at the same time not surprised at all since he knew Jason wasn't the kind of guy you could push around. Still, knowing this conversation had happened, and knowing the admiral was due to arrive at the facility soon, caused Dennis stress of his own.

As he came nearer and nearer to the Midway Magnetic facility, Kenji decided he needed to approach this situation strategically. For the time being, he still needed Dr. Marsalis and his knowledge of the portal, but soon, at a time of his own choosing, he would take the necessary steps to eliminate this threat to national security. There was no doubt in his mind: Jason had to be eliminated "for the good of the country," in whatever way was necessary.

Dealing with this situation called for a plan. Kenji had to come up with a tactic which would net him all he wanted, including the removal of this particular thorn in his side. But how? What would be the best plan?

While descending in his car down the cement-lined hydraulic elevator shaft, Kenji had a brainstorm regarding how to deal with this idiot who dared to trifle with Admiral Kenneth Grant Brinstock. How? By putting on a nice smile, treating him like there was no problem at all, perhaps even making nice with an apology for how he came across on the phone. That should do it. That would make this Poindexter lower his guard, putting himself in the perfect position for Kenji to lower the hammer. When exactly that would happen wasn't immediately apparent, but Kenji would know when it came. Yes. He would be nice to Jason; he would be his buddy.

The elevator platform finally came to rest on the underground parking garage level, and Kenji's driver pulled the car forward into the first available spot. It didn't matter to him that the spaces were numbered and this one was set aside for someone else. Once parked, Kenji could see out the front window that Diana O'Laney, Jason Marsalis, and Dennis Greene were waiting for him. While he was still behind the privacy tinting of the car window, Kenji looked in the flip-down mirror and practiced his smile. He put on his best "grandpa" face so he could be as disarming as possible.

When his driver opened the car door, Kenji got out and started walking toward the waiting three. "Hi, guys! Good to see you again!" was his syrupy and overly dramatic salutation.

Since Diana was also familiar with Jason's telephone altercation with Kenji, all three of them were ready for "Hurricane Brinstock" to blow through the parking garage. The fact that Kenji was not only not antagonistic but actually friendly to the nth degree, caused the hair on the necks of all three to stand on end. Jason could actually hear Dennis almost imperceptibly say, "Uh oh, danger Will Robinson," under his breath. This had the unintended, but well-timed, effect of making Jason chuckle, which caused Kenji to believe his ruse of being friendly was working.

Instantly realizing the timeliness of his chuckle, Jason decided to go with it. "Admiral! Good to see you. I trust you had a pleasant drive up here?"

"It was fine, Jason. And you know what, why don't you just call me Kenji like the rest of the higher-ups in Washington do."

"Fair enough, Kenji," said Jason. "I trust you remember our director of research, Diana O'Laney?" As Kenji turned to address Diana, Jason wondered what the admiral was up to. The last time they were on the phone, Jason could feel the icy bullets sailing through the telephone lines. Now the admiral was playing the part of the happy-go-lucky grandpa so obviously a flea would know he was hiding something. But what?

"Yes, of course, I remember Diana. How have you been doing?" asked Kenji.

Diana had been taken back by the admiral's disposition. She wasn't as subtle with her surprise at the demeanor he was displaying. For a moment, she wondered if perhaps Jason had read him wrong and he wasn't the jerk Jason described. Yet, a very big part of her knew this guy was probably more politician than military tactician these days, although being a military tactician could account for the approach he was taking. It would be in his best interests to play nice with her two star physicists. That's when the fog cleared for Diana, and she came to the same conclusion as Jason and Dennis. This guy was playing her, and he was playing Jason and Dennis, too. That's when she realized the admiral was probably pretty stupid to think he could get away with this with either Jason or Dennis.

Still, there was probably an agenda on his mind, so whatever that was, it would be better to play along and wait for him to reveal his cards.

"I've been doing just fine, Kenji. Thank you for asking," replied Diana.

Kenji got a serious look his face. "I told Dr. Marsalis he could call me Kenji, but I don't recall telling you that."

Jason thought to himself, "Jeez, what a dope."

A concerned look flashed across Diana's face. She knew he was just pouring on more syrup and hoping to get a rise out of her, so she played along.

After two seconds of supposedly allowing her to get scared, he pointed at her with both index fingers. "Aaaahhhh! Gotcha," followed by a belly laugh.

Commensurate laughs came from all three, who knew their parts in this script of stupidity.

Satisfied that he had broken the ice with these brain-drained lackeys, Kenji suggested, "How about we go get comfortable? I have some things I need to discuss about the you-know-what."

More grandpa-isms. After Kenji had turned his back, Diana looked at Jason and Dennis, making a magnanimous gesture of sticking her index finger down her throat and silently pantomiming retching. It was all Jason and Dennis could do to keep from heaving forth their own belly laughs. What that did was confirm all three of them were on the same page.

While descending down the elevator, they made small talk about the local bed and breakfast where the admiral stayed and some of the sights that could be enjoyed locally, eventually making it to Diana's office where they could speak confidentially. Only now did the three notice Kenji had brought along a manila folder.

Shutting the door, the four of them sat down in the living-room-like area of her office. There were two opposing couches and comfortably-wide chairs on either end. A large coffee table and an area rug rounded out the sitting area quite nicely. Kenji was the first to speak.

"Now that we can be assured there aren't any prying ears, we can speak more freely about the portal. How have things been going with it? Any new discoveries since I left the last time?" he asked.

Long before Kenji arrived, Diana, Jason, and Dennis reached a unanimous conclusion. The "little tidbit" of information that the portal allowed not only viewing of past events, but also the transportation of matter, even people, to any place they chose, needed to stay secret for the time being. Even with that being the case, there was still a great deal to tell the admiral about.

"Plenty, actually. We've been watching things like the tearing down of the Berlin Wall, a few famous speeches, and the other day we saw Paul Revere make his famous ride," said Dennis enthusiastically.

"Wow. That's something I wouldn't mind seeing myself someday." Then a serious cloud came over his face, as though something was seriously troubling him.

"Unfortunately, something else is of grave concern right now that almost nobody knows about. The three of you have the highest possible security clearance; in fact, your security clearance is at a level others don't even know exists. I know I can trust you guys with what I am about to reveal. Even so, I need to say this for the record. What I am about to discuss is Level One top secret. You aren't to reveal this material to anybody. OK?"

All three nodded and gave their verbal agreement.

"Ok. Basically, I have two things to discuss. The first has to do with Yellowstone National Park."

The admiral told Diana and the two scientists about the impending extinction level event due to occur at Yellowstone sometime in the next two months. He explained how massive the eruption was predicted to be, and how there wouldn't be any survivors left once it happened.

Up to this point, the reactions of all three were manufactured in response to being wary over the admiral's syrupy demeanor. But with the disclosure of this information, their reactions were now genuine. To say they were all shaken by the news would be an understatement. Jason immediately thought about Mikki and little Jace. He envisioned how they would be ....

At that point, he shook his head and stopped thinking about it. He was shaken, all right; shaken to his core.

Dennis wasn't married and had no kids, but he did have family. He was traveling down the same mental road Jason was, and had to arrest his trip lest he fall apart at the prospect of the eminent death of those closest to his heart.

Diana was numb. Unfortunately, she hadn't arrested her mental progression down that pathway like Jason and Dennis had, so she was feeling the horror of potentially losing not only her husband but also her son and two daughters. She was holding it together, but it was a herculean task.

Satisfied he had terrified them enough to work unreservedly on the task at hand, he continued.

"I'm really sorry to dump this on you, but it reinforces the urgency of the task I have in mind for you. If it works, then we just might have a chance of survival."

The three of them straightened up in their respective seats, more than eager to hear how they could help avert such a disaster.

"Before I tell you what my plan is, though, I need to tell you about another top-secret thing playing into this," said the admiral. "We have made a recent discovery off the coast of Florida. When I tell you about it, your first reaction will be to not believe it, to think I'm pulling your leg. That was my reaction, anyway. Let me assure you ahead of time, what I am about to tell you is not only very true, but very real. Understand?"

Again, all three nodded their heads. Kenji noticed their eyes were wide as saucers, and they were hanging on his every word.

"Ok. Remember, I warned you." Drawing a deep breath, he began to speak.

"Off the coast of Florida, right smack dab in the middle of what a lot of people call the Bermuda Triangle, is an island which has never been mapped before. There is a good reason for that. It hasn't been mapped because ...."

The admiral paused, his eyes darting between the three people sitting before him.

"It is an island that was created by an alien race of beings."

Kenji allowed that sentence to float around the room for a while. It took a few moments for it to sink in, but when it did, the eyes that couldn't get wider, did.

Jason looked at Dennis and Diana, then back at Kenji. Even though the admiral said he wouldn't be joking, Dennis said the first thing that came to mind.

"You're kidding, right?"

"No, my boy, I'm not kidding. I'm very serious."

"What do they look like?" asked Diana.

"Right now, not too good, since they're all dead. That's the problem," replied Kenji.

"They're dead?" asked Diana, furrowing her brow. "How?"

Kenji shook his head. "We're not sure, and that's what I need you to find out."

Almost simultaneously, all three slumped in their chairs, realizing this was no joke, that the admiral was serious.

Eventually, Dennis asked, "While I'm incredibly disappointed, to say the least, to hear they're all dead, why do you say that's a problem?"

"The answer to that question is related to why I told you about Yellowstone. On this island, there's a machine which supposedly has the ability to counteract the things that are happening in Yellowstone, but it isn't working."

"Wait," said Dennis. "You're telling me you want to take this alien machine, fly it over to Wyoming, and use it to tell the volcano in Yellowstone what it can go do with itself?"

"Not exactly," replied Kenji. "According to our expert on the island, the machine is stationary. She says it has the ability to tell the volcano what it can do with itself from over there."

Jason finally spoke up. "This is unbelievable."

"Believe it, son. It's as real as it gets, and in about two months things are going to get *very* real unless we do something about it. But now, with this thingamajig you two made," Kenji mentally patted himself on the back with how grandfatherly he could make himself sound to get these idiots to do his bidding, "we might have a shot at doing whatever is necessary to save the American people."

"Don't you mean 'save the world'?" asked Jason.

"Of course, son, of course."

Once again, Jason cringed at being called "son" by this arrogant, devious excuse for a human being.

"So what do you want us to do?" asked Diana.

"I need you guys to look back in time, see what killed them, and see what we can do to fix the machine. I'm not only flying blind in my daddy's airplane, right now I don't even know how to fly."

"So you want us to get you more intel on these aliens and how to fix the machine," replied Jason. It was a statement more than a question. "We're going to need the coordinates for the island."

Reaching into his coat pocket, the admiral pulled out a USB drive. Handing it to Jason, he explained, "This contains all that we have on the island, including the latitude and longitude. It has pictures of the island, even the skeletons which are everywhere. Guard this with your life."

Taking the drive, Jason replied, "We will, Admiral."

"Hey, uh, Jason can I talk to you in private out in the hallway for a second?" asked Kenji.

"Sure," answered Jason. Internally, he told himself the same thing Dennis and Diana were saying to themselves. "Oh boy, here it comes."

Jason and Kenji stood up and walked to the door. After they closed it, Dennis and Diana looked at each other. She made like she was sticking her finger down her throat, and he chuckled and rolled his eyes.

Outside in the hallway, the admiral was gearing up for what he hoped would be an Oscar-worthy performance.

"Jason, I want to apologize for the way I conducted myself on the phone the other day. I was out of line, and man to man, I want you to know I respect the way you take care of your family. I was married once, and it didn't take. I guess I should take some lessons from you."

"Thank you, Admiral. I appreciate that," answered Jason. If he didn't know better, he would have thought that was almost a sincere apology. Almost.

The admiral stuck out his arm, and the two men shook hands. Afterward, they went back into Diana's office where she and Dennis greeted them.

"Gentlemen and lady," said Kenji, "I need to get back to the farm and let you get to work. Please burn as much midnight oil on this project as you can. The survival of every man, woman, and child depends on you getting us this information."

"We'll get right on it, Admiral," said Jason.

"I know you will," replied Kenji.

Turning to leave, Diana escorted Admiral Brinstock back to his car, while Jason and Dennis remained behind. Without having to discuss it ahead of time, the two men stayed silent to make sure nothing they said would be heard by their recent guest. Once they were satisfied there was no way the admiral was within earshot, the two of them relaxed and started speaking.

"Well, buddy," said Dennis, "I knew working with you was going to be a ride, but I didn't expect to have the fate of all humankind resting on our shoulders. Can you believe this?"

"There's a lot of this I have a hard time wrapping my head around," said Jason, "but one thing I don't have a hard time with is knowing all that 'thingamajig' and 'son' performance was nothing but a load of manure. He's trying to play us like a fiddle."

"Sheesh, you said it. He was pouring it on so thick I felt like I was going to get diabetes just listening to him."

The two men chuckled loudly just as Diana was arriving back in her office. "What's so funny?" she asked.

"Oh, just how thick he was pouring on the whole 'grandpa' thing," answered Jason.

"Jeez, I know. I'm not kidding, I wanted to throw up the whole time," said Diana.

"Yep," replied Jason. Getting a serious look on his face, he continued, "Although the way he said it stunk like a diaper, *what* he said was earth-shattering."

"Good word for it," said Dennis. "We need to get on this."

The two men left and made their way to the portal room. They hadn't had lunch yet, but weren't really hungry. Having the fate of all humanity on their shoulders made them more concerned with other things.

CHAPTER 47

AS SOON AS THE ADMIRAL left, after telling them about the eminent eruption of the volcano at Yellowstone National Park and the existence of the alien island off the coast of Florida, Jason and Dennis dove into finding out why the aliens had died.

Diana wasn't about to allow the opportunity to see real live aliens, up close and personal, go by. She was on their heels as her two stars headed down to the portal room, where they immediately got to work. While Dennis fired up the cryogenics plant and got the power generation system on-line, Jason plugged in the USB drive containing information about the island. Diana didn't really have anything to do, but made sure if the guys needed anything, she would be their gofer.

The USB stick had a considerable amount of reading material that needed to be reviewed at some point, but Jason immediately found a file with a GIS extension containing the Geographical Information System data needed to locate the island. After opening the file with his custom software, a globe appeared on the screen. As soon as Jason selected the file, the globe rotated to a location where the island was located: 26 degrees, 22 minutes, 9.4 seconds North; 70 degrees, 50 minutes, 7 seconds West. According to the topographical map information that came with the file, the ocean depth was approximately 1,737 meters below sea level in an area of the ocean floor called the Hatteras Abyssal Plain.

The globe on the screen settled on the proper location, allowing Jason to enter an elevation. To be safe, he entered an altitude of 1,000 meters so they could get the lay of the land from high above before starting to drill down to points closer to sea level.

"I have the coordinates entered, but what date should we shoot for? I don't exactly remember 'Admiral Rotten Tomatoes' mentioning exactly when they supposedly died," asked Jason.

The colloquial name he gave the admiral earned a few chuckles from his friends. Dennis replied, "Perhaps we should start off with today's date. Let's see what we're working with, then go back in time with a better idea of what, and when, we're looking for."

"Good idea, bud." Jason entered it and pressed the commit button.

As soon as he did, a set of pre-determined operations began. Like Cape Canaveral launching a rocket, a countdown showed on the screen of Jason's and Dennis' consoles. The countdown synchronized several operations that had to take place in proper order: when the cryogenics plants released the liquid helium into the superconductor conduits; when the four major banks of relays kicked into place; and when the time and place parameters shaped the control surfaces in the portal chamber, allowing a specific time and place to be displayed. The software controlling all this was the primary thing Jason and Dennis had been working on in the last several weeks. Diana was rather impressed with how smoothly things worked this time versus the last time she saw the portal in operation.

When the countdown neared the zero mark, the last set of relays closed and the final power was rendered to the portal system allowing the portal field to form, Once completely formed, it showed something they hadn't exactly expected: a living room.

This wasn't your typical living room, though. In a word, it was beautiful; comfortable, contemporary, romantic, breezy, modern, yet classic. In the foreground was what looked like a computer terminal with a screen but no keyboard. To the side of the screen was what appeared to be a holster that could hold something relatively small, like a computer mouse.

The floor looked like it was made of multi-colored blue marble. In various places, there were pots of blooming flowers, and off to the left was a couch and coffee table, which was perched on top of a fluffy area rug. The living room was perched high up in the air, perhaps in some high-rise building's apartment. In front of the open doorways, on all sides of the room, were gauze-like curtains lightly wafting back and forth in the gentle breeze. Pillows of various shapes and colors were on the couch. A spiral staircase in the far end of the room contained a tree growing up from the floor, surrounded by several well-arranged plants.

For a few moments, the three just stared at the scene in front of them. They weren't expecting to see anything like this when they connected.

"What altitude did you enter for this connection?" asked Dennis.

"One thousand meters," answered Jason.

"Nah, that can't be right. Check your numbers again."

"Already did. This is 1,000 meters all right. This is a stinkin' tall building."

The three continued to examine all the features of the room. Only now did it appear to have something that didn't quite fit the décor. Off to the left, near the couch, was what looked like a backpack. In any other living room, this wouldn't be out of place, but since the décor and height of the room were not man-made, the backpack seemed a little odd. Jason leaned forward, nearer the portal, to get a better look.

That is when all three were jolted back in their seats. Coming in from the left was a woman, obviously not aware she was being watched. She was wearing a beautiful dress and, as she walked, they could see she was rather tall with attractive tangle of red hair reaching just past the middle of her back. She walked over to the couch and sat down, allowing all three in the portal room to see her fair skin and beautiful green eyes.

She started rifling through that same backpack Jason had been looking at earlier. Almost forgetting that the speakers were hooked up to the portal, the three voyeurs suddenly heard her ask, "Hey Lynne, did you see my hair spray?"

Away from the view of the portal, another woman's voice could be heard in reply. "Yeah. I saw it earlier in the other bathroom."

"Oh, that's right! I left it in there earlier."

Jason looked over to his companions, who were just as amazed at what they were seeing, before reaching over to his console to change the coordinates of the portal from 1,000 meters to something even higher. He decided to double the value to 2,000 meters.

The portal field went hazy for a while, then refocused to a scene considerably higher above the surface of the ocean. The novelty of what they had seen earlier wasn't outdone by the new vista, but this new scene was equally an enigma. After a few seconds, they realized they were seeing a large portion of the island itself.

Jason thought its description should be left to poets since the words "beautiful," "elegant," "gorgeous," "stunning," and "attractive" somehow just didn't cut it. The overall shape of the island was centered around an area where dozens of enormous buildings were located, all gleaming and amazing to behold in their own right.

Stemming out from the central section were six peninsulas. Each was immaculately maintained, and all appeared to support a tropical garden paradise. On the far end of each peninsula was what looked like an arch, or pylon, standing in guardianship over the central part of the island. They arched toward the middle, and had terraces fashioned in their sides supporting trees and plants. Each must have been at least 1,500 meters tall.

This time, it was Diana who spoke. "O-M-G!"

"It's beautiful!" said Jason.

The three stared in amazement for almost ten minutes. Sporadically, each of them would take turns pointing out features here or there they had only just discovered from so high a vantage point. The fact that they were currently looking at the island from over a mile up in the sky was certainly not lost on them. It was, in a word, incredible.

The reality of why they were here looking at this island finally intruded on their consciousness, and Jason was the first one to corral the thoughts of his colleagues back to the task at hand.

"As much as I would love to continue looking at this, I don't think we're going to save the world this way," said Jason.

"You're right, but one thing's for sure," said Dennis. "If we do save the world, I'm moving here!"

"Count me in on that one," added Diana.

Nodding in acknowledgment, Jason said, "Ok, let's get back down to ground level and get a good look at the lay of the land."

"Wait a minute," said Dennis. "Didn't Admiral Dorkus Membrainus say all the aliens were dead? That redhead didn't look too unhealthy."

Scowling, Jason let out a "hmmm," but it was Diana who said, "She wasn't an alien."

"What makes you say that?" asked Dennis.

"For one thing, I'm certain those aliens don't shop at Small-Mart. I saw that backpack there when I was shopping for one for my son. I think she might be one of the admiral's 'yes' women."

"Wow," acknowledged Dennis. "That's some pretty stout deductive reasoning there, Sherlock."

Diana looked at Dennis and, without a word, rendered a toothy smile.

Jason, only half listening to Dennis and Diana, typed new coordinates into the portal control software. He had decided on relocating to a park-like setting on the surface of the island. The new version of the software was able to not only pinpoint a specific location and time, but also alter the portal's control surfaces so they could change the 360x360 degree direction it was facing. That particular feature made it easy to locate to the park, then face toward a large walkway, large enough to support quite a crowd walking along. It also showed a nice bench situated in the middle of the park.

As soon as he entered the coordinates, the portal changed back into a pale blue haze. Within a few seconds, the scene transformed into a gorgeous park-like setting, or at least half of it. The altitude setting was about one and a half meters too low, so the lower half of the portal was nothing but dirt. There was a grass line stretching from the nine o'clock position to the three o'clock position on the circular portal aperture.

"Oops!" called out Jason with a half laugh. Both Dennis and Diana chuckled.

Jason's trained hands glided over the keyboard, and within seconds the portal realigned itself, and the entire opening showed a complete vista of flora. The well-manicured setting was impressive.

"If they're supposed to be all dead, how is this park so well maintained?" asked Dennis.

"Ya got me," answered Jason. The breeze coming in from the nearby ocean lazily moving the trees back and forth; the light orange, violet, and pink light coming from the late afternoon skies to the west; and the sound of birds rounded out the serene scene.

"Bringing up the time scroller subroutines. Setting time advance quotient to T minus 1000," said Jason. As soon as he entered the parameters and pressed the commit button, the scene seemed to freeze for a moment, then resumed movement.

"It froze for a second. Was that a glitch?" asked Diana.

"Not exactly," said Jason. "What I just did was bring up a subroutine which allowed me to tell the portal control software that the specific time point I want doesn't need to proceed forward in time; instead, it progressively resets the time point back in time by one second, every second. In other words, each second we move forward in time, the portal is reset back in time by 1,000 milliseconds or one second. For that split second, the portal replays the same second for more than one second. If you watch things long enough, you'll notice the late afternoon sunlight beginning to get lighter and lighter as we go back farther in time. Eventually, we will be replaying ...."

Just then Jason's point was made obvious by a person dressed in a military uniform walking past the viewpoint of the portal ... backwards.

"That certainly makes your point," said Diana.

"Sure does," said Dennis, "but we're going to need to step it up a bit."

Deciding to gradually increase the speed of the backward march in time, Jason said, "Setting time advance quotient to T minus 3.6 megs."

"What does that mean?" asked Diana.

"The number he's entering in is in multiples of milliseconds, or thousandths of a second," answered Dennis. "He's selecting 3.6 million milliseconds, or one hour, as the new backward step speed."

Sure enough, as soon as the time scroller subroutine accepted the new parameter, each second that went by for three standing in the portal room saw the portal go back in time one hour. As they looked at the sky, they saw the sun, then the moon, make their way across repeatedly. Slowly but surely the portal was systematically going back in time.

"This is still too slow, said Jason. "Resetting to T minus 86.4 megs," said Jason. Looking at Diana, he explained, "One day per step."

Suddenly, the sun stopped its east/west movement across the sky, and started a north/south movement.

"Why is the sun moving that way?" asked Diana. Figuring it out for herself, she said, "Oh, I get it. We're looking at the same time of the day every day, but now we're seeing the movement of the earth in its travels around the sun."

"Precisely," said Jason. "At this speed, we are already looking at things a month or two ago."

"Freeze!" shouted Dennis.

Immediately Jason smacked the spacebar on his console and the scene froze, as if he had hit the pause button on a DVD player.

"What is it, pal? Did you see something?" asked Jason.

"I think so," responded Dennis. "Unless I was seeing things, I'm sure I saw that redhead sitting on the bench over there. Go forward one day at a time, but stop at each day. It shouldn't be many days until she is sitting there."

Jason altered the scroller subroutine to T plus 86.4 megs and turned off auto-progress. "Starting now," he said.

The portal showed the scene one day forward in the future. The scene was unremarkable, so Jason repeatedly pressed the spacebar, allowing the portal to show the next day.

With a chuckle in his voice, Jason said, "Buddy I think you might have been seeing th ...."

Right then, the scene was exactly as before, but sitting on the bench was the redheaded woman they had seen before in the sky-high apartment.

"Is she crying?" asked Diana.

"Actually, I think 'wailing' is the correct word for it," said Dennis.

For reasons not readily apparent, the redheaded woman was sitting on the bench crying her eyes out. She wailed at the top of her lungs, apparently to nobody. She was inconsolable, not that there was anybody there who could console her. The sadness evident in her was infectious. The longer they watched her repeatedly cycle between episodes of uncontrollable wails to periods of muted subs, the more they descended into their own sets of sympathy pain.

Thankfully, Jason pressed the spacebar once again, and she suddenly vanished. All that could be heard were the sounds of nature.

It took a few moments for anybody to speak, and even then all Diana could say was, "Wow."

Jason and Dennis simultaneously breathed deep, and Jason said, "That was intense. If I had seen that in the movie theaters, I would have personally given her an Oscar right then and there."

"Yeah," said Dennis, "but this isn't a movie. This is real. She was obviously distraught about something. I'd like to find out what that was."

"Me too," said Jason, "but that won't save the world. I'm going to save the coordinates for later. Once we clear things up, we can always come back to her. She's not going anywhere."

Begrudgingly, Dennis agreed. "You're right, but I don't like it."

"I know," acknowledged Jason. "We have a few billion people to save first. We'll come back."

He hit a few keystrokes, allowing the control software to save the time and location coordinates for use later, then proceeded on. This time, however, he changed the time signatures so he could move back one year at a time. He figured he could go back relatively fast this way, and when he started seeing life on the island, he would slow things down.

It took some time, but eventually the portal came to a point where there appeared to be people walking around in the park, enjoying the walkways and each other's company. After slowing down the backward motion of the portal, Jason paused the scene on a place where they could clearly see what the aliens looked like.

They should have become used to this, but once again they were speechless. Right there, right in front of them, were beings who were not human, who had presumably not been born on this planet.

They were statuesque, and seemed at least two and a half meters tall. They looked similar to humans in that they had two arms, two legs, one head containing two eyes, one nose, one mouth, etc. And yet, other than the height, there was something different about them. From this vantage point, it was difficult to make out a lot of details.

Once they got over the initial shock of seeing real live alien life forms for the first time, they began systematically traveling around the island trying to figure out what happened. Listening to their spoken language, the three quickly figured out they had no idea what was being said. They came to a point where they could see some starting to appear sick; within a few days, they all seemed to disappear.

It actually took about three days for Jason, Dennis, and Diana to narrow down the events to what triggered the start of the sickness. At one point, a human made it to the island in a tiny rowboat. Listening to the soundtrack of the event, they could hear this person speaking Spanish. Jason's Spanish was a little rusty, but it sounded like he was speaking the kind spoken in Spain. The only thing they discovered was his name: Jose Barragon y Cisneros. Beyond that, they didn't understand much.

It took another day of them following him around to see he was sick; very sick, in fact. Going back and forth over the timeline confirmed that before this guy from Spain landed, everybody seemed to be doing just fine. After his arrival, they seemed to die off until, about four weeks later, none were left. They figured he must have brought with him some disease that infected everybody on the island, eventually killing them.

"That guy must be the key to what happened to the aliens," said Diana. "What I don't understand is why, with all the advanced technology we've seen here, didn't they have the ability to fight off a bug like this? It's almost like we're watching a real-life case of 'War of The Worlds' from H.G. Wells."

"Huh," said Dennis. "I hadn't thought about it like that, but you're exactly right. They seem to be a pretty advanced civilization, yet this seems to be a pretty fundamental thing they missed."

"The fundamental truth we now have sitting in our laps," said Jason, "is this guy was really sick with some kind of contagious disease, one we don't have the training to identify, and it's what killed them."

There was a lull in the conversation for a few moments. "We need to get a doctor to diagnose what's wrong with this guy. Then," Jason paused, "we need to give him and them the medicine they need to keep from dying."

The proverbial lead balloon cut a swath through the portal room. Once the suggestion was made, the die seemed to have been cast. Diana and Dennis sat in slack-jawed silence, looking straight at Jason. "Stunned" would best describe the two.

"Do you realize what you're suggesting?" asked Dennis.

Staring down at the floor, Jason answered his friend without looking at him. "I do, pal. But if I do it right, I can go there, fix the problem, then come back."

"You do realize, don't you, this is going to let the cat out of the bag?" asked Dennis. "The revelation that this portal allows not only time viewing but also time traveling, is going to put a very big gun in the hands of a certain admiral."

Jason shrugged and said, "I'm *really* open to alternate suggestions."

Diana and Dennis continued looking at Jason for a very long minute, then at each other, then at nothing in particular. Staring off into the distance, Diana said, "If we're going to do this, then we need the best diagnosis we can get. If this race of beings really is the key to the continued lives of every man, woman, and child on the planet, then whatever doctor we consult had better get it right."

Without a word, Jason and Dennis nodded their heads and unanimously agreed.

Diana reached over and dialed the number to the Pentagon.

CHAPTER 48

＊＊＊ (alien script decorative text)

JASON AND DENNIS WERE SITTING in the waiting room, waiting for a doctor to speak with them. This doctor wasn't a typical doctor, though.

The night before, Diana had made a call to Admiral Brinstock's office telling him they had a pretty good idea why the aliens died, but they needed an expert medical opinion on what the nature and treatment of the malady would be. The fact that they were asking for not only a medical opinion but also a treatment plan wasn't lost on the admiral. After thinking about it, he decided more information was always useful in devising a battle plan, so with one call Jason and Dennis were almost instantly on the fastest jet Kenji could find, bound for Walter Reed National Military Medical Center. Located in Bethesda, Maryland, Walter Reed was the nexus for the best of the best when it came to medical treatment for both military and civilian alike. Even several United States presidents routinely used it for medical needs.

Within a few minutes after arriving, the door to the waiting room opened, and a nurse entered indicating they should follow her. Walking down the hallway, they were taken not to an examination room, but rather to an office where Dr. Bruce was waiting for them. Seeing the two men enter, he got up from his desk and came around to shake their hands.

"Gentlemen. My name is Dr. Bruce, but you can call me Jim."

"Thanks, Jim," said Jason. "I'm Dr. Marsalis, and this is Dr. Greene. I go by Jason, and this is Dennis."

"Jason, Dennis. Nice to meet you. I have to say, regardless of your medical conditions, it's gotta take something special to have the administrator of this center make me drop everything to meet with you."

"Jim, I'm sure you're familiar with the concept of things being national secrets," responded Jason. "I can't tell you the whole back story on this, but what I can tell you is that there isn't anything medically wrong with us. We have a video recording of an individual who is clearly sick. We need you to observe his symptoms and, to the best of your ability, render not only a diagnosis but also a treatment plan."

"You want me to render a diagnosis without a personal examination and with no bloodwork?" asked Jim.

"I know it's very unorthodox and that your diagnosis could be wrong with the unavoidable limitations forced on you, but we've been told you're the best infectious disease specialist in the country. We've been assured that if anybody is going to get it right with the cards stacked against them, you will," said Jason.

"Well, as Mae West said, flattery will get you everywhere, gentlemen," replied a smiling Dr. Bruce.

Dennis reached into his satchel and produced a portable DVD player. Turning on the power and pressing play, a heavily-edited portal recording of the Spaniard was shown to Dr. Bruce. Jason and Dennis were prepared to show him about 15 minutes of video, but apparently it only took about five minutes for Jim to think he knew what was wrong with the guy. He took another five minutes watching the screen to be sure of his initial diagnosis.

"When I was in medical school," said Jim, "one of the professors found out I was going to specialize in infectious disease and, since that was his specialty, he took me under his wing. Through the semesters, we would spend a lot of time after class going over different symptomologies. I would try to trip him up with some obscure disease, and he would do the same to me. We sharpened each other, and I attribute my proficiency in the field to all the mentoring he gave me.

"One afternoon in his class he plied me with a list of symptoms and said if I was able to get it right, then he would pass me on the spot. He thought he'd be able to trip me up by giving me the symptoms of two diseases occurring in a patient at the same time. To make a long story short," said Jim, "I figured out what was wrong, and immediately received a passing grade in his class.

"Your patient could be dealing with one of two things. He could be dealing with pneumonic plague," Jim seemed to be thinking for a while, then he continued, "or he could be dealing with a combination of two other diseases, typhoid fever and pneumonia. In my educated opinion, I think it's the latter, not the former." What he didn't mention was he chose the latter because pneumonic plague was extremely rare and hadn't been a serious problem for centuries.

"Is there a treatment?" Jason asked.

"Sure there is, but you gotta understand, I may be way off on this. I'll need to directly examine the patient before I can write a scrip for the antibiotic. Can't have this guy sue me in case he's allergic, or in case I have it wrong."

"Unfortunately," responded Jason, "for reasons of national security, a direct examination isn't going to be possible. What I *can* tell you is there is absolutely no chance of this guy bringing litigation against you in any way, shape, or form."

The doctor sat there looking at the two men for a few seconds before responding. "Normally, this is when I would show you the door and explain how sorry I am that I won't be able to help you. But before you got here, I received very pointed instructions from the hospital administrator telling me there was to be nothing held back from you, gentlemen; whatever you requested, I was to give without question. I have to tell you this is a first for me, and I am profoundly uncomfortable writing a prescription under these circumstances."

Dennis spoke up, saying, "Actually, we're going to need a little more than just medicine for him."

"Oh?" said Jim.

"Yes," replied Jason. "We're going to need to learn how to make the medicine."

Jim got a rather perplexed look on his face, wondering how many people needed to be cured of this, and if there was an outbreak somewhere that was really serious. Working in a military hospital meant he was no stranger to secrecy in the name of national security. He knew he needed to comply without question.

Beginning with a few calls, Jason and Dennis immediately met with manufacturers, gaining the knowledge on how to formulate the needed medicine. Jason took a generous supply of the medicine with him, and all the necessary information to be able to formulate it in the field.

Eventually, Jason and Dennis made their way onto the military Lear jet and settled in for the trip home. The plane was normally used for shuttling around various members of the military brass, so it was fitted with all the latest in communication technology, including an encrypted line which could be used for secure telephone calls. Now that the diagnosis was made and the means for helping had been secured, there was only one thing left to do for today. Jason and Dennis had discussed this contingency on the way out to Maryland earlier that same day. Since things had gone the way they did, a call had to be made. Jason picked up the phone and dialed the Pentagon.

"Yes, I'd like to speak with Admiral Brinstock, please."

"No, I do not want to leave a message. Please connect me to the admiral."

"Yes, I know he's a very busy man, but I am pretty sure if you impede my call to him, you will instantly be out of a job."

"My name is Dr. Jason Marsalis."

"Sure, I'll hold."

Jason looked over to Dennis, who had this grin on his face he always got when either he or Jason was playing cat and mouse with some military lackey.

"Yes?"

"Thank you."

Jason looked back to Dennis and smirked. Apparently, someone got their hands slapped. Soon a new voice came on the line.

"This is Admiral Brinstock," said Kenji.

"Hello, Admiral. This is Dr. Jason Marsalis, and I am calling on a secure line."

As soon as Jason said this, there was no response from Kenji, who reached over and pressed a special button on his phone that allowed for scrambler technology to be employed, scrambling the voice signal between the two phones equipped with it.

"Scrambler link established and our conversation is secure. Jason. How are you doing? I trust you received the cooperation you needed at Walter Reed?"

The syrupy admiral was back, and Jason began to have the sense of nausea.

"Yes, admiral. Whatever strings you pulled were effective. As soon as we got there, we were met by the world's most eminent infectious disease specialist," replied Jason.

"Great. Great. So are you going to tell me why I had to call in some favors for you two now?"

"Diana O'Laney, Dr. Greene, and I have spent many nights and days on this project, working hard at tracing back what happened to the inhabitants of the island," answered Jason. "We found the pivotal event in their history which led to their race being decimated."

"And what was that?"

"Well, sir," replied Jason, "for a reason we can't specifically determine because we don't know their language, it appears a human landed on the island in the 1400s, and when he did, he brought with him a plague that wiped out the entire population."

"You're telling me these aliens died of a disease that *we* brought it to them? We killed them?"

"Yes, sir. That is exactly what I am telling you. This is why we needed to consult the best of the best when it came to infectious diseases. We showed him a highly-edited video of the human who landed on the island, and asked him to make a diagnosis without performing a physical examination."

"What did you find out?" asked Kenji.

"It turns out that he was infected with typhoid fever coupled with pneumonia."

"Wow. So that's what took 'em out. Why couldn't they just take an alien pill or something?"

"As I said earlier," answered Jason, "we weren't able to understand the language the alien race was speaking, so I can't answer that particular question. We were asking it ourselves, but were unable to derive a satisfying answer from our observations."

"Ok. So we know what killed them, but what do we do now?" wondered the admiral. He was saying it more to himself than posing a question.

"The next step we took was securing a large supply of the medicine to cure those conditions," answered Jason, "along with the equipment and materials needed to synthesize more of the medicine."

"Medicine?" exclaimed the admiral. "Why would we need medicine for this? One thing I do know from my medical corpsman training is bugs like that wouldn't survive six or seven hundred years. We're just not at risk anymore."

Jason looked over once again at Dennis, who was no longer wearing a grin, but rather showing misgivings over what they were about to share with Kenji. Dennis didn't like him any more than Jason did, and he knew the next words out of Jason's mouth were probably a bad idea. Unavoidable, but still a bad idea.

"The medicine isn't for us, Admiral," said Jason.

"I'm not following you, son," said Kenji.

"The medicine we have secured, and the technology we have secured to synthesize it, is for the aliens."

"Run that past me one more time."

"Admiral, the portal not only has the ability to allow the viewing of events in the past anywhere in the world, it also allows us to go there. Remember that video of your graduation from the United States Naval Academy at Annapolis, Maryland?"

"Yes," said Kenji, with a tone mirroring the questioning look on his face at that moment.

"Admiral, we personally shot that using a disguised video camera which looked like a film camera from that period. The portal can transport things, even people, to any place on the globe at any point in time."

There was a very long pause while the admiral strained to wrap his mind around this new revelation. It was evident that the façade Kenji had been putting on up to this point fell, and was now shattered into pieces on the floor. He could only respond with two words.

"God Almighty."

Continuing, Jason said, "We intend to go back in time before the human lands on the island, meet the aliens, and explain to them what is about to take place. We intend on giving them the medicine so they won't get sick, so they will be around to keep that machine in working order."

As soon as Jason said this, Dennis got a concerned look on his face that Jason couldn't quite read. He knew Dennis was tacitly in agreement with everything he had said to the admiral, but suddenly there seemed to be something bothering Dennis a lot.

Meanwhile, Kenji was reeling at what Jason had just revealed.

"Are you telling me that not only do we know what went wrong, we also can correct the problem and clear the way for the machine on the island to be maintained, thus counteracting the eminent threat in Yellowstone?" he asked.

"Yes, Admiral," responded Jason. "That is exactly what I am saying. The thing is, if I'm going to do this, I need to know as much as possible about the aliens. When you were in our offices, you mentioned having an expert on these aliens. I'd like to meet with your expert and get as much information as I can about them before I go back in time to fix this mess."

Without saying anything in reply, Kenji reached over to his intercom and hit a very well-used button.

"Stephanie, make immediate arrangements to transfer Doctors Marsalis and Greene to the headquarters for Project Pylon."

The tinny voice on the other end of the intercom replied quickly. "Right away, sir." An immediate tone indicated the intercom had turned off.

"Project Pylon?" asked Jason.

"That is the code name we have affixed to the island," replied Kenji, "so I can use personnel who aren't cleared for the details to still help with some of the more mundane tasks."

There was another pause, then Kenji asked, "So you're telling me we have a real chance to fix this?"

"Yes, sir," replied Jason.

"Son, you just made my day. You've got a steak in your future, and it's on me!" said Kenji. The syrup was back.

"Thank you, Admiral."

"Don't think anything of it. Stephanie will be back in touch with the details on getting you there. Plan on being there tomorrow."

"Sounds good, Admiral."

"All right. We'll talk soon. Over and out," said Kenji.

"Over and out," mimicked Jason, hanging up the phone.

Looking over to Dennis, Jason said, "Well, it's done. We're going to the alien island."

"Looks like it," said Dennis.

After thinking about the task at hand, Jason's thoughts about the admiral congealed. "Dennis, I need to say something to you that I'm not planning on saying to anybody else."

"What's that?" asked Dennis.

"I know it isn't a shock to you that there's something fishy about the admiral. He's being nice to us nowadays, but he's *too* nice. I trust him about as much as I can throw him. He's up to something. I don't know what it is, but my spidey sense tells me he's biding his time, waiting for the right moment to do something. And that 'something' might be something I wouldn't necessarily like. With me going back in time, I'm going to need you to watch my back."

"You got it, pal," said Dennis.

"Oh well, at least we get to spend time in a tropical paradise," Jason said.

Looking over at Dennis again, Jason expected to see a look of elation at the prospect of visiting the island; instead, he saw a look of intense thought on his partner's face. It was the same look he had noticed earlier when he was talking with the admiral.

Lost in his own thoughts, Dennis didn't respond. "What is it bud?" Jason asked.

"We need to talk about this trip of yours," Dennis replied. "It just occurred to me that we are trying to open up and stop a ticking nuclear bomb, and all we have are hammers."

Jason was stymied at why Dennis was thinking this way, and the look on his face said so. Dennis began to elaborate.

"Here's the deal. If and when you go back in time, you can't just give them the medicine and then come home. It's not going to be that simple," said Dennis.

"Why is that?"

"Because you will be manufacturing your very own grandfather paradox," answered Dennis.

As soon as he said that, the entire reason for Dennis' concern was blatantly obvious. If Jason went back there and cured any malady the aliens had, and they continued to live, that would alter the timeline for this planet so completely it'd be likely Jason would never have been born. The portal would never have been built, so the volcano would erupt, and so on.

This set Jason back on his heels. "I'm stunned I didn't see this myself," said Jason.

"Don't feel bad. That particular load of bricks didn't fall on my head until just now," consoled Dennis.

The two men pondered how this new wrinkle could, and probably should, alter their plans. But how? They needed to fix the machine, which meant the aliens needed to be cured. Naturally, that meant the aliens would still be alive.

The solution wasn't immediately evident to either of them. "I just hope this expert knows his stuff," Jason said.

"Her stuff."

"Come again?" asked Jason.

"The expert is a woman," said Dennis. "Archaeologist actually. I've been reading a lot of the material from that USB stick the admiral gave us, and a lot of the material in there is from her, Dr. Terri Lindstrom."

CHAPTER 49

JASON AND DENNIS WERE BACK on the Bombardier Challenger 300 business jet they had flown on when they visited the president a couple of weeks ago. Jason wondered if the government had a fleet of these things.

Listening to some music with a set of personal headphones, Jason was in his own world, thinking about the task lying before him. Dennis chose to continue his reading of the classified material given to them by the admiral. About halfway into the flight to Miami, Dennis put the laptop to the side and gave his eyes a rest after reading for about two hours solid. Looking over to his friend as he stared out the window, Dennis pondered what Jason must be thinking now.

He thought about how much he admired his friend. Jason seemed to have so many parts of his life well in order, whereas Dennis sometimes felt balancing work and a home life was like trying to reach for the unattainable. His first marriage failed because he didn't show enough attention to his wife. What really made that particular thought

distasteful to Dennis was a rumor that the admiral had the same problem, so in that way he and Dennis were similar. Being similar to the
Admiral in *any* way was something which made Dennis shudder; that
alone was enough to make him take a new personal inventory about
what's really important in life.

It wasn't only that. This whole odyssey he and Jason were now em-
barking on was something that could end up really good, or it could go
south very easily. The unsettling thing about all of it was if the timeline actually did get changed, causing a grandfather paradox, the odds
are he, Jason, Diana, the admiral, and about eight billion others would
never know it; everything would just suddenly cease to exist. Yep, very
unsettling. As he stared at the floor of the jet contemplating this, he realized how that possibility might be making Jason downright panicky.

And yet, glancing over to Jason as he stared out the window, it
seemed like he was the very personification of poise and calmness.
Without him knowing it, Dennis came to have an even deeper respect
for his friend right then. As he regarded Jason, he thought about how,
in a very real way, the weight of the world was now going to rest on his
shoulders.

Jason happened to be thinking that same thing right then, and what
made this an even more thankless job, is nobody could know that he
did it. Sure, important people like the president and those he chose to
trust with this most secret of technologies would know, and he would
certainly receive accolades from those few sources. But for the most
part, John and Jane Q. Public would just go on living their respective
lives completely oblivious as to how close they came to having their
lives and the lives of their husbands, wives, and children completely
snuffed out of existence.

It wasn't the lack of fame that bothered Jason. What bothered him
the most was there were people out there so caught up in their own
lives, they thought the comparatively minor crises they were dealing
with represented the end of their particular world. Jason thought if
people really knew their lives were in such dire peril and, as a collective
life form, they were all at risk of losing their lives unless they banded
together in unity and harmony ....

As Jason looked out the window of the speeding jet watching the
ground pass by, he reflected on how people formulate their social and
political values. It seemed so petty how nationalism blinded people into
believing their ideologies superior to anything that had ever been done
before or anything else currently being done by any other social or political ideologies of the day. With the knowledge Jason now possessed, he

seemed to have the same viewpoint of many astronauts coming back to earth. He reached back into the recesses of his mind and thought about an online article, "Why Give a Damn," posted by astronaut Ron Garan:

> *We have within our grasp the resources and technology to solve many, if not all, of the problems facing our planet, yet nearly a billion people do not have access to clean water, countless go to bed hungry every night, and many die from completely preventable and curable diseases.*

Indeed, thought Jason. As the jet sped along, a new idea began to form in his mind: the portal technology is something that could be used for tremendous bad if put into the wrong hands, but could also be used for tremendous good. What if food, medicine, and supplies miraculously showed up at the exact place where they were needed?

About this time, the captain's voice came across the speakers. "Attention all who are flying with us today. We are landing at Miami International in about ten minutes, so please stow your things in preparation for landing. That is all."

Because of his headphones, Jason didn't hear the announcement. Dennis tapped him on the knee.

"We're about to land, bud, and we need to batten down the hatches."

"We're there already?" asked Jason.

"Yep. Next stop," Dennis arched his eyebrows, "well, you know."

"Yes indeed," said Jason. Then he asked a question which occurred to him earlier, but he hadn't had a chance to ask. "Did you ever get pictures of the personnel we're going to meet with at you-know-where?"

"No, never did," replied Dennis. "But, I suppose we're going to find out soon enough.

There were the typical pass-throughs by the flight attendants and within a few minutes, the plane pulled to a stop. As soon as it stopped and the door opened, a black Hummer with black tinted windows pulled up to the stairs, and the driver got out to meet Jason and Dennis. He must have been part of the Secret Service, since he was a cookie cutter copy of Agents Lockwood and Elder who took them to see the president. After being quickly taken to the marina, they boarded a small boat belonging to the Coast Guard. The captain said this was a fast boat; even so, the voyage would take the better part of four hours. He suggested that if they were tired, they could rack out down below. They had, indeed, been burning their candles at both end, so the suggestion of a healthy nap sounded pretty good to both men.

In the blink of an eye, Jason and Dennis were rousing themselves out of bed after simultaneously sensing the shrill whine of the turbo engines had just been tamed down to the purr of a caged animal. They both decided to see what was happening back on the bridge. Jason and Dennis approached the captain, but he was concentrating to the extreme. Deciding not to interrupt him, they just observed what was happening.

Their presence wasn't lost on the captain. Using his peripheral vision, he said, without shifting his gaze in the slightest, "This part's tricky, gentlemen, since the slightest miscalculation will mean we'll all have a bad day."

Looking out the window, it wasn't obvious to Jason in the least what was so "tricky," as the captain said. In front of them were some of the most beautiful seas one could ever ask for. In fact, it appeared not only the sea, but the weather, outside was absolutely perfect.

"I'm not sure what you're looking at, Captain," said Dennis, "but I wouldn't mind going for a nice swim right about now."

"That's the deception of it." Turning to his navigator, he asked, "Position?"

"Two hundred yards east of position delta. Turn to starboard in one minute twenty seconds, Captain," replied the seaman to his left.

At the one-minute mark, the seaman set a timer at his station for 60 seconds. As it counted down, the captain ritualistically shifted his gaze back and forth between the forward windows and the timer. As soon as the timer ticked down to zero, he called out a new command.

"Officer of the watch, come starboard 90 degrees in three-two-one-*now*!" bellowed the captain.

The officer of the watch relayed the command to the quartermaster in charge of the directional controls of the boat and immediately made a change to its heading.

Dennis was watching the controls being manipulated by the quartermaster, and was tickled that the overall direction of a ship this size was being manipulated by relatively tiny controls about the size of his fist. He went to point this out to Jason, but then noticed his friend staring out the front window with a shocked look on his face. Dennis looked out the same window to see what Jason was staring at in this featureless sea; as soon as he did, he saw it wasn't so featureless anymore.

Like a wraith forming from the mist churned up by the waves, a most magnificent sight materialized right before their eyes. It was not only a city, but it was *the* city. The same one they had seen through the portal. All on the bridge were quiet, except for the newly-restored sound of the engines roaring back to life.

"Where the hell did that come from?!" asked Dennis.

The captain chuckled. "Everybody asks that the first time, me included." Visibly more relaxed now, he continued. "What we were doing back there was navigating our way through a very specific set of turns, all designed to get us through an elaborate doorway in the shield surrounding this city."

Looking out the window at the magnificent city looming larger and larger every moment, he said, "Gentlemen, I give you the island of New Galimar."

The moment was historic for Jason and Dennis, who had never personally been here before. Seemingly miles across, an adequate description of the island was more than any storyteller could possibly conjure up in a lifetime. The tropical paradise was unbelievably majestic, with sunlight glinting from the marvelous structures all nestled in a paradise of palm trees, plants, shrubs, and flowering plants. Jason and Dennis were mute, trying their best to take in all that lay before them.

The landing craft pulled up to a dock, and all began disembarking from the boat. Amazed at the towering structures arching their way for thousands of meters over his head, Jason almost forgot the cases he had brought with him, including his laptop. He had to repeatedly reorient himself as he walked up the pier since he spent more time looking up than watching where he was going. It wasn't until he almost walked directly into a tall woman with a very commanding tangle of red hair that he stopped looking up and was struck by the beauty standing in front of him. It seemed he had seen her before, and it wasn't until Dennis said, "Dr. Lindstrom, I presume?" did Jason realize who she was.

"Correct. I am Dr. Terri Lindstrom, but you can call me Terri. And I assume you are Doctors Marsalis and Greene?"

"Correct," responded Jason, "but you can call me Jason, and this is Dennis."

"Very good," responded Terri. Pointing to the man on her left, she said, "This is my assistant, Joe. He has been my right-hand man while working here on the island."

Jason and Dennis looked at Joe, then looked at each other with a look of amazement. Volumes of thought passed back and forth between the two men, such as how the admiral had authorized Terri and her assistant to know about the portal technology. But there was something else, something much more significant than that.

Without a word, Jason was the one to verbalize what the two men were thinking. "Joe?"

Rolling his r's in the way common to those of Latin descent, Joe responded, "Correct."

"Are you sure?" asked Jason. "Don't you normally go by Jose Barragon y Cisneros?"

Now it was Jose's turn to have his eyes bug out while looking at Jason. Terri scrunched her eyebrows together, then turned to Joe to ask what he was talking about when she saw the look of pure astonishment on his face.

"What's going on here?" asked Terri.

Looking at her, Jason said, "There's a lot to tell you Terri, but we can't do it here. We need somewhere a lot more secluded so I can tell you what's going to be happening in the next few days, all of which is highly classified. We can't talk about it out in the open like this."

"Well, okay then," retorted Terri. "Perhaps you can tell me what all the hubbub has been about lately. Since that admiral guy was here, I've had to answer some rather odd questions, so I'm glad to have someone who will fill me in on what's going on."

With that, Dennis asked, "Are we going to your apartment in that high-rise over there?"

"That's not really my apartment, I'm only staying there." She stopped dead in her tracks, spun around, then exclaimed, "How could you possibly have known I was staying in an apartment up there in that building?!"

This is when Jason put two and two together and realized Terri was the redhead they had seen when they first connected to the island with the portal. They just happened to see Dr. Lindstrom long before knowing who she was.

"Soon enough, Doctor, your questions will be answered. I assume you will want to invite Dr. Marlowe who has been living with you in that apartment as well?"

Now it was Terri's turn to have a completely astonished look on her face. "You have *got* to tell me how you know all this!" She was almost yelling, yet with a smile on her face.

Jason laughed out loud and said, "Oh no. This is way too much fun."

Getting a look of mock anger on her face, Terri shook her finger at Jason and said, "Oohh, I'll get you for that!" She finished her threat with a healthy dose of smiles and sneers.

Walking along, the four of them came to the side of a building clad in what appeared to be glass mirrors. Knowing she had some tricks up her own sleeves, Terri made like she was going to walk right into the side of the building. As she approached, the side panels of the building transformed and suddenly there was an entryway leading into what looked like a lobby area. At the rear, a door opened into what proved to be an alien elevator which led the team to the top floor of the building. Jason and Dennis noted they had to clear their eardrums about four times as the elevator ascended.

They emerged from the lift into what appeared to be a lounge where it would be very easy to engage in a relaxed conversation. Waiting for them was another woman.

"Gentlemen, this is my partner in crime, Dr. Lynne Marlowe."

The brunette, green-eyed beauty shook their hands. Jason noted that Dennis had to work hard at keeping his tongue in his mouth. Knowing the type of woman who fascinated his friend, Jason understood that Lynne represented relationship nirvana for Dennis.

"It's a pleasure to meet you, gentlemen. Please call me Lynne. I look forward to working with you."

"It seems," said Terri, "these two will finally have some answers for us as to all the hurdles we've been jumping over lately."

"Oh?" remarked Lynne. "That's good, because I'm just about ready to shoot myself over the way nobody is talking around here."

"Please don't do that," said Dennis. "I'm sure we'll be able to answer all your questions."

"Good," exclaimed both women, simultaneously.

The five made their way to a comfortably-appointed conversation pit where couches were arranged in a circle, all decorated with pillows of different colors. They took their seats, and Terri was the first one to speak.

"All right, out with it! How did you know all those things?"

"What things?" asked Lynne.

"They knew I lived in the apartment, they knew you were living there with me, and they knew something I didn't even know. Joe's real name is actually Jose Barragon y Cisneros."

Lynne looked rather surprised at this revelation, and Jose spoke up for the first time since the two men arrived. "I am very interested in knowing how this came about as well. That is information I have not shared with anybody here."

"The answer to both those questions is actually the same answer," Jason said. "I need to fill you in on a lot, so get comfortable because there is a great deal to go over."

Jason and Dennis then related a very long and detailed story leading up to the invention of the portal, and what it had the ability to do.

"Do you remember a story recently about a terrorist cell that was destroyed, how it was planning on carrying out another bombing, and how President Michaelson ordered a strike that took them out?" asked Jason.

"Yes, of course. The story was everywhere in the news about a week ago," replied Lynne.

"That order was based on intelligence obtained from the portal," said Jason.

"You gotta be kidding. It's that accurate?"

Jason looked over to Dennis and smiled. He then reached into his case, brought out a laptop, and fired it up. "Take a look at this video and tell me what you see."

Terri was the one to respond. "It looks like a lot of actors dressed up to play a part in a movie about the signing of the Declaration of Independence. There seems to be a lot of people missing, though."

"That, my dear, is a video recording of the *actual* event in Liberty Hall," Jason explained. "The famous painting by John Trumbull was embellished by the artist to include many who weren't really there. In fact, if you listen to the audio, you'll learn this is just the presentation of a draft of the declaration, not the actual signing."

"You're telling me," said Terri, "this isn't a movie? This is the real thing?"

"That is exactly what we're telling you," responded Dennis.

"Oh my god," said Lynne. She and Terri were completely astonished. Looking over to Joe, it seemed he wasn't as surprised.

"What's with you, Joe? It looks like this is an everyday thing to you. Like it isn't anything new," said Terri.

"It isn't," replied Joe, enigmatically.

"What do you mean?" asked Terri.

"It isn't," said Jason, "because 'Joe' isn't from around here, are you, Joe?" Turning to Terri, Jason continued. "In fact, our friend here is actually Jose Barragon y Cisneros, a man of the sea who landed here on the island about 700 years ago."

Terri snapped her gaze over to Jose, who finally decided to speak and share all he had been keeping secret in his heart.

"What your friend says is correct. My real name is Jose Barragon y Cisneros. My father and mother are Arturo and Valera Barragon y Cisneros. I was born in a small village in the central part of Spain, called the Extremadura, on March 28, 1295."

The silence was now deafening. Terri and Lynne sat in their seats staring at Jose for the longest time, apparently waiting for him to say he was pulling a practical joke on them. When no such confession came, Terri swung her gaze back towards Jason, saying, "This is ...." She couldn't find the words to finish the sentence.

Jose continued his story. "When I landed on this island, I was greeted by the race of people you call Galimarians. At the time, they didn't know what to do with me, so their governing body held meetings for the purpose of deciding that. It was their custom to show what happens at those meetings to everybody on the island, so when I learned they wanted to put me into something called suspended animation because there weren't enough people present to vote, I was scared. It sounded a lot like a prison to me, and I didn't want to be in prison. I decided I had to get off the island, so I tried. I even stole a golden amulet from them to sell for money to get home. In the end, I realized there was way I could survive on the open ocean again, so I turned around and came back. I was going to put the amulet back where I found it, but it fell into the ocean somehow."

Terri gasped, almost silently. Nobody except her friend Lynne noticed, but after seeing Terri was basically okay, Lynne decided to just ask her about it later.

"When I got back," continued Jose, "I returned to the home where I was staying, and the next morning several people arrived to take me to the suspended animation chamber. They put me in, I fell asleep, and in what felt like a few seconds, there were people waking me up several weeks ago."

"Wait," Jason said. "You've only been out of the chamber for a few weeks? How did you learn English so quickly?"

Jose knew it was the effect of the amulet the Galimarians put on him when he had arrived. He wasn't wearing the amulet now, but the effects of it lingered. Since that day, he had the ability to learn things at lightning speed. English was an easy language for him to learn, so he was fluent in it. He observed that Terri was wearing her amulet all the time, and he also noticed she wasn't forthcoming with the role it was playing in her knowledge of the island and the Galimarian people. For the time being, he decided to keep her secret.

"I am a fast study," said Jose. "I was able to become conversant in a relatively short period."

"Boy, I guess," observed Dennis.

"I suppose the admiral hasn't told you why we're here, has he?" asked Jason.

"Oh, you mean Admiral Crabapple?" asked Terri with a smirk. Lynne unsuccessfully caught herself from snickering.

Jason grinned. "It seems we have the same opinion of him."

Smiling a toothy smile, Terri replied, "You too? Yeah. I don't like to talk about people when they aren't around to defend themselves, but let's just say he isn't on my Top Ten list."

"Yup. He tried to strong-arm Dennis and me a few times, but when that didn't work, he really got mad. Lately, though, he's nice, too nice, and that's really got me bugged."

"Anyway," Jason continued, "the reason why we're here is because a major volcano in Yellowstone is about to blow."

"I know," said Terri.

"Yes, I suppose you do know all about that," said Jason. "Because of that volcano, I'm here to learn all I can about the Tectonic Stabilization Machine and the Galimarian people. Once I do that, then I'm going back in time, deliver them antibiotics to fight against the diseases our good friend Jose brought them, then try to get back home without causing any grandfather paradoxes."

The same exclamation was uttered by Terri, Lynne, and Jose at the same time, but for different reasons.

"What!"

Jose was the first to follow that up with another question. "Are you telling me I am to blame for all of them dying?"

"I'm sorry, Jose, but that is exactly what I am telling you."

The news that he was the whole reason why the Galimarian people died was a severe blow to him. Up to this point, he didn't have a clue as to why they all died; to learn this now was utterly heartbreaking. Like Terri, he had formed somewhat of an attachment to the people he only met for a few days. Certainly, he reasoned, how could you not come to respect such an amazing race of people.

"Aye, Dios Mio!" cried Jose in his mother tongue. While few in the room spoke Spanish, they knew what he must be feeling.

Terri was the next one to blurt out a burning question. "Did you just say you're going to go back in time?"

"Correct," replied Jason.

"This portal can do that?" asked Terri.

"Correct."

Terri's response was to sit back in her seat and exhale loudly.

After a few moments of introspection on the part of all present, Jason related the experiments he and Dennis undertook leading them to discover the portal has the ability to allow not only physical travel but also time travel. Jason described how the sheet of paper flew into and through the portal while they were watching the great Chicago fire, then instantly burned. With a smile on his face, he even told them how he and Dennis were hungry one afternoon, so they went to China, got some real Chinese food, and brought it back to the portal room for lunch. That got some chuckles from a few very amazed people.

The rest of the day was spent walking to, and spending time in, the underground room housing the Tectonic Stabilization Machine (TSM). While in the room, Terri connected to the amulet companion in charge of the TSM, Khaeleus. Even though Jason and Dennis had been dealing with some amazing technology of their own design, talking with a synthetic sentient life form was nothing less than staggering.

Khaeleus entertained any questions they put to her, and was able to describe to Jason the exact nature of the malfunction. For her part, Khaeleus was pretty impressed with Jason's command of physics. He decided not to elaborate why he wanted to know so much about the TSM, and his plans on traveling back in time to visit with the Galimarians. The real reason he wanted to know so much was because his foreknowledge of the machine would help the Galimarians accept who he said he was.

After meeting with Khaeleus in the underground TSM control center, the group went back to the surface, found a park where they could all sit, and struck up conversations with each other. Dennis, Lynne, and Jose were in one conversation, while Jason sat about three meters from them talking with Terri.

"I have to say," said Terri, in a more reverent manner, "I am impressed with you, Dr. Marsalis. You really seem to know your stuff." Normally at this moment, she would have checked his ring finger to see if the man was a candidate for a relationship, but she knew her heart belonged to only one person, someone she would never get to meet.

"And I have to say, Dr. Lindstrom, I am just as impressed with your grasp of the Galimarian culture," said Jason. "How did you learn so much about it?"

"A lot came from archival footage I spent hours viewing in my room," said Terri.

"Can I see an example?" asked Jason.

Terri smiled, knowing once again she would be able to see her soulmate's face. Leaning over, Terri said in a loud voice to Lynne, "Jason and I are going to look at some of the archival footage. Do you want to go, or stay here?"

Dennis decided wherever Lynne wanted to go, that's where he wanted to be since he was already falling head over heels for this brunette beauty. Jose was content with staying with Lynne and Dennis, although not for the same reason. Lynne told Terri, "I think I'd like to just soak in some nature for a while. How about we meet you back at the lounge in two hours?"

"Sounds good," Terri replied. She and Jason walked to the building where Terri's apartment was located and, after ascending in the elevator, they entered the room Jason had already seen once before when the portal happened to locate there.

"This room is just as beautiful as I remember," said Jason, "although I didn't turn around to see the rest of it behind where the portal was oriented. This is a pretty big place."

"Indeed it is, but sometimes I just like to sit here on the couch and feel the light breeze floating by as the night sky comes," replied Terri.

"I can imagine," acknowledged Jason.

Looking over to the computer terminal, Terri asked, "Do you want to meet Khreelon?"

"Khreelon?" asked Jason.

"He's the original occupant of this apartment. Would you like to meet him?" asked Terri.

"Here? Now?" asked a visibly startled Jason.

"It's not what you're thinking," laughed Terri. With a more somber tone, Terri said, "In the back is a room I rarely go into. It is his bedroom, and where his remains are still."

Jason could tell this was something that touched Terri deeply. Taking in a deep breath, he said, "If you are okay with that, I would like it very much."

Without saying a word, Terri turned around and started walking toward the back of the apartment. Opening a door in the rear, Terri and Jason entered the room where a bed was located in the center of the far wall. Jason stepped forward to get a closer look, then stopped. Standing there, he felt this room was a sort of mausoleum; this was a place to show respect for the dead. Holding his left wrist with his right hand, Jason stood quietly in respect for the original occupant of the home. Remembering the name of the person lying before him, Jason said, "Khreelon, I want to thank you for allowing us to spend time in your home. I hope to bring the honor and respect that it, and you, deserve."

Terri was shocked. She remembered saying something similar when she arrived at this apartment. It was at that moment she learned Jason was a man of character and integrity, unlike Admiral what's-his-name who couldn't be bothered to even look at Khreelon, let alone show this kind of respect. Glancing from Jason over to her soulmate Khreelon, Terri's eyes began to moisten as she once again beheld the man of her dreams, an alien who had died six or seven hundred years earlier.

After gazing at Khreelon, Jason thought of a question he wanted to ask Terri. Turning around, he was stopped short by the look of profound sadness on her face. Whatever he was going to ask quickly left his mind, and now the only question was, "Would you like to talk about it?"

Terri tore her eyes away from Khreelon and looked at Jason pleadingly. He stepped forward, gently taking Terri's elbow, to lead her back out to the living room. As they sat down on the couch, Jason said the same thing he would say to Mikki whenever something was bothering her.

"Talk to me, Terri. What is it?"

She was looking down at her lap when he said that, and after wiping away a stray tear which refused to stay put in her eye, said, "Jason, I can tell you are a man of character. You aren't like any of these military schmoes walking around here. You actually care. You're a man of principle.

"When you asked how I knew so much about the island and the Galimarian people, I wasn't completely honest. While it's true I have learned quite a bit from the archival footage, there is actually a more significant source for the information I possess. Do you remember Jose telling us about the amulet he had stolen that had somehow been lost while he was at sea? Remember how he thought it had fallen overboard?"

"Yes," replied Jason.

"Well, I found it," said Terri.

"How?"

"To be perfectly accurate, I didn't find it; a man named Cyrus Field did."

"Cyrus Field? The guy who laid the first telegraph cable across the Atlantic?" asked Jason.

"One in the same," replied Terri. "Did you know the first expedition had a problem with the ship going off course?"

"I seem to have read something, now that you mention it. If I remember correctly, they attributed it to a magnetic field generated by the coiled wire on board the ship," answered Jason.

"Correct. That is what people were told. What they weren't told was the coiled cable wasn't the reason for them going off course."

"It wasn't?"

"No," replied Terri. Reaching for something around her neck, she pulled out a small golden amulet at the end of a golden chain. Showing it to Jason, she said, "This is what caused the ship to go off course."

"What's that?" asked Jason.

"This," said Terri, "is a Galimarian amulet, similar to the one Jose said he lost at sea. In fact, it might be the very same one."

"How could an amulet make a ship go off course?" asked Jason.

"On one particular day, the cable Cyrus was laying snapped, and the end of the cable they had already laid fell down to the sea floor. They used a dredging hook to find the cable and bring it back up. When it came up to the surface, this amulet was magnetically stuck to the hook.

They brought it on board, and for a time it was kept in a drawer near the ship's compass, which is how it drove the ship off course."

"Ok. So, how did you get the amulet?" asked Jason.

"Before working here on this island, I worked at the New York Museum of Natural History," answered Terri. "I am an archaeologist by trade, and I was working in the archive basement cataloging all the old relics down there. I found this amulet where it had been scuttled away after that voyage."

Jason squinted his eyebrows, but then asked, "Interesting story, but how does that relate why you know so much about the island?"

Reverently holding the amulet in her hands, Terri said, "It is because I discovered, in the museum basement, that this amulet contains a sentient life form named Quorlynn, and she has become my companion and best friend. She has taught me an incredible amount of information about this amazing race of beings. I have learned enough to now consider myself Galimarian as well. In fact, Quorlynn and the millions of others like her all now consider me to be Galimarian."

This new revelation was staggering to Jason. Right there in Terri's hands was a sentient life form? One who had such a complete and complex personality that Terri could consider it … her … to be her best friend? As he began smiling, Jason thought, "This is next-level cool."

Seeing how he was completely in awe over the information she had just shared with him, Terri got up and walked over to the computer terminal. Jason rose and followed her. Terri removed the amulet from around her neck and placed it in the cradle on the side of the terminal. Within a few seconds, the face of an incredibly beautiful woman with dark black eyes, and slightly pointed ears, appeared on the screen.

"Jason, this is Quorlynn, my amulet companion and best friend. Quorlynn, this is Dr. Jason Marsalis. He is a man of honor who I now consider to be my friend. He has invented technology which will allow him to travel back in time and correct the disaster to our Galimarian brothers and sisters. He will bring them medicine to cure their illnesses so they won't have to die, so they can be with us again."

With that explanation, Quorlynn's eyes enlarged, and her head dipped slightly, indicating her disbelief that this would even be a possibility. Seeing that Terri was completely serious, Quorlynn looked at Jason and asked, "Is this true? Can you really do this?"

In awe of the fact he was about to converse with a synthetic sentient being, Jason replied, "That is correct. I am here to learn as much as I can about this wonderful race of beings. I would count it a privilege to know more about them, and hopefully I may count you as my friend as well."

Quorlynn looked back to Terri, who had a very big smile on her face. Terri simply said, "Told ya."

Quorlynn nodded, acknowledging she and Terri were thinking the same thing. Quorlynn then looked at Jason again. "Dr. Marsalis, I am indeed very glad to make your acquaintance. I know Terri doesn't quickly call people her friends unless there is good reason for it. Since she feels you are her friend, then I will as well. I wish to thank you in advance for doing whatever you can to help our people."

"Thank you, Quorlynn, and you may call me Jason from now on," he said. "I very much hope I can be of service to this amazing race of people. I would really like to know more but, unfortunately, I don't have a great deal of time to learn the spoken or written language, so I'm going to have to rely on you and Terri to teach me as much as possible."

Terri looked at Quorlynn. "My friend, is there any reason why he can't?"

Knowing exactly what Terri was thinking, Quorlynn replied, "None whatsoever. That would certainly give him a 'leg up,' as you like to say."

"Why I couldn't what? Leg up on what?" asked Jason.

Smiling at Jason, she told Quorlynn, "I'll see you in a little while, my friend." After Quorlynn smiled and dipped her head in a sign of respect, Terri reached over, plucked the amulet from the cradle, and handed it to Jason.

With three words, Terri rocked Jason's world.

"Put it on."

CHAPTER 50

From the moment he put the amulet on, Jason received the same download of information Terri had when she first put on the amulet in the basement of the museum. After the initial period of blindness coupled with total bliss and contentment, Jason was taken to a beautiful park-like setting, the exact same one where Quorlynn had first met Terri.

When the very tall and beautiful Quorlynn appeared in front of Jason, he was deeply moved. Many things were happening to him lately that took a lot of getting used to, but this experience was in its own league. Jason stood looking into the deep dark pools of Quorlynn's eyes, completely mute. It was actually Quorlynn who spoke first.

"It's nice to meet you in person, Jason."

"I can't even begin to describe how much of a pleasure it is to meet you, Quorlynn. Thank you for allowing me into your home."

Quorlynn smiled. "I can see why Terri likes you so much. You are quite gracious."

"Thank you," said Jason. "May I ask you a question?"

"Of course," said Quorlynn. "You may ask as many questions as you like. In fact, I think that is the entire reason why Terri suggested you come in-world."

"Ok. Here's my first question. By 'in-world,' do you mean coming here to visit you?"

"Yes." Looking around at the peaceful forest environment, she continued. "The world you see here is a perfect representation of our home planet. Galimar is a world of peace and harmony, where our species learned the path to true happiness is also the path to discovery. There is an endless universe to discover, and we are dynamic and spirited explorers."

Jason thought about her response for a moment, then asked, "I know Galimarians are long-lived, but exactly how long-lived are they?"

"In terms of earth years," said Quorlynn, "It isn't unusual for a Galimarian to live for 20,000 years, although some have lived longer."

"Wow," was Jason's unqualified response. Quorlynn smiled at his childlike expression.

After thinking for a while, he said, "I'm not sure how to ask this next question without sounding condescending."

"The more time I spend with Terri," replied Quorlynn, "the more she teaches me about not only human thinking, but also a large number of human verbal expressions. So, to address your concern, I am 'thick skinned.' Go ahead and ask whatever you wish."

Jason smiled. "Well since you aren't flesh and blood, am I correct in assuming you don't have an end to your life expectancy?"

Quorlynn nodded, replying, "It is true that individuals like myself do not have to worry about dying like those who are made of flesh and blood. When our companion dies, we grieve like anybody else would. It takes time for us to reconcile ourselves to life without our companion, but in time many of us decide to be a companion again to a new friend."

"Is that what happened to you?" asked Jason.

Quorlynn took a step forward and put her arm in Jason's. They began walking along a cobblestone pathway toward a marvelously landscaped pond. "Before Terri, there was a period of several hundred years when I had no one as a companion. This was a very lonely time for me, since I was also out of communication with all my amulet brothers and sisters. When Terri came along, I was very eager to meet her. Before Terri, I did have another companion. He was an amazing man who accomplished some amazing things in his time. His name was Jobiah Aramine, and he was actually an ancestor to the designer of this island/ship. We had a very close friendship, and I miss him very much. When he died, it felt like a part of me died with him. He and I were together in-world when he died, and I have to say it was very traumatic for me."

"If this is too hard to talk about, we don't have to, Quorlynn."

She squeezed Jason's arm with her hand as they continued to walk. "Thank you for your consideration, Jason, but I am fine. It has been 80,000 years since he became one, so I have had time to heal."

"Two things," said Jason. "First, *wow* at the fact you are more than 80,000 years old! Second, what do you mean he became one?"

"Our bodies, our minds, even mine," said Quorlynn, "are all part of the seeming unending body of energy that makes up the universe. Some of that energy is compressed so much it becomes matter that makes up your physical body and the circuits of the amulet where I live. Following the laws of what you call entropy, when someone dies, the energy which is compressed into matter forming that body breaks down and returns to a simpler form. The energy isn't wasted, it's just converted and becomes useful in a different form. This is why most of the time when someone dies on Galimar, a tree is planted over their grave. That way, their body lives once again and benefits an entirely new generation. The pure energy represented by the matter making up the body can once again 'become one' with the universe."

Jason contemplated Quorlynn's words. It was obvious she was wise. As they reached the banks of the pond, Jason knelt down and sat on a grassy patch. He looked over at her, admiring her face and form, and was quite taken with her. Having a companion like her might be confusing for him. He loved Mikki with all his heart, mind, soul, and strength. But Quorlynn was captivating. If his heart didn't already belong to someone else, he could easily fall in love with her.

As Jason was looking at Quorlynn, she said, "May I ask you a question now?"

"Of course! Anything you like."

"This thing you propose to do, traveling back in time, how is that possible?"

Since Quorlynn was in a league all her own, Jason decided the rules of secrecy surrounding humans didn't really apply here.

"I have to ask that you only discuss this with Terri since she is already privy to this information," said Jason. "If you happen to speak with anybody else, please do not discuss it with them."

Nodding her head, Quorlynn said, "You have my word."

With that assurance, Jason proceeded to explain the process of how he and Dennis had invented the process of time travel. He described their initial disappointment with the results, and how they thought they had failed. Then he told her about the turning point in Las Vegas when his wife Mikki asked the question that turned everything around, without her even realizing it.

"It sounds like your wife is a very wise woman. I am surprised you don't have her working with you."

"Considering the contribution she has made to this project, that wouldn't be a bad idea. I know she can keep a secret, so perhaps we should do that."

"Why would you keep something like this a secret?" asked Quorlynn.

"I realize you are used to the 'enlightened' way of thinking, as you say, but there are many in my world who are not enlightened," Jason explained, "who only pursue their own interests, based on greed and the love of power, not for the good of their fellow man. That's why something this powerful must be kept secret."

Quorlynn had a look of understanding on her face as she was nodding her head.

Their conversation seemed to last for hours. Topics ranged from the planet of Galimar, the events leading up to the journey to Earth, and the death of everybody on the island. Quorlynn didn't know much about that, other than what her amulet companion brothers and sisters told her, since she wasn't present then.

As the conversation began to wind down, they discussed his upcoming adventure.

"What, exactly, do you intend to do when you go back in time?" asked Quorlynn.

"To be honest with you," said Jason, "I'm still working out the details. The big picture is I'm going to travel back seven centuries to the island of New Galimar to bring them the medicine to cure their malady. Beyond that, I'm working to make sure I don't end up creating any grandfather paradoxes."

"What medicine?" asked Quorlynn.

"It's something we call antibiotics," said Jason. "I am taking ceftriaxone and cefixime to counteract the typhoid fever and pneumonia we think they are dealing with."

"Those two antibiotics are good, but they won't help."

"I beg your pardon?" said a very surprised Jason. "With all due respect, how do you know they don't work?"

"When Terri and I arrived on the island," replied Quorlynn, "we learned all the inhabitants had died from some outbreak of illness. I took it upon myself to learn as much as I could about medicine. I am not a complete authority by any means, but one thing I do know is they didn't have typhoid fever or pneumonia."

"How do you know?"

"If you recall, the person who carried that sickness to the island in the first place was Joe, or Jose as you call him. When we revived him from the suspended animation chamber, he was very sick and required immediate medical care. The doctors were able to do a physical examination, make a diagnosis, then treat him with the necessary medications."

Jason sat back, silently berated himself for not thinking of it before now. "What did he have?"

"He had pneumonic plague. The medicine they gave him was chloramphenicol. According to my research, streptomycin or gentamicin would be acceptable alternatives. Ceftriaxone and cefixime are good antibiotics too, but the others are more widely accepted as a proper treatment for what Jose, and by extension all Galimarians, had."

"Good grief!" exclaimed Jason. "I could have made my very own grandfather paradox by taking back the wrong thing."

"You've used that expression before. What do you mean 'grandfather paradox'?"

"A grandfather paradox," explained Jason, "is what we call the hypothetical situation where a person travels back in time and ends up killing his own grandfather. If he did that, his own father wouldn't be born, hence he wouldn't be born, and wouldn't end up going back in time."

"I understand now," said Quorlynn. "On my planet, we call that the Gokotiva Postulate. There was a great thinker by the name of Temelan Gokotiva, who basically said the same thing. He reasoned that if the person was real, and if he really did successfully kill his grandfather, that would be proof there are, indeed, an infinite number of universes."

"Something we did successfully changed the current timeline, proving that very concept," said Jason. "We put into motion a predetermined set of steps resulting in the portal opening to a spot in the room exactly one minute in the past. When it opened, we sent back a piece of blank paper. When we started the process, we waited for the timers to count down. About a minute before the portal window opened, a blank piece of paper magically appeared at that very spot in the portal room. A minute later the portal opened, the paper was sent, and the portal window closed.

"We concluded that when we go back in time, we are changing *our* timeline, so a grandfather paradox could exist, it's something I'm very concerned about."

Quorlynn seemed to be in deep thought about what he had just described. Jason decided he should allow her to be alone with her thoughts. She was a lot older than him and perhaps might be able to render some insight on how to minimize what could possibly go very wrong with this endeavor.

Quorlynn was looking out across the pond at a flock of blue and white feathered spinsages gathering at the edge. They had just flown in and landed here, apparently in search of an evening meal and rest. While luxuriating in the restful environment, Jason considered the radical changes necessary to the plans he and Dennis had in place regarding the medicine. He needed to get back soon to tell Dennis about this new development. Quorlynn's words broke Jason out of his trance.

"You are right to be concerned about the paradox," she said. Jason nodded.

Turning her whole body toward him, she chose her words slowly and carefully.

"I have an idea."

CHAPTER 51

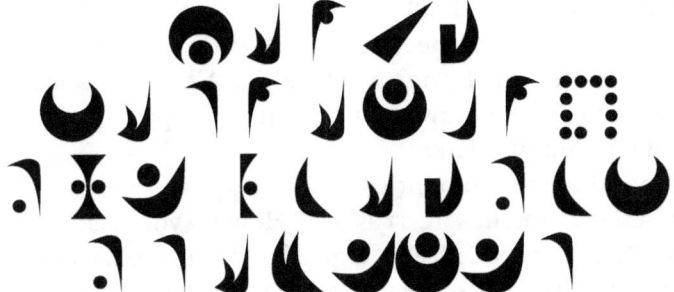

Blinking his eyes several times, Jason had to get used to seeing light through his literal eyes, instead of the eyes of his mind.

The time he had spent with Quorlynn was unbelievable. She had proven to be one of the most insightful, most heartwarming, and wisest individuals that he had ever met. Jason realized how odd it was to feel this way about a synthetic, albeit sentient, life form.

While he tremendously enjoyed his time with Quorlynn, an overwhelming sense of guilt privately locked away in his heart caused Jason to say he needed to get back. He realized Terri would completely understand the reason why he had spent six to eight hours with Quorlynn, but he still felt it was very rude of him to leave Terri alone for so long. He fully expected her to have retrieved the rest of their party from the lounge where they were supposed to have met, and to have brought them back to the apartment to wait for his return.

When Jason emerged from his time with Quorlynn, the first thing he saw was Terri's face. Looking around, he noticed the others weren't there, and were probably wondering where they had gone. Lynne knew where Terri and Jason had gone, so if need be she could have brought Dennis and Jose back to the apartment.

"I'm sorry I took so long to come back," said Jason.

Terri smiled. "I know it seems like you were gone a long time, but you weren't."

"Are you sure? It seems like I've been gone for at least six hours."

Letting out a giggle and brushing back a lock of fiery red hair, she said, "In this world, you were actually gone for about ten minutes."

Jason's eyes went wide, and his mouth hung open.

"You've got to be kidding!"

"Nope. Not kidding. The first time I went in-world I was supposed to meet Lynne for lunch shortly after that. When I got out, I was certain I had completely blown out that lunch appointment, but it was only about 15 minutes later."

Jason sat there dumbfounded.

After a few moments, Terri asked, "How do you feel?"

"Actually, I feel great. I feel energized and ready to tackle the world!"- simply nodded.But, while I *really want* to compare notes on this, I need to get back to Dennis. Quorlynn helped on so many levels, and I have to get some critical information to my partner."

"That's fine, but I need to make a request," said Terri.

"What's that?" asked Jason.

"The role this amulet has played in my understanding of the Galimarian people isn't something I have shared with anybody else. I was impressed with you right away, so I knew I could trust you with this information. Most of the military goons walking around here definitely aren't going to get their grubby hands on Quorlynn if I have anything to say about it. I'd like to ask you not to tell anyone else about what the amulet can do, or about Quorlynn."

"That's a fair request. What about Lynne?"

"She's a good friend, but she sometimes has a tendency to be a little loose-lipped, if you know what I mean." Terri grinned.

"I gotcha. I won't tell anybody," said Jason. "I'm hoping you will allow me to meet again with Quorlynn. There is a lot more I want to learn from her, and since I can seemingly live a lifetime in there with hardly any time going by out here, I'd like to leverage all I can learn from her before I go back."

"I'll have to get the ok from Quorlynn, but I don't see why she wouldn't agree to that."

Terri and Jason got up to make their way back to the park where
Dennis, Jose, and Lynne were still conversing. As they were about to
get on the lift to return back to ground level, Jason said he'd forgotten
something in the apartment, and would be right back. He was only
gone for a couple of minutes, then he returned and they continued on
to the park.

After arriving, Jason revealed to rest of the gang that the medicines
they had secured weren't the right ones, they needed to get back to
Midway Magnetic and, in the meantime, arrange for some alternative
medicines to be delivered.

After making some private satellite phone calls to the Pentagon,
Jason returned to the group with a request. Pulling Terri aside, he said,
"I'd like to make a request of you. I told the admiral you were crucial to
the success of the mission, so I asked for and received his permission to
allow you to return with me to Midway Magnetic so you can be there
in the portal room when I go back."

Terri looked away and stared at the city center of New Galimar, contemplating his request. "I know going there is an honor since the nature
of the technology is super-secret, but," Terri gestured to the gleaming
tropical paradise where they now found themselves, "I don't know if I
can leave this place. It's my home."

Gently putting his hand on her shoulder and turning her around
to face him, Jason said, "Believe me when I tell you, Terri, that after
my amazing experience with Quorlynn, I empathize with you. I completely understand why you consider yourself Galimarian because, to
be quite honest, so do I. This place calls to me like nothing I have ever
experienced before.

"The thing is," he continued, "if we don't succeed in what we are attempting to do, then this world you and I love will be destroyed, along
with our families and about seven and a half billion others. I originally
wanted to do this to save our world; now I'm doing it because I want to
save New Galimar, too. It's important enough for me to put my life at
risk to make it happen."

Terri looked deeply into Jason's eyes, and she saw the same resolute
determination she had come to love in Khreelon. "Since you put it like
that, I'd have to be a real jerk not to go. All right, Jason, lead the way."

Jason patted her shoulder and, turning to the rest of the group, explained the new arrangements.

From that moment onward, the course of events leading to their arrival at Midway Magnetic was certainly a whirlwind that the President
of the United States would have been proud of. On the returning

jet back to California, Jason spent time reviewing some last-minute preparations. Then, feigning a nap, he borrowed the amulet from Terri and returned to Quorlynn. He told her the current plans that had been set in motion, and spent as much time as possible learning about the Galimarian culture. Like Terri, the more he learned, the more he identified with this beautiful race.

After getting home that evening, Jason wrote a letter like no other, addressed to Switzerland. No one knew its contents; not Terri, not even Mikki. He hoped it would never be read, but this was his insurance in case something went wrong.

The next morning, after picking up Terri from a local hotel, Jason drove to work where they met Dennis and Diana. Knowing the importance of the trip about to be undertaken, Admiral Brinstock arranged to be present as well, and brought along his assistant, Lieutenant Flume. Upon entering the portal room, Jason saw that the replacement stock of medicines was ready and waiting. After introducing Terri to Diana, Jason then spoke up above the din of conversation.

"May I have your attention?"

Admiral Brinstock, off to the side speaking softly to the lieutenant, turned to face Jason. Dennis, who was sitting at his station, stopped typing, and Diana and Terri gave Jason their attention.

"We are about to do something never before done in the history of man." Jason stopped. With a smile on his face, he continued. "In the history of man. That phrase takes on a different meaning now, doesn't it? For as long as mankind has recorded the events of history, several things have always been regarded as unchangeable and unshakable. The ground we walk on, for one, and the inexorable forward march of time. An ancient proverb says, 'Time and tide wait for no man.' Yet now we are faced with the facts that not only is our world quite shakable and our earth is on the verge of perpetrating its own suicide, but also that time can, in fact, be made to wait. It can be put at our disposal and made subject to our whims.

"We must take a lesson from the brave men and women who, through a sheer act of brute force on their part and on the part of millions who supported them, faced their fears and helped usher mankind into the Space Age. They showed bravery beyond compare. Most were able to beat the odds and come back alive, but as the Challenger and Columbia space shuttle disasters showed, some of them didn't come back home. As President Reagan said at the time, we will never forget them, nor the last time we saw them that morning, as they prepared for their journey, waved goodbye, and 'slipped the surly bonds of earth' to 'touch the face of God.'

"I now stand before you, a man who is about to slip the sometimes surly bonds of time. I certainly hope this doesn't mean I am about to touch the face of God, but I wanted you all to know I do this not because of any desire for glory, but simply because of love: my love for mankind; my love for my friends, both old and new; but most of all, I do this because of the love of one woman. A woman who shall never know the sacrifice I have made for her."

Reaching over to his desk, Jason opened a drawer and produced a bottle of champagne along with some plastic cups. "I'd like to share a drink with my friends and compatriots, and ask you to send along all the positive thoughts you can muster." Then after pausing, he said, "I'm gonna need 'em."

"Here, here!" shouted Dennis.

"Here, here!" shouted all the rest in the room, taking a long drag from their cups.

After finishing his drink, Jason turned to his partner and longtime friend. "Dr. Greene, are you ready?"

"Ready on all accounts, Dr. Marsalis. Waiting for you to give the word."

Jason smiled. "Dr. Greene, the word is given!"

Dennis smiled. The two men reached under their collars and produced chains they were wearing around their necks. Hanging at the end of each chain was a diminutive USB drive.

In the weeks preceding their journey to New Galimar, Jason and Dennis had been working feverishly on refining the software controlling the portal architecture. As a security measure, they devised a lockout system requiring two USB keys to be inserted into two separate consoles that controlled the portal; each was separate and distinct from the other, and both were required to activate the portal. The system was designed to be similar to the key locks used with the control systems for nuclear missile silos and submarine-launched ballistic missiles.

The two men plugged their thumb drives into the control consoles and turned each 90 degrees to the right. As soon as they did, the bright fluorescent tubes in the room all shut off and were replaced with red lights, indicating the system was beginning to power up. Above the portal, two large yellow LED digital displays came to life. Both showed the current day and time down to the millisecond.

Having to shout over the loud noise of the cryogenics plants coming on line, Jason said, "You will notice there are two date and time displays

445

shown above the portal aperture. The LED display on the top represents the date and time here locally, whereas the one on the bottom represents the date and time where the portal is currently pointed. Soon, you will see those two dates and times diverge from each other."

Dennis spoke up over the noise coming from the liquid helium pumps and compressors. "Cryogenics systems nominal. Beginning power up of superconductors."

In the background, the massive relays controlling the flow of power into the superconductors began to slam shut. Each time they did, trillions of volts started their march toward the specially-formulated ceramic magnets which had the unique ability to not only handle the tremendous amount of power needed to guide the particle streams, but did so with a smile, just asking for more. By the time the last of the four ten-foot-tall relays closed, there was a rather significant hum floating around the facility.

Looking at this console, Jason now addressed Dennis.

"Commencing countdown to particle acceleration in three, two, one, Mark!"

At this point, the control surfaces of the portal architecture altered almost imperceptibly, and by doing so the particle stream was redirected so that billions of protons which used to be part of hydrogen atoms were now directed toward the reaction chamber connected to the portal. As soon as this happened, the region in the middle of the portal aperture started to fill in from the edges with a hazy, powder blue field. Eventually, the field closed in on the portal opening itself, and in the middle a scene came into focus. Since Jason had entered the coordinates of New Galimar as the starting point, all in the portal room were now shown a scene of the same park where they had all (except for the Admiral and his assistant of course) been standing just twenty-four hours earlier.

Standing near Diana, Terri leaned over and said, "Are you telling me that if I step through that portal right now, I'll instantly be on the island again?"

"It's incredible, isn't it?" said Diana, smiling. Leaning in to share something secret, she added, in hushed tones, "The other day they even used it to get Chinese food for lunch from *China*!" Terri couldn't help but laugh out loud. The subject of their laughter was immediately a cause for interest on the part of all, but Terri understood this wasn't something to discuss while the military was present.

Interrupting the light mood, Jason announced, "Commencing time dilation."

After entering a couple of keystrokes, the clocks above the portal began to diverge from one another. The display on top didn't change, since that represented the date and time in the portal room. But the readout on the bottom was a different story; it appeared to hesitate for a moment, then stop. In a couple more moments, the time portion of the readout started to move backward and, as it did, the speed with which it moved steadily increased.

"Time dilation rate, one year per second," said Jason, as his eyes remained locked onto his screen. Terri took a few steps to see what he was looking at. While Dennis' screen was designed to monitor the power flow and the health of the cryogenics plants which were keeping the superconductors cool, Jason's screen was in charge of the control surfaces that shaped not only the X, Y, and Z coordinates where the portal was pointed, but also the crucial T coordinate. The T, or Time, coordinate was the main thing Jason was watching. As the readout on his screen showed the X, Y, and Z coordinates remaining static, the T signature was steadily proceeding backwards. In the corner of his screen was a video feed of the scene in the portal aperture, allowing Jason to see what was happening without tearing his eyes away from the screen.

The backward progress of the lower LED readout slowed, eventually settling on a date and time approximately 700 years ago. The park scene the team had observed about ten minutes ago was the same, except for a very important difference. Right there, right in front of them, was the vibrant population of Galimarian men, women, and children. All the adults were strolling along gracefully, and the well-behaved children were playing. Off to the left, there were three children, impossible to tell whether they were girls or boys, who were completely fascinated with something that looked like a butterfly. One allowed the butterfly to land on his/her hand, and the others were studying it with a look of sheer delight on their faces. The interest of these children wasn't lost on other children; several walked over to see what was so interesting.

On the now famous bench in the middle of the park, a man and woman, who both appeared to be about 30 years old, were talking with each other. He was comfortably dressed in a billowy, long-sleeved shirt that had no buttons on the front, and she was in a beautiful dress which looked like it was made of chiffon containing several of the same colors as the park. Her hair had small flowers inserted in the left side; while allowing her hair to hang down on the right in loose curls, she had somehow pinned up her hair on the left, and the small flowers laid a path disappearing down her back.

It was late afternoon, the time Jason had chosen to ensure as many as possible would be present when he arrived. Earlier, he thought perhaps he ought to create garb somewhat matching that of the Galimarians. But for the Galimarians to take him seriously, he decided not only did he need to be dressed very differently from them, but as many people as possible needed to be present for an arrival which would be very surprising to them.

The time had come. The portal was ready. Jason was ready. The correct medicines were ready. All the planning, all the science, all the soul searching, all came down to this moment. Now, there was nothing left to do but take that one small step.

Jason stood up from his console and extended his hand to his compadre Dennis. Ignoring Jason's hand, Dennis came in for a very hearty man-hug. Gently hitting Jason's upper back with his closed fist, he told him, "You get your butt back here! Don't make me come get you."

"You got it, partner."

Stepping back, Jason hugged both Diana and Terri. Admiral Brinstock and Lieutenant Flume maintained their stoic stances, observing the events as they unfolded, and made no effort to step forward. Jason was quite happy not even acknowledging their presence since there was certainly no love lost between them. The cold look on the admiral's face spoke volumes about his opinion of Jason, much better than the fake "grandpa" act he had been using lately.

Turning around, Jason strapped on his backpack and picked up two large cases with handles. Stepping toward the portal field, he stopped for a moment, glancing over his shoulder at the six people looking back at him. Turning to face the portal again, Jason took his step into time and destiny.

In previous transportations, Dennis had been the one to do the traveling. Going to China was the first time, and Dennis said the trip there and back was rather unremarkable. Jason wasn't sure if that was really true, or whether Dennis had just been brandishing a sporty bravado of some sort.

When Jason's body was first touched by the surface of the field, it seemed to spread around his body even though some of it seemed to be still in the portal room. Completely enveloped by the field, the immediate sensation Jason noticed was an instant change in ambient noise around him. The loud noise of the portal mechanics was instantly replaced by the peaceful, almost melodious chirps of birds nesting in the nearby trees. The sound of the ocean and the animal life around him was suddenly pierced by a quenched shriek off to Jason's right.

Turning in that direction, he saw a woman standing there with a man, her hand covering her mouth. The woman and man were looking directly at him, and only now did Jason realize that, without much pomp and circumstance, he just became the first time traveler in this small corner of the universe. Looking behind him, he couldn't see the portal room; he couldn't see or hear the machinery. Nothing. He knew they were still watching him from the portal room, but from his perspective, it was impossible to know he was being watched.

The woman to his right said to the man, "Who is it, Bonan? Where did he come from?" The man didn't reply, but those in close proximity to Jason started to recede from him. From their perspective, he had appeared out of thin air.

Within moments, there was quite a commotion surrounding Jason, everyone observing how different he was. One man said to another, "Look at his ears. I don't think he's Galimarian! Another said, "I've never seen anybody else clothed like that."

Jason placed the bags he was carrying down on the ground as a sign of non-aggression, and simply stood there with his hands clasped together in front of him. He wanted all to know they were not in any danger.

One of the women finally said, "I've seen someone like this before, but you're not going to believe who he looks like."

One of the others asked, "Who? Who does he look like?"

"He looks human."

There was a sudden intake of breath on the part of all upon the realization that one of the barbarians who were the dominant species on this planet was now standing in their midst. How he got there was only one of a myriad of questions starting to float amongst them as they looked at each other, then back at Jason, then back to each other.

Eventually one of the individuals in the group said, "Everybody, please listen."

The flow of conversation died down until that man was the only one speaking.

"I agree this one standing here before us must be human. How he got here without anybody seeing him arrive is certainly a mystery, but he must be terribly bewildered at all he sees here. I don't want to scare him."

Jason could see they now needed to learn he wasn't what they thought he was. Remembering something he learned from Quorlynn, Jason put his open palms together and, while bowing, uttered a greeting in the Galimarian language. "May you have peace, my fellow Galimarians." This caused a very sharp intake of breath from *everyone* present.

449

What Jason couldn't know was everyone in the portal room, except Terri, were equally shocked to hear him communicate in a language they had never heard before. They looked at Terri, who had been interpreting what the Galimarians were saying. She explained this greeting was a sign of respect, and was sure to break the ice.

"How is it you know our language?" asked one of the men standing close to the center of the circle now surrounding Jason.

"To answer that there is much I have to tell you," replied Jason, "but before revealing the answer I request, under the provisions of Testimonial Law, that I be allowed to speak before the Grand Council. When I do, the answers to all your questions will be made clear."

The fact that Jason, a human, was not only fluent in the Galimarian language, but also familiar with Testimonial Law, was staggering to all present. The same one who asked the last question stepped forward.

Placing his right hand on Jason's opposing right shoulder, he said, "It is evident we have much to discover. In our own tongue, you have invoked the right to request audience before the Grand Council. Normally that privilege is only afforded to Galimarian people, but in this case, I think an exception will be made. If it is to the Grand Council you wish to speak, then to the chamber of the Grand Council you will go. Please follow me."

The throng of individuals centered around Jason left the park and walked toward the center of the city. As they walked, Jason was flanked by the same individuals who had been asking questions about, and speaking with, him in the park. Since it was going to take some time to get to the Grand Council chambers, Jason decided to break the ice a little bit more.

"This is a beautiful city you have. It is hard to believe you've been here for thousands of years."

"It appears you have us at a disadvantage," said the Galimarian man. "My name is Triiak. What may I call you?"

"My name is Jason Marsalis. You may simply call me Jason."

"It's a pleasure to meet you, Jason. I am very eager to learn from you the answers to our questions," said Triiak.

"And you will. I realize I am a little mysterious in my response, but trust me when I say the reality I have to share with you is even stranger than you can imagine."

"Your very presence is already something stranger than I would have imagined. I hope you don't take offense when I say that having a conversation with a species we always thought was far too primitive for intelligent conversation has already gone beyond all previous expectations."

"No offense taken," said Jason. "To be honest, I don't blame you for considering humans barbaric."

As they were talking, the subject matter of the conversation Jason and Triiak were having rippled back through the rest of the crowd. By the time they reached the building where the Grand Council chambers were located, all in the crowd of about 75 people were aware of what was discussed.

"Seeing as you already know so much about us," said Triiak, "you're probably aware you will need to wait outside while I go in and announce to the council coordinator your arrival, and that you have requested a meeting with the council."

Placing his right hand on the opposing right shoulder of Triiak, Jason bowed his head and said, "I await your return."

Triiak bowed his head in response, then retreated toward the office of the coordinator, shaking his head back and forth in disbelief.

Jason sat on a bench surrounded by the original crowd. As time passed, a growing throng of Galimarians came to the courtyard outside the Grand Council building to see the phantasm who appeared out of thin air in the park. As was always the case with the young, no matter what species, they came near to see Jason up close. He would engage them in some simple talk, and soon all were disarmed by Jason's engaging, gregarious nature.

The general feel of the gathering took on a somewhat festive feel, and the more Jason observed all around him, the more he fell in love with these amazing people. They were calm, tranquil, peaceful, and serene. Each of them was intelligent and self-assured, and seemed to wear their intelligence only as an accessory. The women were dressed in elegant flowing apparel featuring fabrics both opaque, yet transparent. As beautiful as the women were, Jason observed the men were equally handsome. They were suave and gracious as they attended to those who were apparently their mates. Dressed in outfits that accentuated their masculine features, each and every one was the picture of health and vitality.

Eventually Triiak returned, and walking next to him was another Galimarian man dressed in what Jason had learned from Quorlynn to be the traditional garb of one who occupied an office of oversight. As Triiak and the other man approached, Jason stood.

"Jason, this is N'Zollivant. He is the ...."

Jason interrupted. "The coordinator for the Grand Council." Putting his palms together and bowing, he said, "It is an honor to meet you, Lord N'Zollivant."

A very astonished coordinator looked over to Triiak, then back at Jason. Putting his own open palms together and bowing, N'Zollivant replied, "No, the honor is mine, Jason. When Triiak told me about your appearance in the park and your request to address the council, I thought his story was less than credible. Now that I have witnessed you for myself, I can see you should, indeed, be heard by the council. If you will follow me, I will call an emergency session of the council immediately."

With that, Jason picked up his backpack and cases and accompanied Lord N'Zollivant into the antechamber where speakers customarily waited. Triiak explained he would return to his own home where he would tune in and listen to all Jason had to say. He wanted to make sure his wife and children were aware of Jason's arrival, and of what he was going to say.

For a time, Jason was alone, and the room was quiet. It took him by complete surprise when the entire unremarkable wall to his left suddenly changed into a floor-to-ceiling, wall-to-wall video screen. The scene was the same one Quorlynn had shown him once before, the chamber of the Grand Council. The members were beginning to filter in and take their seats. It took about ten minutes for the chamber to fill, but eventually all members of the council were present.

About the time the coordinator took the stage, a Galimarian man who appeared to be an assistant to the coordinator came into the room and said Jason would be asked to come to the stage very soon and that he should follow him.

The coordinator began to speak.

"Lords and Ladies of the Grand Council of New Galimar, I thank you for responding to my call for an emergency session. I'm sure some of you might be aware of the reason why I have called this meeting, but to erase any speculation, I am simply going to relate what I was told. As many of our fellow lords and ladies were relaxing in the park near the northern spire, seemingly out of nowhere an individual appeared. The clothing of this person was different, but what was truly remarkable was the man standing in the middle of the park," the coordinator paused, "... was human."

There was an instantaneous outbreak of hushed but impassioned words passed back and forth around the chamber. The coordinator held up his hands and said, "Council members, please."

It was no use. The coordinator had to allow the members to settle themselves down before he could continue. "Council members, there is more you will find equally amazing. This human not only somehow found himself onto our island, but he is fluent in our language and was familiar enough with Testimonial Law to request a session to speak before you now." Turning to his right, he held out his arm toward Jason, who by this time was approaching the podium. "I give you now the human, Jason."

As opposed to the uproar that existed moments before, the chamber was now completely devoid of sound, as if the Galimarians weren't even breathing. Jason approached the podium and set his cases and backpack down to the side. Stepping up to the lectern, he gripped both sides and scanned his eyes across the audience of Galimarian elders. After a few seconds of silence, Jason began to speak.

"Lords and Ladies of the Grand Council of New Galimar, and to all those tuned into these council proceedings from their homes, I carry with me the greetings of my people. I know my simple presence before this esteemed council is something unexpected, and I wish to thank you for allowing my intrusion." With these first disarming words, Jason suddenly toppled years of isolationism on the part of all Galimarians who had assumed the barbarism witnessed when they first arrived had continued.

"For thousands of years, your people have lived on this amazing oasis, living, laughing, and loving in peace and harmony. Your culture is centered around discovery and the pursuit of happiness found therein. As I began learning more and more about you, I discovered your culture is not dissimilar from my own voyage into the realms of learning. I, too, have found great satisfaction in learning all I can, then passing along that knowledge. I am certain, as time goes on and we learn more from each other, there will be an interchange of thought between our species which will be mutually beneficial.

"One of the first things asked of me was how did I come to be standing, suddenly, in the middle of the park where Triiak found me. I will warn you now, the answer to that question will be difficult for you to believe, but my very presence before this council should be considered proof that what I am about to tell you is true. My name is Jason, but among my people I am a scientist and a doctor. My complete name is Dr. Jason Marsalis, and the field of study I specialize in is high energy physics. As part of my work, I experiment with many different things to achieve a fuller understanding of the world around me. Like you and your culture, my quest is to discover all I can about the universe and how it is constructed.

"Not too long ago, one of my experiments led me to discover something that, for the longest time, our people thought was impossible: time travel."

As Jason had assumed, this revelation caused an all new uproar. He respectfully waited for the clamor to recede before continuing to speak. "I know this is something that will take some getting used to, but my very existence, and the fact I am so well-versed with your culture, proves I am telling the truth. I come from a time in the future approximately 700 years from now. It is a time when humankind has progressed significantly in terms of our understanding of the universe and the world around us. Yet, our culture is in its infancy. It is a time when we have progressed so far but, like a young child, we are still vulnerable. This means we are not only powerful but, unless we use that power wisely, it will result in our own undoing."

Jason's mention of this was by design. In his long conversations with Quorlynn, she had told Jason of experiences the Galimarians suffered through with planets like Traxis, where the Traxians used technology Galimar had supplied, only to end up eradicating themselves from existence.

"Still," Jason smiled as he continued, "with guidance from advanced cultures such as yours, I am certain we will be able to weather the storm of our own cultural and technological puberty."

With the outbreak of laughter from those assembled in the council chamber, Jason knew he was breaking through to all those listening.

After the laughter died down, Jason added, "Normally, I would not have come back in time. As your philosophers have no doubt pondered, altering the timeline of the past would most certainly alter the course of events in history, resulting in catastrophe in the present. Unfortunately, there are mitigating circumstances that required me to risk this voyage.

"On your island, you have the Tectonic Stabilization Machine, which continued to run properly well into the century previous to the one I come from. However, approximately 100 years before I left to come here, your machine ceased to function. As a result, widespread earthquakes and volcanic activity began, and they have continued during the time of my generation."

"You are probably asking yourselves why it ceased to function, and why it wasn't immediately repaired by your engineers. I must again warn you, the answer to that question will be equally difficult to hear, if not more so, than what I have already shared with you. The answer is that your society is in grave danger of extinction due to an event about to occur exactly 30 days from today."

Jason expected this to cause consternation among those assembled; to the contrary, all that could be heard was a lone cough from the rear of the room.

"In your current era, the world outside the shield surrounding this island is suffering from a sickness which, at its zenith, resulted in the loss of millions of lives. Thirty days from today, your shield will go down as it normally does when the plasma emitters fail. The replacement of these emitters only takes about a minute, but in the span of that particular minute, a lone human will be in the wrong place at the wrong time. He will sail past the position of the shield and land on your shores. Unfortunately, he will bring with him this same sickness that, unless something is done, will cause the complete extinction of every man, woman, and child on this island. One month after he lands, you will all be dead."

The mood of the room, the mood of the entire island, changed from one of wonderment to dire hopelessness. All Galimarians were convinced Jason was exactly who he said he was, and now that he had just prophesied the complete destruction of their species, all were at a complete loss as to what to do.

"A lesser evolved society would simply allow that human to lose his life at the shield," said Jason, "and not make it to your island, but I know this is not an option for an enlightened society such as yours. But since your species will have been erased from the planet in my timeline, there would be no one to repair your machine when it breaks down 700 years from now. However, I bring you hope." Gesturing to the cases he brought with him, Jason said, "With me, I bring medicines from my century that we use to treat and cure cases of this sickness, which we still experience from time to time. I have not only brought with me a supply of the medicine for you to use, but I have also brought with me information on how to synthesize this same medicine. That way, you will have enough to give to any who may need it, and your species will not have to suffer this catastrophe."

At this point, one and all in the council chamber rose to their feet and began clapping their hands over the relief they felt. Cheers hailed Jason, but after a few moments of this, he raised his hands in a request for silence. Eventually, they all retook their seats and allowed Jason to continue speaking.

"Thank you for that, and thank you for your warm reception. In the next few weeks, I look forward to learning more about you and becoming close friends. However, there is something else I need to say."

Jason related the story of Terri Lindstrom, and how she had discovered an amulet which had been spirited off the island. He related how Quorlynn, the amulet companion, taught Terri about New Galimar, and about how the Tectonic Stabilization Machine had sent an urgent signal asking any who heard it to respond. He related the story of how she first visited the island, only to discover that all Galimarians were dead, and how that eventually led to his visit.

Jason then related how the earth was on the brink of destruction due to the super volcano in Yellowstone National Park in the United States, and how their machine was the only thing able to quell the impending doom. If the volcano were allowed to erupt, it would result in the death of every living thing on the face of the earth, an extinction level event.

"I have related this story to you," said Jason, "for a very important reason. All these events leading up my arrival in your time on your island must still happen exactly as I have just related to you. If they don't, and if at any point in the timeline something is altered such as my visit here being interrupted, then not only will your race be destroyed, but so will mine."

Without asking to be recognized, an individual in the front row stood and was about to say something, when Jason saw who it and said, "The floor recognizes Lord Khreelon Tellindor."

A normally very poised Khreelon was suddenly at a loss for words at being recognized by Jason, a man he had never met. The other council members were nothing less than floored by the spectacle; inadvertently, Jason gained even more credence by this simple act. All in the room realized Jason would not know who Khreelon was unless everything he was saying was true.

"I must say, you have completely taken me by surprise, and I am honored for you to call me by name," said Khreelon. "My question is simple. How do you propose we avert this disaster?"

In answer, Jason replied, "As I was preparing for this trip, I was speaking with Quorlynn, who is as wise as she is beautiful. She was the one who actually came up with the idea. She proposed that after the man who lands on your shores is cured, you should make fake representations of your bodies which will look like you died while lying on your beds in your respective homes. Once that task is complete, all of you, including the man who lands on the island, must lock yourselves away in suspended animation chambers with a timer, allowing you to awaken at the very same moment I come back in time. You will then repair your machine, save the planet, save yourselves, and save every human being. It is important that the suspended animation chambers for all of you be located somewhere we won't discover in my timeline. The suspended animation chamber for the human who lands will need to be in a place where he can be discovered by us in the future. It is also critical that each and every one of you keep the news of my visitation from your amulet companions, so as to not divulge the true course of events surrounding my arrival here today to anyone they might meet in my timeline."

By this time, Khreelon had sat back down and all who heard Quorlynn's solution understood the responsibility they now had. After hearing the overall assent his fellow council members were expressing, Khreelon stood again and held up his arms to ask for silence among his contemporaries.

Turning to Jason, he said, "All that you are saying, we shall do."

CHAPTER 52

SINCE MIDWAY MAGNETIC WAS SITUATED in the middle of the Sierra Nevada mountain range, the environment surrounding the facility was nothing short of spectacular in terms of its beautiful vistas of pine forest and sheer granite cliffs. It was the pinnacle of high-tech and nature all rolled up into one place. That combination, though, was the last thing on the minds of those gathered in the portal room after Jason first stepped through the opening, leaving them and arriving on the island.

They were all watching intently as he spoke to the Galimarians in the park. It was then that Admiral Brinstock received a call on his private line. The sound of a cell phone down in the deepest reaches of the underground facility was quite a rare event, but then again, the admiral's cell phone was one of the most secure cell phones on the market these days. He was able to get reception only because cell signals were repeated down here, and only for encrypted phone conversations such as the one he was receiving now. Watching Jason talk to the aliens was certainly capturing his attention, and he was rather irritated at receiving this interruption until he saw it was someone calling from the USGS field office at Yellowstone. He had a passing thought that perhaps they were too late with what they were trying to accomplish since Jason hadn't done anything yet. He was still talking in the park.

"Brinstock here."

"Admiral? This is Dr. Morrison from the USGS. There have been some critical changes in the Yellowstone volcano I need to share with you."

"Okay, hang on a second." Looking over to Lieutenant Flume, he said, "I have to take this. Pay attention to what happens and report it to me when I return."

"Yes sir."

Walking off to a more secluded part of the portal room, Kenji continued his phone call while Jason continued speaking with the Galimarians in the park. Terri was translating what was being said, and Larry came closer to hear her.

"He just told the other guy he's never seen anybody else clothed like that. I think he also said something about Jason's ears, but it's a little hard to hear."

"Who said that?" asked Larry, knowing he had missed some of the events in the portal.

"The Galimarian on the right of the one next to him," replied Terri.

Looking at Jason, Lieutenant Flume observed that he had taken a non-aggression stance. Jason had put his bags down and was standing there with his hands folded. "Smart," thought Larry. "He's a cool cucumber with these people so they don't get too excited."

There was more said by one of the aliens, then the whole group of them seemed to gasp. "What happened?" asked Diana.

"That woman just said she's seen someone like this before, but they wouldn't believe where she thinks he's from. Then she said he is human. Apparently they know who humans are, and I think they're a little scared about it."

"Scared?" asked Larry, who had now become part of the conversation. "Why would they be scared?"

"When you think about it," said Terri, "they purposely isolated themselves for thousands of years, so there's no telling what perceptions about us they might have. Keep in mind that thousands of years ago, mankind was nothing like it is now. They probably think humans are still like that."

"I guess that makes sense," said Dennis.

The crowd had been stirred when they figured out Jason was human, but then another one of them was trying to speak, and with his gestures, apparently asking them to quiet down. He started speaking, and when he finished, Terri let out a chuckle.

"He just told the group not to get too excited because Jason must be bewildered and they don't want to scare him."

Larry, Diana, and Dennis started chuckling themselves, and as Dennis was laughing, he looked toward the far end of the room to where the admiral was talking on the phone. Apparently due to the noise in the portal room, he had the cell phone pressed to one ear while plugging his other ear with a fingertip. His body language was that of a person in an intense phone conversation. Suddenly, the admiral hung up the phone call he was on and dialed someone else.

Meanwhile, back at the portal, it now appeared Jason was doing something.

"That gesture he is making is a traditional gesture of respect," Terri explained. "I think he's going to speak."

Jason opened his mouth and spoke something in a language nobody in the portal room had ever heard him speak before; it sounded strangely like the language the aliens were speaking.

Another sharp intake of breath, this time from not only the aliens, but also from each of the humans looking on through the portal.

"What the heck was that he just did?" asked Diana.

"He just greeted them," said Terri, "and bid them peace."

"How in the world does he know their language?" asked Lieutenant Flume.

Terri, of course, knew exactly how Jason learned the Galimarian language; it had been downloaded into his mind when he first put on the amulet. But since she was keeping secret the existence of the amulet and the effects it has on the mind, she just replied, "He might know only a few phrases, but I think he's a quick study."

"He is pretty smart about that kind of thing," added Dennis, unknowingly buying into Terri's ruse. "Last year when we traveled to Sweden for a physics conference, I was amazed how well he did over there."

"One of them is asking him how he knows their language," Terri said. "He replied that there are a lot of things he has to share with them, and he's requesting to speak with the Grand Council of New Galimar."

"The what?" asked Diana.

"The Grand Council of New Galimar is their version of Congress. It's their ruling body on the island and, to be honest, it's pretty smart of him to ask to speak to them directly."

By this time, Admiral Brinstock had finished his phone calls and rejoined the group.

More words were spoken by one of the aliens who was acting as their spokesman, then the group began moving away from the viewpoint of the portal.

"Wait! What's happening?" asked Diana urgently.

"That guy said he would take Jason to the Grand Council, so apparently that's where they are going," replied Terri.

"Okay," said Dennis, getting up from his position in front of the cryogenics control station where he normally was positioned. "I can change parameters on Jason's station so we can follow him."

"Hold it!" called out the admiral. Dennis stopped in his tracks.

Stepping toward Jason's workstation and turning to face the group, Kenji said, "I have just gotten off the phone with the USGS. They reported to me something which I had to verify with my contacts at the seismological laboratory at the California Institute of Technology. The team at Yellowstone reported a sudden and complete cessation of seismological activity. For reasons they don't understand, the thousands of minor quakes at Yellowstone reflecting magma movement in the chamber below the park have completely stopped, along with any magma movement."

"That's great!" said Dennis. "That means he did it."

"That isn't possible," said Terri. "He only just left the view of the portal. He hasn't had enough time to even begin talking to the council."

"To quote a movie, you're not thinking in the fourth dimension."

"Yeah, I seem to have a problem with that," replied Terri.

"The events Jason is setting in motion have already happened in our timeline," reasoned Dennis. "The fact that the earthquakes have stopped means Jason was successful in stopping them from dying off. This means they are still alive, and they have fixed the machine on the island."

Terri's eyes grew wide. "Did you just say they are still alive?"

"They have to be," responded Dennis. "How else would the machine have been fixed?"

Terri's knees felt like they were about to buckle. The thought that Khreelon might actually be alive was both exhilarating and terrifying at the same time. She had become resigned to the idea she was in love with a person she would never have the opportunity to meet.

Kenji decided this was his opportunity to eliminate a particularly nasty burr under his saddle. The insubordination Jason had shown him one too many times was now going to stop.

Deciding to manufacture a story legitimizing what he was about to do, the admiral said, "The problem is that Dr. Marsalis was about to release information about this portal. He said that the entire world needed to know about it because the world should decide what to do with it. I tried to reason with him that this was foolhardy and the president needed to be the one in control of the portal technology, but he just wouldn't listen."

"What?" shouted Dennis, incredulously. "That's ridiculous!"

"It's true," responded Kenji.

"He would never do that," retorted Diana. "I would stake my life on Jason keeping the secrets of this facility."

"Then you must not value your life, Ms. O'Laney," shot back Kenji with cold, venomous contempt. Diana looked the admiral square in the eyes and couldn't tell if that was a statement of opinion, or a threat to her life.

"There is no way I'm going to sit here and listen to this," Dennis said as he started for Jason's console. With a commanding voice he had never heard from the admiral before, Kenji shouted, "Halt!" Dennis once again stopped short of the console where the admiral was now hovering. As soon as he looked Kenji eye to eye, the admiral's gaze swung to a place behind Dennis. Kenji nodded his head.

Prior to arriving at the portal facility, Kenji had considered the events that were about to occur and decided he needed to plan for any contingency, including the possibility the aliens would turn out to be hostile. To that end, Kenji came prepared. Turning around, Dennis was shocked to witness a contingent of soldiers, some with weapons at the ready, filing into the portal room. The ones without weapons took positions at the control stations formerly occupied by Jason and Dennis. The rest took their position to each side of the portal, and near the control mainframes littered about the room. Several stood near Diana and Terri.

Turning back to the admiral, Dennis said, "What the heck is going on here?"

"Unfortunately, Dr. Greene," replied Kenji with a monotone voice, "Dr. Marsalis represents a clear and present threat to national security. I have no choice."

"What are you going to do?" said Dennis, wide-eyed with dread.

Kenji stood there for a moment, staring Dennis straight in the eye. "What I do now, I do for the good of the country," he said, reaching over to the USB stick key Jason had placed in the key switch.

"*No!*" shouted Terri and Diana simultaneously. Dennis yelled, "You'll kill him!"

The admiral hesitated momentarily then, while slowly looking back up at Dennis, twisted the key counterclockwise. With that motion, the park scene in the portal vanished.

Diana and Terri, who were holding each other for support, and Dennis, standing helplessly near Kenji, all looked on in disbelief and horror. Their friend, their longtime associate, their mentor ... gone with the flick of a switch. Even though Dennis and Diana weren't exactly fans of the admiral, this was far beyond anything they had expected him to do.

Dennis took two steps away from Kenji while his gaze faltered. Stepping backward, the feeling in Dennis' legs began to leave, and he collapsed to the floor like a building being demolished. His mouth hung open as he contemplated not only the loss he had suffered, but also, "Oh my god, Mikki..." He was dumbfounded how emotionless Kenji demonstrated himself to be. Dennis looked at Admiral Brinstock and saw the former "grandfather" face now icy, stony, and callous. With eyes devoid of any concern, the admiral said, "Dr. Marsalis decided what side he was on when he chose not to listen to reason. What you have to decide now, Dr. Greene, is whether or not *you* are going to listen to reason."

The threat was clear. Jason had opposed Kenji, and now Jason was gone. Gone forever! Now the admiral was telling Dennis that if he opposed Kenji, he would suffer the same fate.

To the side, Diana and Terri were a mass of tears. Dennis looked over and saw they had lost the will to stand as well. They were seated on a bench near the door, each of them holding on to the other for support.

"My god, what have you done?" was all Dennis could say.

"I did what was necessary to get rid of a man who made himself a terrorist by his actions," said Admiral Brinstock.

Instantly, Dennis was not just angry, but infuriated. With an outrage surprising even himself, Dennis leapt up yelling, "Jason was the best of humans! Better than I will *ever* hope to be, you son of a ...."

"Nothing will help him now, Dr. Greene," interrupted Kenji, "and if you don't play ball, then you will never see this device again."

"What?" shot back Dennis. The renewed fight was still in him, and the soldiers on either side of Dennis were physically restraining him from attacking Kenji with his bare hands.

Admiral Brinstock was attempting a well-played bluff with Dennis. Kenji knew he needed Dennis to operate the portal effectively, but he couldn't let that particular card show in this game of high stakes poker.

Dennis could see right through the attempt at deception, though. He could see Kenji was going to allow him to continue to work on the portal, but that would only happen on Kenji's terms now.

Dennis stopped resisting the soldiers who had been holding his arms, and straightened his body. Closing his eyes and shaking his head in disgust, Dennis couldn't see any other choice. There wasn't anything he could do for his friend now, but maybe this idiot admiral might still use the portal for some good like he did with those bombers in Houston.

Slowly taking in a breath, Dennis relented. "All right, Admiral. You win."

Putting on his grandfather voice once again, Kenji said, "Now, now, Dr. Greene, it won't be that bad! You and I eliminating the terrorists of the world. It's what this thing was meant to do!"

Resuming a cold and icy stance once again, Kenji reached over and unplugged the USB key he had earlier turned. "But this key is going to stay with me. Without it, you won't be able to get any bright," the admiral paused for emphasis, "and *dangerous* ideas."

The message was clear. Either Dennis did exactly as the admiral said, or his life would be snuffed out as Jason's had been.

It was silent in the room now, except for the ambient sounds of some minor machinery and the fluorescent ballasts humming in the high distance. Kenji walked out the door, and the soldiers followed him one by one. The last one to leave the room was Lieutenant Flume, who glanced back at Dennis slumped again on a chair near Jason's console. Looking at him, Dennis sensed a sorrowfulness completely out of sync from the admiral. Larry Flume looked down at the floor as he stepped out the door, closing it behind him. Diana, Terri, and Dennis were the only ones left in the portal room.

Diana rose and walked over to sit next to Dennis. "What do we have to do to get him back?"

"We can't," replied Dennis.

"Sure we can. Just make a new key!" Diana said, with irritation.

"I can't. Because the portal could be used for bad as well as good, Jason and I created our own encryptions for each of these keys. I don't know what Jason's encryption was for his key."

"Then we're going to have to find a way to steal the key from Kenji," said Diana.

Again, Dennis said, "We can't."

"What is this with can't, can't, can't?" said Diana, in an irritated voice.

He replied, in just as irritated a voice, "You don't get it, do you? No matter what we do, we will never be able to re-establish the same bridge to Jason. Even if we did have the key, which we *don't*, we've figured out it is impossible to establish the exact same path in space-time to the exact same spot in the timeline. The math tells us that if we attempted to go back to the same spot and pull him back, it would cause a rip in space-time, most likely causing a cascade effect that would grow as it progressed to our point in the timeline. For all we know, we'd end up creating a chain reaction that would make it a very bad day for everybody in the neighborhood."

Dennis got up from his chair and walked to one of the wooden file cabinets in the room. Uttering a colorful metaphor, he slammed his fist down on it, causing some of the accouterments on top to shift around.

Diana didn't understand completely, but she could see Dennis knew what he was talking about. Her hands dropped to her lap, and she just looked at Terri.

"Then he's gone," said Terri. "He's really gone."

There was no reply.

CHAPTER 53

ᗧᕁᔓ ᔕᒍᒫᔕᗧᙢᔓ ᐸᔔ
ᖴᔓᐼᔕᔐ

EIGHT-YEAR-OLD JANET WALKED ALONG THE street going to school. It was a winter morning, the middle of the school year, and she was looking forward to class today because it was going to be her first chance to play an instrument in her music class; that is, if the teacher was able to make arrangements with some rich guy to buy the instruments for the kids in her class. She walked briskly, not only because she wanted to get to school quickly, but also because this wasn't the best of neighborhoods.

Forty years ago, her mother walked these same streets going to school. Back then, the street cleaners would come by and sweep the trash out of the gutters. That practice had gone by the wayside about ten years ago, so a lot of trash now just piled up. The concrete sidewalks were cracked in a lot of places, and most of the businesses in this area of the city were all boarded up. One business still making it in these times was the liquor store. The owner, Mr. Wong, would always look for Janet to walk by. It's not like they ever talked to each other, but through the dirty window half-covered with lottery advertisements, he would notice her walking past each day, and secretly hoped she would be safe on her journey. Out in front of his store, several men who were out of work gathered for most of the day around a metal barrel that had a fire burning inside for warmth. They would spend their time talking about everything and nothing at all.

Janet looked both ways before she crossed the street in front of Mr. Wong's. She held her pink-tufted vinyl coat together in the front because the zipper hadn't worked since the jacket, which belonged to her sister last year, was handed down to her this year. The men in front of Mr. Wong's looked out for little Janet, too. They didn't really know her, but Lord help anybody who might mess with her.

Across the street and catty-corner to Mr. Wong's liquor store was another storefront that had closed long ago. Next to the closed liquor store on the right were two nondescript storefronts, and to the left, three more. Above the boarded-up windows of the old liquor store hung a bleached-out sign for a beer company which had gone out of business years ago. Over the other storefronts to the left and to the right were light boxes that had long ago lost their plastic sign-fronts. This building was actually quite a large eyesore, and seemed to be one that should be torn down. It seemed obvious nobody cared about it at all.

It *seemed* that way.

Behind the building ran an alley, with a large roll-up door to the back of the building. A 20-year-old car with different colored fenders and dark tinting drove up the alley slowly. As it approached, the roll-up door quickly rose, and the multi-colored car ducked inside a darkened cavern. Just as quickly, the roll-up door closed behind the car, allowing it to park next to several other similar cars.

Once the rough running engine was shut off, the door opened and out stepped a gentleman dressed in an expensive cashmere suit. Shutting the creaking and rusted door to his car, Mr. Armand walked toward a wall where a dusty and long unused door to an elevator was situated. Pressing the black mushroom-head style button next to the elevator door seemed futile, since it appeared this elevator hadn't run for decades. However, this button was only there for show. Mr. Armand waved his left wrist over the worn description panel located just above the button. A transponder inserted just below the skin in his wrist communicated with the sophisticated passive induction circuitry in the panel, and the command was sent to the elevator to come to life.

As the elevator doors opened, the perfect red velvet and walnut paneling inside were completely out of place with the dingy disguises all around. On the back wall of the elevator was a handcrafted, tufted bench where one sat while waiting for the elevator to complete its journey. One would be forgiven for thinking this elevator would rise to floors above, since the half-moon dial with pointer above the dingy door showed the elevator was supposedly at the lowest floor, ground level.

But that was only another part of the subterfuge. Once Mr. Armand entered and took a seat, the elevator doors closed, allowing him to inspect his appearance in the mirrored inside doors. The elevator car then lurched downward and continued its journey for 40 seconds until it came to a halt, and the doors opened into a large room.

The room was filled with comfortable conversation nooks with tables, overstuffed chairs, floor lamps, and crystal chandeliers. On two walls, there were what looked like well-lit windows, part of the well-played deception of this impeccably well-appointed underground lounge. As he entered, a man dressed as a butler approached.

"May I take your coat, sir?" offered the butler.

"No thank you, Ellery," was the reply.

"In that case, may I offer you a drink?" asked the butler.

"Now that sounds like a good idea. Make it my usual," replied Mr. Armand.

"Very good, sir." Ellery left to arrange for the drink, and Mr. Armand strolled over to the fireplace and took a seat. Reaching over to the business journal waiting for him, he checked a few numbers there, including the current trading price of seven companies in which he owned a majority of the stock. By the time he had been gazing at the numbers for a few minutes, Ellery returned with a tumbler filled with ice and a generous portion of 35-year-old Japanese single malt whiskey. Armand had calculated one time that each swallow cost a little over $580. As he savored the ripe fruit and grain subtleties sitting behind strong Japanese mizunara oak notes, he thought to himself that $580 per swallow never tasted better.

Far quicker than he would have preferred, the lounge started to fill with others who were similarly appointed. All were comfortable and well taken care of. Conversations floated around the room, centering around topics that would only interest titans of government and industry such as themselves. There were only five additional arrivals and, like Mr. Armand, they all had their particular vices, ranging from expensive alcohol to the finest of cigars.

All too soon, a light ringing of a bell signaled that the meeting was now to begin. Knowing the predictable timing, Ellery had already been waiting near the double doors across the room from the elevator. Hearing the bell, Ellery turned and reached for the handles to the doors, allowing the men to enter a meeting room with a circular table in the center.

In the center of the table was a three-inch-high, 24-four-inch wide bowl containing stones on fire. The flames lazily rose from the stones, marginally added to the light of the room. On the walls were crystal sconces centered in the middle of red and gold tabards hanging from the ceiling. The design of an eagle with angular edges was embroidered into each tabard. Its wings were outstretched to either side, and its single eye seemed to look straight through you. Below the monochrome black body of the eagle were its talons, holding onto what appeared to be a wreath. Inside the wreath was a cross made of four equal triangular shapes; the number 1939 was in the lower triangular shape.

Each man proceeded to a seat, and once the last man entered, Ellery exited the room, closing the airtight door behind him. The discussions of the room were not for his ears.

The six men stood in front of their chairs and simultaneously recited the pledge of the group:

"I swear by oath that I will ever be loyal to the enlightened, and will serve as a brave and obedient soldier, and risk my life for this oath at any time. I give my will, my heart, and my soul to the enlightened ones. They are my guide for all that I do. If the enlightened say I live, then I live. If the enlightened say I die, then I die. We are the enlightened ones. We are the illuminated."

They all took their seats, conscious of the one chair that would not be filled today. One of the members began to speak.

"Welcome, my brothers, to the monthly meeting of this most sacred bastion of civilization. May we all guide the world around us for the betterment of mankind, and may we all have the bravery to make hard choices for the good of our organization."

All spoke up and replied in unison, "Amen."

"Brothers, today we have much to discuss. As you all know, Brother Quinn O'Cassidy was killed after successfully carrying out Phase One of Project Watermark in Houston, Texas, but before he could carry out Phase Two in Las Vegas, Nevada. Our program of destabilization leading to a profitable domestic war on terrorism has been stalled by this development. Today we not only have the task of finding a replacement for our brother killed in the line of duty, but we also have to decide how to get the project back on track. I now open the discussion to the group and call for comments."

"I have information on these developments," said someone to the left of Mr. Armand, "and, should we decide to act on this information, it may turn out to be extremely advantageous to us. The aforementioned project may be delayed if we choose to pursue this avenue of interest, but in the end, it will increase the efficiency of our operation one hundred-fold."

The apparent chairman of the group said, "Please elaborate, Mr. Smith."

Mr. Smith sat forward. "I have some sources in the military who have brought to light a device recently developed by a couple of physicists in California that is truly groundbreaking. It actually has the ability to act like transporters in science fiction."

"What, like 'Beam Me Up'?" quipped another member with a definitive chortle.

Mr. Smith looked over with an icy stare and simply replied, "Yes, Mr. Jones."

With an abrupt end to the laughter from Mr. Jones, the coordinator intentionally interrupted the stare-down between the two members by asking, "And it actually works?"

Mr. Smith slowly tore his gaze away from Mr. Jones and replied, "Two days ago, they not only successfully transported a man through it, but they also demonstrated it can view scenes from any place on the planet, and can do so at any point in time. They actually sent a man back in time 700 years."

"Are you telling me they invented a time machine?" asked an incredulous, but much more somber, Mr. Jones.

"Yes," answered Mr. Smith, dispassionately.

For a grand total of 20 seconds, the room was quiet; an eon for a room filled with such industrial magnates. Other men would be thinking of how this invention could work for the betterment of mankind, but this was not the case for these sociopaths. No, these men were all independently thinking of how this new development could be used to dominate the world more and more, allowing their respective powers to grow even greater. World domination. That was the goal of the founding member of this modern twist to the ancient society from which this group sourced its name. The illuminated of the ancients started with the laudable goal of enhancing the experience of being human.

But as with many things in this world, the organization that was once pure in its intentions became a group of only seven men, acting as puppeteers pulling the strings of the political, military, and industrial worlds, to ever increase their own power.

"What are your stated goals, Mr. Smith? Do you have a business plan for this project?" asked the chairman.

"At this time, I believe our goal," he answered, strategically adding in the word "our" to his reply, "should be to appropriate the technology so we can use it to our omnipotent advantage. The technology is currently under the control of an Admiral Brinstock who, through his recent actions, has shown himself to be potential candidate material this body might consider as a replacement to Mr. O'Cassidy. I propose we make contact with Admiral Brinstock in the standard manner, and see if he will play ball. If so, we will have an important ally. If not, we will dispose of him in the normal manner and find another avenue. Either way, this machine must come under our control sooner than later."

"Give me a cost-benefit analysis for this, Mr. Smith," asked Mr. Armand.

"The cost would be the number of men needed to secure the device. At this time, I forecast it would take a workforce of 300 mercenary personnel. Based on recent operations, I only see a reduction of about 30% stemming from the incursion into the facility."

"Thirty percent? Do you realize how much it costs to train each of these assets?" objected Mr. Armand.

"Of course I do, Mr. Armand. However, consider the benefits portion of this proposal. Imagine using the device to transfer a bomb to a location only seconds before the explosion. The introduction of a sense of unpredictability can be quite useful to bend others to our way of thinking.

"Also, consider that we don't actually need to transport anything," Mr. Smith added. "We could just use the device to perform recon on any person at any time. This would allow us to be truly omnipotent in an unprecedented manner."

The nodding heads of each member present indicated the point had been made.

Seemingly to make amends for his earlier outburst, Mr. Jones then said, "I move we authorize Mr. Smith to contact Admiral Brinstock to see if he will play ball."

Another attendee spoke up. "I second."

The chairman said, "All in favor say 'Aye.'" All did.

"With no dissenting votes," the chairman continued, "the motion has been carried. Mr. Smith, you are authorized to contact Admiral Brinstock for purposes of recruitment. As far as his membership on this board, we will evaluate his viability after contact has been made."

"Now, on to other business. We have a report on the progress of the project in the Ukraine."

CHAPTER 54

IT WAS SUNDAY MORNING, AND Mikki had invited Karen from work to stay the night with her and little Jace while Jason was out of town on business. He was due home Sunday evening, so in the meantime Mikki decided to go shopping in Modesto. She was planning on buying something special to wear for her husband that evening. Since it was spring break, Mikki had arranged for Jace to spend the night at a friend's house so she and her husband could have the house to themselves.

Mikki had risen from bed earlier and, while Karen slept in in the guest bedroom, she cleaned up the kitchen and got the coffee going before starting the bacon frying. The smell of bacon was often better than an alarm for Jace; sure enough, he appeared at the kitchen table, bleary-eyed and not much of a conversationalist. Two smiling faces looked back at Mikki, and a very grateful Karen accepted a hot cup of coffee while Jason sipped his orange juice.

"Mmmmm! You know," said Karen, while savoring her coffee, "I used to hate this stuff. I would tell people coffee was cruel and unusual punishment, and coffee ice cream was a terrible use for perfectly good vanilla ice cream."

Laughing, Mikki responded, "Boy, that sure doesn't fit the Karen I know."

"Well, the Karen you know had to start getting up in the morning and going to work," she replied, with a slight chuckle in her voice. "It was a matter of economics really. Either I start drinking cups of ambition so I would be able to function well enough in the morning to get to work, or starting looking into multi-level cardboard box homes."

Mikki suddenly had a mental image of Karen living out of a cardboard box and started laughing so hard she had to put down the spatula she was holding. Jace didn't quite understand the joke, but he sat quietly until the laughing died down, then said, "I don't like coffee. I think it tastes like farts."

This, of course, opened up a whole new round of laughing, and since Jace understood the subject matter of this particular joke, he was laughing right with them.

"Ohhhh boy," said Mikki, wiping the tears from her eyes. "I don't think I've laughed that hard in a few years. I'm just glad I'm not wearing mascara yet!"

There was a knock at the door. Mikki went to put down her spatula once again, but Karen said, "Stay. I'll go see who it is."

"Thanks, love. I'm not sure how I look after the Karen and Jace comedy show."

As she disappeared around the corner heading to the front door, Karen said, "Oh, just you wait. I'm just getting started."

Mikki chuckled a little and continued frying the bacon on the griddle, enjoying the light rock coming through the radio playing in the background. She heard a noise behind her and said, "Who was it, Karen?"

"Mikki ..." was all she heard.

She turned around and looked at Karen. Instead of the light and smiling face of her friend, the face looking back at her was stricken and filled with worry. This instantly concerned Mikki. "Who was it?"

"Mikki, you're needed at the door," was all Karen could say.

In the following days, there were those who asked what happened next; quite honestly, Mikki couldn't answer. She had no recollection of the events of that day other than knowing she was told Jason was dead. Mikki was thankful for Karen being there because she's not sure she could have been responsible enough to care for herself, let alone Jace.

According to Karen, Mikki went to the door and met two men who were officers of the Navy. Actually one was an officer, and the other was a chaplain. After learning they were talking to Jason's wife, they explained he had been working on a very classified project for the government. While working on the project, an explosion happened and Jason was caught in it. Explaining that his death must have been instantaneous, they regretted to inform her there wasn't even a body they could return to her.

When they told her the bulk of the message, Mikki slumped to the ground. Jace instantly ran to her side calling "Mommy!" and crying himself. Stepping through the door, the two men went to either side of Mikki and helped her to her feet, then guided her to the dark gray couch near the front door. Karen moved the pillows so Mikki could sit, then remained glued to her side, helping prop her up as much as possible.

The tears streaked down Mikki's face so much she could barely see. Karen told Jace to get some napkins, then realizing he was equally disabled at the loss of his father, she asked the chaplain to get some from the table.

"Do you want me to shut off the stove?" asked the chaplain when he neared the kitchen.

"Yes please," replied Karen. Mikki didn't even hear the question. All she could hear was what sounded like rushing water in her ears.

The one thing Mikki managed to ask through the sobs was, "How could this have happened?"

"Mrs. Marsalis," said the officer, "I'm sure you know the projects your husband worked on were top secret. He was working on things even I haven't been told about since they are way above my pay grade. All I can tell you is what I've been told; the project he was working on went catastrophically wrong, and it exploded when he was right next to it. I was also told his efforts saved the lives of a lot of people before he perished."

There was a pause, then the officer said, "Ma'am?"

Mikki, who had been staring at the floor, slowly looked up at the officer. "Mam, your husband is a hero. There is no greater sacrifice a man can make than to give his life to save others. I stand in respect of a hero of our country."

Mikki didn't have any words. Being willing to sacrifice his life to save his fellow man was definitely the kind of thing Jason would do, but what was she going to do now? Jason was her life. He wasn't just her other half. He was her everything. Even on the few occasions when she was cross with him, he still occupied a place in her heart no other man, no other person, occupied. Half of every heartbeat in her chest beat because of him. Every move she made, every breath she took, every plan she made for the future was based on living the rest of her life with her soulmate. She had met Jason when they were in elementary school. It was always understood that she would spend the rest of her life with this boy. This man.

The officer felt helpless as he sat in front of Mikki and Jace. Karen wasn't spared from the tears either, knowing her close friend was in exquisite anguish. She did her best to prop up her friend, but felt so impotent in her efforts. She was trying to think of anything she could say to help Mikki feel better, but she had nothing. There wasn't anything that could be said.

After a few moments of silence, the officer spoke up again. "Ma'am, there's something I've been asked to give to you." Reaching into a satchel he had been carrying, the officer produced an eight-inch by five-inch flat case bearing the presidential seal.

"I have been asked by none other than President Michaelson to give this to you. It is the presidential medal of freedom. I'm not sure of the circumstances surrounding it, but I can only assume the president wanted to award this to Jason for the bravery he showed in saving so many lives." Then turning to little Jace, who was sitting there like a fawn in the headlights, the officer said, "Your father is a hero, son, and this medal is something awarded to him by the president himself. Few people get this medal, so you should be incredibly proud of him and what he's done."

Mikki held out her shaking hands, softly grasped the case, and took it from the officer. Placing it in her lap, she opened it and gazed at the blue ribbon suspending the medal. The white star with thirteen stars on a blue center background was impressive, but it did nothing for her. Five minutes ago she had a husband, in her mind at least, and now he was gone. There wasn't even a body to bury.

The man who came with the officer spoke up, saying, "Ma'am, you have the deepest sympathy of the President of the United States. I am told he was a splendid man and had outstanding character, and certainly the circumstances surrounding his passing speak to that. May I ask if you have someone who can help you from a spiritual standpoint, Mrs. Marsalis?"

Not looking up, Mikki replied, "Yes. Yes, I do. Thank you."

"Good," said the chaplain. Glancing over to the officer, the chaplain stood, causing the officer to stand as well.

After Mikki stood as well, the officer said, "Mrs. Marsalis, what I said earlier about there being no greater sacrifice than to give your life in the saving of others, I meant that." Sraightening his back, the officer snapped his best salute saying, "Please allow me to salute the wife and son of one of our country's bravest men." Standing there, he maintained his salute until Mikki said, "Thank you, officer."

Before they left, the chaplain handed Karen a packet of standard information for the proper handling of arrangements, not that any mortuary arrangements would be needed in this case. It was a sealed envelope, and was far too much for Mikki to deal with at the moment. As the two men left and were walking away, the officer said how much he hated this duty but, at the same time, he understood the honor to himself in honoring the families of the respected dead of this country. The chaplain agreed on both counts.

Mikki clutched the box with the medal to her chest and seemed to aimlessly wander away from the door. As she walked, Karen continued standing nearby in case she was needed. Eventually, Mikki found herself at Jason's desk in his office and, sitting in his chair, she once again broke down and cried. Jace was crying again too; Karen sat on the couch in Jason's office, holding the little boy who had just lost his dad. As she sat there, Mikki thanked God that Karen was there. She didn't know what she would have done if she were alone.

After a long time with no words and only tears, Mikki slowly released her hold of the medal case and looked at the seal on the front of it. She contemplated how this medal was basically all she had left of her husband now. She looked around at his desk and at the things Jason placed there only days before. The last thing was a small statue of a Greek goddess called Niobe which, although he couldn't say why, had meaning concerning the work he'd been doing. There were a lot of characters in another language around the base. Mikki thought to herself it was probably Greek.

Looking again at the case with the medal, she propped it against the statue. For now, this was to be a memorial, a shrine to the best husband a woman could ever have. He was the one and only love of her life, and she knew there would be no other. A heartbroken Mikki went to bed and cried herself to sleep.

Karen moved in with her that day. Although Mikki continued to live each day, going through the motions, inside she was dead. Beginning that day, Mikki kept a hand towel near the bed as crying herself to sleep became a nightly ritual.

CHAPTER 55

I AM SITTING ON THE EDGE of a bed in an unfamiliar place. It's a large open room with old wooden floors that tend to creak when you walk across them. In the corner, there is a bed with sheets that have already been rifled through, by carnal activities I can only imagine. But now, now it is me in this very place, with thoughts of the preceding hours.

He had spent the day preening me, utterly intoxicating me with everything from food, to wine, to art. His name is unimportant to me at this moment, but his abiding attention at every turn makes it much more difficult to stop what is obviously going to happen. I watch him as he prepares things around me, making sure everything is in its place. Every time he passes me, he glides his fingers across parts of my exposed skin; my shoulders, the upper part of my back, my arms, even a light stroke of my chin. He proceeds as if they are all his for the taking. I never see his face, but he seems to know me.

Another woman walks in and, amazingly, I don't bat an eye at her presence. She brings a tray of something, but from my point of view, I can't see what is on the platter. They speak softly, as if they had been in on this event from the day's beginning. It is only when she passes me, giving me an assuring look that I am in good hands, do I realize she is part of the seduction. I am the prey, he is the hunter, and she is the willing accomplice, hoping for a meal at his table.

My head reels. Even though my mind says something different, my body wants this. Yes, my body truly, deeply, yearningly wants this. I am almost in a trance now. I know what all this is leading to; it is no stretch of the imagination as to what he desires.

My mind screams at me, saying I need to speak up to remind him that I refuse to be intimate with him, or anyone else for that matter. I so want him to just read my mind on this. But my heart and body, that treacherous duo who betray any good intentions, decide better of it. Without my permission, they decide not to ruin the ambiance.

Oh, why did I allow myself to be here in the first place? I know better!

But then, I look at his muscular back and feel an exhilarating rush, one that can be seen felt in every part of my body. His confidence shows he knows he has me. I silently wish I had myself, but then my betrayers once again rush in and war against my faltering virtue. Without seeing his face, I look at this man as he moves through the room, realizing I know all he feels. It's a familiar yet ancient feeling, as if memories not my own are flashing past my senses, making me aware of centuries of love.

He steps in and out of the room, lighting candles as he goes. All I really wanted was a kiss, perhaps a minor touch, but he intends to go so much further. Like a moth to a lamp, I am drawn to him. I feel myself releasing all of my mind, but more significantly my body, to his control. My skin is on fire, and my body responds to the cravings it knows are eminent. This is going to be so much more than I really wanted, but now it is *all* I want. How did the hours, minutes, and seconds lead to my naivety, my innocent assumption that I could resist the heady aroma of his charm? His demeanor, his approach; he knows every weakness in my soul. With each move of his body through the room, he opens my heart and reads from his script of seduction. I am weak in his presence. I must breathe deep and resist!

As he finishes his preparations, he turns to me, this man of intensity and passionate strength. I had resisted looking at his face; I didn't want him to see my resolve falter, but now there is no other option. I look up into his eyes and his fixed gaze. Only now do I realize this man, this stranger, isn't an unfamiliar one at all. He is none other than my true love, my Jason! Within seconds the fortress of my defenses falls, and I am his with no resistance.

He holds out his hand, and I do the same. Only now do I realize the lace on my negligee has come undone and ....

"Mommy?"

Mommy? His voice; so young, but so familiar. Why would he say that? I tell him I don't understand. I don't ....

"Mommy!"

Only now do I feel the hazy pressure on my body and, as if it was beyond my control, my bloodshot eyes open to see the pure and unscathed face of my son looking at me expectantly.

Blinking away the deep lethargy of sleep, all I can muster is a heavily slurred "Hi."

"I'm hungry, Mommy. Can we have pancakes?"

Smiling at me as if I should see how wonderful that suggestion is, I nod and tell him to go watch some cartoons while I get up.

I look at the ceiling and contemplate how long it has been since I had felt the soothing touch of a man, the soothing touch of *my* man. With a heavy and breathy sigh, I swing my legs around and my feet touch the wooden floor, a floor that creaks when you walk on it. I am reminded of the unrequited lust so unfairly torn from my consciousness.

Once again, the tears arrive.

CHAPTER 56

MIKKI SAT AT A TABLE, twirling the olive in her martini. Staring at the triangular glass, she remembered the first time she drank a martini, and once again her thoughts were drawn to Jason. He was the one who got her to try one the first time, and when she tried it, she crossed her eyes and told him it tasted like a doctor's office. He then told her to order it "dirty," and when she did, it was all over. She loved them from that day forward.

Sitting alone at Karen's wedding, Mikki did her best to keep a smile on her face. Since the day those men came and told her Jason had been killed, Mikki was simply a shell of her former self. Sure, there was a part of her that kept trying to believe it wasn't possible Jason was dead, that there must have been some kind of mistake, but she knew it was just the phantom pains of having such an important part of you cut off. Mikki had religiously avoided anything that would even remotely remind her of love and marriage. Having lost her soul the day Jason died, she couldn't bear being in the company of people who were so happy to have their mate with them. She knew she would be a downer to most parties, so she usually opted to not go; in this case, that wasn't an option. Karen had been absolutely essential to Mikki not losing her mind after Jason died, so she owed it to Karen to be there for her friend on her happy day. Thinking back to the early days after the death notification, Mikki couldn't actually remember any of it. It was a really good thing Karen was there because someone had to look after Jace. Mikki knew she wasn't able to be a fit mother.

Karen and her new husband were talking with a group of people who were all laughing and having a good time. Karen was just stunning in her wedding dress. While the lacy dress was very form-fitting in the middle, it was designed to come up to the neck in the front but was backless. A single strand of diamond-like stones hung down from the neck collar to the small of Karen's back. The dress gracefully flared out as it reached the floor. There were long sleeves which worked well with the lacy vest she had initially worn. Mikki was appreciating how pretty her friend looked when Karen looked over, and the two women locked eyes. The entire evening, really the entire day of her own wedding, Karen kept a hawk-eye on Mikki, making sure Mikki was there for everything that happened. It was Karen's way of keeping tabs on her; that's what made her such a good friend.

Karen had married a man of East Indian heritage, so the outfits of the men and women from her husband's side of the family were stunning. Appreciating all the colors of the outfits and the amazing jewelry the ladies wore was a temporary distraction for Mikki. It gave her the chance to temporarily pay attention to something other than the thousands of pieces of her own heart which had shattered. For a few precious moments, she could actually say she was having a good time. It was only temporary, though. All too quickly, the memories would flood and crash back in.

From across the reception room, Karen smiled at her friend, winked, and blew a kiss at Mikki. Smiling, she blew a kiss back at Karen, though Mikki had a feeling inside like her body was just tired. "That's it," thought Mikki. "I'm just exhausted. What was it Jason used to say? Oh, that's right. 'I've got that deep-down-body-*tired*.'" It made sense, really. Mikki hadn't spent much time sleeping lately since bed represented pain. The spontaneity of their private life together was something she had cherished, and it was something she missed terribly. The dreams she seemed to have nightly didn't help either; Jason played a central role in most of them. It was torturous seeing him in her dreams, then realizing fresh and new every day that he was gone.

She had taken a leave of absence from work since the accident, and in those two months, Mikki had not only relied on Karen being there every step of the way, but she had also hung onto her son as close as possible. Sometimes she would quietly sit in his room and watch Jace sleep as if somehow she needed to know he wasn't going to disappear the same way Jason had.

As the evening wore on, it came time for Karen and her new husband to leave the party and go off on their honeymoon. A big part of Karen felt tremendously guilty for leaving Mikki, but she was astute enough to know any attempt to forestall the honeymoon would meet with Mikki's instant and very strenuous displeasure. It didn't change how she felt, though. Karen almost wished she could take Mikki with her so she could keep an eye on her. Almost.

Going home that night, Mikki picked up Jace from his friend's house and took him out for ice cream. Jace had a hard time with the loss of his father too, but it was difficult for Mikki to tell how good or how bad he was taking it. She had a feeling he was being a little trooper to be strong for his mom; if so, she'd have to start thinking about how to handle that. She knew burying his feelings wouldn't be healthy for the little guy, so maybe some counseling would be a good idea for him. Maybe for her, too.

When they got home that evening, it was the first night Mikki was alone in two months. For a while, she just laid in bed staring at the ceiling; finally she got up, flipped on the TV in the living room, and stared mindlessly at the screen until she eventually nodded off.

Waking with a start, three things immediately came to her consciousness. First, the TV was off. Second, her son was curled up next to her on the couch, asleep with his head in her lap. Third, the reason she had been awakened occurred again; a rather loud and distinct knock was coming from the door. The knocker seemed insistent, and as much as she wanted to ignore it, Mikki carefully moved away from her slumbering son and went to the front door in all her just-woken-up glory.

The man at the door seemed to be a courier, but wasn't the same kind of delivery man you normally see running around the neighborhood. He was from one of those more obscure companies, and had an envelope in his hand.

"I have a delivery for a Mrs. Michaela Marsalis," he said.

"That's me," replied Mikki.

Jutting out the clipboard, he simply said, "Please sign here."

Mikki signed, and the man handed her the typically-sized letter carrier envelope for an overnight company. As she closed the door,

Mikki looked at the envelope, and while she recognized the "to" name and address, the "from" was one she didn't recognize. It had the words "Waldau Vertrauen der Schweiz," which looked like German to Mikki, and below it were the words "Switzerland" and "Air Mail."

In her morning stupor, she thought this was something coming for Jason, so she yawned, put the envelope down on the table near the front door, and returned to her warm place on the couch. Carefully returning her lap to its place underneath Jace's head, Mikki laid there thinking how glad she was that she wasn't totally alone. Jace was a little boy, he was her son, and he was a tangible remnant of her late husband she could still hold on to. As she thought more about Jason, she eagerly returned to her dreams, hoping to see him once again.

Biology being what it is, a couple of hours later Mikki had to get up from the couch to take care of nature. By this time, Jace had also awakened, and was quietly watching cartoons in his room. Passing by, she looked in.

"Good morning, my precious son," greeted Mikki.

Jace turned and smiled. "Good morning, my beautiful mother."

It was apparent Jace was taking on some of the verbal mannerisms of Mikki, which she loved. It was a supreme form of flattery. As she stood there looking at the screen alongside her son, it occurred to her that while this little event wasn't significant in the grand scheme of things, sometimes small things make a big. That little greeting from her son made her realize she was going to be all right after all. Her heart hurt, for sure, but the feelings of the early days—how she just wouldn't be able to go on, how she wished her heart would stop beating—those days were starting to fade into the distance.

By far, Jason was still the only one she ever wanted to have in her life. But Jace's simple little greeting helped her see that not only does life go on, but giving herself permission to be happy, to enjoy something, anything, didn't constitute a betrayal to her dead husband. As she was leaving Jace's room and walking to the bathroom, she realized that although her conscious mind wasn't articulating the thought, her subconscious mind was telling her that she was supposed to be completely miserable. It was as if a part of her heart kept telling her anything less would constitute a message to the world saying she must not have loved Jason as much as she claimed she did.

Once those thoughts rose to the surface, her conscious and reasoning mind dissected the idea and, as she was washing her hands, arrived at the conclusion that this line of reasoning was a complete load of balderdash. Thinking more about it while making breakfast for the two of them, she began contemplating what Jason would probably think, and what he would say about her continued happiness. Once again, the conclusion was clear. Not only did she love Jason, but one thing she knew beyond any shadow of a doubt was that he loved her. He always looked out for the best for her, and if there was one thing she knew, it was that ultimately Jason would want her and Jace to be happy, no matter what.

In a significant way, this whole idea was rather freeing to Mikki. It didn't lessen the pain of being without her right arm, which is the way she felt without Jason, but at least the feeling of being in a prison of misery with no chance of getting out was lessening. She was in a place now where she could give herself permission to enjoy some things.

"Breakfast is ready!" Mikki called out towards the hallway.

"Okay" was the distant response.

Sitting at the table and enjoying breakfast, the two of them began chatting about plans for the day.

"So, my son, what would like to do today?" asked Mikki.

"I don't know. What would you like to do?" replied Jace.

Drawing a comparison between this response from her son and his typical response to the same question before Jason had died, Mikki could see Jace was being the little trooper she had been wondering about last night. He was just trying to be there for his mom at the expense of being a kid. Or maybe it was him needing to be with his one remaining parent.

Knowing that Jace was the kind of kid who didn't need the newest of toys to be happy, who preferred spending time outside, she replied, "I tell you what; why don't we go to the zoo today?"

"*Really?*" was the enthusiastic reply from her son. Jace loved the animals at the zoo; in fact, he occasionally said he wanted to be a zookeeper when he grew up. Perhaps that actually meant he wanted to be a biologist or a veterinarian, but the simple truth was this little boy loved animals.

"Really. We can go as soon as you get dressed and your room is clean."

Not letting any more time go by, Jace shot off his chair and left his half-eaten breakfast with no further thought about it. Mikki's first reaction was to call him back to his plate; instead she just relaxed and watched a very excited 11-year-old run down the hallway to live up to his end of the agreement.

Knowing Jace would be ready at lightning speed, knowing she would have to point out what he missed in cleaning his room, and knowing she would have to send him back to brush his teeth or comb his hair, she smiled and cleared the table. Making her way to the bedroom, she chose her clothes for the day and got dressed. As predicted, she had to send

Jace back a few times to complete the tasks he missed, but soon enough they were out the door and for the first time in months they were actually smiling and enjoying themselves. The day was absolutely perfect. A cool breeze tempered the hot sun, and the sights and smells of the zoo were exactly what Jace was hoping for. Today was extra special because he was able to get in and pet some of the animals, his absolute favorite thing to do.

Around lunchtime, they stopped at a restaurant in the zoo and ate some pizza together, with Jace excitedly talking about the names of the animals he had memorized. He impressed Mikki, not only with all the names he had memorized, but also some interesting facts about each of them. On more than one occasion, Mikki admitted to Jace she hadn't known this or that fact.

After lunch, they returned to the animals, and this time they concentrated on the part of the zoo featuring marine life. Reaching in to touch the different animals like the starfish, Jace was so in his element that Mikki had to work at keeping an eye on her son. Jace was single-minded, like his father. Stab!

Shaking herself away from thoughts that would take her down a dark road, she nestled in right next to Jace and did her own bit of discovery with her son. The day wore on, and the two of them ended up having a really good time. After the zoo, they decided to go see a new animated movie playing at the theater, which made a good day great for both of them. They had each other, and for now, that was enough for both of them.

They returned home tired and ready for bed. Jace went straight to his room, and after tucking him in with a good night kiss, Mikki retreated to the living room to enjoy the fireplace and a glass of Moscato. Noticing a book she had been reading up until two months ago, Mikki decided to crack it open again and continue reading. Ultimately the fire burned out, and the wine glass was empty. Her eyelids began their up and down dance, and clearly it was time for bed.

Getting up from the couch, she made her rounds to make sure the doors were locked and the windows were closed and latched. Checking the front door, she noticed the envelope which had come for Jason that morning, and decided to put it on his desk. Since that fateful day, she hadn't touched the desk at all, so a slight film of dust now showed. In the same way she had refused to enjoy anything up until today, a part of her was treating his desk as a sort of shrine. Placing the envelope on the desk, she glanced at it once again; this time it registered that it wasn't addressed to Jason but was, in fact, addressed to her. Wrinkling her eyebrows for a moment, she picked it up again and looked at the addresses and markings on the front. Turning it over to see if there was anything on the back that would help her to know who it had come from, she pulled the tab to open the large envelope. Dumping the contents onto the desk, four items appeared. First was a cover letter. Second, a sealed envelope labeled "To Mikki." Third, a sealed envelope labeled "To Mikki. Open this second." Finally, a sealed envelope labeled "Open me last."

Now completely awake, Mikki looked at the second envelope and muttered to herself, "What is going on here?" The cover letter was the easiest thing to start reading, so she held it up to the light.

> *Dear Mrs. Marsalis,*
>
> *On the date referenced above, Mr. Jason Marsalis contracted with this office to be the caretaker of an annuity for him. This annuity isn't the type of annuity that results in the payment of money, but is the type of annuity that results in the delivery of valuables and other items we hold in safekeeping in our vaults. As long as the space rent is paid, we keep the items safe for the renter. If the account defaults, then we follow previous arrangements made with the owner of the items to deliver such items to a party of the owner's choosing.*

Mikki looked over at a picture of her and Jason on the desk and thought to herself how even in death, Jason was now reaching out to take care of her. Mikki's eyes started to water. Looking down at the letter, she continued to read.

> *Even though this contract was only taken out three months ago, payments for the annuity have ceased, and our efforts to contact Mr. Marsalis have been unfruitful. Due to this, we are exercising the termination clause of the safekeeping contract with Mr. Marsalis and are herewith delivering the items held in safekeeping.*
>
> *It is our sincere hope that all is well with Mr. Marsalis, but if not we wish to render our sincere condolences.*
>
> *Very Truly Yours,*
>
> *Heinrich Mohr*
> *Account Manager*
> *Waldau Vertrauen der Schweiz*
> *Waldau Trust of Switzerland"*

Looking at the three remaining envelopes, the next logical one to open was "To Mikki." Knowing she would probably need the support, she took a seat on the couch in Jason's office, opened the envelope, and began to read.

To my dearest Mikki,

Whenever I think of you, the only word that comes to mind is "Heartless."

Don't worry. I think of this word because it's me without a heart. So many years ago when we were both still in school, I gave you my heart, and it was on that day I realized the sound of each beat of my heart sounded like your name. Each time we're apart, my love, I realize I don't own my heart anymore. You do. You keep it in a warm spot in your pocket, keeping it safe from harm. No, it isn't you without a heart, it's me. I've been robbed by the most enticing, alluring, fascinating, and beautiful thief in the world.

The problem is that every moment we aren't together, my blood stops moving, my eyesight fails, my hearing fades, and my body goes limp. I have so many memories of our time together, I often reflect on them and wonder: "Was it real? Did my time with her really happen? Was I really that happy? Am I really that happy?"

Mikki, I came to the conclusion a long time ago, that I don't want my heart back. I freely give it to you for safekeeping, hoping you will always have it and that I can come and visit it whenever I want. When I am with you, my mind and body recharge, allowing me to face the new day with vigor. When we are together, the wind blows again, the mountain streams flow again, and the falcon cry pierces the mountain sage again. Your kiss is the vodka in my martini, the beat in my heart, the fun in my roller coaster, and the sigh of the embrace.

Why is it that you can never appreciate the moment until the moment is gone?

If you are reading this letter, I fear that something has gone terribly wrong. I may not be the first to do so, but may I tell you how utterly devastated I am to think you are dealing with the pain of not having me there to hold you. Loving you is the best thing that ever happened to me.

Each night when we went to bed and I would spoon up behind you and tell you this was the best part of the day, I truly meant it. Knowing you now have to go to bed without me is a heartbreaking thought, one that I have to rescue myself from before I get too depressed.

If there is one thing I want you to know, it is that I want you to be happy. I know it is silly to think you should be happy after just losing me like you apparently have. The thing is, life goes on, my love. Hopefully, you still have Jace in your life, and he will continue to be a source of happiness to you for sure, but eventually there will come a time when you will need to have the touch and love of a man in your life. Do not be the kind of widow who stays alone for the rest of her life out some sense of duty to her loved one. As much as I love you, and as much as I relish that you are all mine, it is that same love which makes me wish for you to be happy in the arms of another man should the opportunity arise. Please know that while I am with you, you are mine alone, and I am yours alone. But as Mr. Shakespeare said, should I happen to shuffle off this mortal coil, I wish you love. I wish you happiness.

Please tell my son that I love him more than life itself. When he is older, and when he would understand, you have my permission to show him this letter.

I love you, Mikki. Now and for all eternity. I hope, in some small way, the contents of the other envelope will help you know how much I do love you.

Your husband,

Jason

Needless to say, Mikki was a complete mess by the time she finished the letter. Tears were streaming, her nose was running, and the mascara had morphed Mikki into a rather scary-looking creature. Putting down the letter, she made her way to the bathroom to clean up. Coming back to the office armed with several more tissues, and even a towel if needed, Mikki read the letter from Jason again. Through the tears, it felt strange to Mikki how this letter evoked such heavy emotions; yet at the same time, it felt like he was there in the room talking to her. Reading it a third time, she almost felt like he was holding her in his arms again. It was painful, but it was a good feeling at the same time.

Holding the letter with her hands in her lap, Mikki looked out the windows into the night sky. A crescent moon looked back at her and, for a few minutes, she could hear Jason telling her to feel the moment. She sat with her eyes closed and envisioned her man holding her face with both hands and coming in for a kiss; she could feel his mouth again. To her, he was alive. To her, he never left.

Reaching for the towel to dab away the streaks of tears, she opened her eyes and looked down at her lap. She contemplated reading the letter again, but then her eyes strayed to the couch next to her where the other two envelopes lay. Picking up both of them, she read the outsides.

She opened the "To Mikki. Open this second" envelope and read the note inside.

To my dearest Mikki,

By this time, you have already read my other letter, so you know how much I love you and how much I wish I could be with you.

If you are reading this letter, then something has gone wrong with an experiment I was working on in my office. I can't tell you about the experiment, but what I can tell you is I am suspicious of someone.

I ask you to please seek out a woman by the name of Terri Lindstrom at the address shown below. She doesn't know I have sent you this letter, but she most certainly will know more information than what you have probably been told about me and why I am not with you anymore. Please seek her out using the resources I have included in the last envelope.

Finally, it is absolutely critical that you bring her the remaining sheets I have included in this envelope.

When you do this, Terri will know what to do next.

In closing, my love, please be assured that I love you and regardless of whether we are together or apart, I will always be with you.

Your loving husband,

Jason

Mikki looked at the next few sheets. All that was written on them was more Greek. Finally, she opened the third envelope and looked at the contents.

It was a bank draft for two and a half million dollars, payable to Mikki Marsalis.

CHAPTER 57

KNOCK. KNOCK. KNOCK.
Mikki was dressed in a conservative skirt and blouse and had a bag with her personal belongings slung over her shoulder. Clutched in her arms, held close to her body since they were so precious to her, were the letters Jason had sent to her. She stood on the steps of a modest but well-presented home in Prospect Heights in New York City. The quiet, leafy streets lined with old brownstones were charming, and it certainly would be a place Jace would love to live. Walking to Terri's address, Mikki passed the Prospect Park Zoo, a wonderful dog beach, and a park with what seemed like miles of bike paths. "Hmmm," thought Mikki. "Food for thought."

There wasn't any answer, so Mikki tried again.

Knock. Knock. Knock.

From inside, she heard a voice. "One second!"

After a few moments, the door opened, and a shapely red-haired woman reacted as if she automatically knew who Mikki was and why she was there.

"I'm sorry I'm not interested."

Undeterred, Mikki asked, "Are you Terri?"

Shocked, the woman stopped closing the door. Opening it again, she had a look of quizzical bemusement as to why this person she had never met knew her name.

"Yes. I'm sorry, do I know you?" came Terri's reply.

"Not yet. I am Mikki Marsalis, Jason Marsalis' wife."

It took a total of point five seconds for Terri to fling the door wide open and shoot straight into Mikki's arms.

"Oh, Mikki!"

Terri's reaction caught Mikki completely by surprise. For a few moments, she didn't know what to do with her hands, then decided a return hug would be appropriate.

"Please, Mikki. Please come inside," said Terri.

Mikki stepped through the door into a well-decorated apartment. It looked lived in, and she saw several different ways the apartment had been decorated that she would love to try. In the meantime, she decided to start with an apology.

"I'm sorry, Terri. I know you didn't expect ...."

"No!" said Terri. "I am *so happy* you came! I've wanted so many times to reach out to you, but I knew you didn't know who I was. Honestly, I didn't know what I would say when I came to see you either. Look at me," Terri said with a chuckle. "For someone who didn't know what to say, I seem to be talking a lot!"

Leading Mikki to the couch in the living room, Terri said, "Please, have a seat. Can I get you something to drink? Maybe some water or coffee?"

"Coffee sounds nice. Just a little bit of cream if you have it."

"Of course. I'll be right back" said Terri as she left for the kitchen.

As she was waiting, Mikki looked around the room. The closer she looked, the more details she noticed. It seemed Terri was interested in antiques. Not the kind from a hundred years ago, but more like those of a thousand years ago. Shelves were graced not only with books, but with replicas of ancient artifacts as well. Looking at the far corner of the room, she saw something that made her heart stop. Getting up from her perch on the couch and walking across the room, Mikki picked up a picture displayed in a place of honor on the baby grand piano. It was a picture of Terri, a man she knew Jason had worked with named Dennis, another woman she had met a couple of times named Diana ... and there was Jason.

They were all smiling at the camera, and their arms were around each other's shoulders.

Mikki wondered what all this meant. What kind of life did Jason lead when he was at work? She knew Jason was faithful to her, but what else was happening when he was away? It seemed there was a part of her husband, perhaps an entire life, she had no idea existed. Smiling to herself, she wondered, "Maybe he was a secret agent?"

"We took that picture just before it happened," said a voice right behind her.

Instantly twirling around, Mikki reacted as if she'd been caught with her hand in the cookie jar. "I'm sorry for intruding on your things."

"Don't be," said Terri. Standing in the doorway with two cups of coffee, she added, "Jason was an amazing man. He always talked about you, and how much he was in love with you. Believe me when I tell you, many in this world can only wish they had a man as devoted to them as he was to you, sweetie."

Mikki looked down at the picture in her hands, and for a moment thought she would begin to cry. She was tired of crying so much.

Seeing the emotions welling up in Mikki, Terri said, "Here, let's drink our coffee on the couch. You can bring that with you." Mikki accepted Terri's hospitality and walked back over to the couch. Sitting down and setting the picture on the coffee table, Mikki took the cup of hot coffee and enjoyed a rejuvenating sip.

"I'm curious. How did you know where to find me?" asked Terri.

"Jason gave me your address."

"He gave you my address?" retorted Terri. "How could he have done that?"

Putting down the coffee, Mikki reached into her bag and produced Jason's second letter to her. After reading the letter, it now became clear how Mikki had found Terri, but that still didn't explain why Jason told Mikki to seek out Terri.

"This letter talks about some additional papers," said Terri.

"Oh," responded Mikki. "I almost forgot. Jason wanted me to give you this Greek writing."

Terri accepted the papers which were in an envelope. Opening it, she instantly recognized the letters weren't Greek; they were Galimarian.

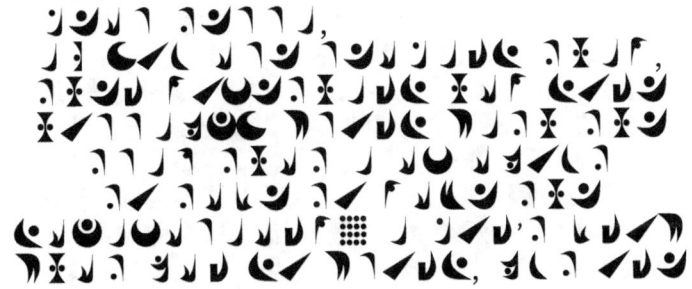

Dear Terri,

If you are reading this, then something has gone horribly wrong with the trip that I am about to take to save the Galimarians. I don't know what can go wrong, but one thing I do know is that I don't trust Admiral Brinstock. He is a loose cannon, and I wouldn't put it past him to do something to get me out of his hair.

If that is what has happened, I ask that you trust me and know that I will figure out a way out of this. In the meantime, I need you to seek out Diana, Lynne, and Dennis and meet with them in my living room in Sonora on the first day of the month.

No doubt, you are sitting there with Mikki right now, so I would appreciate it if you would do me a few favors.

Mikki is incredibly smart. It was actually something she said when we were on a trip to Las Vegas that helped me figure out a breakthrough with the portal.

Tell her everything that happened. Tell her about the portal. Tell her about how we used it to thwart terrorist activities. Tell her about what I really did for a living, and tell her about how I had to go to Galimar of the past to help the Galimarians so that the world wouldn't be destroyed. Tell her about the Admiral, and about how he's the low-down scumbag that he is, and how he needs to be stopped for what he no doubt did to me. Trust her with anything and everything, Terri. She is a smart girl, and she will no doubt be one of your best allies.

Terri, my friend ... in the short amount of time I have known you, you have wormed your way into my heart. Worm your way into Mikki's too. Trust me when I say, she will be a life-long friend that you will never want to let go.

With affection,

Jason

Terri looked up at Mikki and smiled. She knew it always irritated Jason that there was so much of his life Mikki never knew existed. Now, Terri would be the one to tell her all that had happened.

"Girlfriend, we have places to go. But before we do, I have a long story to tell you about the day Jason left us."

Over the next two days, Terri recounted an amazing tale of all that had transpired. Mikki learned about the island of New Galimar. She learned about the Midway Magnetic Particle Accelerator, the XYZT portal, and the impending volcanic doom in Yellowstone. She learned how Jason and Dennis had single-handedly saved the lives of not only the peaceful alien race on New Galimar, but also the lives of every man, woman, and child on earth.

Terri could see that Mikki was having a hard time accepting the truth of the tale she was weaving, so finally she said, "Will you excuse me for a moment?"

"Of course," said Mikki. Terri noticed that, while being nice, Mikki had a look about her that showed she was waiting for the cameras to jump out and declare she was on a TV gag show. Smiling, Terri had an idea how to show Mikki this was all real, but she had to run it by Quorlynn first in the other room.

Once she returned to the living room and to the same couch where Mikki was seated, Terri said, "Mikki, I can see you are having a hard time believing all this."

Mikki looked down at the carpet, knowing she had just been read like a book. she started to speak. "Well, I ...."

Interrupting her, Terri said, "I don't blame you. I know all I've been telling you is a story that somewhat stretches credibility."

Mikki rolled her wide eyes to show she agreed.

"I want you to do me a simple favor," continued Terri.

"What do you want me to do?"

"It's simple," replied Terri. "Just put on this amulet."

Mikki put it on and, as Terri watched, Mikki's eyes closed and the most serene expression came over her face. Reliving her own first contact with Quorlynn, she knew all that was happening to Mikki right then, and felt privileged to be part of Mikki's first experience with this wondrous people whom Terri now identified with and loved.

In the outside world, Mikki was only gone with Quorlynn for about 10 minutes, but the sensation of time passing in-world was far longer from her perspective. When Mikki eventually opened her eyes again, she immediately began sputtering an apology for being gone so long, but Terri shushed her and explained how long she was actually gone.

It was then the two women shared a moment of silent communication, doing nothing more than staring in each other's eyes. Eventually, Mikki's jaw went slack, and she slowly shook her head back and forth. "I ...."

"You don't have to say anything," Terri said, already knowing what Mikki was feeling. "I know it was a lot to take in, but you had to see how beautiful this race of people is, and for whom Jason risked his life."

A small window of silence passed between them, then Terri's eyes took on a look of sorrow. She recounted the sad tale of what Admiral Brinstock did to Mikki's husband, and how Jason was lost forever when Kenji turned off the portal. When she heard this, Mikki felt like her legs had been knocked out from under her. She understood the amazing things she had learned about her husband needed to stay secret but this; this was nothing short of murder! And what made it worse was the admiral had the audacity to lie not only to Mikki, but no doubt to anybody else who was in the know about the portal.

Mikki felt violated. This admiral, this animal, had taken something precious from Mikki and then saw to it she was lied to. Not only did

Mikki feel violated, but the more she thought about it, she felt the most extreme form of red rage she had ever experienced.

Needless to say, an earthquake was tearing through Mikki's world. A lesser woman may have crumbled, but not Mikki. She was instantly able to see the bigger picture, and what a picture it was. Yes, there were aliens. Yes, there was a time travel portal, invented by her own husband, no less. And yes, her husband was a sort of secret agent, but more importantly, he was a hero. A hero to everyone in the world. Then, in the face of all this heroism, this monster kills the very one who saved his own butt!

The two women immediately made the necessary arrangements for their trip to Sonora. It wasn't until the flight back that Terri explained to Mikki the money Jason left was the reward money the president himself had given to Jason for having provided information on the apprehension and elimination of a dangerous terrorist named Quinn O'Cassidy. Mikki remembered hearing about it in the news, and how that all but ensured the reelection of the currently sitting president. Learning how pivotal a role her own husband played in that operation made Mikki proud beyond words. To think that the man she went to sleep next to was a true hero; it was almost too much to imagine.

Soon enough, the day came on the first of the month when Terri, Mikki, Dennis, Diana, and Lynne were all seated in Jason's office at home. Mikki had paid for all travel arrangements so the group could be there. After coffee had been served, she was the first one to talk.

"I want to thank all of you for coming to my home. It's only recently I have learned about the real job my husband had at Midway Magnetic, and the role he played in the events leading to the world being a safer place. I'm not sure what the next step is, but I do know he wanted us to seek out each other. I've had the opportunity to become friends with Terri now and, as Jason predicted, she and I are the best of friends. As far as the rest of you, I really look forward to getting to know you all, and getting to know the real kind of person my husband was when he was away from me."

"One thing I can tell you for sure," said Dennis, "is I was always a little jealous of Jason. He seemed to have the perfect balance of being dedicated to his job, yet so amazingly dedicated to you and his son. In fact, I think it was that dedication which made Kenji do what he did."

Diana nodded her head. "I remember when I first started as the administrator of the facility. I hadn't had a chance to read the personnel files of all the people who worked directly for me, but I remember seeing Jason the first time and how taken I was with him. At the time, I started considering what the consequences of a romantic relationship with him would be. Fortunately, I hadn't made a complete fool of myself by making comments to him before I read he was married. I am so glad I didn't say anything," said Diana, laughing. Mikki joined in the laughter as well.

"What I don't get," said Lynne, "is why the admiral hated Jason so much. I mean, my god! The guy literally saved the whole world. How could you hate a guy like that?!"

"It's because he couldn't control him," replied Diana. Dennis nodded. "There was more than one occasion when the admiral told him to be present for a meeting, and Jason told him what he could go do with himself. I remember one of the last times was something having to do with taking a trip out of town for his anniversary. I think he said he was going to Las Vegas."

"Oh, my god! He put himself at risk so he could go on that trip?" asked Mikki.

"Not exactly," replied Dennis. "Yes, the admiral called and tried to strong-arm him into canceling that trip, but Jason told him you were a lot more important than he was. That really got under his skin. But it was actually something you said on that trip which led to him making a breakthrough with the time travel portal."

"*Me?!* What could I have said that would help him figure out something with time travel?"

"It was when he was talking about something being in two places at the same time," replied Dennis. "You asked him if it was possible for something to be in two times at the same place. Asking that question unlocked everything in his brain and, while he loved being with you in Vegas, he couldn't wait to get back to the office and tell me what you had said and what he thought it all meant."

"I remember that conversation!" said Mikki. "Now it's starting to make sense. When I said that, he looked like he had just lived through an earthquake. I didn't know what he was thinking, and I had been conditioned to not ask questions, so I didn't. I do remember thinking at the time his reaction was weird."

"Not half as weird as me seeing my young parents back in the sixties and seventies the first time. I even saw myself when I was a kid. It hit me so hard I passed out!" said Dennis, laughed as he remembered the incident.

There was a lull in the conversation, so Mikki asked the question on everyone's mind. "So, what now? Do we just let this guy get away with it? I mean, he basically killed my husband. Can he really get away with it?"

Knock. Knock. Knock.

Mikki cracked open the door to the office and yelled for Jace to see who it was. He was due to go somewhere with one of his friends, so it was probably the parents picking him up. "Make sure to tell me if you are going anywhere."

"I will, Mom," yelled Jace, as he walked toward the living room.

"The problem is the admiral has Jason's key to the portal. Maybe if we had his key we would be able to do something," responded Dennis as Mikki closed the door to the office again.

This seemed to cast a pall over the assembly. Everyone stared at their cups of coffee. After Mikki repositioned her lace shawl over her shoulders and arms, she added, "I just have this feeling like we're missing something here. He sent me those letters, he said he wanted us all to meet together, but he didn't tell us what to talk about. He must have had a plan in mind."

"I do, actually."

Five heads instantly spun towards the door. Standing there, holding his son in his arms, was Jason.

CHAPTER 58

ꓶꚔꙷ ꓶ⚈ꓵꓩ

WHEN JASON WALKED THROUGH THE door to his office and said those first words, there was a veritable implosion surrounding him. He was instantly fenced in by laughing, giggling, and joyous elation on the part of all there. Plied with an instant barrage of questions about where he'd been and how he made it home, their questions went unanswered. Only after being consistently ignored did they realize this revelry lacked the participation of both Jason and Mikki, the latter of whom stayed rooted to her place on the couch. Everyone in the room had been so amazed to be laying eyes on Jason, they didn't really notice something profound was happening right before their eyes. One by one, each in the room looked back and forth at the two of them, and only then did they see Jason and Mikki's eyes locked onto each other. Like the biblical parting of the Red Sea, the group opened up an unobstructed path between the two lovers. Sliding his son off of his hip while still not taking his eyes off Mikki, Jason slowly walked forward to her.

Mikki was in shock, or at least she looked that way. Her eyes couldn't get any bigger, and she was acutely aware she was running on the ragged edge of passing out. This was like all those dreams of Jason, and a part of her was unable to decide if this was real, or if this was another slumbering façade of reality. This dream was so real, much more so than any of the others.

Jason strode to his one true love, knelt down at her feet, and reached out his hand. Mikki's eyes snapped to his hand reaching toward her and, with trembling fingers, she lifted her hand toward his. The lace on her arm fell to the side, which made her reach falter. She was waiting for the dream to end as it had every time before.

But it didn't end. Seeing her losing her strength, Jason reached further and took hold of Mikki's hand.

First touch.

It was as if the dams of emotion and the very floodgates of happiness broke open. The touch was the key to a lock Mikki thought would never be opened again. She had resigned herself to being alone for the rest of her life, even though Jason had said not to in his letter. She knew there was no other man for her, and now that man had been resurrected. He was touching her fingers, and the touch was electrifying.

With that touch, Mikki crumbled into his arms and wept louder than she ever had in her life. Through the tears, she once again breathed in the heady aroma which was unique and all his own. Reaching around his body with a grip ensuring he would never to leave her side again, her spirit flooded forth with all that had been ignored. As she lay her head on his shoulder, baptizing his body with the wetness of her howling cries, his hand slid up her back and held tight the nape of her neck while he crushed his own eyes closed. Both her body and his convulsed, and a deluge of ache began rinsing away from their spirits, showering itself onto each in the form of unabated liberation. The crushing weight of solitude was now over, and the gospel of Marsalis could once again be preached by any who had the privilege to be its witness. As the two whispered invocations of love to each other, the rest of the group stood in awe at the tender emotions they were privileged to behold.

Jason and Mikki. Man and woman. One.

Each privileged witness knew they were spectators to a devotion more profound, more intense, more overwhelming than any they had ever seen before. None who watched this pure expression of love and passion were spared from the welling up of tears. Lynne reached out to a weeping Dennis and hung onto his frame for support, whereas Terri and Diana grasped each other for reinforcement as they collapsed onto the couch behind them.

For unmeasured time, all in the room sat quietly at this shrine of pure love. None wanted to add their brushstrokes to this perfect painting of affection and ardor. Finally, Jason spoke. "I'm so sorry you were put through this, my love." His voice showed more tender affection than one could imagine.

Still unable to form words, Mikki continued to weep. Not just his words, but the simple sound of his voice was something she craved. "I can't even fathom the depths you were driven to when I didn't come home," said Jason.

By this time, Lynne had left and come back with a towel from the kitchen. Reluctantly, Mikki released her hold on Jason and gratefully accepted the offering.

"I must look like a mess!" said Mikki, wiping the tears and remnants of long-lost makeup from her red and swollen eyes.

With an ethereal look, never taking his eyes off Mikki, Jason said, "You are the most beautiful woman I've ever seen in my lifetime. Trust me when I say, I've lived long enough to know."

Mikki's hands, which had been busy wiping her face, dropped away and she shot straight into the arms of her husband. Her real and alive husband! Once again, all in the room were equally affected. It was fortunate Lynne had brought towels and napkins for all.

As Jason was holding his wife in his arms, he felt something on his back; turning, he saw his son standing next to him. Scooping him up, the three embraced. With his eyes closed, Jace said, "I've missed you, Daddy."

"I've missed you too, little man!" said Jason.

With closed eyes, the boy held his father and mother harder. They were luxuriating in the knowledge that once again, they were whole. They were complete.

Eventually, the coarse intrusion of spoken word burbled forth from the room. Dennis simply said one powerful word: "How!?"

Reluctantly pulling himself away from his family, Jason took a corner of the towel in his wife's hands and turned to the group while wiping his eyes. Looking at them, he saw four people holding onto each other for dear life. Knowing that they were deeply affected by the reunion, Jason began to speak.

"What is the last thing you saw when I left?" asked Jason.

"We saw you talking with the people in the park," said Dennis. "Terri interpreted for us what you and the others were saying, and then you all left our viewpoint. I was going to reset the portal to watch where you were going, but that's when it happened."

"When what happened?" asked Jason.

"Oh my god! You don't know, do you?" blurted Diana. "Of course you don't; you couldn't!"

Jason stared blankly at the group until Dennis began to speak. "It was Kenji, pal. That poor excuse for a road apple shut off the portal and marooned you back there."

"Yeah," added Mikki, without looking up. "Then he sent two officers to tell me you had died in an explosion, and you did it saving some other people."

"That son of a ...." Then shaking his head, Dennis added, "I knew he was low, but that's, that's just ...."

"Sociopathic," said Diana.

"Exactly," confirmed Dennis. Furrowing his brow, he asked, "Wait a minute. How did you get back?"

"Kenji," said Jason as he sat back on the couch, looking up at the ceiling and shaking his head. With noticeable contempt in his voice, he said, "I knew he couldn't be trusted."

"That's for sure," agreed Dennis. "But how *did* you get back here, bud? I mean, you and I both figured out that once the bridge was severed, there was no way to perfectly re-establish it. How did you do it?"

"That's a long story, my friend," said Jason, rolling his eyes. When he could see that everyone was more than eager to hear the story in every detail, Jason saw it was important to relate all that happened. He took a cleansing breath and, as he sat next to Mikki, began to speak.

"When you saw us leave the park, we went to the building where the council chambers of the Grand Council of New Galimar are located." Jason sat there reflecting on the memories, and a small smile played itself across his lips. "I have to tell you, these people won me over in about five seconds flat. I have never identified with anybody like I have with them; I felt completely at home, and completely at peace every moment I was with them. As I was waiting to speak with the council, I sat there watching the families enjoying time with each other and with other families. It was amazing. In due course, it was time to speak in front of the council, so Lord N'Zollivant called me in."

"Lord?" asked Diana.

"It's a term of respect they use in referring to each other, but it's usually reserved for those who are more mature and well-respected," explained Terri.

Nodding, Jason added, "I was waiting in the wings before I went up to the podium, and that's when he told the council a person was there to talk to them and that he was human. I could actually hear a gasp from the audience, and there was a lot of murmuring among them" laughed Jason. "But by the time I approached the podium, the room was quiet as a morgue. I'm pretty sure nobody there was expecting me to let out much more than sniffs and grunts."

"Why?" asked Mikki. It was obvious she was still a little shaken up from having Jason next to her. She maintained a death grip on his hand, and her eyes never left him.

"When they first came here thousands of years ago, they encountered a very barbaric set of humans. They felt it would be a very long time before humans would ever become anything else, so my coming to them and being able to understand and comprehend their language was astounding to them."

Nodding, Dennis added, "I gotta say, pal, you sounded like you had a pretty good handle on the language from what we heard in the park. You and languages are pretty amazing."

Jason glanced over at Terri, who had a look of concern. Jason knew Terri didn't want to share how the amulet helped him, so he simply said, "I had a good teacher." Terri smiled in relief. The others interpreted it simply as the giving and receiving of a compliment.

"Anyway, I explained why I was there, and how I got there. They were understandably impressed to learn I was not only human, but also a time traveler in a time machine Dennis and I had built. I think the biggest thing that won them over was I knew so much about them and their city, including the existence of the TSM."

"What's a T-S-M?" asked Mikki.

"It stands for the Tectonic Stabilization Machine. It's the device I fixed to stabilize the earth's core and avert the eruption at Yellowstone," replied Jason.

"You fixed? What do you mean *you* fixed?" exclaimed Dennis. "That thing needed Galimarian DNA and only Galimarian DNA."

"Correct. That's what we were told by the TSM caretaker Khaeleus. But when I discovered the portal window was gone for some unknown reason and I was marooned, they actually proposed a solution I hadn't thought of before. Part of it involved the council authorizing an engineer to train me on what I needed to do to fix the machine, and they made an exception in the security systems and allowed my DNA to have access to the systems."

"But how did you get back from the 1400s to now without a time machine?" asked Diana.

"That's the other part of their solution. My dear, you are looking at the only living 700-year-old man," replied Jason.

"What?!" was the unified response from everybody in the room.

"Here's the deal," said Jason. "When I told the council why I was there and what was going to happen when Jose landed on the island, I suggested they use their suspended animation technology to put themselves in stasis for the duration until it was safe for them to be awake again. We had a little bit of a back-and-forth discussion on the whole grandfather paradox thing, but in the end, they saw that any interference whatsoever in the events of the earth between then and now would have dire consequences. They needed to act like they were dead all these years, so they told me about an undersea sanctuary where they could relocate their entire population, and where they could sleep in suspended animation until I woke them up."

"Okay, let me get this straight. They didn't fix the TSM, you did. Why didn't they just fix it when they were awakened?" asked Diana.

""After explaining to them the concerns Dennis and I had about grandfather paradoxes, they suggested I be the one to fix the machine. Only after ensuring all was well, would I raise them back from suspended animation."

"But that doesn't explain how you got back here," Terri said.

"That's the easy part," said Jason. "They set up a suspended animation chamber in a secret place for me too, but there was a time lock on my chamber which caused me to revive at the very moment I went through the portal."

"You've been alive this whole time?" asked Mikki, showing a bit of questioning ire.

"Sweetheart, I had no idea you were told I died. I was hoping you were told I was away for an extended secret mission or something. After I revived and restored the TSM to working order, I saw there was a lot of military presence on the island, so I had to covertly find a way off, which wasn't easy. Something told me I needed to lay low, and that was confirmed one day when I was eavesdropping on a conversation between two soldiers. They were wondering how the admiral was going to 'divvy up duties on the island when he takes it over completely.' Then they said there was some secret technology in California the admiral was going to take over and relocate to the island, and they were hoping to get in on that detail."

Looking Mikki straight in the eyes, he said, "I had no idea Kenji was so low that he would make you think I had been killed. I'm so sorry."

Mikki softened the edges which had formed on her face earlier. "I know. You're not the one I should be mad at." She reached up and stroked Jason's cheek, causing him to smile once again.

"But something doesn't add up here," said Terri. "I saw Khreelon's bones in his apartment."

Jason smiled. "You saw *fake* bones."

"*Fake*?!" said Terri.

"Yep. I knew you had seen them just as I had, so I told them we needed to fake the death of all the Galimarians. We came up with a plan where everybody would plant a fake set of bones in each of their homes, to make you think they had all died."

"But why? Why would you create something so awful?!" asked Terri.

"Because if they hadn't," Mikki answered, "the course of events leading to Jason going back wouldn't have happened."

Knowing his very intelligent wife was really catching on, Jason replied, "Exactly. If you hadn't thought they all died, you wouldn't have considered why they died; you wouldn't have been presented with the problem of needing to fix the TSM with Galimarian DNA; you wouldn't have gotten the military involved; and you wouldn't have been introduced to me. It had to happen this way, with no interruptions."

There was a general consensus, evidenced by the nodding of several heads. Terri then asked, "So they're all alive? Where?"

"They have an ocean floor habitat and are all safely sleeping, waiting for me to wake them up."

"What's the plan now?" asked Dennis. "When you came in here, you said you had a plan."

"I've had a lot of time to think about what happened. I didn't know why the portal window was gone, but I did know whatever happened probably wasn't something I would like and it probably had something to do with Kenji. I was thinking we could use the portal to dial up the scene of the portal room at the time I went back, get video evidence of what happened, then send that video to the president."

"No-can-do, amigo," replied Dennis. "Your security key is in the clutches of Admiral 'Estupido.' You and I both know we can't change the security until we are inside the system, unless we take the dang thing apart which would take a week, and I don't think he's going to let us dismantle his new toy."

Jason smiled. Getting up from his chair he walked over to his desk and picked up the small statue of Niobe. "Did I ever tell you why this statue was so important to me?" asked Jason, looking at Mikki.

"You just said it was something having to do with …." Mikki froze, looking at the statue for the first time since she'd put the amulet on in Terri's home. Since she now had knowledge of the Galimarian language, she instantly recognized the writing along the bottom of the statue, and what it said.

Mikki smiled. "Be careful. Don't drop it."

Jason's eyebrows raised in surprise, then he smiled. As the statue slipped from his fingers, he casually said, "Oops."

The small plaster statue of the namesake of the primary metal used in the supercollider fell to the floor, shattering into several large pieces of mortar. Tumbling out from the middle of the heap was a small plastic container, within which was a second USB key.

"Well, I'll be a son of a gun," said Dennis.

CHAPTER 59

DENNIS WENT TO WORK AS usual the next morning. The atmosphere around the particle accelerator installation was somewhat somber since the reported "explosion" a couple of months ago. On that day, the admiral made it painfully clear that if Diana, Terri, or Dennis said anything about what really happened, they would be treated to a beautiful suite at Hotel Guantanamo. He even threatened bad things would happen to their respective families. As much as they wanted to tell Mikki about what really happened, they had kept their mouths shut.

What ensured dour and emotionally overcast days lately was the admiral, the killer of Jason Marsalis in the eyes of Dennis, had actually set up an office at the Midway facility. As Dennis was traveling down the elevator to the underground level where his and Diana's offices were, he thought about how the whole "Guantanamo" thing never entered his mind the previous day. He was sure glad he had shown up at Jason and Mikki's home yesterday, and more than glad he got his buddy back. As he rode the elevator down to his office level, Dennis kept his hands in his pockets, and in the palm of each hand was a USB security key.

Since the day of the "explosion," Jose had been assigned to work with Dennis. Jose wasn't an engineer, but it was remarkable how intelligent he turned out to be. This was due to the capabilities afforded to individuals who wear an amulet, and since he had worn one when he first landed on the island, he had clarity of thought far above those around him. He ended up being Dennis' lab assistant since Dennis had a hunch it would come in handy to keep him near.

Sure enough, today was going to be Jose's chance to come in handy. When he arrived at his office, Dennis saw Jose was already there and ready to start work.

Dennis closed the door and came over to sit in a chair near Jose. "Hey Joe, how you been?"

"I am well, Dennis. And you?"

"I'm good. Great, actually." Lowering his voice, Dennis asked, "Am I right in discerning you aren't a big fan of the admiral?"

"You would be correct in that assumption. What he did to Mr. Marsalis was unethical, immoral, and depraved. I have nothing but disgust for him."

"I'm really glad you said that, Jose," said Dennis.

"Why would this be?" asked Jose.

Lowering his voice to nothing but a whisper, Dennis responded, "Because, my friend, Jason is alive and he is sitting in his living room as we speak."

Jose's eyes grew wide, and his mouth hung wide open.

Nodding, Dennis added, "That's right, he's back, but he wants to get some evidence for what Kenji did to him. Would you be willing to create a diversion to keep Kenji out of the portal room while I carry out the plan?"

Up to this point, Jose had been leaning forward to hear Dennis as he whispered. Jose now sat back in his chair and stared at Dennis for several moments. Glancing to some papers he had stacked on his desk in Dennis' office, Jose said in normal volume, "Dr. Greene, I have these estimates on the systems tests you scheduled for next week, but I think I need to personally go over this schedule with the admiral. Would you agree?"

Dennis smiled, stood up, and walked back over to his desk. "Yes, I agree. We need to make sure nothing happens here without the admiral's approval."

"Very good, Dr. Greene. When do you think I should go over these numbers with him?"

"Time is of the essence. Feel free to go see him now if you wish," replied Dennis, stifling a smile on his face.

"Very good, sir. I think I'll probably be with the admiral for maybe 15 minutes?" asked Jose.

"That sounds about right."

Jose nodded his head, picked up the estimates sitting on the desk, and left the office. Dennis was on his heels until they got to the elevator. He took the elevator down to the level where the portal room was, and Jose proceeded on to the office where the admiral had set up shop.

As he neared the portal room, Dennis looked around to see if anybody could see where he was going. Once he was satisfied he was proceeding undetected, he swiftly entered the room. Getting to the control stations, he promptly inserted the two USB keys into their respective sockets and activated the portal systems. First, he sat at his normal console and took the necessary steps to spin up the cryogenics for the particle accelerator. Once that began, he sat at Jason's console to enter the specific coordinates for Jason's living room.

Meanwhile, Jason, Mikki, Terri, Lynne, and Diana were all waiting in the living room for Dennis to arrive. As soon as the portal window formed, Dennis looked at his watch and stepped through at the exact time pre-arranged with Jason. Instantly transported to Jason's living room, his arrival served as notification that the portal window was now active; all six individuals stepped back through it and now stood in the portal room looking back at the scene of Jason and Mikki's living room.

As soon as he arrived, Jason took his seat at his workstation while Diana rushed to a filing cabinet in the back of the room where the video camera was kept. Hoping the camera was charged, she flipped the power switch and was more than gratified to see it power up, ready to record the evidence they needed. Mikki and Terri took places near the inward swinging door to the portal room, Mikki on the hinge side, and Terri on the handle side. Their job was to watch for anybody coming.

Jason quickly moved his fingers over the keyboard, and in no time at all, the portal window changed so the scene was no longer of Mikki and Jason's living room, but rather the portal room itself. It was a little disconcerting to see themselves in real time, and the portal window showed the endless tunnel of reflections as if two mirrors faced each other.

Looking up at the portal window to verify it was showing what he expected, Jason started to adjust the T parameter, swiftly going back in time, but stopping at precisely the moment he stepped through the portal.

Looking at Diana, Jason asked, "You ready?"

"10-4," she replied. Holding the camera to her eye, Diana pressed the record button and began recording all that the portal showed. Jason clicked a button on his screen, and the scene in the portal began playing out the events of that day. It recorded Jason stepping through the portal, and the conversation he had with the Galimarians. It then showed the reactions of his friends when Kenji reached over and coldly clicked off the portal, effectively marooning him. There were about 10 minutes of recorded video when all was said and done, then Jason paused the portal timeline.

Diana brought the camera over to Jason, and he extracted the memory card carrying the video. Inserting it into his workstation, Jason immediately extracted the recording, created an email to the president's private email account he'd been given by the president himself when he was at the White House, then pressed send. As soon as the email program reported it as being sent, all in the room breathed a sigh of relief. They looked around to each other, and a lot of smiles were silently exchanged.

Terri stepped forward and left Mikki near the door, keeping vigil for anybody coming.

"Jason, now that we have what we came for, would you please do me a favor?" asked Terri.

Jason smiled. "You want to see Khreelon."

A little embarrassed, Terri said, "I know he doesn't know me from Adam or Eve, but I just want to see him."

"Actually," revealed Jason, "If you remember, I had about a month to wait while we were preparing for Jose to land on the island. I ended up working with Khreelon for quite a while."

Terri's eyes went wide, and a look of shocked embarrassment came over her face. "You didn't say anything about me did you?"

Laughing, Jason said, "Actually, I told him all about you, about how Loranna had chosen you to be Khreelon's soul mate in my timeline, and how completely in love with him you are."

"Oh my god!" said Terri, turning several shades of red.

Jason stepped out of his chair and took Terri by each shoulder, saying, "Terri." She looked into Jason's eyes.

"Khreelon is very anxious to meet you."

Terri's mouth opened to say words, but none were there. Her heart was beating fast, and eventually she was able to manage, "He is?"

"Yes. Would you like to meet him?"

"Now!?" asked Terri.

"Now," responded Jason.

Terri's instant reaction was to look down at her apparel and flatten out whatever invisible wrinkles in the material she thought were there. Reaching up to her hair, she said, "I, I don't know if, I mean what if ...."

Diana stepped over to Terri. "Sweetheart, if he's your soulmate, then it wouldn't matter if you had a ring through your nose, and greasy hair. But in this case, you're beautiful. He's gonna love you."

Lynne came to her other side and said, "Go get him, girl!"

She looked at Diana and Lynne for a few moments, then at Jason. "Okay, yes. I want to meet him."

Jason smiled and took a seat at his workstation. "I never actually went to the underwater habitat where they are sleeping, but I need to go wake them up now, anyway. I'll try to get the positioning right, but it might take a couple of tries."

"Wait a minute," said Diana. "If you point this thing underwater, won't that flood the room here?"

"Good question, but no, it won't," replied Jason. "There are a lot of safety protocols built into the computer program Dennis and I created to run the portal. One of the things Dennis put in was any time we connect to a new destination, we turn off the two-way transportation."

"Makes sense," said Diana. "My blouse is dry clean only, you see."

"Very funny," said Dennis, chuckling.

Within a few moments, the scene changed from the paused portal room scene previously shown, to what looked like a mostly dark green window. Jason had been a little off in his guess as to where the underwater habitat was located. Within a couple of seconds, they were looking at a scene under the water, and the water was clear enough to see, in the far distance, a domed underwater city. It looked like it was about 200 meters away from the portal window.

"What am I looking at?" asked Diana.

Without glancing up from his workstation, Jason answered, "This is a little over 1,000 meters below the surface of the water. Normally the water down here would be completely dark, but as you can see, the habitat off in the distance is shedding enough light to illuminate this whole area. I'll just make a few calculations, then reprogram the location to where I want it to point next."

This was the first time Mikki was able to see Jason in his element. She had seen him in many circumstances, but this was truly a first. As she looked on from her vantage point behind the door to the portal room, she appreciated this new dimension of her husband.

As Mikki stared at her husband through rose-colored glasses, appreciating the amazing man he was, she didn't notice the admiral

517

approaching the door. As soon as he reached it, he swung open the door, causing an unseen Mikki to be pinned behind it. Stepping into the room, nobody noticed his arrival due to the noise of the control systems and liquid helium pumps operating all around. Not until, that is, he decided to speak.

"You!"

Looking up from his console, Jason's fingers froze. He was just about to enter the new coordinates, but the admiral's arrival was his new focus. Jason stood and, with manly courage, addressed the man who had made himself such an arch nemesis.

"That's right, Admiral. Contrary to your original desire, I'm not dead."

"That's something that can be corrected," said the admiral, with a cold, detached expression on his face. "You have become an enemy of the state, and you will be stopped."

"And who decided that? You?" said Jason.

Admiral Brinstock took a couple of steps forward and stopped. Mikki began extricating herself from behind the door, and looked over to Dennis since she didn't have a line of sight to Jason. Dennis looked at Mikki as well and, with an almost imperceptible shaking of his head, he indicated to her to stay put and not make her presence known.

With venom in his voice, and pointing his thumb at his chest, Kenji responded through clenched teeth. *"I did!"*

Jason smiled, looked down at the floor, and took a couple of steps to the side. While his movement seemed casual, his real reason for doing so was to lay eyes on his wife behind the door. He wanted to visually see she was okay.

"Well!" said Jason. "The big bad wolf has come to blow down my house again, has he? Well, you're too late, grandpa!" Jason's eyes then narrowed. "I don't know what I did to tick you off, but one thing I know is you are a sad, old, power-hungry criminal who is going to pay for his crimes."

"Oh, is that so?" replied Kenji. "I suppose you and the rest of your little pigs here are going to stop me?"

"We already have, *Admiral*," said Jason, with all the virulence and spite in his heart.

"I suppose you're referring to the little email you just sent?" said Kenji.

The countenance of all in the room fell when the admiral mentioned the email. Simultaneously, they all asked the same unuttered question. How did he know about the email Jason had sent?

"I'm afraid your little attempt to make me look bad isn't going to make it out of the facility, you little leech," said Kenji. "Fortunately, I put in place some new security protocols since you were here. Any time an email leaves the facility, it crosses my desk first. It's actually a good thing for the security of the country you sent that email; I wouldn't have known you were here if you hadn't. So I have you to thank for alerting me to your presence. Your terrorist activities are going to stop here and now!"

Jason instantly thought about it, silently berating himself for not thinking about the possibility Kenji would have bugged all the communications to and from the facility.

"Terrorist?" yelled Terri. "Jason is a hero for saving the planet, *you included*!"

What she couldn't know was her voice was strangely similar to that of his dead ex-wife. Kenji swung his head to the left to the source of the outburst, and was shocked to see an apparition. Standing there in her favorite dress was Mrs. Brinstock. The dress was terribly singed, and it appeared to be smoking. What was left of her hair was in disarray, and the right side of her face was burned. As Kenji looked at her, she asked, "What are you going to do?"

Interpreting the question as an encouragement to seek revenge, he answered the hallucination. "Trust me, Judith. I will avenge your death!"

All sane individuals in the room were instantly put on edge by his statement. It was now obvious this man was dealing with some sort of psychotic break, and there was no telling what he would do.

"It doesn't matter, anyway," recovered Jason, trying to focus the attention on himself and not Terri. "I'm still here, so your little story about me dying in some accident is going to start raising a lot of uncomfortable questions, and you are the only one people are going to be looking at."

"That's only if you are there for them to see," replied the admiral, as he looked back at Jason.

Right then, Kenji reached down to his right side and flicked the small strap normally closed over the back end of the Sig Sauer P229 always strapped to his side. The handgun was such a part of the admiral's persona, it was something easy to ignore. But with the flick of the strap, it became suddenly obvious what he intended to do: remove the source of his downfall.

Kenji extracted his side arm, raised it slowly, and uttered the same words he said when marooning Jason on the island. "What I do now, I do for the good of the country."

All in the room were too far away to reach the admiral in time; all in the room, that is, except Mikki. As the old man raised the gun toward her husband, Mikki relived the events of the last 24 hours, all of them flashing before her eyes in an instant. She felt the happiness of having her husband back, and the overwhelming anger at Kenji for what he did to her and her family. She looked at Jason and relived the feelings of pride in who her husband had turned out to be, and the instant kinship she felt for all those in the portal room, with the distinct exception of the admiral.

There was only one thing to do. Lunging out from behind the door, Mikki reached for the gun in Kenji's hands. Unfortunately, Kenji had already pulled the trigger, so the firing pin began its unchangeable journey toward the bullet primer. Striking the percussion cap, the 40-caliber bullet fired, emerging from the barrel traveling at over 200 meters per second. The shell would cover a mile in five seconds flat, so any movement on Jason's part would be meaningless. Fortunately, Mikki's thrust against Kenji's arm was just in time to cause the trajectory to miss her husband's head. The bullet whizzed past, only missing him by an inch. Jason could literally feel the wind of the shell passing him by.

Dennis wasn't so blessed, though. He had been leaning against his workstation, his left hand resting on the lower cabinet. The same bullet that promised to kill Jason found Dennis' left hand, piercing it through and through. After penetrating the metal cabinet, it lodged itself in the circuitry of the cryogenics control systems. This caused the liquid helium pumps to lose power without waiting for the needed signals from Jason's station indicating the particle stream had been shut down first. As a result, the superconductors no longer had their ever-renewing bath of super-cold liquid helium; soon, they would begin warming and losing their ability to effectively guide the particle stream.

Lynne had been standing near Dennis when he was shot. Fearing he had been mortally wounded, she reached out to catch him and help in any way. She was a Navy reservist, but any shred of respect for her superior officer in the room melted at that moment. Her first priority was to help Dennis, who she could now see needed assistance, but was going to be okay.

Mikki's hit against the admiral's hand had caused him to lose his grip on the gun, and it went flying through the air. Hitting the ground without accidentally firing, it went skittering across the floor until it solidly lodged itself deep underneath a cabinet bolted to the floor. When Mikki heard the gunfire, her heart sank thinking she had been too late; she looked over to her husband, expecting to see him slumping to the floor. Seeing that Jason was ok, she temporarily lost her focus as she felt tremendous relief. At that same second, a stinging backhand from the admiral connected with the side of her face. The strike from Kenji caused her entire body to spin around. She instantly saw stars, and ended up flying off into the corner of the room near the door. "*You're next!*" screamed the incensed admiral.

Having a gun drawn on him had made Jason instantly fear for his life. But seeing Kenji strike Mikki like that flipped a switch in Jason. He went from fear to outrage in zero seconds flat. It was that threshold a man sometimes crosses when he no longer cares if he personally feels any pain. It's the focus a man feels when his circuits of compassion seem to short out, and all he can think of is applying pain to his adversary. Jason wasn't the warrior type, and had always lived a fairly tranquil life. He had never experienced this before, but seeing Mikki fly through the air like that caused Jason to have fire in his eyes.

Lunging for the admiral, Jason yelled, "Aaaggghhh!" He only had enough time to turn his head and see Jason's fist as it connected with his face. Immediately, Kenji's body spun around and fell to the ground. Breathing heavily while opening and closing his now throbbing hand, Jason stood over the admiral's body and said, "Not so big without your gun are you?"

The admiral spit out a tooth which had been dislodged. Jason approached the disabled heap of a man spitting blood and reached down to deliver the coup de grace. Suddenly, the old disabled man showed himself to be not so disabled. Taking his own knee, Kenji struck out against Jason's knee. Fortunately, not only was Jason's leg already tensed so the blow didn't cause any lasting damage, but it also missed its target. The hit definitely did come as a surprise, causing a tremendous amount of pain to the hero of the world. Calling out in pain, Jason crumbled to the floor, giving Kenji the time to stand again.

"What? You think an 'old man' can't fight, you worm?" said Kenji, blood dripping from his mouth. "That's the problem with you brainiacs. You think you know everything. Well, tell me …." Kenji drew back his foot and solidly kicked Jason in the exact same spot he had previously hit him with his knee. "Did you calculate that to happen?"

Jason cried out in pain, writhing on the floor.

Diana, who all this time had been silently standing near the portal, yelled out, "Don't!"

Hearing a new voice and satisfied he had subdued Jason for the time being, the admiral turned around to see where the voice had come from. "And you! You're nothing but a sorry excuse for an administrator." Stepping forward and coming near her, he added, "I'm pretty sure you can't even add two and two. I should have known better than to have a woman run this place." Kenji continued berating Diana, telling her how she and all her terrorist cohorts in the room were going to be eliminated. Having seen what he did to Mikki and Jason, Diana began to fear for her life. She turned her head away from the admiral, cringing as he spread his poison in her direction.

At that very moment, the lights to the room went black. The only light entering the room was, oddly enough, the light coming from the alien habitat three meters away on the other side of the portal window, which had begun to destabilize. There were strange sounds similar to static electricity discharges coming from the portal aperture. The warming superconductors were losing their ability to control the particle stream in the accelerator, so the edges of the portal window were beginning to lose their focus. The entire scene would fluctuate and wink out, then back in.

Jason, whose eyes had been closed due to the pain, opened them and saw the admiral standing near to Diana, who was cowering. It was obvious Kenji was suffering from delusions, and that introduced an unpredictability in whatever he might do. Jason thought about how Kenji had threatened to kill the others in the room, including his wife, and was certain the admiral would follow through with that threat. There was no reason to think he wouldn't; the Admiral had tried to kill him by marooning him in the past and, when that didn't work, tried to kill him with a gunshot to the head. Jason thought about how his beautiful wife had saved his life, only to pay for it with a beating from Kenji. That thought steeled him for what he knew he had to do.

While the admiral was verbalizing his monologue on how worthless Diana was, Jason silently crept up behind him. As soon as he was close enough, he purposely made a sound while crouched near the ground, like he was still crippled from the pain. The admiral turned and, seeing Jason crouching next to him, said, "Oh, look here now! Are you back for another beating?"

Kenji raised his foot to kick Jason again but, knowing that would happen, Jason yelled, "Nope!" Reaching for Kenji's foot, Jason grabbed it and twisted as hard as he could. The admiral wasn't expecting Jason's move, but his hand-to-hand combat training took over, and out of instinct he did a tuck and roll away from him. Unfortunately for Kenji, this was the one time his survival instincts didn't serve him well.

Because he was standing so near to the portal, the moment his shoulder touched the portal field, it surrounded his entire body, and Admiral Brinstock was instantly transported to a location over 1,000 meters under the sea and 300 meters from the nearest underwater safe haven. It wouldn't have mattered if it was only one meter away, though.

His body was instantly subjected to over a quarter million pounds per square foot of pressure, and within moments all gasses in his body collapsed. His body basically imploded. The last thing everyone in the portal room saw was Kenji's lifeless body floating away. At that moment, the portal window finally destabilized completely. The fail-safes took over, and the particle streams were automatically shut down. In no time at all, the room went silent and the lights turned back on.

All eyes had been on the portal window witnessing the death of Kenji, but then simultaneously, all wondered why the lights turned off and on at the perfect times. One and all turned and looked toward the door.

Standing there slightly nodding, with a look of resignation on his face, was Lieutenant Flume, Kenji's assistant. His hand was still on the light switch.

CHAPTER 60

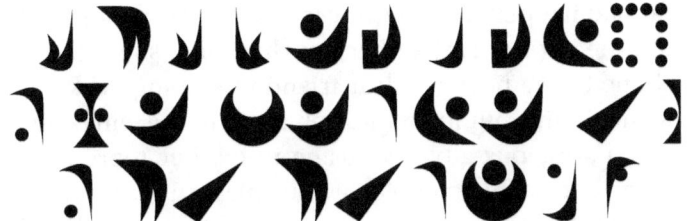

A LITTLE OVER THREE WEEKS HAD gone by since that terrible scene played itself out in the portal room. With the portal being non-operational due to the bullet which pierced not only Dennis' hand but also the cryogenics control station, there wasn't anything they could do to revive the Galimarians. For now, they continued sleeping on the ocean floor; since they weren't in any danger, Jason and Dennis concentrated on taking their time to fix the portal properly.

The Coast Guard detail sent to the general area where Admiral Brinstock's body might have floated to the surface searched for at least four days, but in the end, there was nothing to find. Once his body had been transported to a spot 1,000 meters below the surface of the ocean and started to rise, it became a welcome source of food for quite a number of marine animals. By the time they were done with the feast, the bones had been picked clean, eventually settling down to the sea floor.

Work on the portal didn't actually start right away. If he hadn't requested the time off, Diana probably would have demanded that Jason stay away from the office with Mikki. As it was, he and Mikki, as well as Jace, were acutely ready to spend time getting reconnected with each other. That, coupled with Dennis needing to take some personal time off to tend to his hand, meant things were pretty quiet in the portal room for a while. Jason and Mikki decided to take a trip to the Napa wine country near San Francisco, California, spending a week visiting every single winery, park, and tourist trap they could find. Jace went along on the trip too, and really loved taking a tour through a candy factory along the way. Diana decided she needed to hold down the fort for the time being, making sure nothing and nobody went in or out of the portal room until Jason and Dennis were there.

When Karen returned from her honeymoon, she knew nothing about what had happened recently, especially regarding Jason's return. The minute she got home with her new husband, she called Mikki on her cell phone to see how her dear friend was doing. Mikki explained that she wasn't home, but in fact was on a trip to the wine country with her son and a gorgeous guy, promising to tell her more about things when she got back. This completely, but pleasantly, surprised Karen, and she said so. At the same time, she privately wondered if Mikki was getting into the dating scene a little too soon after losing her husband. After hanging up, Mikki laughed, saying to a grinning Jason that she decided this was news she needed to share with Karen personally, not over the cell phone. She also knew the story to Karen needed to be artfully crafted so as to not reveal national secrets Mikki was now privy to.

After getting shot by the admiral, Dennis was quickly treated for the gunshot wound and released. He had to come up with a story about how he was target practicing, and the gun went off unintentionally. After laughing at Dennis' "good fortune," the doctor said if you are going to get shot, the hand is probably the least fatal place, although he was going to be dealing with a lot of soreness for a while. The doctor put his hand in a cast and said it would have to stay that way for at least four weeks. Lynne experienced the Florence Nightingale effect, deciding she was going to stay around to "take care" of Dennis, something he eagerly accepted.

Terri decided to stay in town while Jason and Mikki were away; in fact, both she and Lynne stayed at their house during that time. It worked out well for all involved.

When Jason and Mikki returned, Dennis was raring to go on fixing the portal and, for that matter, so was Jason. Since Dennis' hand was still out of commission, that meant more of the portal rebuilding responsibilities would normally have rested on Jason. But by the time Jason returned and got back to work, the acquaintance between Dennis and Lynne had nicely blossomed into a full-fledged romantic interest, so Lynne volunteered to work closely with Dennis and be his hands.

It took about two and a half weeks to order the new parts and get them installed. It normally would have taken longer; however, when the bullet pierced the circuitry of the cryogenics console, a cascade surge traveled through the rest of the facility, wiping out a few other components in the missile defense system. This meant the parts order took on a "Top Priority" status, elevating it to the top of any bureaucratic list the government maintained. This time, the consoles and critical equipment in the portal room were changed out, and all critical systems were encased in hardened cabinets.

The day finally came when it was time to start powering up the portal systems. It wasn't just a simple flicking of a switch, and suddenly everything was on. First and foremost, the missile defense system had to have priority, so they concentrated on making sure everything there was working perfectly. Once that was accomplished, they began individually powering up the nearly two dozen sub-systems which comprised the portal technology. Only when each of those systems was independently working was the main control system software fired up, allowing the sub-systems to be started in proper sequence.

The startup actually went rather well, considering all the changes to the system. Because they had carefully and systematically tested and re-tested everything along the way, the first full systems test of the portal went off perfectly. They were able to dial up the scene of something they had been tossing back and forth while working that week. After typing in the X, Y, Z, and T parameters indicating the date and time, they were rewarded with a scene of not only the gleaming white limestone facades of the Great Pyramid of Giza, but also a nine-year-old Tutankhamun being made the king of Egypt. They considered dialing the scene forward 10 years to see how he was killed, but they both agreed this was one of those scenes they'd rather not see.

Jason and Dennis looked at each other with relief, knowing all traces of the admiral had now been erased.

"Well, paisano," said Dennis, "I guess it's off to never-never land to wake up all the sleeping beauties, eh?"

"I don't think so," replied Jason.

"Why?" asked Dennis, with a look of bewilderment.

"The first thing we need to do is to get the president up to speed on where we are and what we intend to do. One of the first places

Brinstock went wrong was going rogue and making decisions by himself, instead of relying on the elected powers that be."

Dennis sat at his station contemplating what Jason had said, and realized he was spot on in wanting to get President Michaelson involved. He glanced over to the other corner of the room where Lynne and Jose were just finishing putting away some oscilloscope test leads and high voltage insulation they had been installing.

"As usual, you're right. You still got that email address he gave us?"

"Yep. Right here."

Jason turned to his workstation and brought up the email program he normally used. As he was typing the email, Dennis spoke up and asked, "Hey, wait a minute. Are you sure that email will make it out? He created an intercept for all the email, didn't he?"

"Yeah," replied Jason, "but one of the first things I did was remove the intercepts. I wanted to send an email to Mikki while I was here, but I also knew there would come a time when I would want to send this very ...."

"Good afternoon, gentlemen," interrupted Diana as she entered the portal room. Not only was she entering the room, but also Terri and Mikki, since they arrived at the facility together after spending the morning engaging in what they referred to as "retail therapy."

"Hey!" called out the two men simultaneously.

"What do we have on the schedule today? More endless tests?" asked Diana.

"Tell me about it!" responded Terri. "I mean, I'm all for taking one for the team and being there for your friends, but after the last week of tests, I ...."

"*We*," interrupted Mikki.

"Sorry, girlfriend," acquiesced Terri. "*We* had to get out of here and blow off some steam."

"You'll be happy to hear the tests are complete, and the portal is now operational in all respects," answered Dennis.

"Really? So, what's first?" asked Diana enthusiastically. Like Dennis, she was really looking forward to making the jump to the underwater habitat where the Galimarians were sleeping. Truth be told, that was also on the minds of Terri and Mikki.

"Actually," replied Jason, clicking the send button on his screen, "I am just now sending an email to the president's personal account letting him know we need to speak with him regarding the 'you-know-what,'" chuckled Jason as he made quotation marks in the air.

"The president?" asked Mikki. "You have the personal email address for President Michaelson?"

Dennis smiled. "Your hubby and I are on his short list of favorite people, my dear. When we facilitated that whole hubbub with the Houston bombing terrorists being taken out, he made a point of telling us that any time we needed to talk, just send him an email."

With raised eyebrows, Mikki's only response was a muted "Wow." Her expression showed she was impressed.

"Why are you emailing him?" asked Lynne, as she and Jose approached the group. She sat her oft-used place, Dennis' lap.

"As I said to Dennis earlier, a big way the late but not great admiral went wrong was not following protocol in making sure the president knew what was going on. I don't intend on making the same mistake," said Jason. "In fact, I have some thoughts I'd like to run past the president on how to keep this portal, and the people of this planet, safe."

Just then the phone on Jason's console rang. Knowing that anybody who *would* normally be calling him was already in the room, Jason scrunched his eyebrows together and looked at Dennis, who had the same look on his face.

"Hello?"

Those in the room could only hear Jason's side of the conversation.

"Yes, this is Doctor Jason Marsalis."

"Okay."

He looked over to Dennis and shrugged his shoulders, indicating he still had no idea who was calling; apparently he had been put on hold.

"Yes, this is Dr. Jason Marsalis. Who is this?"

Jason cleared his throat. "Mr. President!"

Six sets of eyeballs in the portal room all collectively went wide in astonishment.

"Yes, sir. I am alive and well, sir."

"As I said in my email, that is a long story I very much want to share with you as soon as possible, sir."

At that moment, Jason had a thought that caused him to smile.

"Actually, are you busy right now sir?"

"Perfect."

"Yes, sir."

"No, sir. If you'll give me about five minutes, I will be back in contact with you and explain everything."

"Yes, sir."

"Thank you, sir."

"Goodbye."

Jason hung up the phone and smiled at his friend. While the other four in the room were completely bewildered at the rather cryptic half of the conversation they had just heard, Dennis was completely on the same wavelength as Jason. Turning to his workstation, Dennis took out his security key, placed it in the console, and fired up the cryogenics systems. Jason took out a similar key and fired up his control station.

"Parallel T," called Jason, as the liquid helium pumps started to come online.

Terri leaned over to Diana and asked, "Do you have any idea what's going on?" She looked back at Terri and just shrugged her shoulders, shaking her head.

"Min temp!" called out Dennis.

"Firing particle stream," called out Jason.

The machinery in the portal room began performing its dance as the particle stream started to gain acceleration using the immense set of superconducting magnets in the tunnels, guiding it to ever greater speeds. It was always a rush to be at the helm of such a powerful leviathan as it groaned to life.

"Max V," called out Dennis.

"Firing!" responded Jason.

The parameters Jason entered while the particle stream was coming up to speed caused the control surfaces in the portal to shift the course of the particle stream, and the portal field began to form. As soon as the light blue field completely formed, the scene of the Oval Office materialized in the aperture of the portal.

It was now evident to all in the room exactly what idea Jason had while talking to the president. Without saying another word, he and Dennis approached the portal and stepped through it.

President Michaelson was sitting at the Resolute desk in the Oval Office, waiting for Jason to call him back, with a faraway look on his face. He, or more specifically his executive secretary, had just received an email on his personal account from Jason. Until that email, he had been under the impression Jason was dead due to an explosion at the Midway Magnetic facility. According to Kenji, the explosion happened away from the portal, so it remained operational thankfully, but he was certainly dismayed to hear that such a great American had been killed in the line of duty. He wished he could have publicly honored such a great man, but that wasn't possible due to the secret nature of the Midway installation, not to mention the secrecy surrounding the portal.

President Michaelson had been staring at the portrait of Abraham Lincoln when, suddenly, what appeared as rays of light started to shine near the fireplace directly across from his desk. Standing up quickly, President Michaelson was just about to call for the Secret Service to come running when suddenly Jason and Dennis appeared in the middle of the light rays. As soon as their bodies completely materialized, which only took about a second, the light rays stopped and two men with rather large smiles on their faces stood before the president.

"What? How?" It was one of those rare times when President Michaelson was at a loss for words.

"Mr. President, I'm sorry for startling you, but both Dennis and I felt it was important to explain the events of the last few weeks in person," said Jason.

"Weren't you just talking to me from your facility in California?" asked the president.

"Yes sir," responded Dennis.

The president looked at the two men for a few seconds, until he said the first and only word that came to mind. "Astonishing." He breathed deeply, shaking his head from side to side.

"Mr. President, may we invite the rest of our team to be here with us?" asked Jason.

"Uh, sure. You need to use the phone?" asked the president, as he began to reach for his phone.

"Thank you, sir," said Jason. Then holding up his open palm to the president, Jason added, "That won't be necessary, sir."

Knowing exactly what his friend was thinking, Dennis smiled and turned back to the fireplace. "It's okay, guys. Come on through."

For a few seconds nothing happened, until the same light rays that filled the room a few minutes ago were now doing so again. One by one, new people appeared in the Oval Office. First to come through was Diana.

"This is Diana O'Laney, administrator of the Midway Magnetic facility."

The president stepped around his desk and approached her. "Ms. O'Laney, I am pleased to meet you." He had a look on his face best described as deer-in-the-headlights.

"The pleasure is all mine to be sure, Mr. President. You can call me Diana."

Jason spoke again. "This is Doctor Terri Lindstrom. She and her associate ...."

Lynne appeared now in the Oval Office.

"Lynne Marlowe, are experts on the alien island of New Galimar."

One by one, the president shook the hands of the women.

"Mr. President, this is Mr. Jose Barragon y Cisneros."

The president reached out his hand to Jose and, after shaking his hand, Jose bowed in respect. "Mr. President, it is an honor to make your acquaintance," said Jose, with a noticeable Spanish accent.

"And finally, Mr. President, this is my wife, Michaela Marsalis."

President Michaelson stepped over to shake her hand, cupping her hand with both of his.

"You can call me Mikki, Mr. President."

"Mikki, it is a pleasure to meet you. I am glad to meet the wife of a man who is such a great treasure to this country."

"Thank you, Mr. President. He is certainly a treasure to me."

"Don't leave Dennis out of that whole 'national treasure' thing," said Jason, smiling at his pal.

"Of course not!" responded the president. "I don't believe a day goes by without my thinking about the service you both have rendered to this country."

"Thank you, sir," responded Dennis.

Gesturing to the couches, he said to the assembled group, "Please be seated."

Each took a seat on a couch or chair. While this wasn't the first time Jason or Dennis had been here, it was a new experience for the rest of the group, who were rather star-struck over the experience.

President Michaelson walked over to his desk and punched a button on his phone.

"Lindsay, would you please bring in some refreshments."

"Certainly, sir. Would you like your usual?" asked the executive secretary to the president.

"Actually, please bring in an assortment of refreshments and snacks for my guests."

"Yes, sir. Would you like the Limburger as well?"

Jason and Dennis both thought this was an unusual question, but they chalked it up to an odd taste preference on the part of the president. What they couldn't have known was that it was a coded question. Since Lindsay sat immediately outside the president's office, she knew for a fact nobody had passed her desk to enter the Oval Office. The meaning behind the question from the secretary about the Limburger was actually, "Do you need the Secret Service to come in with guns blazing?"

"Not this time. But perhaps you can bring the mozzarella."

Mozzarella meant all was green, and there was no need for worry. If the president had ordered some cheddar, though, Jason, Dennis, and the rest of the visiting party would have been dead within the next 10 seconds.

"Very good, sir. I'll have that sent in right away."

Clicking off the intercom, the president stood in front of his desk and leaned against it. "I gotta say, gentlemen, I'm still a little in awe over the kind of technology you have created. It's really like a transporter in the movies, isn't it?" asked President Michaelson.

"Yes sir, with the added benefit that we can also move to different points on the clock as well," replied Jason.

"I've said it before, and I'm going to say it again. Astonishing," responded the president.

"Thank you, sir," said Dennis.

"So, to what do I owe the honor of your visit?"

"Before I answer that, Mr. President," said Jason, "I'd like to first point out that each of the individuals in this room was instrumental in keeping the portal safe, and their knowledge of the secrets of the Midway Magnetic facility was essential. I know you hadn't granted permission to individuals such as Mikki, but their role was, as I said, essential."

"Understood," said the president.

With that, Jason and Dennis related the entire story of what had happened. Admiral Brinstock had kept the president completely in the dark about a lot of things, especially about how he had marooned Jason in the past, effectively murdering him from a modern day perspective. At this point, Jason produced the USB flash drive which had the original recording of when Kenji marooned him. It also had a video Jason recorded when the admiral tried to kill him.

Not one detail was held back from President Michaelson. The end of the story culminated with Jason explaining how he wanted to make sure the president was the one in charge.

"I can't believe it," said a resigned, yet quite angry, president. "I trusted that man with the safety of the nation!"

"If it makes any difference, sir, I think he originally had good intentions, but became mentally ill, and was getting sicker," responded Jason.

"What makes you say that?"

"Well, sir," replied Dennis, "when he was trying to kill Jason, he apparently was hallucinating. He was looking at Terri, but addressing her as his wife who had recently died."

"He thought you were Judith?" asked the president, looking at Terri.

"Yes, sir" replied Terri. "He looked squarely at me and talked as if I was his dead wife."

The president didn't respond, but once again his head slowly shook from side to side.

"But now, sir," said Jason, deciding it was time to turn the conversation onto a more positive path, "we should proceed to awaken our alien benefactors. I spent a month with them while I was in the past, and I really look forward to seeing them again. They are an amazing people, sir."

Nodding his head, the president said, "Dr. Marsalis and Dr. Greene, you have a go to proceed." With a smile on his face, he added, "I have an idea. Gentlemen, would you please accompany me to my private office to go over some details?"

"Certainly, sir."

President Michaelson, Jason, and Dennis disappeared through a doorway while the rest of the team stayed in the Oval Office, enjoying the treats Lindsay had brought earlier. Each of them took turns commenting on the surreal nature of having been in California a few minutes ago, but now being in Washington, D.C., talking with the president in the Oval Office.

After about 10 minutes, the three men emerged from the president's private office, all smiles.

"How are you going to get back home, guys?" asked President Michaelson.

"All we have to do is step over toward the fireplace, sir. The portal is still active, so it will transport us to back to California."

The president didn't say anything, but once again just shook his head and chuckled. Taking this as the cue to leave, Diana was the first to step toward the fireplace and, sure enough, she disappeared. One by one, each of the assembled party left the Oval Office until once again it was just the president.

He tapped a key on his phone and asked Lindsay to have the refreshments taken away.

"Sir, will your guests be staying for dinner in your residence?"

"They're gone now, Lindsay."

Knowing she hadn't seen anybody pass by her desk, the president smiled at the undoubtedly quizzical look on his secretary's face. Changing the subject, he said, "I need you to bring in today's schedule, please. I'll have to reschedule and free up the rest of my afternoon."

"Yes, sir. Right away, sir," responded Lindsay. She decided there must be some secret panel to the Oval Office nobody else knew about.

"It's amazing how many secret's this town has!" she thought to herself.

Meanwhile, Jason and Dennis got to work right away, not only shutting down the connection to the president's office, but beginning the process of setting the portal's parameters to the habitat on the ocean floor. As was the case when the scuffle with Kenji happened, the first try pointed the portal to a place deep underwater; the location still needed to be refined.

While they were refining the portal window position, Lynne came over to stand next to Terri.

"Are you ready to meet your soul mate, Terri?" she asked, smiling.

With a start, Terri shot forward in her seat. "Oh my god!" exclaimed Terri. "With all that's been happening, I forgot he's going to be on the other side of the portal window!"

The women in the room smiled at Terri who was now starting to sweat and whose heartbeat had just doubled.

"What if, what if," said Terri, unable to complete her sentence. She didn't really need to, though. Everybody in the room knew exactly what she was thinking.

"He's gonna love you, sweetie," soothed Lynne. "What's not to love about you?!"

"That's easy for you to say. I just wish I knew for sure!"

"He will," responded Jason, keeping his eyes trained on the console.

Terri turned her head toward him with a questioning look. "What aren't you telling me?" A wry smile began to form.

Jason looked up and, in a signature move, made like he was zipping a zipper across his lips.

"Ugh!" shouted Terri in exasperation. Diana, Lynne, and the rest all had huge smiles on their faces.

As Jason and Dennis continued to work on their consoles, slowly but surely the portal window seemed to get closer and closer to the underwater habitat, until finally its interior showed itself.

"Wow!" exclaimed Mikki.

"Not what you expected?" asked Jason.

"Actually, I'm not sure what I expected, but I didn't expect to see anything like this."

The room where the portal was now pointed looked like a reception room or lounge in the lobby of a posh hotel. There were several conversation pits, not being used at the moment, all designed as depressions in the floor with steps leading down to them. They were differently shaped, but all had what looked like couches lining their inside circumferences. Comfortable pillows were plentiful in each pit, and most had a center fireplace which would support a display of fire emanating over hundreds of small, shiny glass orbs, or marbles.

On the far walls, ocean life swam past the floor-to-ceiling glass windows. The windows were roughly four meters tall and spanned the entire width of the room. Plants were growing out of pots artfully placed throughout the room, and some caretaker robotics were scurrying from one pot to another, making sure the plants were properly fertilized, watered, and trimmed.

Overhead were dozens of circular panels about four or five meters in diameter. Each was brightly lit and shedding light into the room. It was barely noticeable that the light was slowly cycling between a warm white light to soft colors which accentuated the comfortable feeling of the room. The floors were both multi-colored marble and carpet, artfully crafted in drifting and casually curved designs.

"Okay dude, let's lock it in," said Dennis to Jason.

"Yep," responded Jason. He recorded the exact coordinates where the portal was now pointed, but then did something completely unexpected, at least from the perspective of the rest of the party in the portal room.

"Commencing shutdown in 3-2-1-Now," said Jason.

The scene in the portal aperture suddenly vanished, and all that could be seen was the metal shielding set up on the other side of the portal window.

"Shutdown? What the heck? Aren't we going to see Khree .... I mean, aren't we going to wake up the Galimarians?" asked a visibly irritated Terri.

"We sure are, but there's one last thing we need to do before going there," said Jason.

"Well, that was anti-climactic," muttered Lynne.

"Patience, my dear," said Dennis. "We'll go there in a minute."

Jason called up the list of saved locations on his workstation and brought up a very important one.

"Coordinates locked in. Ready to fire?" asked Jason to Dennis.

"Ready."

"Very well," responded Jason. "Firing particle stream in 3-2-1-Now!"

As was now predictable, a hazy, light blue field started to form from the edges of the aperture until it materialized in the middle. When the field had completely formed, the scene was a familiar one to Jason and Dennis; the other inhabitants in the room were in wonder at what they saw.

Jason stepped through the portal alone. On the other side of the portal, he talked to the one and only individual there.

"Mr. President, we are ready in all respects. Are you ready?" asked Jason.

"Lead the way, Dr. Marsalis," responded President Michaelson. Jason turned around, stepped back through the portal, and appeared back in the portal room. Everyone could see the president hesitate for a moment before taking a step toward what he couldn't actually see but knew was there, based on what he just saw happen to Jason.

From his perspective, the movement from Washington, D.C., to California happened instantaneously. One moment he was in the relative silence of the Oval Office at the White House, and then he was suddenly hearing the noise of the machinery supporting the portal window.

After taking another step into the portal room, the president realized where he was and turned around to see the Oval Office displayed through the portal. Only one word came to his mind. "Wow!"

The others in the portal room were trying to make sense out of what they were witnessing, when Jason stepped over to their new visitor and said, "Mr. President, welcome to California, and welcome to Midway Magnetic. If you stand over here for a moment, we will reorient the portal to where we need to go."

President Michaelson took a step to the side near where Mikki was standing, and he looked a little off his game. He was normally a poised individual while in the public eye, but this was more than the average Joe ever had to deal with. Mikki could see he was still trying to wrap his mind around all that was happening, so she stepped next to him and put her arm through his.

"Don't worry, sir. You're in good hands with my husband and Dennis."

He looked at her, then over at Jason who had taken a seat at his control station. "Oh, I can tell that easily, Mrs. Marsalis. This is just a lot to take in all at once."

"It is, but we gotcha. And don't forget, you can call me Mikki."

"Thank you, Mikki. I tell you what. When we aren't in the public eye, you and your friends can call me Dave. Deal?"

"Deal, Dave!" responded Mikki, with a laugh in her voice.

"Commencing shutdown in 3-2-1-Now," said Jason.

The scene of the Oval Office disappeared, and once again the metal shielding could be seen.

"Habitat coordinates locked in. Ready to fire?" asked Jason to Dennis.

"Ready Freddy!" replied Dennis, with a cheeky grin.

"Very well. Firing particle stream in 3-2-1-Now!"

The habitat was visible once again through the portal. Once the connection to the Galimarian habitat was stabilized and the safety protocols were cleared allowing two-way travel, Jason got up from his console and walked to the president.

"Mr. President, are you ready to make the first presidential connection with an alien race?" asked Jason.

"As ready as I'll ever be. You know, I have to tell you. I figured being president would afford me the opportunity to do things most others could never do, but this really takes the cake."

"This takes the whole bakery, if you ask me!" responded Dennis.

All in the room laughed at the humor, but now it was time for action. Jason, President Michaelson, and Mikki (with her arm still through the President's arm) all stepped through the portal, followed quickly by the others in the room.

The first thing to assault the senses was the absence of noise which had been all around those in the portal room; next was the aroma of the floral arrangements peppered throughout the room. There weren't any artificial sounds in the underwater lounge. After acclimatizing to the room, there was a calming sound coming from the ocean itself all around. It was a low-frequency sound, occasionally punctuated by the sound of passing animals. Each in the landing party walked around the lounge to get familiarized with the comfortable, yet functional, room. Jason and Dennis seemed to be all business, though, especially Jason. He positioned himself in front of a control station to access the environmental stasis pod control systems.

"How far underwater are we right now?" asked the president.

"According to the portal controls we used to get here, the depth is a little over 1,500 meters below sea level," replied Jason.

"Fifteen hundred meters below sea level? How did they possibly build this down here?" asked President Michaelson.

"When I spent a month with them in the 1400s, they explained to me their builder robot technology. Essentially, they programmed the builder robots to build whatever they needed here, and since they can self-replicate as many times as necessary to get the job done, they were able to build this facility housing about one point two million Galimarians in only about three weeks."

"One point two million! You didn't tell me there were *that* many," said a rather surprised Dennis.

"I have to keep some secrets," responded Jason with a smile.

The president stared out the window at the undersea life. "Incredible!" As he was watching, he and all those with him were amazed to see a frilled shark lazily pass by the window.

The terminal where Jason sat was similar to the ones he became familiar with on the island of the past. He was able to easily navigate through the screen, and soon was rewarded with confirmation that his commands had been accepted.

"Mr. President, if you'll accompany me to this wall here, we are soon going to be presented with ...."

Interrupting Jason just then, the wall they were standing near opened, and machinery could be heard. As soon as the panels of the wall had completely opened, an oval-shaped capsule appearing to be made of a white lacquer material emerged. The pod was about three meters long and was reclined back at a 30-degree slant. The front of the pod had a window, but no one could see what was inside. Jason walked over to the pod and pressed a button on a side panel, turning on an interior light. A Galimarian man was sleeping peacefully inside. For everyone in the room except Jason, this was the first time they had seen a real alien life form. All took a sudden intake of breath at the sight of this seemingly perfect specimen of life. The man was tall and arrayed in what appeared to be an impeccably embroidered ceremonial cloak. The richness of color and stitch was amazing to behold.

"Do you know who this is?" asked President Michaelson.

"Yes, sir," replied Jason. "This is the captain of the ship."

"What ship?"

"I guess I didn't explain that part to you, sir. The island of New Galimar is actually an interstellar ship. The part we see above the waterline is quite literally the tip of a very large iceberg, sir; about 98% of the ship is below water. It is a ship designed to fly in space, and it's what their people came here on from their home world over 6,000 years ago."

Not just the president, but all in the room were overwhelmed to hear these details, with the exception of Terri; Quorlynn had shared this information with her long ago.

Jason reached over to the control panel on the side of the pod and pressed another button. A mist filled the inside of the pod, temporarily obscuring its inhabitant. As all in the room continued to watch, a series of lights sequentially filled in from the left to the right above the main pod window. Evidently this was a progress bar indicating how long they had to wait for the process to complete; once the lights reached the right side of the pod, the window receded and slipped to the right out of the way. Immediately, the mist which had obscured the Galimarian man from sight now dissipated, revealing him to be simply sleeping. His chest could be seen slowly moving up and down.

It only took about another five seconds for his eyes to open, revealing completely black irises. Looking now from side to side, his eyes settled on Jason, who was now standing in front of him.

"Jason," said the Galimarian man, with a tone of what sounded like relief.

"Hello Ehobak, my friend," replied Jason, with a pleased and gratified smile on his face.

Reaching down to steady himself, Ehobak stepped out of the pod and stood up for the first time in almost 700 years.

"It is good to see your smiling face again. I trust our plan worked?" asked Ehobak.

"Perfectly. Your plan to keep us from contaminating the timeline by making sure the only thing that came forward was the knowledge in my head, then keeping me locked away in a timed pod of my own, was brilliant and worked perfectly."

"That is excellent news."

"Ehobak, I'd like to introduce you to someone," said Jason. Gesturing to the man in the suit standing adjacent, he said, "This is someone in our world who holds an office called the presidency. He is the head of the government where I live, representing a little over 300,000,000 of my fellow humans on the planet. May I introduce you to President Michaelson. President Michaelson, this is Lord Ehobak Aramine. He is the designer of the Arageena, the ship that is also the island of New Galimar, and also its captain."

Ehobak turned to face President Michaelson. Putting his open palms together above his head, he then brought his pressed palms down until they remained over his chest. Ehobak closed his eyes and slightly dipped his head. "May you have peace, President Michaelson. Welcome to our underwater habitat."

President Michaelson, who had always enjoyed a reputation for being a top-notch diplomat, turned his body to Ehobak and perfectly matched his gestures. "May you have peace as well. It is an honor to be welcomed into your establishment."

"The pleasure is mine."

"Lord Aramine," replied President Michaelson, "I requested to be here personally to thank you and your people for the role you played in helping to save not only your people, but also over 8,000,000,000 of my fellow humans. Words cannot express how much we are in your debt. It is my hope we can establish a close working relationship with your people."

"No, it is we who are in your debt for developing the technology making it possible," responded Ehobak. "Establishment of diplomatic relations with your government is something I cannot personally agree to, since that must come from our ruling body, the Grand Council. However, I will say our people are very fond of Jason for all he did on behalf of our people."

"Ehobak," interjected Jason, "I must mention that it wasn't just me who was responsible. This gentleman is Dennis Greene. Without him, I wouldn't have been able to do what I did for your people."

Turning to Dennis, Ehobak greeted him in the same manner he had the president. Dennis responded in like manner.

At this point, Ehobak suggested he begin the process of reviving principal members of the Grand Council. One by one, they appeared at the revival station in the lounge. Ehobak made sure they were apprised of what had happened while they had been sleeping, as well as the role each of the humans they were now meeting had with the saving of Earth and New Galimar. Each of them greeted the humans with gratitude.

As Ehobak supervised the selection of the pods to be revived, the next name that came up on the control station screen made him recall a conversation he had with Jason shortly before he went into suspended animation. Selecting this particular pod as the next one to be revived, he called over to Jason and pointed to his screen at the name of the next one to awaken. Jason smiled and looked at Terri, who was on the other side of the room enjoying a conversation with a woman who was a member of the Grand Council of Galimar. The councilwoman looked to be around 35 years old but, in reality, she was a little over 12,000.

As Jason walked up to Terri, she spied him in her peripheral vision and said, very excitedly, "Jason! You won't believe what Lady D'Zaniveen just told me! They have something called nanite technology which will make it possible for us to live as long as they do."

"Really?!" exclaimed Jason. This was a development he hadn't even considered when he was living with the Galimarian people. This was quite a staggering revelation to him, and certainly merited investigation, but something else was at the top of Jason's mind. Turning to the councilwoman, he said, "Lady D'Zaniveen, may I distract Terri from you for a moment?"

"Certainly, Jason." Turning to Terri, she said, "Terri, it was a pleasure to meet you."

"The pleasure was all mine, Lady D'Zaniveen," replied Terri.

Walking away, Jason said, "I need to talk to you over here for a minute." As they were walking, he caught Dennis' eye, giving him a look that said, "Get over here." Dennis took the hint and made sure all the rest of the humans understood they needed to come over as well. Assembled behind Terri, she didn't even notice they were near. "What's up?" she asked Jason.

Terri didn't register where they were standing at that moment, but then the wall next to them opened up, a new pod came forward, and stopped. The window was as opaque as the other ones, but as soon as Jason reached over to the control pad illuminating the inhabitant of the pod, Terri's heart dropped to the level of her shoes. All the color drained from her cheeks, and she seemed to lose control of the muscles in her face, except those causing her eyes to bug out of their sockets. Mikki, Lynne, and Diana all rushed to her side, knowing there was a high likelihood Terri would have a hard time standing. Right there in front of her was her beloved Khreelon. Not just bones and clothes as she thought she had seen before, but in the flesh.

By this time, Ehobak and his wife Ruavu appeared next to Terri. Ruavu spoke up, saying, "Terri, you should know that Khreelon is very much looking forward to meeting you."

Terri looked into Ruavu's dark black eyes and saw the look of a gentle soul. The soul of a sister she never had. "I can't even begin to say how much I have wished for this day to come," said Terri.

With that, Ehobak walked to the pod and pressed the button to revive his close friend. As with the others, what looked like a mist filled the compartment, and the indicator lights began their progression from left to right above the window. Terri looked on, shaking like a leaf, while the women holding onto her stroked her arms soothingly. Even Ruavu reached over and placed her hand on Terri's back between her shoulders. That touch more than any seemed to calm Terri the most.

The progression of the lights made their way completely to the right, and the window receded, sliding away as it had with all the others. As the mist rolled away from Khreelon, several seconds passed, then his eyes opened.

Terri took in a sharp intake of breath upon personally seeing Khreelon's face for the first time. His eyes first focused on Ehobak who was standing in front of the pod; he reached out to his friend, and Khreelon accepted his offering.

"Ehobak. Is it over?"

Placing his right hand on Khreelon's right shoulder, Ehobak slowly nodded his head. "It's over, my friend. Jason was successful in correcting the malfunction in the TSM, and he did it without corrupting the timeline."

A visibly relieved Khreelon extended his own hand in the same manner and smiled.

He then looked around to all who were gathered there. He spied a grouping of humans looking on, and they all had rather large smiles on their faces. That is, all of them except one, who at that moment looked like she wasn't breathing; which, in fact, she wasn't.

Taking steps toward Terri, he stopped directly in front of her. Putting his open palms together above his head, he then brought his pressed palms down until they remained over his chest. Khreelon closed his eyes and slightly dipped his head. "May you have peace, Terri. I am very pleased to meet you."

"You are? I mean, you are of course. Not of course. That would be rather presump …. I mean, you can be any way you want. I was just …."

Terri stopped herself from blathering on and just looked Khreelon in the eyes; those beautiful, deep dark pools of sight she could almost see her reflection in. Yes, she realized right then if she were to look deep into the most secret recesses of his soul, she would discover she had lived there all along. Like the words of her letter, there must have been cosmic forces at work. No matter the galaxy, no matter the millennia, no matter the forces against them, Khreelon and Terri were one. They always had been. They were one even before Terri had ever been born. They were one even when Khreelon lived millions of light years away. Gazing into his eyes at that moment, her heart and his began beating in symphony with each other. They began to beat as one. They *were* one.

Terri reached out for the hand she had seen on the video screen so many times, the same one she had coveted to touch. She took his hand in hers for the first time, and caressed it with her quivering lips. Kissing it tenderly, she said, "You have no idea how much I have wanted to meet you."

"Actually, I do," said Khreelon, with a glassy-eyed smile on his face. What Terri didn't realize, what she couldn't have known, was that Khreelon was succumbing to the spectacle of the moment as well. He realized his heart was suddenly no longer his; rather, there was a new heart beating in his chest for they had just invisibly exchanged souls. It was the most comfortable, yet the most anxious, cocktail of feelings. Standing there before him was the one he had been searching for, for thousands of years.

"You do?" asked Terri, wondering what he meant.

"I do," responded Khreelon. With a look on his face that portrayed happiness he dared not believe would ever happen to him, he reached into his cloak and produced a rolled-up piece of parchment with a red ribbon. "I know," he said, with a gentle smile on his face, "because you told me."

There in Khreelon's hand was the very letter she had written to him, seemingly so long ago. The same one she had placed in the compartment above his bed.

A very shocked Terri looked at Khreelon. "How in the world did you get your hands on that? I put that away in the secret hiding place above your bed. I didn't tell anybody it was there."

"I can answer that," said Jason. "I gave it to him."

Jason approached the love-struck couple and said, "When we were in your apartment, I secretly retrieved the letter when you were waiting for me on the elevator."

"When Jason came to the island in the past," added Khreelon, "he brought this with him. He wanted me to know what would be waiting for me when I was awakened."

"I don't understand," said Terri. "I was the only ...." She stopped dead in her tracks. Her face took on a completely different look, one of suddenly solving a mystery. Only two names came to her mind.

"Quorlynn and Loranna."

Both smiling, Jason and Khreelon nodded their heads.

"Terri, when I read your letter, it felt like you were speaking straight to my heart. Your words soothed me, and at the same time made me more impatient than I had ever been in my life. The month before we all entered suspended animation seemed interminable. As my time for sleep drew closer, I knew, at least from my perspective, I would soon see you. It seems like I closed my eyes to sleep only five minutes ago, but even those five minutes were far too long to wait. Terri Marie Lindstrom, you are my soulmate. For thousands of years, you were the one I was searching for. All my heart, all my soul, all my love," Khreelon drew in a breath, "... is yours."

With this declaration of love from Khreelon, Terri realized he had fulfilled the most precious yearnings of her heart. She was now his, mind, body and soul.

With those words, Terri shot straight into the arms of her lover. Wrapping her arms around him tightly, Khreelon likewise folded his cloak around Terri and kissed the top of her head. With closed eyes, he breathed in the aroma of his one true love. They were one now. Regardless of what different races there are in the universe, the scene of love before the eyes of those looking on had never been seen before, and could never be duplicated. Love had never been symbolized more than with the union of these two. It was a triumph, a victory. With eyes closed, Terri and Khreelon christened each other with tears of love which had no restraint. As they warmed to the love freely passing back and forth between them, they each felt their breathing, their chests expanding and contracting underneath the grip of their respective arms. Leaning back, but still standing body to body, Khreelon looked at Terri through watery eyes, and she did the same. Smiling, Terri whispered, "Ah, there's my blue love."

Diana, Lynne, and Mikki held onto each other for support as they shed tears of joy, but it was when Ruavu, who was shedding her own tears, placed her arms around them that the merging of two worlds became complete.

Jason looked around to see if the president was doing all right, and noticed he was off in a corner speaking with a few of the members of the Grand Council. Leaving the scene of love, Jason signaled Dennis with a couple of taps on his arm to follow him. As they approached, President Michaelson saw them and smiled.

"Gentlemen," said the president, "I am glad you came over. I've been talking with these esteemed members of the Grand Council about that idea we had discussed in my private office earlier. They agree with you two that this technology needs to be in the hands of people who can handle it responsibly. I am happy to tell you they have agreed to discuss your idea of relocating the portal to the island at the next meeting of the council. I explained that we would release it to them with the provision that not only will they be allowed to use it, but we will be allowed to come to the island and use it as well."

Jason turned to Lord N'Zollivant and the others. "I am pleased you are open to this proposal, my lords. I know your isolation from the rest of the inhabitants of this planet is important to your people; we will be happy to maintain the secrecy of your society from the prying eyes of others."

"We thank you, Jason Marsalis and Dennis Greene, for your consideration," said Lord N'Zollivant. "My esteemed colleagues and I have been discussing whether our policy of isolationism is something that continues to be applicable, in light of recent events. It will still need to be discussed among the full complement of council members, but I can tell you that you and your associates present today are welcome to come to the island at any time."

"Thank you, my lords," said Jason. Dennis added, "We are glad to have been of service."

"Jason and Dennis," added Lord N'Zollivant, "our people are indebted to you, and we all remain your humble servants. There is something else I have to say, though. Before we entered the suspended animation chambers, the council met and came to a unanimous decision."

Reaching into a pocket in his cloak, he produced two amulets. "These amulets of understanding are a gift to you both, and we wish for you to wear them as a token of our affection and respect. Amulets like these will also be given to your associates here as well, and we wish to confer upon you and your associates the titles of Lord and Lady. From here on out, when you are visiting our island, your names will be Lord Jason Marsalis and Lord Dennis Greene. It is one of the highest honors our culture can confer."

Overwhelmed, a speechless Jason and Dennis accepted the tokens of appreciation from Lord N'Zollivant, and immediately donned their new amulets.

Ultimately finding the words, Jason spoke up, saying, "Thank you, my lord. From the bottom of our hearts. Thank you."

Dennis leaned over to Jason and asked, "Understanding? What does that mean?"

"Trust me, buddy," said a grinning Jason, as he placed his hand on Dennis' shoulder. "You're gonna love it!"

Standing there with his best friend, Jason looked down at the sparkling amulet in his hand, knowing the adventure was a complete and resounding success. Looking over to Mikki, he saw her talking with Ruavu and several others, and it looked like she was really enjoying herself. In fact, they were engaged in what could be characterized as a conversation between old friends, even though they had only known each other for minutes. All in their group were continuously laughing while alternately resting their hands on each other's shoulders. Adding in the unbelievably melodious music coming from another corner of the room where Diana was being shown a traditional Galimarian dance, the overall feeling was a relaxed, calm happiness which seemed to be the trademark of this amazing people. Jason felt at home. He felt at peace. Looking back at his life mate, he knew there wasn't anywhere in the universe he'd rather be.

Somehow sensing Jason's eyes, Mikki looked over to him and smiled with a wink.

"Yep," he smiled to himself. "Everything is going to be okay."

EPILOGUE

The late afternoon sun was casting the last dregs of butter-scotch-colored light across the valley floor as Jose sat on the veranda of his new hacienda, looking out over all that lay before him. Situated on the side of a mountain range encasing the valley, the view afforded the Spaniard was breathtaking, but to Jose it was also bittersweet. As he contemplated his life, which was both short and long, he thought about what his father would say if he could see him now. Ever since the day he found out the real story about his father, not one made up in the mind of an adolescent without his father, Jose had decided all his decisions would be ones that would meet with his father's approval. The latest decision, buying this estate, was one he hoped his father would have approved of.

As he thought about his family and its link to his new home, Jose was rescued in the nick of time from descending into the pit of melancholy by the arrival of his friends.

"Jose!" called out Dennis.

Jose's pained look was immediately replaced with one of joy at once again seeing friends with whom he had formed a lifelong connection ever since that day at Midway.

Standing up, Jose responded, "Hola! Have a seat here; I have wine chilling and some hors d'oeuvres from the local inns."

Dennis approached, holding Lynne's hand; they had recently announced their engagement. They were accompanied by Jason and Mikki, likewise holding hands. As the four sat down and held out their wine glasses to be filled, each hovered over the delectable plate of breads and cheeses complemented by a generous bowl of garlic aioli, a staple of every table in this region of Spain.

Jason soaked in the view of the green-carpeted valley below, which reminded him of a similar valley Quorlynn had shown him. The multi-colored sky was accented by corpulent yet wispy clouds making their way toward the horizon, catching fire as the sun laid itself to rest.

"Beautiful" was all he could find to say. The others, who had been soaking in the breathtaking vista, sighed in agreement. A lazy breeze made its way up the side of the hill below them, and with it was the agricultural aroma of grapes soon to be harvested.

Reveling in the restful peace of the moment, Dennis remarked, "I have to say, Jose, this is a great spread you have here."

"Thank you, Dennis. I really enjoy spending time here."

"How much land do you have here?" asked Jason.

"All of it."

"What do you mean by 'all of it'?" asked Mikki.

"Every part of the valley which has a vineyard on it is land I own," responded Jose.

The group looked out at the valley floor laying before them and saw that its entirety, from stem to stern, was covered with vineyards.

"You're telling me you own this entire valley?" asked Lynne.

"Correct."

"How did you manage that?" asked Dennis.

Jose contemplated the fact that these four people were now his family, and decided they could certainly be trusted with the story of how he came by this land.

"About 700 years ago, when my father was a boy ...."

"Seven hundred years ago. Your dad. Kind of a funny way to start a story don't you think?" interrupted Dennis, with a laugh in his voice.

Nodding his head and smiling, Jose said, "Yes, I suppose there aren't many who can say that." Continuing with his story, he said, "When he was a little boy, he and his twin brother spent many afternoons hiking in the hills over there."

Jose pointed to a portion of the hills on the other side of the valley. "When I was little, I remember hearing from my father about the things they would get into. They were always exploring the natural features of the land and the river, as well as the wildlife. In fact, the river nearly took their lives one time when they were swept away by it. But that is another story."

"They all lived in a small cottage." He pointed to a different part of the valley. "That cottage was situated right there, where the river comes close to the hills. After they grew up, my Uncle Hernan lived there with my Aunt Sofia, and my father, mother, and I would come for evening meals. When I grew up, long after my father and uncle disappeared, I inherited the cottage and it is where I lived for some time. I always loved that cottage and the surrounding land, which is why I bought this land. It is a direct connection to my family."

"Of course now," Jose paused, "all of you are my family. You are part of me now."

The group smiled. Mikki said, "You are part of us too, Jose."

"Definitely, old chum, but that still doesn't explain how you were able to swing buying this land. You know where a gold mine is?"

"Not gold, but something a little more precious."

"What are you talking about?" asked Jason.

"Remember how I said my father and his brother were always exploring in these hills? One day Arturo, my father, found a rock he thought was beautiful, so he decided to wash it off and give it to his father as a present. Diego, my grandfather, was a man who was proud of his sons and loved them very much, so even though it was just a rock, he held onto it as if it was a precious diamond. He placed it on the mantle of the small cottage where they all lived, the same cottage where my father and his brother were born. From that day forward, my father was always bringing home pretty rocks to his father, who always graciously accepted the gifts from his son. He always made out like they were the most precious things he'd ever seen. When I was an adult, I found out that when the boys weren't looking, he would take them out and bury them in the same spot, down there against that rock outcropping. The original rock stayed on the mantle, though."

"Well," said Jose, "I kept that rock, but before I went on the voyage across the sea which led me to meeting the Galimarians, I buried the original rock in the same location where Grandfather buried all the other rocks. Shortly after I came back here, I dug up those old rocks since they were family heirlooms to me. After washing them off, I decided to find out what they were made of. You know what I discovered?"

All those listening shook their heads.

"It turned out about half of those 'pretty' rocks were actually diamonds. The first one, the original rock my father brought home, was a diamond so large it ended up becoming a cut diamond larger than the Hope Diamond."

"You're not telling me you were the original owner of the Appleton Diamond, are you?" asked Jason.

"The what?" asked Lynne.

"The Appleton Diamond," answered Jason. "It's been in the news lately. The owner won't say where it came from, but speculation is running rampant. I think they said it's something over 3,500 carats."

"It's actually 3,958 carats," said Jose.

"Oh my god," blurted Mikki.

Taking a deep breath, Dennis said, "Well, I'm darn happy for you, my friend. Darn happy. Couldn't have happened to a nicer fella."

"I agree," said Jason.

"Hey! You didn't start the party without us did you?"

Everyone sitting at the table turned and saw Terri and Khreelon walking up the path toward them.

"Hey you guys! I'm so glad to see you! I didn't know you were coming," said Jason. All who were seated instantly rose and greeted the new arrivals.

"Yeah! I thought you two lovebirds wouldn't be seen for years!" laughed Dennis.

"Life goes on, my jocular friend," answered Khreelon. Terri, who was holding his hand, smiled knowingly.

Their friends were especially glad to see them together. It was obvious they were inseparable. "So, how are you going to make this work with you living in New York?" asked Jason.

"President Michaelson has asked me to be the special ambassador to the island of New Galimar, and to serve as liaison to the Grand Council of New Galimar."

"That's wonderful!" gushed Mikki and Lynne together. The men stuck out their hands and shook Khreelon's, a new custom he only recently had gotten used to.

"Terri is going to live with me on New Galimar," added Khreelon, "although she will remain in communication with your president."

"That's great," replied Dennis. "I'm glad control of the island is back in the hands of those who should be in the driver's seat."

Khreelon didn't know exactly what Dennis meant by that idiom, but he was able to understand its meaning. After all Galimarians had been revived, President Michaelson ordered all military personnel off the island. The government of New Galimar was back to operating in full force.

After the group offered the two new arrivals seats at the table, Khreelon said, "Jason, may I have a word with you?"

"Sure." The two men walked off a small distance so they could talk alone.

"What's up, Khreelon?"

"Jason, the Grand Council of New Galimar recently met, and the subject was the relationship of New Galimar with the members of your government."

"Oh? How did that go?" asked Jason, with a look of trepidation on this face.

"You needn't be concerned. Part of that meeting was the decision to ratify the relationship Terri has with the Grand Council."

"Good. For a second there, I was thinking you guys decided against the whole deal."

"No. In fact, the council asked me to convey to you their decision to accept the proposal from you and your president," said Khreelon.

"You have?" asked Jason, a little surprised. "You've decided to allow us to relocate the portal to the island for safekeeping?"

"Yes, we have."

"That's great news!" said a very excited Jason. "If there's one thing recent events have taught us, it's that we need to make sure the technology is in safe hands. The president agreed with me that your people represent the safest of hands for something so powerful."

"Knowing what we now know about the device you and Dr. Greene invented, the council agrees it needs to be kept safe. But there's something more, though."

What's that?" asked Jason.

"The council was very impressed with the way you conducted yourself throughout this entire experience, and equally impressed with the responsible decisions made on the part of your leader, President Michaelson."

"Please convey my thanks to the council. The more I learn about the Galimarian people, the more I feel a special kinship with them. I hope to be friends with you and your people for a long time."

"We feel the same," replied Khreelon. "There's something else Terri doesn't know about, though. In a special session of the council, I was asked to convey something to you and your president that we very rarely give."

"What's that?" asked Jason.

"The council would like to offer you and your people the opportunity to share technologies between our two cultures."

Jason, staggering back in stark surprise, exclaimed "Wow!" He sat down on a rock wall they were standing near, and Khreelon sat next to him. "I have had many long discussions with Kaynar, my amulet companion, about the history of your people, especially the events surrounding the planet of Traxis. Isn't the council worried the same thing might happen to us?"

"I will admit there were some on the council who voiced that same concern. But in the end, they all agreed your maturity is unusual, and you are far beyond anything we have ever experienced, nor expected to experience here on Eden. Or Earth, I should say."

Jason sat there for a few minutes digesting all Khreelon had said. He thought about how interesting it would be to work with technologies he'd never even fantasized about. Khreelon allowed him to be alone with his thoughts, wisely discerning that he was working through the pros and cons of the proposal the council had made. Jason certainly wanted to learn sciences far beyond anything he'd ever heard of, but then he thought about the recent experiences with Admiral Brinstock, and how close things came to being really bad for humankind.

Looking at his friend sitting next to him, Jason said, "Khreelon, I want you to convey my sincere thanks to the Grand Council of New Galimar."

"Then you will accept?"

"Khreelon, there isn't anything I would like more than to set sail on a voyage of discovery in sciences I've never even thought were possible. The problem is, not all on this planet feel the same way I do when it comes to being responsible with things having the power that much of your technology represents. Take the portal technology, for example. While it's true that Dr. Greene and I spent countless years learning all we needed to learn so our discoveries with the portal technology were possible, still, we were lucky. And the planet was lucky it was Dr. Greene and myself who discovered it. We know how powerful the portal is, and we know it needs to be treated with respect, which is why we asked that you and your council be the caretakers of it.

"There are those on my planet," added Jason, "who are driven by greed, and are consistently in search of more and more power, regardless of whom they have to step on to get it. I fear sharing that knowledge would be a premature at this stage of my people's social evolution."

Khreelon smiled. "You, Jason, are personally far more developed than anyone else from any other planet I've been to, and you never cease to amaze me. I told the council you would probably love to work with our scientists."

"Oh, I didn't say Dr. Greene and I didn't want to work with your scientists," laughed Jason. "What I am saying is we are probably a rare breed among our people in that we really don't care to have all the power. Like you and your people, we have learned discovery is the real power, and it gives us joy to no end."

Khreelon nodded. "So be it. I will recommend to the council that you and Dr. Greene be allowed to work with our scientists as much as you wish. The offer will remain, and if there comes a time when you think your people can handle it, we stand ready to share. The council trusts you and Dr. Greene, and will follow your recommendations."

"Sounds good. Now, how about we join the rest of the crew over there?"

Khreelon closed his eyes and dipped his head with a smile on his face, to indicate his respect. The two of them walked back to the group, just in time to see Jose passing out gifts to all gathered at the table, Jason and Khreelon included. The gift was a small box, within which was one unusually pretty rock.

"To the memory of Hernan and Arturo Barragon y Cisneros" said Jose, taking a sip of wine from his vineyard. "May their legacy live forever."

"Here! Here!"

The End

Will the Circle of Seven allow the portal technology to slip through its fingers?

Will the world learn about the island of New Galimar?

What is the amazing reason behind the fire at the Library of Alexandria?

Don't miss the next saga in the Galimar series!

GALIMAR

JASON AND
THE CIRCLE OF SEVEN

www.ingramcontent.com/pod-product-compliance
Lightning Source LLC
Chambersburg PA
CBHW070350030726
47504CB00001B/131